D0524771

J. J.

Plough the Furrow
and
Sow the Seed

MARGARET DICKINSON

Born in Gainsborough, Lincolnshire, Margaret Dickinson moved to the coast at the age of seven and so began her love for the sea and the Lincolnshire landscape.

Her ambition to become a writer began early. Her first novel was published when she was twenty-five. This was followed by ten further titles, including *Plough the Furrow* and *Sow the Seed*, the first two books of her Lincolnshire trilogy. Magaret Dickinson combines a busy working life with her writing career.

Margaret Dickinson

Plough the Furrow and Sow the Seed

PAN BOOKS

IPlough the Furrow first published in 1994 by Pan Books
Sow the Seed first published 1995 by Pan Books

This omnibus edition published 2004 by Pan Books
an imprint of Pan Macmillan Ltd
Pan Macmillan, 20 New Wharf Road, London N1 9RR
Basingstoke and Oxford
Associated companies throughout the world
www.panmacmillan.com

ISBN 0330 43271 0

Copyright © Margaret Dickinson 1994, 1995

The right of Margaret Dickinson to be identified as the
author of this work has been asserted by her in accordance
with the Copyright, Design and Patents Act 1988.

All rights reserved.
No part of this publication may be reproduced, stored in or
introduced into a retreieval system, or transmitted, in any form, or by
any means (electronic, mechanical, photocopying, recording or
otherwise) without prior written permission of the publisher.
Any person who does any unauthorised act in relation to this publication
may be liable to criminal prosecution and civil claims for damages.

1 3 5 7 9 8 6 4 2

A CIP catalogue record for this book is available from
the British Library.

Typeset by intype London
Printed and bound in Great Britain by
Mackays of Chatham plc, Chatham, Kent

This book is sold subject to the condition that it shall not,
by way of trade or otherwise, be lent, re-sold, hired out,
or otherwise circulated without the publisher's prior consent
in any form of binding or cover other than that in which
it is published and without a similar condition including this
condition being imposed on the subsequent purchaser.

Plough the Furrow

For Dennis, Mandy and Zoë

Acknowledgements

'Brumbys' Farm' has been modelled on Lincolnshire County Council's Church Farm Museum, Skegness, and the locale of 'Fleethaven Point' now forms part of the Gibraltar Point National Nature Reserve, managed by the Lincolnshire Trust for Nature Conservation. My sincere thanks to Ruth Walker, Museum Assistant at Church Farm, for her interest and help in providing background information, and also to Carl Hawke, the Gibraltar Point Warden.

I acknowledge use of material regarding the First World War taken from the *Skegness Herald* dated Friday, August 7th, 1914, printed and published by the Proprietor Jas Morrill, MJI, at the Herald Press, 19 Lumley Road, Skegness; and also general information from later editions of the newspaper, then printed and published by C. H. Major & Co Ltd.

My very special thanks to my family and friends for their interest and encouragement, particularly those who helped me so much by reading the novel in the early stages – my sister and her husband, Robena and Fred Hill; Pauline Griggs; Linda and Terry Allaway; and my daughter, Zoë, who helped with the final draft.

M.D.
Skegness, 1994

One

LINCOLNSHIRE, 1910

'A GIRL! A chit of a girl is no use to me.'

Esther Everatt stood before the glowering man and ignored his insult. Inside she was quivering, but she wasn't going to let the old man know that. Her firm chin jutted out resolutely. 'Well, mester, it looks like I'm all ya've got. An' from what I've heard, all ya're going to get.'

'Why you cheeky young wench, Ah'll . . .' Sam Brumby raised his hand and stepped forward as if to strike her. The girl did not flinch. Her green eyes stared at him steadfastly. Her feet were planted firmly on the cobbles of his farmyard as if already she intended to put her roots down in this place.

'Aye,' she said softly now, 'ya can hit me if ya like. I'm used to it. One more blow'll mek no difference.'

Sam's arm sliced the empty air inches from her face. 'Be off with you,' he muttered and turned away, but not before she had seen the momentary shame in his eyes. She guessed it was the first time he had ever raised his hand to a woman, but her impertinence had angered him.

'Ah've no use for the likes of you here,' he was saying gruffly as he went back towards the cowshed. 'It's a strong farm lad Ah want – not a lady's maid!'

1

Her laughter rang out clear and sweet in the misty, early morning air. 'Mr Brumby – do I *look* like a lady's maid?' Her mouth softened when she laughed; even so, it was a mouth that could harden into an unyielding line of determination.

Despite his insistence that he had no interest in her, he glanced back over his shoulder. She was still standing there, hands on hips, watching him. There was a feline stillness about her. Her feet were encased in boots which had known better days long before her ownership of them. Dust from the road she had travelled encrusted the hem of her long, coarse skirt. She was slim, yet there was an aura of physical strength about her. Her hair was a dark tangle of curls with strands plastered damply to her forehead. Her hands and face were tanned by wind and sun.

But it was her eyes that caught and held the attention of anyone who dared to meet that bold, green gaze. They were still staring at Sam, willing him to listen to her, holding him from turning away.

She saw his moment of hesitation, could almost read on his face the question that was forming in his mind. Where had a young girl like her come from at this early hour? She saw Sam Brumby open his mouth, then clamp his jaw shut again. He was afraid to show even the slightest interest in such a cheeky baggage – she thought, inwardly amused – in case it gave her more ideas.

But Esther Everatt did not need anyone to give her ideas – she had plenty of her own. As Sam Brumby turned away and disappeared into the cowshed, she picked up the meagre bundle of her belongings she had dropped to the ground and marched after him. Outwardly, she was displaying a confidence she did not feel inside. She was determined that this old man should not guess how desperately she needed work and a place to live. She wanted to tell him that she would work morning, noon and night for him if only he would let her stay. But grovelling was not part of Esther Everatt's nature, nor, she guessed, would it find favour with this gruff old man. He would see it as weakness and despise her for it.

At this moment she knew far more about Sam Brumby than he did about her. He had never married and had no family to carry on the farm now that his once-strong limbs were painfully misshapen with rheumatism.

'He needs help,' Will Benson, the carrier, had told her. 'But the miserable old devil's too stubborn to admit it. He needs someone young and strong and not afraid of hard work. Someone like you, lass. And it would get you away from *this*!' Will had jerked his head towards the cottage where Esther lived with her aunt and uncle and their large brood of children. She had stared up at Will as he sat on the high seat on the front of his carrier's cart, hope rising within her. Threading the reins backwards and forwards through his fingers, not looking at her, he had murmured, 'I've always known what a rough life you've got, lass, with yar aunt, an' I've often wished I could do summat to help you.' He had lifted his head and smiled. 'Then last week when I went on me usual trip out to Fleethaven Point and saw how old Sam's getting more bent and slow ev'ry time I sees him, well, I thought to mesen, "he needs a young 'un about the place" and, o' course, I thought of you, lass.'

Now she was here, had walked all through the night to get here, and with all her being she wanted Sam Brumby to need her.

As she followed him towards the cowshed, he banged the lower half of the door behind him, right in her face, but she merely dropped her bundle against the wall, waited a moment or two then drew in a deep breath, lifted the latch and stepped inside. She stood quite still breathing in the pungent smell of the warm beasts – oh how she loved it! She reached out and touched the back of the nearest cow, making soothing noises deep in her throat, standing quietly while Sam Brumby worked.

At last he stretched his aching limbs and stood up from where he had been crouching to finish milking the first of the two cows. Esther saw him rub his knuckles, swollen with rheumatism.

''Ere,' he growled, 'since you're so keen, you can 'ave a go with her – Clover.'

Was she mistaken, Esther thought shrewdly, or did she detect a wicked gleam in the old man's eyes? Her mouth twitched, but she said nothing and moved towards the cow tethered in the corner. Clover turned wild eyes towards her. Again came Esther's soft, pacifying murmur. She ran her hand over the cow's rump, down her legs and along her rounded sides. Down and round and under the cow's stomach until tenderly she touched the bursting udder, all the while her voice crooning softly. She sat down upon the three-legged stool, leant her head against the beast's belly and began to draw milk with steady, rhythmic movements.

Esther refused to look up but sensed that Sam was

4

watching from under his shaggy white eyebrows that shadowed watery hazel eyes. The white stubble on the old man's face scarcely concealed the hollowness of his cheeks and his wispy hair stuck out from underneath his cap. His clothes – a striped, collarless shirt with the sleeves rolled up above his elbows, black waistcoat and thick corduroy trousers with leather leggings from knee to ankle – hung loosely on him, as if, when new, it had been a much stronger, straighter man who had worn them. Sam was now bent with age, his shoulders permanently rounded, his legs bowed. Each step he took seemed painful; the hobnailed boots too heavy for him to lift.

She heard him sniff and wipe the back of his hand across his mouth. 'You can finish milking her before . . .' he added pointedly, 'you go.' Sam was testing her, she knew it. Esther sensed that Clover was a difficult cow.

'Yes, Mr Brumby, right you are,' she replied, pretending meekness.

As he left the cowshed, closing the half-door quietly behind him, Esther allowed herself a wry smile against the soft hide of the animal. For the first time in her young life she had cause to thank the bad-tempered woman who had reared her. Everything she knew – not only household duties, but all aspects of work on the farm – had been learnt under her aunt's cruel tongue and harsh hand.

Thanks to Aunt Hannah, it would take more than a temperamental cow for Sam Brumby to rid himself of Esther Everatt.

*

Half an hour later, Esther tapped on the back door of the house. It opened into Sam Brumby's back scullery. At least Esther presumed it to be the scullery though it bore no resemblance to her Aunt Hannah's, always so neat and clean you could see your face in the shining copper pans hanging on the wall. This place was filthy; unwashed pots and pans were piled in the deep sink and bits of mouldy food littered the draining board.

In front of her was the door leading into the main kitchen. This room was no better than the outer one. To her right she noticed another door leading out of the kitchen and down some steps into what she guessed would be the pantry.

Sam Brumby was standing at the cluttered kitchen table hacking at a lump of fat bacon. He glanced up. 'You still here?'

Esther eyed the food hungrily. She hadn't eaten since the previous day and even Sam Brumby's unappetizing fat bacon in his dirty kitchen looked good to her.

''Ere, sit down and eat,' he said grudgingly and almost threw her a wedge of meat and a hunk of coarse, grey bread. 'Then you can be on your way, wench.'

'Thank you, Mr Brumby.' All politeness now, she sat at his table and ate the food he offered. When she had finished she thanked him, stood up and left the house. But she did not leave the farm. If Sam Brumby wanted her gone, he would have to carry her bodily off his land — and even then, there would be nothing to stop her returning.

She had nowhere else to go. Not now. Not since she had bundled her few possessions into a square of cloth,

6

and, tying the corners together, had crept from her pallet bed in the draughty loft and out into the night. Esther had walked away from the only home she had ever known without looking back. Now, as she stood near the wall of the cowshed, watching the back door of the house but ready to dodge out of sight when Sam appeared, she thought briefly of her journey through the previous night, leaving the village on the edge of the Wolds that had been her home for the first sixteen years of her life. She had left without a trace of sorrow. There was no one she would really miss; certainly not her Aunt Hannah nor her seven cousins, from Mary, the eldest – a pudding-faced, sullen girl – right down through boys and girls of varying ages to the youngest girl – a spoilt, whining brat! Taking the lead from their mother, they had alternately ridiculed Esther or used her to do their share of the chores.

Perhaps her Uncle George was the only one whom Esther would remember with affection. A strong ox of a man, he was kindly but slow-witted and no match for his wife's sharp tongue. He was even overawed by his growing children. Esther had watched his efforts to be close to his family meet with derision. Somehow, she thought, there was a streak of cruelty in all of Hannah's children – and they did not inherit it from their father!

When she saw Sam come out of the back door and go towards the barn, Esther collected the milk and carried it back into the house. She stood at the top of the three steps down into the pantry and surveyed the long, cool room with its red brick floor. At one end similar red bricks formed a raised gantry. Round the walls were shelves cluttered with all manner of stone jars, earthenware basins and bowls, enamelled jugs, scales and weights, knives, spoons and ladles – the conglomeration of years of neglect. On the top shelf was a row of glass preserving jars still holding fruit that was grey with age, a thick layer of dust lining the greased paper tops. Cobwebs festooned the shelves, looped between the jars and spiders scuttled away at her approach.

Her glance came to rest – with a final expression of disgust – upon the dairy equipment on the gantry.

'It's a wonder the folks drinking this milk don't die of disease,' Esther muttered aloud and with pursed lips set herself to clean the bowls, milk cans and the barrel-shaped butter churn. By the time Sam returned, she was pouring the milk into a spotless separating bowl, broad and shallow for the cream to rise to the top.

'Thought I told you to go?' he said, standing at the top of the pantry steps.

'Just thought I'd do this for you, Mr Brumby. After all, this is woman's work. I'm sure there's something else waiting that needs a man's brawn.'

He gave an angry snort. 'Cheeky young wench!' he growled and shook his fist at her before turning away. 'Just dun't let me catch you still here next time Ah gets back. That's all!'

Esther straightened up and eased her aching back. With one last glance of satisfaction at the change she had already wrought in the pantry, even though it had taken her nearly the whole day, she went outside again. She saw Sam disappearing into the cowshed. She stood outside the back door of the house and looked about her.

Just how, she asked herself, was she going to get this stubborn old man to admit that he needed help about his farm? Her help!

Straight opposite her across the yard were some stables, the cowshed and between the two, a small barn. The stables were littered with an accumulation of rubbish slung in carelessly; tools, empty sacks, a barrow and harness badly in need of cleaning and polishing. So, thought Esther, there've been no horses in here recently.

On the right hand side of the yard was a row of small, brick buildings – three pigsties and a tool shed. Beyond that was a large barn with a hayloft.

Four geese headed by a gander came waddling towards her, protesting loudly. The gander spread his wings. Flapping and shrieking, he thrust out his neck and came rushing towards her, his webbed feet slapping the cobbles. Esther stood her ground, hands on hips and faced the fearsome bird.

'Ya can stop that racket!'

He stopped, his vicious beak only inches from her. The wings settled back and, fluffing his feathers, he regarded her with tiny bright eyes. Behind him his mates squawked encouragement from a safe distance. With one last strident screech of disapproval, he turned and, gabbling to his wives, he waddled away. Dutifully, the geese fell into step behind him.

Esther glanced across the yard and saw that Sam was looking out over the half-door of the cowshed, presumably to see what was causing all the noise. For a moment he stared at her, then, even from this distance, she heard him sniff and saw him scratch his white stubble thoughtfully. He glanced at the departing gander and then back at Esther before turning away.

Already the sun was setting, throwing shafts of golden April sunlight across the fenland fields that stretched westward, flat as far as the eye could see till they touched the glowing sky. As dusk closed in on the farm, the tiredness swamped her. She hadn't slept for over thirty-six hours and though the work she'd done that day had hardly been strenuous even in her own estimation, every bone and muscle in her body ached to lie down and rest.

But the work was not done yet. From the cowshed she could hear the sounds of evening milking. She leant on the half-door watching Sam, listening to his rasping breath as he worked. She saw him lever himself up from the low milking stool and a grunt of pain escaped his lips.

As he moved towards Clover in the end stall, the animal lashed her tail and kicked out sideways with her back leg, catching Sam a painful blow on the shin. The old man swore volubly and then, suddenly becoming aware of Esther's shadow at the door, turned his anger on her. 'Ah told you to clear off. Ah dun't want you here. Ah dun't need no help.'

He snatched a leather thong from a hook on the wall and strapped it round the cow's back legs. Now Clover was forced to stand still an . submit to being milked.

' "Kicker" would be a better name for that 'un, mester,' Esther grinned saucily and, picking up her bundle, she turned away.

She stood uncertainly in the yard for a moment, breathing in the soft air with a hint of the sea in it. The barn, and its hayloft, loomed before her in the gathering dusk and promised warmth and rest. She glanced back over her shoulder. Let him struggle tonight, she thought, but tomorrow — I'll show him! Esther smiled to herself and went towards the barn.

Two

SHE became aware of the early morning light filtering through the cocoon of hay she had made for herself. There was a rustling close beside her. Rats! Esther thought. Her drowsiness vanished. Not that she was afraid of them but she didn't want them running over her whilst she slept.

Without warning the sharp tines of a pitchfork were driven into the hay only inches from her throat. She gave a shriek, flung back the hay covering her and scrambled to her feet. A young man stood there, open-mouthed, the fork he held still embedded in the hay. They stared at each other for a moment before both spoke at once.

'What the 'ell . . . ?'

'Can't you be more careful with that thing? You nearly speared my neck!'

'You shouldn't be 'ere,' he retorted defensively, then as his initial shock faded, he grinned and his gaze travelled up and down her lithe body. 'Oh, I don't know, though.'

He let go of the pitchfork and moved towards her. Esther stood her ground, her eyes challenging him. He was standing close now, too close, but she did not move. He was no taller than she was, but stockily built, the width of his shoulders proclaiming their muscular strength. He wore an open-necked shirt, the rolled-up sleeves showing his arms covered with black hairs. A

12

red kerchief was knotted at his throat, but he wore no waistcoat. His trousers were the usual corduroy with a length of twine tied below each knee. His cap perched uneasily on top of his thick, curly black hair and his skin was swarthy. Three days' growth of stubble darkened his face even more, but his brown eyes glinted as their gaze rested on the gentle swell of her bosom. He ran his tongue around his lips and then grinned showing white, even teeth. He put out his hand to touch her throat where the top button of her blouse was undone. 'It'd be a pity to wound such a lovely neck as—'

Her arm came up smartly to smack his hand away before his fingers could touch her skin. 'Keep ya hands to ya'sen — boy!' She uttered the final word with scathing derision. His eyes blazed and a flush of anger spread across his dark features.

'I aren't going to let a little tramp talk to me like that . . .' he muttered. His strong hands gripped her shoulders bruising her skin and digging into her flesh. Instantly she brought her arms up to knock his sideways, loosening his grip on her. Then she tugged on his right sleeve at the same time as she kicked his shin with her sturdy boot. He found himself lying on his back in the hay, staring up at her. The fall had knocked the breath from him. He could make no answer as she said, 'Next time I'll let you have it where it really hurts — boy!'

With that she climbed down the ladder.

As Esther sluiced the sleep from her eyes under the icy water from the pump, she heard behind her the clatter of hooves on the cobbles of the yard and turned to see Sam bringing two of his three cows through the farm gate and towards the cowshed. She wondered why he didn't milk the cows in the field like her aunt had done, but watching his hobbling, bow-legged gait, she realized it was easier for him to bring the cows to the byre than to be chasing each one around the field to milk it – especially the temperamental Clover.

As he passed her, she thought he hadn't noticed her until he said, 'What sort of time do ya call this? 'Tis half-way through the day. Ah thought the work'd be too much for a slip of a wench.'

Esther opened her mouth to retort, but for once she thought better of it. She wasn't one to make excuses. Let him think what he liked. Instead she said, 'What do ya want me to do, Mester Brumby?'

He was moving away from her now, but over his shoulder he grunted, 'Ah want you to go, that's what Ah *want* you to do!' He paused, one hand on the door of the cowshed, then turning to look at her, added, 'But seein' as how Ah dun't expect you'll tek any notice of me – you can get on with milking this pair.'

He let his hand fall from the door and began to go towards the house. 'When you've done, turn 'em out into North Marsh Field. Ah'll show you when you're ready. Ah'm off up Top End, but Ah'll be back by you're done.'

There was no further sign of the 'boy'. Who was he, Esther wondered, and what had he to do with Brumbys' Farm? She wrinkled her brow thoughtfully. Maybe what Will had told her wasn't true after all. Maybe Sam Brumby had got some help about the farm. If so, her argument about being the only one he could get to stay would lose its effectiveness.

As she leant her head against the warm flank of the beast and began to pull with easy rhythmic movements, she could almost hear her aunt's shrill voice: 'Not like that, girl, you'll 'eve 'er tits as sore as 'ell,' and, obediently, Esther's fingers were gentle on the cow's udders.

Just as she was finishing milking the two cows, a shadow fell across the straw near the pail and Esther twisted her head slightly to look over her shoulder, although her hands never slowed or faltered in their task.

A girl stood there, though Esther could not see her features for the light was behind her, casting her face in shadow, but outlining her rounded form. She stood uncertainly in the doorway, one hand resting on the rough wood of the door jamb.

'Is Mr Brumby about?' she asked, her voice low and husky.

''Fraid not. He's up Top End – wherever that is,' Esther told her, the milk still squirting steadily into the pail.

'It's yon side the Point,' the girl said. 'I must have missed him somehow – I've just come from there.'

Esther stood up and placed the full pail of milk away from the cow's restless hooves and then moved out of the cowshed and into the light so she could get a better look at the newcomer. Long hair – black, now that she could see it properly in the morning light – straight yet sleek and shining. A grey, knitted shawl covered the girl's shoulders and she hugged it about her, folding her arms across her already womanly breast. She was smaller than

15

Esther but her body was rounded and buxom. Her eyes were dark brown with long black lashes. Her face was childishly plump, yet her high cheekbones and smooth brow hinted at the promise of beauty as she grew and matured.

She seemed to hesitate as if uncertain what to do next.

'Are you working here?' The dark eyes regarded Esther steadily. 'Matthew told me he thought Mr Brumby needed more help about the place, so – I've come up to see him . . .'

Esther felt her heart lurch. Somehow she would have to give this girl the impression that the job was taken. Esther adopted her forthright pose: hands on hips, feet planted apart, a stance that refuted opposition. But deliberately she smiled, as if to take some of the sting out of her words. 'I heard that too. Sorry – it looks like I've beaten you to it!'

The dark-haired girl shrugged. 'Oh, well, never mind then. It was worth a try.' She smiled in return. 'I reckon he'd have frightened me to death, anyway. I hope you get on all right.'

Esther was taken aback by her friendliness. The girl was not in the least resentful that Esther had taken what might have been her job.

'What's your name?' she asked as the girl half-turned to go.

'Beth Hanley. I live at the Point in one of the cottages with me dad.'

'Oh.' Esther shook her head. 'I ain't seen the Point yet . . .' She grinned ruefully. 'I ain't been off the farm since I got here.' She did not add that it had been deliberate; she was afraid that if she set foot outside the gate, Sam Brumby would find some way to keep her out. Now, more than ever, if there were others wanting the job, she had to prove herself indispensable to Sam.

But Beth Hanley was smiling again showing white, even teeth. 'Mester Brumby'll work you hard, there's no doubt about that.'

'Well, well, well, look what we've got here, then. *Two* pretty girls . . .'

They both turned and Esther saw the young man whom she had encountered early that morning in the hayloft coming towards them looking from one to the other, a broad grin on his face.

At once the smile disappeared from Beth Hanley's face. Her glance went from Matthew to Esther and then back again. 'D'you know her, Matthew?' The friendliness was gone from her tone. 'Did you tell *her* about this job too?'

'Naw, course I didn't. *I* don't know who she is or where she's come from. I only met her this morning.' His insolent eyes raked Esther up and down. 'But – I can't say I'm sorry.'

Obviously, Esther thought, he bears me no grudge for kicking his shins, even though the bruise must still be sore. Perhaps he thinks he can tame me. Well, Mester Matthew – if that's what ya name is – ya can think again! A small smile flickered on Esther's mouth as she met his impudent gaze.

Seeing it, Beth's dark eyes flashed, any sign of a tentative friendship gone in an instant. 'Huh, might 'ave known *you'd* have your eye on her afore she's been here

17

five minutes. Can't keep your hands off anything in skirts, can you, Matthew Hilton?'

'What would either of you do here anyway?' he asked of them mockingly. 'The ploughing?'

He came and leant casually against the other door frame close to Esther, his arms folded across his chest.

Esther stood in the doorway between them. Defensively now, she said, 'Aye, an' I can plough a straight furrow, an' all.'

Matthew threw back his head and laughed, the sound echoing around the yard. There was a sarcastic smirk on Beth Hanley's face as she said, 'Get away, you couldn't handle them great horses, so don't . . .'

'Got time to stand all day gossiping, have you?' Sam Brumby's voice made them all jump. Esther turned back into the cowshed and in her haste, turning from the bright morning light back into the darkness of the shed, she tripped over the pail and fell sprawling into the dirt. The milk spread across the cobbles, running rivulets of white amongst the cow muck.

'Get back to your work, you idle creature!' Sam roared at Matthew and punctuated his words with a blow to the side of the lad's head. 'And forget ya wenching!'

Sam took no notice of Beth Hanley, who nevertheless scuttled out of the yard and up the lane towards the Point as if a nest of hornets were in pursuit.

Esther cursed herself roundly for her own stupidity. The appearance of first Matthew and then Beth had unnerved even Esther's determination to prove herself useful to Sam Brumby.

And spilling a full pail of his precious milk would do her no good at all.

Three

*B*Y the time she had dealt with the one remaining bucket of milk and had come out into the yard again, Sam Brumby and Matthew had disappeared. She sighed, unsure what to do. She badly needed to prove herself useful to Sam. She had nowhere else to go. She would not go back. Not ever! But now she had probably ruined her chances of staying here. She knew just how precious every drop of milk was to a small farmer who had only three cows; and one of those was not being milked just now because it was due to calve at any time.

Esther was standing uncertainly in the middle of the yard when she heard a scuffling from one of the sties and went to investigate. Esther liked pigs. She loved their pink, hairy coats, their snuffling and grunting, and their noisy troughing made her want to giggle. As she looked in over the first door, a half-grown young gilt squealed and rushed excitedly towards her. She expected Esther to be the bringer of food.

Esther laughed. 'You look hungry. I'll go and see what I can find.'

She turned away from the sty and looked back towards the house. There were two buckets of pig swill standing outside the back door. She fetched them and the young pig scurried around her ankles, knocking against her in its eagerness to get at the food Esther carried.

'Let me get to the trough to tip it in, then,' she laughed.

The next sty was empty, but in the end one she found a large Curly Coat sow pacing up and down. She was heavily in-pig and displayed no interest in the other bucket of swill Esther tipped into the trough. The animal was obviously agitated and frothing at the mouth. From time to time the sow picked up a mouthful of straw and carried it about the sty, each time finally dropping it in one particular corner.

Esther moved towards her carefully. 'Now then, old girl,' she soothed. This pig reminded her of one of her uncle's, a restless animal that had turned vicious at the birth and had tried to eat its own young, succeeding in killing all but two of the litter before her uncle had found them. Esther looked around her for something in which she could put the newborn piglets to keep them safe from their mother. There was nothing in the sty, but in the barn she found a battered old tea-chest. She dragged it into the sty and placed it in one corner, pushing some of the straw into the bottom as bedding.

Esther stayed in the corner near the door watching the sow from a safe distance whilst she waited. She had no idea where Sam Brumby had gone. Perhaps she should try to tell him, but she was rather afraid that if she left this pig alone for very long, by the time she returned there could well be a half-chewed piglet or two.

The youngsters slipped out quite easily one by one. The sow tried to rouse herself each time, but her eyes were wild and her mouth frothing. Esther knew she was not trying to suckle her young. This animal was danger-

21

ous, just like her uncle's sow. She would kill her litter, given half a chance.

Esther went to one of the other sheds. The door squeaked rustily as she opened it and the fusty smell of neglect met her nostrils. Tools and implements had been thrown in higgledy-piggledy to lie dusty and forgotten. She stood a moment to let her eyes become accustomed to the dim interior and then she spotted what she wanted and pulled it from the heap of implements, disturbing a cloud of dust. She carried the garden hoe back to the pigsty and each time a piglet was born, Esther crept forward, keeping well away from the suffering mother, and as gently as she could pulled the wriggling creature away until she could pick it up. She wiped it as clean as she could with straw, over its face to clear the mouth, and slipped it into the tea-chest in the opposite corner. Then she stood up again and moved quietly back near the door to wait for the next arrival.

A shadow appeared across the doorway. '*Now* what are you up to, wench?' came Sam's exasperated tone.

'Yar pig's farrowing, mester, and it looks to me as if she might try to eat her young 'uns.'

Sam snorted. 'That's nothing new with that sow. Lost half the litter last time, Ah did.'

'Well, not this time,' Esther vowed, more to herself than to Sam.

'What? What d'you say?'

'I'll stay with her, Mr Brumby.'

Sam sniffed again and turned away. 'Well, Ah can't stand here all day playing nursemaid to a pig. You do what you like.'

Esther smiled to herself at his oblique reference once more to her sex, but at least this time he had not told her to go.

Esther did not go into the house at midday. Her stomach was rumbling with hunger, but she dare not leave the sow for a moment.

'Ah've brought you a mug o' tea.' She turned to see Matthew grinning at her over the half-door of the sty. He jerked his head back towards the house. 'Mester said you was playing midwife to Curly.'

'Ooh, ta,' Esther said appreciatively, taking the tea. Matthew leant his forearms on the lower half of the door and rested his chin on his arms, watching the sow. 'Awk'ard old devil, she is. You want to be careful – she'll 'ave yar leg off soon as look at ya.'

Esther grinned and held up the hoe. 'That's why I'm armed – and why I'm standing near the door. But I reckon she's a mite busy to be chasing me just now.' They watched together as another piglet thrust its way into the world.

'Here – hold this a minute, will ya?' She moved forward and plucked the tiny animal away, wiped it and popped it into the tea-chest. Then she returned to her place by the door and took the mug back from Matthew, sipping the hot, sweet tea gratefully.

'Well, I'd best be getting back to me hedging and ditching, else I'll have the mester after me again.'

'Thanks for the tea,' Esther said.

'Ya're welcome.' Giving her a saucy wink, Matthew went off whistling.

As the sixth piglet was born – and she could see that the sow was not done even then – Esther heard a familiar shrill whistle and moments later the wheels of the local carrier's cart rattled into the yard.

'Is she here, then?' Will Benson was demanding to know of Sam.

'Who?' Then, understanding, Sam added accusingly, 'Oh, so it's *you* Ah've to thank for landing me with a chit of a girl, is it? Ah can't get rid of the cheeky little baggage!'

Esther heard the carrier's laugh. 'That's our Esther right enough. She's a rare lass. You've met your match there, Sam Brumby. She'll take no notice of your moods and your tempers.'

'What's she to do wi' you then, Will Benson? And what right have you to inflict such as her on me? Ah didn't ask you to bring her. She ain't staying, Ah can tell you that!' It was a long speech for the taciturn Sam, but Will only laughed again.

'*I* didn't bring her, but I admit I told her about you needing a young 'un about the place. I were going to offer to bring her over at least to see you, but when I called at her aunt's – ' he gave a snort of contempt. 'Lord strike me, how I detest that woman – Esther had already left. Set off to walk through the night, her aunt said, so as to arrive by first light.'

''Ow far she come, then?'

'Oh, must be thirteen odd mile, I reckon.'

24

Peeping out of the door, but minding to keep well hidden from the two men, Esther saw the farmer staring up at the carrier and then – a rare thing – Sam Brumby smiled. It twitched the corner of his mouth, unwilling at first, hesitating as if not knowing quite how to form itself after years of neglect, then spreading across his mouth, wrinkling his eyes. From deep within came a chuckle. 'The young . . .' he murmured more to himself than to Will. 'And Ah accused her of being weak because she looked tired this morning. Well, Ah never did!'

The carrier's mouth dropped open. Sam Brumby was actually laughing! It would be a talking point on the carrier's rounds for weeks to come.

Esther saw Sam shake his head wonderingly. He took off the cap he always wore and scratched his balding pate, then pulled his cap on again. 'Well, Ah never!' he muttered again. Esther knew she had, for the moment, earned Sam's grudging respect. And that, she guessed, was not an easy thing to do.

'Ah'll tell you summat else, Will. She got the better of me gander last night. Now, I ain't ever seen old Wellington beat afore – not by anyone.'

'Didn't I tell you, Sam, didn't I tell you she's a rare lass?' the carrier said delightedly.

Will Benson was a dapper little man, dressed more smartly than the farmer. He wore trousers and a striped jacket and matching waistcoat, and the toes of his sturdy boots shone. He sported a ginger moustache which drooped at the corners hiding to some extent the shape of his mouth. Some days he wore a cap and on hot summer days a kind of boater-shaped hat. Esther knew him well for he lived in the same village where she lived — or rather had lived, she reminded herself. She smiled as she saw Will take off his cap. He had a good head of hair for a man of his age, she thought, seeing it smooth and glinting ginger in the sunlight. She liked Will. He had always treated her kindly and even on occasions boldly outfaced her aunt on her behalf. There weren't many who dared to do that, Esther thought ruefully, yet Will Benson always seemed to get away with it.

He was speaking again now. 'She's a good lass, Sam, I can tell you. Treated rough, she's been, by that shrew of an aunt of hers. Mind you, she's raised Esther alongside her own bairns, you can't deny, but only out of a sense of — of *duty*. She never showed the poor lass any affection.' He shook his head and added bitterly, 'She could show it to her own, though. She made the difference between them very obvious, I can tell you.'

Sam said nothing whilst the carrier chattered on. 'She's a hard worker,' and he added a little ruefully, 'she's had to be, with Hannah for her aunt! The lass deserves better. She ought to be given a chance.' Esther felt a blush of embarrassment creep up her face. She had never before heard herself so praised.

'What happened to her folks, then?'

'Her mother, Hannah's younger sister, died giving birth to her,' Will replied briefly.

'What about her father?'

'How should *I* know?' As if to cut off any more of Sam's questions, Will climbed down from his seat. 'I can't sit here chatting all day. I've me rounds to do. I'll

26

just have a word with the lass an' I'll be on me way. Where is she?'

From the pigsty, Esther saw Sam jerk his head in her direction. Even from this distance, Esther heard Sam's dismissive sniff. 'Wasting her time wi' me sow.'

As the conversation between the two men ceased, Esther hung over the half-door of the pigsty. ''Morning, Mr Benson,' she called.

'Eh, there you are, Esther lass.' He gave a wave in greeting and came towards her. 'You settling in all right, then?'

'Ah ain't said she's staying yet,' Sam Brumby raised his voice before Esther could reply.

She grinned at Will. 'He'll find he's a job on 'is hands to get rid of me though, won't he, Mr Benson?'

The carrier laughed, whilst Sam Brumby growled, 'There's nowt Ah want today, Will Benson. You can be on your way.' And with that parting shot, Sam hobbled off.

'Well, lass,' Will said softly. 'Are you all right?'

Esther pulled a wry face. 'I ain't managed to make him see he needs me yet, but I'm working on it.' She grinned suddenly. 'I'm banking on Curly here to help.'

Will Benson poked his head into the sty and a doubtful expression flitted across his face. Esther leant closer and lowered her voice. 'She usually turns nasty with her litter and kills 'em. I'm trying to save 'em.'

Will's expression cleared and he smiled. 'Oh, so that's it – I wondered what Sam meant. Well, lass, it might work. Dun't let that grumpy old beggar get the better of you. Good luck and tek care of yasen. I'll be calling again on Thursday as usual. Tuesdays and Thursdays I come out to the Point.'

'I'll be here,' Esther told him with far more confidence in her tone than she felt.

He turned away, raised his hand in farewell, and went back to his cart.

There were ten strong, healthy piglets by the time the sow had done. The eleventh, a poor, thin little reckling, did not live. Esther bit her lip. She knew the piglets ought to be suckling now. They needed nourishment, particularly that first fluid from the mother's teats, and they needed the warmth of their mother's body, but Esther wasn't sure even yet that the sow's proper maternal feelings had replaced the wild pain.

When the cleansings came away, Esther allowed the sow to eat these. Perhaps that would assuage her unnatural desire, Esther thought. She'd seen it done before and it had worked then. As she watched, the animal seemed to relax. The sow's eyes seemed calmer and she struggled to her feet and went to the trough. Esther smiled. The signs were good.

When the mother returned to the corner and lay down again near the tea-chest, Esther picked one piglet out and placed it to the sow's teats. With inborn sense, the tiny creature nuzzled at the teat to make the fluid come and then began to suck greedily. The sow's eyes closed in contentment and she lay still and quiet whilst Esther placed all the piglets one by one to feed. They'd be all right now. Once the mother had suckled her young, it was unlikely she'd turn on them.

Esther slipped out of the sty and latched the door taking one last look at the now placid scene.

Suddenly, she felt weary. She sank down on to a square of hay and leant back against the rough brick wall and closed her eyes. Already the sun was slanting deep shadows across the yard. She'd been most of the day with the sow without realizing how the time was passing, so intent had she been on saving the piglets. She had not eaten all day.

'All dead, are they?'

Her eyes snapped open to see Sam standing over her.

'Take a look,' she invited and watched as he moved to the door of the sty and looked in. He glanced back at her and then swiftly away again, back to the sow and her litter.

'One of her tits is a windy one,' Esther told him. 'But with only ten young, she's plenty to feed 'em all. One didn't live, but not – ' she added pointedly – 'because she ate it!'

Sam stood looking at the litter as if weighing the piglets she had saved for him against the milk she had lost. He made no comment but as he turned towards the house, over his shoulder he said gruffly, 'Like a bite o' summat, would you?'

Esther grinned as she levered up her tired limbs to follow him. It was the closest a man like Sam Brumby would ever come to a 'thank you'.

Four

*E*STHER spent another night in the hayloft, but the following morning, she made sure she was up very early. She had already brought the two milking cows to the byre by the time Sam appeared in the yard.

"Morning, Mester Brumby,' she called cheerfully. His only reply was a sniff and a deepening of his permanent scowl. But at least this morning he hadn't told her to 'clear off'. Instead he seemed to be leaving her to do the milking, for she saw neither Sam Brumby nor Matthew the rest of the morning.

After finishing the dairy work, she attacked the dust and grime of years in the kitchen. She found a long-handled broom and swept the ceiling and then she washed down the walls. As the dirt came off she found the plastered walls were painted a deep red.

Next she scrubbed the wooden table and one by one she cleaned the pans from the hooks on the wall. Then she washed the piles of plates, cups and saucers from the two shelves at one side of the kitchen. There were four huge hooks in the ceiling for hams, but only a storm lantern was hanging from one of them. Perhaps the half-grown gilt was being fattened for killing?

A torn lace curtain was the only covering on the kitchen window and Esther took it down carefully, spluttering as the dust tickled her nose and throat. She would wash and mend that later.

If I'm still here, she thought ruefully.

It was dinner time before she had finished this one room and there was still the huge black range to tackle. She surveyed the clean kitchen with satisfaction. The back scullery and the range would have to wait. Now she would try to find something to make Sam Brumby a midday meal.

She went out of the house and turned to the right. Adjoining the main house was a low building constructed in the same brick and roof tiles. The first door she opened was the wash-house. She sniffed the damp, mouldy air.

'Sam hasn't done much washing in 'ere lately,' she murmured, wrinkling her nose. I'll attend to that later, she promised herself, leaving the door open to let in the fresh air. Beyond the wash-house, on the corner, was the privy. Esther turned again to the right, round the corner of the building and stepped on to grass. To her left was a pond with a beautiful weeping willow tree straggling its graceful fronds in the water. Five green-headed ducks, wriggling their tails, waddled round the edge then flopped into the water. Hens wandered freely about the yard and the grass, scratching and pecking. At the far side of the pond the gander and his geese paraded up and down. The gander held his head proudly and pretended not to notice Esther.

She moved on beyond the end of the house and round to the front. She found herself in what must once have been a well-tended front garden and orchard, but now the weeds were trying to strangle the few surviving flowers. Fruit trees grew up out of the long, unkempt grass but to one side she found a small vegetable patch which showed signs of recent digging. She fetched a fork from one of the small sheds and dug up a spring cabbage and a few leeks. She even found a turnip that had been left in the ground.

Back in the kitchen she washed and sliced the vegetables and put them together with some of the cooked bacon into a clean cooking pot on the fire in the range. Soon the aroma of a kind of stew filled the kitchen. It was a warm, inviting smell which Esther guessed – and rather hoped – had not welcomed Sam Brumby for some years.

Esther was bending over the fire ladling stew into three bowls when Sam entered the house with Matthew behind him. Wordlessly, she placed one bowl on the table in front of the chair where Sam had sat the previous day. She placed another for Matthew and sat down before the third herself.

'By gum, this is good – a good cook as well as pretty!' Matthew grinned.

Esther hacked off a piece of bread for herself making no outward response to his compliment, though she felt a glow of pleasure.

Sam Brumby concentrated on his bowl; he neither spoke nor looked at either of the other two. Esther rose and poured each of them a mug of tea.

As they finished the meal, Matthew stood up. 'I've to go to Mester Willoughby's after dinner today. Shall you be wanting me tomorrow, Mester Brumby?'

Esther saw Sam glance quickly at her and then look away again. He sniffed. 'Aye,' was all he said.

Matthew grinned at Esther, picked up his cap and, whistling jauntily, left the house. Esther cleared away the dishes and carried them into the back scullery. She drew hot water from the tap in the range. As she poured it into the sink in the scullery, she felt Sam Brumby's presence in the doorway behind her and smelt the sweet-sour smell of tobacco smoke as he methodically packed his clay pipe and lit it.

'There's a room — ' he spoke in short bursts between each puff as he drew deeply on his pipe to get it fully alight — 'above 'ere.' He prodded his pipe stem towards the ceiling of the kitchen. 'You can get to it by a ladder in yon corner. It'll — be warmer — than the hayloft.'

He turned away without waiting for her to speak and went out of the back door.

Esther leant on her knuckles in the bowl of hot water and closed her eyes. Two tears of thankfulness plopped into the washing-up water.

The room above the kitchen was no more than an attic boxroom. When Esther climbed the narrow ladder from the corner of the kitchen and poked her head through the trap door, she was met by the musty smell of rotting apples. To one side, spread on newspaper, were apples from the previous autumn; maybe even the one before that, she thought, by the look of some of them. Several were aged to a brown pulp and covered with a thick blanket of dust.

The small, oblong room with a sloping ceiling was

33

littered with bits of broken furniture, a trunk of old clothes and the general clutter of a family who had lived in the same house for generations. In one of the corners, tied up with binding, was a rolled mattress.

Esther surveyed the chaos grimly but by nightfall when she lay down on the mattress, the room was clean and sweet-smelling.

The following morning, as soon as she and Sam had breakfasted and the latter was away out on the farm, Esther went into the back scullery. She sighed as she stood surveying the scene of neglect. It was the same in the wash-house. A mangle stood in the far corner festooned with cobwebs, and tubs and dolly pegs and washboards had been pushed into an untidy heap. On a shelf above stood four irons, a line of cobwebs linking one to another. In the corner opposite the door was the large brick copper with its wooden lid covering the deep bowl. There was evidence that Sam – or someone – had washed a shirt and a sheet which were hanging on a piece of rope strung between two hooks across the room. But in the copper lay a mound of mouldering, dirty clothes.

'Well, Mester Brumby, there's enough work to keep me here a while yet,' she murmured aloud and bent down to rake out the dead cinders from under the copper. Suddenly she felt a smart smack on her rump which was sticking immodestly in the air as she bent double to her task.

'Ouch!' she cried and, coming up suddenly, banged her head on the fire door of the copper. She turned and saw Matthew standing over her, grinning.

'Oh, it's you again, is it, *boy*? I might've known!' And she turned back to her chore.

'Aw, come on, Esther, 'ow about a little kiss for a feller in a morning?'

'I got better things to do wi' me time,' she snapped and raked vigorously at the ashes, sending up clouds of grey dust so that she coughed and spluttered as it prickled her throat and stung her eyes. She was forced to draw back and stand up.

Matthew only laughed. 'Serves you right for being so unfriendly.' But he pulled out a spotted kerchief from his pocket and wiped the tears from her eyes. 'Don't cry, sweet Esther,' he said mockingly. At his words she slapped his ministering hand away.

'Cry? Me? You'll never see me cry, Matthew Hilton, I'll promise you that!' They gazed into each other's eyes, hers intense with anger, his fascinated by her loveliness.

'You've got beautiful eyes, Esther. Green, they are. I ain't never seen such lovely eyes . . .' Now the playful, teasing tone was gone from his voice and with surprisingly gentle fingers, he touched her cheek. For once Esther was startled into silence.

The moment was broken by a clatter in the yard. Swiftly Matthew turned away and shot out of the door. 'God, he's back,' he muttered as he went, and Esther was left staring after him with smut on her face and grime on her hands.

An hour later she had a fire glowing white hot under the copper and was staggering to and from the water-butt at the end of the house with heavy buckets to fill it. Each

35

time she climbed on to a stool and tippled the cold water into the huge bowl. Satisfied at last that she had enough, she covered it with the wooden lid and, leaving the water to heat up, she came out into the yard. She glanced at the sun and reckoned it must be nearly midday. The rumblings in her own stomach told her so. There was no sign of Sam Brumby or of Matthew but she prepared a simple meal of bacon and bread and left it set on the table. Then wiping her hands down her skirt, she took a deep breath and opened the door leading from the kitchen into the house beyond.

It led into an ordinary living room with an armchair set on either side of the fireplace and peg rugs on the floor. A table covered with a green plush cloth stood in the centre with four straight-backed dining chairs set around it. In the middle of the table stood a blue and white pot holding an aspidistra, long since dead, its withered leaves rotting and filling the room with a pungent mustiness. The window was covered by yellowing lace curtains which were falling into holes and two huge blue velvet curtains, lined with dust, hung from a wooden pole across the top. The wallpaper had once had a pretty green pattern but now it was faded and dirty. Around the room were several pictures – a large one depicting Jesus in the Temple, with smaller landscape paintings around it. On the far wall at the side of the window was a photograph, brown and faded, of a stern-looking woman, her black dress buttoned to the neck, her dark hair parted in the centre and drawn back severely behind her head.

In the corner, diagonally opposite where Esther had

entered, was another door leading further into the house. She moved slowly past the table, letting her fingers feel the soft fabric of the tablecloth, but it was sticky with dust. She opened the door and stepped into a small hallway. To her left was the front door which she knew would lead out into the garden and orchard and to her right the stairs climbed steeply to the floor above. Opposite was another door leading to what she presumed on entering to be the 'best parlour'.

The huge fireplace was ornate and bordered by a brass fender, sadly dull. Dusty velvet festooned the mantelpiece and to one side stood an embroidered fire-screen. In one corner was an organ and in front of the fireplace were chairs, a work-box and a footstool. A tall grandfather clock stood in one corner, its hands set permanently at ten to two. On a round table in front of the window lay a huge family Bible and as Esther glanced round the room it seemed that every surface was cluttered with ornaments and pictures.

She was quite impressed by the size of the farmhouse; to have a living room *and* a best parlour was richness indeed. And yet, Esther felt a sadness sweep over her. It was obvious that this house had once been inhabited by a loving family. Poor Sam, she thought, these neglected rooms echoed his loneliness.

For some reason she could not quite explain, she found herself tiptoeing up the stairs and quietly lifting the latch of a door to her left at the top of the stairs. It was Sam Brumby's bedroom. Her heart pounded in her chest with nervousness. It was one thing to arrive at the farm and worm her way into a job and a place in a dusty attic;

it was quite another to prowl about Sam Brumby's home and go into his bedroom to search for his personal washing. Even Esther, for all her boldness, felt this might be going just a little too far.

The room was surprisingly tidy, though dusty. Sam's Sunday best suit stood on a hanger in the corner, and two faded photographs in silver frames stood on the chest of drawers. Esther bent closer. One was of a man and woman; the woman seated, stiff and straight-backed, her face stern and serious. It was the same face that stared out of the larger picture hanging in the living room. The man, his hand on the back of her chair, had the likeness of Sam about him. Yet it was not Sam. In the other photograph was a solemn little boy, his arm protectively round a smaller girl with a sweet face surrounded by a mass of dark curls.

Esther straightened up and went to the bed. The covers were pulled straight, though the patchwork quilt needed washing. She pulled back the top coverlet and saw that there were no sheets on the bed, only a rough blanket that smelled a little sour. There was no pillow-case on the rough ticking of the pillow either. Her fingers hesitated over a heavy oak chest standing at the foot of the bed. She had no wish to pry into Sam's belongings, but if she were to care for him properly she needed to find fresh bedlinen. Taking a deep breath, she lifted the lid. Inside were sheets and pillow-cases, yellow with age, but neatly folded. She pulled out two of each and bundled them under her arm. The lid dropped with a dull thud and as she was going out of the room she noticed a shirt on the floor behind the door. She scooped that up too. At that moment she heard the back door bang and she scuttled down the stairs without stopping to look at the other upstairs rooms.

Sam was in the kitchen. 'Now what are ya up to, wench?' His words followed her as she rushed past him out to the wash-house.

'Weshing, mester,' she called back over her shoulder. 'Just a bit o' weshing.'

When the sheets, pillow-cases and shirt were bubbling in the copper, Esther went into the barn to search for a length of line to string between two trees in the garden at the front of the house. A good blow in the fresh air was what all these clothes and the linen needed. She glanced down at the coarse skirt and dirty pinafore she was wearing. She wished she could wash her own clothes, but she had nothing to change into and with that cheeky Matthew about, she dare not risk it.

She was possing the clothes in the rinsing tub when he appeared again, startling her as she caught sight of him standing silently in the doorway. She dropped the posser suddenly and cold water splashed her face.

'Oh – ya made me jump!' she said with annoyance. 'What ya doing here? Shouldn't ya be at work?' Sweat plastered strands of hair to her forehead. Her cheeks were red with exertion.

'I've come back to see you.' Matthew grinned and took a step nearer.

She raised her hands, palms outward, as if to fend him off. 'No, there'll be trouble – I dun't want to lose this job. I've come a long way and there's nowhere for me

to go back to, so – so don't spoil it for me, please?'
she pleaded.

Teasing, he said, 'It'll cost you, seeing as 'ow you've
taken it from under Beth's nose,' and without giving her
a chance to argue, he walked away across the yard, a new
arrogance in his stride. He turned once, shouted, 'I'll see
you later,' gave her a saucy wink and a wave and then he
was gone.

Esther felt herself hot all over and knew it was not the
steaming water and the activity of wash-day that had
caused it.

Five

HE was waiting in the yard when she finally finished in the wash-house that evening.

'What are you doin' here? You haven't finished milking, have ya?'

'Haven't started,' he replied boldly, and stood before her to bar her way back into the house.

Esther gasped at his audacity and her green eyes glittered. 'You'll have Mester Brumby after you. It should've been done hours ago!'

'I can handle Sam Brumby.'

Esther was at once sceptical. 'Now you're bragging, Master Matthew.'

'Well now,' he said softly, his eyes roaming over her face. 'At least you've stopped calling me "boy".'

She could feel his breath warm upon her cheek as he added, 'I thought mebbe we could take a little walk. I could show you around, like. I could show you where it's safe to walk on the beach – and where it's dangerous.'

'And how do I know you're not the biggest danger out there?'

Matthew threw back his head and laughed. 'You don't,' he said. 'You really don't know.'

Esther made no attempt to rebuff him further. She felt like taking a walk and she was curious to find out more about this place. Since the morning she had arrived at

Fleethaven Point she had not left Brumbys' Farm. But now Sam was some distance away in the field which lay adjacent to the neighbouring farmer's – Top End, he called it. He would not return until after dark. She could spare half an hour . . .

She fell into step beside Matthew. Whistling through his teeth, he swaggered jauntily across the lane and led her beneath the trees growing on the dunes. They climbed to the highest point and paused to catch their breath whilst Esther looked about her, soaking up the feel of the land. Already, she felt an affinity with this place. She shaded her eyes against the red glow of the evening sun and let her gaze travel round, trying to gauge the extent of Sam's holding.

Brumbys' Farm lay with its front windows facing the flat land that stretched westward. About a mile inland were the tall chimneys of a large house surrounded by trees.

'What's that place?' she asked Matthew. He came and stood close behind her placing his hands lightly on her shoulders and putting his cheek against her hair.

Following the line of her pointing finger he said, 'That's the Grange where Squire Marshall lives. He owns most of the land around here.'

'And over there – those buildings?' Esther was pointing to the north-west now.

'That's Tom Willoughby's place – Rookery Farm. Lives there with his wife and her sister. He's a grand chap – you'll like him.'

To the south-west she could see another farm but it

was further away – a good two miles at least. 'That's Souters' Farm,' Matthew told her.

Directly below where they were standing was the lane running alongside the dunes leading from the town of Lynthorpe to Fleethaven Point.

'Come on,' Matthew said, grabbing her hand and pulling her down the other side of the dunes. 'I'll show you the sea.'

Esther found herself following him across squelchy marshland, jumping the creeks, wading through green spiky grass and skirting stagnant pools until they came to a lower line of sand dunes. Close by them a skylark rose into the air, hovered above its territory and then glided gently down trilling its song, plunging at the last moment towards the ground.

'These dunes are just forming,' Matthew was telling her as they climbed them. 'A few years back the sea used to come right up here. There you are . . .' As they reached the top, he waved his arm, triumphantly encompassing the view before them as if it were all his own handiwork. 'There's the sea.'

The breeze was cool, but Esther lifted her face and sniffed the salt air and listened to the gentle lap-lap of the waves.

They walked along the shore until they came to the place where the sea curved in to form the mouth of the Wash. Matthew led her along the dunes which ended in a promontory of land sticking out into the water. 'We call this the Spit,' he told her. 'The tide's high at the moment so the water comes right in on either side.'

Esther found herself clutching his arm, afraid of

slipping off the sandy bank and into the swirling water.

'It's what they call an intertidal marsh,' Matthew told her loftily, airing his knowledge. 'When the tide's out, all this – ' he waved his arm – 'is thick mud.'

Matthew let go of her hand and bent down at the water's edge, cupped his hands together and sluiced the cold sea water over his face and head. His black curly hair shone. He shook his head, the droplets of salt water flying everywhere. Then he grinned at her and bent to pick up a flat shell.

'Watch,' he said and then holding the shell between his thumb and forefinger, he skimmed it across the water, the shell bouncing three or four times before it sank into the waves.

'Here,' he said, bending to pick up another. 'You try.' He took her hand in his own, shaping her fingers around the shell. 'Now lean down slightly to one side and flick your wrist so that the flat side of the shell hits the water.'

Esther tried to do as he told her, but the shell merely plopped into the sea and disappeared.

'Look, I'll show you again. Like this . . .'

He made her practise until she could get the shell to skim the surface of the water a couple of times before sinking.

'There you are,' he said jubilantly, 'now you can play ducks and drakes as good as the rest of us. Come on, now I'll show you the Point where I live.'

They walked back along the Spit and retraced their steps across the marsh coming out into the lane once more, but nearer the Point than Brumbys' Farm. This line of dunes – formed many years before and now with

44

trees and bushes well established – curved and formed a solid bank over which the road had been forced to rise.

'We call this the Hump.' Matthew grinned. 'Poor old Will Benson always has a job getting his cart up here. Some days in winter, if it's slithery, he dun't make it and the women from the Point have to traipse across here to meet him when he blows his whistle.'

They stood together on the top of the bank and Esther let her gaze take in the view in front of her. Matthew pointed to a building only a few yards to the left below the rise of ground on which they were standing.

'That's the pub – the Seagull. That's where us fellers all get drunk on a Saturday night.'

'I can imagine!' Esther said drily, but Matthew merely grinned again and swung his pointing finger round slightly.

'And that's where I live, in them cottages.' A stretch of grass in front of the row of cottages sloped gently down towards the river bank. 'The Harrises live in the far end one with all their brood – seven kids there were at the last count,' Matthew went on.

Her mouth tightened. Same number as her aunt's large family. If Mrs Harris was anything like her Aunt Hannah, then Esther had no wish to meet her.

'I live in the next one,' Matthew continued. 'Then Beth Hanley lives next door to that with her dad. He's the coastguard and has a look-out station built on the East Dunes. Last cottage this end nearest to us is empty at the moment.'

Esther's glance travelled around until her gaze rested upon the twisting river to their right.

45

'Whatever's that?' she asked. A boat – a large, black hulk – was set up out of the water close to the river bank on poles and wooden sleepers.

'What's what? Oh, that boat, you mean? That's where Robert Eland lives.'

'Lives? Somebody actually lives in a boat? But it's sort of half on the land and half in the river!'

Matthew laughed then wrinkled his forehead. 'I suppose I've never thought about it before. I've lived here all me life and Robert's parents lived in it before him, so,' he shrugged his shoulders, 'I never thought about it bein' odd.'

'What does he do?'

'Who, Robert Eland?'

Esther nodded.

'He's the lifeboat coxswain. The lifeboat's moored about a mile up the road nearer to the town. All the men that live round are in the crew – Mester Harris, Percy Holmes from the pub, and then two or three from the town. Me too, I'm a launcher at the moment, but one day I'll be in the crew.'

'Is there much need for a lifeboat here?'

He looked at her incredulously. 'Don't you know nothing about the sea?'

Esther shook her head. 'I've come from inland.'

'Ah, that explains it, then. This Point is right on the edge of the Wash and the North Sea and you get a lot of boats coming into the Wash to the ports, an' there's lots of sandbanks and tricky currents, and . . .' He shrugged, finding it difficult to explain to someone what he had known from childhood.

'Is that all they do then? Just man the lifeboat?'

'Course not!' Matthew said scornfully. 'They work on the land – for Squire Marshall, mostly. I told you, he owns nearly all the land hereabouts. And Robert Eland, he helps Dan Hanley with coastguard duties, an' all.'

Esther listened, learning more about the people who lived so close to the sea that it was part of their lives just as much as the land. Sea and land, their life was ordered by the two. To a country girl the sea was a mystery, yet it held a fearsome fascination.

'I'll have to be going,' Matthew said, as the dusk deepened around them, 'else I'll have old Sam after me.'

Before she could stop him, he had planted a kiss on her cheek and had dodged out of the range of her hand, raised at once to deal him a stinging slap. As he broke into a run down the slope of the Hump and back along the lane towards Brumbys' Farm, she could hear him chuckling.

Her swift anger at his audacity softened and she found herself smiling. He was just a cheeky lad with an eye for a pretty girl, she told herself sternly, but the feel of his lips on her cheek still tingled and the thought that he found her pretty warmed her.

She took a last look around from her vantage point, then stretched her arms above her head and breathed deeply in the soft air. What a beautiful, *beautiful* place! Such a feeling of space and freedom. Such stillness and silence – and peace!

Such a peace as she had never known before in her young life.

She gave a final sigh of contentment and let her arms

fall to her sides. She ran lightly down the slope towards the farm.

Home to Brumbys' Farm.

Esther had arrived on the last day in April and by the end of May she sensed that Sam was watching for the bloom to appear on his crop of grass. For a small farmer, a good hay harvest together with the corn harvest and root crops which came later meant feed for his stock through the winter.

On the day hay-making began, Esther followed Sam out to the meadow. The morning was bright and clear. Later they would swelter under a hot sun in a clear blue sky.

In one hand Sam carried his scythe and in a holder attached to the back of his leather belt was a honer for sharpening the long, curving blade.

'You bring the forks and rakes out to the field, wench.'

Esther was amazed at the number of workers who arrived. Men, women and even children, from the neighbouring farms and from the cottages at the Point, came to help Sam Brumby bring in his hay. Then in turn Sam, Esther and Matthew would go to work on the other farms. Esther worked alongside the women and children from dawn to dusk and beyond, shaking and spreading the cut grass out to dry during the day and then just before dusk raking it into long rows down the field so as to collect less dampness through the night.

Esther watched Sam at work as he scythed the long grass with easy rhythmic sweeps, moving steadily down the field. The grass seed flew everywhere; it buried itself in Esther's hair and even blocked her nose and made her throat dry and husky.

The next day they spread the cut grass out and collected it again at dusk, until the whole field was cut. Then, after the grass had lain in the field for a few days to dry, it was collected into haycocks.

When all Sam's meadows had been cut into neat rows of haycocks, which were then left to dry in the wind for a while, the time came for loading the hay on to the wagon to be taken to the farmyard. Matthew stood on top of the growing load on the wagon, spreading the grass evenly and expertly as it was thrown up to him on the ends of their long pitchforks by three men below. Under the hot sun Matthew had stripped to the waist, the black hairs on his chest and back glistening with the sweat of his hard work. But he still found time and energy to flirt with the women – young or old, it didn't seem to matter to Matthew Hilton.

Esther, matching his teasing tone, shaded her eyes as she looked up at him. 'Fancy ya'sen up there, don't ya?'

'I'd rather *you* fancied me, lovely Esther.' He grinned down at her, but she noticed that he never paused in the rhythmic swinging of his hay fork, deftly catching the hay as it was swung up to him. For the first time since she had met him, Esther found herself admiring his skill.

Esther herself blossomed under the workload that harvest time imposed and now she felt Sam had really accepted her.

From now on this was her home, this was her land.

When the other helpers left the farm in the evening, Esther went into Sam's kitchen to bake and cook for the next day. Her cheeks were flushed with the heat from the range, her hair straggling in wet wisps around her forehead. Swaying with weariness, late at night she climbed the ladder to her little room.

But the morning found her the first out to bring in the cows and have the milking done before the visiting workers arrived. Mid-morning she would leave the fields and hurry back to the farmhouse to bring out baskets laden with freshly baked meat pies and fruit pasties to the workers in the fields.

All this she did without Sam's instruction, maybe even without his approval.

'Eh, we ain't been fed like this on Brumbys' Farm afore,' one of the workers told her, biting into a juicy fruit pasty. 'This is a rare treat an' no mistake!'

Not a word of praise to her ever passed Sam's lips, but there began a subtle change in his attitude towards her. One morning she overheard him talking to the carrier again.

'She's a way with her, Will,' Sam was saying in one of his rare talkative moods to the man who was perhaps the nearest the reclusive, taciturn farmer had to a friend. 'She laughs and jokes with all the visiting workers, and yet when she wants 'em to do summat, well . . .' Sam paused, lifting his cap and running the back of his hand across the red, sweating mark the band of his cap left on his forehead. 'Well, I don't rightly know 'ow she does it, but she gets t'work out on 'em, and no mistake.'

Will grinned. 'Bit of her aunt in there somewhere, I'll warrant, but Esther wouldn't thank me for saying so. But she's a nicer way wi' her than that old shrew.'

50

Sam Brumby sniffed and settled his cap back on his head. Squinting up at Will he said slyly, 'Mebbe she teks more after her dad, then?'

'Aye, mebbe so, mebbe so.'

And Will's grin broadened.

Six

SAM Brumby's hay was gathered and stacked in the farmyard. Now it was time for Sam, Esther and Matthew to go to the other farms and offer their help in return, but at least this time Esther did not have to provide the food for the workers. This was the task of the womenfolk on the farms where they went to work.

At Tom Willoughby's farm, Esther was surprised to see Beth coming out to the field carrying baskets laden with food.

'What's she doin' here?' Esther demanded of Ma Harris.

Ma Harris lived in the end cottage at Fleethaven Point. She had a horde of children, but there, to Esther's relief, all resemblance to her Aunt Hannah ended. Ma Harris was shorter than Esther and her plump little body reminded Esther of a cottage loaf on legs. Her grey hair was drawn back into a bun and covered by a white frilled bonnet which she always wore. Esther wondered if she even took it off to go to bed. Ma Harris was a motherly woman, with a ready laugh, a kindly word, and although she often delivered a stinging slap if one of her brood misbehaved, it was a swift chastisement made with rough affection and soon forgotten by both child and mother.

'Who, lass?' Ma asked in response to Esther's question. 'Beth Hanley.'

Ma Harris looked across the field. 'She's got a job as dairymaid for the Willoughbys. Posh, ain't she, in her white apron and cap? Gone up in the world, 'as our Beth,' Ma Harris laughed, opening her mouth to reveal almost toothless gums. She turned back to Esther. 'You ought to wear a bonnet, lass, in this sun.'

Esther grinned at the older woman. 'To protect my milky white skin, you mean, Mrs Harris?'

Ma Harris's laugh cackled out across the field at Esther's sarcasm against herself. Of all the women and young girls in the field, only Esther wore no protection of any kind on her head against the heat of the day. Pride would not let her admit that she did not possess a bonnet. Ma Harris, however, was a wise woman and good-hearted and, within her means, as generous as it was possible to be. The following day, she brought one of her old bonnets and made Esther stand meekly whilst she tied it on the girl's head. ''Twill keep all that grass seed out o' your lovely hair, lass. By, I ain't seen prettier hair than yours. Auburn streaks, it's got, when the sun shines on it.'

Esther thanked her both for the bonnet and the unaccustomed compliment. Working the rest of the day at Ma Harris's side, listening to her prattle and smiling as the woman marshalled her children whilst never pausing in her own work, Esther basked in the warmth of her motherly friendliness.

*

The hay harvest was in and there would be a few weeks' respite before a similar process would begin again with the corn harvest.

Her litter of piglets, as Esther thought of them, had been weaned at eight weeks old and sent to market. One morning after feeding Curly and the young gilt, she went in search of Sam.

'Mester?'

His answer was a sniff.

'I reckon Curly is ready for the boar.'

'Eh?' He looked up, startled. ''Ow does a wench like you know about such things?'

Esther laughed. ''Tis nature, ain't it?'

Sam sniffed again, dropped his hedge knife and walked back with her to the sty to take a look for himself.

Esther giggled as she walked along beside him, and added, 'The chap who used to bring the boar to me aunt's always used to ask, "Is the sow ready, is she flushed – just like a strawberry – at the back?"'

Sam stopped and looked at her. Then a slow smile spread across his shrunken mouth and a chuckle from somewhere deep within forced its way out. 'Eh, lass,' he shook his head. 'You'll be the death o' me.'

Esther grinned back at him.

Sam reached the sty, opened the door and went inside, whilst Esther watched from the doorway. He stood behind the pig and leant his hands on her haunches. The sow blinked but did not move away. 'Aye, lass, I reckon you're right.' Sam stood a moment looking down at the huge sow with her wiry, curling coat. 'Well, old girl,' he said as if to the pig, but at his next words Esther knew he intended her to hear. 'I reckon this wench here has saved your bacon. If ya'd killed yar litter again this year, you were fer me knife come autumn.'

Sam looked directly up at Esther and laughed wheezily again. 'Go up to Tom Willoughby's and ask him to bring his boar as soon as he can. Tell him she's as flushed as a strawberry. He'll like that, will Tom.'

Tom Willoughby did like it. He leant back and roared with laughter, his great belly wobbling, the grey whiskers of his long sideburns quivering, his fat cheeks growing redder by the second. He was a huge man, tall and broad and obviously jovial. 'So it's true what I've heard about you, lass?'

'That depends on what ya've heard, mester.' She stood before him, smiling at his infectious laughter.

He drew a large red and white spotted kerchief from his pocket and mopped his brow. 'Will Benson told us that Sam had got a rare lass working for him now. A rare lass, 'ee said. I reckon 'ee's right.'

Esther's smile broadened but she made no comment. She expected that every farm for miles around on Will's route would know she had come to live and work at Brumbys' Farm.

'Aye, lass, tell Sam I'll be over with the boar tomorrow.'

Soon the corn harvest was upon them. The work for Sam was not quite as hard for he did not do the cutting but allowed Tom Willoughby to send his new reaper.

'Newfangled thing,' Esther heard Sam mutter as he

watched the sails of the reaper crossing the field pulled by three heavy horses. "Spect me corn'll be ruined.'

Sam still worked in the field, tying the sheaves and stooking, all the time keeping a truculent eye upon the machine swallowing up his harvest and spewing it out behind. The stooks stood in the fields for a few weeks to dry in the wind that always seemed to blow across this flat land and when the time came for them to be moved, the wagon was loaded so high at times that Esther held her breath thinking a wheel would crack and it would surely tipple over. But when Sam walked behind the last load to leave the field carrying the last sheaf and placed it on top of the final stack, he knew he had never had a better harvest.

The cry went up amongst the workers, 'Harvest home, harvest home.' Then the gleaners were allowed into the fields and one of the first was Ma Harris, wearing a bag apron over her long skirt in readiness. With her tribe to feed, Ma Harris was thankful that the old traditions still survived. She could usually collect enough corn from all the nearby farms for her family's needs through the winter.

When harvest was finally over, Esther noticed that Sam's walking was more painful, that his back was a little more bent and the joints of his fingers were gnarled with rheumatism. He was tired, yet not too tired to give thanks for a good harvest.

One Sunday morning in September, Sam Brumby bade Esther put on her best frock and be ready in the yard in half an hour.

Esther blinked and looked down at the coarse, well-worn skirt in dismay and then back at Sam. Didn't he realize these were all the clothes she had? Didn't he know that when she washed them each week and hung them on the clothes horse so close to the warm range over night that they almost scorched, it was because they had to be dry for the following morning? Esther wrinkled her forehead and smiled at her own foolishness. Of course he didn't know, for she was careful to strip off and take her bath in the tin bath in front of the kitchen range and wash her clothes long after Sam had climbed the stairs.

'I ain't no more clothes, mester,' she said flatly.

'Huh,' was Sam's only comment, but his glance at her, up and down, spoke volumes.

'You'll have to do as you are then, wench. I'll be waiting in the yard – half an hour,' was all Sam would say. Self-consciously and wondering what this was all about, Esther strip-washed in the back scullery, intrigued to hear the boards above her head creaking as Sam moved about upstairs. In her own small attic boxroom, Esther brushed her hair and shook out her only shawl and put it about her shoulders. Then she climbed down the ladder and opened the back door. She stopped. Her mouth fell open with surprise and then widened into a grin.

Sam Brumby was a resplendent figure in a black suit, a gold watch-chain looped across his waistcoat. He had shaved and his thin white hair was plastered down under a black trilby hat. He was standing stiffly by the gate staring down the long lane leading towards the town, looking as if he hardly dared to move in his starched white collar. Her handiwork, Esther thought, with a stab of pride. It took a moment for her to control her laughter, but knowing that at any moment Sam might turn and see her, Esther cleared her throat and strode purposefully across the yard, her boots scrunching on the cinders.

Sam pulled out the gold Hunter watch from his pocket and looked at it, then giving a sniff he set off along the road towards the town. Esther fell into step beside him, but where exactly they were going, she had no idea for not a word passed between them.

They had walked about a mile when behind them came the rattle of the wheels of a pony and trap. Stepping on to the grass verge to let it pass, Esther looked up to see Matthew grinning down at her. Beth, in her Sunday best bonnet and shawl, was sitting beside him.

As they drew level, Matthew slowed the trap. 'Want a lift, Mester Brumby? 'Tis a long way to the church.'

Sam's frown deepened. 'Thank 'ee – no. Ah can still walk two miles, young feller!'

Above Sam's head, Matthew winked at Esther. ''Spect you'd like to ride in style, Esther?'

Esther grinned back at him but, mindful of Sam's feelings, she answered pertly, 'Thank you kindly, sir, but I'll walk with Mester Brumby.'

As Matthew flicked the reins and urged the pony forward, Beth looked back over her shoulder at Esther, a smug expression on her face. With an obvious gesture, she tucked her hand possessively through Matthew's arm.

When they reached the outskirts of the town, Esther looked about her. She had come this way the day she had arrived, but in the early morning light the houses had been only shadowy shapes. Now, in the sunshine of a

September morning, there was a brightness about the neat houses and well-kept gardens.

'By, them's posh places, mester,' Esther broke the silence. Twisting and turning as she walked she pointed excitedly to right and left. 'Look at that 'un – it's a mansion!'

Esther noticed a brass plate fixed to the gatepost. Laboriously she spelt out the name. 'Doctor Blair.'

Sam neither answered nor turned his head. Esther heard his sniff that indicated disapproval. Evidently Sam Brumby had no time for the town-dwellers.

They walked through the town centre, down the main street with little shops huddled together and living quarters above, and on almost out of the town to a small church. Sam walked up the flagged path, gravestones standing sentinel on either side, to the low porch. Esther followed.

Beth was sitting in a pew half-way down the left hand side of the church, her dark head bowed, her eyes closed piously in prayer. On her left against the wall sat Matthew, but on her right was a thickset man with dark hair. His mouth was completely hidden by a full beard so it was impossible to see if he ever smiled. It was unlikely that he did, for there was no laughter in his eyes beneath heavy, dark eyebrows. The visible part of his face was weather-beaten and lined, giving his forehead the impression of a permanent frown. Esther had seen this man before – he had been one of the visiting harvest workers – but she had never learnt his name.

As if feeling her gaze upon him, the man turned his head slightly and looked straight into Esther's eyes.

The frown seemed to deepen.

Wordlessly, Sam motioned Esther to precede him into a pew on the opposite side of the aisle to where Matthew, Beth and the stranger were sitting. Beth seemed not to have noticed their arrival, or was deliberately ignoring them.

The service began and Esther watched and listened. The altar steps overflowed with the offerings from the congregation of fruit and vegetables, flowers and even one or two small wheat-sheaves and corn dollies. The atmosphere was warm and friendly as if the air of thanksgiving pervaded the congregation. She knelt beside Sam and watched covertly as he turned the pages of his prayer book. Esther was no great reader, yet she had learned enough to be able to find the same page in the book as Sam had, and then she proceeded to make a pretence at following the service, moving her lips and miming the prayers, deliberately inaudible.

Esther could not remember having been in a church before. Her Aunt Hannah had been a staunch Methodist and Chapel was the only form of worship with which Esther was familiar.

The service came to an end and Esther stood behind Sam whilst the gentry from the front pews walked down the aisle and out of the church. There was a portly gentleman with whiskery grey sideburns and red-veined cheeks that spoke of too much indulgence of the port. He nodded and smiled to each side as he strutted down the aisle. Esther watched as the men touched their foreheads in a deferential salute, whilst the women smiled self-consciously and nodded. One or two even bobbed at the knee. In contrast to the gentleman's jolly manner, the woman who walked at his side with her hand in the crook of his arm was a thin, miserable-looking creature. True, she acknowledged the greetings of the congregation with a quick, darting look and the briefest of nods, and then her eyes were downcast to the floor as if she almost feared to meet anyone's gaze directly. She looked nervous and ill-at-ease, though why Esther could not imagine, for it seemed her husband was held in high esteem.

Behind them came Tom Willoughby with two ladies whose skirts rustled and swished. One was very large, tall and stately. She sailed along, her breadth filling the width of the aisle. Her face was bloated and the folds of fat beneath her chin wobbled as she moved. The woman with her was thin, with steel-rimmed spectacles perched on her hooked nose. A receding chin and protruding upper teeth accentuated her thinness.

As he drew level with the pew where Sam Brumby and Esther were still standing waiting to leave, Tom Willoughby greeted them. 'How do, Sam? And you, lass?'

Sam nodded briefly and Esther smiled up at the huge figure of Tom Willoughby, causing the two women with him to look her up and down. Their heads bobbed together as they whispered to one another and then they stared at her again. Boldly, Esther returned their scrutiny. As she passed close to Esther, the thin woman pointedly picked up her skirt and pulled it towards herself as if to avoid the merest contact with Esther, even though Sam stood between them.

Sam, Esther noticed, spoke to no one and acknowledged only very few people – the portly gentleman and his wife, Tom Willoughby and the vicar as they left the church – and then only with a sharp nod, a swift pecking movement. All the rest of the congregation Sam deliberately ignored, even those from the Point who were, after all, his nearest neighbours.

As Esther followed Sam from the church the vicar was standing outside the porch shaking hands and exchanging pleasantries with each member of his congregation.

'Ah, Mr Brumby.' He clasped Sam's hand warmly. 'It's good to see you, good to see you.'

'Parson,' Sam murmured.

'And is this the young lady I've been hearing so much about who's come to help you on the farm? Glad to meet you, my dear, glad to meet you.'

Esther smiled broadly at the vicar, her tanned face creasing with smiles, her green eyes twinkling. 'Thank you, sir.'

'Now, come again, my dear, come again. Mr Brumby, you bring this young lady to church again.'

Sam was half-way down the path and made no indication of having heard the vicar. Behind her Esther heard a muffled snort of indignation and a whispered comment between the large woman and her skinny companion. 'Young lady, indeed!' whispered one.

'Fancy,' came the twittering reply. 'Who would have thought it of Sam Brumby?'

Esther whirled around, a stinging reply on her lips, but the retort died as behind the two gossiping women she saw Beth Hanley, her hand on the bearded man's arm.

Esther's gaze met Beth's and she saw the triumph written in the girl's eyes. Esther turned away, sickened by the implications of the two women and Beth's glorying in their insults of her. Still in front of the vicar, Esther turned back to him and said politely, but loud enough for those about her to hear distinctly, 'I'll certainly come back to your church, when your congregation show a little more Christian charity. Good morning.' Ignoring the appalled gasps behind her, she marched down the path after Sam.

It soon became apparent to Esther that Sam Brumby was no regular churchgoer and he had what some might think was a peculiar attitude towards the Being he always referred to as 'The Almighty'. He did not believe in the prayer of supplication; he could never bring himself to pray for things to be given to him. On the contrary his sole purpose in his rare attendances at church was to give thanks. At harvest – good or bad – he would attend the Harvest Service. At Christmas he would celebrate with the Church the birthday of the Son of the Almighty, and at Easter he would give thanks for Christ's sacrifice. But never, ever, would he ask for anything for himself. His lips hardly moved during prayer except to say such words as, 'Thanks be to God'.

Esther was not to attend church again until Midnight Mass on Christmas Eve, but her first visit was not soon forgotten. The very next day when she saw Matthew, she demanded, 'Who was the man sitting on the other side of your girl?'

'Beth's not my girl,' came his swift reply.

'She seems to think so.'

'Well, she ain't,' he muttered and then he grinned. 'You jealous?'

Esther tossed her curls. 'I can do better for mesen than the likes of you, Matthew Hilton.'

'Oh, Miss High an' Mighty, chance'd be a fine thing . . .'

'I asked you who that feller was.'

'Well, you've no chance there, I can tell you. He's eyes for no one but Beth, even though he's years older.'

Esther blinked at Matthew. 'Really? But who *is* he? I thought he were her father.'

'No – Beth's dad never sets foot in a church – not as long as I've known him, an' that's all me life. No – the feller you mean is Robert Eland.'

'Oh, yes,' she said, remembering suddenly what Matthew had told her previously, 'he lives in that boat stuck up on the river bank, dun't he?'

Matthew nodded. 'He's a seaman at heart and dun't really want to live on the land.' He grinned. 'I reckon he tries to get as near to living at sea as he can.'

'Who was the portly gent and the thin woman with him?'

'That's Squire Marshall. He lives at the Grange.'

Esther nodded. She hadn't been required to help out at harvest on the squire's farm. He would employ enough of his own workers, she supposed.

There was silence between them, then Matthew asked, 'Dun't you want to know who everyone else was in church? How about the two women who . . . ?'

'I dun't wish to know who *they* were, thank you very much!' Esther replied.

'The fat one's Martha Willoughby and the thin one's her sister, Flo.'

Rather than display any interest in them, she refused to listen to Matthew any more, picked up two heavy buckets of milk and disappeared into the pantry.

There were others too who would not forget Esther's first visit to the church and two in particular who had no wish to see her there again.

Three days after that first Sunday, a pony and trap bowled along the lane from Rookery Farm, turning sharp right at the junction with the lane running alongside the sand dunes and came to a stop outside Brumbys' Farm. Hearing the rattle of wheels and the horse's hooves, Sam came out from the barn and Esther peeped out of Curly's pigsty, which she was cleaning out.

The two ladies from the church were climbing gingerly down from their trap and coming towards Sam, marching side by side as if confronting the enemy.

'Sam Brumby — Flo and I would like a word with you, if you please,' began Martha Willoughby, taking the lead.

Esther watched the scowl on Sam's face deepen but he said nothing.

'It's about that young girl you have — er — living with you,' put in Miss Flo, but she took care to stand slightly behind her more formidable sister.

'You see, Sam,' continued Mrs Willoughby, 'Flo and I — we don't consider it seemly for a young girl — and one

65

of doubtful character and morals – to be living out here *alone* with you. I mean – did you know what she said to Tom about – about . . .' The woman wafted her hand before her face as if it ill became her to speak of such an indelicate matter. '. . . the boar?'

Flo nodded in dutiful agreement. 'It's all over the town, Sam, just think.'

Esther had heard enough. She came out of the sty and slammed the door behind her. Two pairs of startled eyes turned towards her as she crossed the yard, her green gaze spitting fire, her determined chin thrust forward, the pitchfork she still held in her hands pointing aggressively towards them like a fixed bayonet. Miss Flo gave a terrified shriek and clung to her sister.

Sam put up his hand warningly, as if to fend her off. 'Easy, wench,' he murmured. 'They're naught but a couple of busybodies . . .'

'I'll not be called such names, mester. Not by them nor anyone else. I may be poor, an' I may look like a tramp, but I *ain't* one, an' no one has the right to . . .' Esther jabbed the fork towards them, and Miss Flo began to wail and even the bolder Mrs Willoughby took hold of her sister and stepped backwards. Esther thrust the pitchfork towards them again, so that the two women jerked away. Mrs Willoughby stumbled and fell heavily, dragging her sister down with her.

'I *work* for Mr Brumby on the farm and nothing else. You hear me, missus, *nothing* else.'

She emphasized her statement by prodding the fork ever nearer to the two quivering women on the ground. For a long moment she glared down at them and then, as if satisfied, she lifted the fork away and stood back a pace. The two women, seizing their chance, scrambled up, clinging to each other. Tripping over their long skirts, they scuttled towards the trap. As they went, Esther's anger was turned to laughter. Planted neatly on Martha Willoughby's fat bottom was the perfect brown circle of a cow-pat.

Esther heard Sam's wheezing and she looked sideways at him. He was bending slightly forward, his hands resting on his knees, his head tilted up to watch the two women and laughing until the tears came into his eyes.

'Aye, wench,' he spluttered, 'you'll be the death o' me!'

Seven

'YOU coming to the Supper tonight, Esther?' Matthew was grinning at her over the half-door of the cowshed.

Without pausing in her milking, her voice muffled against the beast's stomach, Esther asked, 'Supper? What Supper?'

'Harvest Supper, of course. Ain't Sam told you about it?'

'No.'

'It's at the Grange. Squire holds a Harvest Supper for all the folks around here. Anyone can go – an' they do. It's a grand night. Aw, do come, Esther. Come with me, if you're frit to go on your own.'

She finished milking Clover and stood up, giving the cow a last gentle pat on her rump. 'Good girl, there now, there's a good girl. We'll have to stop milking you soon, shan't we? Ya'll be calving in a few weeks.'

The cow swished her tail but her kicking feet stayed still at Esther's pacifying tone.

Now Esther faced Matthew. 'I ain't frit to go nowhere on me own, Matthew Hilton.'

'Aw, don't take the huff, Esther. I only meant – well – I meant I'd like you to come with me. There's still a lot of people round here you don't know an' . . .'

'Aye, and some as I'd rather not know an' all, judging

by them two old biddies in church last week,' she countered.

Matthew grinned. 'I 'eard about 'em coming here. But you sent 'em packing by all accounts.'

Esther smiled at the memory and found Matthew staring at her.

'My, but you're bonny when you smile,' he said softly and his eyes darkened with desire as he stepped towards her.

'Oh, go on with you.' She pushed him away from her, laughing as she added, 'I'll think about the Harvest Supper. Now go away, I've work to do.'

Grinning, Matthew went.

'Mester,' she ventured to Sam at tea time. 'What's this Harvest Supper Matthew's been on about? Do you go?'

Sam sniffed. 'I s'pose I'll have to. I don't reckon much to it, but I don't like to snub the squire. Why d'you ask? You going?'

She shrugged and looked down at her rough work-worn skirt and faded blouse. 'I – I dunno.'

Sam sniffed again. There was a long silence between them. He got up from the table and settled himself in his straight-backed Windsor chair by the range. He reached for his clay pipe on the mantelpiece and began to pack it slowly. Without looking at her, he said, haltingly, 'In that room where you sleep . . .'

Esther looked at him.

'. . . there's a trunk of – old clothes. They – they belonged to – to someone – a long time ago. If – if there's

69

owt you can wear, you can have 'em,' he finished in a rush.

Her green eyes were shining. 'Aw, thanks, Mester Brumby, thanks ever so.'

Sam sniffed, settled his aching bones in his chair and puffed at his pipe.

On the night of the Harvest Supper, Sam Brumby was waiting for her in the kitchen when she climbed down the ladder and stood before him in her finery. She had found a cotton print dress, patterned with blue corn-flowers. Its skirt was a little too full to be fashionable and the sleeves too narrow. But, ignoring the fusty smell of material which had been packed away in a trunk for years, she had put it on, pinned up her freshly washed hair with some ivory combs she had found in the bottom of the trunk and arranged her curls to fall over her fore-head. She felt like a princess.

Sam was staring at her. His eyes misted over as if he were seeing not her but someone else standing before him. Perhaps he was remembering the person to whom this dress had once belonged. For a fleeting moment, Esther felt awkward. Then Sam brushed his hand across his face, sniffed and said gruffly. 'You look bonny, wench. Come on, we'd best be off.'

The autumn evening was soft and balmy under a clear starlit sky and merry laughter filled the night air as they approached Grange Farm. Lanterns had been festooned all around the edges of the barn which the squire left free for the Harvest Supper. Long trestle tables had been placed down the middle with squares of hay for the revellers to sit on. The tables were piled high with food and when Esther arrived with Sam, people were already helping themselves. There were hams and pickled tongues, pork pies and sausages and for dessert, junkets and cream cheese soufflés. Esther's mouth watered.

Matthew appeared suddenly at her side. 'Come on, Esther, let's get stuck in or it'll all be gone.'

She took a plate and, following his example, piled it high with food. She reached across the table to pick up a cooked sausage when her fingers touched someone else's reaching from the opposite side. She looked up to find herself staring into Beth Hanley's resentful eyes.

'You with Matthew?' Beth asked bluntly.

Esther straightened up. 'Well – sort of. Why?'

There was hurt in Beth's dark brown eyes. 'Dun't you know we're walking out together?'

'No – no, I didn't. I'm sorry – if he'd said then . . .'

Beth snorted. 'Oh, him, he likes to think he's fancy free. He'll flirt with anything in skirts. I knows that.'

'An' doesn't it bother you?'

She didn't answer directly, but stared Esther straight in the face and said, 'He'll come back to me and I'll be waiting for him. You mark my words, Esther Everatt, *he'll always come back to me!*'

For some inexplicable reason the vehement certainty in Beth's tone sent a shiver down Esther's back.

The dark-haired girl turned away and was lost in the throng of people. Esther too turned away from the table and drew breath sharply for she found herself staring into the disapproving faces of Mrs Willoughby and her sister.

'Well, really!' was all Flo could muster.

'And what, may I ask, are *you* doing here?' demanded Martha Willoughby.

Esther recovered her senses and smiled brightly. 'Good evening, missus,' she addressed Martha Willoughby. 'And, er . . .' she hesitated and then deliberately her gaze searched the left hand of the thin woman, whom she now knew to be Martha Willoughby's sister. Seeing her ringless finger, she added with emphasis, 'And miss.'

Miss Flo gasped. The edge of sarcasm towards her spinster state was not lost on the middle-aged woman.

'Oh, Martha, come away. I won't be seen talking to this – this creature!'

'Quite right, Flo dear. Really, I don't know what the squire is thinking of.'

They picked up their skirts and with one last glance made as if to turn away in a calculated snub. But in that last glance, Flo had looked Esther up and down properly. She gasped and gripped her sister's arm.

'Oh, Martha,' she squeaked. 'Do – do you *see* what she's wearing? Oh, how could he? How could Sam let her wear one of poor, darling Katharine's gowns?' Flo fished in the sleeve of her blouse for a delicate lace handkerchief and held it to her lips, her eyes wide and staring above the frothy white lace. Martha was made of sterner stuff. She merely eyed the old-fashioned gown with distaste.

'It's absolutely . . .' But exactly what, Esther was not to hear for at that moment Tom Willoughby came up behind them and put an arm about the shoulders of the two sisters. 'Now, now, my dears, making friends. That's the way,' and he gave a great bellowing laugh so that his stomach wobbled and his whiskers shook.

72

'Oh, really, Thomas. Friends, indeed!' The two women turned away in disgust, but before he followed them, Tom gave Esther a broad grin and an exaggerated wink. 'They'll come around, m'dear, don't you worry.'

Esther stared after the three of them as they walked away. She wasn't bothered one way or the other whether they ever 'came around', but she was intrigued by something Flo had said.

Just who was Katharine?

Thoughtfully, Esther took her plate and sat down in a corner of the barn.

'There you are,' Matthew said and sat down beside her. 'This is good, ain't it, Esther?' he said, his mouth stuffed with food.

'Mmm,' she murmured.

'There's dancing later. Old Joe usually brings his fiddle and plays for us.'

'Dancing,' Esther was startled into replying. 'I can't dance!'

'I'll show you,' Matthew said loftily. 'There's nothing to it.'

He was indeed right. There was nothing to it – at least not the way these happy folk danced, for no one cared that they all just hopped and jigged about in time to the music. There seemed to be no organized dance steps of any kind. But, Esther had to admit, they all certainly enjoyed themselves. Even Beth was dancing and laughing and seemed to have forgotten her rancour for the moment.

'Oh, stop, Matthew, do stop. I'm puffed. I can't dance

another step,' Esther gasped. 'Really, I can't. Oooh, I've got a stitch in me side.'

Matthew laughed. He was by now none too steady on his feet, for he had been partaking liberally of the ale set aside at the far end of the barn. He pulled her away from the other dancers and with his arm about her waist, led her out of the barn and away from the light. Behind them the music and laughter continued but around them now was the black stillness of the night. He pulled her round a corner and towards a straw stack looming in the darkness.

'Oh, just let me sit down. Me feet are fair aching.' Esther giggled and fell into the straw. Matthew stumbled and fell on top of her and in a moment they were rolling and shrieking about in the straw. Then suddenly he was on top of her, his mouth finding hers as he kissed her roughly and his hand was tugging at her skirt. Then she felt his hand hot upon her thigh and felt his fingers working frantically upwards, upwards . . .

She struggled. 'Stop it, Matthew. I won't—'

'Aw, come on, Esther. You'd like it. I know you would. You're ripe as a plum . . .'

'No!' she almost shouted, and then she heard an ominous tearing sound near her shoulder as the fragile material of her dress tore.

Her sudden anger giving her extra strength, Esther shoved him off her and tried to scramble up. The straw caught at her skirt and hampered her escape, so that he caught her by the legs and tackled her to the ground once more. Now she was fighting him in earnest, fighting for her purity.

'Not 'til I'm wed,' she panted. 'I *won't*.'

Suddenly he stopped and rolled away from her. 'Huh, you're a prude, Esther Everatt. You'll die an old maid and never know what it was like.'

Finding herself free, she struggled to her feet and moved a little way away from him. Then she turned and with a parting flourish shouted, 'I'd rather that than bring your bastard into the world, Matthew Hilton!'

She turned and fled back to the safety of the throng of dancers. She found herself a drink and sat in a corner. She was hot and dishevelled, but hoped that everyone was too busy enjoying themselves to notice.

She felt at the back of her shoulder. The tear didn't seem too bad. She had been thrilled to find the dress and had so looked forward to this evening, but now, what with the contempt of Mrs Willoughby and Miss Flo, Beth's angry eyes, and now Matthew's drunken attempt on her virtue – her pleasure was spoilt. She sighed heavily. His behaviour had soured what she had thought had been a friendship. She had liked being with him, quite enjoyed his harmless flirting if she were honest. But no more than that, she vowed to herself, not until I'm married.

Beth Hanley was standing over her. 'Matthew tried his tricks on you, then?'

Esther looked up. 'He tried, but he got nowhere,' she said tartly.

Beth seemed to reflect for a moment as if unable to decide whether or not she believed Esther's claim. 'Funny, he's not one to give up.'

Esther looked up and then slowly rose to her feet

to meet Beth's gaze on a level. 'You don't mean you let him . . . ?'

Beth shrugged. 'Why not? 'Tis natural.'

Esther's lips curled, and she saw anger spark in Beth's eyes.

'Think you're too good for the rest of us, do you, Esther? Matthew not good enough for you, eh?'

Esther shook her head. 'That don't come into it, Beth,' she said quietly, but with candour. 'I – I always vowed I'd be a virgin when I married – that's all.'

For a moment a look of uncertainty crossed Beth's face as if she were struggling with her conscience. Then her dark head came up defiantly. 'Well, it's a mite late for me now to have such high-minded principles. I'll leave you to your lonely bed, Esther Everatt, and wish ya well on it.' With that parting shot Beth tossed her long hair back and flounced away.

Esther, determined to have the last word, shouted after her, 'You're welcome to him.'

Beth disappeared out of the barn into the darkness to find Matthew.

Later that night, for the first time in her life, Esther lay awake with a strange feeling of restlessness. Matthew could be right, she thought sadly, maybe she'd never know what it was like to be really loved by someone kind and thoughtful. Perhaps no one decent would want to marry a girl with a name; 'my sister's bastard' as Aunt Hannah had constantly reminded her.

All she had ever wanted, Esther told herself fiercely in the lonely darkness of the little attic room, was a place to belong. That was why she had left her aunt's house and

76

walked through the night. That was why she had forced herself upon the ailing Sam Brumby. He needed her youth and her strength. But Esther was honest enough to acknowledge that her need of Sam and his farm was even greater than the old man's need of her.

She had no place in her scheme of things for rolling in the hay with the likes of Matthew Hilton!

With harvest time over, now came the preparation of the ground for next year's crops. The work would continue as the weather allowed throughout the winter months, though Sam told Esther he liked to aim to get the ploughing done by December.

'Ah dun't always manage it,' he told her ruefully, 'and there's the threshing to pull in an' all.'

'We'll manage it, mester,' Esther told him confidently. 'Me an' Matthew between us.'

Sam grunted doubtfully. 'Reckon you can manage them great horses of Tom Willoughby's, d'ya, wench?'

Esther grinned at him, her green eyes sparkling. 'You just watch me, mester.'

So on the first day that Tom brought his pair of heavy horses to Brumbys' Farm, both he and Sam followed Esther as she led the animals out to the field; stood watching her as deftly she harnessed them to the plough. She marked out a rig and then cut her first furrow, true and straight. Her clear voice rang out across the field, 'Gee-back, gee-back,' as she guided the horses on a right turn at the end of the rig and began her way back down the field towards the two men. As she approached, Esther's concentration never faltered, her hands stayed

77

firmly on the plough, yet she was aware of their critical scrutiny.

Tom's rumbling voice carried to her ears. 'By heck, lass, that furrow's as straight as I could do mesen. What d'you say, Sam?'

Faintly, she heard Sam's now-familiar sniff. 'Aye, it'll do,' was all he said.

From Sam Brumby that was praise enough.

So day after day Esther took turns with Matthew in following the horses borrowed from Tom Willoughby, guiding the plough as it carved furrow after neat furrow until her legs ached and her ankles were sore from all the miles she had walked on the uneven ground. Her hands were chafed raw from holding the plough handles but doggedly she plodded on through the rain and mud of autumn. The days seemed to grow rapidly shorter and the weather turned colder. Seagulls shrieked above her diving down on to the freshly turned furrow in search of food. Mile after mile she trudged and then, cold and wet, she would return to the farmhouse at night, but only when the horses had been brushed and fed with corn and chaff did she allow herself any respite. In front of the glowing fire in the range she would fall asleep in the wooden chair in the corner by the hearth, often too exhausted even to eat.

Life at Brumbys' Farm fell into some sort of routine for the three of them — Sam, Esther and Matthew. Matthew did not work full time for Sam, Esther found. He helped out on all the local farms and so several days could go by without Matthew being there. Then suddenly he would appear again, grinning cheekily, winking at her and, given less than half a chance, slapping her buttocks, although he was quick to dodge out of the way of her stinging right hand returning the slap.

With the ploughing, Matthew was needed at Brumbys' more than usual. On Mondays Esther washed and ironed, on Tuesdays and Wednesdays she helped with the ploughing when Matthew was needed elsewhere, then on Thursdays she baked and cooked enough food to last the week. Fridays and Saturdays she worked outside again, sometimes more ploughing, sometimes with the stock. But on Sundays, she found that Sam was quite happy to do a minimum of work.

'It's the Lord's Day,' he said gruffly one Sunday morning when he found her black-leading the range. Even the animals were given as little attention as possible.

'Give 'em a sharpener on the Lord's Day,' Sam told her. 'One feed a day instead of two on the Sabbath – they'll be all the more ready to come to the trough tomorrow.'

So on a Sunday, Esther found she had time for herself.

Walking down the lane from Brumbys' Farm towards the Point one Sunday afternoon, when the winter sun lay low in the southern sky, streaking the fields with a golden glow, Esther hummed to herself and every so often she gave a little skip of sheer happiness. She came to the stretch of grass between the cottages and the river bank. Four of Ma Harris's children were chasing each other in a noisy game of tag. Esther smiled to herself. Sabbath or not, Ma Harris would never manage to keep that brood quiet.

79

'Is yar mam at home?' she asked a boy with a runny nose.

'Nah, she's away yonder,' he pointed inland with a grubby finger, 'there's a babby bein' born at Souters' Farm.'

'A babby?'

'Aye, the missus is having her fifth babby. Me mam allus goes to 'elp when a babby's getting borned.' He wiped his nose with the back of his hand and sniffed noisily.

Esther nodded, said goodbye, and walked on towards the river bank.

Now she had time to take a look around her, at the sea and the sand and the river that joined the sea. She was fascinated to see the little fishing boats moored along the river bank, and she followed its curve until the bank gave way to the sea. Esther paused in her walk to look at the huge boat where Robert Eland lived. It was lodged half on the bank, and shored up by sleepers and wooden poles dug deep into the bed of the river. At high water, it would seem to be almost afloat and yet the vessel was firmly anchored and would not move from its place. There was a narrow wooden jetty built up from the firm ground running on to the boat. Esther stood looking up at it in wonderment. She had never seen anything like it. It was a strange place for a man to make his home, she thought. She accepted, though, that there were those who felt an affinity with the sea as she did for the land she helped to work.

'What are you doing here?'

The voice came from behind her, interrupting her

reverie. She turned to find Robert Eland standing beside her. 'Oh, I'm sorry, I didn't mean . . .'

'You're Sam Brumby's wench,' he stated bluntly.

Esther bristled. 'If you mean I work on Mester Brumby's farm, the answer's yes. If you mean owt more . . .' Her green eyes glinted. 'Then you're quite wrong.'

The expression in his eyes lightened a little, but he did not smile. His mouth was completely covered by his wiry beard. He was a dour man, who saw little humour in life in general and even less in his own. 'Aye, I heard of your little – er – rumpus – with Missus Willoughby and 'er sister.' He was glowering again. 'Aye, an' that's not all I've heard about you. You took the job my Beth went after.'

'*Your* Beth, but – but I thought she was Matthew's girl.'

The scowl deepened. 'Huh, *him*!' Robert Eland muttered. He seemed about to say more, but then turned away angrily. As he brushed past her and headed for the gangway to his home, Esther thought she heard him mumble, 'Ah, what's the use?'

Esther walked on and came to a place where the river widened and joined the waters of the sea. On her left – to the east – was marshland, the beach and the North Sea to the horizon and beyond. To the west lay mile upon mile of flat farmland as far as she could see.

Esther shaded her eyes and looked out towards the sea. In the far distance she could see the Spit jutting out into the water, further out even than where she was standing.

She retraced her steps past the cottages and the boat and took the path leading across the old marsh until she came to the dunes. Pushing her way through thick clumps of spiky marram grass, she came to the Spit and walked along the narrow ridge of scrubland to the end until she was surrounded on three sides by the sea. At high tide, the point of land could afford boats a haven from the treacherous currents and sudden squalls of the North Sea. At low tide the River Lynn still wound its way through the mudbanks.

All around her was a magnificent bleakness. She turned slowly in a full circle, but every view was the same – flat as far as the eye could see. With the land so low and level, the glorious sky seemed to surround her entirely. There was so much space, it gave her such a sense of freedom.

She threw back her head and breathed in the exhilarating air. She closed her eyes as the sea breeze wrapped itself around her, lifted her skirt and ruffled her curls, like a man flirting with her. The sound of the waves gently lapping at her feet was soothing.

Whatever happened in her life, she thought, the waves would continue to break upon the shore and the tide would ebb and flow. It gave her a feeling of constancy, a sense of security. Behind her was the land that she loved already. Before her was the sea that she would come to know, too. She belonged in this place, she would make this place her own. She bent and picked up a fistful of the sand. She revelled in the feel of it in her hand. Then she flung it high into the sky and laughed aloud as the particles showered around her.

Esther – unwanted and unloved all her young life – had found a place to stay, a place to love. She had found her home.

Eight

*T*O Esther's disappointment, Christmas Day in Sam Brumby's house was little different from any other day. She had cooked and baked for most of Christmas Eve, so that there was a chicken and vegetables to be cooked on the day itself, and a pudding to be warmed. Even her aunt had made more of Christmas than this, Esther thought disconsolately, as she remembered the shouting and laughter of her young cousins, her uncle carving at a huge goose and the dinner table loaded with all manner of food that they never tasted at any other time of the year. It was the first – and probably the only – time she would think kindly of her aunt.

That night Esther's sleep was disturbed by dreams of a family of children, her own children, with a husband sitting at the opposite end of the table. At first the man in her dream was just a shadowy, indistinct figure, but then the features took shape and it was Matthew who sat at the head of her table. She awoke early, sweating and breathing heavily, but she could not understand why.

That winter on Sam Brumby's farm was a harsh one. Snow came although it never seemed to stay long, yet the north-east winds from the sea were bitingly cold and whipped savagely across the flat land. Matthew still came for a day now and then to find Esther working about the farm huddled in a thick cloak, her hands chapped and her lips blue with cold.

'You want some warming, Esther,' Matthew told her saucily. ''Tis cosy in the hayloft.'

She tossed her head and turned the barrel churn angrily until she heard the flip-flop of the cream turning into butter. 'You never give up, do you?'

He moved closer. 'No, Esther, I'll never give up.' And he reached across and planted a rough kiss on her cheek.

'Oh, go on with you.' But the protest was half-hearted now and there was a faint tinge of pink to her cheek that had nothing to do with the cold.

There was no let-up in the wintry weather and at the beginning of January there came such severe frosts that everything seemed to be frozen solid. The trees were white with ice and the ground as hard as stone. There could be no more work on the land until the cold spell eased, so Sam sent Esther to ask if they could borrow the threshing machinery.

'I ain't no threshing gear, Esther lass,' Tom Willoughby told her. 'Sam must have meant you to go to the Grange.'

'Oh, mebbe he did, Mester Willoughby. He didn't say, but because we borrowed the 'osses off you, I just thought . . .'

Tom roared with laughter. 'I ain't that well off. But dun't you worry no more, lass. I'll see the squire's bailiff for you and see what we can do.'

'Thanks, mester.'

*

One Sunday morning Esther was surprised to see Matthew appear at the cowshed door as she was finishing the milking.

'Hello, Esther. My, but you look bonny this morning. Your cheeks is all rosy.'

''Tis the cold,' she said tartly to his compliment.

'Esther, can you get time off this after'? The pools in North Marsh Field are frozen solid now. I thought we could go skating.'

Esther almost dropped the pail of milk she was carrying. 'Me? But I can't skate.'

'Aw, it's easy. Come on, Esther. 'Tis time you had a little fun. I'll find you some skates.'

'Well,' she said doubtfully, 'all right. I'll be ready after dinner.'

'See you later, then.' Matthew went off whistling loudly.

As she went to and fro between the kitchen and the scullery clearing away the pots after dinner, Sam settled himself in the chair by the range for his Sunday afternoon nap.

'Matthew says North Marsh Field is frozen solid. He's tekin' me skating,' Esther told him.

Sam's only reply was a sniff as he pulled his pipe from his pocket, but a short time later, when she had finished the washing-up and was reaching for her shawl from the peg behind the door, Sam said, 'Wench, watch ya'sen with that lad.'

Slowly she put her shawl about her shoulders and stared at Sam. It didn't register for a moment that Sam was warning her about Matthew. It was the first time the old man had shown the least concern for her. Strangely, the knowledge warmed her.

'Aye, I'll mind him, Mester Brumby,' she said gently.

Satisfied, Sam nodded and, stretching his feet out towards the glowing coals in the range, went back to packing his pipe.

When they reached the field it seemed to Esther as if half the townsfolk of Lynthorpe were there. Happy shrieks of laughter filled the sharp air.

Esther clutched Matthew's arm, convulsed with laughter. 'Oh, look – do look at her over there, she went a right cropper – and her petticoats flying!'

Matthew laughed, 'Look at him, then, he can't control his feet, they're sliding in all directions!' They clung together hooting with laughter.

'Oh, Matthew,' Esther said at last, tears running down her cheeks, 'I don't think I want to try this after all. I'll only mek a fool of mesen.'

'It's much more fun watching everybody else do that . . .' His voice trailed away, and she felt his arm stiffen under her touch. She glanced up at his face to see his lips pressed together into a hard line of anger. A frown creased his forehead and she followed the line of his gaze across the frozen surface to a couple skating slowly and sedately around the far side.

It was Beth and Robert Eland. He held Beth's hand with his left, whilst his right arm was around her plump waist to steady her.

As the couple passed close by them, Matthew slipped his arm around Esther's waist. 'Come on, Esther. Let's

give it a try.' Without waiting for her to agree he pro-
pelled her forward on to the ice.

They staggered around the perimeter of the ice clinging together, laughing helplessly, aware that they were
every bit as funny as those they had been laughing at
earlier. They were behind Beth and her partner now.
Matthew gave Esther a little push that sent her sprawling on to the ice and sliding into the couple. Beth
shrieked and clung to Robert Eland but he was even
more unsure on his feet than she and he fell on to his
back, clutching at Beth so that she fell on top of him.
Matthew, the only one left standing, could hardly hide
his mirth at the flailing legs of the other three, the
tangled bodies and petticoats fluttering.

Matthew was beside them, holding out his hand to
Beth to help her to her feet, leaving Esther to scramble
to hers as best she could unaided. As for Robert Eland,
Matthew paid no attention to him whatsoever.

'Whatever did you make me go an' do a thing like
that for, Matthew Hilton? I've never felt such a fool in all
me life!' Esther hissed angrily, but Matthew was paying
no attention to her either now.

'Come on, Beth,' he was saying, 'let's show 'em how it
should be done.' Before Robert or Esther had a chance to
make any protest, he put his arm firmly around Beth and
skated off with her.

'Well,' Esther gasped indignantly, 'would you look at
that?' she demanded of no one in particular.

'Aye, I see it,' said Robert Eland, having now regained
his feet. 'I see it all too well.'

Esther saw the look of anger and jealousy in the man's

eyes as together they watched the other two skating quite expertly. Round and round they went, faster and faster, until the other skaters, most of them still unsteady on the ice, began to move out of their way and to smile and nod towards Matthew and Beth in admiration.

'I'm no judge of skating, mester,' Esther said grimly. 'But I'd say them two's done this afore – and together!'

She glanced up at the man at her side and saw such an expression of hatred as he glowered at Matthew that she was quite startled. That look was far more than just pique because Matthew had stolen his skating partner. Then, just as she heard Robert mutter, 'What's the point of stayin' here any longer?' she saw Matthew propel Beth to the side where they were standing and come to a halt in front of them with a flourish and a shower of ice.

They were breathless and laughing. 'There, didn't I say we'd show you how it was done?'

'Showing off, more like,' Esther said cuttingly.

With exaggerated gallantry, Matthew took hold of Beth's hand and offered her back to Robert. 'Here's your partner back safe and sound. Now, Esther, take that mardy look off ya face and let's see if I can give you a twirl. It's one way of getting the ladies to cling on to you, ain't it, Robert?'

Robert had no chance to respond to his saucy remark, before Matthew pushed Esther back on to the ice and away from the other two.

But for Esther the afternoon's fun was spoilt. She seemed to feel Beth's gaze following her wherever she and Matthew went and Beth Hanley's words seemed to ring yet again in her ears.

'He'll always come back to me, Esther Everatt.'

Towards the end of January the threshing tackle arrived at Brumbys' Farm. Soon the yard was hazy with dust and chaff and noisy with another 'newfangled' machine that Sam hated so much.

'I still like flailing mesen,' he muttered to Esther, but she knew he had accepted the squire's help for the work was beginning to get too much for the old man.

As winter dragged on and spring seemed reluctant to arrive, Esther began to notice a change in Sam Brumby. He rose later each morning, coming down to sit before the range whilst she bustled about the kitchen, singing softly to herself.

'Are you all right, mester?' she asked him finally.

His reply was an ill-tempered sniff. ''Tis the cold, wench. Nothing more. I'll be right as ninepence come the spring.' So Esther continued to cope with the farm with only Matthew for help.

As she finished the milking one morning she heard a clatter in the yard and looked out to see a gig drawn by a fine horse which pawed at the ground and tossed its head.

'Whoa, there, whoa.' The man at the reins was Squire Marshall, whom Esther had seen in church.

Rubbing her hands down the side of her skirt, Esther stepped out into the yard. ''Morning, Squire.'

'Good morning, my dear.' Mr Marshall climbed down from the gig and looked about him. 'Sam Brumby – is he – er – about?'

'He's in the house, sir. Would you like me to . . . ?'

Mr Marshall put out his hand, palm outward. 'No, no, my dear girl. Don't trouble. It was – er . . .' He cleared his throat as if in embarrassment. 'I heard Sam Brumby was – er – not well.' Now he looked keenly at Esther. 'Is that right?'

Esther licked her lips. 'Well, he dun't seem quite his usual self, sir. But he says 'tis only the cold; that he'll be all right come the warmer weather.'

'I'll go in and see him.' Without waiting for an invitation, Mr Marshall turned and walked towards the house. Sam would be sitting huddled in front of the range, she knew, with a blanket wrapped around his shoulders. He looked thin and old now, but he refused to see a doctor.

Esther stayed about the yard pretending to be busy, but in truth waiting for Mr Marshall to reappear. She didn't have long to wait. Ten minutes later, the squire came out of the house closing the door quietly behind him. He seemed lost in thought and didn't notice Esther until he was almost up to her. 'Ah, there you are. Er – well now – I don't like the look of Sam at all, not at all. I've tried to persuade him to let the doctor have a look at him but . . .'

He caught sight of Esther's half-smile. 'Ah, I see you've tried already.' He was silent for a moment, then, stroking his chin thoughtfully, he said, 'Well now, what's going to happen to the farm while Sam's ill, mm?'

'I'll manage,' she said curtly, adopting her usual stance when her ability was questioned – feet apart, hands on hips.

'Well, my dear. I hope you can. I'm not a hard man.

I'm not about to turn a tenant out just because he's ill, especially when his family have held this tenancy for generations . . .'

'Tenant? Mr Brumby is a *tenant* of this farm? He – he dun't own it?'

'Oh no, my dear. Didn't you know? I own all the land around here. I have three tenant farmers in all – Willoughby at Rookery Farm, Souter and Sam Brumby. Sam's family have farmed here the longest. So, as I say, I'm not going to turn him out because he hits a bad patch, particularly if you can keep things going till he gets better.'

Esther's head was whirling. Then she remembered Matthew's words when he'd been explaining about the folk who lived at the Point. 'They all work the land round here – they all work for Mester Marshall,' Matthew had said, but she hadn't understood fully what he had meant then. 'He's the squire – he owns all the land hereabouts.'

Now she understood. Sam Brumby was only a tenant farmer. He didn't own the farm, so what would happen if anything happened to Sam, if he should be ill for a long time, or even die? After all, he was an old man, though Esther had no idea just how old he was. What would happen to her, Esther, then?

She squared her shoulders and looked Mr Marshall in the eyes. She had to make amends for her curtness of a few minutes ago. She knew it was important that she should make a good impression upon Mr Marshall, the real owner of the farm.

'Well, sir, I can manage the farm all right.'

His clear gaze was upon her. 'Can you? Can you really?'

'Oh, yes, sir. Matthew — Matthew Hilton — you know he helps out here quite a lot?'

'Yes, yes, I did know.'

'We've managed everything between us. Nothing's been let slip.'

She went on to tell him about what she intended to plant and in which fields, and which she intended to leave fallow. 'I've tried to talk it over with Mester Brumby, but he dun't seem to have the strength to be interested even.'

The squire nodded. 'Well, you seem to know what you're about — your plans seem eminently sensible.' Mr Marshall glanced about him. 'And, I must say, the place looks every bit as good as when Sam *is* around, I'll grant you that.'

Esther smiled at him. 'I'll cope, sir. I'll keep things right.'

'Well, my dear, I admire your spirit. I can see for myself you're a worker.' He nodded at her as if in approval. 'But don't be afraid to come to see me if you have any problems. I'll be only too glad to help.'

'Thank you, Squire. I'll remember that,' she answered him politely, but inwardly she resolved to prove that she could manage things alone — and manage them well.

Even with the spring, Sam made no improvement, in fact, he seemed weaker.

'You ought to call the doctor in, lass,' Will Benson told Esther. 'Ne'er mind what 'ee says, you get the doc in. It'd look bad on you if owt happens to Sam, an' you hadn't done anything.'

'Would you call on your way back through the town at Doctor Blair's house, Mr Benson, and ask him to call as soon as he can?'

'Aye, righto, lass. I don't mind doing that. I don't like to see old Sam so bad. He's shrivelled away to nothing. All skin and bone he is, now.' Will shook his head. 'No, I don't like the look of him at all.'

As the carrier's cart trundled out of the yard, Esther went to find Matthew. 'Will Benson's going to call and ask the doctor to come out to see Sam.'

'Not afore time neither,' Matthew said brusquely. 'He's poorly, you know. But he's such a stubborn old goat!'

They looked at each other, both thinking the same thing. Just what was going to become of the farm — and of them — if anything dreadful were to happen to Sam Brumby?

Nine

THE doctor came to find Esther feeding the pigs. Above the noise of the scuffling and grunting, Esther heard a loud rapping on the sty door and looked up to see a stranger in a tweed suit.

'I'm sorry, sir. They make such a row at feeding time,' Esther said, hurrying outside and closing the door after her.

Fastidiously, the doctor stepped backwards. 'Quite so, quite so.' There was a pause whilst Esther waited. Then he went on, 'You live here with Mr Brumby, I understand?'

'That's right, sir. I've been here nearly a year now.' Esther felt the doctor looking her up and down.

'Well, my dear.' The doctor's voice had a kindly, concerned note now. 'I'm sorry to have to tell you that Mr Brumby is a sick man. I fear he has not many weeks to live. I'm very sorry, but there's nothing I can do to help him.'

Esther stared at the doctor. 'I – I should have called you sooner. I – should . . .'

Doctor Blair laid his hand upon Esther's shoulder. 'It wouldn't have made any difference, my dear. Don't reproach yourself. He's a tired old man who's worked this land all his life. He's worn out – that's the truth of it.

There's nothing I could have done for him, not even if I had come earlier.'

'Is he in any pain?' Esther wanted to know.

The doctor shook his head. 'Not that I can find out. But his breathing's bad – very bad – and will get worse, my dear, before the end.' He met Esther's steady gaze. 'But you let me know, and I'll do what I can to help him.'

Esther nodded and said hoarsely, 'Thank you, sir.'

Doctor Blair gave her shoulder a friendly squeeze. 'Your being here makes his passing a lot easier, my dear. A lot easier than if he were still living on his own. Just remember that.'

'Why?' she asked candidly. 'I seem to be able to do so little.'

'You being here means he can die in his own home, on the land he has always loved. Otherwise . . .' He paused and took a deep breath. 'I would have had to take him away.'

Esther's eyes widened and her lips parted in a gasp. Grim tales of being sent to the workhouse had been hurled at her by her aunt so often as a threat that she understood at once what the doctor meant. She wasn't sure that it was still a reality that unwanted children, the destitute, the old and the sick actually ended up in the workhouse, but the fear itself was enough.

'I'll look after him, mester – I mean, doctor,' she said in a voice that was none too steady.

'Yes, my dear, I believe you will,' he said, with a final pat of encouragement and understanding.

As the doctor turned to leave, she was surprised to feel

a lump in her throat and a prickle of unaccustomed tears. She realized suddenly just how fond she had become of the grumpy old man.

With the news that Sam Brumby was so very ill, and mindful of her promise to care for him until the end, Esther decided to move out of the attic boxroom above the kitchen for it had no direct access to the upper floor of the house. She needed to be nearer Sam.

Stepping into the room on the opposite side of the small landing to Sam's room, Esther found what appeared to have once been a nursery. Pushed into the corner was an assortment of children's toys – a battered rocking horse, a doll's house, a high chair, a doll with a china face and cloth body and in another corner a full-sized baby's cot.

Esther wondered if all these things had belonged to the sweet-faced girl in the faded picture in Sam's bedroom. Perhaps he could not bear to throw anything away; maybe a lot of the old man's memories of happier days were stored away in this room with these toys. Esther could almost see the little girl with her long hair flowing as she rocked to and fro on the wooden horse; could almost hear her childish laughter . . .

Esther shook herself; her worry over Sam was making her fanciful and morbid. She must concentrate on practical matters, she told herself firmly.

Another door led into a long narrow room with a sloping ceiling, beneath which there was just enough room for the iron bedstead to stand. At one end of the room there was a small chest of drawers and a basin and jug stood on a wash-stand. Although the whole place needed scrubbing out and the bedlinen washing, the room was luxurious compared with the attic boxroom. This room had obviously been the nurserymaid's, but Esther chose it in preference to the larger nursery for it seemed warmer. If she left the two intervening doors open, she would still be able to hear if Sam needed help in the night.

Three nights later, when the room was clean, the bedlinen freshly laundered and the dust banged from the mattress with a carpet beater, Esther moved in. For the first time in her life, she was sleeping in a real bedroom and on a proper bed.

Yet, as she lay awake listening to the rasping, laboured sound of Sam's breathing, she wished she was back in the quiet solitude of the cramped boxroom.

Sam Brumby lived to know that another harvest had been gathered but he had not been well enough to take any active part in the work. Just once, when she was returning from the fields, she saw that he had dragged himself to the kitchen window to watch the final wagon load brought home, but this year it was Esther who had to put the last sheaf on top of the stack. As she did so she turned to see Sam watching her from the window and saw him give her a little nod before he turned and went back to his place by the range.

The following morning when Esther came in from the milking, she found Sam seated in his chair. He was leaning forward, his breathing a rasping, tearing sound.

'Why didn't you wait till I could help you down the stairs?' she said hurrying towards him.

He was seized by a spasm of coughing and waved his hand feebly at her. Helplessly she had to stand and watch as the coughing racked his thin frame. He sat hunched in the chair, growing weaker with every passing day.

'Mester . . .' she began again, but he lifted his hand as if to silence her.

'Lass, get Mester Thompson . . .' He could hardly get the words out, and then only in a wheezing whisper.

Esther bent closer. 'Who's Mr Thompson?'

'I – I want to see him.' He lay back in the chair and closed his eyes. The effort of dressing, coming downstairs and speaking even those few words had exhausted him.

Esther bit her lip. She must find this man, but she didn't know who he was. At that moment she heard the familiar whistle heralding the arrival of Will Benson's carrier's cart in the yard and she flew out of the house and towards him, her skirt held high, her curls flying. All formality forgotten in her agitation, she called the carrier the name by which she always thought of him in her own mind.

'Will, Will – oh, thank goodness you've come . . .'

'Steady, lass, steady. What's wrong? Is it Sam?'

She nodded. 'He's much worse, Will. And he's asking for a Mester Thompson. I don't know who he is, do you?'

Will Benson nodded. His face was grim. 'He's the lawyer in town.'

They stared at each other.

'Why should he – want a lawyer?' Esther asked innocently.

'Dun't you know, lass?'

Esther could only shake her head for suddenly there was a funny lump in her throat and she could not trust herself to speak.

'I reckon he wants to make a will, lass.'

'A will? But folks like him dun't make wills . . .'

The carter nodded his head. 'They do if they think they haven't long to go, lass.'

Esther groaned. 'Oh no,' she whispered. 'You reckon he – he knows?'

Will nodded. 'Aye, lass, he knows. He knows all right.'

They stood for a moment in silence. Then Will patted her shoulder in a kindly gesture. 'Go and get yar shawl, or whatever, an' I'll take you back into town and drop you off outside his office.'

'Will, couldn't you . . . ?'

Will was shaking his head. 'Nay, lass, Sam's asked you to go, an' you should do as he's bid. I'll go and have a word with him whilst you get ready.'

She would have enjoyed the ride on Will's cart into town if she had not been so worried about Sam and nervous of presenting herself at a lawyer's office.

'What'll I say, Will?'

Will almost smiled despite the cloud that hung over both of them. He had never seen Esther so irresolute. It was totally unlike her.

'Just go into the office and ask to see Mester Thompson. If he's not available then leave a clear message with – well – with whoever is there. Just tell 'em that Sam

Brumby is a very sick man and that he's asked you to fetch a lawyer out to see him. And could he come as quick as possible.'

'Will he take notice of someone like me?' she asked diffidently.

Now Will did smile. 'Esther lass, just go in there and be yourself. They'll tek notice all right!'

A small smile touched Esther's mouth and her confidence returned. Sam was relying on her.

The young clerk looked her up and down as she entered the office. He moved forward from the tall desk where he was working. 'Can I help you, miss?'

Esther repeated what Will had advised her to say. Without argument the young man consulted a large book. 'I'm afraid Mr Thompson won't be able to come out until tomorrow.' He looked up anxiously. 'Do you think that will be – all right?'

Esther stared at him in surprise. The young man had evidently understood the situation only too well. She relaxed a little. 'Yes, yes, I should think so.'

'Very well, miss.' The young man picked up a pen. 'Mr Thompson will come out to the farm at eleven tomorrow morning.'

'Thank you, thank you very much.'

'Good day, miss.'

Esther hurried along the lane, every so often taking little running steps. She seemed to have been away from the farm and from Sam for such a long time. Even though she worked all day about the farm, she checked on Sam every hour or so. This was the longest time she had left him alone, and because he seemed even worse today, she was anxious.

She turned in at the farm gate at last and hurried across the yard. Beth was standing at the back door raising her hand to knock. At the sound of Esther's footsteps on the cinders, she turned and then let her hand fall.

'Oh, there you are. I've bin knocking for ages.'

'Mester Brumby's very ill,' Esther told her shortly and brushed past her to go into the house, but Beth caught hold of her arm. 'Where's Matthew? I've got to see Matthew.'

'How should I know?' Esther muttered. 'I ain't seen him for days. Just when I could use a bit of help, Mester Matthew decides to do one of his disappearing acts!'

'I thought – he was here – with you.' The statement was an accusation.

'Well, he ain't.' Esther twisted her arm impatiently to release Beth's grasp and added, with a touch of the malice that Beth had used towards her on occasion, 'Mebbe he's chasing a bit o' skirt on one of the other farms.'

The girl turned white and swayed slightly. She put out her hand to steady herself against the wall. With her other hand she clutched at her shawl, pulling it closely around her.

Esther gave her a click of exasperation. Beth's possessive behaviour over Matthew irritated her, and besides she had enough on her mind over poor Sam. She went inside and slammed the door behind her – right in Beth's face.

Ten

MR Thompson, the lawyer, arrived promptly at eleven the next morning. He was a thin-faced, balding gentleman in a pin-striped suit. The broad, stiff white collar seemed too big for his thin neck. His eyes were large behind the thick lenses of his steel-rimmed spectacles, which seemed to be forever slipping down his long, thin nose.

He was closeted with Sam in the front parlour for an hour and a half, at the end of which time he came out into the yard to find Esther talking to Will Benson, who had driven in.

'Come here,' he beckoned her with a long bony finger. 'Would you be kind enough to ask Mr Benson to step into the house for a moment.'

Will followed the lawyer into the house, whilst Esther waited outside in the yard, stroking Will's horses and watching the back door. Will was not required for many minutes for he appeared again almost immediately and climbed up on to his cart.

'Good day, lass. I'll see you later in the week.' He turned his cart around and rattled out of the yard.

'Will . . . ?' Esther called, but he did not seem to hear her shout above the noise of the cart's wheels.

A few moments later, the lawyer too came out of the house, unhitched his pony and climbed into his trap. Touching his hat in a very gallant way to the young girl still standing uncertainly in the middle of the yard, he too turned his conveyance around and left the farm.

Esther watched the cart and the trap disappearing down the lane. Then she turned and went slowly back into the house.

That night it took Esther half an hour to help Sam up the steep stairs to his bedroom and the next day he did not even try to get up out of his bed.

A worried frown creasing her forehead, Esther went out into the pale morning to cope with the milking. She felt more weary than she could ever remember feeling in her young life. Hard work, whatever the weather, had never exhausted her as caring for Sam was doing. Each night she slept restlessly, waking every hour or so to listen to his rasping, painful breathing. Several times a night she would drag herself from her warm bed and, bare-footed, pad across the wooden floors to his room. There was little she could do to ease his suffering, except raise him up on his pillows and give him a drink. Some nights when he seemed even worse, she would go down to the kitchen and heat up some broth on the glowing embers of the range. He scarcely managed more than a spoonful or two and it seemed a waste of time, yet she had to try.

He was so cold that each night she heated three bricks in the range oven, wrapped them in thick, woollen rags and placed one either side of him in the bed and one at his feet.

Now, this morning, he was weaker than ever.

She leant her head against Clover's warm stomach and

closed her eyes. The cow, somehow sensing Esther's distress, stood patiently waiting for her udders to be emptied.

'You sleeping on the job?'

She jumped at the sound of Matthew's teasing voice and, lifting her head, saw his shadowy form in the half-light of the cowshed. Bringing her head up sharply, she snapped back an answer. She was in no mood for his horseplay this morning. 'An' if I am, it's no thanks to you. Up half the night with poor old Sam and all the work to do on the farm. Where've you been? Just when I could use a bit of help, you disappear for days on end!'

Matthew moved forward and now, Esther had to admit, there was genuine concern in his tone. 'Is he worse?'

The anger went out of her as swiftly as it had come. Her voice breaking slightly, she told him, 'He's much worse. He – he had the lawyer here yesterday . . .'

'Oh, Lord!'

'. . . and today he dun't seem to have the energy to try and get out of his bed. Would you go for the doctor, Matthew?'

'Of course, I'll go right now.' He made as if to leave and then, turning back briefly, he added, 'And from tonight, I'll stay here with you and give you a hand with him.'

Esther opened her mouth to protest, but Matthew had gone.

The doctor was sorry but there was nothing he could do. 'I'll leave you this,' he added, handing her a bottle of liquid. 'It may just help him to rest a little at night. Are you sure you can manage, my dear? You're looking exhausted. I could remove him to the cottage hospital, but I very much doubt he would survive the journey into the town . . .'

Esther shook her head vehemently. 'No – no. I dun't want that. I'll manage . . .'

Matthew stepped forward to stand beside her. 'We'll manage, doctor. I'll be staying here now to help Esther.'

Esther saw the doctor glance from one to the other, her own doubts mirrored in his face. 'Well now, I don't quite know if that would – well – be quite right. Isn't there someone – some woman – who could come and help out?'

'If you're thinking of the gossips, doctor, dun't worry. Esther's not one to let their wagging tongues bother her,' Matthew said. For a moment, despite the seriousness of their situation, his cheeky grin was back. 'An' as for keepin' me in me place, well, she's a dab hand at that, an' all!'

The doctor glanced back at Esther and she, seeing that he was still not convinced of the rightness of leaving two young people alone in the farmhouse together, gave him a brief nod. 'We'll be all right, thank you, Doctor Blair. 'Tis Sam we've to worry about.'

Doctor Blair sighed heavily. 'I'm sad to say you're right there, my dear.' He turned away and went out to his gig. 'I'll call again in a day or two, but don't hesitate to send for me if you need me.'

As the gig clattered out of the farmyard, Matthew

said, 'Who's paying for all these doctor's visits, Esther? The likes of us dun't have doctors – not unless we're dying.'

Esther faced Matthew and said quietly, 'Sam is dying, Matthew.'

He stared at her for a moment and then dropped his gaze to look at the ground and shuffle his feet. For once, Esther felt a moment's sympathy for the young man's awkwardness, so she added briskly, 'Besides, I'll see the doctor's paid when the harvest money comes in. Now, let's get back to Sam.'

That night Matthew filled four sacks with straw to form a makeshift bed for himself on the floor in the old nursery between Sam's room and the little room where Esther now slept. 'It's no good me sleeping out in the hayloft, or in that little boxroom you had. I'm no use to you out there.'

'What do you mean?' she asked sharply.

'I'll never hear if you need help, or if Sam gets worse.'

'Oh – oh, er, yes.' Esther turned away but not before she had caught Matthew's grin, and realized that he knew exactly what had been in her mind.

Esther lay in her own bed, every nerve tensed. Any moment she expected to hear the latch raised and Matthew creeping into her room.

He's not stayed here to look after Sam, she fretted to herself, he just wants the chance to climb into my bed and he reckons this is a good excuse to worm his way into the house. She lay there in the darkness, listening. Now that her bedroom door was shut against Matthew, she could no longer hear Sam's laboured breathing. Yet this was worse, she told herself. Now she dare not go to sleep!

But for once Esther was wrong. After some time, she heard Matthew's gentle snoring, and only then did she allow herself to close her eyes and rest.

So they fell into some sort of routine. Matthew rarely helped directly with Sam but he took on most of the farm work, leaving Esther to devote nearly all her time to the old man. Once her initial suspicions as to Matthew's motives had been allayed, she found she was pleased to have him there.

She did not feel quite so alone in the face of death.

When the Sunday of Harvest Festival came, Esther walked the two miles alone to give thanks at the little church as Sam had done all his life. She sat alone in Sam's pew, but as she left the church she found herself being questioned on all sides as to how Sam fared.

'If there's owt you want, lass,' Tom Willoughby boomed, deliberately ignoring the pursed lips of his wife and her sister, 'you just let me know.'

'I'll call and see him,' the vicar promised, and though she nodded agreement, Esther was a little doubtful as to how Sam would view such a visit.

At the church gate she found Beth waiting for her. Her annoyance was tempered by the fact that the girl looked ill. Her face was pinched and although the autumn evening was not cold, she was huddled into her thick winter shawl making her girlish body shapeless. Despite the thick clothing, she still appeared to be shivering.

'He's with you, ain't he?' Beth accused Esther.

There was no point in pretending that she did not understand, so Esther merely replied shortly, 'Matthew's staying to help look after Sam.'

She was surprised to see tears in the girl's eyes. 'I don't believe you. You think you've got him, don't you?'

'I keep telling you, I dun't want him – not that way. But I need his help. I can't manage Sam and the farm on me own.'

'I don't believe you,' Beth whispered again.

Esther shrugged and turned away. 'Believe what you like, then.'

'Esther . . .' Beth cried after her. 'Please – I must see him. Please tell him.'

Esther did not look back or even acknowledge that she had heard the girl's desperate plea, but as she walked along the road from the church, she could almost feel Beth's eyes watching her every step of the way.

Back at the farm, she hurried straight up to Sam's room.

'They all asked about you, Sam,' she told him. 'The parson and the squire. They all sent their regards and wish you well.'

Sam lay in his narrow bed with his eyes closed. It was as if, being unable to go to the church himself, he had given up. He refused all food, and would take only sips of water.

'Parson said he'll come and see you,' she added slyly, hoping that such news would spark some sort of reaction.

But Sam's eyes remained shut and his expression did not alter. Sadly, Esther doubted if he had even understood what she was telling him. His face was like a skull, the skin stretched like dry parchment over the bones. All the ruddy good health of a life working in the open air had gone in the last few weeks. He lay there with his eyes closed, every breath a shuddering, rasping sound, his fingers clutching at the quilt covering him.

'Do you feel worse, Sam?' Esther asked gently, bending down towards him.

There was no answer.

The next morning Esther sent Matthew to fetch the doctor again. 'He's much worse now than when Doctor Blair last saw him.'

Matthew just nodded and muttered, 'I'll go right away.'

It was only when Matthew had disappeared around the bend in the road that Esther realized she had not even thought to tell him that Beth wanted to see him.

Only two nights later, Esther was startled out of her sleep by the sound of the latch of her bedroom door being lifted. At once she was fully awake, lying stiffly, holding her breath.

In the early morning light, Matthew's shadowy form came towards her narrow bed. Ducking his head below the slope of the ceiling, he grasped at the counterpane near her shoulder. She gave a little cry and pulled the cover from his grip. 'Dun't you dare, Mester Matthew . . .'

'Oh, you're awake. You'd better come. I – I can't hear Sam breathing.'

'What?' She sat up suddenly, forgetting the nearness of the ceiling and gave her head a nasty crack.

Fearful of what they were to find, the two young people clung together as they crept through the room Matthew now occupied, across the tiny landing and lifted the latch of Sam's bedroom door.

They found him still warm, yet motionless and silent for ever. He must have died quite peacefully for the covers were unruffled and his hands were folded across his chest, just as he had gone to sleep.

With the dawn, Matthew set off to fetch Doctor Blair to come to Sam Brumby for the last time.

'I'll see the undertaker for you, my dear,' the kindly doctor told Esther as he left the farm later that morning. 'Get Matthew to ask Mrs Harris to come and lay him out.'

Esther nodded, not trusting herself to speak for the lump in her throat. She felt suddenly bereft and very much alone again. She had begun to feel secure and had dared to be happy. Sam had given her a home and had shown her a gruff affection.

Now he was gone.

Sadly, she wandered from room to room downstairs, conscious all the time of poor Sam still lying upstairs and that there was nothing more she could do for him. What would happen to all his family possessions now? she thought. Would his things be auctioned off with people prying and poking amongst his treasured memories? She opened the door into the front parlour – a room she had rarely entered and hadn't even liked to clean properly.

She moved around the room touching the furniture, the ornaments and pictures until she came to the family Bible lying on a small round table under the window. Now, with reverent fingers, she opened the book.

Written on the first blank page was a list of the births, deaths and marriages of the Brumby family.

Esther read the entries and learnt that the first Brumby to farm here had been Sam's grandfather, Joseph. One entry stated that he had been granted the tenancy in 1807. The entry of Joseph's death was in different handwriting, as if the next generation had taken over the duty of recording the history of the family. There was one entry that particularly intrigued her.

'William Joseph Brumby married Sarah Willoughby 27th May 1833.' Her finger moved up and down the page working out the relationships. William and Sarah were Sam's parents. So, she thought, perhaps Sam was some relation to Tom Willoughby.

The next entry was Sam's birth – 'Samuel Joseph Brumby born on 24th August 1833.'

Esther allowed herself a wry smile. There was less than nine months between his parents' marriage and his birth. She closed the Bible and turned away, feeling a little guilty for prying into Sam's secrets. But his parents had married and Sam *had* been born in wedlock, even if only just! Not like mine, she thought bitterly.

Esther sighed deeply. No doubt she'd soon have to leave Brumbys' Farm. But where could she go? No one wanted her.

Tears prickled behind her eyes and the lump in her throat seemed to grow bigger.

Eleven

MA Harris came mid-morning. 'Now then, lass,' she said to Esther. ''Tis all over with the poor old man, then. Aye well, he's been poorly for a while, ain't he?'

'Do – do you want any – help?' Esther asked, not without reluctance. Normally she would tackle anything, but the thought of helping to lay out Sam Brumby made her spine shiver.

'Nay, I'll manage. He were no'but skin and bone towards the end. You get on with yar work. I 'spect you've a lot to do with the funeral, an' all. By, lass, but you've kept this place going, I've got to hand it to ya . . .' and still chattering, Ma Harris heaved her stout frame up the narrow stairs. Esther stood at the bottom and watched Mrs Harris turn into Sam's room and close the door.

So it was late afternoon by the time Esther had finished everything about the farm and had washed under the pump in the yard, changed into her Sunday best frock and pinned up her hair.

When she came down the stairs she found Matthew lingering in the kitchen, warming his hands before the glowing fire in the range. The wood fell and sent a shower of sparks up the flue.

'Thought you'd gone home,' she said abruptly.

He turned slowly and grinned cheekily at her. 'Now –

why would I be wanting to do that, Esther?'

'Well, there's no need for you to stay any longer – not now.' Even to her own ears, her tone sounded more brusque than she had intended.

The smile faded from Matthew's mouth and his eyes glinted in the dancing firelight. 'Oh – dismissed, am I? Just like that, eh?'

Esther gave a click of exasperation. 'Oh, don't be so touchy, Matthew. I've been grateful for yar help, ya should know that.'

He turned away from the fire and moved slowly towards her, almost with a touch of menace. 'No, I dun't know. Perhaps you'd better show me just how grateful . . .'

She put out her hands, palms outward, to fend him off. 'Now, dun't you start that, Matthew Hilton.'

He stopped and regarded her insolently, then said, feigning innocence, 'Start what, Esther? Whatever can you be meaning?'

Esther turned quickly away from him, exasperated. 'Oh, really!' she muttered. Reaching her shawl from the peg, she dragged open the door and was through it and gone before he could say – or do – any more.

The easterly wind whipped across the fields as Esther took the path inland towards the Grange. She stopped to pull her shawl more closely about her as the wind caught at her skirt and tossed her curls. A small smile of satisfaction curved her mouth as she looked around her. Autumn had been gentle and the ploughing was going well, despite her time being taken up with caring for the old man. She smiled ruefully to herself. She did indeed owe

Matthew a debt of gratitude, for without him she certainly would not have kept up the farm work so well. Her smile widened. But it wouldn't do to tell him so, she thought. Matthew Hilton was quite full enough already of his own importance!

The smile faded and she sighed heavily. Everything could be very different from now on. What was going to happen to her now that Sam was gone?

At the Grange, the huge front door was opened smoothly by a tall, thin man dressed in a black suit. His mouth curved downward as if he had a bad smell under his nose. He looked down upon Esther and as she made to enter the house, the man deliberately barred her way. 'I don't think you can have business in this establishment, girl.'

Esther squared her shoulders. 'I am here to see Mr Marshall.'

She waited in vain for any kind of apology from the man, whose expression did not alter. 'I see, and have you an appointment?' He enunciated every word with clipped precision – and with an edge of sarcasm as if deriding the country dialect that was always so strong in her tones.

Esther stood her ground, refusing to be intimidated by him. 'Not exactly,' she said calmly, meeting his cold eyes steadfastly. 'I have come to inform the squire of the death of Mr Brumby.'

The manservant had the grace to look ashamed. But when he left her alone in the hall whilst he went in search of his master, some of Esther's confidence deserted her. She waited nervously, standing first on one foot and

115

then on the other, twisting her fingers together agitatedly as her gaze roamed over the lofty hallway and the elegant sweeping staircase above which hung numerous ancestral pictures of serious-looking men and elegant women. In their company, even in her Sunday best dress, Esther felt like a tramp. The butler emerged from a door to the left of the hallway and beckoned her imperatively. Esther crossed the hall, her boots squeaking on the polished floor. She saw the butler's look of disgust, but the man stood aside for her to enter and as the door closed softly behind her, Esther found herself standing in a book-lined room. In the centre of the room stood a huge mahogany desk, inlaid with a red leather top. The smell of rich tobacco smoke hung in the air. It was undoubtedly a man's room. For a moment Esther thought she was alone, then from a leather wing chair near the fire, Mr Marshall rose and turned to greet her.

'Now, my dear, what is it?'

'I thought I ought to come and tell you, sir. Mr Brumby died this morning.'

'Oh dear. Oh dear me. I am sorry.' Mr Marshall sat down again. 'Come and sit down, my dear girl.'

'Thank you, sir.' Esther sat tensely on the edge of the chair set on the opposite side of the fireplace to Mr Marshall.

'You'll let me know when old Sam's funeral is to be, won't you? I shall attend. As I told you, that farm has been in his family for several generations.'

Esther nodded.

'Is everything all right on the farm? Do you need any help until I can get things sorted out?'

116

Esther bit her lip. She desperately wanted to ask him what was to happen to the farm — what was to happen to her. Huskily, she said, 'I've kept things going, all the time he's been ill . . .'

'I know you have, my dear, you have done remarkably well. I admire the way you've coped.'

Esther opened her mouth, trying to form the right words, but Mr Marshall was standing now and she found herself on her feet and being ushered towards the door.

Mr Marshall gave her shoulder a comforting pat and repeated his offer of help should she need it. Before she had time to say any more she was being shown out of the front door by the butler and the moment was lost.

She walked back along the lane towards Brumbys' Farm, but at the gate she paused and looked up at the shadow of the farmhouse, still and silent in the dusk. Not wanting to go back into the empty house yet, she turned and climbed the bank bordering the lane. Across the marsh, jumping the meandering streams, she climbed the far dunes and came to the beach. She walked out to the very end of the Spit where the sea and the land and the sky all seemed to meet. She sat down on the damp ground, the wind whipping around her. She could taste the salt on her lips. It was lonely and desolate out here, yet she was not afraid. Her eyes scanned the darkening sea and, half turning, her gaze took in the flat land behind her.

She gave a deep sigh of sadness. She felt as if the niche she had deliberately carved for herself in this place had been taken away from her. He had been a strange man, Sam Brumby, yet already she was missing him. She remembered everything that had happened since the morning she had arrived; Sam's initial rejection of her, then gradually his grudging acceptance and finally his need of her. For the first time in her life she had known real happiness living at Brumbys' Farm. She hoped she had repaid Sam by caring for him until the end.

Poor Sam, she thought, poor Sam.

'What happened?' Matthew demanded, as, back in her working clothes, Esther led the cows out of the byre after evening milking. 'Did Squire say what was going to happen to the farm?'

'No,' Esther snapped. Her moments of reverie out on the Spit were gone. There was work to be done, a funeral to organize. She did not pause in her vigorous sweeping of the cowshed. 'Tek them cows back to the field, will ya?'

'Did he say he would come to the funeral?' Matthew persisted, ignoring her command.

'Yes.' She stopped her sweeping and said briskly, 'Talking of the funeral, I'd best get baking.' She banged the door of the cowshed shut and walked towards the house.

'There'll be a few come, I reckon,' Matthew said following her. 'Old Sam Brumby was a funny old boy, but folks respected him. There'll be Mr Marshall an' his bailiff for a start . . .' On his fingers he ticked off the people he thought would attend Sam's funeral. Esther would be responsible for offering refreshment to them all. It was customary for a spread to be put on at the house following the interment, even if it was over two miles back to the farm from the church. 'The vicar will probably come; all the folks who live at the Point, Tom Willoughby, of course, and Will, the carrier.' There was a pause, then Matthew said, 'What's up with you, Esther? You're not listening to a word I'm saying.'

'Everything will be ready,' she said, 'dun't you worry. You just see to them cows.'

'Huh, I was only trying to 'elp,' Matthew muttered and stomped off.

Late that night as she climbed the stairs, her limbs heavy with weariness, she paused outside the closed door of Sam's bedroom, her hand hovering towards the latch. Then she let it fall. Best not go in, she told herself, I shan't sleep if I look at him again. The funeral people would be here tomorrow to put him in a coffin in the front room. It wouldn't be so bad then. But she didn't like to think of him still lying in his bed, cold and silent – and so close. Holding her breath, she scuttled through the neighbouring room where Matthew had slept, not daring to peer into the dark corners. Only when she was in her own small bedroom and leaning against the closed door behind her, did she breathe easily.

She almost wished she had agreed to Matthew staying another night or two.

Whatever's the matter with you, Esther Everatt? she asked herself fiercely. You're not usually so squeamish. But she had not had to deal with death before. It was not so easy to be rational and strong-minded alone in the darkness of the night with Sam's corpse in the nearby room.

For a long time she lay in her bed listening to every sound; the wind whistling around the farmhouse and the old timbers creaking. She was just on the point of falling asleep when the click of the latch on her bedroom door startled her into wakefulness. She lay there breathing hard, her heart pounding, her scalp prickling with fear. Someone stepped into the room, closed the door behind them and began to move towards the bed.

Esther screamed – a loud, shrill noise piercing the blackness. The intruder fell against the end of her bed and she felt strong hands grasping at her legs kicking under the covers. 'Esther, Esther – it's only me.'

She stopped screaming, panting hard. Now she was angry.

'Matthew! How dare you? What—'

'Esther – please. I thought I'd stay another night or two – just till after the funeral. You dun't want to be here on your own, do you?'

'Well . . .' she said, a little mollified. The memory of her apprehension was still fresh in her mind. Still, she did not trust his motives. 'Mebbe not,' she conceded, 'but that dun't mean I want you in me bedroom.'

'Oh, Esther.' His voice was a hoarse whisper and she felt him sliding along the bed towards her.

'That's quite far enough, Matthew Hilton.' She snuggled further under the covers, pulling them up tightly under her chin.

'Esther – stop tormenting me. It's killing me, sleeping – or not sleeping – knowing you're lying just the other side of the wall . . .' His voice deepened with desire. 'Esther – I want you like I've never wanted anyone before. You've got me all twisted up like no other girl ever has ....'

She gave a snort of laughter. 'Aye, only 'cos I'm the first to fend ya off, me lad.'

'No, no, it ain't that, truly it ain't.'

She felt his breath upon her face and then his lips were on her mouth, but gently, pleadingly. 'Esther,' he murmured. 'I love you, Esther.'

She twisted her head away. 'Matthew – I won't. I've told you I won't – not till I'm married.'

'Then I'll marry you, Esther Everatt, if that's what it takes.'

Twelve

ALL the people whom Matthew had listed attended the funeral, plus a few more besides. Esther recognized most of them. There were the two neighbouring farmers – also tenants of Squire Marshall – Tom Willoughby and Mr Souter. All the men from the Point were there and the squire, together with his farm bailiff, and, of course, Will Benson.

All funerals were sad, Esther thought but she felt the pathos of this one. Poor Sam. There were no close relatives, no one to shed a tear into a delicate kerchief for him. Esther and Matthew kept to their places at the rear of the funeral procession, sitting towards the back of the church in the pew Sam had occupied on the few occasions he had attended a service. The flowers from the previous Sunday were withered and dying. No one had cared enough to put fresh ones in their place. The church was cold and musty with the damp.

The vicar said a few words about Sam, about him being a man of the soil, a man close to Nature, whose life had been ordered by the Seasons of God. Much of what he said was way above Esther's head, but he seemed to be speaking about Sam in a kindly and respectful manner, skilfully avoiding any mention of the fact that he had attended church only about three times a year or that he lived the life of a grumpy recluse.

They stood in a little cluster around the grave as the coffin was lowered into the earth, the damp drizzle seeping through their clothes so that as soon as they could without unseemly haste, the mourners moved away from the cold graveyard and back to their conveyances. Esther saw the squire and his bailiff in conversation. They both glanced across at her, then swiftly away again as they saw her watching them. Then Mr Marshall climbed into his carriage.

Esther unhitched the pony and trap Matthew had borrowed for her from Tom Willoughby and climbed up, slapping the reins so that the pony turned homeward. The rest of the mourners followed Esther back through the town and along the coast road towards the farm.

The spread she had prepared did Sam Brumby proud, though she was a little doubtful as to whether he would really have approved of all the fuss. The atmosphere amongst those present was a little strained. There was no common ground between them for easy conversation, though Esther was painfully aware that the squire and his other two tenants gravitated towards each other and sat together talking quietly as they ate. Esther saw Mr Marshall wave his hand at one point as if to encompass the land all around the farm, and she was sure he was discussing the future occupancy of his holdings. Perhaps even the two farmers whose land adjoined Brumbys' Farm were laying claim to it right now.

Only Will, the carrier, seemed at ease. 'He were a good friend to me,' Will said to no one in particular, and he waved his fork towards Esther. 'An' he gave this young 'un a good start. That right, ain't it, lass?'

Esther nodded. 'Yes. I've learned a lot from Mr Brumby,' she said and purposely she glanced towards the squire. But Mr Marshall was deep in conversation with the two farmers and appeared not to have heard.

Replete at last on ham and pork pie, the mourners began to settle themselves to hear the reading of Sam's will. Mr Thompson, the lawyer, began delivering the legal jargon in a respectful monotone. ' "This is the last Will and Testament of me Samuel Brumby of Fleethaven Point in the County of Lincoln, Farmer. I give devise and bequeath all my real (if any) and personal estates and effects whatsoever and wheresoever of which I have power to dispose by Will unto Esther Everatt . . ." '

At the mention of her name Esther gasped audibly and felt the blood drain from her face. For a moment all eyes in the room swivelled to look at her. But the lawyer did not look up or pause in his reading.

' ". . . absolutely and appoint her sole Executrix hereof. I revoke all former Wills by me at any time heretofore made and declare this only to be and contain my last Will and Testament. In witness whereof I have hereunto set my hand this fourth day of October one thousand nine hundred and eleven." ' Here Mr Thompson looked up. 'The will was signed by Mr Brumby and witnessed by myself and –' his glance rested briefly on the carrier – 'Mr William Benson, whom you all know.'

Now Esther felt the lawyer's gaze come to rest upon her, sitting straight-backed in a chair in one corner.

'You, I presume, are Miss Everatt?'

What old Sam Brumby had actually said to Mr Thompson, as the lawyer was to tell her later, had been, 'I want the wench to have it all,' and it had been left to the lawyer to couch his wishes in legal terms.

Esther licked her dry lips and her reply came out in a hesitant whisper. 'Yes – yes, sir.'

'Well, Miss Everatt, I shall be obliged if you will present yourself at my office tomorrow at ten in the morning for the signing of some documents. Of course there are legal procedures to be gone through, but I see no reason why you may not take it that everything that belonged to Sam Brumby –' he paused for effect – 'is now yours.'

Esther could not stop the words from tumbling from her lips. 'Even the tenancy of the farm – I can stay on at the farm?'

The lawyer held up his hand as if to fend off her eagerness. 'That's quite another matter, Miss Everatt. Presumably –' the lawyer glanced towards Mr Marshall for confirmation – '. . . the tenancy would cease with his death.'

Esther too looked towards the squire and saw him nod in agreement. 'That is correct, Mr Thompson. It is written into all my tenancy agreements.'

'Quite so, Mr Marshall.'

There was a general shuffling in the room as the others present began to lose interest in the finer points of what Sam Brumby's will meant. Not one of them had the right to have expected anything from Sam Brumby, and yet there was an air of displeasure that the girl who had arrived out of the mist one morning from God alone knew where, had got it all.

125

Only on Will Benson's face was there a smile of satisfaction on Esther's behalf.

Esther noticed Matthew staring at her, as if not knowing quite how to accept the news. She was no longer the waif who had arrived from nowhere and with nothing. Now she was in possession of some valuable belongings and, possibly, even the future tenant of Brumbys' Farm. She saw a slight frown of thoughtfulness appear on Matthew Hilton's young face, but then, as if with silent agreement the gathering made to leave. Esther forgot about Matthew.

She followed Mr Marshall out to his carriage and held the reins for him as he climbed up.

'Mr Marshall – sir – about the tenancy of the farm . . .'

Mr Marshall looked down upon the anxious girl, but his expression was hard and cold. 'This is hardly the time or the place to discuss matters of business. If you wish to see me, come to the Grange.' Without a further word he took the reins from Esther's hand and clicked to the horse to move on.

Esther stared after his retreating back, cursing herself for her mistake. Had she ruined her chances through, in Mr Marshall's eyes, a lack of proper respect for Sam Brumby's funeral day?

The following afternoon – after her morning visit to the lawyer's office – found Esther trudging the muddy lane towards the Grange. There was a fine drizzle and by the time she had walked the distance between Brumbys' Farm and the Grange, the cold dampness was seeping through her cape. Her face and hands were wet and her hair straggled in dripping strands down her face and neck.

'Have you an appointment?' the sour-faced butler asked her loftily. Obviously he had forgotten – or would not acknowledge – the discomfort of his last meeting with Esther Everatt.

'No, but Mr Marshall told me to come and see him.'

'I see.' The man looked her up and down, sighed audibly and then said with pained resignation, 'Then you had better come inside. But please, do wipe your – er – boots.'

She stood just inside the doorway whilst the man walked towards the heavy oak door to the study and knocked. He disappeared inside and closed it behind him.

It seemed an age before the man reappeared, time enough for the rain to seep from Esther's boots on to the polished wooden floor and leave tell-tale puddles. Returning, the man sighed again and then said, 'Would you follow me, please?'

Mr Marshall was sitting behind the huge desk. 'Do sit down.' With a vague wave of his hand the squire indicated a hard wooden chair which had been placed on the visitor's side of the desk.

'Now,' he leant on his desk and his sharp eyes bored into Esther's, 'what was it you wanted to see me about?' It was an oblique reference to Esther's impropriety the previous day. Rather than embarrassing the young girl further, it now made the courage flow into her. 'Mr Marshall, sir, I have come to ask you if you will please grant me the tenancy of Brumbys' Farm. After all, Mr Brumby put in his will that he wanted me to have everything of his and—'

'Whoa there, steady, my dear girl!' The squire put up his hands, palms outward, as if to slow down a galloping horse. 'Not so fast.' He sighed and then leant back in his leather chair. 'The tenancy was not Sam Brumby's to pass on. It reverted to me on his death, to be reassigned as I think fit.'

Eagerly, Esther leant forward. 'But, sir, you know I've managed that farm since Mr Brumby was ill, all this last spring and summer, through haymaking and harvest. You've seen for yourself . . .'

The squire spread his hands in mock helplessness. 'I don't deny it, my dear, you've done a good job, a wonderful job, considering you're a woman. But you see, that's the problem, we don't grant tenancies to women. I have checked with my lawyer and there is a specific clause in the agreement drawn up by my great-grandfather that the tenancy must be in the name of a man.'

'Oh,' she said flatly. Then again, 'Oh.' There was silence in the room between them. Then Esther lifted her head defiantly. 'But why, Squire? Why won't you let a woman have your farm? Can't *you* change the – the clause?'

The squire blinked in the face of her boldness. He had never before met a young woman quite like Esther Everatt and for all his breeding and position, he did not know how to deal with her.

'Well, we never have, in all these years, changed any

thing. I really don't think—' He broke off, as what he thought could be a better idea came to his mind. 'Now, my dear,' he leant forward, 'if you were married, then it would be a different matter entirely.'

'Married? Why?'

'Well, we could put the tenancy in your husband's name.'

Her green eyes flashed, her mind working busily. She too leant forward eagerly, her voice becoming slightly breathless. 'You mean — if I were married, you'd grant the tenancy to me — to my husband?'

The squire nodded. 'Yes, I'd be prepared to do that.'

Again there was a silence between them as they stared at each other. The girl's mind was working feverishly, the man's wondering what was going on in hers.

'There's no one else asked you for the tenancy of Brumbys' Farm?'

'Not exactly, though my other two tenants whose lands adjoin Brumbys' have discussed the idea in principle of splitting it between them. There's no outsider come forward — not yet anyway. Though word may not have got around yet that it's become vacant.'

'How long could you give me before you need to decide?'

The squire shrugged. 'Three weeks or so.'

Esther nodded, her eyes glinting. She stood up and held out her hand. After a moment's hesitation, the squire shook it.

'Three weeks, Squire Marshall. Three weeks it is.'

*

She was hanging the washing on the line when she suddenly saw Beth standing uncertainly at the corner of the house leading round from the yard into what Esther called the front garden.

'Is Matthew here?'

Esther stared at her for a moment then looked away. The girl's face was white and there were dark shadows beneath her eyes. She stood huddled into her shawl, her shoulders bent, her arms folded across her body as if protecting it.

'Where is he?' Her voice rose shrilly when Esther did not answer her first question. 'I've got to see him.'

Esther shrugged. She avoided looking directly at Beth and concentrated on stretching out the clothes and pegging them to the line. 'I dun't know where he is.'

'Yes, you do,' Beth said with a flash of her usual vitality. 'He's been here all the time with you since old man Brumby took ill. I thought at least once he were dead . . .' The spark that had flickered briefly died and she sank back into lethargy, almost pleading with Esther. 'Please – tell me where he is. I – I've *got* to see him!'

Esther eyed Beth shrewdly now – she looked dreadful. But if what Esther had in mind was going to work, then she didn't want Beth to meet up with Matthew. She jabbed a clothes peg firmly over a sheet on the line. 'Well, I dun't know where he is. He went off early this morning and I ain't seen him since!'

The girl stared at her, the last vestige of any colour draining from her face. Esther looked away from her again and bent to pick up another sheet from the washing basket. When she looked back, Beth had disappeared.

Esther worked through the day's chores, Beth's visit forgotten, for her mind was busy with her own problems, her own plans.

'Cat got yar tongue?' Matthew appeared in the washhouse doorway as she folded and mangled the sheets from Sam's bed.

'Eh?' She looked round at him. 'What? Oh, no. I was thinking, that's all.'

'You think too much, Esther me girl.' He came up behind her, put his arms about her and nuzzled her hair. For once she did not pull away from him and, encouraged by her lack of rebuff, he kissed her neck.

Esther's eyes darkened. He wanted her, she knew. But did he want her enough to marry her? Had his rash statement in her bedroom the night after Sam had died been made only in the heat of his rough desire for her?

His lips were searching for her mouth, his fingers reaching for the fastenings of her blouse.

'No, Matthew, no!'

'I want you, Esther, I'm goin' crazy for you. Let me love you, Esther, please – please . . .'

'I've told you before, Matthew Hilton, no man's goin' to touch me till I'm married!'

He looked deep into her eyes, his own burning with undenied passion for her. 'Then marry me, Esther, marry me?'

For a long moment they gazed into each other's eyes;

his fervent, blazing with a frustrated passion that threatened to spill over and engulf them both. But Esther's eyes were troubled. She liked Matthew – she liked him a lot. And he worked hard. Without his help she could never have coped over the last few months. But was it really enough for marriage? Could she really spend the rest of her life with him, working side by side on the farm? The farm! She felt a shudder run through her. How could she bear to leave Brumbys' Farm now, the only real home she had ever known?

Mistaking her involuntary shiver for excitement, Matthew murmured in her ear, 'Oh, Esther, you're lovely. I want you so. Please say yes!'

'All right then,' she said at last, 'if you're sure . . .'

'Do you mean it?' His eagerness was almost pathetic.

'Yes, course I mean it. I'll marry you, Matthew.'

His eyes were afire, and his arms were about her again, hugging her, longing to love her. 'When?'

She smiled up at him. 'As soon as you like,' she whispered huskily, clamping down hard on any feelings of guilt. It wasn't just to get the tenancy of the farm, she persuaded herself, she really did like him.

She put her arms about him in genuine gratitude and kissed him.

He groaned as he returned her kiss ardently. 'Esther, oh, Esther!'

It wasn't until a lot later that Esther remembered with a little stab of shame that neither of them had spared a thought for Beth.

*

132

Mid-morning about three weeks later found Esther dressed in her blue cotton dress and Matthew, stiff and awkward in his Sunday best suit, walking down the lane towards the Grange. They walked side by side in silence, companionable yet not touching.

The grim-faced butler opened the door once more and ushered them reluctantly into his master's study.

'Well, well, Miss Everatt, and to what do I owe this pleasure, my dear?' the squire greeted them.

They stood before him.

"Tain't Miss Everatt now, Mr Marshall, 'tis Mrs Hilton. We were married by special licence at half past eight this morning at the church.' Esther's look challenged the squire boldly. 'Mr Marshall, this is my husband.'

133

Thirteen

*T*HERE was silence in the squire's study, broken only by the steady ticking of the grandfather clock in the corner.

Mr Marshall recovered his senses, stood up and came around the desk holding out his hand to Matthew. 'Well, well, my boy. Congratulations indeed!'

He turned to Esther and held out both hands to her. 'My best wishes for your happiness, my dear. I'm not a man to go back on his promise, dear me no.' He beamed at them both. 'You've got yourself a farm.'

Esther glanced at Matthew but he was staring at the squire, his mouth slightly open.

'This calls for a celebration.' Mr Marshall went to the side of the fireplace and pulled a red silk cord. When the door opened and the butler glided into the room, he ordered a bottle of Madeira and three glasses. 'My wife would join us, I'm sure, but I believe she has taken the carriage into the town.' He smiled again at them both, his glance flitting from one to the other.

'Well, well,' the squire rubbed his hands together. 'This has all worked out very nicely. I had no idea you two were intending to be married. This is splendid, really splendid news.' He looked towards Matthew and added, 'I'll have the tenancy agreement drawn up by my lawyer and let you know when to come and sign it . . .'

Matthew stared dumbly at the squire, who cleared his throat and turned to Esther for reassurance. 'You must come too, seeing as how really it was you . . .' He coughed in embarrassment and stopped, glancing again at Matthew. The door opened and the butler carried in a tray of glasses and the wine. With obvious relief the squire turned to pour out the wine himself, dismissing the manservant, and handing the glasses to Esther and Matthew. Mr Marshall raised his glass, 'Here's to a long life of happiness and success in your new venture.'

Esther felt that one of them should speak, say something, and since Matthew seemed to have lost his wits, she said, 'Thank you, Mester Marshall. We'll do our best to run the farm right, won't we, Matthew?'

Matthew took a gulp of the wine, spluttered slightly and nodded. He opened his mouth to speak but a fit of coughing overcame him as the wine caught the back of his throat.

Not until they were half-way down the lane leading back to Brumbys' Farm did Matthew speak. They had come out of the big house and walked side by side down the drive and out of the gate. Without even looking at him Esther could feel the rigid anger of Matthew's body as he took huge, furious strides, so that she had to take a little running step every so often to keep pace with him.

Well away from the Grange under a clump of trees that overhung the lane, he stopped and turned to face her, gripping her upper arms with his strong hands so that his fingers dug into her flesh. 'What's going on, Esther?'

'We – the squire's giving us the tenancy of the farm, Sam's farm.'

'Oh? And when was all this worked out, eh?'

'I – I asked him after Sam died, after his funeral. You know I did.'

There was a pause and then his blue eyes narrowed. 'But what did he mean when he said he wasn't a man to go back on his promise? What promise?'

Esther hesitated.

Matthew shook her. 'What did he promise you?'

The words came out in a rush. 'He promised me the tenancy of the farm if I was married.'

It seemed he stared at her a long time, just stared and stared not releasing his hurtful grip, not speaking, just holding her gaze with his own hard, wrathful eyes. His breathing became deeper.

'You mean – you married me – just to get the bloody farm?'

Her chin came defiantly higher and she returned his gaze brazenly. 'So? What if I did? If we dun't take the farm on, what's going to happen to us, eh?'

'You – you – scheming *whore*!' He was beside himself with rage, and could think of no worse insult to fling at Esther who had always held off his amorous advances with such puritanical, virginal fervour. He pushed her so violently from him that she lost her balance and fell on to the grass verge at the side of the lane. He seemed taller in his fury as he stood over her. As she lay on the grass, she felt completely at the mercy of his menacing power. 'You used me,' he spat at her. 'You knew I was crazy to have you, and you used that to get me to marry ya, just to get the farm.'

'Matthew – you dun't understand, t'aint like that . . .' She scrambled to her feet to face him, but he made no attempt to touch her now.

'Ain't it?' He seemed calmer for the moment, yet his composure was perhaps even more frightening than his white hot anger. 'You think I'm stupid, dun't you, Esther, some stupid farm *boy* . . .' He emphasized the derisory name she had first used upon him, as if the implied insult still offended him. 'I 'eard you at the funeral, soon as he'd read the will leaving you everythin' – everythin' in that house – an' still you was after more. "What about the farm? Can I stay on the farm?" you said.' He raised his voice in high-pitched mimicry of a woman's tones, mocking and insulting her now. 'An' you chased out after the squire as he was leaving to ask him the same thing. Oh, by heck, but you're grasping, Esther Everatt.'

In his anger he had forgotten that only a few hours previously she had changed her name to his.

Now Esther's temper was rising to match his own, sweeping away any vestige of fear. 'What about you, then?' she demanded, determined that he should accept his part. 'Why did *you* marry *me*? You asked me, remember?'

'You know why. I wanted you that bad, I'd have agreed to anything . . .'

She stepped nearer to him, her green eyes sparking with fire, her lips parted. Huskily, she said, 'An' dun't you still want me, Matthew? I ain't one to break my promises either. I'll be a good wife to you, Matthew Hilton. You'll not have cause to complain.'

He shook his head wonderingly. 'What is it about you, Esther? God, I hate you for what you've done this day, yet I can't stop mesen wanting . . .' His lips were on hers, crushing, bruising, revengeful, but Esther did not flinch or try to pull away as he half-carried, half-dragged her beneath the trees. He put his hands into the bodice of her dress and ripped the thin material the full length from neck to hem. He took her for the first time, there on the roadside, in a mixture of passion and rage, the culmination of months of pent-up frustration and longing. Esther lay submissively beneath him with her eyes closed, the only sound she uttered being a gasp as he thrust deep within her and she felt a searing pain shoot through her groin. The damp ground was cold to her naked back and small stones bit into her skin. In a final humiliation, as the breeze rippled through the undergrowth, she felt the sting of a nettle on her cheek.

Esther did not see Matthew the rest of that day. Her wedding day, she thought, and here she was milking the cows, feeding the pigs and churning the butter like any other day of the week. Thoughtfully, she rubbed her cheek. It had not been the way she had imagined becoming a wife, the way she had pictured giving herself to her husband and certainly not the way she had wanted it to be.

By nightfall, Matthew had still not returned to the farm. A little after ten o'clock, when Esther was about to give up waiting for him and take her candle up the stairs, she heard his footsteps in the yard. He stopped outside the back door and it seemed a long time before he opened it and stepped inside.

She was sitting near the table mending her stocking by the light from the oil lamp. She looked up as he appeared in the kitchen doorway. They stared at each other. Then Matthew shifted his gaze and moved, a little unsteadily, towards Sam's Windsor chair at the side of the range. For a moment he stood looking at it and then, as if making up his mind, he turned around and sat down in it. Slowly he turned his head and looked towards Esther.

'Well, are we having any supper, then?'

Esther laid aside her mending and moved to and fro between the pantry and the kitchen laying out bread and cheese and mashing a pot of tea. She glanced across at Matthew but he made no move to come to the table, so with a small smile of amusement – for it was obviously Matthew's way of assuming his role as master of the house – she cut him a slice of bread and a lump of cheese, poured a cup of tea and took it to him.

He took the plate and the cup and saucer from her and, placing the tea on the hearth, bit into the cheese.

'Suppose I'd better make a start on the ploughing at Top End tomorrow.' He paused, his gaze on the dying embers of the fire. 'That all right with you?'

Taking her cue from him, Esther said, 'Yes, fine. We'd do well to make the best of the mild autumn weather. Can ya borrow the horses?'

Matthew nodded. 'I saw Tom in the Seagull tonight. He'll bring 'em over in the morning.'

There was silence between them again, whilst Matthew ate and Esther merely nibbled at a piece of bread. She was wondering what was going to happen when they went upstairs. She realized that she should have made preparations for their wedding night, for their first night together in the home that was now rightfully and legally theirs.

She cleared her throat nervously. 'Er – I'll go up. You'll see to things down here, then, will ya?'

Matthew did not look round, but merely grunted.

Upstairs, Esther stood in the room where Matthew had slept on a makeshift bed on the floor. Then she moved into the small narrow room leading off it where she had been sleeping in the single bed. She undressed quickly and then, hearing Matthew's footsteps on the stairs, she scuttled on bare feet back into his room and lay down beneath the rough blankets on the straw-filled sacks on the floor.

As he reached the top of the stairs, she heard him open the door into Sam's room, pause and then close it again.

She was holding her breath as he stepped into the room where she lay. He came and stood over her, the candle in his right hand as he looked down at her. For a long moment, in the eerie shadows cast by the flickering light, they stared at each other. Then he blew out the candle. She heard the rattle as he set it down. In one swift movement the blankets were pulled from her and she felt his weight come down on top of her.

The daily demands of the farm forced them to settle quickly into a routine. The following morning Matthew fetched his belongings from the cottage that had been his home at the Point, and Esther scrubbed and cleaned the bedroom that had been Sam's. Now it was Matthew's Sunday best suit that stood on the hanger in the corner, Matthew's boots set ready beneath. There was fresh linen on the bed and on cold winter nights there would be a fire in the grate.

But Esther did not try to remove every trace of the old man to whom she owed so much. She put Sam's family pictures on the mantelpiece and that night, as they undressed for bed, Matthew padded across the floor to look at the faded photographs.

'By heck,' he exclaimed. 'Is that his pa? He's the spitting image of him!'

'I never dare ask him – but I 'spect so. It's not Sam. I reckon that one's Sam as a younger man.'

Esther pointed to the other photograph in a silver frame. Matthew looked closely at it. 'Not a bad looking fellow, was he?' Then he pointed at the pretty young girl with a cloud of curls. 'Who's this?'

'I reckon that's Katharine Brumby, Sam's sister. There's an entry about her birth in the old Bible in the front parlour – and did you notice at the funeral where Sam was buried?'

'No, can't say I took any notice. I dun't like funerals. I wanted to get out o' there as quick as possible.'

'Sam was buried alongside his parents, but on the other side was the grave of Katharine Brumby, his sister. She was only forty when she died. She can't ever have married.'

Matthew leant forward and peered closely at the faded

picture. 'She looks like you, he murmured. 'That explains it, then.'

'Explains what?'

'Why he took a fancy to you, of course.' He came and stood in front of her. 'You probably reminded him of her or summat. But then—' Suddenly he grabbed her round the waist and lifted her bodily off the floor and tossed her on to the bed, so that the old springs squeaked and protested. 'Who wouldn't fancy you, Esther?'

He could not quell his hunger for her, yet now there was a look of resentment deep in his eyes.

'Wait a minute, Matthew. There's something else I want to show you.'

He was on top of her, his dark eyes so close, his breathing rapid. She could feel his desire.

'Dun't start mekin' excuses, else I'll . . .'

'I'll not break me promise,' she said quietly, 'but there's something I want to show you.'

'What?' he demanded roughly, his tone still suspicious.

'Let me up, then.'

After a moment's hesitation, he rolled off her on to his back. Esther slid off the bed and bent down to pull out a heavy wooden box from under it. As she lifted the lid, Matthew reared up on one elbow and peered over the side of the bed. His jaw fell open. Inside were a great many coins, more money than either Matthew or Esther had ever seen in their lives.

'The old miser!' Matthew grinned, but there was admiration for the old man, not insult, in his tone. His ill-temper was smoothed away by the sight of so much wealth. Wealth that was now Esther's and – by rights – his too. 'Who'd have thought it?'

Esther let the lid fall and pushed it away. Then she climbed back into bed.

Esther kept her part of the strange marital bargain. Never once did she refuse Matthew his demands upon her body, day or night. He took her whenever and wherever he wanted. In the hayloft, in the wash-house as she bent over the dolly tub, out in the fields where anyone might have seen them – almost as if he were trying to punish her, trying to make her refuse him, just once, so that he could turn on her and accuse her afresh. Certainly, he was trying to humiliate her. But Esther remained stoically docile to her husband's demands. Not a word of complaint or protest passed her lips. Matthew had not reckoned on her strength of will. Nothing he could do to her physically would break her resolve. She had got what she wanted – the farm – and she had been willing to pay the price. And the price was to be a dutiful wife to her husband.

For a time there was an uneasy truce between them, but a week after their marriage, that tentative pact was threatened almost before it had begun.

Beth came to the farm.

From the wash-house Esther saw her talking to Matthew and as she stepped out towards them, drying her hands on her apron, they both turned to look at her. Matthew's face was set in an angry glare, whilst tears trembled on Beth's black lashes. As Esther came closer the weeping girl whispered, 'So it's true, ya got yar way at last?' She turned her tearful eyes to look up into Matthew's face. 'She dun't love you, Matthew. She – she's used you. Mester Willoughby, 'ee told his wife that the squire said he never gives the tenancy of his farms to a woman. She had to be married – to get the farm.'

'Beth, I—'

'It's true!' Her voice was becoming shrill. 'I love you, Matthew, I've always loved you and I thought we was . . .'

'Beth, I'm sorry, I—'

The girl shook her head. 'Mebbe it's me that's the fool. I let you . . .' her voice broke and she took a deep, trembling breath. 'But she – she got you by holding out, didn't she? *Didn't she?*' She screamed at him now, pummelling her fists against his chest and then falling helplessly against him, sobbing hysterically.

'Aw, Beth.' His voice was an anguished whisper, and for a moment his arms were around her holding her tightly against him, whilst Esther stood watching them. She heard Beth give a gulp and saw her pull away from Matthew. Beth turned, her head bowed, as if to walk away, but with a final fury that shuddered through her body, she turned on Esther and came close to her, shaking her fist in her face.

'You'll suffer for this, Esther Everatt, you'll—'

'Esther Hilton now, Beth,' Esther corrected her with brutal calmness.

The girl gasped and the colour flooded into her white cheeks. 'You'll suffer for this,' she spat again so that

Esther actually felt Beth's spittle on her face. 'You an' yours will never know happiness!'

It was like a curse being laid upon her.

'If you plough a crooked furrow an' sow a bad seed, you mun reap a bitter harvest.'

Fourteen

'YOU heard the news then, lass?'

Ma Harris placed her milk can on the floor of Esther's spotless pantry and watched whilst Esther filled it with creamy milk.

'No, what's that?'

There was a triumphant note in Ma's voice as she said, 'Beth Hanley's married Robert Eland, all quick-like. Yesterday, it were. What d'ya think to that – an' only four weeks after yours, eh?'

Esther almost dropped the small churn she was holding. Slowly, she straightened up to meet Ma Harris's keen gaze. Levelly, Esther said, 'I'm very pleased for her, I hope they'll be very happy.' She forced a smile to stretch her mouth. 'Mr Eland has been – fond of her for a long time, I believe.'

Esther felt Ma's shrewd glance studying her, but skilfully she avoided meeting those perceptive eyes. 'Aye, that's right,' the older woman acknowledged. 'Strange how things work out, ain't it? Young Beth married to a man old enough to be her father . . .' She cackled at her own joke. 'Well, not really, I'm exaggeratin' a bit. He's thirty-summat but she's only nineteen. An' she's gone to live in that monstrosity of a boat thing – I don't reckon it's safe, mesen,' she added musingly. 'An' there we was all thinking . . .'

146

Esther picked up the full can and held it out to Ma Harris, holding out her other hand for the coppers in payment. 'Shall you want any eggs this week, Mrs Harris?'

'Eh, but call me Ma, lass, everyone else round here does.' The toothless gums widened into a smile and Esther found herself unable to resist smiling in return. 'I'll have half a dozen,' Ma said, 'and they'll want a dozen at the pub.' Slyly, she added, 'An' shall I ask Mrs Eland if she wants to place a regular order for milk and eggs?'

Esther, having recovered her composure after Ma's piece of news, raised a quizzical eyebrow and returned Ma Harris's gaze steadily. 'I dun't reckon the new Mrs Eland will want to get her milk and eggs from me – from us.' She shrugged. 'But ya can ask her, if ya like.'

Ma turned and waddled back through Esther's kitchen. 'Eh, but you've worked wonders with this place. It's spotless. I ain't never seen old Sam's place look so clean. He's a lucky young feller, that Matthew Hilton. Fallen right on his feet, 'ee has, what wi' you gettin' the farm, an' all.' Again she shot Esther a knowing glance. Nothing, it appeared, got past Ma Harris's astute understanding. With what sounded like a note of disapproval, she added, 'But I don't expect he realizes it. Same with all the fellers, lass, they don't know a good thing when they've got it!' She chuckled at her own philosophy. 'But they know when they've lost it.'

As Esther closed the back door behind Ma Harris, she was wondering how Matthew would take the news of Beth's marriage to the man he had always disliked.

Would he start to think about what he, Matthew, had lost?

Esther could not bring herself to speak of Beth to her husband, yet the black-haired girl lay like a shadow over any chance of happiness that their marriage might have had. She guessed Matthew must have heard of Beth's marriage, for the same night that Ma Harris had imparted the news to Esther, Matthew ate his meal in silence and left the farmhouse without a word to her. He had still not returned when Esther banked down the range, took her candle and went upstairs to bed.

She awoke with a start.

A loud crash had disturbed her. Her heart pounded. She heard someone moving through the kitchen, as if they were lurching from side to side, colliding with the table, knocking over a chair. She swung her legs over the side of the bed and reached with fingers that trembled to light her candle. Her mouth was dry with fear as she reached the top of the stairs and heard the door from the living room into the small hall smash open, thrown back against the wall. She held the candle high to see who had dared to invade her home.

'Matthew! Whatever——?'

'Hello, Esh-ter, my beeootiful darlin'. Your husband's come home to hish lovely wife . . .' He hiccupped and reeled backwards falling against the front door behind him. He slithered down into an untidy heap on the floor. In the flickering candlelight, she could see the silly grin on his face.

'You're drunk!' she accused, rather unnecessarily.

Matthew giggled. 'I think I musht be.'

She turned and carried the candle back into the bedroom, leaving him in total darkness. She climbed into bed, blew out the light and lay there shaking with anger as she listened to every blundering step he made, pulling himself slowly up the stairs, muttering to himself then giggling foolishly.

'Esh-ter, bring the candle back here, woman. I can't see a thing. I'll fall down and break me – me neck.'

Grimly, Esther lay still and stared with wide eyes into the blackness.

He gained the top of the stairs and fell into the bedroom, the door thumping back against the bed.

He lay on the floor laughing stupidly. 'Ya know, I reckon I've had – hic – a bit too much.'

Esther said nothing.

She heard him pull himself to his feet and sit heavily on the side of the bed. She listened whilst laboriously he took off his boots. Slowly and with careful deliberation, he took off each item of clothing and laid it across the bottom of the bed. She could feel the heaviness of his clothes across her feet. Then he tugged at the bedclothes and scrambled his way beneath them. For a few moments he lay beside her, breathing heavily. Then suddenly, he rolled over towards her, flung one arm across her, brought up his knee and thrust his right leg over her body.

Although the smell of drink on his breath made her feel sick, she lay rigidly still. He tried to pull himself up to lie astride her, but in his befuddled state the effort was too much. He nuzzled his head against her shoulder and then gave a huge sigh, sending waves of ale fumes into her face.

His breathing became regular and soon he was snoring heavily. After a few minutes she gently eased herself out from under his heavy limbs and pushed him on to his back and on to his side of the bed. She turned her back to him and lay as far to the outside edge of the bed as she could. Her fingers gripped the thin mattress and her eyes stared sleeplessly into the darkness.

What have I done? she asked herself. What *have* I done?

The New Year brought its own problems. January was one of the wettest that the old farmers could remember. The ploughed fields became a quagmire and the swollen river spilled over its banks on to the fields that bordered it. The bitter winds whipped across the flat land, howling around the exposed farmhouse in the dark of the long nights. The winter ploughing was a long way from being finished, but there was no way they could get on to the land.

'We ought to have our own 'osses, two at least,' Matthew said to Esther. 'When the weather lets up, Tom Willoughby'll want his 'osses for his own ploughing. I reckon he's further behind than us.'

Esther nodded. 'He's more acreage than us, he'll not want to be lending us his team when the weather does get better, will he?' She was thoughtful for a moment. 'Do you think the squire would lend us a couple of his?'

Matthew shrugged. 'We could ask, I suppose, but Souters' Farm always has first call on Mester Marshall's 'osses. We ought to try to get our own, Esther,' he persisted. 'Could we find the money to buy a couple of carthorses?'

Esther pulled a face. 'We-ell,' she said slowly as if thinking aloud. 'Last year's harvest was good. We've enough and more to see us through for winter feed. Then there's seven pigs almost ready for market, still leaving us a couple for our own use.'

'What about that money you found under Sam's bed after he died?'

Esther looked up sharply and her eyes narrowed. 'I didn't want to use that. I wanted to hang on to that in case we ever hit a bad time and needed it for the rent and – well – just livin'.'

Matthew appeared to consider. 'Yes, I suppose that's sensible.' There was disappointment in his voice.

Esther looked across at him. It was the first time since their marriage that he had shown positive interest in the running of the farm. Oh, he worked hard, she couldn't deny that, but he seemed determined to remain the hired hand, rather than take his rightful place as the tenant farmer of Brumbys' Farm.

It seemed to her as if he was always angry, as if there was a brooding resentment simmering just below the surface ready to flare into anger at the slightest provocation – particularly towards her. His once merry, ready-to-laugh face seemed to have a perpetual frown, where before there had been laughter lines around his brown eyes. Now those same eyes were often resentful and shadowed with bitterness.

The day they had gone to the Grange again to meet

the squire and his lawyer, who turned out to be Mr
Thompson, Esther had felt that Matthew had been deliberately awkward. As they had entered the squire's study,
Mr Thompson had risen and come towards them, holding out his hand and smiling at Esther. 'My dear Mrs
Hilton, what a pleasure it is to see you again. How are
you settling down into married life?'

She had glanced at Matthew in time to see him
glowering truculently at the lawyer, and when Mr
Thompson had placed the Tenancy Agreement before
them, Matthew had pushed it roughly away from him,
almost shouting, 'I can't read all that complicated stuff.
You'd better ask my wife to deal with all this. *She's*
the "mester"!'

Patiently, Mr Thompson had read the lengthy legal
document, pausing to explain the obscure parts in sim-
pler words, at last saying, 'Despite all the involved legal
jargon, Mr Hilton, I can assure you – both – that this is
the standard form of Agreement which Mr Marshall has
with all his tenants. There are no catches.' He had
beamed across the desk at them.

'Quite so,' Mr Marshall had put in. 'Just sign it at the
bottom, my boy, and let me shake you by the hand as my
new tenant.'

Matthew had made a great play of signing the Agreement with big scrawling letters, as if he could barely
write properly, whereas Esther knew he could sign his
name quite easily. She had felt that this behaviour was all
part of his punishment of her for having trapped him
into marrying her so that she could secure the tenancy of
the farm.

Now, as they stood in the kitchen discussing the possibility of buying a pair of horses, for the first time he was showing real enthusiasm in planning their future.

A thought struck her. With a calculated subtlety that was normally alien to her candid nature, she said, 'Why don't you have a word with Tom Willoughby? He would probably know how much a pair would cost. He might even know of some for sale?'

Matthew grinned at her, and for a moment he was the old Matthew. 'Eh, but you're a sharp one, Esther Hilton. Why didn't I think of that?' Then, remembering suddenly, his eyes clouded over. 'Aye, you're a sharp one, all right, an' don't I know it.' He turned away abruptly, the tentative signs of a burgeoning co-operation dying instantly.

'I'll see Tom some time,' he said casually over his shoulder and went out to feed the pigs.

Esther sighed and returned to churning the butter, venting her disillusionment by thumping the wooden barrel of the churn over and over vigorously.

With February came the snow.

It fell heavily and almost continuously for three days. A strong wind sprang up off the sea from the north-east, a bitingly cold wind, drifting the snow and cutting off all communication with the town and even with the other farms.

As the snows began, Matthew brought all the cows into the farmyard. As the weather worsened the animals kept to the byre, munching their way through the hay and watching the white world outside with soulful eyes.

On the first Sunday in the month, as they sat either side of the kitchen table eating the roast beef dinner with no word of conversation passing between them, there came a thumping on the back door. They glanced at each other in surprise. Sunday was not usually a day for callers and no one could get down the coast road from the town. Not even Will Benson had been able to get through on his usual calls during the past week.

'What the . . . ?'

'I'll see who it is.' Esther rose and went to open the back door.

One of Ma Harris's children stood there, his thin frame shivering in the cold, the snow resting on his cap and clinging to his coat.

Esther gasped, 'Aw, Ernie lad, come in, do. Ya look like a snowman!' She laughed and pulled the boy into her warm kitchen. 'Look at him, Matthew—'

'I can't stop, missus, me ma sent me to fetch mester . . .'

'Who? Me?' Matthew rose from table and came towards the boy. 'What is it, lad? Summat wrong? Is it a shout?' Mr Harris was a member of the lifeboat crew too and often the Harris children were sent running to the neighbouring houses, to the pub and to the farms to fetch the crew, and the horses from Tom Willoughby's, when there was a launch.

The boy shook his head, scattering the snow over Esther's floor, where it melted and lay in little puddles. 'Naw, mester, 'tis Mrs Eland. Me mam's with her . . .'

'Beth? What's the matter with Beth?' Matthew's voice was sharp with anxiety.

154

'She's come to her time an' me mam says things aren't straightfor'ard. She—'

'What d'you mean – she's come to her time?' Matthew rapped out.

The boy gaped at him, his mouth falling open. 'She's havin' her babby.'

'*Baby!*' Matthew's voice was a strangled whisper. 'Beth – is – having a – baby?'

'Oh, yes, didn't ya know?' The boy's tone was matter-of-fact, but he was glancing nervously now from Matthew's dark face to Esther's, unable to understand the tension in the air.

The colour drained from Esther's face as Matthew swung round towards her. 'Did *you* know about this?' he hissed at her accusingly.

She hesitated a moment too long. 'No, no, I didn't!'

Matthew's hand shot out and his strong fingers gripped her chin, digging painfully into her cheeks. 'You lying bitch, you did know! It's mine, ain't it? It's got to be! Did you know before we was wed?' He shook her roughly, hurting her neck. '*Did* you?'

'No, no,' Esther cried, but she was remembering Beth coming to the farm asking for Matthew at the time when Sam had been so ill, dying in fact. Twice Beth had come, looking pale and wretched, huddled into a shapeless shawl she must have worn to hide her growing belly. Esther remembered now the desperation in Beth's eyes and how she had pleaded with Esther to tell her where she could find Matthew.

Esther should have guessed, but she had shut her mind – deliberately – to the obvious. She hadn't wanted to

155

know. Then again, after Matthew had married Esther, Beth's hysterical outburst had been caused by much more than just her love for him. She had been pregnant – and desperate!

'I – I swear I didn't know, Matthew,' Esther faltered. But her words sounded unconvincing, even to herself.

'I don't believe you,' Matthew said, through gritted teeth.

The boy, who had been watching them open-mouthed with astonishment, seemed suddenly to remember the urgency of his errand. He tugged at Matthew's sleeve. 'Mester – ya've got to fetch the doctor from town. Me mam can't manage the birthing. The babby's wrong road on.'

Matthew seemed to have forgotten young Ernie Harris's presence. Suddenly he flung Esther away from him and turned back to the boy.

'What? What d'ya mean?'

Patiently, seeming suddenly older than his fourteen years, Ernie explained to the uncomprehending man. 'The babby's coming feet first, like calves do sometimes, mester. Y'know.'

Matthew nodded grimly. Esther saw him close his eyes and heard him groan. She knew what he was thinking. She had seen him have to put his arm inside a cow and pull out her calf, with the animal in terrible pain and the man, fearing for the life of the unborn, heaving and sweating and covered in slimy birthing fluid. She could sense his agony. If it was anything like that – half as bad – for Beth . . .

Esther watched as Matthew pushed the lad aside and

156

lumbered towards the back door, snatching his coat from the peg on the back door as he went. Ernie too, darting a glance at Esther's face, scuttled outside after Matthew.

Slowly, Esther moved to the scullery window. She saw Matthew reach the farm gate and turn towards the town, wading his way through the knee-deep snow, his arms flailing from side to side in an effort to keep his balance as he went.

Out to the east, over the sea, the sky was low and heavy with more snow as Esther stood alone by the window watching her husband trudge determinedly towards the town to fetch the doctor for the woman who was about to give birth to his child.

It was almost twelve hours later, gone midnight, when Esther, still huddled over a dying fire in the range where she had sat for most of the day, just staring into the glowing coals, heard a loud rapping on the back door.

The sudden noise in the silence of the night made her start suddenly and her heart began to pound.

'Matthew . . .' She jumped up and, snatching the lamp from the table, hurried to the door to open it. But it was Ernie Harris standing there again.

'Missus, me mam sent me to fetch ya.'

'Why, what's wrong? Is it Beth? Mrs Eland?'

'Naw, that's all over.' Even in the pale flickering light from the lamp, Esther could see the delight spread across the young boy's face. 'She had a lad, missus. Doctor were there. Yar man fetched him, but . . .' The smile faded now. ''Ee's bin in the pub ever since, an' now . . .' The

157

voice faltered and the boy dropped his gaze as if embarrassed to look into Esther's eyes.

She put out her hand and gripped Ernie's shoulder. 'Tell me, what is it? What's happened?'

The boy looked up again, the words coming out in a rush. 'Yar man's roaring drunk, missus. An' he's standing outside the boat – Eland's boat – shouting and carrying on. There'll be a fight, missus, if ya don't come. Me dad and some of the other men at the Point have tried to pull 'im away, but . . .' the boy shrugged. 'He's fighting mad, missus. Do come.'

Esther turned back into the house and took down her cape from behind the door and pulled on her boots. Taking the lamp, she snecked the door behind her and bending her head against the sleeting wind, she trudged out into the snow.

Luckily, there had been no further heavy snowfalls so she was able to follow the path trodden by the comings and goings earlier in the day. She followed Ernie's wiry form as he leapt and bounded through the snow. Long before they reached the Point, she could hear Matthew's voice.

Then, as Ernie helped her clamber up the slippery Hump, she saw him.

A small group of people from the Point cottages were standing in a huddled semi-circle behind him, holding lanterns high as if to light the drama going on before them.

Matthew was at the foot of the wooden jetty leading up to Robert Eland's boat. At the top of the gangway stood Robert Eland, shaking his fist at Matthew below.

'Come down here, Eland, and fight like a man – if ya call ya'sen a man. That bairn's mine. There's a cuckoo in ya nest, man . . .'

'Go home, you fool, to your own wife and let mine be,' Eland shouted back.

'Beth's mine. Her bairn's mine, an' ya know it, Eland. I'll not have my son live on a rotten boat that might get swept out to sea wi' the next tide.'

Esther drew in a breath to shout his name, but before she could utter a sound, Robert Eland had run down the gangway and from about half-way up had leapt down upon Matthew, falling on top of him and tumbling him to the ground. They rolled in the snow, grappling to get a hold, trading punch for punch. They staggered to their feet, holding on to each other in the effort to rise. Then they swayed back momentarily and came at each other again, fists swinging. Matthew caught Robert Eland high on the side of the head, whilst in the same second Eland's knuckles found Matthew's nose, and blood, black in the fitful light from the lanterns, spattered the snow.

Esther pushed the lantern she carried into Ernie's hands and ran forward. 'Stop it – stop it, Matthew. You have no right. Robert – please . . .'

Matthew swung his arm back to aim a punch at Eland, but caught Esther full in the chest, knocking her into the snow. She lay there winded, but her attempt at intervention galvanized the other men amongst the onlookers to take action. They moved forward as a body, some to take hold of Matthew, others to grasp Eland. The women amongst the group rushed to help Esther.

'Ee, lass, what a to-do.' She heard Ma Harris's warm voice in her ear.

'I'm – fine,' Esther gasped, not quite truthfully, as they helped her upright. 'Just help me – get him away from here – home.'

She looked across at her husband. He was slumped forward, only held up from falling into the snow by the other men. He was sobbing now, a wretched, distraught figure.

'Beth – oh, Beth. I'm sorry. I didn't know. Ya should have told me . . .' He talked to the empty air because, of course, Beth was not out there in the snow to hear his anguish.

Esther moved forward, resolutely pushing away the memory of Beth's stricken face asking to see Matthew, of her distress at hearing of his marriage. Now Esther put her shoulder under her husband's arm and felt his weight sag against her. She swayed a moment and then straightened.

'Thanks, Mester Harris. I've got him now.' Esther braced her shoulders and half-dragged, half-carried her husband up the lane towards their home.

As soon as they were some distance up the lane, Esther said firmly, 'Shut up now, Matthew. What's done is done. Ya mekin' a right fool of ya'sen.'

He lifted his head briefly. 'Ya made the fool o' me, Esther Everatt. I hopes ya satisfied.'

Still, she thought, he thinks of me by my maiden name and not by the one he has given me in marriage. More than anything, this seemed to accentuate the bitterness he felt towards her.

They stumbled their way through the snow, Matthew still rambling about Beth and his son, and venting his anger upon his wife. By the time they reached the back door of the farmhouse, Esther was exhausted. There was a pain in her chest from Matthew's blow and his weight seemed to grow heavier and heavier. Inside, she pushed him thankfully into the chair by the range and sank down on to the rug herself. The coals still glowed with a little welcome warmth. It was several minutes before she could drag herself upright and move towards the kitchen to fetch a rag to wipe away the blood still trickling from his nose. Two dark shadows were swelling beneath his eyes.

She fetched a bowl and spoon. 'There's some broth here still warm.' Her tone was sharp. 'Come on, Matthew. Stir ya'sen. It'll do ya good.'

There was no response. Matthew leant his head back against the wooden chair and closed his eyes.

'Please ya'sen,' Esther muttered impatiently, but nevertheless she fetched a blanket and wrapped it around him.

Then she went upstairs alone to her bed.

Fifteen

WHEN she came down the following morning, the blanket had been tossed aside and Matthew was not in the house.

Esther cleaned out the range and relit the fire. She laid the breakfast table and was about to go out and start the milking, when he came in. He sat down at the table, picked up the spoon laid ready for him and began to eat the porridge which Esther had spooned into a bowl.

'Ya know,' he began between mouthfuls, his eyes cast downward. 'I reckon we could just afford a pair of 'osses. I was talking to Tom Willoughby at the pub last night an' he reckons he knows of a chap who's got a couple of crossbreeds for sale.'

Esther almost gasped in astonishment. Matthew was acting as if yesterday, and more especially last night, had never happened. She looked closely at him. There was no way he could forget last night's escapade though, she thought grimly, with two black eyes and a bruise across the bridge of his nose. Esther shrugged slightly. Oh, well, she thought to herself, if that's the way he wants it, it suits me. Aloud she said, 'They might be a bit pricey for the likes of us, but there's no harm in 'aving a look, Matthew.'

'Right, I'll go an' see Tom later on today.'

A little later he left the house without ever looking directly at Esther or meeting her eyes.

'By heck,' Ma Harris shook her head. 'Ah dun't want many of them type of birthings. Poor lass were fair worn out, and torn – eh dear!' She clicked her tongue against the roof of her mouth and cast her glance skyward in an expression of regret and shook her head again. ''Ee were a big lad an' wrong road on. She had a bad time, did poor Beth.'

Quietly, Esther said, 'She had a son, then?'

She felt Ma Harris's perceptive gaze upon her, watching her. 'Aye, a fine lad. She's calling him Daniel after her father. The babby's none the worse, just Beth. She'll get over it. She's young enough to have plenty more bairns.' Ma Harris cackled. 'She'll have to go some to catch me up, though, won't she? Me eldest, Ernie, he's nigh on fifteen and the little 'un, Alice, she's just turned three – seven in all livin'.'

Esther smiled and nodded as if in congratulation.

'Ya'll be next, if Ah'm not mistaken,' Ma said. 'How far on a' ya?'

Esther stared at her. 'How – how did you know?'

'Lass – 'tis written in your face.'

'But I scarcely know mesen – I mean – I can't be sure yet . . .'

Ma nodded sagely towards Esther's stomach. 'Ya've one in there, me lass. Ah can tell.'

'Don't – don't say anything, will ya?'

Ma's knowing eyes narrowed. 'Not telled him yet?' she murmured.

Esther shrugged evasively. 'Well, I didn't want to until I was sure.'

'Aye, all right, lass. I'll say nowt.' A look of concern crossed the older woman's face. 'But are you all right, lass? Ya took a nasty knock last night. Ya've no pains, a' ya?'

Esther shook her head and managed a thin smile. 'No, Ma, I'm fine. Really. I'm tough as owd boots!'

Ma Harris nodded, satisfied.

As swiftly as it had come the snow melted and a wintry sun and a sharp breeze seemed to do their best to dry out the land. Nevertheless the ploughing was still way behind until the day that Matthew came home triumphantly leading a pair of heavy horses.

'They're getting on a bit. Fourteen they are, but there's four or five good years left in 'em yet. The chap said he'd got some young 'uns broken in, but he didn't want to split this pair up. Been together years, they have.'

The horses stood patiently in the yard, submitting themselves to Esther's scrutiny. Their chestnut coats shone and the flaxen socks gleamed. 'They're lovely,' Esther said, smiling and patting their necks. 'Have they got names?'

'This one with the little white mark just below his forelock is Prince and t'other's Punch,' Matthew told her. 'Ya know what, Esther? I can't hardly believe it mesen. The chap as sold 'em to me said Tom 'ad told him all about us. About you and Sam Brumby, and us getting wed . . .' His eyes flickered away a moment, but the excitement of the moment was too great to allow even his bitterness to spoil it. 'An' he said he liked to hear of youngsters working hard and having a go and he wished us well and said we could have a month or two to pay for the 'osses. I give him half as a payment now and . . .'

'I don't like owing anyone money, Matthew,' Esther said firmly, adopting her determined pose; hands on hips, feet planted apart. She saw Matthew look at her, saw his glance falter and flicker away.

'But—'

'Ya'll take the young pigs to market this week and tek the man his money as soon as you get it.'

Matthew's face darkened. 'Dun't mek a fool out o' me, woman.'

Esther's own eyes sparked with anger. 'No need for me to do that, Matthew Hilton, ya make a good job of that ya'sen.' They glowered at each other.

'I'll not be in debt to anyone, Matthew. An' it'll not make a fool of you as long as *you* go and pay the man. But,' she lowered her voice and there was a threat in her words, 'if you don't do it – I will!' She turned on her heel and marched back into the wash-house. Within five seconds the clothes were taking a vicious pounding in the dolly tub.

She heard Matthew leading the horses into the stable. Esther tried to calculate in her head. Would they have enough feed to last through a long, hard winter with two great horses now as well as the cows and other livestock?

In their bed that night, for the first time since before the birth of Beth's child, Matthew took Esther roughly and swiftly, with a bitter fury, as if he bore her a deep resentment and yet he still wanted her. He could not quell his desire for her, yet he despised himself for succumbing to his physical need and for being rendered defenceless by her nearness. His young, virile body could not deny itself the pleasure which she, whilst taking no pleasure herself, never denied him.

Esther was deliberately keeping her part of the marriage bargain.

During the weeks that followed, Matthew worked long hours at the ploughing. He stayed away from the Seagull and the Point – and Beth.

Some days Esther took her turn behind the plough. She came to love the great plodding horses with their gentle eyes and shaggy manes and tails. They were strong with broad, muscular backs and massive hindquarters that pulled the plough through the hard ground as easily as drawing a knife through butter. They were a team and they seemed to know without being told what they had to do. They would turn at the end of a furrow, never faltering, plodding steadily around the rig she had marked out, seeming to slow imperceptibly whilst Esther lifted the plough, ran it along the top edge and then let it down again. Up and down the long straight furrow they plodded, one horse walking in the hollow of the furrow, the other on the unturned turf. Up and down, up and down, whilst above their wise old heads, seagulls screeched greedily and swooped down behind the plough on to the newly turned earth to search for morsels.

One morning Esther caught sight of Will Benson's

cart coming down the lane and heard the blast on his whistle to herald his approach. She halted the horses near the edge of the field that bordered the lane. As the carrier's cart slowed to a stop she could see Will's grinning face. He was wearing a greatcoat over his suit, for it was bitterly cold riding on the front of his cart.

'Eeh, Esther lass,' he said climbing down from his seat high up above the rump of his horses. 'It's good to see ya again. My, it seems ages since I was out this way. What wi' all that snow.' He looked her up and down, and then searched her face more closely, holding her gaze with his own steady eyes. 'How've ya been, lass? How's married life?'

Esther smiled determinedly, 'Fine, Will. Look . . .' She took hold of his arm and turned him to look into the field. 'Matthew bought a pair of horses. Aren't they fine, Will?'

'By, lass, they are an' all.' He looked at her again. 'But should you be doing the ploughing, lass? Ya husband should—'

'Oh, he does his share, Will, and I likes to tek me turn. I ain't no slacker.'

Will's laugh rang out. 'No one could ever accuse you of that, lass. No one.'

'If ya going to the Point first on yar calls, I'm nearly done in this field. I'll come back to the farm and ya can have a bite of dinner with us, Will.'

'Ah'd like that, lass.'

So it became a regular thing that Will had his dinner with Esther and Matthew on the days he came to the Point on his rounds. Soon he was taking their produce to the town markets and selling it for them, bringing the money he made for them on his next visit.

'Why dun't you come into the town on the cart, Esther?' he would ask her. 'Ah could always bring you back if it's too far . . .'

'It ain't that – I ain't keen on the town.' She grinned. 'Tell you the truth, Will, I'd be lost.'

Will smiled indulgently. 'All right, lass. But you'd enjoy a trip now and then. Get that husband of yours to take you.'

'Mebbe, Will,' she hedged, 'mebbe – some time.'

When the ploughing was done and the seed safely sown at last, Matthew suddenly said, 'We should go to church again, Esther. We'll go tomorrow.'

She nodded. 'I'd been thinking the same, it's what Sam would have done after such a bad winter. He'd have wanted to give thanks that we'd got the crops sown, even if we are a bit late.'

Matthew looked at her a little strangely then smiled and nodded. 'That's right, Esther, just what I'd thought.'

He went outside whistling. Esther watched him go, a thoughtful look on her face. She had readily agreed to his suggestion, though she was surprised that the idea had come from him.

The following morning Esther came downstairs in time to set off for church to find Matthew waiting for her in the living room. Her mouth fell open.

'Matthew, what on earth . . . ? That's a brand new suit. Where did ya get that?'

'I went into town yesterday afternoon an' bought it.'

His face clouded ominously. 'Can't a man buy himself a new suit without being answerable to—?'

'Don't fly off the handle,' Esther snapped back. She glanced down at the old dress which had belonged to the long-dead Katharine Brumby. It was already getting very tight around her expanding waistline. Her head came a little higher and her chin jutted out. 'If ya can afford a new suit, Matthew Hilton, then I reckon yar wife deserves a new frock, don't you?'

'Suit ya'sen.' He turned back to the mirror, trying to smooth down his unruly curling black hair but without success. He had shaved, but his dark colouring still gave his jawline a blue tinge however sharp his cut-throat razor.

'I've got to admit it, Matthew,' Esther said, 'ya look very smart.'

He turned to look at her again and suddenly he grinned and she glimpsed the old Matthew; the Matthew who had pursued her, who had tried to tumble her in the hay.

'Ya dun't look so bad ya'sen.' His eyes roamed over her, taking in her long, glossy hair which she had piled high on her head and fastened with the pearl combs; then down her slender neck and lingered on the generous curves of her bosom. He moved towards her, his eyes glinting wickedly.

'Matthew . . .' Esther held out the thing she was carrying in her hands to steer him away from the direction his thoughts were obviously taking. 'I thought you might like to – to have this. Remember? It was Sam's. He always wore it to church.' She held out Sam Brumby's gold Hunter watch. 'Would ya like it?'

'Like it?' Matthew's eyes shone. 'Aw, Esther, it's a fine watch . . .' He slipped it into the pocket of his new waistcoat and looped the chain across his chest and stood there proudly, puffed out like a pouter pigeon.

Esther smiled at him. 'It looks grand, Matthew. Real grand. Well, shall we go?'

The smile faded a little from his mouth and for a moment she thought he looked uncertain.

'Esther,' he began, 'let's not go to church, let's . . .'

Remembering the look of desire which had flared in his eyes a few moments ago, Esther tapped his arm sharply, yet with an air of playfulness, and retorted, 'Oh no you don't, Mester Hilton. You wanted to go to church, so we're going!'

'Esther, mebbe . . .'

'Matthew, do come on, or we'll be late.'

She saw him hesitate, give a shrug of resignation and then he offered her his crooked arm and murmured, 'Very well, but just remember – it was you insisted we go.'

They walked the two miles to the church, Esther's arm through Matthew's. She was wondering if now was the right time to tell him her news, but decided to leave it until they returned home. She was loath to spoil this moment, for she had no idea how he would take the fact that she, too, was to bear him a child.

In the church porch they met the Willoughbys and Miss Jenkins. Tom Willoughby greeted them jovially, asking how their horses had settled down and were they pleased with them? Had they got all their ploughing and sowing done? It was the general talk of the neighbouring farmers greeting each other. A determined smile stretched upon her mouth, Esther glanced at Martha Willoughby and her sister, Flo Jenkins. Their heads were bent close together, whispering.

She caught the odd snatch of their conversation. 'Sam's watch . . . new clothes . . .' And then something she could not understand. 'Fancy him daring to come today of all days.'

Esther's fixed smile faded and her chin came up a little higher. Loudly she said, 'Come, Matthew, we'd best take our place in Sam's pew. I know he'd 'ave liked us to take his seat.'

With satisfaction, she heard the gasps from the two women and a 'tut-tut' as she stepped through the church door, walked up the aisle and took her place in the pew Sam had occupied. Matthew followed her in and sat beside her.

Just before the service began there was a slight commotion in the porch and the sound of a young baby crying. At her side, Esther felt Matthew stiffen. She turned her head to see the colour suffusing his neck and creeping slowly up his face. He stared fixedly straight ahead at the altar. Esther looked behind and saw Robert Eland and then Beth carrying her child wrapped in shawls into the church and taking a seat near the font. Tight-lipped, Esther too turned back and fixed her gaze upon the altar. Morning service began, but Esther was hardly aware of it. Mechanically, she rose and opened her lips to the hymns, mouthing the words. She knelt and whispered the prayers, yet all the time she was uncomfortably aware of the three other people at the rear of the church.

At the end of the service the beaming vicar announced that Robert and Beth Eland had brought their baby son to be christened and that all the congregation would be very welcome to stay if they so wished.

Esther made to stand up to leave, but Matthew gripped her arm and pulled her back down on to the seat. 'We're staying,' he hissed. ''Tis the reason we came.'

Esther gasped. 'Ya knew? Ya . . .'

Heads were turning towards the angry whispers between husband and wife.

'Hush,' someone demanded.

The vicar cleared his throat and raised his voice above the whispering and the shuffling and began the opening words of the service of baptism.

Seething with fury, Esther sat where she was. Not because she was afraid to walk out, far from it, but she was not going to be forced into causing a scene in front of the squire and his family, and the vicar, to say nothing of the Willoughbys. By so doing, she realized, it would be she, Esther, who would be made to look foolish.

When it came to the point in the service where the vicar addressed the parents of the child, Esther felt Matthew make an involuntary movement as if he were about to respond. Now it was her turn to grab his arm and hiss at him, 'Oh no, ya don't. Ya sit where you are.'

He shot her an angry, hate-filled glance, but did as she bid.

Just you wait, Matthew Hilton, she thought savagely, till this is all over.

By the time they were half-way along the lane towards home, Matthew did indeed begin to wish he had never thought of attending his son's baptism uninvited. His wife castigated him, her voice rising. shrilly, echoing across the fields until he felt the whole parish must hear her.

'How dare you, Matthew Hilton? Ya knew, didn't ya, that it was his christening today? Didn't ya?' she insisted until he admitted grudgingly that he had overheard the men talking in the pub and had learnt that Beth Eland's son was to be christened that Sunday after morning service.

'I almost changed me mind this morning, when you gave me that watch. But you,' he added, trying as ever to lay the blame on her, 'insisted on us going – if you remember.'

'Whatever possessed you to do such a stupid thing? How could you think you'd be welcome there? Ya've made a fool of all of us.'

He stopped and turned to face her. She stopped too and they stood either side of the narrow lane, the wind whipping loose sand from the dunes around them, the sound of the sea in their ears, and the gulls screeching above as if the wheeling, diving birds were joining in their heated quarrel.

'What d'ya mean?' he argued belligerently. 'Ah've a right to be there. Daniel's my son.'

He uttered the name he had heard the boy given with

pride in his voice and his tone was not lost on Esther. But it served only to fuel her outrage.

'Aye, ya bastard son!' Her country dialect became even more pronounced in her blazing anger. 'Ya've made a fool of ya'sen, and me! An' if that dun't mean nothing, did ya stop to think what Beth must feel to see ya there? And what about Robert Eland — what must that poor feller be feelin'?'

'Beth? Why would Beth mind?' He touched his nose as if remembering Eland's punch. 'And Ah dun't care what *he* thinks! He's leaving me out of the lifeboat crew now on purpose,' he added in an aggrieved tone.

Esther cast her eyes to the scudding clouds above them. 'Are ya so stupid? Can't ya see?' She leant towards him, trying to make him understand. 'Everybody *knows* he's your child, *you've* made sure of that! But you shamed her and she had to marry another to give her bastard a name . . .'

'If that's anybody's fault, it's *yours*, Esther. You knew before you got me to marry you . . .'

'I didn't *get* you to marry me, an' well you know it. You asked me and I said yes, that's all.'

'Only because you held out on me, because you wouldn't . . .'

'Aye, but Beth would and did,' Esther said quietly now. 'And look where it left her. I was always honest with you, Matthew. I always told you I wouldn't bring a bastard into the world, and I meant it.' She paused a moment and then added softly, 'But I'm carrying your child now, Matthew. Your child conceived and born in holy wedlock!'

He stared at her, but his face was expressionless.

'So,' he said slowly. 'Ah'll have sired two calves in a year, eh?' A smile twisted his mouth, but it was a sardonic cynical smile, with no pleasure at her news showing in his eyes. 'Quite the young bull, ain't I?'

Sixteen

*I*T was not the way Esther had imagined giving her husband the news, but it was done now and over the days and weeks that followed Matthew made no mention to Esther about their coming child. He made no enquiries after her health, nor any deference to her condition by trying to help ease her workload. Not that Esther expected anything different. She had seen her aunt work in the fields until a few hours before the birth of a child. She had been brought up to regard such a condition as perfectly natural and not an illness or an excuse for idleness.

Matthew was right about being left out of the lifeboat crew deliberately by the coxswain, Robert Eland. Privately, Esther could well understand why and yet Matthew was a good crew member; whenever the maroons went up throughout that following summer, she would see him start forward as if to race down to the boat-house for the launch. Then angrily he would return to his work but it would unsettle him. He would be watching the lane to see the men return, to catch someone to ask what the shout had been, and had it been successful, and more importantly, had they had a full crew? But no request ever came for Matthew to join them again; no sound of Ernie Harris's flying feet across their yard to pound on the door shouting for 'the mester'.

In the evening following a shout, Matthew would go down to the Seagull to try to join in the chatter and the talk of the rescue. But he was on the fringe now, not welcome amongst the crew members. On such nights he would come reeling home drunk, shouting and singing, only serving to exclude himself further from their number.

At harvest time, their neighbours came to Brumbys' Farm once more to help. Mrs Harris and her brood of children, and workers from Rookery Farm, all came.

This year Robert Eland stayed away.

'He goes out in his little boat cod-fishing more and more now, missus,' Ernie Harris told Esther. 'Mester Eland reckons the land's not for him. His life's the sea, he ses.'

Ernie now helped out frequently at Brumbys' Farm. As Esther's time approached, he would slip in quietly to have the milking done before she came out in the morning. He would arrive again in the evening, often milking the cows out in the field before she came to herd them to the farmyard. Esther smiled to herself. If her own husband had no thought for her welfare, it seemed that the young boy was doing his best to help her.

Ernie was a thin, wiry lad of fifteen now. His brown hair flopped forward over his eyes and he had the habit of flicking his head back and grinning at Esther from under the unruly lock of hair. His face was thin, almost gaunt, but his hazel eyes were bright and he was a quick, ever-cheerful lad. Esther, as her belly swelled, came to rely on Ernie's help more and more. At the end of each week she would pay him for the hours she knew he had worked and then she would add a little for good measure, for the boy never asked for payment, and she was for ever finding jobs that had been done when she knew Matthew could not possibly have done them.

'He's a good lad, our Ernie,' his mother agreed readily when Esther praised Ernie's kindly actions. 'Ah dun't know what Ah'd do wi'out him sometimes. He keeps an eye on the younger ones. Anyway, enough about my brood. How are you feeling, lass? Ya can't have long to go now. Want me to tek a look at ya some time?'

'I'm hoping I can hang on till harvest's safely in.'

Mrs Harris laughed. 'Only if young 'un decides to let ya, lass. They have a will o' their own. They'll come when they'm ready and there's nowt ya can do about it.'

'It's been so wet this year – it's going to be a difficult one. Some of the fields are flooded.' Esther wrinkled her forehead worriedly. 'I'm sure we're going to lose some of the crops.'

'Aye, Ah've seen it happen here afore. Some years back Sam had to take his oats over to one of Tom Willoughby's fields – one of them way over yonder' – the older woman waved her hand westward – 'to spread it all out to dry afore we could stack it.' She glanced again at Esther and said as if warning Esther not to be too hopeful, 'Late we was, that year, gettin' it all in.'

Esther's child decided to wait, however, and when the last sheaf was stacked after a very difficult harvest, Esther heaved a great sigh of relief.

Now nothing could spoil the birth of her child.

*

It was another two weeks, well beyond the time that Mrs Harris had predicted, before Esther felt the tell-tale pain low down in her groin. She carried on milking Clover, murmuring soothingly to the cow as she always did. The pain subsided and died, and Esther pulled steadily on the beast's udders, never slowing, never losing her easy rhythm. She stood up slowly and eased her back. Then she covered the two pails of milk with the wooden lids and picked them up.

She had begun to walk across the yard towards the house, when a second pain struck suddenly and with such intensity that she gasped aloud and doubled over, the bottom rims of the pails catching on the floor and tippling forwards. She gave a cry and tried to pull them upright, but the lids toppled forwards and the milk gushed out on to the yard.

'Oh, no!' Esther cried aloud. The pain was receding now, leaving her vexed and angry with herself for spilling the milk. Half the contents of each bucket was lost and, pursing her mouth, she picked up the two pails and went quickly into the house. If they were to keep up the supply to their regular customers, her own household would have to go short for a day or so. She stroked her swollen belly and glanced down at it.

'But there'll be enough of my milk for you, little one,' she murmured. Already her breasts were tender with ready ripeness for the birth of her child. 'I'll see you never go short – not of anything – if I can help it,' she promised softly.

She left the milk in the dairy. She would have to ask Mrs Harris if one of her girls, maybe Enid, would come and do the dairy work for a few days. And of course Mrs Harris herself would attend her at the birth. She went out again into the yard. The September day, which already had the hint of autumn gentleness about it, was warm and sultry.

'Huh,' Esther said aloud. 'Never anyone here when ya wants 'em.' The yard was silent save for the occasional stamping of a hoof from the cowshed. Esther gave a click of exasperation at herself. She had quite forgotten that she had not yet turned the cows back out into the field after the morning milking. As she opened the byre door, she was forced to lean against the wall as another pain, beginning low down, gripped her in its vice-like severity. As the wave passed she loosed the cows from the cowshed and drove them across the yard and into the lane where they idled along the verges, tearing at the grass and beginning the whole process of milk production once more.

Again Esther looked about her and chewed at her bottom lip with uncertainty. She did not want to have to go to the Point herself. Ma Harris's cottage was overlooked by the Elands' boat and the last person Esther wanted to meet at this moment was Beth Eland.

She was still hesitating, debating whether to go into the house and upstairs and prepare the bed for herself, trusting to luck that Matthew would come home before . . .

Another pain clenched her abdomen, more strongly than ever and she could not prevent a low grunt escaping her startled lips. The pain was so swift and intense, like nothing she had ever before experienced. She found herself doubling over and squatting down on to the verge panting until the pain began to ebb away. Sweat trickled down between her breasts and for a moment she closed her eyes as the heat of the day danced and swam before her eyes.

In the distance she heard a shrill whistle and the faint rattle of cart wheels coming closer and blissfully closer. Esther licked her dry lips and made as if to pull herself upright, but another pain was already beginning, swelling and pulsating, so that she gasped again and toppled forwards on to her knees.

Will Benson's cart appeared round the bend in the lane and drew to a halt. She heard, rather than saw, for her eyes were still squeezed tightly shut against the pain, Will scrambling down from his seat and running with uneven footsteps towards her.

'Aw, lass, what is it? Is it the bairn? Ya shouldn't be out here on yar own. Where's that husband of yours? Where's Matthew?'

Esther almost laughed – if the pain had not been so bad, she would have done – at the flurry of anxious questions.

'Stay there, lass. I'll go on to the Point right away and fetch Ma Harris. Now, don't you move, lass.'

She wasn't planning on going anywhere, she would have said, but she just nodded and bent over her throbbing belly, hugging it with her arms. Will hobbled back to his cart and pulled himself up, catching the reins and flicking them to urge his horses forward. The cart trundled past with Will's anxious eyes upon her as he went by. The pain had subsided a little now and she was able to look up and give him a weak smile. Heartened, he slapped the reins again and drove on.

By the time Ma Harris was puffing up the lane towards the farm, Esther had managed, between the pains, to get back to the house. She paid a visit to the privy next to the wash-house and was at the back door about to go in, when she heard Mrs Harris's voice.

'Here I am, lass, and not afore time, by the look on ya.'

Esther thought she had never been so pleased to see Ma Harris's toothless grin as she was at that moment. She could feel the sweat glistening on her face now, and her hands and legs seemed to be shaking. She felt Ma Harris's firm, comforting grasp upon her arm and thankfully she leant against the older woman.

'There, there, now, ya'll be fine. Just do as Ah tell you, and everything'll be fine.'

It was. The most difficult part, Esther thought afterwards, had been heaving herself up the stairs, with Ma Harris lending a helping hand from behind.

Once she was lying on the bed, propped against pillows, with the older woman taking complete charge and issuing orders, all of which Esther did her best to obey, the birth was surprisingly quick and easy.

'Ya doing wonderful. Child-bearing hips ya've got, me lass. By, but you'm lucky. Push, lass, now a deep breath and push. There – good lass – that's the head.' Esther heard a little whimper and Ma Harris's raucous laugh. 'Aye, that's it, young 'un, let us know ya coming. Now, Esther lass, wait a bit – wait a bit – now push, lass, push.'

Esther gave a little cry as her belly emptied and her child thrust its way into the world.

'Eh, Esther lass, it's a lovely little girl.' Ma Harris's capable hands wrapped the baby in a shawl. 'No need to slap this one,' she laughed above the now squalling infant. 'She means showing ya she's a good pair o' lungs.'

As she laid the baby in Esther's arms, she asked, 'What ya going to call her, lass?'

Two bright spots of colour burned in Esther's cheeks from her efforts, and sweat still shone on her face. There were dark shadows of exhaustion under her eyes, but she was smiling. 'I don't know, Ma, we – we haven't talked about it.'

She heard Ma Harris give a soft sigh, but it was more the sound of understanding than of disapproval. 'Men are never very good at making up their minds. Ya'll end up deciding, lass, Ah can tell ya. So ya might as well think about it now. Just while I gets you sorted out. Now, we've got to get this afterbirth. Can you give a cough?'

Esther looked up in surprise. 'What?'

'Cough, lass. Just cough.'

Obediently, Esther coughed and felt the afterbirth slither from her. 'Aye, that's it. All nicely away. Good, good.'

Esther began to giggle helplessly, the emotion manifesting itself in a gentle hysteria. 'I – I feel like Curly the pig,' she spluttered.

Ma opened her mouth and laughed too. 'Aye, lass, but I hope you're not going to present me with as many as her.'

The two women shook with mirth, their happy laughter mingling with the wondrous sound of the newborn baby's wails.

Some time later, when Mrs Harris had washed her and the baby, and both were lying in clean linen, the infant in the crook of Esther's arm, they heard the back door slam and Matthew's voice. 'Esther. Esther! Where are you, woman? Where's me dinner?'

Ma Harris lifted the latch on the bedroom door and went out on to the top of the stairs. 'Matthew,' she called down. 'Ya'd best come up here.'

Esther heard her husband come to the bottom of the stairs. 'What? Oh, it's you,' she heard him say, then she heard his heavy footsteps mounting the stairs, almost reluctantly, it sounded to her. Ma Harris popped her head round the door.

'Ah'll be away now, lass, but Ah'll be back later. An' dun't you fret, our Ernie'll see to the milking and the dairy work.'

Her head disappeared and Esther heard her say to Matthew, 'In ya go, lad, Ah'll let her tell ya 'ersen.'

Slowly the bedroom door was pushed wider open and Matthew stepped into the room. Esther looked up at him and smiled. His face was expressionless as his glance passed over her and to the small bundle, now quietly asleep, in Esther's arms.

'You have a daughter, Matthew.'

She saw his mouth twist into a wry smile. 'Huh, is that all ya can give me? A girl! What use is a girl?'

Esther gazed at him, conflicting emotions struggling

184

on her face. But she said nothing. His reaction to her news had, for once, left her quite stunned and bereft of any answer.

He sniffed and passed the back of his hand across his mouth. 'Well, 'tis a good job someone's given me a son, ain't it? What good is a girl to any man?'

He turned and went out of the bedroom.

Esther laid her cheek against the soft ginger-coloured down of her baby girl's head. Her eyes glistened with unshed tears at his unkindness. Yet suddenly his brusque words reminded her of Sam Brumby on the day of her arrival here, and a smile trembled on her mouth at the memory.

She rubbed her cheek gently against the baby's head. 'That's what I'll call you, my little one. I'll name you after old Sam's sister, Katharine. Though perhaps,' she added reflectively, 'Kate would suit you better. Yes, that's it. Kate Hilton.'

The baby stirred, wriggled a tiny finger in the air, and slept on.

Seventeen

TOWARDS the end of November, a sudden storm blew up. Lightning split the sky and thunder crashed directly overhead. High winds gusted the sea into a fury and the farmers rushed out to tie down their stacks before the wind tore them apart and scattered them. Doors and windows rattled and the cows moved towards the gateway leading from their field into the farmyard as if pleading for shelter.

'Let 'em in the yard, Matthew,' Esther said, 'an' leave the cowshed door open. Poor things. They don't like the wind. Neither do I, come to that,' she added, shuddering. It was the only weather she really didn't like. She hated the way the wind clattered the roof tiles and shook the doors and windows. It sounded a live, vengeful, relentless being that wrought damage and disaster.

'Sneck the door and come away in to the fire,' she begged Matthew at dinner time as the wind howled around the lonely farmhouse. 'Ya can't do much out there in this lot until milking time. The bairn won't stop crying. I reckon the wind is bothering her, too.'

Matthew slapped his hands together and blew on them to warm them, before sitting down on the wooden chair near the range to pull off his boots. He glanced towards the wicker cradle in the corner of the kitchen and then grinned up at Esther. 'Her wind, or the gales, d'ya mean?'

Esther laughed. 'Fool!' she chafed him, but secretly she was pleased. It was the first time he'd made any sort of comment about the baby or taken any notice of her. Ever since her birth, Matthew had ignored her existence, even though the child had played her part in trying to arouse some sort of response from him by crying half the night. Resolutely he always turned over in their bed, pulled the covers over his ears and left the child to Esther.

'I mean that racket outside. It's enough to upset anyone.' Esther shuddered. 'I pity anyone who's got to be out in this lot when it gets dark.'

They had eaten their midday meal and Esther was scuttling backwards and forwards between the kitchen and the draughty scullery with the pots, whilst the wind battered at the back door and blew in underneath it, when they heard a loud knocking.

Esther turned wide eyes on Matthew. 'What . . . ? Who . . . ?'

'How should I know, woman? Go an' answer it.'

The wind snatched the door out of Esther's hand as she unsnecked it, and almost lifted their visitor bodily and blew him into the house.

'Ernie!' Esther exclaimed. 'Whatever's the matter?'

'Where's the mester?' the boy panted, his eyes dark with anxiety.

Esther pointed into the kitchen and then followed Ernie as he went through.

'Hello, Ernie. What's up?' Matthew asked.

'Me dad sent me to ask ya . . .' He paused, shifting uneasily from one foot to the other.

'Yes,' Matthew prompted. 'What?'

'Well, he knows – well, he feels awk'ard asking you like . . .'

'Get on with it, Ernie.'

The words came out in a jumbled rush. 'It's Mester Eland. His fishing boat's about two miles offshore with a distress signal hoisted . . .'

Matthew was on his feet in a moment.

'He's out cod-fishing. Two fellers on the front saw his sails whipped away by the wind. Nobody knows what to do, 'im being coxswain, like. Me – me dad wants to launch the lifeboat. It'll be hard work rowing in these seas, he ses, and – well – he needs you to – to make up the number.'

Matthew and the boy stared at each other whilst Esther gasped aloud. 'No, oh no, not in this lot!'

'Shut up, Esther, and go and get the 'osses ready. We'll need them, and ours are nearer than going all the way to Willoughby's. Ernie, run and tell yar dad and the others to get up to the station and I'll come with me 'osses.'

Ernie's eyes glowed. 'Me dad says I can come on the boat if you agrees?'

Matthew regarded the young lad steadily for a moment. 'You sure?'

Ernie nodded, unable to speak with excitement.

'Right, then.'

Esther opened the back door and bent her head to the wind. 'Fancy being fool enough to go fishin' in this weather,' she muttered to herself. To be fair, she realized, the gales had blown up suddenly and unexpectedly. At milking time that morning, which would have been roughly when Robert Eland had set sail in his boat, the weather had been deceptively calm.

Punch and Prince were reluctant to leave the warmth of their stable. They flattened their ears and bent their heads as Esther pulled on their harness and then coaxed them outside. They tossed their heads and clattered their hooves on the cobbles and tried to pull backwards into the stable again.

'Stand. *Stand!*' she bellowed, but the wind whipped the words from her mouth and hurled them away. Matthew appeared in the yard dressed in warm clothes. He came close to her, his mouth against her ear, so that she could hear him above the gale. 'Ya'll have to give me a leg up.'

She bent down and cupped her hands and as he put his knee in them, she hoisted him on to the back of the nearest horse. Taking the reins of both horses in his hands, he urged them out of the yard and turned to the left up the lane towards the boat-house set in the dunes nearer the town.

Esther shivered and went back into the house to be met by the wails of her baby girl. She picked her up and opened the front of her blouse for the child to suckle, crooning soothingly. For once, however, Esther's thoughts were not on her hungry child, but on her husband.

As dusk fell the wind seemed to get even stronger, raging around the lonely farmhouse as if it would pluck it from the ground. Esther laid the now sleeping child in her cradle in the corner of the kitchen and pulled on her coat and boots. She checked the fire in the range and then went out into the wild night and across the yard to the byre. The cows were huddled together wild-eyed and restless, disturbed by the storm. With a calmness she did not feel inside herself, Esther crooned softly to each of the beasts in turn, dreading the moment when she would come to Clover who, in the end stall, was already lowing and stamping her feet. But strangely, when Esther came at last to the stall, and ran her hands caressingly over Clover's rump and uttered guttural noises deep in her throat, the animal seemed to quieten at once. The wind still rampaged and rattled the door and the rafters, yet inside the cowshed it seemed safe and warm. Docilely, Clover stood to be milked and as Esther rose and moved the milk away, the cow turned sorrowful eyes upon her.

'I know, old girl, I don't like this storm either, but ya'll be all right snug and warm in here for the night. I aren't going to turn you out into the field.'

Esther chuckled as the cow, seeming to understand, turned back to pluck some hay from the stall and chewed on it placidly.

Back in the kitchen where her baby slept soundly now, Esther threw more wood on the range fire and warmed her chilled body. She had quietened her child and soothed the restless animals. Now that there was nothing to busy herself with, it was Esther who felt unsettled and worried. There had been no word of how the rescue was going. Every nerve in her body seemed to be twitching so that she could not keep still. She paced the small space that was the hearth, walking across to the cradle and back again to the fire, hugging her shawl around her for comfort as much as for warmth.

Why didn't someone come and tell her what was happening?

She paced the floor again. It was no good. Afraid as she was of the storm, it was far worse waiting here alone and not knowing what was going on. She glanced across at the cradle and bit her lip with indecision. There was no way she could take the child down to the shore on such a wild night, nor could she leave her here alone in the house.

The waiting was dreadful. In the darkness with the storm still raging round the farmhouse, Esther's imagination ran riot. What if they were all drowned – Robert Eland and the men who had tried to rescue him? What a devastating effect it would have on this small community. Only widows and fatherless children would be left, and poor Ma Harris, she would lose both husband and son.

'I know,' she said aloud at the thought of Ma Harris, 'she'll look after her.'

If she wrapped the baby warmly, Esther told herself, and carried the wicker cradle to the cottages at the Point, Ma Harris would keep an eye on Kate, just for an hour or so whilst Esther went down to the beach.

'I can't bear this dreadful not knowing what's happening any longer,' she muttered.

Once her decision had been made, within minutes Esther was pulling the door to behind her. Hugging the cradle close to her, she struggled against the wind along the lane towards the Point and Ma Harris's cottage.

The door was opened reluctantly by a thin-faced girl of about fourteen or so. It was 'our Enid' as Ma always called her. Esther smiled, 'Is yar ma in?'

The girl shook her head. 'Naw, she's gone to the beach to see if she can see me dad . . .'

'Aren't they back yet?'

Another shake of the head.

'Oh.' For a moment Esther was uncertain.

'What did ya want?' the girl ventured.

'I – I just wanted to go to the beach mesen, and I wondered if Ma – if ya mother – would keep an eye on the bairn for me.'

The girl's white face broke into a smile. 'Ah'll look after her, missus.' She opened the door wider inviting Esther to step inside. 'The young 'uns are all in bed, so they'll not disturb her and . . .' She led the way into the living kitchen and pointed to another cradle set on a chair in the corner by the range, 'Ah'm already looking after young Danny.'

Esther stopped abruptly in the doorway and drew breath sharply. She had never stopped to think that she might encounter Matthew's other child.

'Come in, missus,' the girl was saying, her eyes on Esther's face. 'It'll be all right, honest it will.'

Esther managed a weak smile, torn by conflicting emotions. She could hardly retreat without looking foolish, and she couldn't bear to return home to continue that awful, lonely waiting.

She sighed and came to a decision. Living so close, she could not hope to avoid meeting the Eland family for ever, she supposed. Pressing her lips together she stepped determinedly into the room and placed her cradle on a chair in the opposite corner of the room. She stood a moment looking towards the other cradle.

'Want to have a look, missus?' Was there a note of slyness in the young girl's voice? Did she know the full story? Esther sighed inwardly. She supposed so, and thought ruefully, who around here didn't know?

Esther nodded and stepped closer as Enid drew back the blanket from the baby.

'He's a grand lad. Black hair, 'ee's got, and the darkest brown eyes you ever saw in a bairn. He'll break a few hearts when he's grown.'

Esther said nothing as she looked down upon the child and saw for herself that there was no mistaking who his father was. Matthew could never have denied his paternity of this boy even if he had wanted to, nor could anyone else. She felt a moment's pity for Robert Eland who seemed to be the only really innocent person in all of this.

She turned away abruptly. 'I won't be long, but I – I just have to go and see . . .'

The girl nodded understandingly.

Leaning into the howling wind, Esther dragged herself up the last dune. As she ran down the other side and on to the beach, she gasped in surprise. There was a large crowd gathered on the sands, several holding lanterns so that the lights shivered and shook in the wind, but showed a welcoming light for the lifeboat to come home.

Esther threaded her way amongst the crowd, glancing

into the dark faces for someone she knew. Before them huge waves crashed on to the sand and rushed up the beach. People were standing near the water's edge, but from time to time were driven back when the waves raced towards them.

'Esther, lass, over here.' In a brief lull in the noise of the wind, she heard Ma's voice calling to her. Esther looked about her and then felt a grip on her arm and turned to see Ma's face, for once not beaming, but serious and anxious.

'Is there any news?' Esther put her mouth close to Ma's ear. 'What's happening?'

Ma lifted her shoulders and shook her head. 'We dun't know nothing. Hours they've been gone now.'

It was then that Esther saw Beth standing a little apart from the rest of the crowd; a silent, motionless figure, hugging her shawl around her and gazing steadfastly out across the black, heaving waters.

Who, Esther wondered, filled Beth's mind? Whose safety twisted at her heart? Her husband's – or Matthew Hilton's?

'A light! There's a light – I saw it,' someone in the crowd shouted. Suddenly there was a buzz of excitement and everyone moved forwards, craning to see.

'There! There it is, did you see it? Only a flash, but it was there.'

'Aye, I saw it. Come on, lads, they'll want a hand.'

Men moved forward out of the crowd, splashing into the thundering waves, reaching with willing hands to help the boat – whatever boat it was – coming ashore. Then Esther saw the lifeboat, riding the crest of a wave, being borne almost on to the beach and coming to rest finally in the shallows. Urgent hands grasped the boat and held it steady, reached in to help the crew climb out. Strong shoulders were offered to the cold, exhausted men of the lifeboat. The onlookers surged nearer, holding their lanterns aloft to give more light.

At that moment Esther saw Matthew.

He was half-carrying, half-dragging Robert Eland ashore, his arms grasping him strongly about the waist. Robert Eland's arms were draped about Matthew's neck and his head lolled forward in a semi-conscious state. Esther did not need to be told that a few more hours out in his boat would have been the death of Robert Eland.

She saw Beth waiting, still standing in the same place on the sands. Beth had not moved even a step forward. In the eerie, flickering light from the lanterns, Esther could see Beth's gaze fixed upon Matthew as he brought her husband back to her from the sea.

As Matthew drew near to Beth, even from here Esther could feel the intensity of their gaze upon each other. She saw Beth reach out with fingers that shook towards the two men. But to whom she was reaching in that tentative, thankful gesture, no one could have said, for her gaze never left Matthew's face. When he gently gave over her husband into her arms, and watched as she took the man's full weight upon herself, it was Matthew's face Beth reached up and touched. Matthew grasped her hand and held it to his cheek for a timeless moment before the crowd surged forward to help, and they were forced to draw apart.

'Here, lass, let us help ya.'

'Is he alive?'

'Matthew – you're a hero. Ya mun be exhausted ya'sen, lad.'

'Here, drink this, Matthew, 'tis rum. 'Twill warm ya.'

'The doctor, get the doctor for Robert Eland.'

Unobserved, Esther slipped away from the back of the crowd, the dark beach enfolding her as she hurried away to collect her child from Ma Harris's and be home before Matthew.

She would never, she vowed, tell him that she had even been on the beach. She could never tell him what she had seen pass between Beth and him that night.

For a while Matthew basked in the glory of being a hero. The local paper recounted the courageous rescue and stated quite categorically that Matthew Hilton, and the rest of the lifeboat crew, had saved Robert Eland's life. It was Matthew, the paper reported, who had plunged into the icy waters and battled his way through mountainous seas to Robert Eland's little boat when they found it drifting helplessly towards a sandbank. Robert Eland, weak with exhaustion and only semi-conscious, could not rouse himself to climb into the lifeboat as it had come alongside in such treacherous, swelling seas. Had it not been for the bravery of Matthew Hilton, the small fishing boat would have been grounded on the sandbank and probably would have capsized, plunging the fisherman to his death. The journalist who wrote the report was unstinting in his praise, though of course he knew nothing of the strange connection between the two men which, had he but known, made the gallant rescue even more praiseworthy.

From that night, Matthew was welcomed back into the lifeboat as a permanent member of the crew. He was fiercely proud of the place he had earned in the lifeboat and even though there was still guarded wariness between Robert Eland and Matthew, whenever there was a shout the two men seemed able to leave their differences ashore. Esther found this difficult to understand and yet she could not help but feel a grudging admiration for men who could hate each other and yet still work as a team to help someone else in distress.

From the time that Matthew had undoubtedly saved his life, Robert, magnanimous in his own quiet way, came back to help out with the harvest on Brumbys' Farm. Matthew still went down to the Seagull at the Point from time to time but he caused no more drunken scenes and whilst they never could be friendly towards each other, there seemed to be an uneasy truce between the two men.

Esther did not know – nor did she enquire – whether or not Matthew ever saw Beth and his son, Daniel. Esther had her own growing child now and always she had the farm.

Through the months that followed, they settled into a routine. Matthew, despite his bitterness against her which sometimes surfaced, nevertheless worked very hard on the farm – and his physical need of her never diminished. Even though now words of love never passed his lips, he still wanted her as much as he had ever done. As for Esther, although she had never pretended to love

Matthew, she had believed that they could find some sort of happiness together. But resentment had changed Matthew and now Esther knew herself to be locked in a loveless marriage.

Nevertheless, she reminded herself resolutely, she had what she had always told herself she wanted most – a place of her own and a family. Now she had someone to cherish and to love – her baby daughter.

If Matthew took little interest in his daughter, there was someone else besides Esther who made up for his deficiency.

From the moment he saw Esther's child, Will Benson was besotted by the little girl. Whenever his cart drew into their yard, it became a ritual for him to climb down and go in search of Kate. Finding her, he would pick her up and, as she grew, offer his pockets for her to delve into with her tiny hands and searching fingers. She would giggle and pull out sweets and pretty ribbons and trinkets one after the other.

'You spoil her, Will,' Esther would admonish, but she would smile as she said it. It was difficult not to spoil the bright-eyed child, though she was not always as cherubic as she appeared to Will. Sometimes there were childish tantrums if she did not get her own way, and it was left to Esther to administer the sharp smack of correction. At such times, Matthew would frown and turn away, irritated by Kate's naughtiness.

'She only does it when you're around,' Esther would say. 'She does it to get your attention. If only you would take a little notice of your own daughter sometimes . . .'

Matthew would be gone, slamming the door behind

him. With Will Benson, however, Kate had no need to provoke his attention – it was hers without asking. For him, Kate was all smiles and dimples and angelic behaviour. He fussed over Kate like a hen with one chick and when she began to walk it was as if he would like to cocoon her against all hurt.

'Should you be letting her play in the yard, Esther?' he asked one bright, breezy washing day, when Esther let the child play whilst she moved between the wash-house and the clothes line in the front garden. 'Won't she get dirty?' A worried frown creased his forehead.

Esther laughed as she slapped the wet clothes on to the mangle and turned the handle rapidly, the suds flowing back into the dolly tub. Then the garments fell into the cold rinsing water in a tub on the other side of the mangle. 'A little dirt won't hurt her. Let her play,' and added softly as she remembered her own harsh child-hood, 'children need to play.'

'But what about the pond? What if she fell in?'

'Oh, I'll mind she doesn't get near that,' Esther promised him. 'I'll have it fenced off by she's really walking.'

The subject of their conversation turned solemn eyes from one to the other as they spoke and Esther smiled as Will squatted down and pulled a tiny doll from his jacket pocket. At once Kate scrambled to her feet and tottered towards him, her chubby hands outstretched. A smile of satisfaction spread across his face.

Esther shook her head. 'I dun't know, Will Benson, you've a way with the women even yet,' she teased him, as he swung Kate up into his arms and walked round to the front of the house with Esther as she carried a basket of wet clothes to hang on the line.

'Eh, lass, I ain't been round the front here lately. You've done wonders with this garden.'

The trees had been pruned and promised apples and pears and plums in a few weeks, and the grass beneath had been neatly cut. At the far end, an oblong had been dug to make a kitchen garden and already Will could see potatoes, cabbages and carrots growing.

So the year of 1913 and the first half of 1914 passed peacefully enough for the small community of Fleethaven Point and Brumbys' Farm prospered under Esther's hard work and common sense.

It was a time of calm before the storms that were to follow; storms that were to tear asunder the fabric of their lives.

Eighteen

AFTER morning service on that first Sunday in August 1914, Esther was gratified that not only did the vicar now greet them warmly, but the squire took the trouble to stop and shake Matthew's hand and ask how they both were and was everything going well on the farm. 'Old Sam would have been very pleased, very pleased,' he boomed. 'Almost three years now, isn't it? It doesn't seem it. How time flies.' He smiled benignly down at Kate's upturned face and tickled her under the chin. 'What a sweet child.'

Kate dimpled at him and pulled in her chin playfully, already artful in the ways of attracting and receiving attention. The squire looked up and winked at Matthew. 'And plenty of time to add to the brood, eh Hilton?'

He glanced back with pride at his own two sons escorting their mother from the church. 'Nothing like family life, Hilton. Nothing in the world to beat it. My eldest boy is going up to Oxford in October. We've just heard he's got a place.'

Matthew nodded as if he fully understood and murmured, 'That is good news, sir,' and hoped it was the right thing to say. There was no mistaking the pride in the squire's voice that must suggest a great achievement on the part of his son.

'What's he mean, "going up to Oxford"? It's a place,

ain't it?' Esther whispered as the squire passed out of earshot.

Matthew shrugged his broad shoulders.

'I'll ask Will,' Esther murmured, 'he'll know.'

She was smugly satisfied to see that the Willoughbys, walking down the aisle only a few paces behind the squire and his family, could not have failed to overhear the conversation, but as usual Martha Willoughby and her sister swept past them, holding their skirts with delicacy and all but sticking their noses in the air.

Walking home, Matthew said, 'It's a Bank Holiday tomorrow, Esther. I'll tek ya on the pier.'

She looked at him, their eyes on a level for Matthew was no taller than she was. 'The pier? What's the pier? I ain't never seen one. Where is it?'

He stopped in surprise and turned to face her in the lane. 'Dun't ya know what a pier is? Why, we've a fine one off the main beach,' he said, jerking his head backwards towards the town. He looked at her closely. 'You pulling my leg, Esther? You must have seen it.'

She shook her head. 'No, honest.' She gave his arm a little shake. 'Tell me, Matthew.'

They walked on slowly. 'Well,' Matthew began hesitantly. He was not adept at describing things. 'It's a long wood and iron thing built out into the sea. Ya can walk down it, an' at the end is a saloon where they have music concerts on a Sunday afternoon. I 'spect there'll be one tomorrow too. I thought you might like to go.'

'I've heard of concerts, Matthew, but I've never been to one. I'd love to go, I really would.'

'Well, we'll go, Esther,' Matthew said generously. 'We'll go tomorrow.'

'Have you been before?'

The moment the question was asked, Esther realized her mistake, for his eyes clouded over and his brow creased in the familiar frown. 'Yeah, a few years back,' he muttered shortly.

He must have taken Beth, Esther thought, and now I've reminded him of her. She sighed inwardly. It was not the first time during the three years of their marriage that she had unthinkingly said something that had reminded him of Beth, or his son, Daniel. It was impossible to go through life trying to avoid saying or doing anything that would remind him of them. So in the end, Esther had given up worrying. How could any of them ever forget when they all lived so close to each other? They just had to live with it.

Esther had thought that Matthew would forget his promise to take her on the pier, but the following morning he said, 'Well, aren't you ready? You're not going into town dressed in yar pinny, are ya?'

'What?'

He was already dressed in his Sunday best suit, the gold watch-chain looped proudly across his chest. With a great play at being a gentleman, he pulled the watch from his pocket and let it rest in the palm of his hand. He looked at it, then lifted it to his ear to listen to its tick. 'Get a move on, Esther, if Ah'm taking you to the pier, else it'll be dark by we gets there.'

Esther's eyes glowed with excitement as she hurried

upstairs to put on her best dress and bonnet and to dress Kate.

So on Bank Holiday Monday, the third day of August 1914, a hot summer day, with just a light, friendly breeze blowing in from the sea, they walked towards the town along the lane that was now so familiar to Esther. Kate walked a good distance on her sturdy legs, but when she cried that she was tired, it was Esther who humped her on to her hip and carried her.

When they reached the outskirts of the town, Matthew turned up one of the avenues leading to the dunes, through a pathway bordered by prickly sea-buck-thorn and on to the beach itself.

Esther gasped at the sight before her. In the distance she could see the pier, a long arm extending right out into the water, with a building at the end. She could see tiny ant-like figures moving along the pier. Then on the sands there were roundabouts and swings and stalls selling whelks and mussels.

A smile curved her lips and she gripped Matthew's arm. He laughed at her excitement; she was just like a child on a Sunday treat. Wasn't that just what she was? A child who had never known anything but cuffs and knocks and hard, grinding work, with never a moment given over to sinful pleasure, as her aunt would have called this outing. But Esther wasn't giving a thought to her aunt today. Today was for fun.

'What is it, Matthew? What are all these people doing on the beach? Won't the tide come in and wash away their stalls and such?'

'The sea dun't come up this high, not in summer.

Mebbe in winter or spring when the real high tides come and the winds whip 'em up too. But these folks is all gone by the winter. These are summer folk.'

'Look at all these people — where are they all from? From the town?'

Matthew laughed again. 'Naw, they're the holiday-makers and the day trippers. They come on the trains.'

Esther shuddered. 'Ah dun't like trains.'

'Why, have you been on one, then?'

'Not me!' she cried. 'But the railway ran through the village where I lived before. Great noisy thing — an' dangerous too. Killed a sheep once.' That, to Esther, was sacrilege.

'Ah've never bin on a train,' Matthew mused. 'Ah'd like to tek a ride on one some day.'

'Well, dun't ask me to come with ya,' she said resolutely, and Matthew laughed at her again. She did not take offence but laughed with him. They wandered around the stalls, watching the folk. Women dressed in their Sunday best and carrying parasols, their long skirts sweeping the sand; the men sweating in their dark suits and starched white collars and bowler hats. A little boy, dressed in a sailor suit, skipped past them bowling a hoop. A small girl in a frock with such stiff petticoats that she hardly dared to move, walked sedately by her mama. Esther watched the child enviously, imagining her Kate in such a pretty dress. But the subject of Esther's daydreams lay heavily in her arms now, asleep against her shoulder, oblivious to all the shouting and laughter of the holiday-makers.

'Look,' Matthew pointed out to sea. 'See the paddle

steamer just leaving the landing-stage at the end of the pier. It takes trips out to sea. D'ya want to go?'

Esther shook her head. 'I'll keep me feet on dry land, Matthew, if it's all the same to you.'

Matthew shrugged. 'I dun't mind. I gets all the sailing I want on the lifeboat.'

They walked on in silence for a time, watching the crowds thronging the beach and the pier. Merry laughter filled the air and the shouts of children at play mingled with the sounds of the sea.

'Come on, let's go on the pier then,' Matthew said and, taking hold of her hand, he led her up to the entrance, through the barrier and out on to the pier, laughing as Esther caught at her bonnet which was in danger of being whipped from her head. 'The wind seems stronger out here,' she gasped.

They walked on and soon the waves were breaking beneath them. Esther looked down between the gaps in the planking to see the water swirling below. She clung tightly to Matthew's arm. 'Oooh, I feel as if I might fall in.'

'Dun't be daft, woman, how could ya fall through them little cracks?'

Esther grinned at her own foolishness. 'I know, but – but it *feels* as if I could.'

She shifted the sleeping Kate to a more comfortable position and the child stirred and whimpered. She rubbed her eyes, gave a huge yawn and then smiled prettily at her mother. She wound her chubby arms round Esther's neck and pressed her pale pink cheek to her mother's.

'Mamma,' she murmured.

Esther patted the child's back. 'There's my clever girl.'

At her side she felt Matthew stop suddenly and having moved on a pace herself, she stopped and turned to look back at him. He was staring at the child incredulously. 'She's talking. She – said a proper word.'

'Well, I should hope so!' Esther pretended indignation. 'She's almost two.'

Matthew moved closer. Kate turned her face towards him and smiled, her cheeks dimpling, her green eyes laughing and her red baby curls dancing in the breeze. She unwound her arms from her mother's neck and, with a child's artfulness, held them out to her father. 'Dadda, Dadda.'

Matthew's gasp was audible. 'She – she called me Dadda,' he exclaimed unnecessarily.

Esther almost giggled but then as she watched the softening expression on Matthew's face, her mirth turned to a deep pleasure. Matthew reached out to take the child from her. He held her carefully, almost like a china doll, his large hands encompassing her waist. He lifted her up to look at her properly. The child gurgled and laughed and repeated the word that had won her such attention. 'Dadda, Dadda.'

Matthew grinned suddenly and settled his daughter in the crook of his arm. 'Ah'll carry her for a bit, if you like. She must be heavy for you after a time.'

'She is,' Esther admitted and eased her aching shoulders thankfully.

They could hear the music from the saloon now, music such as Esther had never heard before. Inside, they sat down to listen to the sweet melodies from violins and then a man with a strong, vibrant voice began to sing. She couldn't make out the words, but she enjoyed watching him waving his arms and closing his eyes and tossing his head. He knows what he's singing about, she thought, even if I don't. Then at the end everyone stood whilst the orchestra played 'God Save the King' and even some members of the audience were singing now, Esther noticed. Then it was over and they all went out once again on to the pier. It was cooler now than when they had gone in, and the breeze was even stronger so that Esther had to hold on to her bonnet and bend her head against the wind.

'We'd best get back, Esther. Looks as if it could turn to rain.'

Esther smiled up at him. 'It'd be worth a soaking. I don't know when I enjoyed mesen so much.'

Playfully Matthew doffed his hat towards her and made a little bow. 'We aim to please, ma'am.' Then, still carrying Kate in one arm, he put the other around Esther's waist and held her close to him as they hurried along the pier and towards home.

Esther was to look back on that day with a sense of regret. There had been, on that bright August Bank Holiday, the tentative hope that things could be better between herself and Matthew; that with a little time, they could become a family.

But the happenings in the weeks that followed were to smash any chance they might have had of a lasting happiness.

Nineteen

*W*HEN Will Benson's cart rattled into the yard on the following Friday morning, Esther called out from the back door, drying her hands on a towel as she went to meet him, 'Whatever are you doin' coming on a Friday? You was only here yesterday.'

Instead of answering her question, he asked her another. 'You heard the news?'

'News? What news?' Esther was shocked by the solemn expression on his face. She couldn't remember ever seeing Will Benson without a smile beneath his moustache and a twinkle in his eyes. 'Will – is summat wrong?'

He climbed down slowly, a folded newspaper in his hand, and came towards her. Fleetingly she thought, something must be very wrong. He hasn't even looked around for Kate, or asked about her.

'We're at war, Esther lass.'

'War? What d'ya mean, war?'

Will unfolded the newspaper he was carrying. 'It's in the paper.' He glanced up at her. 'Dun't you get the local paper that comes out on a Friday?'

Esther shook her head. 'No, I dun't bother with it, though I reckon Matthew sees it at the pub on a weekend. He's sometimes mentioned bits of news – like a lifeboat rescue he was involved in, that sort of thing.' A smile flickered briefly on her mouth, but died when there was no answering response from Will.

He spread the paper out and began to read slowly but unfalteringly. ' "War declared. Note rejected by Germany. The following statement was issued from the Foreign Office at twelve fifteen this morning: 'Owing to the summary rejection by the German Government of the request made by His Majesty's Government for assurances that neutrality of Belgium will be respected, His Majesty's Ambassador at Berlin has received his passports and His Majesty's Government have declared to the German Government that a state of war exists between Great Britain and Germany as from eleven p.m. on August the Fourth.' " '

Esther gasped. 'But – but the fourth – that was Tuesday.'

Will nodded.

'But on Monday, we – we were on the pier with – with all the holiday-makers. We – we had a lovely day . . .'

Will nodded again. 'Ah know, lass, and so did a lot more all over the country, never thinking that the very next day we'd all be at war. Oh there's been talk and rumour for a bit now, but Ah dun't think anyone – well, not the likes of us, anyway – took it serious. But the town . . .' He jerked his head in the direction of Lynthorpe, through which he had just passed. 'It's fair buzzing with rumour and gossip. They reckon there's boats patrolling along the coast. They say Lynthorpe Territorials left by the eight o'clock train this morning and that boy scouts over thirteen are being required for running despatches and such.'

'What will it mean? It – it won't make any difference to us, will it? Not here at the Point?'

'Ah dun't know what it'll mean, lass.' He shook his head sadly. 'It might all be over very quickly, but – ' he sighed heavily – 'on the other hand . . .'

'What?' Esther prompted, her tone sharp with anxiety.

He looked at her with sorrowful eyes and added gravely, 'It could change all our lives.'

They were still standing together, poring over the newspaper and the snippets of news about the war, when Matthew came into the yard a hedge knife in his hand. He had been working in the fields, trimming hedges. His forehead glistened with sweat and there were dark wet stains on his shirt under his arms.

'Ah've just heard. Is it true, Will?' There was an air of excitement about him.

Will nodded and held out the newspaper towards him. Matthew took it eagerly and scoured the page. 'It says there's a rumour there's been a naval engagement off Flamborough Head.' He looked up at Will. 'That's up north from here, ain't it, on the Humber?'

Will nodded. 'Aye, just north of the mouth of the Humber.'

Esther glanced in the direction of the sea, as if she suddenly expected to see soldiers appearing over the sand dunes and advancing in steady lines across the land – her land. She shook herself and said firmly, as if by doing so she could refute the possibility, 'Oh, come in and have a cup of tea, Will. It'll not affect the likes of us.'

Just as she turned away she saw the two men exchange a knowing look. The older man sombre and afraid,

211

the younger with an air of anticipation and exhilaration.

It seemed to Esther that the days that followed were filled with nothing but the talk of the war. Even young Ernie Harris, his eyes bright with excitement, came with news for Matthew.

'The squire's leading a recruiting rally tonight in the town. Shall ya tell the mester for me?'

Esther swung round to stare at him, her eyes dark with anger. 'Ah'll do no such thing, an' you're not to think of going, Ernie Harris!'

He grinned at her cheekily, a newborn confidence in his manner. 'Just try and stop me!'

'You're not old enough, Ernie. Ya can't—' But the boy had turned and was running out of the yard, giving a little hop and jump every so often, capering almost, as he ran home.

Esther shook her head. 'Madness,' she murmured. 'Sheer madness.'.

When Esther found out that her husband planned to attend the recruiting rally in the town on the first of September, she asked Ma Harris if Enid would come to the farm and look after Kate so she could attend too.

'Aye, she can come, lass,' Mrs Harris said, but added doubtfully, 'Yar man'll not like it. Men dun't like women interfering in such things.'

Esther snorted. 'Then he'll have to lump it. If he thinks he's got any grand notion of volunteering, he's got another think coming.'

Instead of laughing, as Esther might have expected,

Ma Harris merely shook her head and sighed. 'Dun't mek a fool of him, lass, ya'll regret it.'

Esther stared at her. 'Ya not letting Ernie go, are ya?'

Ma shrugged. 'Can't stop the young 'uns, lass. Nor the old 'uns, come to that.'

Tuesday evening was clear and fine when Esther watched Matthew walk out of the yard dressed in his best suit, his watch-chain looped across his chest, and set off purposefully in the direction of the town. She saw Ernie Harris running down the road from the Point, saw him draw level with Matthew and fall into step beside him. She watched them until they turned a bend in the lane and were lost from her sight. At that moment, Enid arrived to sit with Kate, and Esther put on her coat and hat. Pulling the back door to behind her, she set off across the yard. As she drew level with the barn she heard footsteps in the lane and, not wishing to be seen, she hid behind the corner of the building, peeping out to see who it was. She almost gasped aloud. A group of men from the Point, all dressed in their Sunday best, were walking towards the town. She spotted Robert Eland with the landlord of the pub. There was Mr Harris and Beth's father, Dan Hanley, too.

Esther clicked her tongue with exasperation. Now she would have to wait until they were well up the lane before she could set out. When they too had taken the curve in the road, she left her hiding place and followed them at what she hoped was a safe distance.

'Esther – Esther, lass. Wait for me!'

She turned to see Ma Harris hurrying towards her as

fast as her little round body would allow. 'You going to the meeting, lass?'

Esther nodded grimly. 'I don't want Matthew to see me though.'

'Huh, I don't want my old man to see me either,' Ma Harris replied with feeling, but tonight there was no toothless grin, no attempt at humour.

On a green stretch of grass on the sea front, a huge crowd had gathered. At one end on a raised dais were a table and several chairs where some of the local dignitaries had gathered. When Esther arrived and joined the throng, weaving her way through the crowd in order to hear better, Squire Marshall was on his feet addressing the meeting, shaking his fist in the air.

'We are fighting for our very existence, for freedom and democracy. In Belgium ordinary men are being shot and their women violated . . .' A horrified gasp rippled amongst the crowd. 'And when they have overrun Europe they will turn upon us, upon Britain. We must unite for God, for our King and for our country . . .'

Cheers broke out all around Esther, as the squire thumped the air with his raised fist. Then he turned and gestured towards a middle-aged man in army uniform, with several medals on his chest. He was introducing him to the crowd. 'We are privileged to have Major Langley with us this evening. He is a recruiting officer for Lincolnshire. Major Langley, I invite you to address the gathering.' The squire almost bowed towards his honoured guest as he rose and stepped forward.

The major's booming voice rang out over their heads, echoing in the dusk of the evening. He entreated all the local men between nineteen and thirty-five to enlist. 'You all stand and sing the National Anthem or Rule Britannia, but now we ask you to prove your patriotism by your sense of duty.' His voice suddenly softened, and yet it still carried out into the night air. 'I pay tribute to the great self-sacrifice of the women of our country during the past few weeks. Bravely, they have waved goodbye to their loved ones who have given themselves – their very lives – in the service of their King and country.'

His voice rose. 'No young woman should allow herself to be seen with a man between the ages of nineteen and thirty-five unless he wears the King's uniform.' A few in the crowd applauded and he leaned towards them. 'For any man who does not wear the uniform will make a rotten lover . . .' the crowd cheered – 'and a very much worse husband.' The cheers grew louder.

Oh, he's clever, thought Esther, he's very clever. First he fosters a sense of outrage by his stories of the violation of women and children in Belgium, then he appeals to a man's pride and sense of honour and as a final weapon he states blatantly that only a man in uniform is worthy of a woman's love and pride. He's making it a matter of a man's virility.

Major Langley was speaking again, issuing a veiled threat. 'If the young men of our country do not answer the call, the same fate will befall our women and children as those in Belgium. I know our fine young men cannot – will not – let that happen!'

Loud cheering and applause broke out and there was a

surge towards the platform as from all sides young men moved forward to volunteer.

To a great roar from the crowd, the squire's elder son, Rodney Marshall, was the first to step up on to the platform and be greeted by a vigorous handshake from the major. The squire beamed and surveyed the crowd, holding out his arm to show off his boy, as if it were the proudest moment in his life.

Others were following, climbing up on to the platform to be greeted by Major Langley.

Esther grabbed Ma Harris's arm. 'Oh no,' she breathed. 'There's Ernie! We've got to stop him.'

Ma Harris, though her eyes were fixed upon her son, remained motionless.

'Come on, Ma. We've got to—'

Ma was shaking her head. 'No, lass,' she said quietly, so softly that Esther had to bend her head closer to hear what she said above the excited hubbub. 'No, let him be. He'll not thank me for interfering. Neither would his dad.'

'Ma, you *can't* let him go. He's not old enough anyway.'

Ma shook her head ruefully. 'That'll not stop him – nor them taking him.'

'Then I'll tell them,' and Esther made as if to push her way through the crowd towards the platform.

''Ere, who you shoving?' The man in front of her turned round to see who was trying to elbow their way through. 'Wait ya turn . . .' When he saw it was a woman, he grinned and his tone changed. 'Hello there, darling,' he leered. 'Want to do ya bit for King and country, eh?'

'Let me through,' Esther said, outraged. 'One of the volunteers on the platform is under age and I mean to stop him.'

'Oho, I can't let you do that, me darling. If the lad wants to go, then—'

'Get out of my way,' Esther spat and pushed the man in the chest with the flat of her hand.

'Esther, don't—' Ma Harris tried to intervene, but no one was listening to her.

At once anger replaced the man's teasing tone and he grasped Esther roughly by the arms. 'Oh no, you don't . . .'

Esther cried out, more in frustration than in pain. She struggled and kicked the man's shins. He gave a yell of pain and those close by now turned round to watch the scuffle.

'Not a German, is he?' some wag shouted, 'having a go already?'

'Let me go!' Esther yelled again.

Suddenly there was Matthew standing before her. The fight went out of her instantly as she looked into his face. His eyes were dark with fury.

'Leave her alone!' Matthew said in a low, controlled voice that held more menace than if he had roared.

'What's it to do with you?' asked the stranger, still holding Esther.

'She,' Matthew said with deliberation, 'is my wife.'

The man let go of Esther as if she had burned him. 'Aw, mate, I'm sorry, I didn't know. I'm sorry . . .' He turned and shouldered his way through the crowd, escaping before the vengeful husband could retaliate.

Matthew was not concerned about the man. He was glaring at Esther, who was rubbing her forearms where the man had gripped her. 'What the hell are you doing here?'

She returned his glare with equal rancour. 'Making sure you don't do anything stupid, like volunteering.'

Colour suffused his face and his eyes bulged. 'Christ, you've got a bloody cheek, woman! You'd do anything – anything to make me look small, wouldn't ya? I've a good mind to go up there this minute and—'

'That's right, mate, you tell 'er. Don't you hide behind a woman's skirts,' a voice from those nearby joined in their quarrel. Neither Matthew nor Esther took any notice.

She put out her hands and took hold of his shoulders. 'Please, Matthew, don't do anything foolish, anything rash. You're needed here, on the farm. You have a family now . . .'

Matthew's mouth twisted sardonically. 'Aye, the farm! Always the farm, isn't it, Esther?'

He brought his arm up and knocked her hands away, twisting out of her grasp at the same time. Then he turned and blundered away through the throng. In a moment he was lost from her view.

'Oh, Esther,' mourned Ma Harris. 'Ya've done it now, lass. He'll join up just to spite ya.'

Twenty

MATTHEW did not join up, but he did not arrive home until the early hours of the following morning, staggering up the stairs to tumble into bed beside her and fall into a state of drunken unconsciousness rather than of sleep.

Talk of the war dominated everyone's conversation and seemed to rule their lives, even though it was happening hundreds of miles away in another country between peoples whom Esther had only heard of in her days at the village school. Foreign places became part of everyday speech, and when lists of casualties began to appear in the local newspaper, suddenly it was very real and very close.

Ernie Harris came to say goodbye, looking somehow bigger, more filled out already. All at once, he was a young man going off to war.

'Oh, Ernie!' In a sudden surge of emotion, Esther put her arms about him and hugged him to her. 'Do you really have to go?'

The boy wriggled with embarrassment at her unexpected display of sentiment. 'I want to go, missus. I'm a soldier now.' His thin face beamed at her as she stood back to look at him. She shook her head sadly and murmured again, 'Oh, Ernie, I – we shall all miss you.'

'I'll be back, missus, when we've taught these Germans a thing or two. Besides, everyone says it'll be over before Christmas.'

As she followed him to the gate, it seemed as if everyone who lived at the Point had turned out to wave Ernie off to war. They shouted after him as he walked proudly down the lane, a slight figure growing smaller and smaller. At the curve in the road, he turned and gave a final wave. Then he was gone. The gathering dispersed, leaving the lonely figure of Ma Harris standing in the road staring at the place where her eldest son had disappeared from view.

Esther went over to her. She put her arm about the older woman's plump shoulders. 'Come and have a cup o' tea with me, Ma.'

It took some considerable urging to make Ma move, but at last she allowed Esther to lead her into the farmhouse.

On the Sunday following Ernie's departure, Esther insisted that they should attend church. As they might have expected, the service revolved round the war. The hymns the rector had chosen were full of patriotic fervour and self-sacrifice, and the prayers appealed for God's help on the side of righteousness and the fight for freedom from oppressors. Stubbornly, Esther refused to mouth the words she could not believe in. However, when the prayers took on a more personal note, and the vicar prayed for all those from this parish who had volunteered, Esther was glad to join in. Fervently she added her own prayers, closing her eyes and pressing her hands together.

As she stood up at the end of the service and looked about the church, she was saddened to see, already, so many empty spaces. The squire and his lady now had only their younger son in attendance, and yet it was their absent elder son who was the main topic of interest. As Squire Marshall passed down the aisle he was stopped at every pew to be grasped by the hand and congratulated.

'A fine boy, Squire.'

'You must be so proud.'

'Good luck to your boy, sir.'

A few pews in front of where Esther, Matthew and Kate were sitting, and on the opposite side, the Willoughbys waited their turn to greet the squire.

'My best wishes to your boy, sir,' Tom Willoughby's voice boomed around the church. 'He does our little community proud and no mistake.'

The squire shook the man's outstretched hand. 'Thank you, Willoughby, thank you.' He nodded towards Martha Willoughby and her sister, Flo Jenkins.

Martha's shrill voice echoed down the church. 'There's some here as might take a lesson from your boy, Squire.' Her glanced swivelled towards Esther and flickered to envelop Matthew. The gathering still in the church had all fallen silent to listen to the exchange. It was as if the congregation was holding its breath.

'And you, ma'am,' Martha was addressing Mrs Marshall. 'What a fine example you have set all women. So brave, so patriotic, ma'am.'

Flo was leaning forward over her sister's shoulder. 'There's some — far be it from me to name names — but there's some who'd keep their men at home, making out they can't be spared from the work on the land.'

Martha nodded vigorous agreement. 'Aye, and the men are all too willing to stay at home. Slackers, they are, ma'am, and worse!'

Flo pursed her already thin lips to a slit. 'Cowards, Squire, that's what *we'd* call them. Cowards!'

A gasp rippled through the listeners and shocked whispering broke out. Beside her Esther heard the hiss of Matthew's breath and felt it on her cheek.

It sent a shudder of premonition down her spine.

She turned to look at him and saw that colour had suffused his face and that his dark eyes were fixed upon the Willoughby family.

'Take no notice, Matthew. It's all right for her to talk. She's no sons to send and she knows Tom Willoughby's too old to be expected to volunteer. *She* can talk — she's safe.'

Through clenched teeth, Matthew muttered, 'Shut up, Esther. What do you know about it, anyway?'

Irritated and angered by what she saw as a misplaced patriotic fanaticism, Esther swept Kate into her arms and stepped out of the pew. She hurried from the church before the squire and his party had reached them. No doubt that would give the congregation further cause to speculate about her and her family. It was an unheard-of discourtesy for anyone to precede the squire and his family from the church. Even the vicar, as she swept past him, gaped at her open-mouthed and did not gather his wits in time to speak to her before she was down the cinder path and out of the gate.

Esther walked home alone, alternately carrying Kate and getting the child to walk a short distance.

The smell of roasting beef greeted her from the range oven as she stepped into the house. Esther sighed. She doubted her husband would return until very late, and more than likely he would be in no state to eat a Sunday dinner.

At ten thirty that night, Esther was about to turn down the lamp and go up to bed when she heard singing in the yard. She hurried to the back door and opened it. In the bright moonlight, Matthew was standing in the middle of the yard, holding on to the pump for support and waving a bottle in one hand.

' "Rule Britannia, Britannia rules the waves, Britons never, never, never, never . . ." ' He sagged against the pump. 'Hello, Esh-ter. Come and kiss your soldier husband.' He slithered down to sit on the ground propped against the pump.

Esther moved forward slowly. '*What* did you say?'

' "Britons never, never, never . . ." ' he began again.

'No, no, not that. After that.'

His head wobbled from side to side. 'I – I forget.' He took another swig at the bottle as if he wanted to obliterate the remotest chance of remembering.

She took the bottle from him and flung it across the yard with all her strength. It smashed against the hen house and the frightened birds set up such a squawking that it sounded as if a fox had got in amongst them.

223

She bent over him – as always when she was angry, hands on hips, feet spread apart. 'Matthew Hilton, have you gone and volunteered?'

Suddenly he seemed painfully sober. 'I – I think I must have done, Esther.' Slowly from his pocket he pulled a piece of crumpled paper. Awkwardly, he dragged himself to his feet, but Esther made no move to help him. Instead she took hold of his arm roughly and pushed him towards the house. 'Then you'd better go back and un-volunteer.' Inside she steered him into the kitchen. 'Just you sit down there, me lad, and let's have it. Just what have you done in your drunken state?'

Matthew fell back into the wooden chair and passed a hand, which shook slightly, across his forehead. Beads of sweat glistened on his face. 'Oh, Esther, I don't know what I've done.'

'*Have* you volunteered?'

Matthew raised apologetic eyes to look at her. Slowly he nodded.

'Whatever made you do such a stupid thing? You can't go. What about the farm? I can't manage the farm on my own.'

Matthew's smile was without humour. It was a smile of sadness. Soberly now, he said softly, 'You don't need me, Esther. You never did.'

'Of course I need you, Matthew. Don't be so stupid. If you can't think about me and the farm, what about your daughter? What about Kate?'

'Kate?' He spoke her name almost as if he didn't remember who she was. 'Oh, Kate. Well, she dun't need me either. You're mother *and* father to her. We both know that.'

'Matthew, will you stop being so – so deliberately stupid,' she screamed at him.

As her tone grew shriller, his by contrast grew softer and more patient – more resigned to what he had done. 'Stupid? Yes, I'm stupid. At least I was.'

He sat staring into the glowing embers of a dying fire. Esther, stunned by his manner, was quiet now.

'I knew you only married me to get the tenancy of this farm, Esther,' Matthew was saying quietly. 'At least I didn't give much thought to it afore we was wed . . .' The ironic smile twisted his mouth again. He had sobered swiftly, yet he was more talkative, more expansive and confiding than she had ever known him. She sank down on to the rug watching him as he talked, his face half in shadow illuminated only by the red glow from the fire.

'I – ain't been quite fair to you, Esther. I know that now. I blamed *you* for tricking me into marrying you, when really I – I should have married Beth.'

There, it was said now, Esther thought, but she remained silent, sitting on the rug, hugging her knees up to her chest and staring into the glowing coals.

'I wasn't being fair to you, Esther,' he repeated. 'You were right when you said it was me who asked you to marry me. I did – 'cos I was mad to have you. I wanted you as I never wanted anyone before – not even Beth – in that way.' He leaned forward and touched her cheek with unexpectedly gentle fingers. 'Oh, Esther, I still want you – that way.'

225

She bent her head and for a moment pressed his hand closer to her cheek, but she could not speak.

'But I – I never stopped to really think things out,' he went on. 'Beth was always there, had always been there for me, and – ' he sighed and moved restlessly – 'and daft-like, I suppose I thought she always would be somehow. I never realized, y'see, that Beth was the only one who really loved me.' His voice broke as he added hoarsely, 'I'm sorry, Esther. I've not done right by you – or Beth. Mebbe, just mebbe, I've chance now to prove I'm not all bad.'

She moved then, knelt in front of him and put her arms around him and leant her head against his chest. 'Oh, Matthew, you're not bad, not wicked at all.' She hugged him tight. 'Don't go, Matthew.'

He buried his face in her hair and for once held her close in an embrace that was affectionate rather than lustful. 'Oh, Esther, I've no choice – now. It's too late.' His voice broke on a hoarse whisper. 'Too late.'

They clung together in a timeless moment, closer, now that they were to part, than they had ever been.

The following morning when Esther opened the back door to go out to do the milking she saw that a swirling fog was rolling in from the sea, enveloping the farm, cutting it off from the outside world. How she wished that they could stay like that, cut off from everything outside the farm gate, a little island of their own, safe from the war and the cruel tongues of neighbours that had driven Matthew to prove himself not a coward.

As she finished milking and was carrying the pails

across the yard, Matthew came out of the back door, dressed in his Sunday best suit. Sombrely he met her gaze. Slowly he drew the Hunter watch from his pocket and unhooked the gold chain from his waistcoat. He held it out to her. 'Here, Esther – ' he cleared his throat – 'you'd best keep it till – till I come back.'

Carefully, she set the pails down and took the watch from him. 'Of course, Matthew, I'll keep it safe for you – till you come home again.'

They stared at each other wordlessly.

She saw Matthew swallow, saw him pull in a deep, shuddering breath.

'I'd best be off then.' He tried to smile, but it did not reach his eyes. 'I – I don't want 'em to think I've changed me mind.'

'Have you seen Kate?'

He nodded. 'Aye.' He glanced away and said gruffly, 'Look after her – and ya'sen.'

'Do you want me to come into town with you?' she asked softly.

He shook his head. 'No – no, thanks.'

'You'll write, won't you?'

He shifted his feet. 'I'm not much for writing, Esther. But I'll try to let you know where I am and, well, if I'm all right – if ya want.'

'Of course I want.' She was about to add 'don't be stupid', but for once she bit back the sharp retort in time.

There was an awkwardness between them as if neither knew what to say and yet didn't want the final moment to come.

He bent and picked up the pails of milk. 'I'll carry these in for you.'

Surprised, she merely nodded. She followed him into the house but stood in the scullery whilst he took the milk through to the pantry. She leant against the wall at the side of the window, her hands still cradling the watch. He came back and stood before her.

'I'll be off, then.'

She nodded. 'Take care of yourself, Matthew.'

He nodded and stepped out over the threshold. Esther stood by the window near the back door watching Matthew walk across the yard and out of the gate. She could just see his shape through the swirling mist as he pulled the gate to behind him and turned towards the town. Then she saw him hesitate and stop. Slowly he turned around and took a few steps in the opposite direction towards the Point.

Beth, she thought, he's going to say goodbye to Beth – and to his son.

She saw him falter and stop again. He stood in the lane, a lonely figure, gazing towards the Point, straining to see the Elands' boat home through the mist.

Esther closed her eyes and laid her forehead against the cool glass.

'Oh, Matthew, Matthew,' she whispered.

When she opened her eyes and looked again, he had disappeared from view.

Twenty-one

*L*ETTERS had always been rare amongst the small community at the Point. The arrival of one used to cause anything from delighted surprise to worried consternation, and everyone knew about its coming within minutes, sometimes even before the real recipient.

Now, letters, cards – news of any sort – were eagerly awaited and pounced upon. The first card, delivered by Will Benson on his rounds, came from Ernie Harris telling his parents he was still in training and had not yet heard of being posted abroad.

A month after Matthew had left, a postcard arrived from him addressed to his wife. As Will handed it to her, Esther read the words Matthew had written so laboriously. 'I am well. I hope you are too. Matthew.' As an obvious afterthought, he added at the bottom, 'And the child'.

Esther sighed and a wry smile twitched her lips. Which child was he really thinking about, she wondered. Kate? Or his son who lived in the boat on the river bank?

She pulled the back door wider. 'Come on in, Will, ya dinner's on the table.'

'Eh, ya're a grand lass and no mistake.'

'You've always been good to me, Will. An' I never forget those that's done me good turns.'

Will grinned amiably, and said shrewdly, 'Aye, an' I reckon you dun't forget those that's done you a bad turn either, eh, lass?'

Esther laughed aloud, her bright eyes glinting. 'How well you know me, Will Benson.'

'Aye,' Will murmured more to himself than to her. 'I reckon I do at that.'

Esther handed Matthew's postcard back to Will for him to read. He smiled. 'Not much of a letter writer, is he?'

'No, but at least he's actually written to me.'

They exchanged a glance of understanding. Will nodded but said nothing more, deliberately concentrating on the meat and potato pie she had placed before him. As always, after the first few mouthfuls, Will made a pretence of looking around the room as if he had just remembered. As usual, he said with careful casualness, 'Where's the little one, then?'

It had become a ritual between them. Esther replied, 'Sleeping upstairs, but I'll fetch her down before you go.'

Satisfied, Will nodded. 'I've got a present for her.'

'Oh, Will, really! You spoil the child. You really shouldn't bring her something every week.'

Will grinned. 'Well, if I can't spoil me – ' he cleared his throat and finished – 'me favourite little girl, then I dun't know who can.'

Gently, Esther said, 'Didn't you ever have any children, Will?'

There was a long silence whilst Will kept his eyes downcast, concentrating on his plate as he mopped up

230

the last vestige of gravy with a piece of bread, savouring every morsel. Esther thought perhaps she had trespassed too far on his privacy, that he was going to ignore her question, but at last he raised his head slowly and looked directly into her eyes.

Choosing his words carefully, he said, 'It never happened with me and the wife, and then not very many years after we was wed she – well – she didn't like that side of things. Y'know . . .' Their eyes held together in a steady gaze. 'But she were a good wife in every other way, *every* other way. And I – never wanted to see her hurt. I still don't.'

Slowly Esther inclined her head. 'Yes,' she whispered. 'I can understand that. You're a good man, Will Benson.'

Colour suffused his cheeks and his voice was a little husky with emotion. 'Mebbe I ain't always been.'

Esther stood up, not wanting to embarrass him any further. She grinned. 'Not many of us are perfect all the time, Will. I reckon we're all allowed a little slip now and again.'

Will laughed, blowing away the moments of awkwardness between them.

'I'll go and fetch Kate down to see you.'

Minutes later as she sat her sleepy daughter on Will's knee and watched as he pulled a toy from his pocket, his head bent towards the child, Esther knew for certain what had lain hidden in the recesses of her mind, and her heart, for years. If only Will would say the words she longed to hear. But from their conversation a few moments before, it looked as if she would have to wait a long time – maybe for ever.

There were a number of familiar faces missing at the Harvest Supper that year. All the young men had gone to war, and the last of the harvesting had been left to the old men, the women and children. Esther found herself meeting new people from more distant farms whom the squire had prevailed upon to help, and she in turn had to go some considerable way to help out in turn.

'By, but we're late getting it all in this year. How's things with you?' Tom Willoughby asked her.

'Not too bad, Tom, thanks. We got it all in just before Matthew volunteered.' Her mouth was grim at the memory of that night, nor could she forget the part Tom's wife and sister-in-law had played. Esther was fair-minded enough, however, to know it was none of Tom's doing.

'Come up to my place in the morning, Esther, lass,' Tom was saying, 'and hitch a lift with my workers. We're off to Browns' Farm tomorrow and it's five miles or more. You can't be carrying your little girl that far.'

Esther smiled her thanks and the morning saw her and Kate perched on the front of the wagon beside Tom Willoughby under the malevolent glare of his wife as the cart trundled out of the yard of Rookery Farm. Tom Willoughby never seemed to worry what his wife and sister-in-law said or did. He was far too intelligent, Esther thought, to be ignorant of their mischief-making, but no doubt long ago he had decided that the best way to treat it was to ignore it. Well, thought Esther, if he can then so can I, though inwardly she had to admit that she still felt resentment towards the two women for having goaded Matthew into volunteering.

Esther found that her horses were much in demand too, and she received payment from some of the farmers for their use of Punch and Prince.

'You'm lucky you've still got yar 'osses,' Mr Souter told her. 'They took the team I reckon to borrow from the squire in the first month of the war.'

'What d'ya mean, Mr Souter? Who took them?'

'This government official came – from the War Office, or whatever they call 'em. Commandeered them for service, he said.'

Esther gasped. 'Can they do that?'

'Huh, can they just!' Mr Souter said grimly.

'Well, ya're welcome to borrow mine, Mester Souter.'

'Thank 'ee, Mrs Hilton. I might at that – while ya've still got 'em!'

So it was not quite such a shock for Esther the day a thin-faced, hunch-backed little man with steel-rimmed spectacles and clutching a sheaf of papers under his arm knocked on the back door of Brumbys' Farm.

'I am sorry to inform you that you are required to give up your two farm horses, Mrs Hilton.'

'I ain't no 'osses,' Esther said boldly, but at that moment, Punch decided to kick his stable door.

The man's eyes narrowed and he smiled thinly. 'Really, Mrs Hilton,' he said. 'Well, I am informed—'

'Oh, yes, and who informed you, might I ask?' Esther said belligerently and added beneath her breath, 'as if I didn't know.'

The man cleared his throat nervously. 'There is another little matter, Mrs Hilton.'

'Oh, yes.' Her tone was uninviting.

'Yes – it's about your grassland. Meadows.'

'What about it?'

'We need you to plough up some of your grassland for—'

'I ain't ploughing me grassland up and that's final!' Esther's eyes sparkled with defiance and she stood, hands on hips, facing him.

'Well – er – Mrs Hilton – the Government . . .'

'If the Gov'ment want to plough me land up, the Gov'ment can come and do it! And . . .' she added menacingly, 'I'd like to see 'em do it without 'osses.'

'But, Mrs Hilton—'

She flung her hand out to encompass the cows munching happily in the field to the left of the farmyard. 'Where are you goin' to get milk from if the cows ain't no grass to feed on? You tell me that!'

'Er – well, I don't rightly . . .'

'Exactly! I've never heard anything so daft in all me life. An' if I lose me hay harvest, I can't feed my livestock through the winter. If you tek me 'osses, I can't bring either me hay in nor me corn harvest.'

'Well, I do take your point about the grassland, but the horses, I really must insist—'

'And I must insist,' Esther said, her tone heavy with sarcasm, 'that you leave me farm. This is private property.'

'Madam.' The man's tone became lofty. 'There is a war on.'

'Dun't I know it. Where do ya think me husband is? Out in France more than likely, when he should be here helping with the ploughing and the threshing.' She took a step towards him and the little man backed away.

'Well – er – I'll see what I can do. I'll – er – bid you good-day, Mrs Hilton.'

'Good-day, mester.'

Through narrowed eyes, she watched him go.

Early the next morning, as the dawn stretched fingers of light across the sea, Esther led Punch and Prince across the marshland towards the East Dunes. Finding a sheltered hollow, she tethered them to a sturdy elder bush and left them, returning at night to lead them back to the farm to feed and again in the early morning leading them back again into the dunes. So, during the second week when the official came back with two men to lead her horses away, Esther was able to say, quite truthfully, 'They ain't here. They've gone.'

'You mean someone's taken them away?'

'That's right,' she said, deliberately misinterpreting his meaning.

'Well, really,' muttered the little man. 'I really do wish my colleagues would keep me informed of what they're doing. Good day, Mrs Hilton. I apologize for having wasted your time.'

Not until the little man and his helpers were safely out of earshot did Esther laugh aloud. It had been worth all the loss of sleep with her early morning and late night treks to the dunes to keep her horses!

*

Life for Esther had never been easy nor did she expect it to be, but caring for her child, running the farm and helping others in return for their help was beginning to take its toll even upon her strength and determination.

'You're losing weight, lass,' Will told her, and not for the first time, 'and you look tired.'

Esther tried to smile but found that her brave act didn't fool Will Benson anyway. 'I am, Will. I'm very tired,' she admitted to him as she would not have done to anyone else. 'But,' she added stoically, 'what else is there to do? I made me own bed, an' now I'll have to lie in it.'

'Aye, I know, lass, I know. But ya didn't reckon on lying in it on ya own.'

At that moment, Kate came toddling towards Will on her chubby legs, her arms outstretched to him asking to be picked up. Fondly, Esther watched them together, the greying wisps of Will's hair, which still glinted red in the sunlight, close to the bright red-gold curls of the child as she wrapped her arms about his neck.

'You'll never guess, Esther, who came on the cart with me this morning.' Will rocked Kate back and forth in his arms. She chortled and played with his watch chain.

Esther wrinkled her forehead. 'No one I know, was it?'

Will nodded. 'Young Ernie Harris.'

Esther's eyes lit up. 'Ernie! Oh, that is good news. Is he home from the war? Home for good? He's not hurt, is he?'

Will laughed. 'Whoa there, steady, lass.' His face sobered. 'No, he's got a bit of leave because he's to be sent out to France very soon.'

'Sent to France?' Esther's voice dropped to a bewildered whisper. 'They can't send him out there. He's not old enough!'

Will shook his head. 'He'll have to go, Esther. He signed up.'

Esther stared at him in disbelief.

Later that day, Ernie arrived at the farm to see Esther. When she opened the back door to his knock she scarcely recognized the young man in army uniform. He seemed to have grown taller and certainly he had filled out. But his face still beamed at her with the familiar grin of Ernie Harris.

''Evening, missus. I couldn't go again without seeing you.'

'Oh, Ernie, how fine you look in your uniform. And how well, too.' She laughed. 'The food can't be as bad as they make out, eh?'

She held open the door as an invitation for him to step inside. He pulled his cap from his head and manoeuvred his pack through the doorway and into the kitchen.

'Are you leaving already? I thought you only came this morning.'

'I did – but I've got to catch the train back tonight.'

'Train! Have you been on a train, Ernie?'

Ernie nodded. 'All the troops are moved about by train.'

So, Esther thought irrationally, Matthew would be getting his longed-for ride on a train. I hope he thinks it's worth it.

Ernie looked bulky and awkward standing in full kit in the cramped space of her kitchen. 'Lynthorpe is a bit of a difficult place to get to by train and be sure to be back in time,' he was explaining. 'I mustn't be late reporting back to camp or I get put on a charge.'

'A charge?'

'Yeah, they're very strict. You have to stick to all the rules and reg'lations. It's a good life, though. I dun't regret going, missus. I'm seeing a bit more of life and I've met some great fellers.'

Esther nodded, her gaze travelling up and down the figure before her.

His eyes were bright with excitement. 'I'm really off to France.'

'You – you want to go?'

'Oh, yes, missus, I do.'

'I – I don't suppose you've seen anything of Matthew?'

Ernie shook his head. 'I did ask about him. We're in the same regiment – the Fifth Battalion the Lincolnshire Regiment – but in different companies. I reckon Mester Hilton's in the same company as Master Rodney, the squire's son. If I ever bump into him, missus, I'll tell him I've seen ya.' There was no mistaking the pride in Ernie's voice as he talked about his regiment.

'Will he – will they be going to France too?'

Ernie wrinkled his forehead. 'I suppose so. I don't know if we all go together or what, but I'll keep a look out for him, missus,' he promised finally.

There was a moment of awkwardness between them before Ernie said, 'I'd best be off. Goodbye. I hopes everything goes well on the farm for you. I've told our Enid to come and help you when she can. I hope that was all right, missus?'

Esther nodded. 'Thank you, Ernie. I'd be glad to have

her.' It would be a little bit of Ernie Harris close to her, she thought.

Esther had been surprised by her feelings after Ernie had gone. She missed him about the farm, missed the help he had given so willingly, and was lost without his cheerful good nature to lighten the days. Especially the days when Matthew had sunk into one of his dark, silent moods.

With an unaccustomed lump in her throat, Esther said, 'Goodbye and – and good luck. Take care of yourself.'

He put on his cap, placing it carefully at the right angle, pride in every movement. 'I will, missus. I'll be seeing you again.'

With a cheerful wave, he was gone. Across the yard and out of the gate, where he turned to wave again and then set off up the lane towards the town.

It was to be the last they saw of Ernie Harris.

Twenty-two

CHRISTMAS that year – the time by which they had all believed the war would be over – came and went. It lacked the usual festive feeling. The adults had to force themselves to make merry for the sake of the children, but a cloud hung over everyone.

A small package came for Esther who, never having received anything like that before, fingered it nervously before opening it. Inside was a Christmas card from Matthew. There were also two copies of a photograph of him in uniform. On the back he had written, 'Some of the lads had their pictures took, so I did too.'

From the photograph, Matthew's solemn face stared up at her. He looked very grand in his uniform. It looked grey on the photograph, but she knew from having seen Ernie that it would be khaki, buttoned up to the neck. He stood stiffly, with his feet set slightly apart, his legs encased to the knees in a sort of bandage – there must be a name for them but Esther didn't know what it was. On his feet were sturdy boots. Well, she thought, Matthew's used to wearing them, but he looks thinner in the face. His eyes, staring straight into the camera, held a scarcely concealed fear. He had been plunged into a strange and violent world, and he must now be seeing sights and experiencing tragedies he had never before imagined even in his worst nightmares. Already he looked a very different man from the one who had left Fleethaven

Point only a few months ago. He looked as if he had aged ten years in as many weeks.

The photographs were identical and Esther wondered why he had sent two. Perhaps it had been a standard fee for so many and, not having had anyone else to send one to, he had sent them both to her.

The thought struck her suddenly, flashing unbidden into her mind. Perhaps he wanted Beth to have one, but did not like to send it to her direct because of Robert Eland.

Esther sniffed. Well, he's had that! she thought with a trace of belligerence and tucked the spare photograph into a drawer, slamming it shut with an air of finality. She carried the photograph of Matthew upstairs. Taking the old picture of Sam Brumby's parents out of its silver frame, she found that the new one of Matthew fitted perfectly in its place. Downstairs again, she stood it on the mantelpiece in the kitchen. Alongside it she placed the pretty Christmas card. It was the first card she could ever remember having received.

She picked Kate up and pointed to the photograph. 'Look, Kate, that's your daddy.'

The child pointed. 'Dadda,' she said obediently. 'Where Dadda?'

'He's away, darling,' Esther murmured. 'Maybe for a long time.' As the child wriggled to be set down to run outside to play, Esther was left staring at the photograph of her husband.

Three months later on a blustery Friday in March, the news made headlines in the local paper which Will

Benson now brought out to the Point each week. Alongside a notice of yet another mass meeting for recruitment with the clarion call to 'Come and Join His Majesty's Forces' were the words:

BRITISH CASUALTIES

Local squire's son and estate worker killed on the same day.

The sad news has reached our town of a tragic loss to our community. Corporal Rodney Marshall, of the Fifth Battalion, the Lincolnshire Regiment, son of Mr and Mrs Marshall of Fleethaven Grange, has laid down his life for his country. Corporal Marshall was one of the first from this district to enlist when Major Langley gave his stirring address at a meeting in the town at the beginning of September last, only a month after hostilities had broken out.

Corporal Marshall was born at the Grange and had attended a boarding school in Lincoln where, only this year, he gained a place at Oxford, which, but for the outbreak of war and his immediate courageous enlistment, he would have taken up last October. A fine young man who undoubtedly had a brilliant career ahead of him, has made the greatest sacrifice of all. Our deepest sympathy is extended to his parents and brother, but we share in their pride at the great sacrifice he has made.

Killed also on the same day and from the same Regiment as Corporal Marshall was Private Ernest Harris, a worker on Squire Marshall's estate.

'Oh, Will.' Esther looked up from the newspaper she held in her hands, having laboured over the printed words, needing to read for herself before she could believe it true. 'Oh, Will, I must go to Ma. Does she know?'

242

He nodded sadly. 'It were me that telled her, lass. Eeeh, but I thought they'd have been told – that they'd have had one of them awful telegrams.' He took off his cap, ran his hand through his greying hair. 'But they hadn't. Oh Esther, lass, they didn't know till I showed 'em the paper.' His eyes were troubled, almost tearful. 'I never thought.'

Esther put her arms around Will and for a moment they clung together. 'Don't, Will, don't. It ain't your fault. It's the – the authorities. They should have told them.'

She felt him shake his head against her and his words were muffled against her shoulder. 'Aye, but there's that many, Esther. That many.'

He pulled away from her gently and patted her shoulder, a little embarrassed at his emotional display.

'What do you mean?' Esther whispered, her eyes wide.

'The main newspapers give lists of casualties every day. I 'eard as how lots of families learn of the death of their relatives that way. Then a telegram arrives a few days later. It ain't really anyone's fault, they're just snowed under with the number that they've to deal with.'

Esther gasped. 'You mean, there's that many getting killed every day?'

Will nodded but could not bring himself to meet her eyes.

Esther sighed. 'Poor Ernie and poor young Rodney Marshall, too,' she added as a dutiful afterthought. She glanced at the clock on the mantelpiece behind which there were now three postcards from her husband. They came about every five or six weeks, always with just

243

the same brief message and whilst Esther had toiled painstakingly over her letters in reply, asking questions, telling him news from home, he had never once answered any of her direct comments.

I wonder, Esther thought to herself, if Matthew is still alive or whether somewhere, sitting on someone's desk, is a telegram waiting to be sent to me?

Ma Harris accepted the news of her son's death in the stoic manner with which she met all life's tragedies.

'I knew when he went, lass,' she told Esther sadly, 'that I might never set eyes on him again. I love all my bairns, lass, all seven of 'em – an' even the two babes in the churchyard that died before they scarcely drew breath . . .'

Esther hadn't known before of that particular heartbreak in Ma Harris's life. But now was not the time to be asking.

'But Ernie was me eldest. The man of the family – after his dad. I'll miss him.'

'We all will, Ma, truly we all will.'

There was a memorial service held in the church for the squire's son, Rodney, and where the newspaper had given only two lines to Ernie Harris's death, Mr Marshall, even amidst his own grief, was more generous. He gave explicit instructions to the vicar that the service should give equal recognition to both young men and he sent his own carriage to take Mr and Mrs Harris and all their family to the church.

For the first time in her life, Esther warmed to a member of the gentry, whom she had always believed cared little or nothing for her and her kind. Squire Marshall, his wife and one remaining son sat in their family pew, the empty place beside them a poignant reminder.

Mrs Marshall's sobs could be heard throughout the service. She left the church clinging to her husband's arm, her face, covered by a black veil, buried against his shoulder. By contrast, Ma Harris, though there was deep sadness in her eyes, seemed to be the mainstay of her family, shushing the weeping little girls, Enid amongst them. Taking her husband's arm, she walked down the aisle and out of the church with dignified pride. Her indomitable spirit was battered but certainly not broken.

Now that a soldier's death had touched Esther in the loss of her young friend, her anxiety for Matthew's safety grew. Although cards still arrived from him, they were spasmodic and Matthew never thought to write the date on his cards, so Esther had no way of knowing how long they had taken to reach her. She had no idea where he was, except that he was definitely in France now. Every day she feared the arrival of a telegram, became more afraid for him if the time between his postcards seemed too long. Every week she had to compel herself to read the growing list of casualties in the local paper.

So 1915 passed and soon the war was a whole year old and there was another Christmas to face – this time knowing that Ernie would never come home.

Although her anxiety for Matthew's safety was never far from her thoughts, the farm took up all Esther's strength and time. Another harvest was safely over but there was the ploughing and the threshing through the winter. Without Tom Willoughby's help, Esther doubted she could have coped. He sent men and machinery to help her whenever he could, so that all her ploughing was done to time in readiness for the spring sowing. The squire rarely visited now, but it was understandable, Esther thought. If the gossips were to be believed, it seemed his wife had taken to her sick-bed since the loss of their son and the poor squire had virtually lost his wife too.

Esther was always tired and had no time for anything now except her work and caring for Kate. Yet there was after all a strange security in the changing seasons and the demands of the farm which must be met no matter how she felt. She could not just give up. The war had robbed her of her young friend, Ernie, and had enticed her husband away; she would not allow it to take away her home and her livelihood too. She must keep everything going until Matthew came back . . .

Enid Harris, and now one of the younger boys, Luke, coming up to thirteen, helped her. Willing though the girl was, Enid was not Ernie and certainly she could not do the work Matthew had done. Esther suggested that Enid should take over the dairy work and looking after Kate. The child adored the older girl and began to run after her towards the Point as Enid went home.

The first time it happened, Esther rushed out of the stable where she had been putting the harness on Punch and Prince, and called after them. 'Come back, Katie, you're not to go with Enid just now. She's going home.'

The child pouted and shook her curls, which glinted in the sunlight. 'I want to go an' play.'

'No, stay here.'

'It's all right, missus. She can come and play with our young 'uns. Me ma won't mind.'

Esther bit her lip. She had no objection whatsoever to her daughter playing with Ma's children, but she knew that Danny Eland often played with the Harris brood.

Esther sighed deep within herself. How could she hope to keep Kate and Danny apart for ever when they lived only a few hundred yards from each other and in such a small, self-sufficient community? She bit her lip and wondered what Beth too felt about the matter.

'All right then, but only half an hour, mind.'

'I'll bring her back for her tea, missus,' Enid promised and held out her hand to the child who trustingly put her own small hand into it.

Esther watched them go, then turned away and went back to lead the two horses out into the early spring sunshine. She groomed them, brushing away the last shreds of the winter coats they were shedding until they gleamed.

'My, you pair have got fat through the winter,' she said and was rewarded by Punch tossing his head and butting her gently. She laid her head against the horse's neck, drawing comfort from its warmth. 'I don't know what I'd do without you two now Matthew's gone,' she murmured. Silently, she acknowledged that her husband had indeed done her a favour when he had bought the pair. She drew back and patted their necks in turn.

'But, me lads, it's work for you tomorrow.' Tom

Willoughby had promised to lend Esther his seed drill and another of his horses for sowing the fields at Top End.

She screwed her mouth up thoughtfully. 'I hope he remembers I need at least another feller to help me. That's one thing I can't manage on me own,' she told the two horses as she led them out of the farm gate and along the lane into the first grass field.

It was as she was closing the gate to the meadow and about to turn back towards the farm gate that she saw a distant figure striding purposefully along the lane towards the Point. She stared, straining her eyes to see if she could recognize him. She saw that the man was carrying a pack on his back and that he was in uniform.

'Matthew?' she whispered and involuntarily took a step towards the approaching figure.

It was not Matthew. As the figure came nearer she saw that the man was a stranger to her. He was taller than her husband and his fair hair fell forward in a gentle flick over his forehead. His skin was a smooth light brown, but his face was thin, his cheeks hollowed. As he walked along he seemed to be deep in thought, for he was frowning slightly. As he drew level with her, he looked up and saw her standing there. A smile crinkled his face and lit up his blue eyes.

'Good afternoon, ma'am.' His voice was deep and soft, with a well-spoken gentleness in it. 'I wonder if you can help me?'

Esther ran her tongue over her lips and smoothed her palms down her skirt. She felt suddenly hot and dirty – and ridiculously shy.

'I – I'll try.' Her mouth was dry and her voice came out in a croak.

His face sobered as he said quietly, 'I'm looking for Mrs Harris. I understand the family live at the end of this road?'

Esther nodded. 'The – the end cottage at the Point itself. There's a row of four.'

He smiled again, but there was a sadness that did not leave his eyes this time. 'I've – er – come to see her about Ernie?'

There was a moment's silence between them as they stared at each other. 'Did – did you know him, then?' she asked.

The man nodded. 'I was with him . . .'

Esther drew breath sharply. 'Not – you mean – when he – he was killed?'

The man nodded. 'Yes. I've – er – brought her a letter from him. At least – I wrote down what he asked me to tell her. I've not been able to get here before now, and I particularly wanted to bring it to her myself. I didn't want to just send it. Perhaps I can reassure her' – there was pain in his eyes as he remembered – 'that he didn't suffer – not too much.' His glance flickered away and Esther wondered if he were being quite truthful. But his good intentions could not be doubted.

There was a lump in Esther's throat as she said, 'It's kind of you to come and see Ma . . . I mean, Ernie's mother.'

He shrugged. 'It's no more than we do for each other all the time – out there.' There was a trace of bitterness in the final two words.

Esther did not argue, although she could not imagine Matthew sitting beside a dying boy, listening to his last message home, and then travelling to a remote part of the country to deliver that message in person to his mother.

Esther continued to gaze at the stranger and he returned her trance-like stare. He seemed to be searching for something to say, anything to say, that would keep him here, talking to her.

At last he said reluctantly, 'Well, I suppose I'd better be getting on. Maybe I'll see you when I come back?'

Esther nodded. She was conscious of her ruffled hair, her face shiny with sweat and the smell of horses still on her hands and clothes.

'Thank you for your directions.' He smiled again and began to walk away, glancing back once to give her a cheery wave, to which her hand fluttered nervously in response.

Close by her, just beyond the gate, Punch stamped his feet, lifted his head and whinnied loudly. Esther jumped, startled from her reverie by the sudden noise. She moved slowly down the lane towards her own farm gate, watching the striding figure as he reached the Hump and climbed to the top of the bank. She saw him pause, turn and look back once more towards her. Then he disappeared down the other side and was gone.

Esther hurried into the back scullery and sluiced cold water over her face. She ran lightly up the stairs and brushed frantically at her tangled curls until her hair gleamed. She bit her lip as she glanced down at her working clothes. Pulling open the top drawer of the chest she took out a clean white blouse and a starched pinafore.

He'll be there now, she thought, meeting Ma Harris and being asked into her kitchen. She'll sit him down and bustle about making tea and bringing out scones and cakes, wanting to hear his news, wanting to talk of Ernie and yet putting off the moment, postponing the renewal of the pain the visitor's news must bring.

She'll be sitting down too now, Esther imagined as she went downstairs and stood in the scullery looking out into the back yard, and beyond, into the lane. Ma would sit down at the scrubbed table and face the stranger across it and listen to what he had to tell her about Ernie.

How long would they talk? How long would it take for him to impart his message? And how long afterwards would he stay?

Esther rubbed her palms down her clean apron, turned away from the window and went back into her kitchen, but a moment later she was back at the window. She went outside and stood in the centre of the yard, biting the edge of her thumb uncertainly. She didn't want to intrude, yet she wanted to go down to Ma's cottage.

She wanted to meet the stranger again.

'What on earth's the matter with you?' she said aloud. 'You're a married woman!'

Still her feet would not take her back indoors to start getting Kate's tea ready – which was what she should have been doing. A strange fluttering somewhere under her ribs would not let her dismiss the smile of the stranger quite so easily.

Then she realized she had a ready-made excuse to go to

251

Ma's cottage. Kate was not home. She was still down at the Point with Enid. Eagerly Esther almost ran towards the gate and out into the lane. She must fetch Kate, she told herself, trying to justify her action. It's way past her tea-time.

There were no children playing outside the cottages; no sign of Danny Eland or – thank goodness – of his parents.

Outside Ma Harris's cottage Esther hesitated, feeling diffident about being here. She clicked her tongue against her teeth, impatient with herself. She was still trying to decide what she ought to do, when she heard a tapping at the window and she turned to see Kate's beaming face pressed against the pane, jam smeared around her mouth. The door opened and Enid beckoned her in. 'Kate's all right, missus. I'm sorry I didn't bring her back, but this feller's come to see me ma . . .' Her eyes were shining, and her voice dropped to a whisper. 'Ooh, he's a lovely feller, missus, real handsome. Come in an' meet him. He knew our Ernie.'

Shyness swept through Esther – an unaccustomed feeling for her. 'Well, I don't want to intrude, I just came to fetch Kate home . . .'

'She's had her tea.'

'Yes, but . . .'

'Oh, do come in, missus, please,' Enid urged her, and Esther needed no more persuasion.

Twenty-three

A S she had imagined, they were sitting around the kitchen table, the stranger in the place of honour in Mr Harris's Windsor chair at the head, whilst Ma sat at the opposite end. Mr Harris had come in from work and in deference to his honoured guest had sat down at one side of the table. The children stood together, wide-eyed and curiously silent, just staring at the visitor.

As Esther came in, the man glanced towards her and rose politely. Their eyes met and the wonderful smile spread across his face.

'Hello – we meet again,' he said in his rich, deep voice.

Esther smiled self-consciously. She felt Ma Harris looking from one to the other in puzzlement, but Esther's own gaze was fixed upon the stranger's face.

'You know Esther – Mrs Hilton?' she asked him.

Did she imagine it or did the faintest trace of disappointment flicker across his face?

'Not exactly,' he was saying evenly. 'We met in the lane and – er – Mrs Hilton directed me to your house.'

Esther found her voice. 'I'm sorry – I didn't mean to butt in. I came looking for Kate.'

'Nay, lass, you ain't butting in. How could ya? Sit down a minute and have a cup of tea.'

'Well . . .' she murmured, but the stranger, still standing whilst she remained so, was already pulling out a chair near him and inviting her to join them around the table. 'If you're sure.'

For a few moments there was an embarrassed silence, covered by Ma busily rattling cups and saucers and filling the teapot.

'Are – are you on leave?' Esther asked him, remembering that he had said in the lane that he had not been able to come to see Ernie's mother before now. In a few more weeks it would be a year since they had heard the news of Ernie's death and it seemed strange that it should have taken quite so long for him to make his visit. His reply soon answered her question.

The smile twisted a little wryly. 'Sort of. A few days after Ernie was hit, I was injured and eventually sent back home to hospital.'

Before she could stop herself, her gaze roamed over his body. A lean, lithe body, now he was divested of the uniform's shapeless greatcoat.

As if reading her thoughts, he said, 'Don't say it – I don't look injured.'

She looked up to meet those brilliant blue eyes watching her with amusement. She drew breath sharply and laughed, 'How did you know what I was thinking?'

'It was written on your face.'

Ma pushed a cup of tea in front of her and Esther gave a little start. She had forgotten that there was anyone else in the room. The kitchen was crowded with people – Mr Harris and Ma, six of their children and her Kate, yet for a few moments she had felt herself completely alone with the stranger.

'Mr Godfrey—' Ma began, but was interrupted by the soldier saying, 'Please – call me Jonathan.'

Ma rewarded him with her toothless smile and nodded. 'Jonathan,' she corrected herself, 'is going to stay with us a few days, Esther, at least he's going to stay at the pub . . .' Ma grinned. 'Ah dun't reckon he fancies sleeping with all my brood!' The family all laughed together and two of the younger boys started a rough-and-tumble on the hearth-rug which earned them a quick cuff from their mother. Suddenly the kitchen was full of noise, for although the soldier had come on a sombre errand, he had somehow lifted their spirits and helped to ease their loss.

They could not bear to let him go – not just yet – and so had prevailed upon his good nature to stay a while in their midst.

Carefully – though her heart was beating in a most peculiar manner – Esther said, 'That's nice. Where – where are you from?'

'Lincoln. You know it?'

Esther shook her head.

He was smiling at her again. 'Well, I've never been to Lynthorpe before, and to be honest—' the laughter lines around his eyes crinkled – 'I'd never even heard of Fleethaven Point until I met Ernie.' His voice dropped a little as he added, 'He made it sound like the most wonderful place on earth.'

'It is!' Esther replied without thinking.

The stranger, who was by the minute becoming less of a stranger, threw back his head and laughed. '*Now* I know who you are. You're the missus from Brumbys' Farm, aren't you?'

Esther felt the colour rising in her neck and flooding up her cheeks. 'Is that what Ernie called me – *the missus from Brumbys' Farm*?'

'He talked a lot about you.' The blue eyes were teasing her gently and yet she knew by his tone that Ernie's tales of her had been flattering. Very softly, he added, 'I had to come and see –' he paused as if deliberately – 'for myself.' Louder he added, 'Everything – the sea, the marshes, the farms . . .'

'We'll show ya, mester, we'll show ya.' The two boys were either side of him, both talking at once. 'We'll tek ya crabbin' and shrimpin' . . .'

'That would be nice,' he answered the boys, placing an arm across each of their shoulders, but his gaze never left Esther's face. 'I'm looking forward to seeing the sea.'

Esther liked the way the newcomer spoke, his voice was deep yet gentle and to her his words seemed well pronounced.

'Esther had never seen the sea before she came to live here,' Ma was telling him, 'had you, lass? Now ya can't keep her away from it. Always up at the Point she is, staring out across the water.'

Esther coloured with embarrassment and could think of nothing to say. She pushed back her chair with a scrape on the stone floor. 'I'd best be goin'. It's way past Kate's bedtime.'

As she rose, the soldier got up too.

'Goodbye, Mr Godfrey,' she said, a little breathlessly, wanting to add 'I hope we meet again' but not daring to in front of the Harris family. Then the thought struck her – Esther Hilton not *daring* to do something because of what someone else might think? It was unheard of. What had come over her?

But the stranger had no such inhibitions. There was a twinkle in his eyes as he held her hand in his and said, 'I hope I see you again whilst I'm here, Mrs Hilton.'

As she walked home, Kate skipping along at her side and hanging on to her hand, Esther could not stop the tiny thrill of pleasure from flooding through her at the thought that Jonathan Godfrey would be staying for a few days at least.

She would see him again.

Esther thought about him several times during the following morning.

About mid afternoon she saw his tall figure coming along the lane, the two youngest Harris children hopping alongside him. They were carrying home-made shrimping nets. The soldier was bending his head slightly to one side to listen to their chatter whilst a small smile played on his mouth. Watching them, Esther moved towards the gate. He looked up and saw her and raised his hand in greeting. His smile broadened, crinkling the laughter lines around his eyes. It was impossible not to return his smile.

'Georgie and Alice are taking me shrimping.' His blue eyes danced with merriment. 'We wondered if your little girl – Kate, isn't it? – would like to come along.'

'I'm sure she would. Please come in a moment.' She opened the farm gate and they followed her into the farmhouse. 'Would you like a drink of milk, Georgie – Alice?'

'Yes please, missus,' they chorused.

Esther turned to Jonathan Godfrey. 'Please – sit down. Can I offer you anything – a glass of home-made wine perhaps?'

'Thank you – as long as I'm still sober enough to wield a shrimping net!'

The children giggled and the sound of their laughter brought Kate downstairs from her room.

'You comin' shrimpin' with me an' our Alice an' Mr Godfrey?' Georgie asked her, a rim of milk on his upper lip.

There was pleasure on Kate's face, but then it faded. 'I – I ain't got a shrimpin' net.'

The Harris children exchanged glances. 'Ya can borrow ours,' Georgie offered generously. 'We can take it in turns.'

Kate brightened again and as Jonathan stood up, she slipped her hand trustingly into his. 'Can Danny come too?' her piping voice asked and she smiled winningly at the tall man, her red curls dancing.

Jonathan glanced at Esther. 'Danny? Who is Danny?'

Before Esther could answer, Kate spoke for herself. 'He's my friend. He lives at the Point – in the big boat.'

'You know, mester. He was playing cricket with us this morning.'

Above the children's heads, Jonathan exchanged a glance of wry amusement with Esther. Laughing, she said, 'It sounds as if you're in great demand.'

'He's bin teaching me an' Danny to bowl overarm,

258

ain't ya, mester?' Georgie turned back to Esther, awed admiration in his tone. 'He's played cricket afore the war with a proper team in Lincoln.'

'Fancy!' said Esther, dutifully echoing the young boy's respect.

Kate was tugging at his hand. 'Well – can Danny come too?'

'Of course he can.' Jonathan looked again at Esther. 'I'll take good care of them,' he promised her.

As she watched them go, Esther felt disappointed that she had not been asked to join them. Just for once, she thought forlornly, she would have liked to have left her work and responsibilities for an hour or so and joined in the childish games on the seashore.

Suddenly, she felt very much older than her twenty-two years.

He brought Kate back to Brumbys' Farm at tea time, carrying her in his arms, her head lolling sleepily against his shoulder. Esther met them half-way across the yard and as she took the child from him, she saw him wince.

'You shouldn't have carried her. She could have walked.'

He smiled wryly. 'Poor little mite's tired out.' He drew the back of his hand across his eyes and yawned. 'Oh, I'm sorry, but that sea air's strong.'

'They've worn you out, that's what it is,' she teased him, and was surprised at how easy it was to talk naturally to him, as if she'd known him weeks or months instead of just two days.

'You could be right there,' he smiled ruefully. 'Perhaps I'm not as fit yet as I thought I was.'

'What – happened? I mean – where were you hurt?'

'My shoulder.' He gestured to his left one. 'A piece of shrapnel was lodged in it. I was shipped back to this country to have it removed. They think they've got it all out, but the wound seems to be taking a long while to heal properly.'

'I'm sorry.'

His smile broadened as he said candidly, 'I'm not. It gives me an excuse to stay here a little longer.'

Esther was surprised to feel a strange excitement just below her ribs.

'Well – I suppose I'd better let you put the little one to bed.' There was no mistaking the reluctance in his voice. 'Maybe I'll see you tomorrow?'

Esther nodded.

It was as she emerged from one of the pig sties early the following morning that she caught sight of him passing the farm gate, walking towards the town. Involuntarily, she made a move towards him, to shout after him, but she checked herself. Jonathan Godfrey was leaving and he had not even bothered to call to say goodbye. As one of the growing pigs from a recent litter pushed past her legs and scampered about the yard, grunting and snuffling in its excitement at being free, Esther gave a click of annoyance. Seizing a broom, she chased the pig back into its sty.

Fool! she chastised herself, getting dreamy about a handsome face and smiling eyes.

'I'm off to play with Danny, Mam,' Kate came skipping across the yard, her pinafore on inside out.

'Oh no you're not,' Esther began and then seeing the child's disappointment, she forced a smile. She picked her up and swung her round and round till Kate giggled. Then setting her down on the yard again, Esther added, 'At least, not until you've collected the eggs for me. You're getting a big girl now, Katie, you'll soon be four and I need you to help with little jobs you can do.'

'Then can I go and play with Danny?'

Exasperated, Esther sighed, but relented. 'Yes, then you can go.' As the little girl skipped away to fetch a basket, Esther shouted after her, 'And don't break any, Katie.'

'No, Mam, I won't.'

But when Katie had left the farm, running on her sturdy little legs towards the Point, Esther's thoughts turned once again to Jonathan Godfrey. Her irritation stayed with her all day. She was angry with herself for having read more into his glances, his smiles, his words. How could he just go off like that, without a word? He was just another flirt – like Matthew, she told herself crossly.

Then she sighed. Only the stranger had been so very good-looking and so kind. How many other men she knew would have spent the whole afternoon shrimping with four small children? Certainly not Matthew! He had hardly ever taken any notice of his own daughter, let alone anyone else's.

Despite her vexation, she still found herself glancing

up the lane, half-hoping she would see Jonathan Godfrey walking along it, back towards the Point.

But the lane was deserted – not even Will was due for a visit today.

When Kate returned at dinner-time, Esther questioned her eagerly. 'Has Mr Godfrey gone?'

The child wrinkled her smooth brow. 'Dunno. Nobody said.'

'But – he's not there now?' Esther persisted.

Kate shook her curls. 'He was nice, wasn't he, Mam?'

'Yes, Kate,' Esther murmured, more to herself than in answer to the child. 'He was nice.'

Twenty-four

AS Esther spooned stewed apple into a bowl and placed it before Kate, there came a knock at the back door.

Mother and child exchanged a glance.

'Mebbe it's Danny.' Kate picked up her spoon and as Esther moved to answer the door, the child added, 'Tell him I'll come when I've had me dinner.'

But it was not Danny.

Esther found herself gazing into a pair of blue eyes, the laughter lines crinkling around them. Then her glance went to something he was holding out to her.

'I made this for Kate. Is she here?'

Esther nodded. 'I – thought . . .' she began, then, gathering her reeling senses, pulled the door wider open to invite him in.

Esther saw her daughter's eyes light up and she gave a little squeal of delight. 'A shrimpin' net! Is it for me?'

Jonathan nodded. Kate jumped down from her place at the table and took the net from him. 'Ooh, it's lovely. I must show Danny—'

She was gone, rushing out of the back door, her feet flying across the yard.

'Kate! Kate, what do you say to Mr Godfrey?'

But Jonathan only laughed. 'Let her go. Her delight is thanks enough.'

'Mebbe so –' Esther pursed her lips – 'but she shouldn't forget her manners.'

His smile disarmed her chagrin at her impulsive daughter, and in an instant dispelled the feeling of disappointment that had lingered all the morning.

He had not gone away. He had not left without so much as a goodbye, as she had believed. They were standing in the kitchen, just looking at each other.

Esther was searching for something to say but could think of nothing. She smoothed the palms of her hands, suddenly moist, down her white apron.

'Well, I'd better be off,' he said. 'Robert Eland is taking me out in his boat, fishing.' But still he made no move to go.

There was silence between them as they stared at each other.

'Well, er . . .' he said at last. 'Maybe I'll see you later?'

Esther nodded. 'Don't fall in the sea,' she teased him.

Esther went about her work during the afternoon in a daze. Ever before her mind's eye was a smiling face with brilliant blue eyes. By dusk, when Kate was in bed and Esther began the evening milking, she had given up hope of seeing him again that day.

'Hello,' came the soft, bass voice, and Esther looked around Clover's rump to see a dark shadow framed in the early evening sunlight leaning over the half-door. She felt a sudden flutter beneath her ribs, and her fingers stopped their gentle pulling on the cow's teats and involuntarily she tightened her hold.

Clover, unused to such ungentle treatment particularly from Esther, lashed her tail and kicked out sideways with her hind leg. The cow's hoof struck Esther's knee and the swishing tail cuffed her cheek. Surprised, she toppled backwards on to the cobbles of the cowshed.

In an instant he was bending over her, dropping to one knee in the slurry, his blue eyes clouded with anxiety.

'Are you hurt?' He put his arm under her shoulders and bent as if to put the other under her knees to pick her up, but, more startled than hurt, Esther struggled to rise.

'No – no, really. I'm fine.' She gave a nervous laugh as she gained her feet, disturbingly aware that he was still supporting her, standing very close and holding her arm.

Clover had turned her head and was looking at Esther with soulful eyes. Esther reached out and patted the cow's back. 'It's all right, old girl, it was my fault,' she crooned gently. Embarrassed, she looked up into Jonathan Godfrey's face and explained, 'She – she's temperamental and needs a lot of coaxing . . .' Feeling an unaccustomed foolishness, she let her voice trail away.

Gently, he said, 'It was my fault entirely, I startled you – and her.' Tentatively, he put out his hand and stroked Clover's hide. The cow moved under his touch, but it was a movement of pleasure rather than of restless irritation.

Esther laughed in surprise. 'She likes you. You must have a special touch.' Immediately the words were spoken, she flushed with embarrassment, and more so when she realized he had still not let go of her arm.

She pulled away and bent to pick up from underneath the cow the pail of milk, which, miraculously, was still upright.

'Here, let me,' he offered and without giving her chance to refuse, gently but firmly, he took the pail from her hands. 'Where do you want it?'

'In the house, please,' she said a little breathlessly. 'In the pantry.'

'Right you are, Ma'am,' he teased, then added more seriously as he noticed her limping slightly as she left the cowshed, 'Did she hurt you?'

'Not much – but she caught me right on my knee.'

He pulled a face as if he shared her pain. 'Ouch!' he murmured with feeling.

Esther laughed wryly. 'Too true! But it'll soon go. It's not the first kick I've had by a long way, an' I don't expect it'll be the last, either.'

Whilst he set the milk carefully in the pantry, she lifted the kettle from the hob and mashed a pot of tea.

He came back and stood before the range, spreading out his hands towards the warmth of the fire, for the early spring evening had grown chill. He gazed into the flames and there was a far-away look in his eyes.

Esther came to stand beside him, holding a cup of tea. She looked up at him, watching his profile in the flickering light, the straight nose and smooth, firm chin, the well-shaped mouth that smiled so readily. But now there was no smile upon his lips. Whatever his thoughts were, they were grave. Slowly he turned to look at her and for what seemed an age they just stood there looking deep into each other's eyes.

At last Esther stammered, 'Er – would you like a cup of tea?'

He started visibly as if she had woken him from a

daydream. Perhaps she had, but in the next instant he was taking the cup from her and as their fingers touched, she felt a tingle run through her.

Alarmed that the touch of a stranger could arouse such a feeling in her, Esther stepped backwards and put the distance of the hearth rug between them. As if realizing what her action meant, there was a fleeting look of disappointment upon his face that this time she did not imagine. He smiled sadly and, taking a mouthful of tea, looked around him. His eyes rested upon the silver-framed photograph and the several postcards stacked behind it.

He nodded towards it. 'Your husband?'

'Yes – yes. That's Matthew. He's – he's a soldier, like you. I think he's somewhere in France. He sends me a postcard every six weeks or so, just to let me know – he's – he's all right. He doesn't write much.'

'We're not allowed to say much at all,' Jonathan Godfrey defended Matthew. 'You're lucky to hear anything, believe me.'

'What's it like out there?' Immediately she had spoken the words aloud she wished them unsaid, for the haunted look of anguish that came into his eyes filled her with guilt.

'I'm sorry,' she said at once. 'I shouldn't have asked. You want to try to forget for a time, while you're home.'

He shook his head sorrowfully. 'There's no way of forgetting. Not ever.' His voice was a hoarse whisper and once again he just stood gazing down into the fire.

He was not seeing the fire in the range in Esther's kitchen. He was seeing flashes of gunfire and mangled flesh, hearing the thud, thud, thud of the guns and the screams of his comrades.

'Oh, you try to push it out of your thoughts,' he said slowly, 'but then it all comes flooding back when you least expect it – or want it. At night, just when you're falling asleep. Or in quiet moments like this. Moments that should be peaceful and – ' he raised his head and looked directly into her eyes – 'savoured.' There was a long pause then he added, flatly, 'But back it all comes to torment you.'

Now she moved back closer to him. 'I'm sorry,' she whispered again.

'It's – all right. It's natural that you think you want to know. But you don't, believe me you really don't.'

Esther returned his gaze steadily. 'I'm not afraid of the truth, however bad it is.'

'No – no, I don't believe you are.' His eyes roamed wonderingly over her face, her hair and then came back to look once more into her eyes. Those steadfast green eyes that returned his gaze so directly. He leaned forward, lifting his hand to touch her cheek with gentle fingers.

For one breathless moment, she thought he was going to kiss her, but as his fingertips brushed her cheek, he jumped physically as if he had been stung and stepped back abruptly. In the fading light of the evening, the firelight glinted on his hair and highlighted his cheekbones, his fine nose and firm jawline. His eyes were shadowed, but she could hear his rapid breathing.

Brusquely he said, 'I shouldn't be here – I must go.'

He turned, went out into the scullery and wrenched open the back door.

Esther followed him, the words bursting from her lips before she could contain them, 'How long are ya staying?'

He stood very still, his hand on the latch, but he did not turn round. Muffled, the words came to her in staccato jerks. 'I don't know – but I must leave. Tomorrow – I'll have to go – tomorrow.'

She felt the disappointment flood through her. 'But I thought you were going to stay longer – a few days, you said.' The words were out of her mouth before she thought to stop them. They were like a reproach. 'Why must you go so soon?'

'I must. Goodbye, Mrs Hilton.' He dropped his hand from the door and the action was like a gesture of despair. He took a step forward, but still he did not look back. He walked away from her and though she stood watching him through the dusk all the way to the gate and into the lane, not once did he turn or wave.

By the set of his shoulders, it was as if he were afraid to look back at her.

Esther lay awake for most of the night haunted by the feel of the feather-light touch of his fingers on her cheek and then his sudden brusqueness.

She could not bear to think of his leaving in the morning, knowing that she would never see him again. She groaned aloud and buried her head in the softness of her pillow. What was she thinking of? What was the matter with her? She was a married woman with a child.

She had only just met him and yet when she closed her eyes, she could see his face so vividly; his smile, the kind blue eyes, and yet his jawline was firm and his handsome face showed strength and honesty . . .

The following morning seemed to drag and Esther found herself watching the lane leading from the Point to the town. The lane he must walk down when he left. She snapped at Kate every time the child tried to catch her attention. She raced through the milking, even shouting at Clover and slapping her rump sharply when the cow moved restlessly, to be repaid by the cow kicking over the pail of milk and wasting it all.

Common sense would have told her she was being foolish and very unfair to Kate – and the animals.

But common sense seemed to have deserted her.

By lunch time when Enid arrived, Esther was so irritable that she decided that the only thing to do was to go up to her favourite spot at the end of the Spit to see if the place where the land and the sea and the sky became one would soothe and calm her – and maybe bring her to her senses.

Beyond the lane she climbed over the bank and crossed the marshland towards the East Dunes heading for the beach.

He'll have gone by now, she told herself firmly. She must have missed seeing him pass by her farm gate. Yes, she reminded herself sharply, her farm gate. That was all that mattered. Her farm, her land.

She reached the Spit and walked the length of it, breathing in the sea air deeply. She bent and picked up a handful of earth, clutching it in her hand, holding it close to her body in that space beneath her ribs where she had felt, and still felt, that peculiar fluttering of nervousness when she saw Jonathan Godfrey – or even thought of him.

'This land is mine,' she said aloud to the sea and the sky as if daring them to refute her words. She threw back her head and closed her eyes and swayed with the soft breeze, wrapping the place around her like a cloak or, more to the point, a suit of armour. Nothing and no one mattered to her more than this land.

His face was still before her; she could not blot out the memory of his smile . . .

'Mrs Hilton – Esther.'

The deep voice spoke so softly behind her that for a moment she thought she had imagined it carried on the wind, brought to her ears by her thoughts.

'Esther?' There was uncertainty in his tone now when she did not respond, did not move.

She opened her eyes and slowly turned to face him, tilting her head to look up at him. The wave of hair flopped forward over his forehead on which now there was an anxious furrow. Involuntarily, her fingers fluttered to smooth away his worry, but she fought off the desire, clenching her hands together and squeezing the earth she already held.

'I – thought you were leaving. Have you come to say goodbye?'

He shook his head slowly, as if he didn't quite believe it himself. 'No. No, I'm not going yet.'

For a timeless moment they stood and stared at each other whilst the tiny waves lapped at their feet and the seagulls wheeled and dived and screeched above them.

Slowly she dropped the handful of earth she was holding and brushed the dirt from her fingers.

'I saw you from my bedroom window in the pub, crossing the marsh, coming this way,' he was saying. 'I was all ready to go – to leave, then I saw you walking out here all alone. And I couldn't go,' he ended simply.

He held out his hand to steady her as side by side they walked back along the narrow strip of land.

After a moment's hesitation, for something told her that she was about to take a step from which there would be no turning back, she put her hand into his.

Twenty-five

THEY met every day. At some point in every day, they were together. Sometimes for a few snatched moments, sometimes for an hour. And for the rest of the time, he filled her mind.

'When must you go?' she would ask, fearful of the answer yet needing to know. 'How long can you stay?'

'A few more days,' he would answer gently, 'then I should go.'

The few days stretched into a week and then two and soon she ceased to ask 'how long?'. She could make him stay, she told herself, she would make him stay. He had no need to go back to France. He'd been wounded, hadn't he? He'd done his bit in anybody's book!

They walked the seashore, side by side, not quite touching, and yet the closeness between them was like a physical embrace. They walked the dunes and they found a sheltered hollow that became their special place to sit and talk.

'Where is it you come from?' she asked him. 'Lincoln, did you say? It's a city, isn't it? I've never been to a city.' There was a wistful note in her voice.

'Should you like to go?' Jonathan asked softly.

She leant against his shoulder and looked up at him coyly. 'Maybe – with you. Tell me about it?'

'Well,' he began, idly tracing lines in the sand,

drawing a rough sketch-map to illustrate his words. 'There's a cathedral high on the hillside – built by the Romans, would you believe? It dominates the city. Wherever you are, you can see it standing proudly over-looking us all. Then the houses and streets sort of radiate out from it. There's a steep hill climb with old houses built close together on either side – buildings so old you'd wonder sometimes how they still stand.'

Esther watched his face as he talked. Watched the memories of his home flitting across his face. Memories in which she had no place. She loved the sound of his deep voice. There was little trace in his speech of the Lincolnshire dialect that was so prevalent in the country-side, and so strong in hers.

'Quaint little shops,' he was saying, 'and old book-shops – dusty and musty, but fascinating – all huddling together on the hillside. Near the cathedral there's a castle with dungeons. It's old too, though I can't remem-ber when that was built.' He grinned at her ruefully. 'I expect I was told at school, but somehow in your own home town you take things for granted. They're there. You expect them always to be there, so you don't bother.'

Esther nodded eagerly. 'It's like the sea here. It fasci-nates me. I love to stand on the Spit and watch it come swirling in around me, but the folks no've lived here all their lives never come to look at it. They just know it's there.'

Jonathan nodded. 'All the same, I bet if you took them away from it – inland – they'd soon miss it.'

'Do you miss the city?'

He looked up from his sand drawing and gazed out

across the wide expanse of beach, across the water as far, if he could have seen it, as the foreign shoreline. 'Not while I'm here, no. But when I was over there – oh, yes, I missed my home town – my home country.'

Esther's gaze followed his own as she murmured, 'I suppose they all do.'

By saying 'they' and not 'you' it was as if she was separating him from the men still over there, trying to make him believe he need not go back.

He was so totally unlike Matthew – like no man Esther had ever known. He held her hand and raised it to his lips, kissing each work-roughened finger with such tenderness that tears sprang to her eyes. He made no demands upon her. He never tried to touch her intimately, to fondle her breast or unbutton her blouse. He didn't even kiss her mouth. He didn't lunge at her in a frantic, boyish manner. He was courteous and caring and undemanding. But there was a look in his eyes when she met his intense gaze. Such a look as she had never seen before in any man's eyes. There was desire – oh, yes, she knew that look – but with Jonathan there was more, so much more.

Esther was bemused and spellbound by him.

If they had not met during the day, as darkness fell Jonathan would slip away from the Seagull and come quietly into the yard of Brumbys' Farm.

'Look,' he told her, holding out his hand to her as they stood in the shadows of the barn. On the flat of his palm lay a door key. 'The landlord said I should have a key in case I wanted to go into the town and see a bit of night life.'

They smiled at each other. Now he could come and go freely from the Seagull, with no awkward questions asked.

Esther moved close to stand looking up into his face. She wanted so badly to put her arms about him, to lean her head against his chest, to feel his arms holding her tightly. The desire was so strong it was almost a physical pain. She steeled herself deliberately not to touch him.

'Oh, Esther, Esther,' he whispered hoarsely and touched her cheek with tender fingertips. 'Every morning I get up and I say firmly to myself, "Today, I must leave."' He smiled ruefully, 'Yet by nightfall, I'm still here.' He shook his head in disbelief at his own actions. 'I would never have believed that a woman could make me shirk what I know is my duty. But you're . . . ' He hesitated, searching for the right word. 'You're something very special. Do you know that?'

She reached up and pressed his hand against her face, holding his gaze with her own intense eyes. Slowly his head came down, as if he were fighting the impulse and yet losing the battle. Their lips touched, a gentle, feather-light brush. She heard him make a low sound in his throat. His lips moved against hers, his eyes closed and his arms came about her drawing her into his embrace. She put her own arms about his neck and pulled him even closer to her.

He lifted his head and loosened his embrace. He shook his head. 'We shouldn't. We mustn't . . .'

His green eyes blazed. 'Why? I love you, Jonathan, and you love me, don't you?' The words – never before spoken to anyone by her – came so easily and so naturally

to her lips that she never paused to wonder, to savour the
sound of them and to revel in the meaning behind them.

He gasped at her directness, then smiled, won over by
her honesty.

'Don't you?' She was insisting on an answer from him.
When he didn't give one, she too released her hold on
him and stood back, away from him. Quietly, she said,
'Say ya don't love me, and I'll turn around and go. And
ya can walk away from here – and never think of me
again.' She saw the pain in his eyes. She stepped closer
again. 'Say it – say ya *don't* love me . . .' She was daring
him to deny her. In a whisper, she added, 'If ya can.'

He groaned, reached out for her and enfolded her in
his arms. 'You know I can't. I didn't know it was possible
to fall in love so quickly, so easily and – so completely.'

Triumphant, she laughed softly against his ear, standing on tiptoe to nibble his lobe with gentle teeth until he
buried his head against her neck. 'Why did I come here?
Why did I ever have to meet you?' he murmured.

'Do you wish you hadn't? Do you wish we'd never
met?'

He lifted his head and cupped her face between hands
that were gentle. 'Oh, no. Never that! Maybe it would
have been better if we hadn't. But whatever happens, I
shall never say I wish I hadn't known you.'

He began to help her about the farm. She taught him
how to milk the cows, how to harness and drive the
horses into the fields.

'I've told Mrs Harris that I'm staying on to help out a
bit with the spring sowing,' he told Esther. 'I'm still on

sick leave from the army . . .' His voice trailed away and he avoided meeting the enquiry in her eyes.

Esther had to bite her lip to stop the question being spoken aloud. How long? How long have we got left?

'It'll look better if we're working together, if . . .'

'Jonathan, I don't care what it looks like.' She spoke sharply, trying to hide her fear of his leaving. At least she was determined to make the most of every minute. 'I don't care what people think – or say.'

He shook his head sadly at her. 'Oh, Esther, but I do. I care for your sake. I wouldn't harm you for the world and when I think what people must be thinking, must be saying, about us – about you . . .'

'Let 'em!' Esther faced him squarely, her chin jutting forward. 'It isn't anyone else's business. I'm not liked around here, except mebbe by the Harrises.' She shrugged her shoulders. 'So what's it matter?'

'It matters to me.'

'Well, it shouldn't. Besides,' she added and was unable to stop the note of sarcasm creeping into her voice, 'there's nothing to know really, is there? For all your fine words, ya don't show me ya love me!'

She turned away from him and with an abrupt 'walk on' to the horses, she moved away down the field leaving him staring after her. When she turned at the far end of the field, he had disappeared.

'Will you stop that silly crying, Kate,' Esther shouted.

The child's weeping was quelled but she continued to hiccup uncontrollably. 'Stop that noise, or I'll give ya something to cry about.'

278

'I (hic) can't. Danny Eland pulled my hair ribbon off and wouldn't give it back.'

Esther stiffened. Danny Eland! Her impatience at her daughter died. She was being so unfair to take her own irritability out on her child.

Where was Jonathan? Why had he gone off like that the previous afternoon and not come back? All the morning they had been together mucking out the stables and polishing the harness and then leading the horses out to the field.

'You'll have to show me what you want me to do to help with the sowing,' he had grinned, and then she had made that stupid remark and off he'd gone. Why did she always have to open her mouth and let it say what it liked? she groaned inwardly.

All the evening she had watched for him. She had moved restlessly about the yard, going out to the field to do the milking instead of bringing the cows into the shed so that she could watch the lane. Any minute she expected to see his tall, slightly stooping frame appearing at her gate.

As darkness had fallen she had hustled Kate to bed and then she had stood most of the evening by the scullery window near the back door overlooking the yard and the lane.

He did not come.

Didn't he love her any more? Had she driven him away so easily by her bluntness? Was he disgusted because she had hinted she wanted more from him – that she wanted him physically? She had not realized just how naïve and inexperienced in matters of love she was, even though she was a married woman and a mother. She didn't know what was expected of her, how a man like Jonathan expected her to behave.

And there was no one she could ask. There was no one she could confide in. Not even Ma Harris and certainly not Will Benson – not this time.

Now, this morning, when Jonathan had still not appeared, she was venting her frustration on her innocent daughter.

'There, there, Katie, Mamma didn't mean it.'

She sighed, picked up her daughter and carried her outside the back door and round to the front of the house to sit on the grass in the sunshine. Taking the child on to her knee, her arms about her, her cheek resting against Kate's hair, Esther gave her mind over to the problem of Danny Eland.

She should have guessed it would happen. He was only behaving just like the brother to Kate that he was. She prayed that they should never find out about their relationship to each other.

'Boys are like that, Katie,' she explained, stroking the little girl's glowing curls, remembering her own boy cousins pulling their sisters' hair and her own if they had half a chance. 'You'll have to learn to stick up for yourself, darling.' As I had to do, she thought. For a moment the life she had led in her childhood came flooding back – the taunts of the other children about her bastardy, her aunt's harsh tongue and rougher hand. Only for her gentle-natured Uncle George had Esther any kindly memories.

'When you go to school there'll be lots of boys like

Danny Eland. You'll have to learn to put up with being teased.'

Kate looked up at her mother. She had stopped crying now, though salty lines still streaked her face. 'I don't think I want to go to school, Mamma.'

Esther smiled down at her. 'You'll like it when you get there. You'll learn all sorts of things – how to read and do sums and . . .'

'But I don't want to be teased – I don't like being teased.'

'No,' Esther murmured. 'No one does, but if you greet their taunts with a smile and a cheeky answer back, they'll soon give up. You see, they're only trying to upset you, to make you cry. If you don't cry but laugh at them instead, they'll give up.'

Kate seemed thoughtful, solemnly analysing her mother's advice in a peculiarly old-fashioned way for one so young.

'When do I start school? Danny says he's going next year.'

Esther sighed. Danny, Danny, Danny – always Danny Eland. 'About the same time, I think, though you're a bit younger than him. I'll have to see the teacher.'

'But Danny and me – we'll go to the same school? We'll be together?'

'Yes,' Esther was obliged to tell her. 'You'll be going to the same school as Danny Eland.'

Kate scrambled up from her mother's knee and ran across the grass towards the yard and the gate into the lane.

'Kate. Kate, where are you going?'

The child shouted back over her shoulder as she skipped across the cinders, 'To tell Danny I'm going to school with him.'

'Well, really!' Esther said, half-exasperated, half-relieved that childish quarrels could so soon be forgotten. Yet Kate's association with Danny Eland brought Esther no comfort, no peace of mind whatsoever.

It was late afternoon before she saw Jonathan.

She had walked across the marshland beyond the road opposite her farm and up the rise of the far dunes. From here she would be able to see the houses at the Point and the Seagull. She could see the children playing round Ma Harris's cottage, Kate amongst them and undoubtedly Danny Eland too. She could see Robert Eland on board his boat home spreading his nets, examining them for holes that would let the fish slip through.

She thought briefly of Beth. It was strange how they never seemed to run into each other. She could remember having seen her only once or twice since Danny's christening, then only in the distance and Danny was four now. Certainly they had never met and spoken even though they lived only a few hundred yards from each other.

Then she saw Jonathan.

He was standing at the end of the Spit – her own special place. A lonely, motionless figure just staring out to sea.

As she watched him, the familiar fluttering began just below her ribs and she felt as if, even though she was out in the open, there was suddenly not enough air to breathe.

282

Then she was running, running. Bounding over the tufts of grass, jumping the sandy hollows, splashing through the rivulets winding across the marshy ground.

A little way from him she slowed, panting hard, watching him. Now she moved slowly towards him.

'Jonathan.' She breathed his name like a prayer. A prayer for forgiveness, for understanding.

He did not move.

His name caught in her throat on a sob. 'Jonathan!'

She saw him jump physically and turn swiftly. She caught a fleeting glimpse of the sadness that was in his face before his joy at seeing her there filled his eyes with love.

He held out his arms to her and she ran into them. In that moment both of them were oblivious of the fact that they could be seen plainly from the cottages even though they were quite a distance away – and even more easily seen by Robert Eland on his boat if he cared to shade his eyes against the dazzling water and look in their direction.

Jonathan was kissing her mouth, her eyes, holding her fiercely in his arms.

'I thought you'd gone,' she gasped. 'Gone away and left me. Forgive me . . .'

Between urgent kisses, he murmured, 'We shouldn't – we'll be seen . . . Come – let's go in the dunes.'

They ran along the narrow bank, clutching at each other, laughing with nervousness, with mutual joy. They gained the dunes and came to their special place, a natural hollow, sheltered from the sea breeze and safe from prying eyes, hidden even from the coastguard's look-out.

They sat down in the sand and she snuggled against him. He wrapped his arms around her and laid his cheek against her hair.

'I couldn't sleep last night,' he said. 'I stood at the window of my room in the Seagull, looking out towards your home.'

She giggled nervously. 'I stood at me scullery window half the night watching the lane. I didn't sleep a wink.'

He stroked her hair.

She rested her head on his chest. 'We won't quarrel ever again, will we, Jonathan?' she murmured sleepily, for the sun was high and here in the hollow it was sheltered and warm. They lay back in the sand.

After the sleepless night tormenting herself that he no longer loved her, Esther just wanted to stay here safe and warm and happy for ever.

When they awoke the fickle sunshine had disappeared and a cold mist had crept in from the sea and surrounded them as they slept.

'Jonathan – oh, whatever time must it be? There's the milkin' to do. And Kate will be looking for me!' Esther scrambled to her feet and rushed headlong towards the twisting track which led back across the marsh and the dunes to the lane.

The mist swallowed her.

'Esther – Esther, wait.' He was instantly fully awake. 'You're going the wrong way. Esther!'

She could hear his voice but she could not see him.

The mist swirled about her obliterating her sense of direction completely. 'Jonathan,' she shouted, 'I can't see you. Where are you?'

Suddenly Esther knew real fear. She had never been lost like this. She heard his voice just once more. 'Now just stand still, Esther, and keep talking to me and I'll come to you.'

There was silence.

'Jonathan,' she shouted. 'Jonathan! *Jonathan!*'

There was no answering shout.

Twenty-six

*E*STHER called his name until she was hoarse. She stumbled over thick tufts of grass, fell into sandy hollows, until she was almost weeping with fear. Her heart was pounding and her breathing painful. She ran first one way and then stopped, unsure, turned and ran another way. Prickly sea-buckthorn loomed out of the mist and scratched at her hands and forearms. She thought she had found the footpath which led back across the marshland to the lane and began to follow it, still calling his name all the time. She shivered in the dampness of the mist and yet she was sweating with fear.

She trod in a rabbit burrow and twisted her ankle, giving a cry of anguish as she fell to the ground. She pulled herself up again and plunged on blindly. The path she was following gave way to a stretch of sand and she knew she was on the beach. She turned around and began to go in the opposite direction which she now knew must lead her back to safety. Then she stopped. What about Jonathan? She could see nothing but the grey, clinging mist all around her.

Suppose Jonathan, who didn't know the beach and the ways of the sea at all, were to wander in the mist out towards the sea? What if he was caught by the incoming tide as it swirled inward, forming creeks and sand islands? That much at least she had learnt about the sea and the tides since coming to live here. Jonathan knew nothing. He would be cut off, caught by the rushing water . . .

'Jonathan,' she cried, fearing more for him now than for herself.

There was silence all around her, the mist wrapped itself about her like a shroud.

She stood still and listened intently. Was that a seagull crying?

Suddenly it was clearer, though faint. 'Eeestheer!'

'Jonathan, Jonathan – I'm here. Where are you?'

His voice was nearer and now she continued to call his name and steadily he was coming closer and closer, the sound of his voice in answer to her own becoming stronger and louder. 'I'm coming, Esther. Stay where you are and I can come to you.'

The mist cleared a little and his dark shape came towards her. She was so thankful to see him that she flung herself against him, winding her arms about his neck, kissing his face, crying and laughing all at the same time.

'I thought you'd gone towards the sea. I thought you could have drowned.'

Jonathan's arms were about her, tight and protective and thankful. Their mouths were warm against each other, whilst the cold mist enclosed them.

'Oh, darling, my love, my dearest love,' she was murmuring, her endearments echoed by his deep voice. She was shivering as much from fear as with the cold. Jonathan took off his jacket and wrapped it around her, hugging her close to him. He kissed her, soothing away her terror. His lips were gentle, but as she returned his kisses, his mouth became more urgent.

'Esther, oh, Esther,' he whispered and they sank down together into the sand.

In their relief at finding each other safe, having for a few brief moments believed each other in danger, their longing overwhelmed them and they were lost. They yielded to the hunger that had been between them almost since their first meeting – an inexplicable craving that had shocked and engulfed them both.

And now their bodies came together in a flood of ecstasy. It was as if they were the only two people in the world. Swept away on a tide of emotion, there was no Matthew, no Kate – even no farm. It was as if for the whole of her life, Esther had been waiting for this moment, for this man. Her need of him was a physical pain. Her body ached for his. Nothing and no one else mattered . . .

'I never knew it could be like that,' she said, lying back on the sand.

Jonathan kissed her forehead, her eyelids and then her mouth, his lips gentle and caressing. 'Oh, my dear love, neither did I.'

She opened her eyes to find his blue eyes, full of concern, searching hers. She could feel his breath upon her face as he whispered, 'You're not – sorry?'

Her own eyes widened. 'Sorry? How could I be?' She reached up to trace the line of his jaw with her fingertips. 'I love you,' she said simply and no other explanation was needed.

His arms tightened around her and his lips kissed her neck, moving down, down to her breast and she felt the flutter of desire begin again. They made love again, slowly now, exulting in each other, murmuring endearments until again the waves of passion bore them to the heights of exquisite happiness.

Afterwards they still lay together in the sand. The mist enveloped them, but they were oblivious to the searching damp, reluctant even yet to leave. Holding her, Jonathan said, 'Esther, what about your – husband?'

Esther, her cheek against his chest, said, 'Matthew doesn't love me. He never did.'

'What?' There was astonishment, and disbelief, in the one word.

'I think,' she said slowly, 'it's time I told you the truth about my marriage.' She shivered suddenly, as if for the first time becoming aware of the cold and, noticing, he wrapped his jacket around her and held her close, warming her with his body.

'I suppose,' she mused as much to herself as to him, 'we should not have married. I—' She stopped as realization came creeping unbidden into her conscious mind. 'I didn't know what love was.' She heard the surprise in her own voice and paused, as understanding at last flooded through her. 'But now I do,' she added. There was a sadness too mingled with her present happiness. A sadness for Matthew – and even for Beth. She sighed deeply and began to tell Jonathan from the beginning.

'I was born a bastard,' she began bluntly, and felt his arms tighten about her. 'My mother died at my birth, refusing to name my father.

'My mother's sister – my Aunt Hannah – brought me up. She didn't love me, though I have to admit she taught me all I know and her harshness has made me a survivor. But as soon as I was old enough, I left.'

She told him how she had come to this place, walking through the night to arrive out of the early morning mist at Sam Brumby's farm. How she had made herself useful to Sam and how, by the time he died, she believed that the old man at least had had some affection for her in his gruff way.

'From the moment I arrived here, Matthew was – well – after me. I always vowed I'd never give way to any man before marriage.' Bitterness crept into her tone. 'I wasn't going to bring another bastard into the world!'

'Oh, sweetheart,' she heard Jonathan murmur.

'I knew there was something between him and Beth but when the squire refused to give me the tenancy of Brumbys' Farm in my own name just because I'm a woman . . .' At the indignation in her voice, he raised her hand to his lips and held it against them. 'I just never stopped to think. Matthew wanted me, asked me to marry him and I agreed.'

There was silence. 'But – but why, darling, if you didn't love him?'

'I liked him well enough. He was the only one of my own age round here who'd been friendly. But it was the farm. I wanted the farm – a home of my own. Somewhere I could belong, and I had to be married to get the tenancy. It was the only way. The only way.'

'Then he – he must have loved you, Esther. He wouldn't just ask you to marry him for no reason.'

She buried her face against him, aware of a kind of shame only now when she had learnt the difference between real love and mere physical lust. 'He – he only wanted me – physically.'

There was a long pause, then Jonathan said quietly, a little ruefully, 'Well, I can hardly blame him for that, now can I?'

She curled up against him, winding her arms around his waist, pressing her head against his chest. 'I think Beth truly loved him, and at the bottom of him I think he loved her. But you see Matthew's the sort of man . . .' She hesitated for a moment searching for the right words to express a knowledge that she was only just becoming aware of herself. 'He's the sort of man who can't resist a challenge – any sort of challenge. Do you know what I mean?'

'I think so.'

'Poor Matthew. It was the same when he volunteered. It was only because Martha Willoughby and her bitch of a sister made loud remarks in church about cowards and that Major Langley . . .' She paused. 'God – I'll never forgive that man! His speechifying altered all our lives. He whipped up such patriotism in his speech at a rally in the town, well, poor Matthew, he couldn't resist it, could he? If something was out of his reach or denied him, he wanted it all the more. At first I was that challenge, whilst Beth was always willing. When he had married me, he had me whenever he wanted. I never said no. Maybe,' she mused thoughtfully, 'it would have been better if I had said no now and then.'

She let out a long sigh and continued. In the circle of

Jonathan's arms, his cheek against her hair, Esther was quietly remembering just how her marriage had been, seeing it clearly for the first time. For now, in this moment in the dunes, she had learnt the difference.

'Matthew seemed to change. I know he was bitter about the farm and why I'd married him. He knew that it was really me that Mr Marshall gave the tenancy to – not him in his own right but only because he was my husband. It sort of – lessened his manhood. In his own eyes, if no one else's.'

'That's understandable,' Jonathan murmured.

'Before we married, when I held out against him, all he could think of was getting me, even if it meant having to marry me. When at last he'd got me, he began to hanker after Beth again. I think he had some funny idea that Beth would still be his even after he'd married me, would always be his. So when she married Eland and was out of Matthew's reach, it made him want her all the more. Then, of course, she had Matthew's baby.'

She felt Jonathan's whole body stiffen and she raised her head to look up at him as he asked, 'Little Danny is *Matthew's* son?'

'Yes.'

'I – see,' he said slowly, trying to comprehend how it must affect the close-knit community of Fleethaven Point. 'It must be difficult for you – for everyone.'

Esther shivered suddenly. 'I'll have to get back to the farm.'

She got up from the sand and held out her hands to him. 'Let's try and find our way back to the road and this time I'm keeping tight hold of you,' she laughed artfully, 'in more ways than one.'

They stood together for a moment, gazing deeply into each other's eyes, sharing again that special intimacy.

'You'll come to the farm tonight?'

'Esther, I don't think . . .'

She placed her forefinger against his lips to still his objection, and whispered urgently, 'Promise me you'll come?'

He nodded, his breath touching her fingers in a soft sigh. 'But only after dark. I don't want the gossip to start.'

'I don't care . . .' she began, but firmly he said, 'It would hurt you, my dear. You — and Kate. I don't want that.'

They parted just before the bank of grass bordering the lane, he to turn off towards the rear of the Seagull and Esther to cross the road to her farm.

She walked as if in a dream. All round her the familiar scene seemed unreal and yet suddenly so much more vibrantly alive. The pungent smell of the yard met her. She breathed deeply revelling in the air around her.

How wonderful it was to be alive — and to be loved.

A smile curved her mouth, softening its hard, set line to tenderness. She hummed softly beneath her breath, and every so often she gave a little skip of sheer happiness.

The farm seemed quiet and unusually still as if waiting for her return. There was no sign of Kate. She would be at the Point with Enid — or Danny.

As she pushed open the back door, she saw it.

Lying on the floor, delivered whilst she lay in Jonathan's arms, was a postcard from Matthew.

Twenty-seven

*S*HE stood holding the card in her hands, tensing herself against the expected flood of guilt. But it did not come. It was as if the card was from a stranger, or from someone she had known a long time ago – a person from another life.

She moved jerkily into the kitchen, and raised her head slowly to look up at the photograph of Matthew on the mantelpiece. She stared at it, but she could not even summon up memories of the real person; she could not hear his voice in her mind, or feel his touch.

To her, now, Matthew was only a face in a photograph.

It was Jonathan who was real. It was Jonathan's face she saw in her mind every waking moment; how the laughter lines crinkled round his eyes when he smiled. The way his mouth was a little lopsided, but how his blue eyes sparkled when he looked at her. How the flick of blond hair fell continually over his forehead so that she longed to brush it back and to feel his face beneath her fingers. It was his deep voice she heard, not Matthew's. It was Jonathan who loved and held her. It was his touch she craved.

Esther tucked the latest card behind the picture at the back of the others. She would tell no one of its arrival, she thought, but then remembered ruefully, doubtless everyone at the Point would already know of its delivery if the postboy had cycled all the way from town.

'Where's my little girl, then?' Will asked climbing stiffly down from the front of his cart as Esther came running around the corner of the house from the front garden, a wet shirt in one hand, clothes pegs in the other.

'Oh, it's you, Will. I thought . . .'

'Aye, lass, it is.' He eyed her shrewdly. 'Expecting someone else, were ya?'

'Yes – no, no of course not.'

His gaze dropped to the man's shirt she was holding in her hands. His eyebrows rose fractionally. 'Matthew home, is he?'

It was an odd question, and there was a peculiar tone in his voice, as if he already knew the answer. There was more behind his remark than the mere words implied.

Esther looked down at the garment she carried, and then she tried to hide it behind her back. 'Er – no, but I'm just doing a bit of weshing, that's all.' Will was the only person, other than perhaps Ma Harris, whose opinion mattered to her. Suddenly she was angry for allowing herself to feel that way. In her own estimation it was weakness.

She overcame her moment of confusion and glared at him, her chin coming higher, defying him to question her further. She turned away and strode round to the front of the house again, her back rigid against his prying. Will followed her and stood watching whilst boldly she shook out the shirt and pegged it wide on the line.

'There's talk, lass,' he said gently.

Esther whirled around to face him, a sharp retort on her lips. She met Will's steady gaze and read in his eyes not the malicious meddling of the Willoughby women, nor the gossipy tittering of the Harris family, but a genuine concern for her. The anger went out of her. She walked slowly towards him and put her hand on his arm.

'Will,' she whispered, as if sharing a secret, as indeed she was. 'I am happier than I have ever been in me life – than I ever knew it was possible to be. Don't begrudge me a little happiness, Will. Not you – of all people!'

She saw his old eyes water. 'Eh, lass, Ah'd never do that, you should know that. But Ah can see you getting hurt. Real bad.'

She nodded. 'I know – I know it can't last for ever. One day, he'll walk away from me down that lane and maybe I – I'll never see him again. But for the moment . . .' she shook her head almost in disbelief at herself – 'I can't help myself.'

'We've all bin young, lass. An' who am I to judge?' A small smile quivered on Will's mouth, then he was serious again. 'Be careful, Esther lass, dun't get hurt. And don't give them vicious tongues the chance to wag all the more.'

She sighed. 'I think it's too late for that warning.'

They stood together for a moment and then Will repeated his initial question. 'Where's my little Katie?'

In the daytime, Esther met Jonathan on the seashore at his insistence. He was still hoping to protect her from the prying eyes of those at the Point.

'I think they know anyway,' Esther told him.

He sighed. 'I was afraid of that.'

Esther didn't care about the gossips, but she loved Jonathan all the more for his concern for her. Theirs was a love that would not – could not – be denied. Sometimes they walked quietly hand in hand at the water's edge, sometimes they cavorted in the shallows like children, splashing each other, till their clothes were wet and clinging. Their eyes would meet and desire would flash between them and they would fly into each other's arms, the salt water mingling with their kisses. Then they would run towards their own hollow in the dunes, pausing to kiss and running again, eager for the moment their bodies would entwine, their souls meet and they were the only two people in the world.

All through that summer of 1916 he stayed. She tried to keep the war news from him, clinging to the hope that if he was cut off from how things were, he would not be forced to go back by feelings of guilt. But he must have seen the newspapers at the Seagull for some days he would come to work on the farm silent and solemn. She would watch him at work, seeing deep in his eyes that he was reliving the horror.

Nineteen sixteen was a year of killing. Daily, terrible reports appeared in the papers and names that were to become synonymous with tragedy – Ypres, Verdun, the Somme and Passchendaele – were on everyone's lips. The people of the little community of Fleethaven hardly knew where these places were and yet they became as familiar on their tongues as their own home town.

Still Jonathan stayed.

Through haymaking and into the corn harvest, he

worked on Brumbys' Farm and at night they made love in the loft in the barn, warm and snug in a sweet-smelling bed of hay. Late at night they took reluctant leave of each other, lingering in the soft starlight, the sound of the sea music to their love, the salt air its perfume. Esther would creep back into the farmhouse whilst Jonathan sneaked in the back door of the Seagull.

One night as they lay in each other's arms in the aftermath of their passion, Esther said, 'You still haven't told me about yourself. You know all about me. What you don't see for yourself, I've told you.' She ran her fingers across his chest. She revelled in the feel of him – his smooth, slightly bronzed skin, marred only by the bandage wrapped around his shoulder covering the wound he refused to let even her see.

'What kind of house do you live in?' Esther asked him. 'I can't imagine what it's like to live in a big city.'

She felt the laughter rumble in his chest. 'It's in a little side street; what they call a terraced house. You know, all the houses in one long row, like the four cottages where the Harrises live, but a whole street of houses on either side. Three small bedrooms upstairs and two rooms down with a back scullery and a privy across the yard.'

'No garden?'

'No. No grass, no trees, no flowers. Just the back yard where my mother pegs out the washing and brings it in all covered with smuts from the works' chimneys.'

'Do you live with your parents?'

'Yes – and my sister, Peggy.'

'What does ya dad do?'

'He's a schoolmaster. He teaches at a boys' school in

299

the city. And my mother's a dressmaker. The front parlour in our house is always littered with paper patterns and pins.' But he was smiling fondly as he said it. It sounded to Esther a genteel sort of occupation for a woman. She imagined Jonathan's mother would be a real lady with soft, smooth hands spending her days sewing fine garments. Not like Esther – out in all weathers with red and roughened hands.

It was obvious to Esther that Jonathan came from a warm and loving family and she felt envious. How she would love to belong to such a family – to Jonathan's family. She was eager to hear all about them. 'You said you have a sister. Tell me about her. How old is she?'

His eyes clouded as he murmured, 'Almost twenty. Poor Peggy.'

Esther checked the question that sprang to her lips. Why 'poor Peggy'?

'She's going through an awful time,' Jonathan told her. 'She was engaged to a young chap who worked with me. We were friends – that's how Peggy met him. We volunteered together.' He was silent, remembering. Memories in which Esther had no part. 'He – he was killed only a month after we went out there. Poor Peggy,' he murmured again. 'She used to be so jolly, always laughing and teasing. Now she's thin and so unhappy.' He stroked Esther's face with the tips of his fingers. 'I wish you and she could meet. You'd be so good for her. You're so strong . . .'

Esther kissed his cheek gently in a gesture of comfort. 'I would love to meet her, too. And your mother and father – they sound wonderful.'

Jonathan drew her into his arms and as she leant her head against his shoulder, he stroked her hair, pulling out the pins and combs so that it tumbled down her back. Then he buried his face in the rich tresses. 'You've such beautiful hair . . .'

Somewhere there was suddenly a loud banging and a shout, 'Missus, missus!'

'What is it?' Esther whispered and scrambled to her feet, pulling the front of her blouse across her exposed breast. 'Where's me skirt? Quick!'

Jonathan too was buckling his trousers and reaching for his shirt.

'No,' she whispered urgently. 'You stay here. I'll – I'll see who it is.'

She almost fell down the ladder from the hayloft and ran out of the barn.

'Enid, what is it?' She hurried across the yard, hastily brushing the tell-tale wisps of hay from her clothing.

Enid turned and, closer now, Esther heard the girl's gasp of surprise. 'Where've you – ?' the girl began and then seemed to think better of it.

'What's the matter?' Esther asked again.

'Me dad sent me for yar 'osses. There's a ship been sunk out at sea. He's got to take the lifeboat out.'

'Right,' Esther said, 'come on, we'll . . .'

As they moved to go towards the stable, they both heard, thinly through the walls of the house, the wailing of Esther's child.

Esther gave a click of exasperation through her teeth, 'There now, your knocking has woken Kate.'

'I'm sorry I'm sure,' Enid said, her tone stiff with

301

sarcasm. 'But I heard her crying as I got to the door, afore I even knocked.' She tossed her head and glared defiantly at Esther, as if to say 'the fault's not *mine*'.

Ignoring Enid's attitude, Esther snapped, 'You go in to Kate and I'll see to the horses.'

Prince and Punch were reluctant to leave the warmth of their stable. They didn't take kindly to a night shift as well. Punch let out a whinny which echoed through the night air then he kicked his huge hoof against the door as Esther struggled to harness them.

'Whoa there, stand, damn you,' she shouted, so unlike the gentle tones she normally reserved for the animals that the horse only kicked all the more.

'Esther, here, let me.' All at once Jonathan was beside her in the stable, stroking the animal's mane and speaking in soothing tones to them. Silently, he harnessed Punch, whilst Esther dealt with Prince, the more docile of the two. Then they each led one out. At that moment Enid came out of the house carrying a lantern. She held it aloft and in its light Esther could see her glancing from one to the other.

'I'll stay with the bairn whilst you both take the 'osses,' the girl said and added with an unmistakable note of censure, 'She's wet through and been crying for ages. But you go on, *I'll* see to her.'

Esther pursed her lips. Their secret was well and truly out now. Not that she cared, but she was very afraid of the effect it would have on Jonathan. Already he felt guilty for seducing the wife of a soldier at the front, a man who was one of his comrades. And he liked and respected the Harrises. What would he do now?

They led the horses up the lane towards where the boat-house lay amongst the dunes. As if reading her thoughts, Jonathan said quietly, 'She'll tell her mother, won't she?'

'Aye, an' anyone else who'll listen. An' they'll all be only too willin' to listen.'

'Esther – I'm sorry . . .'

'Don't be,' she retorted swiftly. ''Cos I'm not. And don't let it spoil things between us.'

'But your daughter, little Kate, we shouldn't have left her alone.'

Even in the middle of all this, Esther was gratified to notice that he said 'we' and not 'you'. How readily he shared the blame. She loved him all the more for it, if that were possible.

More gently, she said, 'No, no, we won't leave her any more. You'll come into the house . . .'

'No, Esther, I – '

'Oh, I'm not asking you into me bed,' she said swiftly, knowing that Jonathan would flatly refuse to go into the bed Esther had shared with her husband. She smiled in the darkness and there was coyness in her voice. 'There's a nice soft peg rug in front of me hearth.'

'Oh, Esther, you're the giddy limit!' She heard the responding laughter in his voice and knew he could not resist her any more.

When Esther returned home a little while later she opened the back door to the sound of her child still crying.

'Oh no!' she breathed. Had Enid gone home and left

Kate alone again, even though she had promised to stay? Esther ran through the kitchen and up the stairs, Kate's wails growing louder to her ears.

In the gentle glow from the night-light, Esther could see her child sitting up in the narrow bed, tears coursing down her red cheeks, her eyes tightly screwed up, her small hands balled into fists beating the patchwork counterpane. Enid was there, sitting on the bed, trying to take the child in her arms to comfort her. Kate was hysterical.

'I can't do nowt with her, missus. I've tried.'

'It's all right, Enid. It's not your fault.' Esther sighed. No, she thought, it's all mine.

She sat down on the side of the bed and wrapped her arms around the child and rocked her and soothed away her night terrors. Kate was wet and frightened and lost. She had cried out and her mother had not come.

'I haven't even been able to change her bed, missus. She won't let me . . .'

Esther nodded. 'You run along home. Enid . . .' she added as the girl paused at the door and looked back at her. In the dim light they faced each other. 'Enid, thanks for staying.'

Enid nodded but said nothing and as Esther listened to the girl's footsteps going down the stairs, she knew that by the morning, Ma Harris would be regaled with all the sordid details of the night's events.

As she changed Kate's nightgown and bedding, Esther felt the first real stab of guilt despite her brave words to Jonathan. Whilst she had been making love with Jonathan in the hayloft, her little girl had been crying for her.

Anything could have happened, she told herself fiercely. Kate could have been sick, or choking to death – and you wouldn't have known. Or cared. Yes, yes, I would. Of course, I care. I'm not that bad, I'm not wicked.

But, said a nagging little voice inside her, you left a small child alone in the house whilst you . . . Now you've been found out and you'll have to take the consequences.

'I can't give him up,' she whispered, as later she lay sleepless in her own lonely bed, 'I just can't.'

The following morning Ma Harris arrived as usual to collect the milk and eggs from Esther. But her manner was nothing like as usual.

'Well, lass, this is a fine how d'ya do, ain't it?'

Esther faced the older woman's stare boldly. There was no point in feigning misunderstanding. Besides, Esther was never one to tell lies.

'You don't understand . . .'

Ma Harris nodded, her toothless mouth pursed to nothingness. There was no familiar cackle of laughter this morning. 'Oh, yes, I do, lass. I understand only too well. I know you hadn't the perfect marriage with young Matthew. But you made yar bed, lass. Ya shouldn't be lyin' in it with another, now should ya? Specially not when yar man's away fighting the war.'

'I didn't want him to go, you know that,' she replied belligerently. 'In fact I begged him not to go – *if* you remember?'

'I remember all right. I suppose the next thing you're goin' to tell me is that none of this would have happened if he hadn't gone?'

'Well, it wouldn't, would it?'

'Dun't lay the blame at Matthew's door. This ain't his fault.'

'Oh, I suppose you're like everyone else around here,' Esther responded heatedly. 'Blaming me for tricking Matthew into marrying me. Matthew should have married Beth, we all know that now, don't we? But wicked Esther Everatt stole him away from poor, innocent Beth. Poor, innocent Beth indeed! She lifted her skirts for him, didn't she, let him have his way with her and bore his bastard? But of course, it's all *my* fault.'

'I ain't talkin' about all that, lass. That's all over and done with.'

'Over it may be,' Esther retorted, 'but I dun't reckon it'll ever be done with. People's got long memories round here for minding other folks's business.'

'So – what's going to happen when Matthew gets back and he hears about – about this feller? What's going to happen then, eh?' Ma Harris persisted.

Suddenly the fight went out of Esther and she sank down on to the cold stone of the gantry where the milk stood in its churn. 'I haven't had a card from Matthew for months, Ma. I – I dun't reckon he's ever comin' back.'

She raised her eyes to meet Ma's and watched the fleeting expressions on the woman's face as she tried to come to terms with what Esther was now telling her, tried to find it within her to understand Esther, to forgive her even, but failing, as she said, 'Well, it still dun't give you the right to take up with another man. And worse, leave yar bairn alone in the house whilst you're – you're . . .'

306

For all her bluntness, even Ma Harris could not bring herself to put it into words.

Esther stood up. 'On that score, I happen to agree with you. It won't happen again.'

'Ya mean . . .' For a moment there was a hint of relenting in Ma's expression. 'You mean you're going to end it?'

'No, no, I don't.'

Ma Harris sucked in air through her sunken mouth. 'Esther – you dun't mean you – you'll take him into yar bed? Not Matthew's bed!'

Esther faced her brazenly, then yielded. She didn't care what any of them said about her, but she couldn't bear them to think ill of Jonathan. She shook her head. 'Jonathan would refuse anyway. Whatever you think of me, you shouldn't blame him, he's a gentleman.'

Ma shook her head grimly. 'I dun't blame him. Ya can't blame a man. I blame you.' With that she turned and went out of Esther's pantry and out her house. Esther followed her to the back door. Half-way across the yard, Ma turned and shouted back, 'I'll be sending Enid for the milk and eggs in future, Esther Hilton.'

She was surprised just how the older woman's attitude hurt her. She had thought herself tough and hard and totally resilient to the opinions others had of her. But she had always liked Ma Harris, had valued her friendship and, at times, her help. Now Ma had literally turned her back on her.

Determinedly, Esther shook herself. I'll survive, she told herself. Of course she would – but still, it hurt.

*

Esther was sure Jonathan would feel obliged to leave, but still he stayed. Now, however, he came into the farmhouse. Some nights they just lay quietly together in each other's arms. Too tired by the day's work to make love, yet wanting to be together, just close to each other.

As the summer grew older, workers from the neighbouring farms began to arrive to help with Esther's corn harvest. She knew they whispered about her and Jonathan, for she saw them in little huddles, nodding towards her. Sometimes a guffaw of laughter would echo across the field. Sometimes she would catch the fleeting disapproval in their eyes, especially amongst the women. There were many more women helpers now on the farms than ever before, for their menfolk were gone. There were a lot of new faces too, but the one familiar face she wanted to see did not come. This year there was no Ma Harris rounding up her brood and setting them to work.

It was obvious that all these workers had heard about Esther Hilton and the soldier. Her chin would go a little higher, and deliberately, she would move towards Jonathan. She would touch his arm and look up into his face then glance towards the whisperers coquettishly, defying their disapproval.

'Esther, you shouldn't . . .' he would murmur, but she would not listen.

'I dun't care,' she would tell him, her eyes flashing rebelliously. 'I'll give 'em something to tittle-tattle about.'

Towards Jonathan, however, the workers' manner was deferential. The men – the few who by reason of age or ill health were left – would gather round him, watching him and quietly helping him. It was like a silent accolade on their part for his suffering, for his bravery. Perhaps it was also a wordless apology for the fact that they were still here, whole and almost untouched by the war.

Doggedly Jonathan kept pace with them and Esther watched with concern as the sweat poured down his face and his shirt clung damply to him. But she knew he would hate her to fuss over him, particularly in front of everyone.

She was returning from the farmhouse to the field with cool drinks for the workers when Kate came running towards her across the stubble. 'Mam, Mam! He's bleedin'. Come quick!'

Esther glanced to where the younger children were playing at the edge of the field. She squinted against the bright sunlight. 'Who? I dun't see—'

'Not them – him!' Kate was pointing, not in the direction of her playmates, but towards the menfolk further down the field.

They had stopped work and were gathered around one of their number lying on the ground.

Jonathan! She couldn't see Jonathan.

'Oh, no!' Esther breathed and began to run.

Twenty-eight

'WHAT is it? What's happened?'

Esther pushed her way through the group. Then she dropped to her knees beside Jonathan. He was sitting on the ground, bending forward, holding his injured shoulder.

'Let me see . . .' she began.

'No! It's just the wound – opened up. Don't fuss, Esther.'

She gasped at his sharpness and sat back on her heels, staring at him.

Immediately, he was contrite. 'I'm sorry,' he murmured softly, and as he raised his head, she saw his face was grey with pain and streaked with sweat.

In her anxiety for him, she had been oblivious to the fact that the gathering were standing silent and watchful, listening for every word that passed between them. Yet even in his pain, Jonathan had not forgotten.

She stood up. Stiffly, she said, 'You'd better come to the farmhouse.' Then she turned to Ben Harris. 'Perhaps two of you would help him?' Then she marched away across the field towards the farm without looking back.

But her eyes were brimming with unshed tears.

When they were alone in her kitchen Esther bathed and dressed the jagged line of the wound which had opened up a little at what had been its deepest point. 'Why didn't ya tell me it was as bad as this? Ya shouldn't be doing *anything*, let alone heavy farm work.'

'I'm not going to be beaten by a little scratch.'

'Please, Jonathan . . .' she began and took his hands in hers. She saw him wince and slowly she turned them over. The edges of his forefingers were covered with blisters.

'What on earth . . . ?' she gasped.

'It's tying the sheaves.' He grinned ruefully. She put her arms around him and he nestled his head against her breast.

Kate's running feet sounded on the yard and Esther moved away from Jonathan as the child appeared in the doorway. Her eyes were wide with alarm. 'Danny ses you was hurt. Are you?'

Jonathan smiled at her and his face softened. 'A little – it's nothing.'

'Nothing, indeed!' Esther muttered.

Kate moved towards him and as he held out his good arm to her, she climbed on to his knee.

'You mustn't do any more work on the farm, you—' Esther began.

'Oh, yes, I will!' His mouth was a firm, determined line. Above the child's head they glared at each other.

'Oh, you're so stubborn. You're just like . . .' Esther bit back the words. She had been going to say 'just like Matthew' but instead she finished lamely, 'You're all the same, you men!'

She was aware of Kate's glance shifting from one to the other. 'If you can't help Mam on the farm, mester,' the child said, beaming up at him with a beatific smile, 'then you can take me shrimpin' tomorrow.'

The look of defeat on Jonathan's face was so comical that Esther turned away and smothered her laughter with her apron. Then she heard his deep chuckle as he ruffled Kate's curls. 'All right, you win. I can't beat the two of you!'

But on the third day, Jonathan was back in the fields doggedly keeping pace with the other workers.

Despite his grief at the loss of his elder son, Squire Marshall was determined that life on his estate should go on as near to normal as possible.

'We shall hold the Harvest Supper as usual,' he told each of his tenants in turn. 'I expect you all to come and bring whatever friends you like.' He paused a moment reflectively and added, haltingly, 'There'll be too many empty places.'

Visiting Brumbys' Farm, he said to Esther, 'And this is the young man I've heard about who's visiting poor Mrs Harris.' He held out his hand to Jonathan and gripped it warmly. 'Did – did you know my boy?'

His voice deep with regret, Jonathan replied, 'Not personally, sir, but by sight, yes.'

'Well, my boy, I trust our good air is returning you to full health. I expect you'll – er – be going back soon, will you?'

Jonathan's normally steady gaze flickered away for a moment. He took a deep breath and then looked back to meet the squire's gaze squarely. 'Yes, sir,' he said softly, but nonetheless firmly, 'I will be going back.'

Esther, hearing the exchange, felt as if the breath had been knocked from her body. Her whole world seemed to crumble and even in the sunlight she shivered. Mechanically, she stretched a smile on to her mouth when the squire wished her good day. She stood staring after him as he mounted his horse and rode out of the farmyard gate.

When he was out of sight, Jonathan put his arm about her and led her into the barn. 'I know what you're thinking – feeling,' he said gently. 'But you've known all along that I must leave eventually. I'm well now – that's obvious to anyone who sees me working in the fields. I shouldn't be here. Every day I'm on borrowed time.'

She looked up into his face. 'But your wound isn't healed properly. You know it isn't.'

'It's – well enough that I ought to be going back. If I don't report back very soon, they'll come looking for me.'

'You could hide here. No one from the army knows where you are, do they?' She flung her arms about him crying, 'Don't go. Stay with me. Please!'

He held her close. 'A little longer, my love, just a little while longer.' More than that he would not promise.

Later she asked, 'You'll come to the Harvest Supper with me?'

'I'll go to the supper – but not with you.'

'Whyever not?'

'Esther, we'd be flaunting our – our affair in front of all your neighbours. We'd only be asking for more trouble. These people care for Matthew. You must go to the squire's supper as the wife of a tenant farmer, the wife of a man who is a soldier at the front doing his duty for his country – as Matthew's wife.' Despite his reasoned argument, his voice wavered a little on the final words, but Esther was too angry to notice.

'Don't be stupid,' she began hotly. 'Matthew only went because he got drunk and volunteered when Martha Willoughby called him a coward.'

'For whatever reason, he's there – in the thick of it. I'll go with the Harrises. That is, if they'll have me.'

For once Esther could not shake his quiet resolve.

Esther dressed with care on the evening of the Harvest Supper. She was as nervous as a girl on her first outing with a young man.

She had to take Kate along, for on this night there was no one who wanted to miss the supper to stay at home with Esther's daughter.

'Will Enid be there? And the others?' Kate chattered incessantly, catching some of Esther's excitement.

'I expect so. Do hold still, child, whilst I tie this ribbon in your hair. Such thick curls you've got, just like mine.'

'Will Danny be there?'

Esther's fingers were stilled a moment. Then she brushed Kate's hair vigorously.

'Ouch, you're pulling.'

'I really don't know,' Esther said, answering her daughter's question but unable to keep the sharpness from her tone. 'But I'll be there tonight to make sure he doesn't pull your hair again.'

'Oh, he doesn't pull my hair any more,' Kate said airily.

'I'm very glad to hear it.'

'No – now he tries to kiss me.'

'What! For heaven's sake, child, you're only four! You shouldn't be kissing little boys . . .' Esther pursed her lips and muttered, 'He's his father's son, all right, and no mistake.'

'What did you say, Mamma?'

'Nothing for you, missy. You stay away from Danny Eland, d'you hear me?'

'He's my friend. I like Danny.' The small mouth quivered and tears trembled, but Esther hardened her heart.

'You'll do as I say, Kate.'

The merriment was in full swing when they arrived at the huge barn at the Grange. At least on the surface it appeared to be, but after a few moments there, Esther could feel that the atmosphere of gaiety was forced. Although everyone was doing their best to put on a show of enjoying themselves, there were so many faces missing now, so many who would never be coming back. Every day the casualty lists grew longer and news of fearsome battles, won and lost, dominated the newspapers.

She scanned the bobbing heads for sight of him and saw him deep in solemn conversation with the squire. She felt Kate's hand tug itself from her hold.

'Kate, you . . .'

The child was gone, darting between the dancers to the stack at the end of the barn where several children were playing, sliding down and tumbling each other. At least, thought Esther wryly, I can't see Danny Eland amongst them. Then forgetting the children, her eyes again sought Jonathan.

Drawn towards him, she threaded her way through the throng, coming to stand a little way off, just watching him. Her gaze roamed over him, drinking in every feature. The flop of golden hair, the smooth skin tanned to a healthy bronze now by all his outdoor work. Reluctantly, she had to admit that he looked the picture of health – not a wounded soldier on sick leave. The realization terrified her.

As if feeling her close by, he lifted his eyes and met her gaze. She saw the fire burn in his eyes, saw the hunger in them as he took in her appearance. He had never seen her in her best dress, for he never accompanied her to church and that was the only time she ever wore it other than for the Harvest Supper. Suddenly, another memory pushed its way unbidden into her mind. She had worn this dress on that last Bank Holiday – when Matthew had taken her on the pier. So long ago, it seemed now. Another world, another life away.

Squire Marshall, following Jonathan's gaze, greeted her. 'My dear Mrs Hilton.' He held out his arm to her as if to draw her closer, to include her in their conversation. 'I'm so glad you've come. Of course you two know each other. I was forgetting – I met you at Brumbys' Farm the other day, didn't I?'

Esther looked sharply at the squire but the remark had been made so innocently and without guile. So, she thought, the gossip hasn't reached the squire's ears, or at least if it has he's choosing to ignore it. She glanced at Jonathan and that special look of a secret shared passed between them.

She held her hands clenched at her sides, willing herself to resist the urge to go up to him, to put her hands against his chest and reach up and touch his lips with her own. Instead she said, 'How is Mrs Marshall, Squire?'

The older man's face seemed to age before her. 'Ah, my dear, she's frail and weak, I fear. She's never recovered from our great loss, you know.'

Esther's green eyes filled with genuine sympathy. 'I am sorry, Squire,' she said softly.

'Thank you, my dear, thank you.' He smiled, making a great effort to play out his self-appointed role as host of the party alone. 'Ah, there's Tom Willoughby. Willoughby, over here a moment.'

Tom Willoughby's huge bulk came towards them.

'Squire,' he greeted his landlord cordially but with due deference. 'Hello, Esther lass. Any news from Matthew, then?'

Esther drew breath sharply and avoided looking at Jonathan. 'No – no, I'm afraid I haven't heard from him – in ages.' She had told no one about the last postcard from Matthew, but even that had been several weeks ago now, so her answer was not exactly a lie. Yet Esther, always truthful, felt it to be. Her heart thudded a little faster, and she was sure her cheeks grew pink.

'I'm sorry to hear that, lass, real sorry,' Tom was saying.

There was a moment's awkward silence between them, then Tom Willoughby and the squire both began to speak at the same moment.

'I wanted—'

'How—?'

'Sorry, sir, after you . . .'

'No, no, Willoughby, it was nothing really, just idle conversation. If you'll excuse me I'll get round to some of the other guests.'

He nodded and smiled at the three of them and as he moved away, Esther said, 'What were you going to say, Tom?'

'I was about to say that I wanted a word with you, Esther. I've a bit of bad news. I don't know if you'll be able to borrow the threshing tackle the squire lends us. It's at my place now, but I'm having the devil's own job wi' the blessed traction engine! The man we usually get when it plays up has volunteered and I don't know of anyone else who knows about engines.'

'Oh, no,' Esther groaned. 'With so many hands short, I was relying on that.'

'Er, perhaps I might be able to help,' Jonathan's deep voice put in quietly. 'What sort is it?'

Tom Willoughby told him. A smile spread across Jonathan's face. 'I'll take a look for you, Mr Willoughby, if you'd like me to?'

'Well, if you think you can do owt, young feller, I'd be chuffed. Er, 'ow do you know about steam engines, then?'

'Made in Lincoln, wasn't it?'

Tom Willoughby nodded.

'That's where I worked before I joined up. I maybe even worked on it, Mr Willoughby.'

'Well, I'll be damned!' exclaimed Tom Willoughby

with such a comical look on his face that both Esther and Jonathan burst out laughing.

It was the only unfeigned laughter heard all evening and then it was heard by many only with disapproval.

Later the following day, Esther went to Rookery Farm to find Jonathan up to his elbows in grease and oil, clambering all over Tom Willoughby's huge traction engine.

She had not seen him all day. Frustrated and feeling neglected, she had guessed that was where he would be. She didn't stop to think of the consequences that parading her friendship with Jonathan before Martha Willoughby and her spiteful sister could bring.

She had to see him.

It was like a craving that would not be assuaged until she was with him. Even then, when he was near, all she wanted was to be in his arms, lying with him, being loved by him . . .

'Have you mended it, then?' she asked, truculence in her tone. His face wore a rapturous expression.

'Oh, hello, Esther, what are you doing here?' Without waiting for her answer, almost as if he were uninterested in it, he had turned away and bent his head once more into the workings of the great machine.

'Good evening, Mrs Hilton.' Martha Willoughby's voice spoke behind her, with an underlining accent on the 'Mrs'. 'And to what do we owe this particular pleasure?'

Esther turned and her chin went a little higher. 'I came to see how Jonathan – Mr Godfrey – was getting on with repairing the engine.'

'Really?' There was a simulated sweetness to Martha's tone. 'I hadn't realized that his – er – services were your particular property.' The sarcasm was evident and Esther was left in no doubt that Martha Willoughby knew exactly what the relationship between Jonathan and herself was.

Esther smiled with false amiability in return. 'I'm sure Mr Godfrey is pleased to be able to help. In fact . . .' She glanced over her shoulder at the two men laughing and talking together, gesturing to the internal workings of the engine, and there was a note of jealousy in her voice. 'He seems to be thoroughly enjoying it.'

Martha nodded, a malicious smile on her mouth, the fold of fat beneath her chin wobbling. 'Yes, he seems to enjoy his life here. Made himself quite at home, so I gather. Nicely hidden away from the war.'

'He came to see Ma – Mrs Harris – to tell her that he had known her Ernie, *if* it's any business of yours, Martha Willoughby, which it ain't. And he was wounded, you can see that for ya'sen.'

Martha smirked. 'Convenient though, ain't it, that he can hide in a little out-of-the-way place like Fleethaven Point where the authorities won't find him in a month o' Sundays?'

'Well, at least he's done 'is bit. I see you hang on to your man well enough. You ain't goaded him into joining up. Though I'm surprised the poor man hasn't – if only to get away from you!'

'Dun't you get high 'n' mighty with me, *Mrs* Hilton. We all know how you come to be where you are. A tramp from the Lord knows where who took old Sam Brumby for the poor old idiot he was . . .' She wagged her finger in Esther's face. 'Getting him to change his will when he was on his deathbed.'

Esther gasped. 'I never did—'

Martha's tirade continued. 'My Thomas's family was related to old Sam's way back. All that should have been ours, by rights, not left to a scheming hussy like you!' Martha was in full flow now, enjoying having Esther at her mercy. 'To say nothing of how you tricked young Matthew into marrying you. Telled him you was pregnant by him, I don't doubt. 'Tis the oldest trick in the book, that one.'

'That's not true,' Esther shrieked, 'and you know damn well it ain't. My Kate was born nearly a year after we was wed.'

Martha cackled. 'Huh, ya dun't have to *be* pregnant to catch 'em. Only tell 'em you are.'

Esther's eyes narrowed. 'Oh,' she said, her tone heavy with sarcasm, 'is that how you caught poor old Tom Willoughby, then?' It was a particularly cruel remark considering that the Willoughbys had no family.

Martha's fat cheeks, already marked with tiny red veins, grew purple. 'Why, you, you—'

At that moment behind them the great steam engine spluttered into noisy life and drowned Martha's abuse.

Esther turned on her heel and marched away from Martha and off their farmland. She returned to Brumbys' Farm. It *was* her farm, and everything in it, no matter what Martha said.

Esther wished now she had never gone up to Rookery Farm, particularly as Jonathan had hardly seemed to

321

notice her. His indifference had hurt her far more than Martha's scathing attack.

So, Esther thought furiously, if he prefers a smelly old engine puthering steam and smoke to me, then he's welcome.

Nevertheless, she found it impossible to sustain her anger for long, for when he came back to the farm, his face was grubby with oil and smuts and his eyes were shining like a little boy's on Christmas morning.

'It was good to get me hand in again, Esther,' he told her as he sluiced away the grime under the pump in the yard. 'Eh, but I've missed it – my work. I hadn't realized just how much until . . .' He spread his hands out before him and looked down at them and laughed. 'Until I got them all mucky with oil and grease again.'

She watched his lean body rippling in the sunlight and longing burned inside her. Again she saw the bandage covering the wound on his shoulder; that jagged, purple scar that was a constant reminder of what he had seen and suffered.

It was a reminder to her too that he was still a soldier and that the war was not yet over. Not for either of them.

That night their love-making was as tender as ever and when they lay together quietly afterwards, she cried against his shoulder, and kissed the scar with tender lips, her tears falling on to it as if to wash it away if she could. But it would always be there. It was as if the scar on his body was like a scar on their happiness. An unceasing reminder that it all must end.

Twenty-nine

*E*STHER watched the rotund figure of a man on a bicycle riding with solemn concentration along the lane towards the Point.

The sun glinted on the silver buttons of his black uniform and her heart gave a lurch of fear as she saw him dismount and lean his bicycle carefully against the gate.

A policeman! Why was a policeman coming to her farm?

He walked slowly across the yard towards the back door of the house. 'Mrs Hilton?' he greeted her.

She nodded and ran her tongue over lips that were suddenly dry.

'We've – er – reason to believe that there's a soldier staying hereabouts, Mrs Hilton.' He paused, but she returned his gaze steadily and remained silent. Her heart thumped so loudly she was certain he must hear it. She was praying that Jonathan would not appear out of the cowshed.

'Well, now . . .'

At that moment there came a clang from the cowshed and the sound of a man's voice. 'Steady, girl. Steady, Clover.'

The policeman raised his voice so that it carried across the yard. 'This 'ere soldier, been in these parts a while now, so we understand. And – er – whilst he might have

323

been on sick leave at first, if you understand me, well, time's gone on, so to speak, and if he's fit and healthy enough to be working on a farm, then . . .' The man spread his huge hands palms upwards.

Esther caught her breath. Over the man's shoulder she could see Jonathan emerge from the cowshed and walk across the yard towards them. She made an involuntary movement to stop him, to try to prevent the inevitable. But purposely Jonathan avoided noticing her gesture and came to stand quietly beside the policeman. The older man turned slowly to look at him as Jonathan asked, 'Could it be me you're looking for?'

'I really couldn't say, sir.' The policeman was polite with a hint of apology in his tone. 'I have to follow up these – er – reports we get, you know. People get some funny ideas, about deserters and such.' He lifted his huge shoulders in a shrug. 'Ugly name, isn't it, for a man who's probably done more than most for his country and rightly deserves a bit of respite, but – well – you know how it is, sir?'

Jonathan nodded, his mouth set in a grim line. 'I do indeed,' he said quietly. 'You have your duty to do.'

'I'm glad you see it that way, sir.' He paused, his keen eyes searching Jonathan's face. 'So may I take it,' he added quietly, 'that you will be reporting back to your unit in the very near future?'

Jonathan nodded. 'Yes, officer, you may.'

'Perhaps you'd call in at the station when you go for the train?' He paused, glanced towards Esther, and back again to Jonathan. 'Shall we say in a couple of hours?'

There was sympathetic understanding in his tone, but nevertheless an underlying firmness.

Esther gave a little cry and her hand fluttered to her mouth to still the sound. She watched, wide-eyed, as Jonathan slowly nodded agreement.

'I'll bid you good day then, sir.' The policeman touched his forefinger to his helmet in a gesture of farewell, nodded to Esther and turned away.

As the man mounted his bicycle and rode off, a little unsteadily, Esther could contain her anger no longer.

'How dare he? How dare he come here . . . ?' She was shaking with fear. Fear that the moment she had dreaded had come. Now Jonathan would leave her.

Jonathan put his arms about her. 'Don't, my darling, it had to come.' He put into words her dread. 'We both knew that one day I would have to go. I'm lucky it was not the military who came looking for me. They would have arrested me on the spot.'

'Why?' she cried. 'You've done nothing wrong? They—'

'Esther, my darling. I should have gone back weeks ago. But I—' His voice broke with emotion and he buried his face in her neck, his words becoming muffled. 'I couldn't tear myself away from you.'

'You mean – you mean you'll be in trouble when you get back?'

Jonathan did not answer her.

She tightened her arms about him, as she realized at last how much he did love her. He loved her just as much as she loved him. She knew what it must have cost this man in terms of pride and principle to have overstayed his term of sick leave and run the risk of being put on a charge.

'Oh, my love, my darling,' she murmured.

At that moment over his shoulder, parked a little way along the lane Esther saw a pony and trap. Sitting in the trap were two women, one tall and stout and the other thin and angular.

Esther stiffened and as Jonathan lifted his head to look at her, she gave a low growl of rage and tore herself from his grasp. She was running across the yard, her skirts held up in one hand and shaking her other fist and yelling at the two women in the trap.

'You bitch! You fat old beezum, Martha Willoughby. And you, Flo Jenkins, you wizened old maid—'

Martha made valiant efforts to turn the trap around in the lane, but Esther was upon them before she could do so. She grasped the side of the trap and shook it, making it rock precariously.

The two women screamed in terror, but Esther's frenzy had driven all sense and reason from her mind. All the fury she had held against these two women for years was unleashed.

If it had not been for Jonathan reaching her at that moment, she would have tipped the trap over on to its side, throwing the two women into the road and undoubtedly causing them physical harm. He took hold of her, pinning her arms to her sides so that she struggled and kicked against him and continued to mouth insults at the two women, but no longer could she hurt them.

Jonathan raised his normally quiet voice above Esther's screeching. 'Go, Mrs Willoughby, just go!'

Martha, red and flustered, scrabbled in the bottom of the trap for the reins and sat up. She cast one anxious look back at Esther and then flicked the reins and the pony moved forward. As the trap moved off down the lane, the two women stared back at Esther, fear in their eyes.

As if to confirm that there was reason for the trepidation on their faces, Esther yelled after them, 'I'm not finished with you two old biddies yet. You'll pay for this day, Martha Willoughby!'

He took her back to the farmhouse and into the kitchen. He made her sit down near the range whilst he poured her a strong cup of tea from the pot on the hob.

Esther was still shaking with rage and now with fear, as the realization overwhelmed her. She moaned and closed her eyes and rolled her head from side to side. 'Don't go. Please, don't go!'

He knelt in front of her and took hold of her hands. 'My darling – I must. But I want you to remember that wherever I am, I shall be loving you still. If we never meet again . . .'

Her cry of anguish broke into his words, but he stroked her hair and held her even closer, comforting her as he might a child. 'If we never meet again,' he repeated bravely, 'our love will last for ever.'

'I love you, I want us to be together. Don't go back. I'm begging you!' Her tears flowed, and she clung to him. 'Don't leave me, I can't bear it.'

He eased himself back from her clinging arms and gently held her tear-streaked face between his hands, forcing her to look at him. He brushed the strands of hair, wet with her tears, from her eyes.

His own sorrow and his heartache for her misery filled his eyes with compassion. 'My own dear love, my only love, you don't mean it . . .'

'I do, I do!' she sobbed wildly.

He shook his head. 'No, you don't, not really,' he insisted with a quiet firmness. 'If I were to stay, I'd be a deserter – a man always running from the authorities. See how easy it is for the local bobby to track me down?'

'They've reported you – I know it! Then they couldn't resist coming to gloat . . .'

'Hush, my love, hush.' He put his arms about her once more. 'I couldn't run for ever. Eventually, I'd be caught and probably sent to prison—'

'You'd be alive!' she cried bitterly.

'What kind of life would that be? A life of shame. You'd come to despise me . . .'

'Never! I just want you here with me – alive. I don't care . . .'

'But I do, Esther,' he said, giving her a very gentle yet nonetheless deliberate shake. 'I'd hate myself. I couldn't live the rest of my life like that – not even with you, my own darling.'

Hysterical now, she pulled away from him and stood up, moving backwards behind the chair, deliberately putting a barrier between them. 'You don't love me. Not as much as I love you – you can't do, or – or you wouldn't go.'

In her passion, she didn't see the hurt in his eyes that her words inflicted. But the pain was in his tone. 'Oh,

Esther, don't say such a thing – not to me. Not to me, my love.'

She stood before him, holding on to the back of the chair, her whole body shaking, racked by heaving sobs. Taking a handkerchief from his pocket, he moved closer. Tenderly he wiped away her tears. Even as he did so, more came to take their place. He could not stem the flow of her misery.

Gently he released her grip on the chair and enfolded her once more in his arms, just holding her close until she was exhausted and her sobs subsided to a forlorn, childish hiccuping. All the while, he murmured soothingly and stroked her hair.

When at last she was calmer, he said again, 'I could not live a life of dishonour, my dear, not even for you.' He tensed waiting for her crying to burst forth again, but she was quieter now, drained of the passion and resigned to his going.

'Esther, you must be strong. We must get through this and then, when it's all over, well, we'll see how things stand.'

It was the only hope he could, or would, give her. She would perhaps never quite understand, never quite accept his reasons, but she realized that despite all her courage, her forthright, strong will, this gentle man was made of even stronger mettle than she.

Jonathan's arms tightened about her and, against her hair, his voice was deep with poignant longing as he whispered, 'Love me one more time, Esther, before I go.'

*

Later, she watched him walk away from her, down the lane and out of her life.

When he reached the bend in the road that would hide him from her view, she gave a cry of agony and began to run after him. Not yet, she told herself, I must see him still. Reaching the bend in the road herself, she stopped and stood watching the figure striding away from her, growing smaller and smaller.

Not once did he turn and wave, not once did he look back. In her heart she knew why. If he looked back now, he would not be able to go.

'Jonathan.' She breathed his name like a prayer. 'Look at me, Jonathan. Turn around, my darling.'

But the figure grew smaller and smaller until, through the blur of her tears, she could no longer see him.

Thirty

*T*HE days following his going were long and lonely.
Ironically, when Jonathan left, it was two years
almost to the day since Matthew had walked away into
the mist down the same road.

'Danny ses that nice man's gone away. Has he, Mam?'
Kate wanted to know.

Esther swallowed the lump that rose in her throat. She
took Kate on to her knee, the child leaning her head
against Esther's shoulder. 'He had to leave suddenly.'

'But he didn't say goodbye to me.' Kate's mouth
quivered.

'He asked me . . .' Esther added, inventing the lie, 'to
give you his love.'

'Is he coming back? I want him to take us fishing
again.'

'I – don't know. Maybe some day.'

'I hope he comes back. I liked him – and so did
Danny.'

'Yes,' Esther murmured. 'So did I, Katie. Oh, so did I.'

Mechanically, Esther went through the motions of living.
The demands of her daughter and the farm were all that
kept her going. There was a numbness in her mind and
an ache in her heart that was an actual physical pain in
her chest. She worked till she dropped, hoping to find

oblivion in exhausted sleep. The nights were the worst, when she lay alone in the darkness and relived the times she had lain in his arms. Even tears would not come to give vent to her misery.

Her grief was too deep for tears.

In the cooling days of autumn she walked the shore close to the water's edge, hearing the ghostly laughter they had shared. She sat in the sandy hollow, the place where they had made love, her arms wrapped around herself, her body aching for his touch. Now, all she felt was a gnawing emptiness below her ribs. Even her favourite place at the end of the Spit failed to bring her solace. It seemed forsaken and lonely, and the wailing seagulls overhead seemed only to echo her own isolation. It seemed as if all feeling had gone, even her love of the land failed her now.

Without Jonathan, her world, the land she had once loved so fiercely and fought so hard to win, had become a desolate and melancholy place.

Now she watched for the postboy, praying that Jonathan would write to her. Was he missing her as much as she missed him?

No word came. As the days passed she found resentment against him growing. He hadn't loved her. He couldn't have done – or else he would have written. He would have found some way to send word to her – to let her know he was safe, to tell her he loved her still.

She heard nothing.

What had happened to him when he reported back to his unit? Maybe he was safe, she tried to tell herself, in prison for his wrongdoing, but safe. But in her heart she knew that even if he faced charges, eventually they would send him back out to the war front.

Why, oh, why, hadn't he written to her? He didn't love her, not really, she tormented herself. Already he had forgotten all about her. Letters and cards came through from the front. Even if he had been sent out to France again, he should still have been able to write to her. Then cold fear would clutch at her heart. He hadn't written because he couldn't — because he'd been killed. And here she was hating him for deserting her so coldly, whilst he was lying dead on some battlefield.

Yet she could not, would not, believe that she would never see him again, that he was gone from her for ever. It was the only shred of hope she had and she clung to it with all the tenacity that was in her nature.

One November night about a month after Jonathan had left, a night so calm and still that the sound of the sea drifted in clearly over the land, Esther came wearily down the stairs from seeing Kate into bed when she heard the strangest noise, faint at first, then growing louder. A cacophony of banging and clattering, like copper pans being beaten, rattling pots and whistles and horns. Nearer it came. She stepped outside her back door and saw lights bobbing in the lane outside the gate to her farmyard. Then, distinctly in the black stillness of the night, she heard the sound of chanting voices:

> 'Her husband's gone to war,
> 'So she becomes a whore.
> 'She leaves her work, she leaves her child

'Her husband's name she has defiled.
'Her sins to the world we'll tell,
'Come out, come out, you Jezebel!'

Esther stepped back inside and slammed and bolted
the door. She leant against it breathing hard. She closed
her eyes and moaned aloud. They were ran-tan-tanning
her! Her heart was pounding in her breast. Then a hot
anger surged through her. She had not stayed outside
long enough to see who was in the group, but now in
comparative safety she looked out of the scullery window
overlooking the yard. In the fitful light of the swinging
lanterns, it was almost impossible to discern the faces,
yet there were two figures which were recognizable by
their shapes. The tall, looming bulk of Martha Willoughby and the stick-like thinness of her sister, Flo
Jenkins, were in the forefront of the mocking group of
ran-tan-tanners. Behind them, the other figures, laughing and chanting their crude verses, remained anony-
mous in the shadows, though she suspected there were
one or two from the Point.

As the noise and shouting continued, echoing all
around her farmhouse, she heard the frightened wail of
her daughter from upstairs. She was about to turn away
from the window to go up to Kate, when, for a brief
instant as the lanterns swayed, she caught sight of a still,
silent figure set apart from the rest, standing on the bank
on the opposite side of the lane. Motionless, with her
hand clutching a black shawl around her head, taking no
part in the proceedings but just standing and watching –
was Beth Eland.

For a long moment, Esther stood looking back at the woman, although she knew Beth couldn't actually see her inside the darkness of her home.

Why was she there? Esther wondered. Had she thought up this escapade? Or had the Willoughby woman and her sister dragged Beth along to see her rival's humiliation?

At that moment, Esther heard Kate's sobs closer and turned to see her daughter standing in the doorway.

She went forward now and gently pushed Kate back into the kitchen. Closing the door behind them blotted out some of the noise.

'What is it, Mamma? What's that noise?'

'Just some people had a mite too much to drink, and acting very silly. Tek no notice. Come . . .' she offered, sitting down in the wooden chair and opening her arms to her daughter. 'Come sit on me knee near the fire till they've gone.'

They sat together, their arms about each other, Esther's tightly around her daughter's shaking body, whilst Kate wound her sturdy, childish arms about Esther's neck and leant her head against her shoulder.

'I wish that nice man was still here with us,' she murmured. 'He'd make them stop. He'd make them go away.'

Esther stiffened and held her breath. 'Who – who do ya mean, Katie?'

The noise still went on outside, but the child seemed less afraid now. She wrinkled up her smooth brow as if trying to remember. 'The man who made me a shrimpin' net – I don't remember his name.'

Esther said quietly, 'You mean J— Mr Godfrey.' To herself, she added, and he's the reason that mob's outside yawping their heads off. Thank goodness you can't understand what they're calling your mother!

Suddenly the noise ceased. The woman and the child sat up, glanced at each other, then Kate slid to the floor and Esther got up. Hand in hand they tiptoed out to the back door. Making as little noise as possible in the silence that followed the din, Esther slid back the bolts and lifted the latch. They were still there, the lanterns swaying, feet shuffling, but they were quiet. All the banging of pans and whistling and chanting had stopped. In front of them stood the huge, avenging figure of Tom Willoughby.

'. . . Get away to yar homes. Ashamed of ya'sens, y'ought to be. As for you, wife – if you ever, ever, do this sort o' thing again to this lass and her bairn, I'll tek off me belt to ya. Aye,' he wagged his finger in the faces of those grouped behind Martha and Flo. 'Aye, and then you'll have cause to ran-tan-tan me as a wife-beater, won't ya?'

'She's a bad 'un, Tom, is Esther Hilton,' came an unidentifiable man's voice from the back. 'No better than a tramp when she came and—'

Tom knew the speaker. He raised his voice. 'Oh, aye, young Percy Souter. Does yar ma and pa know yet that you'm got a lass in Lynthorpe in the family way, eh?'

There was a ripple of embarrassed laughter amongst the crowd, but no answer from the youth. Tom was not finished yet. 'And what about you, Joe Bridges? Why, I remember when we was lads together . . .'

'Eh, steady on, Tom lad. Fair's fair, no need to rake up a young feller's wild oats, not when he's a respectable married man.'

'Respectable married man!' Tom threw back his head and let his roar of laughter ring out into the night. 'Eh Joe, that's the best yet!'

'All right, Tom, you win. We're off home. Come on, lads, let's get away afore he ses any more. You know a mite too much, Tom Willoughby, a mite too much.'

'That I do,' Tom said, his tone grim now. 'There's not one here amongst you that has the right to cast the first stone at her. Not one!'

It was as if the biblical reference finally shamed them all, for one by one they melted away into the blackness until only Tom was left to take a none-too-gentle hold of his wife and sister-in-law and march them off up the lane back towards Rookery Farm.

The weeks and months dragged on. Christmas was a hollow sham for Esther. She had hoped that she and Kate might still be invited to the Harrises' as they had been on the two previous Christmases since Matthew had gone to war.

'It'll be company for the bairn being with my lot and I expect you could do with the company, lass,' Ma Harris had said that first year in her warm, all-embracing way.

This year, no invitation came.

Since their quarrel Ma Harris had never come near Brumbys' Farm, though she still allowed Enid to help Esther with the dairy work and to look after Kate. Even the younger boys helped about the farm and Enid still took Kate to her home. By what Esther could gather from Kate's chatter, Ma treated the child no differently.

It's just her mother she's no time for now, Esther admitted ruefully.

She had thought that even Ma might relent in her coldness towards her at Christmas, if only for the child's sake, but on Christmas Eve Kate hung her stocking on the kitchen mantelpiece and went alone to her room, whilst Esther sat in front of the range and thought of Jonathan. There was a goose cooking slowly in the oven and holly decorated the living room. There were mince pies and puddings in the pantry and only the two of them to share the festive fare.

How stupid and useless it all seemed, yet she had to try, she was obliged to try, for Kate.

But all she wanted was to go down to the beach, even in the cold of the winter, to their special hollow and try to relive those stolen hours in Jonathan's arms.

Esther was relieved when Christmas was over. In the first few days of the New Year the weather had suddenly turned bitterly cold and, still struggling alone with the ploughing, Esther was in a state of near exhaustion each evening.

'Esther, Esther!'

From the depths of fatigue she was roused by a loud banging on the back door and someone calling her name. She must have fallen asleep on the rug in front of the range, for the fire had gone out and the ashes were cold.

She shivered and pulled herself to her feet, staggering

almost drunkenly with the tiredness that never seemed to leave her now, to open the door.

Robert Eland stood there in the darkness. 'Esther, I'm sorry – but one of Tom Willoughby's stacks is afire and the others are in danger. We need everyone we can get to help put it out. Will you come?'

'Oh – of course,' she hesitated, 'but I must make sure Kate's all right first.'

Robert Eland nodded and hurried away whilst Esther ran lightly upstairs to check on her sleeping daughter. Kate was not given to night terrors any more. Esther stood over the bed looking down upon the angelic face of her child. She bit the edge of her thumb and glanced around the room. The night-light! She dare not leave that burning. She put it out and then drew back the curtains. It was a clear, frosty night and the moonlight flooded the room. Kate would not be frightened now, even if she awoke.

Downstairs Esther checked that the fire in the range was out. Now everything was safe, she reassured herself. Within minutes she was half-running, half-walking up the lane towards the Grange and branching off towards Rookery Farm. The coldness of the night banished all sleep from her eyes. Ahead of her she could see the figures of the other men and women from the Point, all hurrying towards the glow in the sky that all farmers dread to see. As she neared the farm, she could smell the acrid smoke and see sparks showering into the night sky, dancing against the blackness and drifting dangerously towards the other stacks in the yard.

Between the burning stack and the well, they formed

two chains, one to pass the water and one to return the empty containers for refill. They used anything they could lay hands upon. Two boys – Peter and Luke Harris – worked the well bucket, and the women and children made up the human chains, whilst Tom Willoughby and Robert Eland were nearest to the burning stack.

'I don't see Martha and that sister of hers taking their places,' Esther remarked to the woman nearest to her and, turning to glance at her, found herself looking directly into the dark eyes of a familiar face illuminated by the flickering light from the fire.

Esther caught her breath. 'Beth!' The name escaped her lips before she could stop herself.

'Hello, Esther,' Beth said quietly. As she passed a full bucket of water to Esther, their eyes met and held for a moment, until Esther turned away briefly to pass on the bucket. Her gaze was drawn back to the woman at her side standing patiently waiting for the next bucket to reach her.

Esther searched about her mind for something to say. But it was Beth who asked, scarcely above a whisper, 'Have you heard any news from him lately?'

There was no need to ask who she meant.

'No – no, I haven't had a card for months now.' Esther paused, but she felt Beth was waiting for her to say more. 'They can't always write, you know. It dun't mean that anything awful's happened to him. Besides, if it had, I'd have heard from the authorities . . .' She stopped, suddenly aware of the strange circumstance. Here she was standing in a farmyard in the middle of the night whilst the flames of a burning stack leapt and danced and cast eerie shadows and grotesque shapes, trying to comfort Beth of all people! If it hadn't been so heartrending, it would have been comical.

Beth said nothing. Esther watched her, wondering about her. There was a calmness and a quietness about Beth now. She seemed so much older than the girl who had shaken her fist in Esther's face and laid a curse upon her for taking the man she loved. It was as if Beth had grown old in the space of a few short years. The promise of beauty that had been in her young, round face had never flowered. She was much thinner than Esther remembered, the high cheekbones and hollowed cheeks giving her a gaunt look, accentuated by the flickering shadows. Her eyes were dark, unfathomable pools of loneliness.

Was that what the loss of true love did to a person? Esther wondered. Would she, Esther, grow old, too, waiting and longing for Jonathan?

There was nothing else Esther could think of to say so they just carried on working side by side to save what they could of Tom's stack.

By the time dawn was spreading cold fingers of light across the flat land, the fire was out and the helpers were trudging home, smut-faced and weary. Esther turned away, sickened by the sight of the blackened and smouldering hay which the men were still spreading and turning to make sure it would not blow up again into a blaze.

She felt someone grasp her arm and as she began to turn to see who it was, a hand slapped her face hard. Caught off balance by the sudden attack, Esther fell to the ground.

Martha Willoughby stood above her. 'So, you thought you'd have revenge for your ran-tan-tanning by setting light to our stack, did you?'

Esther opened her mouth to protest, but the tirade was not finished. 'Well, let me tell you, Esther Hilton. They all know you now round here for exactly what you are. A scheming hussy who tricked a dying man into leaving her everything that rightly belongs to others; who stole another girl's sweetheart and her baby's father and then – to cap it all – when he went to fight for his country, took another man, a deserter no less, into her bed. You're a trollop, Esther Hilton. A whore and—'

Anger flooded through Esther and she struggled to her feet. She stood facing Martha, her eyes flashing fire, her hands on her hips. But before she could utter a word, Tom's booming voice rang out in the early morning light.

'That's enough, Martha.' He stepped between them, but his face was in shadow so that Esther could not see his expression. When he spoke his voice was so hard and cold that Esther was shocked. 'Ya'd better go home, Esther.'

She stood before him now, swaying slightly. This was too much. Martha's malice she could take, but not Tom's animosity. Never Tom's. The fatigue of the night's work, her own very personal misery and now this threatened to overwhelm her. Esther's shoulders sagged and her arms hung limply at her sides. All her strength drained from her. She looked up at Tom and tears welled in her eyes as she whispered, 'Not you too, Tom. You don't believe I'd fire ya stack? Surely you don't!'

Tom shook his head as if not knowing what to believe. 'Just – go home, Esther. It'd be for the best, lass.'

Martha was quiet now, watchful and triumphant. For a moment it had seemed as if her husband was going to take Esther's side, but he had not. Even though he had not exactly taken his wife's side either, Esther could feel Martha's sense of victory.

She turned away hurt and sick at heart.

One day merged into another, each the same as the last. The work she had once loved, had revelled in, became drudgery.

Where was the reason to go on living now that he was gone?

She wandered the shore, grieving as if Jonathan were already dead, lost to her for ever.

During the time that he had been with her she had attended church infrequently. It was as if she had been afraid of retribution, for her early childhood had been spent beneath the flailing arms and chest-beating, fire and brimstone preacher in the pulpit, who had instilled fear of eternal damnation into the young child, which even the maturity of later years and reasoning found hard to dispel completely.

Now she returned taking Kate with her and hoping to find comfort and understanding. Unashamedly – though only in the silence of her own heart – she prayed for Jonathan's safety.

'If only I could know that somewhere he is alive and safe, then I could find the will to go on living.'

She emerged from the church to shake hands with

343

the vicar and nod to the members of the congregation she knew.

'Ah – er – Mrs Hilton. Good morning. Er – so nice to see you.' The vicar greeted her, but he seemed oddly ill-at-ease, and his handshake was swift and too brief. He seemed to snatch his hand away after the merest contact with hers, and turn away quickly to greet, with an exaggerated enthusiasm, the couple walking behind her.

Esther nodded to two or three people she knew by sight, but there was no courteous raising of hats by the gentlemen or answering smile from the ladies. One or two pointedly turned their heads away, deliberately cutting her. Esther held her head high, her chin jutting forward defiantly as she marched down the pathway and out into the road. It was obvious they had all heard about her and the soldier who had come to the Point, no doubt thanks to Martha Willoughby. So what? What did they know about falling in love and being loved by such a man as Jonathan Godfrey! Never, ever, would she allow anyone – least of all these people she hardly knew – to make her feel ashamed of loving Jonathan.

Esther walked all the way home, her anger making her quicken her pace until Kate begged her to slow down.

'I'm getting a pain in me side, Mam,' she wailed.

'I'm sorry, Katie,' Esther said, immediately contrite.

Kate, soon sunny-natured again, asked, 'Can I go and play at the Point when we get home?'

'Yes, yes, you can,' Esther decided suddenly. 'I'll come and see Ma, too.'

When they reached the stretch of ground between the cottages and the river bank, they saw three of the

344

younger Harris children and Danny playing soldiers, marching up and down with sticks on their shoulders for rifles.

'You can't play, Kate,' shouted Georgie Harris. 'We're going to war. War is men's work.'

Esther looked down at her daughter to see the child's lower lip quivering.

Then Danny was standing in front of them. 'Dun't cry, Katie. Course you can play. You can be a nurse when we gets wounded – like Mester Godfrey.'

Esther felt a lurch in her chest at the mention of his name, but Danny, unaware of the effect his words had upon her, was taking Kate by the hand and leading her into the game.

Esther wandered towards Ma Harris's cottage. She tapped on the door, opened it and was about to step inside when Ma's ample frame appeared in the doorway. Esther gasped aloud as she looked into Ma's set face. Her eyes were cold and her mouth set in a hard line.

'Well?' she asked shortly. 'What do you want?'

Esther shrugged. 'I just came – to – to see you.'

Ma stood her ground, making no move to invite Esther in. 'Well, Ah dun't want to see you,' the older woman said harshly.

'Ma, I . . .'

Ma Harris turned away. 'Please go, Esther. We've nowt to say to one another. Not any more.'

Esther turned and blundered away before anyone might see her tears. She picked up her skirts and ran and ran across the marshland and along the Spit. Running, running until she felt her lungs would burst. At the end of the Spit, close to the water's edge, she picked up a handful of stones and hurled them one by one into the water.

Angry tears blurred her vision.

Why was she being punished for having loved Jonathan? When at last she'd tasted – oh, so briefly – real happiness, it had been cruelly snatched away. Now, even her tender memories were being soured by the condemnation of those around her.

Down the years, in brutal mockery, came the echo of Beth's curse.

'You an' yours will never know happiness.'

Thirty-one

*I*T seemed incredible to all of them that the war had been going on for over two and a half years. Mothers dreaded the passing of the months as their sons who were still at home grew older, nearer and nearer the age when they could volunteer, or be called up. Esther heard — through Enid — that Peter Harris, now fifteen, was already planning to volunteer. Esther shuddered and, despite Ma's present coldness towards her, she prayed that the woman who had once shown her such friendliness would not lose yet another son to the war.

As men were killed and went on being killed in their thousands, the Military Service Act had been passed the previous February and all men between the ages of eighteen and forty-one who did not have special exemption were being conscripted. Wives feared that any day their husbands, who had believed themselves too old, would have to go too. Would Robert Eland and maybe even Mr Harris and Tom Willoughby be next? Esther wondered.

She dragged herself through the weeks and months, through the ploughing, through the spring sowing. Now no one came to offer to lend her their machinery, horses or manpower. Whether it was because they were no longer able to offer the help or because they no longer wished to help Esther Hilton of Brumbys' Farm, she did not know. She managed most of the ploughing with her own pair of horses, but the seed drilling was beyond her strength and she was obliged to go back to the old way of broadcasting the seed from a carrier hung around her neck and shoulders.

'Thank you, Aunt Hannah,' she said to herself, grudgingly admitting that the reason she at least knew how to do the sowing this way was once more due to her aunt. How was it, she mused to herself as she walked up and down the fields, casting the seed from side to side as she went, that she could not bring herself to think of her aunt with any shred of affection? Yet she was forced to acknowledge that all the learning and the know-how she was now drawing on in her lone struggle to survive, she had acquired from her aunt. Even her stubborn resilience – going to bed each night to sleep the sleep of the exhausted and rising still as bone-weary to face another lonely day – had been fostered by her aunt's harshness. Esther had survived a loveless childhood and grown the stronger for it. But having known love, Jonathan's love, and for that matter Ma Harris's friendship, it was harder now to live without affection. She had the farm, Esther told herself sternly when weakness threatened to overwhelm her. She had Kate and always, she had Will. He still came each week, as faithful and uncritical as ever.

Esther never spoke of Jonathan to anyone – was never able to say his name aloud. Not even to Will, for whilst he stood by her, defended her sometimes in the face of the censure of those around, she knew that even he had disapproved of her love for Jonathan.

Her heartache and her loneliness had to remain locked silently within her own heart. The days stretched ahead, unendingly desolate. She would face them — and she would survive — but, oh, how she missed the feel of Jonathan's arms around her!

On a bright summer morning in 1917, Esther woke with a sense of foreboding. It stayed with her through milking. The animals were restless and obstinate, and later, in the dairy, the heat of midday affected the milk and the butter would not come. She churned and churned until the sweat prickled her armpits and ran in rivulets down between her breasts.

'Mrs Hilton, Mrs Hilton.'

'Now what?' she muttered, passing the back of her hand across her damp forehead. Giving the churn one last vicious turn, and then letting the handle swing loose, she stepped out of the pantry, through the kitchen and out of the back door into the sunlight. She screwed up her eyes against the glare and shaded her face with her hand trying to see who the caller was. A dark uniformed shape stood before her, thrusting a white square of paper into her hand.

'It — it's a telegram, missus.' The young man's tone was apologetic.

Esther stood staring at it, not moving, until he thrust it towards her again, anxious to be gone before she read what awful news it must contain.

Jonathan! Oh no! Her lips formed his name, but she made no sound. With trembling fingers she reached out and took the telegram. The young man turned, mounted his bike and pedalled away quickly.

The words blurred before her and she had to blink

349

and read it several times before the truth penetrated her consciousness.

Beneath the heading 'POST OFFICE TELEGRAMS' and some small printing which she did not trouble to read, the message was handwritten, the wording terse and impersonal:

OHMS. War Office, London. To Hilton, Fleethaven Point, Lincolnshire. Deeply regret to inform you that Sgt M. Hilton, Lincolnshire Regiment, was posted missing 21st May. Secretary War Office.

There was not even the name of the sender to soften the harsh, dispassionate wording.

For a long time Esther looked down at the piece of paper in her hands, reading and re-reading the words until they blurred before her eyes. She walked slowly into the house. In the kitchen she stood, dazed, in front of the mantelpiece. With shaking fingers she reached up and took down the photograph of Matthew in its silver frame. The postcards stacked behind it slithered down and scattered around her, floating down on to the floor like falling petals. She picked each one up and sat down at the table, resting her arms on the plush green tablecloth. She placed his photograph in front of her and then read and re-read every postcard he had sent.

'Oh, Matthew,' she murmured aloud, 'Matthew, I'm so sorry. I never wanted this to happen.'

She stayed a long time in the house on her own, coming to terms with the news. Learning to live with the knowledge that now she was really on her own. Thoughts of Jonathan intruded, but resolutely she pushed them away. Now was not the time to think of him.

At last she sighed and heaved herself up from the table. She replaced the photograph and the postcards on the mantelpiece and then gently touched the face in the picture with her forefinger. 'Poor Matthew,' she murmured.

She went across to the sideboard and opened the drawer. Lying face upwards was the companion photograph to the one in the frame. She took it out and closed the drawer. Picking up the telegram from the table, she left the farmhouse and turned towards the Point.

There was something she had to do.

Esther walked the short distance from her farm to the Point. At this time of day there was no one about outside the cottages or the pub and for this she was thankful. She didn't yet want to face the inevitable questions. She stood on the bank below the towering bulk of the Elands' boat home. She waited uncertainly. There was no one in sight and she did not want to venture up the gangway uninvited and unheralded. She heard a footstep on the wooden planking of the deck and saw Robert Eland appear at the end of the wooden jetty.

With the hand that still held the telegram Esther shaded her eyes against the sun and met Robert Eland's gaze unflinchingly. She saw his glance switch to the piece of paper rattling gently in the breeze, then come back to her face.

Levelly she said, 'Robert – can I speak to Beth, please?' She heard him draw in breath quickly between his teeth and for a moment his eyes seemed to widen.

He nodded briefly, turned away and disappeared, leaving Esther standing on the river bank below.

It seemed an age that Esther waited, and yet it could not have been more than a few moments that she stood in the sunlight, staring at the black bulk of the boat in front of her. Her eyes took in the peeling paint exposing rotting wood. Poor Robert, she thought, he hasn't had time to keep his own home in good repair. Being one of the few able-bodied men left, Robert Eland always helped out on the estate when needed. And he was often needed.

I wonder why no one has called him a coward for not volunteering? she thought and then answered her own question in her mind. It would be difficult for anyone to accuse Robert Eland of cowardice; many times he had risked his life out at sea in the lifeboat rescuing others. The war had brought a greater number of tragedies at sea. She bit down hard upon her lip as she remembered it had been just such a reason that had brought Enid rushing to the farm for the horses; the night the girl had seen Esther emerging from the barn, her clothing in disarray. I mustn't think of him, she told herself, not now!

She waited in the hot sun, breathing in the scent of the countryside, yet unaware of it. Seagulls screeched overhead, bees hummed busily and butterflies fluttered aimlessly. But the bright day seemed only to mock her. How can it be such a beautiful day, how dare it be, when I . . . ? She closed her eyes a moment against the glare and when she opened them again she saw that Beth was standing at the end of the planking.

The two women stared at each other and then Beth

came slowly down to stand in front of Esther.

Neither of them spoke, yet their eyes held each other's. Wordlessly, Esther held out the telegram for Beth to read. The woman, who had borne Matthew's son, reached for it with shaking fingers.

Dragging her gaze away from Esther's she lowered her eyes and read the words. At last she raised her head, eyes closed and a low moan of anguish escaped her lips. 'Oh, no! *No!*'

Gently, Esther eased the piece of paper from Beth's rigid fingers. 'Beth – I know how you feel. I never – understood – not before. Now I do.'

No more explanation was necessary. The two women regarded each other sadly. In that moment of mutual loss, they came the closest they ever would to understanding one another.

Esther had not known love before Jonathan, but if Beth had loved Matthew in the same way, then there was room for compassion.

Esther held out the photograph. 'I thought you might like to have this. Matthew sent me it soon after he – first went.'

Beth took his likeness and stared at it and then held it to her breast. 'Don't you want it?' she whispered.

'There were two,' Esther explained simply. 'I have the other in a frame on the mantelpiece.'

Beth nodded. Her eyes filled with tears that spilled over and ran down her pale cheeks. 'Thank you, Esther. And thank you for coming to tell me.'

Beth turned away and, like an old woman, dragged herself back up the slope of the gangway.

Thirty-two

*T*HE small community was shocked by the news.

The squire rode over in person to visit Esther. 'Of course, my dear,' he said taking her hand and patting it comfortingly, 'it does say "reported missing". There is room for hope, my dear. It must be chaos out there, you know. Maybe he's been wounded and carted off to some field hospital and not able to tell them who he is. Anything like that can happen. You must – we must all – continue to hope that he is alive somewhere. It's not definite – you must cling to that hope.'

Esther tried to smile. 'Thank you, Squire, you're very kind.' She bit her lip. She wanted so much to ask him what was to happen about the tenancy of the farm, but suddenly the picture of his angry face and his censorious words after Sam Brumby's funeral made her bite back her question. Now was not the time!

Life continued much as before through the summer of 1917 – day after day the same. What had she to look forward to now? What had she to hope for? Indeed, with this dreadful war snatching all the young men from their midst, fathers, husbands – and lovers, what hope for the future had anyone?

The day that Esther had dreaded arrived without warning and before she could take the evasive action she had

354

done the last time. The little man with the sheaf of papers under his arm arrived so unexpectedly that she had no chance to move Punch and Prince from the meadow.

'I am quite aware, Mrs Hilton,' he began without preamble, 'that on the occasion of my last visit you were able to deceive me. I don't intend to make trouble for you.' His voice softened. 'I'm not really the hard-hearted villain you take me for – but I have a job to do and I am afraid I really must commandeer your horses.'

'How am I to get the harvests in? There's no fellers and . . .' She stopped and bit her lip. She had been about to tell him that she no longer had the usual help from her neighbours now that they were ostracizing her at the instigation of Martha Willoughby and – yes, she had to admit it – even Ma Harris.

'I really am sorry,' the official was saying again. 'The squire has been allowed to keep three horses on condition that he loans them out to anyone nearby who has real need . . .'

'How do you think just three horses can cope with all the work around here at harvest? The grass and the corn dun't wait, mester.'

The man sighed. 'I do understand . . .'

'No, ya don't. Ya can't!' She turned away before he should see her tears. Before she would let any man – other than Jonathan – see her cry, she turned her back on him. With an angry gesture she waved him away. 'Oh, take 'em, then. Only, don't let me see.'

She sat in the kitchen, her hands lying idly on the table, staring out of the window that faced on to the front garden, determined not to risk catching sight of her beloved horses being led out of the meadow and up the lane towards the town.

Two pairs of small feet pounded across the yard and Kate, followed by Danny Eland, came bursting into the kitchen.

'Mam, Mam, they're taking Punch and Prince. Mam, stop them.' Tears ran down her daughter's face and even the boy seemed to be having difficulty in holding his mouth from quivering. Esther held out her hand and Kate came and stood at the side of her chair. The child leant her head on her mother's breast and the tears flowed. Esther held out her other hand to Danny and he came and stood close beside her, and rested his head against her shoulder.

'It dun't seem fair,' he muttered. 'They're old, yar 'osses, anyway. What use can they be in – in the war?'

'I know,' Esther murmured. 'I can't rightly understand it myself, Danny. But there it is, they've got to go.'

Through the open back door the three of them listened to the distant sound of clopping hooves going up the lane, growing fainter and fainter until they could hear them no more.

So many leavings, Esther thought sadly. How many more beings she loved – human and animal – were to walk away down that lane never to return?

Danny twisted his head and looked up into her face. 'I'm sorry about the mester.'

Esther looked down into the boy's dark brown eyes and for a moment rested her hand on his black curly hair. He was so like Matthew that one day, as he grew older, he would surely have guessed just who his sire was, if Matthew had still been around. Now Matthew would not be returning. Would Danny ever know who his natural father was?

Quietly she said, 'Thank you, Danny,' then more briskly she added, 'I've some scones in the oven. Would you like one with some fresh butter?' She was rewarded by a replica of Matthew's cheeky grin, and as she rose and went to take her baking from the range oven, she spared a moment's thought for Beth.

How the sight of her son must twist at Beth's heart every day of her life!

'Tom – they've taken me 'osses.'

'Eh, Esther, lass, I'm sorry to hear that.' He shook his head. 'You did well to hang on to them the last time they came. I didn't,' he added with feeling.

They were standing in Tom's stack yard. 'I'd help you if I could, lass, but I've none mesen, now. I have to borrow the squire's. You'll have to do the same.'

'Aye, but I'll be at the end of the line, won't I?' she added bitterly.

Tom faced her squarely. 'No beating about the bush, lass. I dun't reckon the squire holds anything against you, personal like.'

'Not like the rest of you, ya mean?'

Tom's huge shoulders lifted fractionally as he said truthfully, 'You're not perfect, Esther Hilton. You've made mistakes and takin' up with that young feller whilst your husband was at war hasn't gone down too well with the folks round here . . .' He held up his hand

357

as she opened her mouth to protest, speaking for her the words she had been about to utter. 'Aye, I know, it's no one else's business. But folks around here, I'm afraid, will always make other people's business their own. It's the penalty you pay for living in a little community like this. Matthew was one of us, an' you were a stranger here.'

Stiffly, she said, 'I'm sorry if you think badly of me, Tom, but there's – things you don't know . . .'

Tom nodded. 'Eeh lass, I've been around a long time. I don't think badly of you at all. And maybe I understand a lot more than you think, but there's some as don't.'

'Tom—' she said, suddenly needing to know. 'You never thought I fired your stack, did you?'

Tom pushed his cap back and scratched his head, but did not answer.

'How can you believe that of me, Tom? How can anyone believe I'd do a thing like that? Me, who loves the land more than I—' She stopped. She had been about to say 'more than I love people'. Once, not so long ago, that would have been a valid statement. Since she had known Jonathan, it was no longer true.

'Besides, I wouldn't hurt you for the world, Tom – even,' she added with embittered truthfulness, 'if I ain't much time for yar wife and that sister of hers.'

'I know, lass, I know. But she reckons you swore vengeance on her and Flo for reporting your – er – friend to the authorities. Then after that ran-tan-tanning they give ya . . .' Once more Tom's huge shoulders lifted in a non-committal shrug.

'Aye, I did threaten her.' Esther faced him squarely, courageously admitting her faults but stoutly defending

358

herself against false accusation. 'And in that moment when her and Flo were in their trap in the lane, gloating over the policeman payin' us a visit, I would have done her a mischief an' no mistake. But – ' her voice softened, not at the memory of Martha and Flo but at the mention of Jonathan's name – '*he* stopped me. Jonathan held me from tippling the trap over.' She met the older man's gaze steadfastly. 'Tom, I'm not vindictive. Yes, I bear her a grudge. I'll never forgive her for what she's done to me. First goading Matthew into volunteering, then reporting Jonathan . . .' She shook her head again in disbelief. 'But I would never, ever do a thing like firing yar stack! Please believe me, Tom?'

As Tom pulled his cap back on his head and opened his mouth, there was a loud squawk of rage from behind him and Martha came striding across the yard waving her fat arms and shouting at her husband, closely followed by Flo Jenkins.

'Thomas – how can you let this creature on to our farm after what she did?'

'What's she doing here?' Flo demanded and her voice rose shrilly with a touch of hysteria. 'Martha, she's come to kill us – kill us all. It wasn't enough to try to set fire to our farm. She's a whore and a trollop. Set the dog on her, Martha!'

Tom turned to look at them both. 'Now look here, Flo Jenkins,' his deep voice boomed as he stepped forward. Esther saw Flo's face turn a funny grey colour and her thin hand fluttered to cover her mouth. 'I've let you live in this house nigh on ten year and in that time you've done nowt but cause trouble between me and me wife

359

with your tittle-tattle. You've a poisonous tongue on you, woman.'

'Thomas . . .' Martha began to plead.

'And you can hold yourn, else I'll leave the pair of you and join up.'

Martha gave a cry. 'No, Thomas. You wouldn't. You couldn't – you're too old.'

'Too old be damned!'

'Thomas!' Martha still had enough spirit to admonish him for his language, but the farmer took no notice. 'There was a piece in the paper last week saying that they'll take anyone – anyone, mark you – who'll volunteer to dig trenches.' He leaned towards her and said slowly and deliberately, 'Now that I could do, Martha, as you well know, for I've dug a few in me time.'

'Thomas . . .' Martha wailed. 'How can you side with – with her against your own wife?'

'Now come, Martha my dear. You know me better than that. I'll not take your part if I think you're wrong – and this time, you are. I never did believe that Esther fired that stack and I still don't.' He laughed suddenly, throwing back his head, his great belly wobbling. 'She's more likely to come an' give you a good hiding, but set fire to a stack? Never!'

Martha all but stamped her foot. Her face grew puce. She turned and, grabbing Flo's bony arm with her fat hand, she hustled her sister away and back into the house slamming the back door behind them.

Unperturbed, Tom merely rubbed his huge hands together and smiled again. 'She dun't like to be beat,

Esther lass, and that's put her in her place this time – and that sister of hers – and no mistake.'

'Oh, Tom, I'm sorry. I didn't come to cause you trouble, but I'm glad you believe in me.'

It was a comfort to Esther to know that she had Tom's support, for apart from the ever faithful Will, she saw no one now. Even Enid came less and less to the farm to help out and Luke, one of the younger Harris boys who had for a time tried to take Ernie's place, had stopped coming. But Kate was still welcomed at the Point cottages to play with the Harris children – and with Danny Eland.

The only person in whom Esther could confide was Will Benson. She looked forward to the days when he visited Fleethaven Point and had his dinner with her. Sometimes she never spoke to another soul – apart from Kate – from one of his visits to the next.

'Y'know,' he said between mouthfuls, 'I miss my little lass on me visits, now she's at school. How is she? Does she like it?'

Esther frowned. 'Oh, yes, she loves it. Getting quite the saucy minx now. All the children from the Point walk to the school in town together.'

She felt Will's perceptive eyes upon her. Quietly, he said, 'An' you don't like that because she's with Danny Eland.'

She glanced at him and pulled her mouth into a grimace which implied agreement.

'I shouldn't let it worry you none, lass. They're only bairns. No harm can come of it.'

'Mebbe, mebbe not. I still don't like it, though. They

361

– they seem drawn to each other, Will. She thinks he's wonderful. It's all "Danny says", and "Danny did this" with her.'

Will shrugged. 'Well, they are brother and sister . . .'

'*Half* brother and sister,' she corrected.

'Half brother and sister, then. Perhaps there's a kind of closeness – kinship, if ya like – that won't be denied.'

'Yes – and it worries me,' Esther said, heaving herself up from the table. She gathered up the empty plates and took them out to the scullery. 'Though there's not a lot I can do about it, I suppose.'

'You'll find the more you try to stop 'em playing together, the more they'll want to. Even at this age, they'll rebel against you, given half the chance. I'd let them be, lass. Really I would.'

'I expect you're right, Will.' She grinned at him with affection. 'You usually are. I should listen to your wisdom sometimes.'

He stood up and laughed wheezily. 'Mebbe you should, me lass, mebbe you should.'

They exchanged a knowing glance, but still the words she would have liked to hear him say were not forthcoming.

The months dragged on and it was only the needs of the animals and the land that kept Esther going. She was saddened to think that Matthew was dead, for, three months after the telegram, another official form arrived. The words were just as informal and impersonal:

It is my painful duty to inform you that no further news

having been received relative to Sgt Matthew Hilton, the Army Council have been regretfully constrained to conclude that he is dead.

This letter was not such a shock as the telegram had been for despite what the squire had said, she had not thought that the War Office would send such a telegram unless they really believed that there was little hope of Matthew still being alive.

Poor Matthew. He hadn't wanted to die. He hadn't even expected to die, like many of them had done when they volunteered for the glory of it all.

She realized now that although she had never felt for her husband the overwhelming passion she felt for Jonathan, still in a way she had loved Matthew. She owed him a debt of gratitude and the loyalty that any man ought to be able to expect from his wife. But now, having known the intensity of falling in love with a man, of being loved and desired and almost worshipped by that man in return, there was a tinge of sadness in her memories of Matthew. She had no doubt that Beth had loved Matthew like that, and, too late, Matthew had come to realize that he loved Beth. Then he had felt cheated and trapped by his marriage and had vented his unhappiness upon Esther.

Carefully, she placed the letter in the sideboard drawer and closed it. Matthew was gone and she could not alter what had happened in the past. Even so, it had not been all bad, she comforted herself. They'd had the farm and they had created a daughter.

Now the farm and Kate were all she had left.

*

One blustery afternoon, Esther went into her meadow which adjoined Tom Willoughby's land to check the bloom on the grass. She sighed. This field was ready for cutting now — in fact it had been ready for two weeks. Somehow she was going to have to cope completely alone with the harvests this year, for no one would come to help her. She looked about her at the long grass rippling like waves on the ocean in the stiff breeze that blew in from the sea. Clouds scudded across the sun and their shadows travelled across the fields. Suddenly she was filled with a desire to go to the end of the Spit — just to get away from the never-ending workload, if only for an hour.

She left the fields and walked back down the lane away from the borders of Rookery Farm and towards the sand dunes and the marsh beyond them. She had climbed the bank and was about to run down the other side to cross the marsh towards the Spit, when she heard the rattle of wheels in the lane behind her. She turned to see Martha and Flo in their trap, their smart bonnets suggesting they were heading for Lynthorpe. Not wishing to become embroiled in yet further argument with Martha and her sister, Esther ran quickly down the bank and out of their view.

The tide was high and the wind drove waves against the Spit as she walked along it, but she was determined to get to the end where she could find solace and peace surrounded by the sea and the sky with only the birds to share her loneliness.

Seawards, she could see a small boat making towards the haven. Perhaps it was Robert Eland returning from a day's fishing. No doubt, as he drew closer, he would see her standing there, but he would be too intent upon threading his way between the markers he himself had placed in the marsh at low tide to bother himself with Esther Hilton. The poles, sticking up out of the water when the tide was high and the sea covered the marsh, were to guide him up the deep channel of the river bed.

How long she stood there, she didn't know, nor did she know what made her turn suddenly to see Martha and Flo only a few feet away from her, for no sound of their approach had come to her ears above the sound of the sea and the wind.

Suddenly, Esther was filled with an unaccustomed dread. She was standing on the end of the narrow strip of land with her back to the swirling, rushing water and before her, advancing with menace in every step, were the two women who hated her most in the world. Perhaps even more than did Beth Eland.

Esther was trapped. There was no place to run. Young and strong though she was, she would be no match for the two of them.

They had stopped and were standing side by side on the narrow strip of land, effectively barring any chance of escape towards the marsh. Exultation showed on both their faces. The sea, splashing against the bank, showered their best skirts with salty spray yet they didn't seem to care, didn't even seem to notice.

They had Esther Everatt Hilton at their mercy.

Thirty-three

MARTHA was speaking. Her mouth, twisted into an ugly sneer, was moving, but her words were snatched away by the wind before they could reach Esther.

Together they moved forward and Esther felt the fear rise in her throat. Even out here in the cold wind she found she was sweating with terror. Behind her the sea, once her solace, had become a malevolent monster waiting to devour her. The water was not deep but Esther could not swim, and there were hidden channels and pools that were always water-filled even at low tide. If she should fall into one of those . . .

The two women moved forwards again, coming closer, ever closer . . .

There was no escape for Esther.

Suddenly, with one accord, they lunged towards her hitting her in the chest and sending her falling, arms flailing helplessly, backwards into the sea.

The waters closed over her face and there was a gurgling in her ears. She struggled, thrashing with her arms, trying to find the bottom with her feet, striving to bring her head above the water. She broke the surface and drew great gasps of air into her bursting lungs. She could not open her eyes for the stinging salt water. A wave hit her in the back and sent her tippling forward again, face down in the water. She lost her footing and now she could not feel the bottom, could not feel firm earth beneath her feet. She twisted and writhed and tried to push herself upwards. Her sodden clothes were now dragging her down and she felt as if her lungs would rupture. She tried to open her eyes but all she could see was murky, swirling sand. There was a glimmer of light above, but so far away, too far away . . . Water filled her nose and mouth. Her heart was pounding, there was a drumming in her ears. She had never felt so frightened in her life. She knew herself to be drowning and she so desperately wanted to live. She must live – for Kate – for Jonathan. In that moment she saw his beloved face in her mind – the smile crinkling his eyes, the flop of fair hair falling across his forehead – and then there was darkness . . .

Suddenly strong arms were lifting her and she was hauled upwards until her head was above water. She was being shaken and her face was being slapped and suddenly she was coughing and spluttering and clinging on to someone. She coughed and dragged in gulps of air and coughed again until she was sick. Hanging over her rescuer's strong arm, she retched until she had brought up all the sea water that had entered her lungs. Esther was clinging to a man's arm and being pulled along. She felt herself bump the side of a boat.

'Come on, Esther,' said the man's voice. 'I can't lift you in, you'll have to help me.' She brushed her hand across her face and blinked. Her eyes were sore and swollen so that she could scarcely open them. But she knew his voice. Her rescuer was Robert Eland.

She tried to speak but could make no sound. Her breathing was still painful and there was a dreadful ache in her chest.

'Come on,' he was urging her again. 'Put your arms over the side of the boat. Try and grasp hold and I'll heave you in.'

They struggled for a few moments until a helpful wave gave an extra buoyancy to her tired limbs and she found herself sprawling in the bottom of the fishing boat. She was scarcely aware of Robert somehow getting himself back into the boat and rowing away from the Spit towards the mouth of the river and the Point. She neither knew nor cared what had happened to Martha Willoughby and her sister.

It seemed a long time before the boat bumped gently against the river bank, by which time Esther was shivering uncontrollably. Her head ached and her chest still hurt. She kept blinking her eyes to clear her vision. It felt as if she had a barrow-load of sand in each eye.

But she was safe.

Robert was bending over her. 'Can you get up, Esther?'

Valiantly, she made the effort to pull herself up and he supported her, taking her arm and helping her to step out of the boat and on to the wooden landing stage.

'Oh, dear Lord,' she heard a woman's voice exclaim. 'Whatever has happened?'

Still with Robert's arm to support her, Esther staggered on to the land and fell to her knees. She had never been so thankful in her life to feel the firm earth beneath her.

'What happened?' came the voice again.

Slowly Esther raised her head to see Beth standing over her, bending down towards her and even holding out her hands to help her rise.

After only a moment's hesitation, Esther grasped the outstretched hands and hauled herself to her feet. She stood swaying and then she felt Beth's arm about her waist, supporting her, urging her forward. 'Come on to the boat, Esther. I'll get you some dry clothing. Whatever has happened?' she demanded yet again.

Now, relinquishing the care of Esther to his wife, Robert said, ''Twas them two old biddies from Tom Willoughby's farm. They pushed her into the sea off the Spit. God knows what would have happened if I hadn't been near enough to get to her in time.'

Though she could not yet speak, Esther echoed his sentiments. God alone knew!

Esther did not go to the Elands' boat home. She wanted to get to the farm as quickly as possible and Beth took her. Only when she had seen Esther stripped of her wet clothing and sitting before the range with a cup of hot tea, did Beth leave Esther in Kate's care.

Esther recovered quickly and all she told the child was that she had been foolish enough to walk along the Spit on a blustery day and at high tide, and had fallen into the sea.

'And Mr Eland rescued you?'

'Yes, yes – he did,' Esther croaked, for her voice was still ragged. 'I – I think he saved my life.'

Kate, full of importance, said, 'I must go and find Danny and tell him.' In the next moment the child had rushed from the house and Esther had not the strength to stop her.

The following day, Esther opened her back door in answer to a knock and was surprised to find Tom standing there.

'Tom – come in,' Esther invited, her voice still croaky.

Tom hesitated a moment and then eased his bulk through her scullery and into the kitchen.

He pulled his cap from his head and stood twisting it in his huge hands. 'Esther, lass,' he began, 'Eland told me what happened yesterday. I want you to know – I'm sorry.'

'Tom . . .'

'No, lass. Hear me out – please. They'll not bother you again, I've seen to that. But I'd just ask ya to keep away from me farm for a while – an' mebbe church an' all. Just for a time, like.' The cap was still revolving through his restless fingers. 'I've never in me life raised me hand to me wife an' I dun't intend to, but, by God, when Eland told me – I came close to it, lass.'

Esther shook her head sadly. 'Tom – I've told you before, I never wanted to cause trouble between you and your wife . . .'

'I know, I know.' He shook his head, wonderingly. 'I just dun't understand her mesen. You're like a red rag to her, Esther, an' that's a fact.'

'Tom,' Esther asked, suddenly remembering, 'were you related to Sam Brumby? Is that what started it all?'

'Oh, aye, but years back. Now let's see – my grandfather's sister was Sam's mother.'

Esther nodded. 'There's an entry in Sam's old family Bible. I did wonder.' She sighed. 'Martha thinks all this –' she waved her arm to encompass all Sam's belongings in the house – 'should have come to you.'

Tom shrugged. 'Mebbe, Esther. To tell you the truth, I never give it a thought.'

Esther believed him. It was only Martha and her grasping sister who resented her.

She also believed Tom when he said that their persecution of her was at an end. For that, she was thankful, yet his advice to stay away, not only from his farm but from the church too, would isolate her from the community more than ever.

Like Ma Harris, but not as bluntly, Tom was saying they wanted no more to do with Esther Hilton.

A few days later, when she had fully recovered, Esther went to the point in search of Robert Eland.

'I came to thank you, Robert. You saved my life.'

The man looked up at her from where he was sitting on the river bank, mending his fishing net. He nodded briefly in swift acknowledgement of her thanks. Then, looking back down at his nets, he said, 'I reckon we're equal now, then. For yar man saved my life that night.'

She knew she was referring to the time Matthew had gone out in the lifeboat and had rescued Robert.

'Please – thank Beth for me, will ya?'

There was a pause, then Robert nodded and muttered, 'Aye, I will.'

There was no more to be said. To say any more would have been an embarrassment to them both. Robert Eland might have saved her life but it had changed nothing in the attitude of the people of Fleethaven Point towards Esther Hilton. Not one thing.

It was the farm that devoured Esther's time and strength through the rest of the summer, autumn and even the winter of 1917. Thankfully, her growing daughter, happy at school and always welcomed by her friends at the Point even if her mother was not, was little trouble. Kate never seemed to suffer from childish illnesses, she was sturdy, strong for her age, and healthy. If anyone's health was in question during those months, it was Esther's.

Apart from Will Benson, she saw no one but to say that she was utterly alone was not quite true for she had two very willing helpers, and for their age and strength they were remarkable.

Kate – and Danny Eland. Without their help she would have lost more of her crops than she did, for when winter set in with a vengeance there were still two fields uncut. As for the rest, Esther cut the corn with a hand sickle. She had tried Sam's scythe but found it too heavy and unwieldy. Day after day she moved slowly down the field locked into a stooping position, grasping a bunch of corn in her left hand and cutting it with the sickle in her right. Day after day until she thought she would never walk upright again, until every limb in her body ached and cried out for rest. Still she drove herself on. On and on until the pain in her body drove out the ache in her heart and left her mind dulled and unable to think of

Jonathan. At night she fell into bed exhausted and slept at once.

The children took on the job of raking, tying the sheaves and stooking. Esther cut down the handles of two rakes to make them more manageable for them and their merry laughter as they worked was the only sound in the fields, normally alive with noisy chatter from the numerous harvest workers. The fields at Brumbys' Farm were silent, waiting their turn under Esther's lone sickle – and some would wait in vain.

'Ya'll kill ya'sen, lass,' Will told her bluntly.

'What else can I do, Will? I can't lose it all. I won't lose it all.'

'Ask the squire for help, Esther. After all, it's his land.'

'I dun't want him to think I can't cope. I don't know what he intends – now Matthew's not coming back. He might only need the slightest excuse to take the tenancy off me.'

Will was silent, scratching his head in defeat.

'And,' she added bitterly, 'I dun't want him to know why none of the others are helping me this year.'

'I 'spect he knows,' Will muttered under his breath, but Esther's hearing was sharp.

'I suppose you're right. I can't understand them,' she said angrily. 'They all came last year, when Jonathan was actually here. They liked him – everyone did. So why are they punishing me now?'

'They didn't blame him, Esther lass,' Will told her gently, unknowingly echoing Ma Harris's words. 'At first he was a hero in their eyes. A soldier wounded in the war and going to go back. But then *you* kept him here. To their way of thinking it was *you* turned him into a deserter. They blame you for everything.'

Esther closed her eyes and swayed slightly as her loss swept over her again. Tiredness made her vulnerable. Whilst for the most part the hard work blotted out her memories, when those same memories did intrude, she had no resistance to the hurt. She groaned and sank down into a kitchen chair and leant her head on her arms on the table.

'Why was it so very wrong of me to fall in love with him?'

'Because you were married – are still, for all we really know – and to one of their own. More than anything else, they can't forgive you for that, Esther.'

'It's different for men, isn't it?' Her voice was muffled, but there was no mistaking her resentment. 'They get away with it. They can have affairs, even bring – bring bastards into the world and are just thought "a bit of a lad". Even envied by other fellers. But a woman! Oh, no, she's a trollop and a whore . . .' She stopped, appalled that she was talking to Will in this way, that she was thrusting the knife of her years of resentment into him of all people.

Will Benson sighed but said nothing. What was there that he could say to her accusation?

'Me husband's dead,' Esther went on. 'Am I supposed to live the rest of me life alone, just because . . . ?'

'No, of course not, Esther. You jumped the gun, that's what's caused the resentment. You hadn't even had word that he was missing before you took up with Jonathan Godfrey.'

It was a fact that she could not deny and it was that fact the people of Fleethaven Point could not forgive.

Through the long winter, Esther threshed the corn in her barn by hand with Sam's old flail, spending long hours in the cold, with the wind whipping between the two sets of open doors, blowing away the chaff and leaving her the precious harvest of grain.

There was no news of Jonathan. Was he dead too, like Matthew? Or was he still out there in the muddy trenches? Did he ever think of her? she wondered. Did he remember Fleethaven Point and the warm sand and the soft, lapping sea, music to their love-making?

By the spring of 1918 the news from the war front seemed no better – worse if anything. The newspapers which Will still brought each week were gloomy. The Germans had launched massive attacks on the Western Front and British-held trenches were overrun and captured. The British faced defeat and fresh fears swept through those left at home. Had they lost so many young men in vain?

Then, like the turn of the tide, the British and their allies were marching forward, breaking through the Hindenburg Line and marching on and on and people began to speak as if victory could be a reality.

One morning she heard Will's whistle; not one blast as usual to herald his arrival, but three shrill notes piercing the air. Esther set down the egg basket she was carrying and ran to the gate. Will was standing up on the front of his cart, excitedly waving a newspaper and climbing

375

down before his horses had stopped. 'Esther – Esther lass. It's over. It's really over.'

Esther stood at the gate staring at him as he came towards her.

'The war, Esther. It's over.' Wordlessly, she put her arms up and he hugged her to him. 'It'll be all right now, lass. Things'll get better – you see.'

At the eleventh hour on the eleventh day of the eleventh month, it was indeed all over. Of course there was rejoicing and in some towns and cities there were joyous celebrations, but amongst the community at Fleethaven Point there seemed only relief, their happiness tempered by the losses their small number had sustained. The squire's son, who would never step into his father's place; Ernie Harris, Ma's firstborn – and Matthew. In the months since Esther had received the final letter from the Army authorities there had been no further word, no hint that there was any hope that he could still be alive.

Now that it was finally all over, Esther clung to the hope that Jonathan had come through, that perhaps he would come home, that he would come to the Point to see her and, maybe, finding her a widow, just maybe . . .

During the weeks which followed the Armistice, Esther grew increasingly restless. There was little she could do on the land in December, nor could she seem to generate any enthusiasm for Christmas preparations. Once again she had struggled virtually alone with her harvest, though this year she had use of the squire's horses for a week and the loan of one of his men. Yet again, no one from the Point had offered help, nor even Tom Willoughby. And Ma Harris, whose coldness hurt more than anyone's, kept stubbornly away from Brumbys' Farm – and Esther.

Wandering around the farm watching the pigs, the hens, checking on the cows, Esther felt as if she were waiting for something to happen, only it didn't seem to be happening.

She sighed and walked towards the farm gate, leaning on it and looking up the road towards the town. If only he would come walking back round the bend. But the lane was empty. There was no sign of a tall, fair-haired soldier marching towards her.

Her gaze travelled round and came to rest on the rise in the road – the Hump – beyond which were the cottages at the Point. Before she fully realized what she was doing, or had even stopped to think, she was moving out of her gate and down the lane towards the Point. She knocked on the door of Ma Harris's cottage and stood waiting, her heart thumping. It was strange that she should feel afraid. She had missed Ma's warmth, her chatter, her friendship so much. As she stood there she could hear the sound of children laughing and shrieking as they played on the scrubland beyond the cottage.

The door opened and Ma stood there, wiping her floury hands on her apron.

'Oh – it's you,' she said, turned away abruptly and went back to her kitchen table to her pastry-making. But she left the door open. At least she had not slammed it in Esther's face.

'Ma – can I come in?' This was a new Esther, a tentative, penitent Esther.

'If ya must.'

'Ma – can't we be friends again?'

The older woman glanced at her and then back to her pastry, thumping it over and over, rolling it out with the wooden rolling pin. For a long time she didn't answer.

'Ya know what the Good Book says, "As ye sow, so shall ye reap." There'll come a day of reckoning, lass. Somewhere, some time you'll be made to pay.'

An angry retort rose to Esther's lips, but for once she literally bit back the words, pressing her teeth into her bottom lip to suppress them.

Ma Harris let out a long sigh and now there was more sadness than censure in her tone. 'Oh, Esther lass, part of me does understand why you were drawn to that young feller, but it's hard for me to forgive you. Young Matthew has always been part of our lives. I helped bring him into the world in that cottage next door,' she nodded her head beyond her own cottage wall indicating the adjoining house. 'He were like one of me own and after he'd lost both his parents, well, he more or less did become one of me family. But more than that even, it was you leaving your bairn in the house on her own that really riled me. Ya know how I am about bairns?'

'I – I know you think badly of me and I'm sorry, real sorry. As for Kate, yes, I felt guilty about that and it never happened again.'

Ma cast her a sideways glance but said no more. To Esther her look said, 'So, you took him into the house then – into Matthew's house.'

Esther's chin came a little higher, but she kept her tone submissive. 'There's a lot I'm sorry for now – a lot that's to do with Matthew — and Beth. But I'll never, ever, say I'm sorry I met Jonathan.'

Ma gasped and stared at her. Esther met her gaze levelly. 'Eeh, lass, you're honest, I'll say that for ya. An' though I dun't hold with what ya've done, ya didn't skulk about it. Ya didn't try to hide what was going on between you and Jonathan from us all, even knowing we wouldn't like it. You're a strange one, Esther Hilton, an' no mistake.'

Then slowly, like the sun appearing as a cloud passed away, a smile began to spread across Ma's shrunken mouth. She shook her head, almost as if in disbelief at herself for what she was about to say. 'I can't go on being mad at ya — an' the Lord knows I've tried. Truth is, I've missed ya, lass. Missed talking and laughing with ya, I really have.'

Now she was smiling broadly and Esther was smiling back.

'So, you'll both be here for Christmas this year, will you?'

'Try and keep us away!'

So it was a merry Christmas that year of 1918 which Esther and Kate shared with the Harris family once more, for Mr Harris and all their brood took their lead from Ma. Her word was law. If she wanted nothing to do with Esther Hilton, then they obeyed, but if Ma forgave and welcomed her back, then they were ready to do that too.

And their country was no longer at war — it was time to forgive and to make new beginnings. They all went to

Midnight Mass together, walking the long lane in the frosty, moonlit night, the children, far from sleepy, skipping and dancing and chasing each other; the grown-ups, walking arm in arm, smiling and content and thankful. Yes, thankful, Esther thought, that despite what they had all lost, there would be no more killing and maiming. Their soldiers were coming home.

Oh, dear Lord, she prayed silently, let one of them be Jonathan.

It was in the New Year that Esther's restlessness grew and became unbearable. She could find no solace in the farm. Even her favourite place on the Spit and the peaceful scenery brought no comfort and serenity. Her anxiety over Jonathan festered until she was sleeping badly and could not eat.

There should have been some word. Surely the soldiers were coming home from France now? He would have got in touch somehow. Perhaps he was still in France. Perhaps he was wounded and in hospital, or – heaven forbid – perhaps he was dead and lying in a grave in foreign soil, alone and forgotten by everyone but her.

It was Will Benson who gave her the idea that there was something she could do.

'Have you heard the latest?'

She was listening with only half an ear to his chatter, but his next words commanded her immediate attention. 'Squire's going over to France to see if he can find his boy's grave. Course Mrs Marshall ain't going. Poor lady – she's never got over the lad's death, y'know. Just the squire and his younger son are going.'

Esther stared at him. Her heart began to beat a little faster and she felt herself go breathless with excitement. 'How's he managed that? Can anybody go? When's he going?'

'Eh, steady on, lass. 'Ow should I know? All I know is, he's got in touch with that there Major Langley. You know, 'im as gave that speech in the town just after the war started.'

'Oh, I remember him all right!' Esther said grimly.

'Now, lass, the man was only doing his duty—'

'Never mind that now, Will,' she cut him off sharply. 'Do you know when Squire's going?'

'Next week some time I think. He found out from the major where young Rodney's company was when he was killed.'

'Oh, next week, eh?' Esther muttered, her mind busy. Jonathan must have been in the same company as the squire's son. She remembered the squire asking Jonathan if he had known his son and Jonathan had said that he knew him by sight. They'd all been in the same regiment, Rodney Marshall, Ernie Harris, Matthew – and Jonathan! Perhaps . . .

'Esther Hilton – what are you up to?' Will was eyeing her shrewdly.

She grinned at him, feeling alive and hopeful for the first time in many months. 'Never you mind, Will Benson, just never you mind.'

'Mr Marshall – please, I want to come to France with you.' Once more – as if time had taken a tilt – Esther was standing facing the squire across his huge desk.

'Eh? What?' The squire's mouth all but dropped open. 'Come to France? My dear Mrs Hilton . . .'

He was patronizing her. Her green eyes flashed and her jaw tightened. She saw that he had noticed, for his protestations died. He ran his hand through his thin, greying hair. He sighed deeply and said, more kindly, 'I can well understand your desire to go out there. Indeed, it must match my own.' He glanced at her shrewdly. 'More so, if you still hold on to the belief that perhaps your husband may be alive.'

Esther opened her mouth and then shut it firmly against what she had been about to say. She made herself swallow hard before she said, 'Exactly!'

Silently she begged forgiveness for the lie.

The squire spread his hands in a helpless gesture. 'My dear, I really don't think it's a place for ladies . . .'

'But the war is over now. Why don't they come home? Why have we heard nothing?' Deliberately, she allowed him to think she was referring all the time to Matthew, when in her heart she was silently crying the name, 'Jonathan, Jonathan! JONATHAN!'

With quiet determination, she said, 'Squire, please help me. I *have* to go.'

He sighed and looked at her steadily. Esther was sure he could no longer find it in his heart to argue with her. He was determined to go, but knew he would discover only a grave. She could read his thoughts, transparent upon his face. How can I refuse her, when perhaps she seeks the living?

All he did not know was the true identity of the person she sought.

Thirty-four

'*GO* where?' Ma Harris's tone was scandalized. Esther might as well have said she intended to fly to the moon. 'But – but what about yar bairn? And the farm?'

Esther smiled her most winning smile, but before she could utter a word, Ma nodded. 'Oh, I get it. The Harrises'll no doubt help out. Tek care of young Kate and all the livestock! Is that it?'

'Well –' Esther eyed the older woman with a coy look, the smile still twitching at her mouth – 'I was hoping . . .'

Ma's laugh cackled. 'Eeh, but you're a bold one, lass. Is that why you came to get round me again?'

'No, it isn't, Ma. You know me better than that.'

'Aye, I suppose I do at that. We'll help ya.' Then her eyes narrowed as she added perceptively, 'What exactly are ya going for?'

Ma Harris was not as easily deceived as the squire.

For a long moment the two women stared at each other. Esther sighed. 'Ma – please try to understand. I – I have to go.'

'You're going to try and find him – Jonathan – aren't you?'

Esther sat down suddenly at Ma's kitchen table and laid her arms on its scrubbed surface. All her strength, all her resolve ebbed away. She felt her mouth quiver and tears spring to her eyes.

'Oh, Ma, don't be angry with me. Not again, please.'

Ma sat down opposite and patted her hands as they lay, trembling a little, on the table. 'Eh, lass, dun't tek on so. I meant no harm. I didn't mean to upset yar, but I dun't want to see ya hurt . . .' She paused a moment, before adding wisely, 'Or bring more trouble on ya'sen. Ya'd do better to forget all about him and get on with yar life.'

'Oh, Ma, I'm hurting now. I've never stopped hurting since the day he went. I don't know what's happened to him. I've never heard a word of him since he walked down that road away from me.' She flung her arm wide in a vague gesture towards the road leading to the town. 'I've got to know, Ma. I've just got to find out. At least, I must try.'

Ma shook her head sadly, but still held Esther's hands. 'Eh, lass, lass,' was all she could say, but Esther knew by the older woman's tone that whilst she might not condone Esther's intentions, at least she had now forgiven her enough to help her.

'Go where?' Will thundered. 'Are ya daft, girl? What about ya bairn? What about little Katie? Not thinking of draggin' her along with ya, were ya?' It was the first time Will had ever been angry with her.

'No, of course not, Will.' She had never seen him so incensed. He was almost shaking, and his hands, straight down by his sides, were clenching and unclenching.

'Oh, I see, going off an' leaving her, are ya?'

'Ma Harris is going to look after her . . .'

'A fine thing, running off after a feller and leaving your child. Don't try to deny it, girl. I've held me tongue these past months, but I knew what were going on. I didn't like it, but I could feel for ya, aye, I could. But to go off and leave yar child,' he repeated as if he could scarcely believe it possible. 'I thought better of you, Esther.'

'I have to go, Will.'

He flung his hand towards her in a gesture of dismissal almost. 'Aye well, perhaps ya'd better go and get it out yar system.' Then as another thought struck him, his frown deepened. 'You're not going with just the two of them, are ya?'

'Well – yes.' Esther was puzzled. 'You told me yourself, poor Mrs Marshall ain't well . . .'

''Tain't right. 'Tain't fitting for you – a young woman to go off with two men.'

Esther laughed. 'Oh, Will, really! Do you think that bothers me? Besides, from what I've read in all them papers you've kept bringing, in the war women have been doing things they never dreamed of; nursing, working in factories – all sorts of things. I reckon the days of chaperoning have gone – and good riddance, I say!'

'You would,' Will muttered, unable to argue with her. However, he was not going to let her have the last word. He faced her then, his eyes boring deeply into hers. 'Ya'll come back? Ya will come back?'

'I'll come back, Will,' she promised him quietly, but that was the only thing she would concede.

'Huh,' he was muttering almost to himself, 'and to

think it were me that was daft enough to tell you about the squire going out there. I could kick mesen.'

The journey, even in the company of the squire and his younger son, Arthur, was for Esther a nightmare. She had never been anywhere other than the village in the Wolds where she had grown up and Fleethaven Point. Now she found herself being pushed on to a huge steam train that hissed and chugged and puthered smoke. She sat on the seat in the carriage at the side of the squire, her hands clenched around the holdall carrying her few belongings, her eyes tightly shut against the scene flashing past the window.

'Do look at the countryside, my dear. It's very different from our Lincolnshire, but every bit as beautiful.'

Esther took a peep, forcing her eyes beyond the rushing hedgerows to the fields further off, rolling by at a more sedate pace. 'Oh, you're right, Squire. It's lovely. Where are we?'

'We're travelling south towards London. We're in Cambridgeshire now, my dear.'

Esther smiled briefly, but said nothing. She was trying desperately to remember the picture of England divided into its counties in her school atlas, but she could not recall where any other county was except her own. She leaned back against the plush seat. Never mind, she told herself, it's all beautiful, no matter where it is.

When they alighted at the huge, bustling station in London, fear washed over her again. It was a world such as she had never seen before — all metal and brick and stone. Not a blade of grass nor a tree to be seen. The engine gave a roar and belched out a jet of steam. Esther squealed in fright and clung to the squire's arm.

Mr Marshall laughed. 'There, there, my dear. Don't be afraid. We'll take good care of you. Just mind you don't get separated from us, that's all.'

There's no fear of that, Esther thought grimly. I'm hanging on tight to you, mester.

They stayed the night at an inn in Dover, although Esther could not accustom herself to someone else waiting on her. As soon as the maid appeared in her bedroom with a jug of hot water for her to wash, Esther made to take it from her. In the dining room, when the waiter brought her food, she stood up to help him. At the end of the meal she began to clear away the crockery. Blushing, she realized her mistake and sat down again. The squire, noticing her confusion, kindly made no comment, but merely patted her hand and exchanged a word with the waiter, thoughtfully taking the attention away from Esther.

The following morning as they took their leave, she was carefully counting out her coins to pay the landlord, when the squire whispered, 'Put your money away, my dear, the bill is all settled.'

She looked up at him, 'Oh, Squire, you are kind.'

Esther was quite relieved to leave the inn, having felt very out of place.

There was worse to come. The ship crossing the Channel rolled and tossed and Esther was sea-sick. The squire was solicitous, but, she noticed, even he looked a little pale by the time they landed in France. Then, what they saw in this strange land obliterated any memory of the fearsome journey. Their own minor discomforts paled into insignificance compared with the destruction and desolation they now beheld.

How the squire found a means of transport, Esther did not know. It was a dilapidated trap pulled by a scrawny pony, yet better than anything owned by the inhabitants of the towns and villages through which they passed.

The people she saw were hunch-backed with misery. Little groups, whole families with children in tow, seemed to be on the move, pushing all their worldly belongings in carts, going somewhere, but not seeming to know where, or to care. As they passed through villages, Esther realized why. Houses and cottages lay in ruins, some reduced to a mere pile of rubble, whilst others had every window broken, the glass hanging jaggedly from the woodwork. Doors hung drunkenly off their hinges, open to the street and huge holes gaped in the sides of houses. People sat about dejectedly, the spirit pounded out of them by the four years of relentless war being fought all around them. Small children wandered alone, dirty and unkempt, their feet bootless even in the cold of winter. These people had watched their homes being shot to pieces, their land ravaged.

Esther glanced at Squire Marshall and saw there were tears in his eyes. Forgetting, amidst all this horror, their relative positions in life – he the squire and she his tenant – she put her arm through his and squeezed it tightly. Seeking some kind of comfort himself, she felt him grip her hand and hold on to it, whilst they looked around them. They didn't speak, their throats constricted by the sights they saw. Beside them young Arthur sat white-faced and silent.

The pony plodded on slowly, making for the area where the squire had been told some of the biggest battles of the war had been fought, the place where he believed his son had died. The sky was grey with heavy cloud and a fine drizzle clung to their clothes and seeped through making them feel chilled. At last they crested a rise in the ground and there it lay before them, stretching as far as they could see through the mist and the gloom, the land ravaged by years of war.

Wordlessly, the three of them climbed down from the trap and leaving the pony standing, they walked forward, drawn by the awful sight before them, mesmerized by the destruction they were witnessing.

No birds flew overhead, no cattle grazed the land. As far as Esther could see there was not a speck of green. No blade of grass, no living leaf, only thick, greasy mud. Shell-torn trees, blasted limb from limb, struck out grotesquely like burnt sticks. Esther looked down into the trench below where she was standing. In the bottom was at least six inches of murky, stagnant water and the slimy, sloping sides were littered with empty cans, discarded weapons, even items of muddy, torn clothing. A single boot stuck up out of the mud. Everywhere ran the rats. A huge brown one came running down the trench, stopping every now and then to sniff and search. It paused just below Esther and sat up on its haunches, staring up at her boldly. The rats back at home in her barn would have scuttled away at her approach but this monster was tame — frighteningly tame. It dropped down on to all fours and sniffed at the boot then pushed its head into the top and with sharp teeth began tearing at the grey, slimy pulp oozing from the boot.

Esther gave a gasp and clamped her hand over her mouth as the bile rose in her throat. The rat was pulling at rotting human flesh.

She turned away, closing her eyes and her mind against an appalling thought.

Supposing that had been Jonathan's boot. Reason told her not to be foolish. But it had belonged to some young soldier just like Jonathan – some young man whose foot had been blasted away by a shell and left to rot in the trenches.

The trenches ran everywhere, twisting and turning, deep ravines gouged out of the ground, like a gigantic warren where men had lived for months and years. Here they had eaten, slept, laughed and cried with only each other – and the rats – as companions. Here they had died.

A low mist hung a few feet above the ground like a shroud. The smell of death was all around them.

It was as if the reaper of death had laid waste the fields of young corn, destroying not only that harvest, but ravaging the land so completely that there could be no future growth. A generation of young men had been wiped out and with them generations of unborn sons.

She turned and with eyes that were suddenly opened to the world that lay beyond the safety of Fleethaven Point, she looked towards the two men. 'Oh, Squire, oh, Squire!' She shook her head. 'I never thought – never in a million years – did I imagine anything like this.'

The squire blinked his eyes rapidly and pulled a large kerchief from his pocket. He blew his nose noisily. 'Nor I, my dear. Foolish old man that I am . . .' He glanced at his son, standing speechless with shock beside him, and then back to Esther. 'I should have known better than to bring you two young people . . .'

Esther ran to him and grasped his arm. 'Don't say that, Squire. It's – dreadful – awful, but I'm glad I've seen it. Now I understand.'

He looked at her questioningly. 'What do you mean?'

'I was so naïve, so innocent,' she said. 'I thought when that Major Langley was whipping up the young men to follow the call of arms, it was just a game to him, to all of them. I was angry, irritated, that they were going off in a blaze of glory, leaving us to cope as best we might. All that talk of honour and duty and – oh, you know what I mean. But this – this is real. This is what they came for – to stop this happening in our land – in England. All this destruction . . .' she waved her hand to encompass the ravaged land as far as they could see. 'It's just sheer wickedness. And they – our men – came to try and stop it. This land won't be fit to grow anything for years, will it? I mean, what are these poor folk who live here going to do?'

The squire shook his head and gazed about him almost in a trance as if he were overwhelmed by the enormity of the devastation. 'I don't know, my dear, I just don't know.' He paused and then went on more to himself than to the other two with him. 'I had this stupid notion that I should find Rodney's grave on a grassy hillside, a pristine white cross above it, and that I'd be able to lay flowers on it and . . .' His voice broke and Esther, still holding his arm, gave it a comforting squeeze. 'How very foolish I've been,' his voice dropped to a husky whisper.

Esther looked across at Arthur. He had said nothing for a long time. His face was pinched, his lips blue with cold and he was shivering visibly.

'Come, Squire,' Esther said gently, the first of them to recover their senses. 'We'd best find some shelter for the night. Your boy looks about done in.'

'Eh?' Roused from his ghastly reverie, the squire looked at his son. 'Oh, dear me, yes. Come along, let's leave this dreadful place.'

Together they walked back to the tired-looking pony and climbed into the trap. The squire turned the convey-ance round and they made back towards the nearest village.

Along the road they passed a family – a man, wife and three children. The man was pushing a handcart loaded with all their possessions.

'Excuse me.' The squire halted the trap. The man paid no attention but trundled the cart along the side of the road.

'I say – excuse me. Do you know if there are any British soldiers still here?'

The woman glanced up and the children stared at them, wide-eyed with fear.

Nervously, Arthur cleared his throat and asked the same question in his halting, schoolboy French. One of the children – a girl, barefooted and ragged – ran forward and plucked at the man's coat, but the man trudged on. Arthur jumped down from the trap and followed the man a short distance along the road, and though they could no longer hear what was said, it appeared Arthur was still asking questions.

Esther saw the man let go of one of the handles of the cart and gesture briefly to the road behind him, but he neither stopped nor slowed his pace.

Arthur came back to the trap. He climbed in and sat down. 'I think – though I'm not sure,' he added apologetically, 'he said "at the hospital back there".'

'Never mind, my boy. You tried. We'll just keep going.'

As the trap moved on, Esther took a last look at the forlorn little family, homeless in their own country.

It was growing dusk by the time they came to the village. A huge building loomed up before them; impressive, but bleak and dismal. Miraculously, it was still standing, comparatively unscathed. 'That must be the hospital they told us about,' the squire said. 'I'm sure this must be the one where – where Rodney died. That's why I've come here. I thought he might be buried close by.'

'I never knew where Matthew was,' she murmured and added in the secrecy of her own thoughts, or Jonathan. 'They – ' she began and then corrected herself swiftly. 'He – Matthew – was in the same regiment as your son, Squire.' And so, she thought, was Jonathan. 'Do – do you think they might have records of any sort about what happened to people or . . . ?'

The squire was looking at her. 'Do you really think there's a chance that Matthew's still alive?' ·

Esther drew breath – it was the closest she had come to having to tell the squire a deliberate lie. Fixing her mind, for the moment, on her husband and not on Jonathan, she answered, 'It – it was only – presumed.'

'Well,' the squire said slowly, 'I understand there are still some of our men here.'

'Still here?' Esther repeated, sudden hope flaring in her breast. 'In this hospital, you mean? Why? Why haven't they been sent home?'

The squire shrugged. 'Several reasons, I suppose. Some may be too ill to travel yet. Maybe – maybe they don't know who some of them are, if their identification papers were lost. I've heard of that happening.'

'Really?' Esther gazed up at the square, grey building. It looked more like a prison than a hospital. It was a gruesome place. There was such a mixture of feelings within her, a sudden dread of what she might find.

They were made welcome by a nursing sister at the hospital. She displayed surprise, though not displeasure, at their coming and bustled about making ready a narrow bed for Esther in her own quarters. Embarrassed, she said, 'I'm afraid all I can offer you gentlemen will be a bed in a ward.'

'Don't mention it, dear lady. Are you sure you can spare us that? I mean, are you sure we won't be taking up a bed you need for patients? I wouldn't want to do that.'

'Oh we've the room now, sir.' Her eyes were weary and sad and there were shadows beneath them that told of long months of soul-destroying nursing of the wounded, sick and dying. 'We've a few patients left, of course.

394

Those still too ill to make the journey home,' she said, confirming what the squire had already thought. She sighed heavily, 'Of course there are several who are so shell-shocked, they don't know who they are or where they come from. Naturally, we shall repatriate them as soon as we can but . . .' She shook her head. 'Oh, dear me, it's so sad, so very sad.'

Esther's heart leapt and plummeted all in the space of a second. Hope soared and then died. Jonathan might be alive, he might be here. Yet if he were it meant he was so ill that he was scarcely alive.

'Could we – could I see the patients?' She knew there was longing in her voice and desperation in her green eyes as she looked at the sister.

'Well,' the woman said doubtfully, looking Esther up and down. 'Most of them are very ill, you know. Not – not pleasant sights . . .' Then she must have caught some of the pleading in Esther's tone, for she added more gently, 'Are you looking for someone? Is that why you've come?'

Esther swallowed the lump that had risen in her throat, and, not trusting herself to speak, she nodded.

'Ah, well, of course, that makes a difference. Perhaps in the morning . . .'

Esther grasped the woman's wrist. 'Now, please. I beg you . . .' There was no mistaking the urgency in her plea.

The sister nodded. 'Very well,' she said, relenting. 'This way. Please be as quiet as you can.'

Holding a lamp high for them to see their way, she led them along cold, dank passages. Stone walls on either side ran away into the darkness, further than the light showed. Their footsteps echoed eerily on the flags as they passed from room to room, and between the rows of beds on either side. Many were in use, their occupants, lying swathed in bandages, motionless and silent, or tossing restlessly, muttering in delirium. Some sat up in their beds staring fixedly ahead of them, taking no notice of the people who came and went, still trapped in their own world of horror, reliving the nightmare played out in their mind again and again and again.

Esther peered into each face, almost holding her breath each time, then letting it go with a mingled feeling of disappointment and yet relief.

Jonathan, oh, Jonathan. I want to find you, but not here, not like this, not maimed and crippled, or deranged. I want you alive and whole and . . .

She stopped at the foot of one of the beds and the sister, glancing back to see if she were following, came back and held the lantern higher.

The man in the bed was sitting up, rocking backwards and forwards, his head nodding continuously as if he had no control over it. His arms were clasped around his own body, and his eyes stared unseeingly into the darkness. From low in his throat came a whimpering sound, like an animal in pain and suffering.

Esther drew in a breath and held it as she stared at the man in the unsteady light from the flickering lamp. His hair was cropped short to his head and there was a growth of stubble masking the gaunt jawline and yet there was something about him that made her pause instead of moving on.

She saw him become aware of the light, conscious that

there were people standing at the foot of his bed. She saw him blink and run his tongue over swollen lips, saw his gaze flicker and come to rest on her. For a long moment they stared at each other. She saw the frown on his forehead as he struggled to remember.

Then he held out his arms to her, arms that trembled. His voice was a hoarse, pleading whisper, 'I knew you'd come. I've been waiting for you. Take me home. Take me home!'

'Goodness me!' the sister said in a stunned voice. 'That's the first time I've ever heard him speak. We don't know who he is — he had no identification on him and he couldn't tell us — couldn't seem to speak.' She looked at Esther. 'Who is he?'

Esther looked down at him. She was overwhelmed with compassion. In that moment as she stood in this makeshift hospital ward, a dark, cold, damp place, she remembered him as he had been. Once so strong and vibrant, his life had now been destroyed. He was no more than a trembling wreck. In that moment, Esther Hilton passed from girlhood to womanhood. Gone in an instant were all her naïve, immature dreams of happiness, all her hopes for the future. Before her, grim reality stretched down the years and became her future. Loyalty and duty and yes, love, but a very different kind of love, must, of necessity, come before the desires of her own heart.

After a moment's hesitation she put out her own hands and grasped his outstretched, shaking fingers.

With infinite gentleness, she said, 'Yes, my dear. I came to find you. I'll take you home.'

The man's thin shoulders were shaking with racking

sobs and he pulled her hands up to his cracked lips and kissed her fingers.

As she leant towards him, only she heard the name he whispered.

'I've been dreaming about you. Oh, Beth, Beth – thank God you've found me.'

'Is he the man you're looking for?' the sister asked.

'I—' Esther hesitated fractionally, trying to evade answering the woman's question directly, then added, 'I – know him.'

'What's his name, then? Who is he?'

'His – his name is Matthew Hilton. He's my husband.'

Thirty-five

*I*T was a difficult journey home, and without the help of Squire Marshall and his son Arthur, Esther acknowledged she would not have managed. Though the hospital had been thankful to release Matthew into his wife's care, being one less burden on their dwindling resources and supplies, he was by no means fit to travel or to be in the hands of someone without proper medical experience. He seemed constantly to be running a fever. Every limb in his body seemed plagued by shaking fits, whilst his head nodded continuously in a nervous tic.

'Whatever's causing that?' Esther whispered to Squire Marshall.

'I think,' he answered soberly, 'it's what they call shell-shock. The continual sound of gunfire and shells explod-ing all around them for months, years even, finally shat-ters their nerves.'

He shook his head with infinite sadness. 'To think I sent my boy into all that. With such pride – with such damned, stupid, ignorant pride.'

As the squire blew his nose noisily and cleared his throat, Esther patted his arm. Out here amongst all this carnage, she felt the squire's equal in a way she never would back at Fleethaven Point. 'Don't blame ya'sen, Squire. They all wanted to go. He'd still have gone, your lad, whatever you'd said.'

He sighed heavily. 'I suppose you're right, my dear, but it doesn't help me to think that I actively encouraged him to go.' He was silent for a moment, still watching Matthew. With an almost fatherly concern for her, he covered her hand which was still resting upon his arm. 'I'll tell you something else, my dear, that I never thought I'd hear myself say. Looking at poor Matthew here, I'm almost glad my son didn't survive, not if he were to live a life like – like that.'

They watched Matthew's hands fluttering in the air, uncontrolled and without purpose, watched his nodding head and the saliva dribbling from the corner of his mouth.

'Oh, my dear, I don't envy you your task ahead.' He shook his head. 'You may have your husband back, but at what cost?'

What cost indeed – more than the squire could ever know! Esther thought, though she said nothing.

Those thoughts must remain her own.

Once they were home and when Matthew was settled in bed and asleep exhausted by the journey, Esther slipped away to the Spit. Despite her frightening experience at the hands of Martha Willoughby and her sister, Esther still loved the place, still found comfort and solace there. She didn't blame the sea for having almost taken her life – she blamed the people concerned. The Spit was her special place and she wrapped the serenity of it around her like a cloak.

She walked the full length and at the very tip where the water lapped at the edge, she sank down and dug her hands into the shingle and sand, the sharp stones cutting her palms. She didn't notice the pain. She was so thankful to be home, so grateful that her land and this place were still whole and untarnished. She looked about her, drinking in the tranquillity. The sea lapped softly at her feet. Behind her the land stretched smooth and flat towards the pale gold of the wintry sunset.

Young men had died to keep this land – her land – whole. Perhaps one of them had been Jonathan. Tears blurred her vision and spilled over but she let them run down her cheeks unchecked. They were tears of sorrow for what might have been, and now would never be. For a few moments she allowed herself the luxury of self-pity. Never again would she see Jonathan, yet she still prayed that somewhere he was alive and whole, that he had somehow, by some miracle, survived that slaughter.

The memory of that ravaged land would never leave her. If she closed her eyes she could still see all the horror. She had only been there for minutes; how then had it been for the men who had spent four years there, trapped by circumstance and awaiting inevitable death?

No wonder her husband had come home a broken man.

She knew now what she had to do. She knew where her duty lay. Gone were all her romantic hopes and dreams. Before her lay a lifetime of caring for her sick husband, of running the farm single-handed and bringing up her daughter without the love and support of a robust, healthy man in her life.

She prayed as she had never done before. 'Dear Lord, give me the strength. And – please – please – let *him* be alive somewhere. Somewhere in this same world as me, just let Jonathan be alive and well and – and happy.'

If only I could know, she thought, one way or the other, then I could go on. But her reason told her that it was best she did not know, for if she knew that he was somewhere, maybe back home in Lincoln, not all that far away, wouldn't she want to see him, to meet him secretly? The voice of reason told her that cruel though it was, it was best that she did not know what had happened to Jonathan Godfrey.

Now her duty, her loyalty and her compassion lay with the man who was her husband, for all that he did not truly love her any more than she was in love with him. It was Beth he had been dreaming of, Beth's name he had whispered in his befuddled state, confusing his dream world of longing with reality.

Esther had a kind of love for Matthew. He was the father of her child and the maternal spirit that was within her would always hold a place in her heart for the man who had sired her child. And it was she, Esther, he now needed. A broken wreck of a man, it was her from whom he could draw strength. She could not desert him, whatever the desires of her own heart might be.

She could almost hear within her head Ma Harris's words, 'As ye sow, so shall ye reap.' And down the years Beth's shrill cry still echoed, 'Ya'll reap a bitter harvest . . .'

Oh, what a bitter harvest she must now reap.

Esther waited for the solace of tears, but now they would not come. Not any more. Her time for weeping was over. The future stretched before her, bleak and lonely.

With heavy limbs she dragged herself upright and taking one more look at the calm sea and the gentle sky streaked by the setting sun, she turned away and walked back along the Spit towards home.

As she did so, she knew she was turning her back for the last time on all her dreams of love.

They all came to see him. One by one and from all around, those who knew Matthew, hearing the news, came knocking at the door, a joyous smile of welcome upon their lips. But they went away sick at heart, no longer smiling, no longer rejoicing at such a homecoming.

Yet out of every sadness, usually there's some good comes. Esther smiled, thinking of Ma and her sayings. 'It's an ill wind that blows nobody any good.'

All the gossip about Esther and the soldier stopped just as if it had never happened. The community drew in around itself to protect its own. Not one of them would ever tell Matthew how his wife had taken up with a soldier even before she had been told that he, Matthew, was presumed killed. For how could you tell the poor gibbering idiot such a thing? Besides, wasn't she the angel of mercy herself the way she was looking after him now? And the young soldier – what was his name? They couldn't rightly remember – he'd never come back nor by all accounts had he even written to her. For didn't they all know exactly who had cards and letters at the Point? No word had ever come to Mrs Hilton except the telegram and the official letter about Matthew. Esther guessed – and guessed correctly – at what the talk would be over the pints in the Seagull.

Without a word being spoken directly, Esther felt the change towards her, and, most gratifyingly, the last vestige of any lingering animosity between herself and Ma Harris was swept away.

'Eh, lass, Ah said ya'd have to pay, but Ah wouldn't have wished this upon ya. Not in a million years!'

'I know, Ma, I know,' Esther said sadly.

But it was a comfort to have Ma Harris's robust friendship once more.

Three days after they had arrived home, Esther, washing up in the back scullery, heard the shrill sound of Will Benson's whistle in the lane. Three times he blew on it, just as he had on the day the war had ended. Had he heard already that Matthew was home, she wondered, and it was his joyous greeting to someone they had all believed lost?

Will pulled his carrier's cart into the yard and climbed down from his seat, a broad grin on his face. 'Esther, lass, I've got news for you. Wonderful news!'

'Have you, Will? That's nice,' she said, drying her hands on her white apron. Outwardly she appeared calm, but inside her heart was thudding in her chest.

Will was coming towards her, his arms outstretched as if to embrace her, though normally he was an undemonstrative man. 'Wait till you hear what I've . . .' His glance went beyond her, towards the back door of the house. His gaze became fixed, the smile faded from his face and his arms dropped limply to his side. Esther knew why, for behind her she heard the shuffling, unsteady gait of Matthew's footsteps on the cinders of the yard.

Esther stretched a smile upon her mouth. 'We've got news for you, Will,' she said quietly. 'Look who I brought home from France.'

She turned and went towards her husband, taking his arm and gently leading him forwards. 'See, Matthew, here's Will come on one of his visits. He's come all the time, right through the war.'

She leant forwards putting her mouth close to Matthew's nodding head. 'He spoils our Kate summat rotten, given 'alf a chance. Now, come and sit on this seat against the barn wall. Ya can sit a few moments, but not long. It's not warm enough yet to sit out. Come the spring, we'll all feel better.'

Will was still standing in the middle of the yard, just staring at Matthew.

'You taken root there, Will Benson?' Esther forced herself to laugh. 'An' close yar mouth, ya'll be catching flies.' The older man still continued to stand and watch as Esther lowered Matthew tenderly on to the bench seat against the barn wall.

'Mr Marshall sent this across yesterday, from his own walled garden, so his man said. Weren't that kind? He said he thought Matthew would be able to sit in the garden when the weather gets warmer. I've put it here for the time being, as it's more sheltered near the barn. Later on we'll move it near the pond.'

She kept up the bright, inconsequential chatter, but behind her she heard Will murmur hoarsely, 'Lass, eh me

405

lass!' She did not turn round, did not respond to the sympathy in his tone. She dare not, for the lump that rose in her throat threatened tears. She refused to let anyone except Jonathan see her weep.

Her mind latched on to other thoughts. 'What was your news you were so anxious to tell me, Will?'

'Oh, er, yes, that.' He shuffled his feet on the cinders. 'Oh, 'twas nothing really. Just – er – just that I got a better price for your eggs than usual at the market last week.' His voice faded away. 'It – it was nothing – really . . .'

She glanced at him, but his eyes flickered away and would not meet hers. 'Ya'll stay for your dinner, Will, as usual?' she asked quietly, knowing full well that the price of eggs had not been his news. She had never before seen Will Benson so excited about having secured another couple of pence on her eggs. But it was obvious that he was not going to tell her now – not once he had set eyes upon Matthew.

All through dinner, whilst Esther patiently fed Matthew, Will could only look on helplessly. He picked at the food on his own plate, his anguished gaze going from Matthew to Esther's face and back again. Will seemed, time and again, to try to speak, to try to think of something to say. Easy, natural conversation would not come. Esther could sense that he did not know how to handle this new and uncomfortable situation.

'Where's Kate?' Will asked suddenly.

'At school, of course.'

'Oh – oh, yes. I forgot.'

There was silence, then Will whispered, 'Is she – I

mean – how has she . . . ?' His glance flickered towards Matthew.

'All right.'

When Will's expression showed scepticism, Esther added, 'No, really. She's very good. Fetches and carries for him. Almost mothers him.'

'She's – she's not afraid, then?'

'Not a bit. First time she saw him, she just stared at him for a while and then went and fetched a picture she'd drawn at school to show him. Not that he takes a lot of notice, but she chatters away to him. Sometimes he seems to listen – sometimes not.'

Will was silent again.

At last, almost with a sense of relief, he stood up and pushed back his chair. 'I – er – I must be going, Esther lass. Me wife – she's – not well. I dun't want to be late home.'

Esther, a spoonful half-way to Matthew's mouth, said, 'I'm sorry to hear that, Will. Nothing serious, I hope.'

He shuffled his feet. ''Tis this influenza that started last year, Esther. It's the very devil. Two in our village have died of it already.'

'Really. I hadn't heard of it. It dun't seem to have come round here.'

'Well, you'm lucky then.'

'I hope she'll soon be well again, Will.'

'Aye – well – yes, thanks, Esther.'

He still seemed ill-at-ease, more so than could be explained by his awkwardness with Matthew. She glanced up at him, an unspoken question in her eyes. Again Will avoided meeting her gaze.

'Your – your Aunt Hannah's been very good. Came and nursed the wife.'

Esther smiled. 'Then I'm sure she'll soon be well. The 'flu wouldn't dare defy Aunt Hannah!'

Will laughed but shook his head. 'She's been good. Very good. I've not had much time for her in the past, but she's been a godsend to us these last few weeks.'

Esther nodded. 'I know, Will, I know. She's a good woman, I'll not deny that.'

Satisfied with her acknowledgement of her aunt's virtues, Will backed away from the table, taking a last, almost despairing look at Matthew.

'I'll see you next week, lass. 'Bye, Matthew.'

Matthew did not respond.

Esther laid down the spoon she had been using to feed Matthew and stood up. 'I'll come out and see you off.'

'No, lass,' Will said quickly. 'I mean – you stay with Matthew.'

'He'll be fine for a moment or two,' Esther said firmly and followed Will out into the yard.

Standing by the cart as he climbed up on to his seat she said quietly, 'Will – what was your news?'

He sat down on his seat high at the front of his cart and took up the reins. 'I've told you, lass. I got another tuppence on yar eggs.'

'Will – that wouldn't warrant *three* blasts on yar whistle coming down the lane.'

'I'd 'ave thought you'd 'ave been pleased of a bit extra in these hard times,' he snapped and clamped his jaw shut.

'Will, please – tell me . . . ?'

'Esther lass – there's nothing more I can tell you. Now, will ya let me get on me way to the Point or I shan't be home to the wife before dark.'

Reluctantly, she stood back whilst he turned the cart round and left her farmyard. She followed him as far as the gate, leaning on it to watch him go towards the Point.

Will neither looked back nor waved.

There was something – she knew – that he wasn't telling her. And by the stubborn look on his face, he wasn't ever going to tell her either.

Will did not come the next week, or the week after. In all the time she had lived at Fleethaven Point, Esther had not known Will Benson to miss his regular visits, except during the snowy weather. Now he had missed two weeks running. Esther felt concerned for him. Perhaps he had caught this dreadful 'flu from his wife and was too ill to work. Another week went past but no one at the Point knew anything about Will. She was also distressed by his absence because they had parted on heated words. Surely he wouldn't stay away deliberately just because of that? Or was it because he didn't want to face her further questions?

Then Tom Willoughby came home from market with the news.

'His wife's died, Esther. Never recovered from the 'flu, so they say. And Will, he was took bad, though I hear as how he's better now. But with the funeral an' all, he just ain't got back on his rounds yet.'

'Oh, poor Will.' Esther bit her lip, holding back

further comment. Her feelings for Will Benson were her own secret. Gently, Esther told Kate the reason for Will's prolonged absence and the child listened solemnly to the news. With equal gentleness Esther tried to get the news across to Matthew though she wasn't too sure whether he understood. She was unsure too whether word of another death, when he had lived for so long with so much killing and death around him, would make him even worse. There was no outward sign, however, that Matthew even understood. He sat in his chair by the fire, his eyes staring, unseeingly she thought, into the glowing coals. His mind, if it functioned at all, seemed miles away from Fleethaven Point.

Another week had passed when at last she heard the trundling of cart wheels coming down the lane and the carrier's whistle as he rounded the last bend. Esther ran to the gate to meet him. Slowly Will climbed down and she held out her hands to him. 'Oh, Will, I'm so sorry.'

He seemed to have aged several years in the few weeks since she had seen him. He stooped a little more and his hair showed fewer red glints amongst the white.

'Aye, lass, thank'ee. But – but it's not all that's happened.'

'I know you've been ill, too, Will. Are you feeling better now?'

He shrugged and sighed heavily. 'I'm better, aye, but I get tired, very tired.' His eyes met hers. 'It's yar aunt, Esther. She caught the 'flu nursing the wife and me.'

'Aunt Hannah?' Esther's voice was incredulous. She had never known her aunt to have a day's illness. Even giving birth to each one of her large brood had been over and done with in a matter of days.

'It's a natural thing, childbirth, not an illness.' Esther could almost hear her aunt's clipped tones.

'Aye, she's bad – real bad,' Will was saying now.

'And – Uncle George?'

'He had the 'flu a while back. He's fine again and looking after yar aunt. The girls help, of course. The eldest two are away in service now, but Rachael's taken charge.'

'Rachael! But she's only a child, she . . .'

Will was shaking his head. 'She's seventeen, lass. You forget,' he added as Esther gasped in surprise, 'you've been gone nearly nine years.'

Esther nodded slowly. 'So I have, Will, so I have. you're right, I had forgotten just how long it's been. I've been picturing them to be just the same as when I left.

'Well, you've changed, so – why shouldn't they?'

'Yes – of course.'

It was difficult for Esther to imagine how things must be now. How the children she had known were grown up and working and – most difficult of all – that her aunt was now laid low by illness.

'But,' she asked at last, 'they're – managing all right?'

'Aye.' Will was silent for a moment. Then he put his head on one side and said quietly, 'But if you were thinking of paying them a visit, I reckon they'd be pleased.'

Esther shook her head vehemently. 'No, no, Will, I can't. I can't ever go back.'

'Surely you don't still bear a grudge against Hannah?'
Esther turned away and did not answer him.

The following week the news Will brought was even worse. 'She's over the 'flu itself, Esther, but it's brought on some sort of seizure. She just sits in a chair now, lolling to one side. She dun't speak or do anything now.' He shook his head sadly. 'She's a pitiful sight . . .'

He glanced towards Matthew sitting by the range, his hands shaking, his head nodding continuously. Will looked away, but Esther could read his thoughts. The condition of her aunt was much the same as Matthew's, though brought about by a different cause.

'I feel very guilty, Esther,' Will was saying. 'She caught that 'flu coming to help me and the missus. If she hadn't . . .'

'Now, Will, don't be foolish,' Esther told him briskly. 'She'd have caught it some time if not from you.'

'But she nursed George through it and a couple of her own young 'uns. I don't understand it.'

'There's no telling with illness, you know that.'

Will's face was still distressed. 'I've brought trouble on them two sisters an' no mistake,' he murmured.

'What did you say, Will?' Esther prompted, but Will shook himself and said, 'Nothing, lass, nothing at all.'

She took his arm. 'Sit down and 'ave yar dinner, Will.'

He lowered himself into the chair and looked down at the piled plate she put in front of him. 'I dun't know if I can manage all that, lass. I ain't quite mesen for eating yet.'

'Dun't worry,' Esther assured him cheerily. 'What you leave, the pigs won't!'

Over the following weeks Will brought news of her aunt. 'She's better from the 'flu, but she ain't making any more progress. She just sits all day long and George has to dress and undress her. I dun't reckon she'll ever be right again.'

If the news of her aunt was hopeless, at least day by day there were tentative signs that Matthew was improving. Esther's tender and devoted care seemed to be soothing away his shakes. He made no husbandly demands upon her and she was grateful for that, for her thoughts were still with Jonathan. At night when they lay together in bed, she would put her arms around Matthew and pillow his head against her breast, stroking his hair until the shaking stilled and he fell asleep. She would be left staring into the blackness dreaming of bright, sunlit days in a sandy hollow on the beach.

The breakthrough that seemed to set Matthew on the way to recovery came from a most unexpected quarter, and one about which Esther was not altogether happy.

For one day in the early spring, Kate brought Danny Eland home to see her father.

Thirty-six

*T*HE two children stood in front of Matthew sitting on the garden seat against the barn wall and regarded him solemnly.

Esther, coming out of the back door, stopped in surprise and caught her breath as she saw them. Quietly she moved forward to stand a little way to one side of them so that she could observe them, but, unless they turned, they would not see her. She could see all their faces in profile and she saw Matthew staring up at Danny. His head nodded and his hands fluttered helplessly. Slowly a smile spread across the young boy's face, though there was no answering smile on Matthew's.

Esther saw Kate give Danny a sharp nudge in the ribs with her elbow. 'Don't you laugh at him, Danny Eland. Just don't you dare . . .'

The boy turned to look at Kate, their eyes on a level, staring into each other's.

'I weren't. I wouldn't do that, Katie. I was only being friendly-like.' He turned his gaze back towards the pathetic man sitting before them. 'I wouldn't hurt him for the world. He's been hurt enough. He went to war an' I reckon he ought to have a row of medals. You ought to be proud of him, Kate. *I'd* be proud of him if he were *my* father!'

Esther drew in a sharp breath through her teeth and

held it. Then slowly, as she continued to watch, she released her breath. It had been a statement made in childish innocence, but for a moment it had startled her. What was it Ma Harris was always saying? 'Out of the mouths of babes and sucklings!'

At that instant, Kate turned and saw her mother watching them. Esther saw a look of fear flit across her daughter's face, as if she expected to be in trouble for having brought Danny to see her father in this pitiable state.

Esther smiled quickly to show that she was not angry. 'Hello, Danny. You're just the chap I need to give me a hand.'

Kate was not to know of the connection between Danny and Matthew. If Esther had her way, Kate would never know.

The young boy turned to grin up at Esther, puffing out his thin chest importantly.

'I need to carry this garden seat around and put it near the pond,' she explained. 'Now the weather's better, it's a nicer place for Mr Hilton to sit.'

'I'll 'elp you carry it, missus,' Danny said, taking charge. Turning back he leant towards Matthew with a gesture of solicitude that was strangely touching in one so young. Watching, Esther marvelled that the boy, instead of ignoring the sick man and directing his questions to Esther to answer for her husband as so many of the adults had done, actually addressed Matthew.

'Can you stand up, mester? Lean on my shoulder . . .' and as Matthew struggled to his feet, 'that's it, lean on me. Kate, fetch us a chair out of the house for yar dad to sit on whilst we move the bench.'

Kate, ever Danny's willing slave, scuttled off to do his bidding.

Esther stood by as Matthew shuffled across the yard, his hand on the boy's shoulder. She wondered if Matthew had realized who Danny was. It was difficult to guess just how aware he was, for although he made sounds sometimes, since those first words of greeting in the hospital when he had imagined her to be Beth he had not uttered a word. She had no idea if he understood what was being said to him or if he recognized the people around him, even those he had known all his life.

Danny settled Matthew into the chair which Kate had brought out and then, with Esther lifting one end and Danny the other, they carried the bench seat to a place beside the pond.

'There, that's better. Now there's something for you to look at, Matthew. The willow tree and look, there's still a few snowdrops round the pond and soon there'll be the crocuses and daffs.'

'And the ducks,' Danny added, grinning as two ducks waddled towards the pond and splashed into the water. Now the two children stood back looking at Matthew. Slowly, Matthew turned his head and looked directly at them. His gaze, now obviously intent upon them as if he were really seeing them, went from one to the other. His head still moved in that awful nodding tic, yet at the moment it didn't seem quite so bad. A tentative smile flickered on his mouth and his fluttering hands reached towards them.

416

'I think he wants you to go and sit beside him,' Esther said quietly. The two children glanced up at her, as if for permission, and when she nodded, they went and sat on the bench, one either side of him.

Esther watched as Matthew looked down at them, first to one side and then the other. Then she heard a deep sigh escape his lips, as he leant back against the seat. She could almost see his tortured limbs relax and the shaking lessened visibly. Before her eyes she was witnessing the beginning of Matthew's recovery.

She was truthful enough to admit that it was down to Danny Eland.

Once the healing had begun, each day saw an improvement, so much so that on Will's very next visit, he remarked upon the change. 'He looks better, lass. That awful nodding's not so bad and I reckon his hands aren't shaking so much.'

Esther told him what had happened the day Danny had come. 'The lad's come every day since, Will.'

Will eyed her sharply. 'Dun't you mind, Esther?'

She shrugged her shoulders. 'How can I if it's helping Matthew to get better? I'm not *that* spiteful or petty-minded!'

'Does Matthew — er — ever see . . . ?' Will made a gesture with his head towards the Point, towards the Elands' boat home.

'Beth, you mean?' Esther said quietly.

'Aye.'

'To be honest — I don't know. Danny and Kate have started taking him for little walks now. You know, a little further each day. They've got him as far as the pub . . .' she paused and gave a grimace, 'though I'm not sure that's such a good idea,' she added with a tartness in her tone. Then she shrugged, smiled and said, 'Ah well, if it helps, why not?'

'I dun't expect landlord'll let harm come to him — y'know, let him tek too much.'

'No, you're right, of course. Matthew sits outside when it's warm enough and watches the children play on the grassland near the pub and the cottages . . .' She stopped and did not add 'and the Elands' boat'.

There was a triangular piece of grassland which lay between the Seagull and the cottages and on the third side ran the river bank where the boat was moored. From the deck of their boat home the Elands had a clear view of the cottages and the pub and beyond them across the marshes towards the sea.

'Of course, all the fellers come and talk to him,' Esther made herself chatter on. 'They're getting a little less embarrassed now.' She smiled musingly, 'Funny, isn't it, Will, how those two bairns weren't afraid or awkward around him, and yet some of the grown-ups — they couldn't get away fast enough when they first saw him.'

'It was a shock for us to see him in such a state, Esther, remembering how he used to be afore he went to war. A fine strapping lad, brought down like that.' He shook his head in disbelief. 'It's wicked, that's what it is. I must admit,' he added, a little shamefacedly, 'I didn't quite know what to do or say that first time.'

There was silence between them and then Esther, struggling with an inner conflict that she could still not quell, said haltingly, 'How's – how's me aunt, then?'

'No change, lass, no change. George – poor chap – he's wearing himself out.'

Again there was a long pause, then Will said softly, 'Won't you go and see them, lass? Even if only for George's sake. He's always asking after you – has done ever since you left. Won't you go?'

Esther, wrestling with her conscience, pressed her lips together, and shook her head. 'I can't, Will, I just can't.'

Matthew made rapid progress. Soon he could walk unaided. Then, hesitantly at first, he began to speak again. Just one word and then two or three, like a child learning to talk for the first time.

Esther would shake her head, a small smile on her mouth as she watched the three of them together. The two children, one on either side of him, skipping and dancing, chattering, glancing up at him, Kate slipping her hand into his, and Matthew placing his hand on Danny's shoulder, not so much now for support as just in affection. Esther watched and smiled and in her heart she was glad. Glad for Matthew, compassionate enough to rejoice that he had perhaps, after all, some sort of life ahead of him. She was still a little fearful of the closeness between Kate and Danny. Yet what harm could it do while they were so young?

So some of her burden eased, at least some of the physical hardship, now that Matthew did not need quite so much help. Yet the farm work still lay fully on her shoulders. Matthew made no effort to do even the simplest tasks. He just wanted to spend his days with the children, and when they were at school, he would sit by the range or near the pond and gaze into nothingness.

Although Esther gave thanks for Matthew's steady recovery, in her innermost heart Jonathan was never far from her thoughts.

She still slipped away to stand on the end of the Spit, to put her face up to the sky and the wind, to close her eyes and let the peace of the place surround her. This time of solitude she allowed herself was her only way of renewing her strength of purpose. Her iron resolve would not let her do any other than what she had vowed to herself to do; to turn her back on dreams and face reality. She would care for her sick husband and she would not let her longing for Jonathan eat away at her and destroy her. Her pledge renewed, she would turn away from the place where the sea and the sky and the land seemed to meet and once more take up the burden of caring for Matthew and Kate and running the farm single-handed.

With the coming of spring came a surprise for Esther. Suddenly, there were willing hands to help with the late ploughing and the spring sowing. Labourers from neighbouring farms appeared unasked and unheralded, sheepish grins on their faces. 'Thought you could use a hand, missus, just till yar man's well again, like.'

Esther held back the bitter retort that she had desperately needed their help during Matthew's absence, but she knew that the reason they had stayed away towards the end of the war was solely because of her association with Jonathan. Now they had come back and she was far too sensible to turn away their help, however much her prickly pride might have liked to do so. Maybe they had talked it over amongst themselves, or maybe they'd just drifted back automatically now that her husband was home and the soldier gone. She had no way of knowing and she was certainly not going to ask.

Matthew made no effort to help, not even with light jobs that in Esther's opinion he could have managed now. He sat in the spring sunshine or outside the pub on a bench and watched the rest of his little world at work or at play, apparently apathetic, locked in his own private existence.

Then something happened which gave him a new interest. At first Esther was gratified to see a spark of enthusiasm for anything, but as time went on she was to rue the day that the squire brought his brand new motor car down the lane to Brumbys' Farm.

This strange chugging noise came nearer and nearer. Esther, in the process of stabling the horses she had on loan from the squire, had a job to calm the younger one. His eyes dilated with fear and he stamped and whinnied and backed away from his stable as if he thought the sound was coming from in there, and then just as suddenly, as if realizing his stable offered refuge from the noise, he shot forward almost knocking Esther over.

The chugging grew louder and Esther stared up the lane towards the town. Coming round the bend she saw a motor car bowling along the narrow lane and to her surprise turning in at her gate. She stood back against the wall of the cowshed, her hands spread against the brickwork behind her, staring wide-eyed as the vehicle, puthering smoke, came to a juddering halt in front of her. She saw the squire lean forward and then the engine died.

He climbed out of the vehicle. 'Good morning, my dear. I hope you don't mind, I thought I'd take Matthew for a little drive in my new acquisition. I thought it might – well, you know – perk him up a bit.'

Esther glanced towards the seat near the pond and saw that Matthew had already risen and was moving, with that peculiar, shambling gait, towards the motor car.

'That was kind of you, Squire,' Esther said.

Matthew was now standing near the motor car, his gaze roaming over it, his hands reaching out to touch the shiny metal.

'If you'll excuse me, Squire,' Esther murmured.

'Surely, my dear, surely. You have no objections to Matthew taking a spin with me?'

'Of course not, Squire, it's very kind of you to think of him,' she repeated. And it was. It was kind of him and unusual for a man in the squire's position to concern himself so with Matthew's welfare. Perhaps, Esther thought intuitively, looking after another victim of the war is helping to ease the loss of his own son.

From the pantry she heard the car start up again and winced as the loud throbbing once more shattered the peace. Gradually the sound died away as the squire drove down the lane towards the town.

There he goes, she thought of Matthew not without a little bitterness, her lips pursing in disapproval. Gallivanting off with the squire, riding in a grand motor car and not even trying to lift a finger to do a few simple jobs. She sat down suddenly on the cold slab of the gantry.

'Esther Hilton,' she said aloud to the empty house. 'You'll become bitter and sharp-tongued just like your Aunt Hannah if you dun't watch yourself!'

She remained sitting where she was for some time, finding herself in a strangely pensive mood. Maybe, she thought reflectively, it had been the responsibility of her family and the sheer drudgery of her life in caring for them that had made her aunt as she had been. For, despite the fact that her uncle had been a gentle, good-natured lump of a man, Esther could see now that he had never taken responsibility upon himself. He had worked hard but it had been her aunt who had made decisions, she who had carried the burden of bringing up the family.

Maybe I'm more like her than I care to admit, Esther thought ruefully, and tried to imagine what her aunt must be like now, struck down by a paralysing seizure. And her uncle, how would he cope? Hannah had ruled her family and organized their daily routine. Without her hand on the plough, the furrows of their lives would be crooked and uneven.

Again Esther wrestled with her conscience, but still the festering resentment clouded her vision and her emotions. She could not forget – nor yet forgive – the sharp tongue and the feel of the rough hand. Never a word of affection or encouragement had come her way.

The cold of the stone gantry struck through her clothing and reminded her that she had been sitting idling away her time. What would Aunt Hannah have said to that? she thought wryly. As she pulled herself upright and went about her work her feeling of guilt could not so easily be dismissed.

Not yet, I can't go yet, she answered her nagging conscience. Maybe one day . . .

When the squire left Matthew at the farm gate and drove away, Esther came out of the back door to see her husband standing staring after the receding vehicle. Drying her hands on her apron she moved towards him across the yard. 'Well, did you enjoy that?'

When he turned to look at her, she could see that his eyes were shining. He pointed with fingers that no longer shook, after the car. 'It's a Ford, the latest model,' he told her and there was no denying the excitement in his voice. And, Esther realized with a shock, he had put together a proper sentence for the first time since he had come home.

'Very nice,' Esther agreed, forcing herself to be thankful for the obvious pleasure the ride had given Matthew, and for its undoubted beneficial effect. She pushed away uncharitable thoughts of how she carried the burden of the farm work alone. How strange it was, she thought, that such a simple thing could lift him out of his despondency and bring about such an immediate improvement.

The squire came every Friday to take Matthew into the town to the market. The first week, Matthew just got up from the bench seat by the pond and climbed into the vehicle and off they went, but the second week, Esther found him in the bedroom pulling on his Sunday best suit. She opened her mouth to say sharply, 'And where do you think you're off to in that, m'lad?' then pursed her mouth against the sharp rebuke. Aunt Hannah was surfacing again, she reminded herself. Her fleeting resentment against his 'gallivanting', as she termed it within her own mind, died when she saw how unshapely his best suit was now. It hung on his emaciated, stooping frame, a pathetic reminder of his suffering and a reprimand to her uncharitableness.

'Why, you 'aven't fastened your collar stud, Matthew. Here, let me.'

'It's – stiff,' Matthew murmured, but Esther knew his fingers, still without strength, could not cope with fastening the collar on to his shirt.

'It's me starching,' she laughed. 'I always get yar collars too stiff. Now put yar jacket on.'

She held it for him whilst he struggled to put his arms into the sleeves. Then she stood back to look at him. 'Let me brush it down for you. It's a long time since you've worn this. I hope the moths haven't got at it.'

Matthew stood meekly whilst she flicked the clothes brush over his shoulders and down his back. 'There now, that's better.'

She stood watching them go until the car disappeared around the bend in the lane, listening while the chugging grew fainter.

Esther was preparing supper in the scullery by the time she heard the chugging sound of the motor car coming nearer and nearer. Outside it was almost dusk and Kate had been in bed over two hours.

Esther glanced at the clock on the mantelshelf above

the range. Almost nine o'clock. Where on earth had they been until this time? She heard the car stop at the gate, and watching from the small scullery window, she saw Matthew climb out and lurch unsteadily towards the gatepost and lean against it. The car reversed into the gateway and then, with a grating of gears, it swung out again and up the lane towards the road leading off to the Grange.

Esther opened the back door. Matthew was still standing clutching the gatepost as if he needed its support to keep him upright.

Esther clicked her tongue in exasperation and walked towards him across the yard. He was lolling against the post, his arms wrapped around it and as she drew near, she realized just why. Even from a few feet away she could smell the ale on him!

She pursed her mouth. Now she knew why the squire had driven off so quickly. He had not wanted to face her anger.

She sighed heavily. What's the use, she thought. He's in no fit state to understand anything I say. Aloud she said, unable to keep the sharpness from her tone, 'Come on with you. Let's get you to bed.'

In his drunken state, the nodding and the shaking had returned. The squire might be trying to help, Esther thought grimly, but he was doing Matthew no favours at all by getting him like this. No favours at all.

Nor her either.

Thirty-seven

*T*HE Friday jaunts into town with the squire continued and there was nothing Esther could do to prevent them – though she tried.

'You're doing yourself no good, Matthew,' she railed at him. 'The drink makes you bad again.'

'Shut up,' Matthew growled, struggling to fasten his collar, too angry and proud to ask for her assistance. 'Ain't I – a right – after what I've been through?'

'You're getting so much better – when you don't drink.'

He raised his hand and swung round as if to strike her. It was a long time since anyone had hit her, yet Esther stood her ground. Quietly, she said, 'Aye, go on then. Hit me if it makes you feel better. If it makes ya feel a man again.'

She knew the words were cruel, after all he had been through, yet she had to try to make him see sense.

Before her, Matthew swayed, his arm dropping uselessly to his side. There was no strength in him now to deal her any kind of a blow.

The gesture had been a futile one and they both knew it.

A bright spring turned into a warm summer and with each day Matthew improved – at least in some ways. He still refused to do anything remotely connected with work and spent his days between the two children, the Seagull and the squire and his contraption, as Esther called it.

He would sit outside the pub in the early evening and watch the children playing on the stretch of grass. Esther found this out because almost every evening she was obliged to go and stand on the Hump and shout her daughter home for bed.

'Why dun't you come when you know it's your bedtime? I won't let you go playing up at the Point again if you're not going to come home on time,' Esther said, almost dragging the reluctant child home.

'Aw, Mam, but I'm looking after me dad.'

'Danny Eland, more like,' Esther muttered to herself. Her daughter's sharp hearing had caught the name.

'Yes, he looks after me dad an' all. He likes me dad, does Danny.'

Esther's mouth became a thin line as she compressed her lips together to prevent the words tumbling from them. Of course he likes your dad, she wanted to shout. He's his dad an' all!

But the words remained unspoken; they were words that must never be spoken – at least not to Kate.

Aloud she said, 'Yar dad can look after himself now.' Her tone was laced with a bitterness she could not prevent.

'He still dun't walk properly sometimes, Mam.'

'Huh,' Esther gave a disapproving grunt, opened her mouth to explain and then closed it again. Inwardly she sighed. How could she tell Kate that Matthew's

428

unsteadiness was caused not by his illness now, but by drink?

The child must have felt her mother's controlled anger for she said no more and walked meekly beside Esther.

Each evening Kate slipped away to play with the Harris children and Danny Eland and however much Esther upbraided her, she could not stop her daughter, short of locking her up somewhere.

So time after time Esther had to leave her work and climb the Hump and shout to Kate. Then one evening as she crested the rise in the lane and stood on top of it, she saw the children playing on the grass near the cottages and her husband sitting on a bench seat outside the pub. Standing motionless on the deck of her boat home, looking down on the scene below her, was Beth Eland. Esther swivelled her glance to look at Matthew and saw that his face was upturned and his gaze was fixed upon Beth. Below, on the grass, quite oblivious of the grown-ups, Danny bowled a ball to Kate who hit it high in the air, shrieking with laughter.

'Catch it, Enid, oh, catch it!'

Esther turned away and, unobserved, returned to the farm. For once she would let Kate come home of her own accord.

Back in her kitchen, Esther set the kettle on the hob and sat down at the table. For a long time she just sat there, staring out of the window that faced out over the front garden and across the flat land she now farmed. Her gaze was unseeing, for before her mind's eye was the poignant picture of Matthew and Beth.

There was a dull ache of loneliness inside her, but the

release of tears would not come. It was a pain — like Matthew's and Beth's — too deep for tears.

When at last Kate came home, Matthew was with her, leaning heavily on the child's shoulder. Esther, busying herself in the pantry, stayed out of the kitchen until she had heard Kate scuttle quickly upstairs to her bed. When she stepped into the kitchen it was to find her husband sitting in the wooden chair at the side of the range, his head lolling back. His mouth wide open, he was snoring noisily.

The summer was well advanced. The hay was gathered and the corn ripening. Soon they would have to think about the next harvest, Esther thought, and her mind fluttered back to the harvest when Jonathan had been here. Working all day side by side in the fields and then lying together in the soft hay . . .

Esther wandered through her fields of corn, splitting open an ear of wheat here and there. Almost ready, but not quite. She heard the rattle of cart wheels in the lane and glanced up in surprise. Today was not one of Will's days for a call. As she shaded her eyes against the glare she could see that it was Will's carrier cart right enough, but he had not blown his whistle to announce his arrival.

He saw her in the field and waved. She returned his greeting and went towards the gate where he pulled the cart to a halt. He climbed down stiffly and leant over the gate waiting for her to reach him.

She smiled a greeting. 'This is a nice surprise, Will. What brings you out here today?'

There was no answering smile on his face. 'Esther lass,'

he said at once. 'It's yar aunt. She passed away last night.'

Esther laid her hands upon the gate, feeling the rough wood beneath her palms. She could think of nothing to say.

'Yar uncle wanted me to come and tell you. He asked me specially to ask you to come to the funeral . . .'

Esther drew in a sharp breath.

'He asked me special-like,' Will insisted, and Esther found her eyes held by his intense gaze. Softly, he said, 'Ya'll not refuse yar uncle, lass, will ya?'

Slowly, almost against her will, Esther found herself shaking her head. For a moment a look of anger flitted across Will's face, but as she said, haltingly, 'No, no, Will, I'll not refuse him, this time,' his anger died and he covered her hand with his own as it lay on the gate.

'I knew you'd not let me down, lass. I knew it.'

They stood a few moments like that until Will seemed to rouse himself and opened the gate for her to pass out into the lane. Briskly now he made the arrangements, and Esther found herself with no chance to withdraw her promise.

'I'll come for you early on Friday morning and bring you back again when it's all over.'

'But Will, it's one of your busiest days, a Friday . . .'

'I'll work the Sunday, then. The Lord'll not mind for once.'

Esther felt the corner of her mouth twitch. There was no arguing with Will when he was in a determined mood.

*

431

Dawn on the Friday morning found Esther climbing up on to the seat of the carrier's cart beside Will. She was dressed in a new black costume, with a neat black hat to complete the outfit.

'Eh, lass, if it weren't the wrong thing to say on such a sad occasion, I'd tell you that you look right bonny!'

Esther had bought the outfit the previous day on a rare visit to the town. She had pondered long and hard, biting her lip in indecision, counting her savings coin by coin, trying to justify the expense. She still kept her money in the box Sam had left under the bed. Over the years, little by little, she had added to the hoard. Every penny had been hard earned, every coin represented a tiny achievement on her part. She had scrimped on new clothes for herself, making do and mending, as Ma Harris put it. As for Kate's dresses, Esther made most of them herself, sitting up far into the night stitching tiny neat seams by hand as her aunt had taught her until her eyes ached in the flickering lamplight.

There was quite a sum now and it gave Esther a feeling of security.

Now, as if in honour of the woman who, Esther was obliged to acknowledge, had taught her all the practical capabilities she possessed, she had spent a small part of her savings on a mourning outfit to attend her aunt's funeral.

'I ain't never spent any of this money – not even when we bought the 'osses,' she told Matthew as she pushed the box back under the bed. 'I've been saving it all these years. Even when it were tough in the war, I managed not to dip into it. I want to hang on to it just in case we gets a bad harvest, or – or . . .'

Matthew was sitting on the edge of the bed to pull his boots on. 'For that rainy day, eh, Esther? Dun't feel you have to – explain it to me,' he added and then hesitated, as if feeling suddenly awkward. 'If anyone deserves a new dress – I reckon it's you.' He paused again as he still did when striving to put sentences together. 'Pity it's got to be black though.'

Esther rose from crouching down to shove the box back into its hiding place, and stood looking down at him. He was a strange mixture of moods and temper, this husband of hers, and it wasn't all down to the shell-shock either.

One moment he was laughing and jovial, swinging Kate up into his arms now that daily he was growing stronger, or kicking a ball about with Danny and the next he would be growling in anger, raging against the unfairness of his life as he saw it. His mood swings were like the see-saw that Kate and Danny had made in the meadow across the fallen trunk of a tree.

Still Matthew made no effort to work. Today though, Esther had deliberately asked him to try to do the milk-ing for her. 'Enid'll be over later, but try, Matthew, won't you?'

He had held out his hands to her, spreading his fingers wide, frowning down at them. 'How can I – with this shaking?' he had asked her morosely.

She had sighed and bitten back the retort that sprang to her lips. She had the sneaking feeling that Matthew often played upon his disabilities now; that he wasn't really as bad as he still liked to make out when it suited him. His hands didn't shake when he climbed into the squire's car and bowled away to the town to get drunk, she thought resentfully.

'You'm quiet, lass.' Will's voice broke into her thoughts now and she turned to give him a quick smile.

'You've no need to feel – well – awk'ard, Esther,' Will went on. 'Yar Uncle George is looking forward to seeing you again.' She felt Will take a sly look sideways at her and knew he could not resist adding, 'Pity it's taken this to mek you go back to visit.'

Esther said nothing.

Thirty-eight

AS Esther climbed down from Will's cart in the yard of the low cottage that had been her home for the first sixteen years of her life, time seemed to spin around her. It was all so familiar and yet at the same time so strange.

Little about the place had altered, except the people. When the door opened and Esther found herself staring into the eyes of her uncle, she scarcely recognized him. The huge bulk of the man she remembered seemed to have shrunk away. His clothes hung loosely on his thin frame, and he stooped now, his shoulders hunched. His face, the skin yellow and wrinkled, was drawn and care-worn. It seemed he did not recognize her either for it was not until she said tentatively, 'Uncle? Uncle George?' that his expression lightened and tears welled in his faded eyes.

'Esther, oh, Esther. How – how you've changed. Come in, come in. The children are all in the parlour.'

Esther followed him through the kitchen she remembered so well. Here she had stood on a stool at the sink to wash the dishes. Here she had blackleaded the range and polished the brass fender. These rugs were the ones she had shaken each week and the red stone flags were the same she had scrubbed. And all the time her aunt had scolded her. She could almost hear her Aunt Hannah's shrill voice now in this room.

Esther shuddered. She glanced at the empty wooden chair by the range. Her aunt's crocheted shawl lay across the back, and in front of it was the hassock where she had rested her feet. Esther looked away and followed her uncle into the best parlour.

He held open the door for her and as she stepped into the room, her resolve faltered and she put her hand on the door jamb for support.

The furniture which Hannah had polished lovingly herself every week, allowing no other hand to touch her best possessions, had been pushed back against the wall. In the centre of the room on two trestles lay the coffin with a posy of wild flowers upon it.

Esther drew breath sharply. She had not expected that her aunt would still be lying in the house.

She blinked and dragged her gaze away from the wooden box with its brass handles and glanced towards the family who stood in a semi-circle around the coffin.

Esther experienced another shock. Instead of the seven little faces of her cousins as she remembered them, there were five grown-ups to greet her. Well, almost, for only Ellen at thirteen seemed still a child. Two were missing, but now was not the moment to ask. Surely Will would have told her if . . . Then she remembered. Will had said the eldest were away in service. Surely, she thought, they would have been allowed to come home for their mother's funeral?

Her uncle's voice interrupted her thoughts. 'Here's your cousin Esther. You remember Esther, dun't you?'

George was saying. Four heads nodded but the youngest girl merely stared at Esther, her eyes large in a pale, pinched face.

There was an embarrassed silence. No one seemed to know what they were expected to say. They stared at her and suddenly Esther felt shy in her finery. She felt out of place as she noticed Hannah's own family were dressed in their Sunday best clothes, a black armband the only sign of their mourning.

She felt the flush of embarrassment creep up her neck. She was overdressed, as if she had put on a lavish display of prosperity, when in truth all her wealth – her very little wealth – had come from Sam Brumby or her own hard work. As if to add to her chagrin – though unwittingly trying to compliment her – George said, 'Doesn't your cousin look fine? You look real handsome, Esther. Your aunt – ' he made an almost reverent gesture towards the coffin – 'would be proud of you, wouldn't she?'

The poor man, trying to do his best to ease a difficult situation, was turning to his family for support, for their approval of their cousin.

It was not forthcoming.

Rachael, the eldest present, pursed her lips and tossed her head. It was the gesture of disapproval that Esther had so often seen her aunt give. In an instant the years fell away and for a moment she was again the young girl at her aunt's bidding, the bastard niece in Hannah's household under sufferance.

She was no longer that child, Esther reminded herself. She was a young woman, a married woman, with a farm of her own, a husband – such as he was – and a child. Esther's head came higher and her chin jutted forward. She had no need now to cower before their disapproval. She opened her mouth but at that moment, out of the corner of her eye, she caught sight of the pain and sadness on her uncle's ageing face. She closed her mouth, bit back the sharp rejoinder and smiled tenderly at him.

'Thank you, Uncle,' she found herself saying instead, and nodded to her cousins, before sitting down on the chair her uncle held out for her.

Will Benson, following her into the room, came and stood behind her chair. They waited in silence, the awkwardness in the room growing with every minute. No one had anything to say. There was so much they could have said, and yet so little. Hannah, even from her coffin, seemed to dominate the gathering.

It seemed an age that they remained in that small, stuffy room, everyone nervously on edge, awaiting the arrival of the undertakers. A sigh of relief wafted through the parlour when there was a knock at the door and the village carpenter, dressed in his funereal garb, entered the room, and he and George carried the coffin out and on to the cart waiting in the yard.

The family, with Esther and Will bringing up the rear, fell into procession behind the cart. Last as always, Esther thought wryly, and most definitely least in Hannah's estimation, even at her funeral.

After the service in the village church and the committal in the churchyard, Esther found herself alone for a few moments whilst George shook hands with all the villagers who had attended the funeral. His children

438

stood dutifully in line beside him to receive the condolences of their neighbours, but Esther felt she had no place there now.

She wandered amongst the gravestones, reading the inscriptions, recognizing some of the names of the elderly of the village she remembered from her childhood. Some of the not so elderly too, for death was no respecter of age. Not all were allowed their three score years and ten. Even her mother . . .

Esther's footsteps had brought her to that part of the churchyard where she knew her mother lay in an unmarked grave.

'I've no money to spare for fancy gravestones, not for the likes of your mother, girl . . .' Aunt Hannah's voice echoed from the past.

Esther stopped in surprise. In the place she knew to be her mother's grave, there was now a small, white marble headstone, simple yet quite beautiful in its simplicity.

She bent closer and read: 'In loving memory of Constance Everatt who fell asleep 9th June 1893, aged nineteen years. The Lord giveth and the Lord taketh away.'

So, Esther wondered, had her aunt relented? If so, it was only in recent years since she herself had left.

She stood up and looked about her. Next to her mother's grave there was an empty space, the ground flat, the turf unturned. But beyond that there was a mound of recently dug earth, on which lay a fresh bunch of flowers. At the head of the grave was a headstone which matched the one on her mother's grave. A simple, white marble stone.

'In loving memory of Rebecca Benson, beloved wife of William Benson, departed this life 30th March 1919, aged 62 years. Her reward is in Heaven.'

Esther stood back and looked at the two identical headstones. First at one and then at the other. A small gasp escaped her lips. Had Will really had the nerve to . . . ?

A voice spoke behind her. 'So you've found them then?'

Esther swung round to see him standing there.

They stared at each other. Silently Esther pointed, first at the stone on her mother's grave then at his wife's. 'Will, you didn't?'

Will Benson grinned, a wicked glint in his eye. 'Oh, but I did, Esther lass, I did. No one would have put up a stone to yar mam, if I hadn't. I bought these two plots at the side of yar mother after she was buried.' His voice dropped. 'God rest her.' He paused and then nodded at the empty space between the two graves. 'That's my spot when I go, Esther lass.'

He looked at her keenly then. 'Can I rely on you to see to it, lass? To see I'm put where I want to be . . . ?'

'Will, dun't talk so, I . . .'

'Promise me, Esther. I mean it.' His tone was insistent – and serious.

For a long moment, Esther gazed into his eyes. She knew, beyond doubt now, just what her relationship to this man was, and yet even now he would not say the words she longed to hear.

She sighed. Even so, he was asking her to undertake

something which was important to him. It was better than nothing, she supposed.

She nodded. 'I promise . . .' she said, biting back the name she so longed to call him but did not dare. It was strange, she thought, here he was almost proclaiming to the world his affection for her mother, and yet still he would not acknowledge his relationship to Connie's daughter.

What if she, Esther, had been wrong all this time? What if, as her aunt had always implied, her mother had really been that cruel name they had called her and had not known which one of several men had fathered her daughter?

No, no, Esther's heart cried within her. She wouldn't believe it – not of her own mother. She glanced down for one last time at the spot where her mother lay. Poor Connie Everatt, whose only sin had been to love too much. And wasn't she, her daughter Esther, now guilty of that same sin for loving Jonathan Godfrey so passionately? Her mother had paid for her sins with her life, a life cut short. Esther, too, was paying, trapped by duty to her husband.

She turned away and saw that her uncle was beckoning to them to rejoin the family as the villagers drifted away. 'You'll come back to the house, Esther – Will, for a bite afore you go?'

'It's very kind of you, Uncle,' Esther began, 'but we should be getting along . . .'

'Oh, you must come back, even if only for a moment,' said her uncle, catching hold of her hand. 'I have something for you.'

'Something for — for me?'

He was nodding eagerly. 'Yes, you must have it. Hannah was always most insistent that she wanted you to have it.'

'Aunt Hannah? Me?' Now she could not keep the surprise from her tone. She felt Will's warning grip on her elbow from behind and said no more, merely nodding agreement.

They walked down the village street back to the cottage, George and Will one either side of Esther, the others a little way behind, whispering together.

'Come in, come in,' George fussed. 'Rachael, make the tea, girl. We can't let Esther travel all that way back without a cup o' tea.'

Esther smiled inwardly. When she had left this house the last time, there had been no one to bid her goodbye, to make her a farewell cup of tea. No one had seen her go, or seemed to care about her going.

Her uncle was delving into the far corner of the kitchen, picking up a heavy oblong shape and bringing it to the table.

With a gasp, Esther recognized it. Her gaze met her uncle's eyes. He nodded, smiling in answer to the unspoken question. 'Yes, it's yar aunt's sewing machine. Her pride and joy. She wanted you to have it.'

'Oh, Uncle — no! You must be mistaken. Aunt Hannah wouldn't have wanted *me* to have her sewing machine.' The words were out of her mouth before she stopped to think. Her uncle did not seem to take offence, instead he merely said, 'She did, Esther lass, really she did. Ask our Rachael, if you dun't believe me.'

442

Esther glanced briefly over his shoulder to look at her cousin. The glowering expression on the girl's face and the pursed lips were enough to tell Esther that her uncle was indeed speaking the truth.

He was smiling fondly and shaking his head, running his hand over the smooth wood of the lid of the machine. 'She used to say – after you'd gone, Esther – "She's to have my sewing machine, George, you hear me?" And I'd nod and say, "I hear you, love, I hear you." But I never – ' his voice broke a little but he carried on – 'never thought she'd go afore me, Esther.'

Now Esther, feeling embarrassed by the generous gift, leaned forward and spoke softly. 'What about her own daughters, Uncle? Surely . . . ?'

Now he was laughing openly. 'She always said they were all thumbs when it came to sewing. "Esther's the only one with my gift for needlework and dressmaking," she used to say. Oh, she meant for you to have it, Esther, and no mistake.'

Esther sighed and stood back, looking down at the machine. With tentative fingers, she too reached out and touched the wooden lid. She looked up again at her uncle. 'Then, if you're sure, thank you, Uncle George. I'm real glad to have it.'

As Will's cart rattled its way back to Fleethaven Point, she heard him chuckling softly to himself.

'She's heaping coals on yar head still from the grave, Esther lass,' Will said.

Even Esther had to smile.

Thirty-nine

W *HEN* Will Benson pulled his carrier's cart into the yard and Esther climbed down, she thought at once that the farm seemed unnaturally quiet. No sound of children's laughter, even though by now Kate should have been home from school. There was no sign of Matthew, nor sounds of the cows being milked in the byre.

Esther clicked her tongue against her teeth in exasperation. She went to the cowshed and swung back the door. The building was empty. Esther frowned. Had Matthew done the milking early and gone down to the Seagull already?

She went to the end of the barn. There in the meadow the cows were clustered near the gate dolefully watching for someone to come and open it and bring them to the farmyard. Even from this distance, Esther could see their unmilked udders bursting for relief. A pitiful lowing reached her ears.

'Where on earth is he?' Esther muttered crossly to herself.

'What is it, lass?' Will was shouting, lifting down the sewing machine and carrying it into the kitchen. 'Is owt amiss?'

Esther marched back across the yard and followed him

into the house, pulling off her gloves and struggling to unpin her hat as she went.

'Matthew's not done the milking. I'll 'ave to get them cows in, Will, but make ya'sen a cup of tea afore you set off back. And Will . . .'

'Aye, lass?'

'Thanks – thanks for everything, for – for taking me and bringing me back – and that . . .'

Will grinned. 'I could have wished to have taken you on a happier jaunt, lass, but I'm glad you went. For George's sake and, if it comes to that, for your own. Though you might not think it now, I reckon in years to come, you'll be glad you went.'

'Aye well, mebbe . . . I – I must get on, Will.' With that she hurried upstairs to change into her working clothes.

Opening the door and stepping into her bedroom, Esther stopped, her hand still on the latch, her mouth wide in a shocked gasp, but eyes staring in disbelief. Then a sudden spurt of intense anger flooded through her.

On the patchwork counterpane of the double bed lay the wooden box – Sam's wooden box – which held the money she had found after his death. His hoard of savings which had then become hers and to which she had added, coin by coin, by scrimping and saving over the years through her own hard work. All the money she had in the world had been in that box.

Now the box lay open on the bed – empty.

She leant forward and grasped the box, flinging it to

one side, then she dropped to her knees and scrabbled under the bed.

The money was gone.

'Will,' she screeched, 'WILL!'

She stood up again just staring down at the empty box lying open on the bed.

She heard Will come to the bottom of the stairs. 'Esther lass, what is it? What's the matter?'

'Here, Will, come up here!'

'Aw, lass, it's not Matthew, is it?' she heard him say, as he pulled himself up the narrow, steep stairs. As he came through the doorway of the bedroom, she glanced up at him to see his face lined with worry and anxiety at what he was to find.

'My money, Will, all my money's gone. Stolen!' She made a futile gesture towards the box. 'It was in that box – the one Sam left under the bed. Someone's been here and – and found it.'

'Good Lord!' Will muttered.

'Who'd so such a thing, Will? Who round here would—?' Her eyes widened as she whispered, 'I bet it's Martha Willoughby and that sister of hers. They're the only ones who—'

'Now steady on, lass, steady on. You can't go accusing people like that. You'll get ya'sen into trouble. They'd not steal, Esther lass, not them. I know they ain't no time for you, but nay, they wouldn't do that.'

She bit back the retort, 'Aye but they tried to drown me once,' for Will knew nothing of that.

The fight went out of her and she sank down on the bed. 'Then who . . . ?'

Will shuffled his feet awkwardly and murmured, 'Esther, lass, where's Matthew?'

Slowly, Esther lifted her eyes to meet Will's unhappy gaze.

'Oh, Will, no . . .' she began, then she remembered. Only three days ago Matthew had eyed the money in the box as she took out a few precious coins to buy herself a mourning dress for her Aunt Hannah.

Surely, surely he would not . . . ?

'Oh, Will, no!' she moaned again, and let her head fall forward.

By the time she had done the milking and Will was long gone, there was still no sign of Matthew or of Kate, though Esther had a shrewd idea her daughter would be at the Harrises.

She went to the gate of the farmyard and stood looking up the lane towards the town, watching through the gathering dusk, her mouth set in a grim hard line. The lane was silent and empty.

She sighed and set off towards the Point to fetch Kate home to bed.

'There you are then, lass,' Ma Harris's kindly round face greeted her. 'Kate's with the bairns. They've gone shrimping in the pools on the beach. Our Enid's with 'em, they'll come to no harm. I know it's past the young un's bedtime, but I thought you wouldn't mind this once.'

Esther nodded and, suddenly weary, sat herself down at Ma's scrubbed kitchen table and dropped her head into her hands.

'Not been an easy day for you, I 'spect,' Ma said gently, and the sympathetic tone threatened to overwhelm Esther.

She felt the tears prickle and a lump come into her throat. 'Oh Ma. It's just – everything.'

'I know, lass, I know.' Ma's fat hand patted Esther's shoulder. 'Funerals aren't easy at the best of times, and, well, if you ain't seen yar family – for whatever reason – for a long time, then there's bound to be – well, awkwardness.'

Esther raised her head and looked up at Ma. How strangely perceptive and wise this simple country woman was, Esther thought. 'She left me her sewing machine, Ma. Me aunt left me her precious sewing machine.' Esther shook her head, still uncomprehending.

'She must have thought summat about ya, then, lass.'

'To be honest, I can't take it in yet.' Esther sighed heavily and added, 'Then when I get back home, Matthew's gone . . .'

'Oh, he'll be all right, Esther lass. He went off this afternoon as usual with the squire.'

'Of course,' Esther murmured, 'I'd forgotten,' and added cynically, 'It's Friday and nothing – not even doing the milking while I go to me aunt's funeral – must stand in the way of his Friday jaunts into town with the squire!'

'Eh, lass, ain't the milkin' been done?'

'It has now, Ma,' Esther replied grimly.

'I'm sorry, if we'd known, we could have . . .'

'No, Ma, it's not right. Matthew's quite capable now of doing a bit of milking. He does little enough . . .'

'Aw but, Esther, he's a sick man.'

'Not too sick to go jaunting into town – spending money!' she finished bitterly.

Ma shook her head. 'Dun't be too hard on him. He's had such a dreadful time,' Ma pleaded his cause.

Esther opened her mouth to tell Ma Harris about her missing savings and then decided against it. She probably wouldn't believe it of Matthew.

But Esther did.

It was almost midnight and Esther was still sitting before the dying embers in the range, a shawl huddled about her shoulders, her anger keeping her weary body wide awake and rigidly upright, when she heard the familiar chugging noise of the motor car echoing across the flat fields long before it reached the farmyard gate. Esther pulled herself up, her face set in hard lines of resentment as she opened the back door and went out into the yard. She stood waiting whilst the car swung in at the gate. Instead of stopping to let Matthew alight and then reversing out again, the motor car came right into the middle of the yard before it stopped. The engine died and the headlamps were turned out.

Esther blinked in the sudden blackness, unable to see anything for a few moments after being blinded by the light. Then she saw only one person climbing out of the car – out of the driver's seat: Matthew.

'Hello, Esther. Look what I've got! Go and get yar bonnet, and I'll take you for a drive. It's a car, Esther, I've bought a car.'

Matthew must have thought he was back in France

449

under bombardment from the Hun by the time Esther had finished with him.

'How could you do it? How could you spend all that money on a useless object like a car? Who do you think you are, the next squire? We ain't in that class, Matthew Hilton. Just because he's been kind to you since you came back from the war, just because he lost his son and is trying to make up to you because of it, it dun't put you in his class . . .'

On and on she railed and shouted, stormed and raged.

'Oh, I know you've had it tough in the war – none knows it better than me. But you're alive – you're back home with your family. But do you care?' She flung out her hand to encompass the whole of the land around them. 'Do you lift a finger to help me? I've struggled all that time to keep things going, and looking after you when you came back. You're getting better now, Matthew. You could help, but you dun't want to, do ya? You think you've done your bit for evermore. Life ain't stopped, Matthew, it goes on, day after day after day.'

'Maybe,' he said quietly, 'maybe it would have been better if me life had stopped – out there. Ya'd be better off if I had died out there.'

Though she heard the words, she didn't listen to their meaning – their real meaning – and she retaliated impulsively, 'Aye, mebbe it would . . .' Her mouth fell open and she stared at him, stricken with swift remorse for allowing the cruel words to spurt, unchecked, from her lips.

Even to her own ears, her words, shrill and venomous, had the ominous ring of her Aunt Hannah venting her

450

frustration on the young girl for whom she had grudgingly taken responsibility. In the same way that, deep down, Esther resented the burden of a helpless husband which the war had thrust upon her.

She saw his hands start to shake and his head twitch and her shrill tongue was silenced.

He was struggling to speak, to explain. 'I just thought the kids – we live a long way from – school – and town. I just thought . . .'

Aye, she might have known, she thought bitterly, his life revolved around Kate and Danny now – and his jaunts into the town with the squire. Jaunts that had resulted in this last act of madness.

Why? She railed, turning her anger inwardly on herself now, rather than on Matthew. Why hadn't she had the sense to hide her money? Even before the war, he'd hardly shown signs of thrift. He had cajoled her into agreeing to buy the horses. Then he'd come home with a new suit without so much as a by your leave or can we afford it! And that because he had wanted to attend his son's christening. Now, it was even worse, he was scarcely stable in his mind. What a fool she had been! She should have realized something like this might happen. Esther blamed herself. She was responsible for him. It was like looking after another child. The man she now called her husband bore scarcely any resemblance to the old Matthew. Except, she thought ruefully, when it came to spending money.

His whole body was now convulsed with the shaking and Esther had to put her arm about him and lead him into the house. He dropped into the chair by the range and she knelt down in front of him and took his hands in her strong work-worn grasp. 'Don't fret any more. I'm – I'm sorry for the things I said, but – well – you made me mad . . .'

Matthew grinned lopsidedly, but she was relieved to feel the shaking ease a little. Even in the midst of her anger, she had no wish to make him ill again.

'It's not a new one, Esther,' he was saying hesitantly. 'A chap had it afore the war and – well – he didn't come back . . .' He struggled to continue. 'His widow was – glad of the money.'

Esther said nothing, but wryly she thought, well, I suppose it's an ill wind that blows nobody any good.

She had the grace to smile at herself. Why did Ma Harris's sayings always pop into her mind at such times?

She got to her feet and sighed as she did so. 'Ah, well, Matthew, 'tis done now.'

Forty

ESTHER stood in the middle of the yard, her hands on her hips, watching as the squire drew his motor car to a halt at the gate and climbed down. She kept her face expressionless. When he stood before her, she saw that he had the grace to look shamefaced.

'Mrs Hilton – Esther – I am sorry. I feel it's all my fault . . .'

Tight-lipped, Esther nodded. 'Not *all* your fault, Squire, but a part – yes.'

He twirled his hat nervously through his fingers. 'What can I do to make amends, I . . . ?'

'There's nothing that can be done now, Squire. Matthew's bought the car – and what's done's done.'

The squire spread his hands. 'He went off on his own, you see, in the market. I lost him completely and when I found him again, he was tipping all this money into this chap's hands and the deal was done. I couldn't do anything about it without making Matthew look – well – very foolish in front of a lot of fellows stood around.' He paused and looked at her keenly. 'I didn't want to do that, Esther.'

'No,' she said slowly. 'No, Squire, you couldn't have done that.'

'Won't you let me make amends in some way? Let me pay for part of the motor car. After all . . .'

'No, certainly not!' Esther snapped and then remembering just who it was she was talking to, she made a great effort to control her seething anger. 'I'm sorry, Squire. I know you mean it kindly, but we'll manage.'

'Well . . .'

With a supreme effort she forced a smile on to her mouth. 'Please come in, Squire,' she now invited, 'and take a glass of home-made wine with me. I have a nice elderflower just right for the tasting.'

'Why, thank you, Esther, thank you.' Mr Marshall actually looked relieved and accepted her offer at once. 'I'm partial to home-made wine.' As they went towards the farmhouse he added, 'Have you ever tasted Mrs Willoughby's home-made wine?'

Now Esther threw back her head in genuine laughter. 'Oh, Squire! Does she make it from deadly nightshade, because that's the only one she'd give me?'

'Eh? Oh – er – yes, I was forgetting . . .' He grinned. 'You're not exactly bosom friends.'

Again Esther chuckled, though to herself now, to think of the times she had caused Martha Willoughby's ample bosom to heave in anger, not affection.

'To be fair,' she said as she set two glasses on the living-room table and poured out a glass of the clear liquid, 'we haven't clashed much of late. She was almost civil to me the last time I went to church.'

Tom had kept his promise, she thought to herself. His wife and Flo were obeying his command.

'She's not a bad woman, Esther,' the squire was saying. 'Just a bit of a gossip and full of – what shall we say?' He

454

looked up at her somewhat coyly. 'Righteous indignation?'

It was in her power to disillusion him, but instead Esther sat down opposite him and, taking a sip from her own glass, said, 'Aye, well, Squire, I s'pose I did cause a bit of a stir when I came here.'

The squire chuckled. 'You were a trifle – headstrong, shall we say? And I'll tell you something else, Esther Hilton.'

'What's that, Squire?'

'This wine's damned good!'

Across the table they smiled at each other.

Of course Matthew's new and expensive toy created a lot of interest amongst those at Fleethaven Point. From the adults there was incredulity.

'Have you gone quite mad, Esther?' Ma Harris demanded. 'Did you ought to let him be driving around – in his state? He'll kill himself – or someone else in that – that – thing!'

'I've told you what I think about it, Ma,' was Esther's reply. 'But there's not a lot I can do – not without making Matthew look a fool. I dun't want to do that even though I'm mad as heck at him.'

'But to spend all yar money on a car, Esther lass.' Ma Harris shook her head. 'Eh, what will become of him? Ya've got yar work cut out with him, an' no mistake. Ya'll 'ave to keep yar eye on 'im, lass. There's no telling what he'll do next!'

Amongst the young people of the small community, however, there was wholehearted approval for 'Mester

455

Hilton's motor'. It caused great excitement, and most days would find Matthew at the wheel and the motor car overflowing with children begging a ride. Always in the front seat rode Kate and Danny Eland with beaming faces and lording it over their friends.

Esther could not be persuaded to ride in the motor car, not even to be driven to church.

'You're just being plain awkward, Esther,' Matthew growled. 'You're still trying to make me feel bad for taking yar money and buying it.'

Esther pursed her mouth. 'You know I'm not one for dragging up the past. We had our quarrel about it at the time, so there's no more to be said. But I can't bring mesen to perch up there on that great noisy thing. Now if it could pull the plough or drive the threshing drum, then it'd be some use. As it is . . .' She flung out her hand towards the car standing in the yard, a constant reminder as to where all her hard-earned money had gone and why she was now terrified that the coming harvest would not be a good one.

None of these fears did she ever voice to Matthew. He neither helped with the work nor seemed to care what happened to the farm. She carried the burden alone and knew she would have to go on doing so and reproach him no more, but that didn't mean she had to succumb to his foolishness.

She leant towards him. 'I ain't riding in the thing, Matthew, an' that's that!'

'Please ya'sen,' he shouted. 'There's others that'll ride with me. Aye, an' they mean more to me than you ever could.'

As he went from the house and slammed the door behind him, she leant against the table. Suddenly an intense longing for Jonathan swept over her and the loneliness of her life engulfed her. Even though she had husband, child and friends close by she always felt herself to be alone.

It seemed to Esther this year that no sooner had the harvest been gathered in than Christmas was upon them. To her immense relief the harvest had been a good one – not abundant, but good enough. They would not go short through the winter, despite the disappearance of her savings.

The bad weather seemed to close in earlier than normal. Heavy rain made the late ploughing difficult, and blustery winds whipped bitingly across the flat land. The animals huddled in the farmyard and even Esther found excuses to stay in her warm kitchen and cook and bake ready for Christmas rather than face the dreadful weather.

Come the spring, she told herself, it'll be better.

It turned out to be the happiest Christmas she could remember. Matthew seemed more even-tempered and much better in health. He even made an effort to help with the preparations. He stirred the puddings, urging Kate to make a wish. 'Dun't tell what you wish, not to anyone, Katie, for then it won't come true.' He was smiling down at her as the child shut her eyes and screwed up her face.

457

Matthew was chuckling. 'My word, that looks as if it's a wish and a half.'

He plucked, drew and dressed the goose ready for the oven – a job Esther hated.

'We must put up the trimmings, Katie, and tomorrow we'll drive into town and get a Christmas tree.'

'Oh, yes, Dad, yes. Like the one in the square in the town.'

'Well, perhaps not quite as big as that, but . . .'

'They're expensive to buy, Matthew. There's some fir trees on the old marsh. You get one of them,' Esther began and then she saw the disappointment written plainly on both their faces.

'They're not the same as a real Christmas tree off the market, Mam,' Kate said.

'It's me first Christmas back home, Esther. Let's have a proper tree, just this year,' Matthew added.

She sighed inwardly. Really, she thought, half-amused, half-exasperated, it was like having two children instead of one. Aloud she said, 'You pair! Ya reckon ya can twist me round ya little fingers!' But she was smiling as she added, 'Oh, very well, then, but dun't you go mad, Matthew. Promise?'

'I promise, Esther.'

When they arrived home the following day, Esther could see at once that his promise, so lightly made, was also easily broken. Kate was dancing around him in excitement and the tree was so large that Danny, who had been invited to go with them into town in the motor car, was having to hold one end whilst Matthew struggled to drag the tree through the door, the full extent of the

458

branches being wider than the doorway. But seeing the children's joy and Matthew's pride in his purchase, Esther hadn't the heart to spoil their fun by scolding.

They set it up in a tub in the corner of the living room and Kate hung paper decorations and painted fir cones on its branches.

'Teacher showed us how to make these at school, Mam. There, doesn't it look pretty?'

'Yes,' Esther nodded. 'I must admit it looks splendid.'

She felt Matthew's arm around her waist and involuntarily she stiffened. He did not seem to notice as he said close to her ear, 'You're not such a bad old girl, Esther Hilton, in spite of your shrewish tongue.' He planted a swift kiss on her cheek, turned away, took his cap down from behind the door and winding a muffler round his neck, he left the house and headed in the direction of the Seagull.

Esther watched him go. Shrewish tongue, eh? Was she sounding to Matthew like her Aunt Hannah had seemed to her? Only concerned with work and duty, and devoid of any capacity to enjoy herself?

Kate interrupted her thoughts. 'Mam, when can I hang me stocking up on the mantel?'

It was late when Matthew staggered in – too late to help Esther fill Kate's stocking with an orange, some nuts and sweets. And lastly, just one main present – a doll with a china face and a cloth body for which Esther had painstakingly made the tiny clothes on her Aunt Hannah's sewing machine.

They had Christmas dinner at the farm – just the three

of them with Matthew sitting at the head of the table carving the goose.

They were invited to join the Harrises' noisy Christmas in the cottage at the Point for the evening, so during the afternoon she had made an over-excited Kate rest on her bed. Matthew, too, was stretched out in the front parlour, snoring in front of a blazing fire which Esther had lit in honour of Christmas. So whilst the others dozed, Esther snatched a few quiet moments to walk alone to the end of the Spit. The tide was high and lapped at the ridge of land along which she walked, but she had no fear of the water now.

As always her thoughts turned to warm, sunlit days. The memory of Jonathan's blue eyes and gentle mouth was so vivid she almost felt that if she turned quickly he would be there, walking towards her. Sometimes, he seemed so close . . .

Pushing away such foolishness, she bent and picked up some flat oyster shells. Leaning sideways she held the shell between her thumb and forefinger and flipped it across the water. It scudded over the surface bouncing three or four times before it sank beneath the waves. She sent three more skimming after it and smiled to herself as she remembered Matthew teaching her the game.

Ducks and drakes, he'd called it.

Her mind was filled with both the men in her life: Jonathan, her lost love, no more now than a sweet memory, and Matthew – poor Matthew – still suffering from his dreadful ordeal in the war. He needed her and deserved her compassion at least.

But would there ever be real happiness for any of them?

She sighed. Pulling her shawl closely around her she took one last look at the bleak, lonely sea and bending her head against the wind, she went back home.

At the beginning of January north-easterly winds blew in from the sea, combining with the highest tides of the year which pounded the coastline and flooded over the Spit and on to the marsh, swelling the haven and the mouth of the River Lynn.

On the first Saturday after New Year it seemed to reach a climax. The gale howled around the farmhouse, battering the windows and rattling the tiles, and the rain lashed against the glass.

Esther, who had never liked storms, blocked the back door with a chair against it. 'It's like that day you went out on the lifeboat. Remember, Matthew,' she said as she came into the kitchen where he was sitting by the range. 'When Robert Eland was out in his fishing boat and—' She broke off as Matthew got up from his chair and stared at her with wide, stricken eyes.

'Why, whatever's the matter, Matthew?'

He stumbled across the room towards the door.

'Matthew!' she cried again. 'Matthew, what is it?'

'The boat,' he mumbled. 'The boat – I must . . .'

'Don't be silly, Matthew.' She pushed against his chest, trying to calm him, to make him sit down again. 'There's no boat out there on a night like this. Sit down . . .'

Suddenly there was surprising strength in his hands as he gripped her arms, his eyes wild. 'No, no – their boat,

Elands' boat. It's not safe – not in this storm. Beth – Danny – they're on that boat.'

'Matthew, listen to me – Robert'll have brought them off. He wouldn't . . .'

'He'll not take care of them.' Matthew was ranting now, panic and terror in his frenzied eyes. 'He'll not care for my son. Or for Beth . . . my Beth. He's let that boat go to ruin. The wood's rotten now – I've seen it.'

Esther opened her mouth to argue, but suddenly a memory flashed before her – a memory as clear as if she were seeing it before her eyes right now. It hadn't really registered at the time, yet now amidst Matthew's wild babbling, she knew he was speaking the truth.

It had been when she had received the telegram about Matthew and she had gone to see Beth. It was the only time she had been really close to the Elands' boat home – and now in her mind's eye she was seeing once more the rotting, unpainted wood of the boat and the poles and stays that supported it on the river bank. All had been allowed to fall into a state of decay.

She gasped as realization hit her. In such a storm those poles, rotten with neglect, would give way.

'They won't have stayed on the boat, Matthew,' she insisted. 'Not in this lot . . .'

He wasn't listening to her rational statement. All he was thinking of was Beth – and his son.

With sudden, inexplicable strength – the strength that fear gives for those few vital minutes – he pushed her aside, not caring that she lost her balance and fell to the floor. Reaching the back door, he flung aside the chair and the door blew open, the storm raging into the house.

'Matthew, Matthew—'

But he had gone out into the storm.

Esther dragged herself to her feet and staggered after him. The wind blew her shawl from her shoulders and tossed it into the air. The rain soaked her blouse within seconds and plastered her hair to her head. Leaning against the wind she struggled towards the Point. She saw Matthew crest the Hump and disappear from her view.

As she reached the top of the steep rise and came down the other side, she saw he was striving to reach the boat. Already the swollen river was flooding on to the bank, the water swirling around his ankles. The boat seemed to have been lifted up off its supporting poles and looked to be floating, heaving from side to side, and yet it had not yet broken adrift from its mooring.

Matthew arrived at the wooden jetty and reached out to grasp the rope.

'Matthew! No!' Esther shrieked, but the sound was snatched and tossed away by the gale. She could not even hear her own voice let alone be heard by Matthew.

He was pulling himself up the gangway as she reached the water. Lifting her skirts, she waded through it to reach him. She must stop him. This was sheer madness.

She had reached the bottom of the gangway and had even put her hand on the rope. Looking upwards, she saw him jump from the end of the gangway on to the boat, saw him stagger for a moment and then right himself, though the boat rocked beneath his feet.

Then he disappeared from her view.

As she tightened her grip on the rope and steadied

herself to step on to the swaying planking, she felt herself pushed to one side. Above the roaring wind she had heard no one behind her and so the push, catching her off guard, sent her sprawling into the shallow flood-water on the bank. Gasping and gulping she staggered up again, thinking, irrationally at such a moment, that she seemed to be spending more time on all fours than on her feet this night.

When she looked around it was to see that Beth had taken her place. Now it was Beth's fingers which grasped the rope, Beth's face which was upturned to the boat, her eyes wide with anguish and terror. Her mouth was moving and although Esther could hear no sound above the noise of the storm, even this close, she could see that it was his name Beth was shouting.

'Matthew! MATTHEW!'

Esther too glanced up again, but he had vanished, gone below in search of his other family.

Beth made to heave herself up the gangway, and Esther, too, grasped the rope and made to follow her.

Strong arms seized them, pulling them backwards. Robert Eland's arms were around Beth's waist, but still she clung tenaciously to the rope. Esther felt herself held by Mr Harris.

Close against her ear he shouted, 'Nay, lass, ya'll all be killed. Have some sense, Esther.' Suddenly the fight went out of her and she leant against the huge comforting bulk of Ben Harris. She closed her eyes and dropped her head momentarily against his shoulder as a shudder convulsed her whole body. The man must have felt her fear, for his arms tightened about her. Esther took a deep

breath, raised her head and opened her eyes again to see
Robert Eland trying to drag Beth off the landing stage.
Her hands gripping the rope were grazed and bleeding,
but still she clung on, her mouth wide open, her eyes
frantic, her face the colour of death itself.

Then from the mouth of the river, a huge tidal wave,
blown in from the sea, came rolling up towards them,
sluicing on to the banks on either side, sweeping aside all
that lay in its path. Esther felt herself lifted from her feet
and carried by Mr Harris away from the bank, and only
when they were against the shelter of the cottage and
Ma Harris too had taken hold of her, did they turn to
look back.

They stood in a petrified trio, Esther in the centre with
Ma Harris and her husband on either side. They clung
together watching the bizarre and awful scene played out
before their eyes. The wave came nearer and nearer, yet
Beth would not relinquish her hold upon the rope of the
gangway, and Robert Eland would not leave her.

The horrified watchers saw Matthew appear at the side
of the boat above the gangway. Seeing them below, he
seemed about to step over the side to come down. But in
that split second he must have become aware of the surge
of water bearing down upon him for he half-turned,
looked down river and was stilled. His hands resting on
the side of the boat, he was motionless. He looked down
– just once – at Beth. He had time only to raise his hand
as if in final farewell, before the wave crashed against the
boat, lifting it like a cork, tearing it from its mooring
and wrenching away half the landing stage with it. For a
timeless moment, the boat seemed suspended above

them, and then with slow finality it rolled over on its side into the river.

They saw Matthew flung backwards, saw his arms flail wildly and then he and the boat plunged beneath the torrent, sending huge waves washing on to the shore, bowling Beth and Robert Eland over and over on the river bank.

The waters subsided and drained back into the river as the wave, lessening with each yard it travelled, rolled on up the river. Then Esther saw the two of them – Robert with his arms still locked around Beth – lying on the ground.

The Harrises and Esther struggled towards them. As they did so, with a cruel irony the wind dropped suddenly. Now they could hear another dreadful sound.

The sound of Beth's shrill screaming that went on and on and on . . .

Forty-one

*M*ATTHEW'S body was washed up three days later, ironically on the place which Esther had called her own; the place where so often she had found comfort in her solitude and yet the place where she too had almost lost her life – the end of the Spit.

The storm had blown itself out. It had calmed almost at once after the tragedy, as if it had exhausted its cruelty and was appeased.

Beth and Robert Eland were safe, yet Beth, they told Esther, had retreated into a world of her own, neither speaking nor eating. She sat in Ma Harris's kitchen just staring out of the window at the river, at the place where her home had been. At the place where Matthew had died.

Esther was tormented by feelings of guilt. I should have stopped him, she told herself over and over, and even voiced her feelings to Will. 'I should have gone up after him . . .'

'Aye, then there'd have been two deaths, lass. Where would me pretty little Katie have been then, without father or mother?'

'But . . .'

'But nothing, lass. I've heard it all from Ben Harris. He says you'd have gone up if he hadn't held on to ya.'

'I should have stopped him here, before he went out.

He – he wouldn't listen, Will. I tried to tell him they'd have come off the boat, but – but he didn't even seem to hear me, let alone believe me. He was gone so quick, before I really realized what he meant – what he was going to do.'

Will, not often given to displays of open affection, put his arms about her, and likewise Esther, not used to giving way to emotion, laid her head against his chest and her voice was muffled as she said, 'Oh, Will, I feel so – so guilty.'

Will stroked her hair and she heard his words deep from within his chest as he said, 'Dun't blame yourself, lass. We all feel guilt when someone dies. It's not his death you feel the guilt about, it's the life, all that went before. All the things you've done or haven't done. Now you're denied the time to put it right.'

Esther listened to his wise words of comfort. 'You shouldn't need to feel the guilt, lass, because since you brought him home from the war, no one on this earth could have been a more devoted wife than you.'

His voice dropped to a whisper as he added, 'An' I know, more than anyone else, just how much it's cost you to do it, lass.'

She heard the catch in his voice and she lifted her head a little and, her own eyes brimming with tears, she looked up into his face.

'Thank you . . .' the name she longed to call him hovered on her lips but she ended, 'Will.'

*

They all came to his funeral. Everyone from the Point, and from the surrounding farms: the Harrises, the Willoughbys, the Souters and the Squire.

And Beth came.

Supported by her husband, she stood at the end of one of the pews half way down the aisle, her eyes fixed upon the coffin. By her side stood Danny, solemn and white-faced.

The young boy had lost his friend, a man he had helped towards recovery. The man he knew as Kate's father.

Would he ever know, Esther thought, just how much more he had lost?

Following the coffin out of the church as chief mourner, with Kate on one side and Will Benson on the other, Esther paused in the aisle as she came level with Beth. She felt a soft sigh run through the congregation and knew they were watching herself and Beth in this moment.

Esther glanced at Robert Eland – this compassionate man who had borne so much in the face of his wife's love for another man. Yet even now she read the silent consent in his eyes to her unspoken question. She put out her hand towards Beth and Danny and gestured that the Eland family should take the place in the funeral procession directly behind herself, Kate and Will.

It was a gesture she knew might find censure amongst some and would certainly cause gossip amongst many. But as always Esther Hilton flouted convention, cared nothing for how things looked or what others might say or think. She owed this to Beth and to Danny.

Most of all, she owed it to Matthew.

The two women in his life, who had loved him each in their own, but very different, way, stood side by side as the coffin was lowered into the ground.

Esther heard a sob and she reached out and took Beth's hand in hers. It was like ice. She held it between her own, trying to warm it, trying to comfort the woman at her side. There was nothing she could say that would lessen Beth's pain, nothing that could turn back time and make everything different.

The vicar intoned the words over the grave and then Matthew's family and friends threw handfuls of earth on to the top of the coffin.

Danny and Kate stepped forward, their faces solemn, feeling the importance of the moment. They stood close together and Esther saw Danny take hold of Kate's hand. Together they bent and picked up a handful of earth and together they threw it on to the top of Matthew's coffin. They stood in silence for a moment and then Danny turned to look at Kate, concern for her on his young face.

They were only children, Esther told herself fiercely, and yet in that look there was something she had feared to see. There was a closeness between them that had grown innocently, unaware as they were of their blood relationship.

It was a closeness that put dread into Esther's heart.

The house was strangely quiet without Matthew, and Kate was doleful and lethargic. Esther too felt listless and tired. All the spirit and energy that was her nature had been drained out of her. The hard work and the worry she had known since she had brought Matthew home were now reaping their own toll upon her vitality and strength of will. To say nothing of the sadness locked within her own heart. There was no doubt that she had drawn on her reserves of strength this last year – and long before that too, if she were honest.

She walked along the shore deep in thought. Part of her longed to go to the place she had loved. The end of the Spit. But she could not yet face the spot where they had found Matthew's body. She feared her special place despoiled by the tragedy in a way that it had not been by her own traumatic experience there. That, she could rise above, but with this last disaster she was not so sure – not yet.

She had not seen her husband's body in death – the men had told her she should not. In her imagination she had visualized it bloated and battered, and shuddered at the thought. To think that he had survived the horrors of the trenches only to die in the place that was his home.

Matthew had died trying, so he had thought, to save the woman he loved and his own son. But in that last split second, he had seen Beth on the bank and had known she and Danny were safe. Esther believed that was all he had wanted. He could have saved himself then, he could have jumped towards the willing arms stretched out to help him. Instead he had just stood there, gazing down at Beth. He had indeed gone back to her just as Beth had always predicted. At the moment when death was inevitable – and he must have known that it was – hers was the last face Matthew saw.

Esther sank down on to the sand and gazed out across

471

the calm water. How deceptively tranquil and innocent the sea looked now, as if it could never have been the foaming fury that had taken Matthew.

She stayed there a long time, until the winter afternoon grew cold and dusk came creeping across the water. Then forcing her cramped legs to stand, she turned her back on the sea and lifting her head she turned homeward – back to Kate and the farm.

Always, there was Brumbys' Farm.

Forty-two

*T*HREE weeks after the funeral when the demands of the farm had forced Esther to return to her routine, she steeled herself to open the big doors of the barn that housed the contraption, as she still called it, which Matthew had bought in his moment of madness.

She stood, hands on hips, looking at the motor car, her mouth pursed with indecision. A shadow fell across the doorway and she looked up to see the squire standing there. It was the first time she had seen him since the day of Matthew's funeral.

He cleared his throat – nervously, it seemed to her. 'Good morning, my dear. I – er – I've been meaning to come and see you, but well, I thought it only respectful to leave – ahem – matters of business, for a little while after . . .'

His voice trailed away. Esther stared at him. At his words, cold fingers of apprehension touched her and her heart began to beat a little faster.

Matters of business! That could mean only one thing. The farm! Now that her husband was dead – and known to be dead – was he going to force her to leave the farm, just because she was a woman?

Where could she go? What could she do? What about Kate . . . ?

The squire was speaking again. 'I realize I was partly

to blame for Matthew squandering your hard-earned money on — ' he gestured towards the motor car — 'this. I wondered — if it is of no use to you — if you'd like me to try and sell it for you, my dear? I know someone who deals in motor cars and I'm sure I could get a good price for it. If not quite all your money back, I could certainly recoup most of it.'

Esther felt herself smiling as relief flooded through her. Was this the 'business' he had meant? He had not come to throw her out of Brumbys' Farm after all, but to put right a folly in which he had played no little part.

She felt sorry for the squire in that moment. He looked so anxious, so genuinely concerned. All he had tried to do all along was appease his own conscience and loss by taking Matthew out with him. Yet his kindly actions had backfired when Matthew had become obsessed by the motor car.

'I'd be very grateful, Squire, for anything you could do. This — thing — is no use to me. I couldn't drive it, and even if I could, well, it's not quite what people of my class ride about in, is it now?'

The squire had the grace to smile. 'I tell you what,' he said, as an idea came to him. 'What you could well do with is a smart little pony and trap. You could drive that, Esther. You could drive into the market, and take your little girl to school. What about it? Will you let me sell your car and sort out a nice little pony and trap? Needn't cost very much,' he added hastily, as her face showed doubt.

She smiled again. 'Very well, Squire, and thank you.'

'My pleasure, my dear, my pleasure.' He bowed a little

towards her, put on his hat and marched away across the yard, more purpose in his step than she had seen for some time.

Esther stood in the doorway of the barn, her hand on the rough wood of the jamb, and watched him go.

He had said nothing about the tenancy of Brumbys' Farm. The way he had talked – about her driving to market and taking Kate to school – it sounded as if he took it for granted she would be going on living here at the Point.

But would she be the legal tenant of the farm?

Now that the thought was in her mind, it would not let her rest and so it was that, three days later, she put on her best black costume and walked up the lane towards the Grange.

When she was shown into his study, the squire rose from a deep leather armchair by the long window overlooking the lawns and held out his hand to greet her. 'My dear, come and sit down. I haven't forgotten about the car, but I have not yet had the opportunity to strike a deal . . .'

Esther shook her head and remained standing in the centre of the room. 'It isn't about that, Squire.'

'Then what is it, my dear? There's nothing wrong, I hope? Please, do come and sit down here.' He indicated a similar chair to his own set on the opposite side of the window.

Esther hesitated and then did as he bade.

How very different was her reception now, she was thinking as she settled herself in the chair, to the first time she had come into this room with wild, flying hair and muddy boots. She smiled inwardly at the memory, remembering her belligerence, her youthful indignation. Now she was older, and more than a little wiser, yet the sense of injustice was as strong as ever.

'Squire,' she began, picking her words carefully, surprising even herself at her deliberate tactfulness. 'Like you I thought a lapse of time was appropriate, but I'm sure you will understand that I must know what my position is now.'

'Your position, my dear? I don't quite understand.' He seemed genuinely puzzled.

She leant forward a little, towards him. 'As regards the tenancy of Brumbys' Farm, Squire. The agreement was in Matthew's name.'

The squire's expression cleared. 'Oh, that. Oh yes — well — of course. Yes, I see what you mean. I really hadn't given it a thought. In fact, I'd forgotten all about it. You see,' he sighed heavily, 'with Matthew going to the war, and you carrying on so admirably on your own, I accepted the fact that you were running the farm.'

He lifted his shoulders in an apologetic shrug. 'With Matthew being posted missing, then coming home and yet not being well enough to run things, well, I'd completely forgotten we hadn't legalized things from your point of view.'

Esther bit her lip, stopping the words from bursting out. But what's going to happen? she wanted to cry. What's to happen now I'm really alone?

At his next words, all her questions were answered and all her fears allayed.

'The war changed a lot of things for us all, Esther my

476

dear. The biggest change it has brought about has been for women. They've proved they can do men's work when the men are no longer there. And you, more than most, have proved you can run that farm, single-handed if need be.' His keen, knowing eyes met hers and then he glanced away and cleared his throat.

So, Esther thought, the squire had known all along how her neighbours had ostracized her over her affair with Jonathan. He had known how she had struggled to cope alone. Yet he had never censured her, never used his power to oust her as he could well have done.

Now the jovial man in front of her was slapping his knees and beaming at her. 'Well, my dear, I intend to put all this right. You shall have the tenancy of Brumbys' Farm in your own name. Just as you wanted it all that time ago.'

Esther smiled at him in return and expressed her gratitude. She could not let him know that if only he had agreed to this almost ten years earlier, a great deal of unhappiness might have been prevented.

There was a cruel irony in the fact that after all this time she had what she had then wanted most in life. Now, it was not what she wanted the most. Not now, not since she had known real love.

She sighed softly to herself. Once the squire's change of heart would have filled her with ecstasy. Although she did still feel a deep satisfaction at the knowledge that her future, and that of her daughter, was secure, the thrill, the pinnacle of all her dreams as she had once supposed securing the tenancy of Brumbys' Farm would be, was no more.

She was standing shaking the squire's hand and he was saying, 'I'll not forget the business of the motor car, my dear. Just give me a few days . . .'

True to his word, the following week the squire fetched the motor car.

Esther dusted her hands together. 'I'm glad to see the back of that,' she muttered, as the vehicle, coughing and spluttering, disappeared up the lane. But in her own mind she was doubtful she would see her money back.

Esther was wrong.

Two days later a smart pony and trap driven by a beaming Squire Marshall turned in at the gate of Brumbys' Farm. Esther, rolling pastry at her kitchen table, dusted the flour from her hands with her apron and went out to meet him. She walked around the trap and patted the sprightly pony on its neck.

The squire climbed down and stood beside the trap, confident of her approval.

Esther looked up at him. 'Oh, Squire, 'tis lovely, but I don't know whether I really ought to spend the sort of money this must have cost.'

'Now, now, my dear, before you decide . . .' As he spoke he was reaching into an inside pocket of his jacket and pulling out what seemed to Esther to be a sheaf of papers. Holding them out, he added, still smiling broadly, 'Just count that first, and if you're still not happy then I'll take this back and recoup all the money for you.'

Esther held the thin, white pieces of paper in her fingers. Puzzled she glanced up at the Squire. 'Is – is this money?'

'Oh I'm sorry, my dear. Of course, I hadn't realized. Yes, each of those white pieces of paper is worth five pounds.'

'Five pounds!' Esther exclaimed. 'Each?'

The squire nodded. 'Yes, my dear.'

Swiftly Esther counted them, and then looked up once more. 'There's more money here than ever Matthew took from my box, Squire.'

The older man shrugged and avoided meeting her direct, questioning gaze. 'Ah well, I don't know about that, my dear. All I know is, I managed to get a good price for the motor and that is what is left.'

'Is the pony and trap paid for?' she asked sharply.

'Yes, yes . . .' He fished in another pocket. 'Here's the bill of sale. Now, Mrs Hilton, are you happy – or not?'

'Well . . .' Esther frowned over the money and the receipt she held in her hand. She could not be anything but happy, although she had a shrewd suspicion that the squire was not being entirely truthful with her. Had he really got such a good price for the motor car, so much that he had paid for this magnificent pony and trap and still left her with more than Matthew had taken in the first place? Or had he put in some money of his own? There was no way she could know without risking offending him. For once, if her suspicions were founded, she would have to swallow her prickly pride and accept the squire's good intentions with equally good grace.

She looked up again at him, a smile spreading across her face. 'I'm overwhelmed, Squire. Really. I don't know how you've managed it – ' there was a veiled hint in her

tone that perhaps she guessed what he might have done –
'but I'm truly grateful. Thank you.'

Relief spread across Mr Marshall's face and he patted
her shoulder benevolently. 'Don't mention it, my dear,
don't mention it. About that other little matter – if you
care to come up to the Grange tomorrow afternoon, Mr
Thompson will bring all the papers to be signed.'

'That other little matter', he called it. If only he knew
what havoc that 'little matter' had caused in her life.

Forty-three

*E*STHER Hilton was mistress of Brumbys' Farm —
the legal tenant in her own right.

She had the land she loved, she had a healthy, growing
daughter and a smart new pony and trap to take Kate to
school and herself to the market and to church.

She had good friends; Will still came twice a week,
and treated her and Kate as if they belonged to him even
if the words of acknowledgement were not forthcoming.
She had the Harris family; wonderful, motherly, laughing Ma Harris in whose eyes Esther had exonerated herself for her past indiscretions by her tender care of
Matthew, and Mr Harris, quieter than his voluble wife,
but always there to lend a hand when needed. And the
Harris children — what would she do without Enid and
the younger boys helping on her farm whenever they
knew she needed extra hands, without her ever having
to ask?

And then there was Danny Eland.

Oh, Danny, Esther would say countless times to herself watching him about the farm with Kate, or doing
little jobs for her, you're the growing image of Matthew.
What am I to do about you?

Despite all this if there was still an aching loneliness
in her heart, a secret sadness which she could share with
no one, then she would tell herself sternly that she had

much to be grateful for and that she couldn't expect to have everything she wanted in life.

Nevertheless, there was a restlessness about her, a longing that even the work-filled days and exhausted nights could not subdue.

'Our Enid's getting wed, Esther,' Ma greeted Esther one morning.

'Oh, Ma, how wonderful. I didn't even know she was courting. Who is it?'

Ma's round cheeks wobbled with pleasure. 'It's a young feller who's come back from the war – Walter Maine. Lost a leg, he has. He's got a wooden one but you should see him get about, Esther. I couldn't believe it. Before I met him,' Ma clasped her hands in front of her ample bosom, 'I have to admit I was a bit doubtful. I thought he'd be a cripple, like. Not a bit of it! One crutch he uses but can he move!' Her laughter cackled so loudly that the hens, pecking in a leisurely way in the yard, squawked in alarm and scuttled for cover. 'He's not idle either.' There was pride already in her tone for her future son-in-law. 'Learning to be a blacksmith, he is, so's he'll have a trade.' Her tone dropped. 'You know our smithy's lad never came back from the war . . . ?'

Esther nodded and Ma went on, 'So I reckon he's glad to have a young 'un to take on.'

So many lives altered by the war, Esther thought, but aloud she asked, 'When's the big day?'

Ma shrugged and stretched her mouth into the famil-iar toothless grin. 'We thought Midsummer Day – they've no reason to wait any longer. There's attic rooms above the smithy they can have and the smith's wife says she'll be glad to have Enid's help, and,' Ma added, 'our Enid'll even help out in the smithy itself if need be. She ain't afraid of work.'

Esther smiled. 'No, I can vouch for that.'

Ma's round face took on a dreamy expression. 'Eh, but what wouldn't Ah give to see me girl in a fine white dress on her wedding day?' She sighed and then added in a more matter-of-fact manner, 'Ah, well, there it is – frippery's not for the likes of us. She'll have to have a new costume that'll serve her after her wedding day.'

As Ma waddled away down the lane towards the Point, Esther watched her go, a plan forming in her mind.

The sewing machine she had brought back from her Aunt Hannah's was now in constant use. She made smocks and dresses for Kate and simple skirts and blouses for herself. Could she, Esther asked herself, make a wedding gown for Enid?

It would be the most complicated thing she had ever tackled, but she could afford to buy a length of material out of the extra money the squire had got for the car – or that he said he had got.

Esther smiled. The squire had been good to her, so why should she not pass on a little of that kindness to someone else? She owed the Harris family so much. First young Ernie, and now Enid and the younger boys. And Ma herself. Even though there had been a time of estrangement between them over Jonathan, now it was as if their differences had never happened.

The very next day found Esther bowling along the lane towards the town in her smart pony and trap. It gave her a sudden thrill to be driving her own trap, to be dressed in a smart costume – even though it was the one she had bought for her aunt's funeral and therefore black. But she was still in mourning for her husband and only the ruffle of her white blouse showed at her throat in the open neck of the close-fitting jacket.

On her arrival in the busy main street, however, some of her newfound confidence ebbed away. She was not used to coming shopping, frequenting what were to her the smart shops in the town.

As she entered the largest drapery store in the main street, the bell clanged loudly, heralding her arrival. She felt that everyone in the shop turned to look her up and down and suddenly Esther felt very much the country mouse come to town.

For a moment her nerve almost failed her completely when a woman customer at the counter turned to leave and saw Esther standing uncertainly just inside the door. As she came towards her, Esther recognized her as a member of the church congregation and a woman of whom Martha Willoughby always made a great fuss.

Esther drew a sharp breath and waited for the woman's scathing look and sarcastic remark. In readiness to do battle, Esther's chin came a little higher and her green eyes sparkled with defiance.

The woman was on her way out, but as she drew near to Esther she said, 'Good morning. Mrs Hilton, isn't it? How nice to see you in town.' The woman did look her up and down, but there was no disdain in the glance. To Esther's astonishment, it was more a look of admiration.

'G-good morning,' Esther managed to stammer in

reply and then she gazed about her almost in awe of the large shop with its shelves of bolts of cloth, its prim woman assistant behind the counter.

The customer, her hand resting lightly on the door handle, made no move to leave the shop but stood, her head slightly on one side, watching Esther. There was a friendly smile on her mouth.

Esther felt she could confide in her. 'I – er – I'm looking for some material suitable for a wedding gown.' As she saw the woman's eyebrows rise Esther added hastily, 'Oh, not for me! It's for a friend of mine who's getting married and I thought – well – I'd like to try and make her a wedding dress.'

The woman's smile broadened. 'Then I know just the person to help you.' She turned and led the way back towards the counter and Esther followed.

'Miss Davenport, would you be kind enough to assist Mrs Hilton with the choosing of a fabric suitable for a wedding gown?'

'Certainly, madam.'

The woman turned back to Esther and made her farewells. 'Miss Davenport will look after you. She is a fine dressmaker herself – ' she leaned towards Esther with a conspiratorial air – 'she'll give you a few tips, my dear.'

Esther smiled. 'Thank you. You've been very kind.'

'A pleasure, my dear. A pleasure. I'm so glad we met.'

Esther watched her go as the doorbell clanged behind her. How friendly she had been, and yet Esther was sure that the woman – whose name she still did not know – must have witnessed several of Martha Willoughby's sarcastic remarks towards Esther in the past.

'If you'd like to come this way, madam, perhaps I can be of assistance.'

'Of assistance' Miss Davenport certainly was and when Esther finally left the shop, she couldn't think when she had last enjoyed herself so much.

Her arms were full of material and lace trimmings, and her head was bursting with advice and suggestions.

'Do come back and see me again, Mrs Hilton, if you have any problems,' Miss Davenport insisted as she held open the door for Esther.

When her work was finished that evening and Kate safely in bed, Esther spread out the creamy silk material on her parlour table. She wrinkled her brow thoughtfully. Now, she thought, Enid's slightly shorter than me, but her size and shape are much the same as mine. So I reckon if I make it to fit myself, I shan't go far wrong.

The most anxious moment was actually putting the scissors into the lovely fabric, but once she had cut out the pieces and begun to pin and tack them together, Esther's confidence grew.

Two weeks before the wedding, the dress was almost finished. Esther chewed her thumb thoughtfully as she stood looking down at the gown which she had spread out on the narrow bed in the little room beyond the nursery that so long ago had been her bedroom when Sam Brumby had been ill.

She heard voices from downstairs and carefully shutting the door, Esther went down to find Ma Harris and Enid sitting in the kitchen talking to Kate. Esther jumped visibly at seeing them there, thinking for a moment they had found out about her making the dress.

They were both smiling up at her as she looked from one to the other.

'We've come to ask you summat, Esther lass,' Ma began. 'Go on, Enid, you ask her.'

Enid giggled nervously. 'I – we – was wondering if you'd let Katie be me bridesmaid . . .'

At this Kate jumped up and down clapping her hands. 'Oh, Enid, Enid! Oh do say I can, Mam.'

'Now wait a minute, Kate,' Esther said. 'Be still, child. Let me talk to Enid.' She turned back. 'I don't understand, Enid. What about your own sisters?'

Ma Harris and Enid exchanged a knowing look and shrugged their shoulders.

'That's the very reason we're asking your Kate,' Ma said. 'And we're asking Danny Eland to be a page boy. Just the two of them, that's all we want. Enid dun't want a lot of fuss and you should hear the squabbling that's been goin' on in our house over who's to be her bridesmaid. She can't have 'em all and so we thought this was the best way to settle it. That way none of 'em's noses is out o' joint!'

Ma and her sayings, Esther thought irrationally, and then she murmured, 'Danny, you say?'

It was strange how circumstances seemed always to contrive to bring those two – Kate and Danny – together, however much she might wish it otherwise.

Kate was tugging at her mother's skirt. 'Mam, do say I can be bridesmaid and wear a pretty dress, can't I?'

The smile on Enid's mouth faltered. She glanced at her mother before saying quietly, 'Yes, lovey, you shall have a pretty dress.' There was a slight emphasis on the 'you' which did not pass unnoticed by either Esther or Kate.

With a child's directness, Kate said, 'Why, you'll be having a lovely wedding dress, won't you? Like in the picture books?'

Enid shook her head a little sadly. 'It ain't practical for the likes of us. You can't wear a wedding dress for anything else afterwards, Katie.' She forced herself to laugh. 'Can't see me helping Walter at the anvil in a wedding dress, can you?'

The wistful tone in the girl's voice was not lost on Esther.

'Wait here a minute, Ma – Enid. There's something I think I ought to show you.'

She turned and ran upstairs to fetch the wedding gown that was all but finished apart from the final seams. It's only sensible she knows, Esther told herself, and besides, I can fit it on her properly now.

The look on Enid's face as Esther held up the gown before her was thanks enough. Tears of joy ran down her face and all she could say was, 'Oh, missus, missus!'

'I was trying to keep it as a surprise until a night or two before your big day, but I think you should know now.' Esther laughed, 'Especially as it looks as if I'll have to tackle a smaller dress for Kate.'

Enid reached out with fingers that shook. 'It's beautiful, missus. How kind you are – I dun't know how to thank you.'

Even Ma sniffed noisily and, not trusting herself to speak, just nodded at Esther and beamed.

*

Enid's wedding was a joyful affair. There seemed to have been little fun and merrymaking for so long. The long years of war, the loss of Ernie and then the homecoming of an invalid Matthew and the deprivations the war had caused even in this small, close-knit community, had weighed heavily upon them all. And finally Matthew's death.

Now they had something to celebrate. Enid looked beautiful in the wedding gown and Kate was quite the little show-off in her flounced pink dress. Even Danny puffed out his chest and strutted down the aisle behind the bride and her father.

He was growing so like Matthew it was uncanny, Esther thought, and glanced across the aisle towards Beth. He was a living, daily reminder of the love between Beth and Matthew.

Esther's glance rested upon Robert Eland. What an unusual man he was to care and go on caring for his wife's child by another man. Esther sighed. Robert Eland must love Beth very much, and it must hurt him to see how she still pined for Matthew.

Always there was an air of quiet sadness about Beth. Though she looked after her husband and son – they were now living in one of the cottages at the Point – and though she smiled and talked, the sadness never quite left Beth's eyes. Yet Robert still went on loving her and her boy. He was a remarkable man, Esther thought.

Will stood at Esther's side in the church, beaming with pride as he watched Kate in her pretty dress, her red curls glinting in the shaft of sunlight slanting through the stained glass window.

Will – a favourite with all the folk at Fleethaven Point, not just with Esther – had been invited to the wedding. He had arrived that morning leaving his carrier's cart in Esther's yard and setting his horses loose in her meadow for the day.

'Kate's just like you were at that age, Esther lass. A bonny bairn, you were, an' so is she.'

Esther put her hand through Will's arm as they walked behind the merry wedding group. 'Known me all me life, haven't you, Will?'

'Yes, lass, I have. Watched you grow – and watched over you, though you might not always have known it.'

Esther wrinkled her forehead. 'I remember climbing up on to yar cart when you came around the village and me aunt never shouted at me for it. I could never understand that. She shouted at me for everything else.'

Will laughed. 'Aye, well, she knew better than to cross me.'

Esther glanced at him and bit her lip. Will stared straight ahead as they walked together down the lane towards the Point. The bride and groom rode in Esther's pony and trap whilst all the other guests walked behind them.

'I remember you always used to listen to me and talk to me as though I *was* somebody. No one else ever did that, Will. Not when I was little, anyway.'

Briefly his hand covered hers where it rested on his arm. 'You were always special to me, Esther lass, always.'

They had reached the Hump and once over it were enveloped in the wedding celebrations and her moment of intimacy with Will was lost.

From her little cottage, Ma Harris produced the biggest spread that the people of Fleethaven Point had ever seen. Luckily it was a fine, warm afternoon and so the guests played and danced on the grass outside the row of cottages. Trestle tables had been borrowed and the wedding feast was held out of doors.

Enid's new husband was a tall, thin young man, with a slight stoop caused by the loss of his leg. In some ways he reminded Esther poignantly of Jonathan. When the light glinted on his hair or he stooped down to speak to Enid, his head slightly on one side, his eyes smiling into hers, he was so like Jonathan in his actions.

Watching the young couple in the church and now here sitting side by side at the wedding reception, shy and not a little embarrassed, but so happy, Esther felt again the aching loneliness. She ought to be content, she told herself fiercely, she had so much and today she was surrounded by so many happy people. All the Harris family were there, the young ones capering and chasing one another in a noisy game of tag after the wedding feast was finished whilst the adults chatted amongst themselves.

There were new faces too amongst the small community: the bridegroom's family. Ma introduced them to her friends and neighbours. 'This is Walter's mam and dad, Mr and Mrs Maine, Esther, and this is his grandad.'

Esther found herself shaking hands with an old man with a long white beard, who leant heavily on a walking-stick, his legs as bowed as she remembered Sam Brumby's being. At her side, Kate gazed up at the old man with trance-like fascination.

The old man laughed wheezily and grasping his long beard, he tickled Kate under her chin with its wispy ends. 'Now, little girl, ain't you ever seen a beard like this 'un afore?'

Kate shook her red curls. 'No, Grandad,' her little voice piped and she put out her hand and gently stroked the silky waves of his beard. 'It's lovely.'

'Kate,' Esther admonished her daughter swiftly, 'you call this gentleman "Mr Maine". He's Walter's grandad, not yours.'

'She can call me grandad if she wants,' the old man laughed. 'Lots of folks do – even though I ain't their grandad – just 'cos I'm as old as Methuselah.'

'Who's Methoosy?'

At that moment, Danny interrupted Kate's question and, grabbing her hand, pulled her away into the game of tag.

'You've a lovely bairn there, missus.' Old Mr Maine's bright eyes followed the child skipping and hopping amongst the rest.

'She is that,' murmured Will who, standing next to Esther, had heard the exchange of conversation. His eyes were thoughtful as he watched Kate.

Mid afternoon the bride and groom took their leave, riding into town in Esther's pony and trap to their new home above the smithy.

''Tis kind of you, Mrs Hilton, to lend us the trap,' Walter said in his low, soft voice. 'I'll see you get it back in the morning.'

Esther put out her hand to shake the young man's.

'Don't worry. So long as the pony is fed, I dun't mind if you keep it a day or two. Perhaps you could take Enid out tomorrow.'

The young man nodded. 'Aye, well, if you're sure. It'd be nice, being Sunday, but I'm back at me work on Monday.'

He smiled and his blue eyes crinkled, reminding her so keenly of Jonathan that her heart turned over. She squeezed his hand in hers and there was a catch in her voice as she said, 'Good luck to you, Walter. To you both.'

The bride and groom were waved off and the other guests began to drift away. Esther looked around for Will and saw he was in earnest conversation with Ma, who was nodding and smiling. To Esther's astonishment, she saw Will plant a kiss on Ma's cheek and then Ma laughed aloud and smacked him playfully on his arm. 'Get away with you, Will Benson, and do what you have to do.'

They turned and saw Esther coming towards them and for a moment she thought they looked a little sheepish, for they glanced at each other and then quickly away again. Coming to meet Esther, Will said, 'I'd best be on me way, lass.'

'Oh, Will, you dun't have to go yet, d'ya? It's only early and I've a bite of tea ready for you at home afore you set off back.'

Will shifted uneasily from one foot to the other and twisted his hat round and round in fidgeting fingers. 'I'll get off, lass, if ya dun't mind. There's something I've – er

– to see to, like.' He glanced at Ma Harris, who grinned and nodded.

'You get off, Will. He'll be back again afore you know it, lass.'

Esther felt a stab of disappointment. This had been such a lovely day and she didn't want it to end. She didn't want to let Will – of all people – go. Oh well, she supposed, his next call on Tuesday wasn't so long away.

'Goodbye, Mrs Harris,' Will was saying, 'and thank 'ee for asking me. It's been a grand wedding.'

Ma beamed broadly, nodding her head towards him as if sharing a secret. 'Mebbe it won't be the last, eh? Goodbye, Will. We'll be seeing ya again very soon, eh?'

Esther was sure she saw Ma Harris wink at Will.

When Will had gone, Esther, seeing Kate still intent in her game with Danny, slipped away to the shore.

Mechanically her footsteps brought her to the Spit and she was drawn, unwillingly at first, to walk along its length, the water lapping on either side, to its very end, to the point where they had found Matthew's body. She had not visited this place since, but she knew she must face it again.

It had been her favourite spot and she expected it to be haunted by the tragedy and robbed of its tranquillity. As she neared the very tip she found she was holding her breath. She stared down at the shingle where his body must have lain. Slowly she released the breath and lifted her head. Her gaze scanned the gently rolling water. She closed her eyes and lifted her face to the sky, feeling the warmth of the sun.

Everything was just the same as it had always been.

Nothing was spoilt. The peace of this place was almost tangible. She felt she could reach out and embrace it.

She sank down on to the shingle and felt the balm of tears which blurred her vision, so that the water danced before her eyes.

'Oh, Matthew, I'm so sorry, sorry for you and for Beth,' she whispered. 'Sorry I – couldn't make things right.'

She allowed herself the luxury of a few moments of self-pity. After seeing the happiness of Enid and her new husband, after being part of a large and loving family even if only for a few hours, the loneliness of her life ahead overwhelmed her.

'Oh, Jonathan, Jonathan, where are you?' Tears ran down her cheeks and, as she bent her head forward, dropped and were lost in the vastness of the ocean.

Forty-four

WHEN she returned to the wedding party, most of the guests, other than those who lived at the Point, had departed. Only Mr and Mrs Maine and Grandad Maine were still there. Old Mr Maine was sitting outside Ma Harris's cottage watching the sun sinking into the flat horizon, streaking the sky gold and pink. On his knee, her cheek against his silky beard, was Kate.

Esther stood before them and the old man looked up at her with twinkling eyes. 'We've become good friends, yar little lass an' me. Ya'll have to bring her to see my cottage. 'Tis only a few miles inland – nowt for that smart pony and trap of yourn.'

Esther smiled. 'We'd love to come. Thank you.' Gently, she added, ''Tis time you came home now, Kate.'

The child's eyelids were already heavy with tiredness, but like Esther she didn't want this lovely day to end.

'A bit longer, Mam, then I'll come.'

'All right, then. Only a few minutes, mind, just whilst I get yar tea ready.'

'I'll send her home, missus, in a little while.'

Esther nodded and said, 'Goodbye, Mr Maine. It's been lovely to meet you.'

As Esther walked up the lane towards home, she passed the meadow, the rippling grass just ripe for harvest.

'We'll be able to start this week,' she murmured and smiled to herself. 'My first haymaking as the tenant of Brumbys' Farm in my own name.' Shading her eyes, she stood in the lane and looked towards the farmhouse silhouetted against the setting sun, her gaze travelling over the house, the orchard, the barn and other buildings and then beyond to the fields of ripening corn. She sighed. How beautiful it all was and yet that very beauty brought a lump to her throat.

In the distance she heard three shrill, excited blasts on a whistle and the rattle of cart wheels.

Will? But he had only just left an hour or so ago. Was something wrong? Why was he coming back?

Her heart leapt. Three whistles – why three?

As the cart rounded the bend in the road, she could see that there were two figures on the front of it. As it slowed, one jumped down and began to run towards her. A tall man with an unruly lock of fair hair that glinted in the sunlight and fell forward over his forehead . . .

'*Jonathan!*' She couldn't even take so much as a step towards him, her legs refused to move. 'Oh Jonathan!'

But he was coming towards her, that dear, familiar smile crinkling his eyes. Then he was taking her face gently between his hands and kissing her forehead, her eyes and at last her mouth.

'Oh, my love, my dearest love,' he was murmuring.

And all the time, Esther had not moved. Breathlessly, she whispered, 'Is it really – really you?'

He put his arms about her and drew her close against his chest and she felt the solid reality of him.

She was vaguely aware of the cart wheels rattling on towards the Point, and then they were alone.

'But where've you come from? How . . . ?'

'Later.' He stilled her questions with his lips and she clung to him, knowing he would never leave her again.

They drew apart for a moment, their eyes shining with joyful devilment. They both spoke at once. 'The hollow!'

Hand in hand, they were running, across the lane, over the dunes and across the marsh to their special place . . .

Much later they came back to the farm and were standing in the middle of the yard, their arms around each other, when they heard the wheels of the cart returning from the Point. Perched beside Will sat Kate.

'Mam, Walter's grandad's gone home now . . .' Kate began, as the cart drew to a halt in the yard. Then she stopped, her eyes widening, at the sight of the stranger standing there with his arm about her mother's waist.

Will climbed down from his seat and held up his arms to Kate. The child allowed herself to be lifted down, but all the time her gaze was on the tall stranger.

'Will Benson,' Esther began with mock severity, though she could not hide the happiness from showing on her face. 'You have some explaining to do!'

Will was grinning happily as he set Kate down on the ground. She made no attempt to leave him and go to Esther, but stood close to Will, leaning against him and slipping her hand into his. But all the time her eyes were intent upon Jonathan.

'Do you remember,' Will was saying, his expression more sober now, 'the day I came all excited with some news to tell ya, and then I found you'd brought Matthew home?'

Esther nodded. 'Yes, I remember,' she said quietly. 'When you saw Matthew, you said your news was another tuppence on me eggs.'

'That weren't true, lass.'

'No, I knew it wasn't.'

'You did?'

'But you wouldn't tell me. You – you got almost angry when I tried to press you.'

Will shook his head at the memory. 'I didn't dare to tell you – not after I'd seen Matthew.'

There was sadness in Will's eyes now and a look too that begged for her understanding and her forgiveness.

Jonathan took up the story. 'When I got back from France, I went to see Will. I knew he'd know how things were with you. He said he'd come and break the news that I was alive and – coming back to you.'

'Oh, Jonathan,' she breathed.

'Then,' Jonathan added gently, 'he came back and told me that you'd found your husband in France. Of course, I couldn't – wouldn't – come then. But I've kept in touch with Will ever since.'

It didn't surprise her that this man of principle, who despite all her desperate pleading had put duty and honour before everything else, had kept away when he'd heard Matthew had returned.

'I couldn't tell you, lass. You do understand?' Will was saying, anxiety in his tone.

Her voice broke as she reached out and patted Will's arm. 'Of course I understand.'

'I brought Jonathan as far as Lynthorpe this morning . . .'

'We didn't think it right that I should arrive at the wedding. After all it was their day, and besides, I wasn't really sure what my welcome from the folk at the Point would be!' Jonathan added with a rueful smile.

'But everything's going to be all right.' Will grinned broadly. 'I had a chat with Ma Harris at the wedding. Asked her if she thought enough time had gone by since – well – you know . . .' He broke off, cleared his throat, and continued. 'She was that pleased, said you'd earned a bit of happiness and that I'd better get off and fetch the young man as quick as I could.'

'Oh, so that was what all the whispering was about?' Esther smiled.

Esther became aware that all the time they had been talking, Kate had been standing quietly, holding Will's hand and still staring solemnly up at Jonathan.

Jonathan's blue eyes twinkled down at her. 'And just who is this very grown-up young lady?'

Suddenly, Kate beamed.

'Kate, I don't suppose you'll remember Mr Godfrey. You were only little when he was here before . . .' Esther said.

'Yes, I do,' Kate said promptly. 'You made me a fishing net, didn't you?'

The three grown-ups gaped at her.

'Fancy you remembering that, Katie,' Esther said.

The girl wrinkled her smooth forehead and added, with candid honesty, 'It's all I do remember.'

They all laughed.

Kate was still eyeing Jonathan, her head on one side as if surveying him. 'I dun't suppose you're me grandad, are ya? You're not old enough.'

Jonathan looked startled and glanced towards Esther for explanation.

Esther laughed. 'No, lovey, he's not yar grandad.'

The child looked disappointed. 'I did so like Walter's grandad. Mam . . . ?'

Esther held her breath, knowing what was coming next.

'Have I got a grandad?'

Kate's clear gaze was directed at Esther, who, for once, did not know how to answer her daughter.

It was Will who answered the child, saying in a strong vibrant voice, 'Yes, Katie, you have. I'm your grandad.'

Kate gave a little squeal of delight and threw her chubby arms around him. 'Are you really? I *am* glad!'

Above the child's head, Will's eyes met Esther's. 'Yes,' he said at long last, speaking more to Esther than to Kate. 'I'm your mother's father.'

Tears filled Esther's eyes and ran unashamedly down her cheeks but she was smiling as she reached out and clasped Will's hand. 'Oh, Dad, oh, me Dad . . .' was all she could say.

A happiness such as she had never before known flooded through her.

Now, at last, she had everything she had ever wanted.

Sow the Seed

This book is a work of fiction and is entirely a product of the author's imagination. Although specific settings have been used in the interests of authenticity for a regional saga, and duly acknowledged, all the characters are entirely fictitious and any similarity to real persons is purely coincidental.

For Dennis, Mandy and Zoë

ACKNOWLEDGEMENTS

Although 'Suddaby' airfield is fictitious, I would like to acknowledge that the Lincolnshire Aviation Heritage Centre at East Kirkby, owned by Fred and Harold Panton, has been a valuable source of information. The fully restored Control Tower and the magnificent Lancaster B Mk VII NX611 were an inspiration.

My very special thanks to Cyril Barker, of Skegness, a Dunkirk veteran, who relived painful memories of that time in order to help me in my research.

I am also deeply indebted to Mrs Fiona Ryan, of Skegness, for the loan of her personal notebooks and papers written during her service as a WAAF.

My sincere gratitude to Mrs Betty Watson, of Skegness, an ex-WAAF, not only for sharing her memories with me but also for her wonderful help in reading through the final typescript.

And last – but never least – my love and thanks to all my family and friends especially those who read the novel in the early stages – my sister and her husband, Robena and Fred Hill; Pauline Griggs; Linda and Terry Allaway; and my daughter, Zoë, who again helped with the final draft.

M. D.
Skegness, 1995

Part One

One

'IF I say ya'll go away to boarding school, Missy, then go ya will.' Esther Godfrey wagged her finger in her daughter's face. 'And I'll have none of ya chelp neither! Not from a thirteen-year-old, I won't.'

Kate faced her mother, her insides churning. 'I'll be fourteen soon. I can leave school then. You know I can. Please, Mam . . .?' Her boldness was fading now, almost before it had begun. She could hardly believe that she had actually dared to argue with her mother. No one, but no one, defied Esther Godfrey when she stood like she was standing now; feet set apart, hands on hips and green eyes flashing fire.

They were so alike; long, rich auburn hair, the mother with hers piled high on her head, the curls held in place by combs with only escaping tendrils to soften the firm jawline; the girl with hers flying wild and free, her mouth clenched mutinously.

Esther Godfrey was a striking-looking woman, beautiful some might have said, with a smooth forehead and a well-shaped mouth. She had still retained her slim figure despite the recent birth of a child, though her breasts were rounded with the ripeness of a nursing mother's.

Hers was an expressive face; her smile could brighten the day like the sun appearing out of the clouds, but her anger was every bit as threatening as the gales that raged across the marshes from the sea.

3

And at this moment her face was like a menacing thunder-cloud.

In the wicker cradle in one corner of the kitchen, the baby began to whimper.

'Now see what ya've done – woken her up after I've spent the last hour settling her.'

Kate flung out her hand towards the cradle, with a last spark of defiance. 'It's 'cos of her you want to send me away, in't it? You don't love me any more – not since you got Lilian!'

As she saw the colour drain from her mother's face and watched her reach out to grasp the corner of the kitchen table to steady herself, Kate felt a stab of guilt. Strong though Esther was, she had given birth only three weeks ago.

'Oh, Kate . . .' The anger, too, was gone. Now there was reproach in Esther's tone. 'That's not true . . .'

With a sob Kate rushed from the kitchen, through the back scullery, wrenched open the back door and ran across the yard.

Ignoring her mother's voice calling her name, Kate ran on, across the lane and up the slope of the sand-dune. Reaching the top she paused a moment, her glance sweeping the flat marshland in front of her. Beyond the marsh was a second line of sand-dunes and then the beach and the sea.

Maybe Danny was on the beach.

She was running again, down the sandy slope and across the marsh, jumping the creeks, bounding over the tufts of grass until she gained the crest of the eastern dunes. Her gaze scanned the wide stretch of sand.

Then she saw him.

Head down, hands thrust into his pockets, he was following the high-water mark, searching for anything left by the ebbing tide.

'Danny,' she yelled. 'Danny!'

4

He looked up, waved and began to run towards her.

Breathless, she sank down into the sandy hollow that was their own special place. It had been their den, their boat, their desert island, and always, it was the place they met.

Danny took a flying leap into the hollow, landing with a thud and showering her with sand. He sat down beside her and held out his hand. On the flat of his palm sat a huge whelk shell.

'Just look at that, Kate.' Gently he blew the remaining grains of sand from the shell. 'Did ya ever see such a beauty? It's the biggest I've ever found.'

Kate stared at it, but when she made no response, she felt Danny looking at her more closely. 'What's up, Katie? You look funny – ya face is all red. You bin crying?'

'I've had a row with me mam.'

'Oh, heck! What about?'

'School.'

Danny looked puzzled.

'She's sending me to boarding school in Lincoln come September.'

'Boarding school!' He gaped at her. 'Whatever for? I thought ya'd be leaving school, like me.'

'I can't leave till I've passed me fourteenth birthday. And *that's* not till September!' Kate said moodily.

There was silence between them, then Danny grinned, sudden excitement in his voice. 'I say, guess what? I saw Squire Marshall yesterday and he's tekin' me on from next Monday. What about that then?'

She looked at him, this boy whom she had known all her life. His curly black hair shone in the spring sunlight and although his chin was still boyishly smooth and his voice had not yet broken, he seemed to be changing before her eyes almost. She couldn't get used to seeing him in long trousers. He wore a pair of proper braces now – men's braces

– but his thin arms stuck out like sticks from the rolled-up sleeves of his open-necked striped shirt. Suddenly, he seemed to be growing up – and growing away from her.

'That's nice. I'm glad.' She tried to sound pleased – for Danny's sake – but her own misery destroyed her delight in his news. 'I want to get a job too.' There was longing in her tone. 'I don't want to go to school any more.'

He was avoiding her gaze now. She watched as he picked up handfuls of sand and let it run through his fingers. He seemed so intent on what he was doing that Kate thought he had forgotten she was even there.

She prodded his bony shoulder. 'Don't ya care if I go away?'

He looked up quickly then. 'Of course I care. Ya know I do!' He leaned forward and bumped his nose against her cheek in a clumsy attempt at a kiss. 'I'll always care for you, Katie Hilton.'

Kate wasn't quite sure why he whispered it when there was only a lone black-headed gull soaring above them to hear. She giggled, embarrassed, but his gesture had banished her tears.

'Here, ya can have this.' He held out the whelk.

'Are ya sure?' Kate knew the huge shell would have taken pride of place in his collection.

'Yeah, go on, I want you to have it. Just – just so's . . .' A faint redness crept up the boy's neck. He thrust it into her hand and then stood up suddenly, pushing his hands into the pockets of his trousers. Embarrassed, he scuffed at the sand with the toe of his sturdy boot. 'So ya dun't forget me when – *if* – ya go away.'

She held the whelk to her ear and heard the sound of the sea. 'I'd never forget you anyway,' she said softly, slipping the shell into her pocket. 'Not as long as I live, I won't.'

He sat down again and resumed his sand-sifting. 'Why

does yar mam want to send you to boarding school anyway? T'ain't for the likes of us.'

Kate sighed. 'She says she dun't want me staying on the farm all me life – that she wants something better for me. But I reckon—' She hesitated and then plunged on. 'I reckon she – she wants me away from here. Away from Fleethaven Point altogether.'

He looked at her hard now. 'Why?' came the blunt question.

She smoothed her white pinafore over her knees drawn up under her chin. 'Ever since the baby came, she dun't – want me any more.' Her mouth trembled dangerously again.

'Don't be daft, Katie, 'course she does.'

'Well, it dun't feel like it.' She paused, then with a note of belligerence added, 'How would you know anyway, Danny Eland? *You've* no brothers or sisters.' She tossed her long auburn hair which fell in shining waves down her back to below her waist.

'No,' he mumbled in reply. 'But I wish I had.'

'Ya can have our squealing Lilian then – and welcome!'

They sat in silence for several moments while Danny sifted sand into little heaps and then flattened them with the palm of his hand, only to begin the process over again. 'Does . . .?' he began and then stopped.

'What?'

'Does Mester Godfrey want you to go?'

'Me dad?'

'He's yar *step*dad,' Danny reminded her pointedly.

'I know, but he's like a proper dad.'

Danny looked up. 'But ya remember yar real dad, dun't ya?'

Kate wrinkled her smooth forehead. 'Sort of. In – bits.'

They sat in silence, each trying to remember Kate's father.

But their memories were fragmented, like a jigsaw with pieces missing.

'I can just remember him coming back from the war,' Danny said. 'He was in a terrible state, wasn't he?'

'Can't remember that. But I do remember him tekin' us to town in his motor car to buy a big Christmas tree off the market.'

Danny was laughing. 'Oh, yes – we could hardly get it in your back door. I'd forgotten.'

There was another silence before Danny said softly, 'I remember his funeral though – after he drowned.'

'You held my hand when we stood at the side of the hole.' She shuddered. 'I remember that all right. Wish I could forget it, sometimes.' She frowned. 'We threw something on top of the coffin, didn't we? What was it – flowers?'

Danny shook his head. 'Just earth.'

Another silence.

Kate hugged her knees. 'Then Mr Godfrey came and married me mam and we all lived happily ever after.' She pulled a wry face. 'At least, till Lilian was born.'

'Came back, ya mean,' Danny muttered.

'Who came back? Me dad?'

'Mr Godfrey – yeah.'

'What d'ya mean – came *back*?'

'It was just – summat I heard me dad say once.'

'What?'

Danny said nothing.

'Come on, Danny, *tell* me,' Kate insisted. She scrambled up and grasped his shoulders, shaking him. 'Tell me or I'll . . .'

He caught hold of her arms and they struggled with each other like a pair of playful puppies, just as they always had throughout their childhood. Kate shrieked with laughter, her anguish forgotten for the moment as they rolled over and over, her petticoat flying, her black stockings wrinkling around her ankles. Danny was on top of her, pinning her arms back against the sand. They stared into each other's eyes, panting hard, their breath mingling.

Faintly, borne on the wind, there came the sound of a whistle. Immediately, Kate began to struggle. 'Let me up, Danny. That's me grandad coming. I'll go and meet him. He'll not let me mam send me away. He'll tell her!'

Danny released her and stood up. He held out his hands to pull her up from the sand, but before he had regained his breath, she was up and out of the sheltered sandy hollow racing down the slope of the eastern dunes. Across the flat marsh she ran, jumping the winding creeks, squelching through the mud, her long hair flying free.

'Katie – Katie, wait for me,' she heard him calling behind her. But as always she was darting ahead of him. He was still splashing through the streams as she was climbing the line of sand-dunes which ran parallel to the road leading from the town of Lynthorpe to Fleethaven Point. Then she was beneath the elder trees, slithering down into the lane.

'Grandad – Grandad!'

The rattling wheels of Will Benson's carrier's cart came to a halt. 'Why, Katie, me little lass, what are you doin' at home? Ah thought you'd be in school.'

He leaned down from his high seat on the front of the cart above the broad backs of his two horses and held out his hand to her. 'Up you come then, me lass.'

'It's still the Easter holidays, Grandad.' Kate settled herself on the narrow seat at his side and smiled up at him, tossing back the strands of hair which fluttered across her face.

'O' course it is. Ah'd forgotten. Why, here's Danny an' all,' Will said, as the boy came crashing down the wooded slope of the dunes and into the lane. 'Come on, lad, climb up. There's no room on the seat, but you can stand on the shaft. Hang on, mind.'

Danny grinned up at the carrier, caught hold of the side of the cart and pulled himself up. 'Thanks, Mester Benson. Just as far as the gate. I'd best be off home mesen.'

'Ow's it feel to be a working man, then, eh, Danny?' Will Benson laughed wheezily. There wasn't much that escaped the carrier. News travelled on his cart alongside the pots, pans and provisions.

'He dun't start till Monday, Grandad,' Kate said.

'Holiday, is it, lad, 'afore you even start? Eh, but Ah dun't know what things is coming to. Why, in my day . . .'

'Oh, Grandad!' Kate giggled and wriggled her fingers against the old man's ribs to tickle him, but she could not feel his body beneath the thick coat he wore. Although spring had arrived, it was still cold riding on the front of his cart in all weathers when the wind whipped across the flat Lincolnshire fenland. Kate loved her grandfather. As long as she could remember, he had spoilt her and could be relied upon to take her side, even against her mother. He always looked so smart, Kate thought looking up at him now, with his black trousers and pin-striped jacket and matching waist-coat, a gold watch-chain looped across his narrow chest. She only had to ask for him to pull the watch out of his pocket and hold it to her ear to listen to its tiny tick-tick-tick. And his boots, resting on the foot-board, shone so that she could almost see her face in their hard, rounded toe-caps. She liked it in summer when he wore a rakish boater-shaped hat, but today he still wore his winter cap against the cold. His smooth hair was almost completely white with only a few strands of the ginger colour it had once been still showing. Will Benson's old eyes twinkled down at her and he wiggled his white moustache. 'You'll be losing yar playmate then, eh, Katie?'

10

Remembering suddenly, the smile fled from her face.

'Grandad – ya've got to speak to me mam. She's going to send me away. To boarding school. Ya won't let her, will ya, Grandad?'

Will Benson slapped the two horses with the reins and above the rattle of the cart's wheels he asked, 'What? What's that you say?'

Raising her voice, Kate repeated, 'Me mam's sending me to boarding school in Lincoln, come September. I dun't want to go, Grandad. I'll hate it!'

'Huh!' Will made a disapproving noise and muttered something that sounded like 'We'll see about this'. Above the noise of the cart-wheels, however, Kate could not be sure exactly what he had said.

But she was sure the moment he opened the back door of the farmhouse and stepped into the back scullery.

'Esther,' he bellowed. 'You here, Esther?'

'In here, Dad,' came her mother's voice. Kate followed her grandfather into the kitchen.

Esther Godfrey was standing at the large kitchen table. A thick blanket was spread upon it and an old sheet, worn to transparent thinness, on top of that. Two flat irons were heating on the range while she worked with a third ironing the previous morning's wash. From the wicker cradle in the far corner came the baby's mewling.

'Oh, there you are, Missy! And just where did you disappear to?' her mother began and Kate was sure she added under her breath, 'As if I need to ask!'

Peeping round the comforting figure of her grandfather and using his presence as a buffer against her mother's wrath, Kate said, 'I've been on the beach with Danny.'

She saw her mother's mouth tighten. 'I thought as much. Into the scullery and wash yar hands. Dinner's in ten minutes, now yar grandad's here.'

Kate obeyed, but left the door ajar so that she could peep through the crack and listen to their conversation.

In a tone that Kate could not remember having heard him use before, Will said, 'What's this Katie tells me about you sending her away to school?'

She saw her mother glance up in surprise, the iron suspended in mid-air before it thudded down on to one of the baby's white frocks.

'Well?' Will Benson's tone was sharp.

The iron came up again, the tiny dress was flicked over and the iron thudded down once more. In the grate of the huge black range a log fell, sending a shower of sparks up the flue.

'I'm thinking about it – that's all.' Her mother's tone was terse. 'Nothing's settled – yet.'

'Ya shouldn't be even *thinking* about sending the bairn away. A country bairn in a *city*! Lass'll pine away. Besides, how can you afford the fees them fancy schools charge?'

'I've scrimped and saved – that's how. I've still got me box under the bed and there's not a week goes by but I don't add a shillin' or two. I can afford it, Dad, I've minded that.'

Will grunted, casting about for another objection now that one had been foiled. 'Ya trying to turn her into something she's not . . .'

'Dad – I've got to get her away from here. Now she's growing older. You know why. It's for her own good.'

And although Kate strained her ears, it seemed as if her grandad made no reply to her mother's puzzling statement.

Two

'Kate. Kate, where are you?'
        'Here, Dad, in the wash-house.'
    Jonathan Godfrey appeared in the doorway. 'Samphire's about to calve. Do you want to watch?'
    'Me mam's set me to mash these 'tates for the little pigs. Then she said I'd to go to bed.'
    'Bed? This early?' His blue eyes sparked with mischief, the tanned skin around them wrinkling with laughter-lines. He brushed back the lock of fair hair that fell in a gentle flick over his forehead. 'What have you been doing to deserve such dire punishment?'
    Kate breathed in the smell of steaming potatoes, just out of the copper in the corner of the wash-house. As she thumped the wooden masher down, splitting open the brown skins and releasing the creamy potato, her hair fell forward like a curtain, hiding her face. 'I was late back from the beach,' she muttered.
    'And?' he prompted. 'There's got to be more than that.'
    'I forgot to feed the hens 'afore I went to play with Danny.'
    'Ah – with Danny.' She thought she heard him sigh softly, but his eyes were twinkling at her as he added, teasing gently, '*And* forgetting the hens. Dear me, that explains it.'
    She smiled ruefully and continued mashing the potatoes with a steady, easy motion.
    'Well,' he was saying, 'I could do with a little help . . .'

13

She tossed back her hair, her eyes shining. 'Aw, thanks, Dad.'

He put his forefinger to his lips. 'Not a word to your mother.' He turned to go. 'Samphire's in the little barn, Kate. There's more room there than in the cowshed.'

The girl nodded, understanding immediately. This particular cow out of their small herd of four was temperamental at the best of times. She had to be hoppled sometimes just to be milked; calving, she'd be even more difficult. They'd need plenty of space to avoid her kicking hooves.

A little later Kate crossed the yard to the small barn lying between the cowshed and the stables. As she stepped into the dim interior and pulled the door closed behind her, a rat scuttled along a rafter above her head. She glanced up and smiled briefly.

'I ain't time to be chasing you, Mester Rat. You're safe from me big stick just now!' she murmured, thinking of all the times she and Danny had made a game of chasing rats. As her eyes became accustomed to the gloom, Kate moved softly across the thick carpet of straw towards where her stepfather stood beside the cow. Samphire was making a dreadful noise, bellowing and stamping. Suddenly she pushed sideways towards Jonathan Godfrey, pinning him against the brick wall.

'Dad!'

'Keep back, Kate,' he gasped. 'Don't get near her back legs – whatever you do.'

With all his strength he shoved at the cow and, gaining a little space, moved swiftly out of the way.

'You all right, Dad?'

'She's winded me a bit, that's all,' he said, wiping the sweat from his forehead with the back of his hand. 'I can't seem to pacify her, Kate. Your mother's the only one who can quieten Samphire.'

14

After a moment's hesitation, for it would mean she would be banished from the barn, the girl asked, 'Shall I fetch me mam?'

'You can't. She's gone to the Grange to see Squire Marshall. It's rent day.' He glanced down at her and for a moment the worried expression on his face lightened as they exchanged an amused glance.

Esther Godfrey was meticulous in money matters. Her quarterly rent for the tenancy of Brumbys' Farm, which was solely in her name, must be paid exactly on the day it was due.

Turning back to watch the restless cow pulling at the rope which tethered her to the wall, Jonathan's face sobered again as he said, 'I'm rather afraid the calf is breech.'

'Ya'll have to turn it, Dad.'

She saw the beads of sweat standing out on his forehead. Again he swept his hand across his brow. He took a tentative step towards the cow and stopped. Kate watched him. It was obvious that her stepfather was unsure what he needed to do. After all, she thought, with sudden sympathy for him, he had only been involved in farmwork since marrying her mother four years earlier. His trade had been building traction engines in Lincoln.

Kate touched his arm. 'Ya need to put yar arm inside her and . . .'

The sweat was running down the side of his face now at the mere thought.

'I've watched your mother – but . . .' His anxious glance flitted towards the cow and back again to Kate. His anxiety was becoming almost fear.

'Wait, Dad, just wait here and watch her. Dun't do anything . . .' Kate turned and ran towards the door.

'Kate – wait! Where . . .?'

15

But she was out of the door and running round the corner of the building and out of the yard gate.

Danny – she must fetch Danny. He would know what to do. In the lane she turned to the right and sped towards the Point. Arriving at the top of the steep incline, known as the Hump, over a natural bank in the road, she paused to catch her breath and survey the scene below her. To her right the setting sun slanted golden streaks across the fields harrowed smooth and flat after the recent spring sowing. The River Lynn meandered through the fields to the Point where it joined the sea. To her left was the pub and beyond it, the marsh and then the sea. Directly in front of her was a stretch of grass between the river bank and the line of four cottages where Danny lived.

The three Harris brothers, Peter, Luke and Georgie, were playing cricket on the grass, but Kate could not see Danny among them.

She plunged down the bank and, lifting her skirt to her knees, sprinted across the grass. 'Georgie – Georgie! Where's Danny?'

'Hello, young Kate. Come to play cricket, 'ave ya?'

'Dun't let her play again, Georgie,' shouted Peter, though he was grinning as he said it. 'She batted our ball into the river last time,' They were all older than Kate and Danny; fine, strapping young men with broad, muscular shoulders and faces tanned a healthy bronze from working out in all weathers. None of them had married as yet and still lived at home with their parents in the end cottage. 'Can't find a lass to match me mam's cooking' was their unanimous verdict, but if the snatches of conversation Kate overheard sometimes were true, they all three had 'an eye for the lasses' but preferred to stay fancy-free, at least for the present.

'Where's Danny?' she demanded.

The young man clasped his hands over the place where

he believed his heart to be and dropped to his knees on the grass. 'Danny – always Danny! And here am I pining for one little kiss . . .'

'George – me dad can't manage Samphire. She's calving.'

At once the young man stopped his teasing. 'He's up near the Point helping his dad mend the nets, I reckon . . .'

But she was gone like the wind, calling back over her shoulder, 'Thanks, Georgie.'

She ran along the curving river bank until she came to the place where the river widened out into intertidal mudflats, channelling a wandering route to the sea. Moored on the river bank was Robert Eland's fishing boat, and on the headland, the very Point itself, father and son bent their heads over the nets, examining them for holes.

'Danny, Danny!'

The two men looked up and Danny waved. 'Summat up, Katie?' he asked as she reached them.

'Hello, Mester Eland . . .'

The older man nodded briefly.

'Can you come and help us, Danny? Me dad can't manage Samphire. Her calf's coming breech.'

'Oh heck!' Danny muttered and then glanced at his father. 'Dad . . .?'

The older man was silent, threading the nets expertly through his fingers. His eyes were downcast and his mouth was completely hidden by a thick, grey-speckled beard and moustache, so that Kate had no way of reading any expression on his face. It was impossible to see if he ever smiled, and the visible part of his face was weather-beaten and lined, his forehead seeming to have a permanent frown. He was a quiet man who gave the impression of being dour, even moody. Though Robert Eland rarely came to Brumbys' Farm – hardly ever did he help with the harvest for he preferred the sea to the land – Kate's stepfather would often meet him in the Seagull to play dominoes over a pint or two. 'He's a good man when you get to know him,' Jonathan would say, to which Esther would reply, 'You never see bad in anyone', and Kate's gentle stepfather would smile fondly at his wife.

Danny thought the world of his father; he was forever saying, 'Me dad ses' or 'It was summat me dad said'. And that – for Kate – was good enough.

'Where's yar mam?' Mr Eland was asking Kate now.

'Gone to the Grange. We don't know how long she'll be and the cow's in a bad way . . .'

There was a moment's pause before he said, 'All right, then. Off ya go, lad.'

'Thanks, mester,' Kate called over her shoulder for already her feet were flying across the grass back the way she had come.

'Wait for me,' Danny called after her, but, as always, he arrived at Brumbys' Farm hot and breathless and a minute or two after Kate.

'Get me – some hot – soapy water, Katie,' he commanded, still trying to regain his breath, but having summed up the situation in the barn at a glance. In a few moments Kate was back with hot water from the side boiler in the kitchen range and a scattering of soap flakes from the wash-house dissolving in it.

Danny had taken off his shirt. His braces hung loosely down the sides of his trousers. He looked very thin, his shoulder-blades and ribs sticking out, but Kate knew his slight physique belied a wiry strength. He might not be able to run as fast as she could but he could beat her at arm-wrestling any day of the week.

'We'll have to hopple her, Mester Godfrey,' Danny was saying, 'else she'll kick me shins to bits!'

18

Kate reached for the leather thong from the wall and handed it to Danny.

'Kate – we'll need some thin rope. Plough line'd be best, if you can find any.'

Kate screwed up her mouth and wrinkled her smooth brow. Then her thoughtful expression cleared. 'Wait a bit . . .'

In the stable next to the barn the two cart-horses tried to nuzzle Kate as she squeezed past them. 'Move over, Boxer. No, I ain't no sugar – not this time. I'm busy. Oh, move over, do – I need that plough line on the wall.'

She pushed at the huge horse's flanks and obligingly the animal side-stepped and allowed the girl into his stall to reach the line. Giving him a swift pat on his nose, Kate said, 'I'm sorry, old feller, I can't stay. Poor old Samphire needs help.'

Closing the stable door, she ran back to the barn and, stepping inside, saw Danny standing on a box pushing his thin arm, made slippery with the soapy water, into the cow. Samphire lowed and tried to move but because of the thong looped around her back legs she could not kick. Sweat ran down Danny's forehead and his face was contorted with pain.

'There – ain't much – room in here,' he gasped. 'If I can – just . . . aaah.' As he spoke one small back leg of the unborn calf popped out.

'Well done, Danny.' Jonathan Godfrey moved forward as if to help, but as he did so the cow jerked her rump and knocked against Danny, causing him to lose his precarious footing on the box. He let out a gasp of pain as his arm, trapped deep within the cow, was twisted into an awkward position.

'Get back, Dad,' Kate hissed and darted forward to set the box straight and help Danny back on to it. 'You okay?'

she said softly. Anxiously, she looked up into Danny's brown eyes, full of pain. He bit his lip but nodded resolutely.

Again he was moving his hand deep inside the cow, trying to release the unborn calf's other back leg. Danny took a deep breath and grunted with the effort. Slowly Kate moved closer to the cow. She began to murmur soothingly to the animal as she had heard her mother do so often. At the same time she ran her hands gently up and down the cow's back. 'There, there, old girl. We're trying to help you. Soon be over.'

'Aaah,' Danny gave a gasp of pleasure and relief as the second tiny back leg appeared. Thankfully, the boy eased his arm out of the cow. As he did so, he grabbed the tiny, protruding legs.

'Quick, Kate. Give us the line.'

Kate handed it to him and swiftly he tied one end round the calf's legs and passed the other end to Kate.

'Hold it taut, Kate, we don't want him tucking 'em back in.'

Danny stepped down from the box. There were red pressure bruises all the way down his arm and he winced as he bent over the bucket of soapy water to wash away the blood and slime.

'Have you hurt your arm, Danny?' Jonathan Godfrey asked in concern.

'It'll be right, mester. Just twisted it a bit when I fell off the box.'

'That was my fault,' the man said with contrition.

Danny stood up and Kate could tell that the grin he gave was a little forced. 'Right then, let's have a go.'

All three of them grasped the line and, with one accord, pulled on it. As if sensing that they were trying to help her, Samphire appeared to pull in the opposite direction, though her lowing sounds became more frantic and high-pitched.

'It's no good,' Jonathan Godfrey gasped as they paused for breath. 'You'll have to fetch the vet.'

The two youngsters looked up at him askance. 'The vet?' They both spoke at once, and Kate added, 'Me mam'd have a double-duck fit if we was to waste money on a vet.'

The man gestured helplessly towards the cow, now looking round at them reproachfully. 'But we can't manage. We'll lose calf *and* cow if we don't get some expert help soon.'

'Let's give it just one more try, Mester,' Danny urged. 'Then I'll go for the vet.'

'Me mam'll go mad!' Kate muttered, grasping the rope and pulling with every ounce of her strength.

'Come – on!' she heard Danny gasp and echoed his entreaty in her mind.

Suddenly there was a loud sucking sound and the calf slithered out on to the mound of straw beneath the cow's hind legs. The man and the two youngsters, still pulling hard, fell back together in a heap. They disentangled themselves and sat up. In front of them was the newborn calf lying in the straw. Samphire, her cries of pain stilled, looked round in surprise as if to say, 'Where did that come from?'

Kate laughed aloud and scrambled on all-fours to where the wriggling creature lay. She picked up handfuls of straw and wiped the calf.

'Oh, he's lovely. Look, Dad, he's . . .'

At that moment the door of the barn was flung open and her mother stood there. 'What on earth . . .?' began Esther Godfrey. Her glance rested briefly on Danny and her mouth tightened noticeably, but she directed her anger at her daughter.

'Kate! I thought I told you to go to bed. How many times do I have to tell you . . .?'

'Esther,' Jonathan's deep voice interrupted in gentle

21

reproach. 'The youngsters have been helping me. I couldn't have managed without them.'

Kate saw her mother open her mouth but at that moment she saw the calf struggling to its feet, and whatever sharp retort she had been about to make was stilled. Then once more her gaze came to rest upon Danny's head, bowed over the plough line he was looping into a neat coil.

'Thank you for your help, Danny.' Her mother's tone was stiff and unfriendly and as Danny's head jerked up, Kate saw that there was puzzlement in his dark brown eyes and a red flush of embarrassment creeping up his neck.

Handing the coiled line to Jonathan Godfrey, he nodded briefly to Kate and went towards the door.

Once more Jonathan's deep voice prompted gently, 'Esther, the lad saved the calf and probably your cow as well.'

Esther seemed to be struggling with some inner conflict, but as Danny passed by her, she reached out her hand, touched his shoulder briefly and said, 'I *am* grateful, Danny, really.'

The boy hesitated and, for a moment, stared up at her. Then with a muttered 'Missus', he moved on out of the doorway.

As they heard his boots crunching across the cinders in the yard, Esther's attention came back to Kate. 'I don't want you to see so much of Danny from now on, Kate. He's growing up and come Monday he'll think of himself as a working man. He's no longer a boy.'

Kate stared wide-eyed at her mother, her mouth slightly open in shock. Why was her mother behaving so strangely? Danny had always been her friend. He was only a few months older than she was and they had both lived all their young lives at Fleethaven Point.

'Why have you gone all funny with Danny, Mam? You've never stopped us bein' friends before. I can't just . . .'

22

'Mebbe that's where I made me mistake – I should have put a stop to it a long time ago!' her mother muttered, then she raised her voice and added, 'Dun't argue with me, Missy, ya'll do as I say. Now off to bed with ya.'

'Mam...?' Kate began but her protestations were cut short by Esther flinging her arm out and pointing towards the house.

'Bed!'

Three

The next morning at breakfast, Kate was subdued and silent. Had her mother really meant what she had said about Danny the previous night?

'Look after Lilian while I get the dairy work done, will ya, Katie?' her mother asked, bustling between kitchen and pantry where the milk stood waiting in churns. 'Just wheel her up and down the lane, mind. No sneaking off to the Point.'

So – she had meant it. Kate bit her lip, but decided not to argue – at least, not at present.

'Can't I c'lect the eggs, Mam?' Kate hated wheeling the baby in the black baby car; its handle was too high for her and it was heavy to push on the uneven surface of the lane.

'Later – when you've got the baby to sleep for the morning.'

There was no escape. For the remainder of the Easter holidays, it seemed as if her mother deliberately kept her busy. Collecting eggs, feeding the hens, fetching the cows from the meadow for milking twice a day and running errands – anywhere except to the cottages at the Point. And, of course, wheeling Lilian. The baby's blue eyes stared resentfully up at her from inside the huge hood of the baby car, the tiny mouth puckered, ready to whimper.

'Talk to her, Kate,' her mother would say. 'It'll soothe her.'

But Kate could not bring herself to talk to the baby like her mother did. To the young girl it sounded daft!

She had no opportunity to see Danny. Now he had started work and she would soon be back at school, Kate realized there would be even less chance of meeting him.

'Look sharp,' her mother shouted from the bottom of the stairs as Kate dressed on the first morning of the new school term. 'Yar dad's getting the trap ready to take you.'

Tears threatened as Kate realized afresh that only she needed taking to school now. This morning there would be no Danny appearing on top of the Hump and running down towards Brumbys' Farm for a ride to school in their trap. There would be no playing their usual game.

'Go on, Dad, get going. Mek him run. 'E shouldn't be late.'

Smiling, Jonathan would flick the reins to make the docile pony inch forward, the animal seeming to know it was all in the game and that he shouldn't set off too quickly but give the boy a fair chance of catching them.

'Come on, Danny, faster, faster . . .' Kate would stand up in the trap shouting back to him, her merry laughter bouncing on the breeze. 'We'll leave ya and ya'll be late an' get the canc.' Then she would say to Jonathan, 'Let him catch us now, Dad, he's out o' puff.'

Jonathan would ease back on the reins to halt the pony and the boy would clamber up into the back of the trap, breathless and red in the face, but laughing. Always Danny Eland seemed to have a broad grin on his tanned face.

But this morning there would be no game and no laughter because there would be no Danny.

Kate sat stiff and silent in the trap, looking back down the empty lane. Her gaze took in the flat fields stretching westwards as far as she could see, trees dotted black against the low horizon. The lane wound gently following the natural line of the sand-dunes all the way to the outskirts of Lynthorpe.

25

Just before they reached the first houses, Jonathan turned the trap to the left and took a lane leading inland. 'We mustn't forget to pick Rosie up.' He smiled down at Kate, but her normally happy face was solemn.

She felt lost without Danny.

When the trap pulled up outside the smithy, however, and little Rosie Maine came running up, Kate's spirits lifted a little. It was impossible not to be cheered by Rosie – she was such a bright chatter-box, with white-gold bouncing curls, merry blue eyes and a round chubby face that always seemed to be smiling. Jonathan held out his hand and the child climbed up the step into the trap. She flung her arms about Kate's neck and hugged her hard. Then she sat down and pulled her skimpy dress over her knees. Already, the shapeless shift dress seemed too short for her. Over it, she wore a grey hand-knitted jumper that had been washed so many times, the wool stitches had matted together.

Rosie swung her bare legs and giggled as she pointed at her canvas shoe. 'Look, me big toe's poking through. I got a new pair at Easter, but me mam ses I'll only spoil 'em if I wear 'em for school.'

She wriggled closer to Kate and slipped her hand through the older girl's arm. 'Ooh, I 'ave missed you, Kate, these holidays. I didn't even get down to see me Grannie Harris and to come an' play with you. Me mam's been a bit poorly. She's having another babby, y'know.'

Rosie's mother was always having another baby, Kate thought. Rosie, at five, already had two younger brothers and now there was another child on the way.

'She's been sick ev'ry morning this week, but that'll go after the first three months,' the child added, frighteningly knowledgeable for one so young. Rosie paused and looked about her as the trap rattled on. 'Funny without Danny, in't it?'

'Yes,' Kate mumbled, but could not trust herself to say any more. Rosie was the last person she wanted to see her tears. The child idolized her and Kate loved Rosie as she might a younger sister – more, if she were honest, than she loved her real sister, well, half-sister.

Rosie chattered on. 'We might be coming to live at the Point, in that cottage that's empty near me Grannie Harris's. I'll like that.'

Jonathan Godfrey looked down at the excited little girl. 'Your father will still work at the smithy, though, won't he?'

Rosie's father, Walter Maine, had been wounded in the war and had lost a leg. When he and Enid Harris from Fleethaven Point had married some six years earlier, Kate had been their bridesmaid, and the newly married couple had made their home in the two small rooms above the smithy where Walter worked.

'Oh yes.' The bright curls bobbed as Rosie nodded vigorously in answer to Jonathan's question. 'But there bain't room there for all us lot now, Mester.'

Kate saw the slow smile on her stepfather's face, and despite her unhappiness at missing Danny, she wanted to smile too. She well knew the cramped conditions the Maine family lived in, even though they had brought it upon themselves by having so many children. But it would be nice to have little Rosie living nearer.

'You tell your dad and mam that if they want to borrow the horses and a wagon to move, they'd be most welcome.'

The child's pink cheeks shone and her pretty mouth stretched wide in a grin. 'Thanks, Mester, I will,' and as the trap pulled up outside the school gate, Rosie jumped down and was gone, running into the playground.

'She's like a little whirlwind,' Jonathan murmured, and Kate smiled thinly in return.

'Bye, Dad. See you tonight.'

'Kate?' The soft tone made her look back at him. 'Be careful coming home tonight.' He paused, as if knowing that what he felt obliged to say would cause her more pain, 'You – you'll be on your own when you leave Rosie at the smithy.'

Kate closed her eyes against the tears and swallowed the lump in her throat. Not trusting herself to speak, she nodded, turned and ran into the playground without looking back.

All through the long morning, Kate's glance kept wandering to the place where Danny used to sit, now occupied by a fat, spotty-faced boy. It gave her a shock every time she glanced across, half-expecting, half-hoping to see Danny, to see instead the ugly boy sitting at Danny's desk. She didn't want anyone else sitting in the place that had been Danny's. She would have preferred it to remain empty rather than that anyone else should sit there. At playtime she sat morosely in the corner of the playground, refusing to join in any of the games, dreading the end of afternoon school when she must face the long walk home alone.

When the bell clanged for the end of the school day, Rosie skipped and hopped at her side, keeping Kate company as far as the smithy, chattering incessantly. Kate made no reply and finally the younger child looked up and said, 'Kate, a'ya cross with me?'

''Course not.'

'Then what's the matter?'

'Nothing.'

'Yes, there is.' Rosie danced lightly around Kate. 'You bin in trouble at school?'

'No.'

Silence.

They had reached the blacksmith's, Rosie's home, but

28

the child grasped Kate's hand and tugged at it insistently. 'What, then?'

The pent-up emotion of the last few days and the loneliness of this day burst out. 'I dun't want to go away to school. I dun't even want to go on going to school. I want to work – like Danny. I want to *be* with Danny.'

She saw Rosie's eyes widen and her mouth open, but Kate snatched her hand away and ran, leaving the child standing in the lane staring after her.

Kate ran and ran until she came to the lane alongside the dunes, but instead of following it, she scrambled up the slope, catching hold of the tough, spiky marram grass, and down the other side. Across the flat marsh, jumping the creeks, frightening a skylark into the air to defend its territory against her pounding feet, until she crested the rise of the easterly dunes and came to the beach. Her heart was pounding as she gulped air, her lungs bursting, but still she forced herself onwards, across the soft, dry sand until she came to the water's edge where she sank down, sobbing and breathless. She pulled her knees up to her chest, wrapped her arms around her legs and buried her face against her skirt.

The incoming tide came closer, receded and then crept closer still, its waves probing with gentle frothy edges until she became aware of its coldness soaking through her skirts. Sudden anger spurted and she smacked the flat of her palm on the encroaching water, sending a shower of salt water over herself. 'I won't be sent away. I won't go – I won't!' Now the tears that she had kept locked inside all day long spilled over.

The sea retreated but came again; a stronger, bigger wave catching her unawares so that she lost her balance and fell backwards into the shallows. Soaked to her skin, Kate scrambled to her feet. Sobbing, the sea-water squelching in her shoes, she began to run.

'Why, lovey, you're wet through!' Beth Eland reached out with gentle hands and pulled Kate into her warm kitchen. 'Whatever happened? Did ya fall in a creek?'

Kate sniffled and shook her head as she allowed herself to be led towards the rickety wooden chair set before the glowing range. A log settled in the grate sending up a welcoming shower of sparks.

Kate hesitated before she sat down, glancing up at Danny's mother. As if reading the girl's thoughts, the woman smiled gently and said, 'Go on, Mester Eland won't mind you sitting in his chair this once. Now, off with these wet things.'

Mrs Eland slipped the shawl off her own shoulders and wrapped it round Kate. 'I'll rinse ya pinny out and hang it on the line, else that mud'll stain it. Eh, dearie me, even ya shimmy's wet through.'

She took Kate's salt-stained clothes to the deep white sink under the window and worked the handle of the pump. Water splashed into the sink.

'I dun't know how I'm to get these dry in time for you to go home, Katie,' Mrs Eland murmured worriedly, taking an enamel jug from a shelf of pots and pans running along one wall and coming back to the range to ladle hot water from the side boiler.

Kate, her teeth chattering, held out her hands to the log fire, and wriggled her toes into the worn peg rug that covered the hearth. She felt the woman's anxious glance on her.

'Eh, ya shivering. I'll just get these clothes in to steep and I'll make you some hot milk with a spoon of honey in it.'

Kate nodded and sniffled. She was still unable to speak.

After her drenching in the sea, she had run along the beach. Sobbing and breathless, she had climbed the easterly dunes, crossed the marsh and come to the Point, deliberately avoiding going anywhere near her own home.

Danny, she must find Danny.

Now she lifted her tear-streaked face, her long hair straggling down her cheeks, to look up at his mother. 'Where's Danny?' she asked.

Mrs Eland bent over her as she gave Kate a steaming mug of milk and honey. 'There now, drink this. It'll warm ya. Danny? Why, he's not home from work yet.'

Kate wrapped her cold hands round the mug and sipped the hot liquid. 'How long will he be?'

The woman stood looking down at her, her brown eyes full of concern and something else Kate could not quite understand. There was more than just sympathy for her bedraggled state; there was a sadness in Beth Eland's eyes. 'Katie, ya'll have to forget our Danny now and make new friends at school. Ya going to a new school soon, aren't ya?'

The child's green eyes flashed with renewed vigour. Her mouth was set in a line of rebellion. 'I dun't want to go. I won't go!'

Mrs Eland sighed heavily. 'If it's what yar mam wants . . .'

Kate gazed up appealingly at the older woman. 'Couldn't you speak to me mam? Mebbe she'd listen to you . . .'

'No!' Beth Eland's sudden sharpness startled Kate and the mug she held wobbled, splashing hot milk on to her bare leg. The woman's eyes softened, but there was still a deep-rooted pain in their depths. 'Yar mam and me dun't talk to each other, child. Ya know we don't. Not since – not for a long time.'

She turned her back on Kate and went back to the sink, plunging her hands deep into the water and wringing out Kate's dress and pinafore, twisting the fabric in her grasp with a pent-up anger.

'But . . .' Kate began and then fell silent. Mrs Eland's back was rigid; it was obvious that further pleas would be fruitless.

*

'Where on earth have you been?'

Kate faced her mother's anger squarely. Inwardly she was trembling but she clenched her jaw stubbornly, her bottom lip pouting.

The tirade continued. 'We've been worried sick. Your father's been up and down that lane three times searching for you, right as far as the school. He even knocked on the school-house door to ask the headmistress . . .'

Kate's insides quivered afresh. That would mean more trouble at school in the morning. She lifted her chin defiantly. 'I got me clothes soaked and I – I . . .' She hesitated but there was no point in lying. Her mother was sure to find out the truth. Mrs Eland wouldn't tell her, but Grannie Harris very well might.

When Danny's mother had rinsed her clothes and hung them outside in the wind to dry she had come back into the cottage and stood before Kate once more. Her eyes were gentle and concerned again; the sudden, unusual hostility of a few moments before gone as swiftly as it had come.

'You ought to be going home, Katie. Yar mam will be worried.'

Kate had looked away, staring into the flames. 'I dun't reckon she'll miss me, not now she's got the babby.'

She felt the soft sigh on her cheek and was surprised to feel the touch of the woman's lips brushing briefly against her forehead. 'Oh, Katie love,' Beth Eland murmured and then, more briskly, 'I'll just nip next door. Mebbe Grannie Harris has some old clothes her girls have grown out of . . .'

A few moments later Mrs Eland returned with her arms full of an odd assortment of clothing. Panting slightly, she dumped the bundle on her kitchen table and for a moment the anxious look in her brown eyes was lifted as she laughed. 'Eh, Katie, Grannie Harris is such a hoarder. I reckon some of these clothes are Enid's!' Enid was Grannie Harris's daughter and Rosie's mother. Kate knew the garments must be years old!

Mrs Eland held up a shapeless dress. 'It's a bit big, but it might fit you. Fancy her keeping it all this time . . .'

They giggled together when Kate, a few moments later, stood before Mrs Eland, the long dress flapping around her ankles, the waistline somewhere around her slim, girlish hips. The older woman put her hand to her mouth as if to stifle her laughter. 'It looks dreadful, Kate, but it'll have to do. Ya can borrow my shawl and a pair of woollen stockings. You'll look like a scarecrow, but at least it'll get you home . . .'

The laughter faded for they both knew what awaited Kate then.

And now she was standing before her mother's wrath.

'I am waiting for an answer, Missy.'

'I – came home on the beach and fell in the sea. I went to the Point.'

Her mother's frown deepened and some instinct made the girl bend the truth a little and omit mentioning Danny's mother. 'Grannie Harris lent me these clothes,' she finished, praying fervently that neither Mrs Eland nor even Danny would bring her own clothes back to Brumbys' Farm when they were dry.

'Ya'll get ya'sen to bed this minute and no tea or supper.'

'But Mam . . .'

'I dun't know what I'm going to do with you, Kate Hilton. You've grown so wilful and disobedient, ya'll be the death of me. Mebbe your new school will mek you toe the line.'

Four

'Kate? Kate, are you asleep?'

It was her stepfather whispering from the doorway. Kate lifted her head from under the bedclothes. 'No, I'm not asleep, Dad.'

The door creaked as he pushed it wider open and stepped down the one step into her bedroom. He was carrying a glass of milk and a plate with a wedge of crusty bread spread thickly with fresh butter.

In the dimness of her bedroom – it was dusk outside her window now – he smiled down at her. 'Your mother's busy outside with the milking. Don't you tell her I've brought you this, will you?'

Kate sat up and reached for the milk eagerly. Crying had dried her mouth and left a salty taste on her lips.

'I'm sorry,' she said between gulps, 'you – went looking – for me.'

He sat down on the bed, holding the plate ready for her. 'You should have come straight home, Kate. I told you this morning. It was the first time you've had to walk all that way on your own . . .'

As his words reminded her, fresh tears started.

'We were worried, that's all.' His tone was firm, making her understand that she had been thoughtless, but he stroked the hair back from her forehead with a gentle gesture that took the sting from his reproach.

'Me mam's not really going to send me away to school,

34

is she?' Kate asked, her green eyes wide and appealing. She struggled inwardly, wanting to ask if it was because of the new baby. But Lilian was his child – and she wasn't. Even though this gentle, kind man was as good to her as any real father could have been, Kate thought, still she was not his child.

She bit deeply into the thick bread and butter and filled her mouth to stop it speaking.

He sighed and stroked her hair again. 'You're growing up, Kate. You're almost a woman and – and your mother's worried about you spending so much time with – with – well – boys.'

She saw him hesitate and thought that perhaps he was embarrassed to touch upon delicate, feminine matters.

A mischievous grin quirked at her mouth even through her recent tears. 'Me mam has told me about the birds and the bees. I mean, I know I mustn't let boys do to me what the old boar does to the sow when he visits.'

Her grin widened at his shocked gasp. 'Kate!'

'Oh, I've often watched,' she said airily, wiping the crumbs from her mouth with the back of her hand.

'You shouldn't talk like that. It's not the sort of talk for young girls . . .'

He paused and she saw he was staring at her through the gloom. 'What?' she prompted.

He sighed and she felt the waft of his breath on her face. 'Maybe,' he said slowly, thoughtfully, 'that's what your mother means. You need to learn to be more – more ladylike.'

Kate gave a snort of laughter and then clapped her hand over her mouth to stifle the noise. 'Me? Ladylike?' The thought was so comical that for a moment it drove away her tears.

'Your mother's only trying to do what's best for you.' Her stepfather patted her hand, picked up the empty plate and glass and stood up. 'I'll see what I can do, Kate. But I can't promise to make her change her mind, you know that, don't you?'

'Yes, Dad. But if you'd try.'

'I'll try,' he agreed, but she knew that was as much as he was able to promise.

There was one thing about her mother, Kate was obliged to acknowledge, she didn't bear malice and stay angry for days on end. The next morning when Kate appeared at the breakfast table, washed, dressed and ready for school, Esther Godfrey greeted her daughter with a smile and planted a kiss on her forehead. 'Ya lunch box is ready on the side there. Dun't forget it. D'ya want more milk on ya porridge?'

'No thanks, Mam.'

Kate sat at the kitchen table and ate while her mother picked up the baby from the cradle in the corner, sat in the Windsor chair by the fire in the range and opened her blouse front. The baby nuzzled greedily and began to suck loudly. Deliberately, Kate concentrated on her porridge.

'Shall ya come to church with me on Sunday, Katie? It's time I was churched after having Lilian. Ya Dad'll mind her for once.'

Eagerly, Kate said, 'Ooh yes, Mam. I'd like that.'

She was rewarded with one of Esther's radiant smiles. 'That's settled, then.'

Happily, Kate finished her breakfast. On Sunday, for a few precious hours, she would have her mother all to herself.

She didn't see Danny again until Morning Service on the Sunday. He was sitting in his usual place beside his mother on the opposite side of the church. Kate, being first in the pew and landing up against the white-washed wall, knelt on the hassock and covered her face with her hands. Slowly she spread her fingers a fraction and peeped between them to study Danny's bent head. Although he was dressed in his Sunday best suit, the collar of his white shirt stiffly starched, his face looked thinner than just a week ago and there were dark shadows under his eyes.

All local children worked from an early age – it was the way of all their lives – but Kate guessed that Danny's first full week as a working man had been tough and exhausting. It was written on his young face.

As the congregation stood to leave at the end of the service, Kate shifted from one foot to the other impatiently.

'Stand still, Kate, and stop jiffling. I've to see the vicar about our Lilian's christening,' her mother whispered. 'Just be patient, will ya?' Behind her mother's back, Kate pouted. Now she would not be able to catch Danny before he left with his mother to walk the two miles home.

The vicar greeted Esther Godfrey warmly and patted Kate on the head with annoying condescension. 'So, Mrs Godfrey, you want to bring your little one to be baptized.'

'We thought between harvests, Vicar. About the end of July.'

'Mmm, yes, yes, I think we could fit you in after Morning Service. Shall we say the last Sunday in July?'

Kate watched her mother nod agreement, shake the vicar's hand and walk swiftly down the path to their pony and trap.

Kate skipped beside her. 'Walk properly, Kate. You're no longer a child.'

Kate sighed, but obeyed.

It was a fine, warm morning and once on the coast road the pony trotted smartly, the breeze lifting his silky mane.

'There's Danny – and Mrs Eland. Can't we give them a ride home, Mam?' Kate shouted above the noise of the wheels. The only reply her mother made was to slap the reins to make the pony go even faster. Esther Godfrey stared straight ahead, not even glancing down as they passed the pair.

Kate saw Mrs Eland and Danny step on to the grass verge to allow the trap to pass. Danny looked up at Kate, grinned and waved, but Mrs Eland – just like Kate's mother – stared stonily ahead and made no acknowledgement that the trap had even passed near them.

The day Kate had so looked forward to had ended in disappointment.

'We're moving to the Point on Saturday.' Rosie's cherubic face was one broad grin as she clambered up into the trap for her daily ride to school with Kate the following morning. 'We're coming to live in the end cottage.' She flung herself against Kate. 'Won't we have fun? I'll be able to come and play every day and help you on the farm, c'lecting eggs and feedin' the hens, won't I? Do say ya'll let me, Katie?'

Kate could not prevent tears filling her eyes.

'What's the matter? Dun't you want me to come and live near you?' The merry smile died and Rosie's lower lip quivered.

Swiftly, Kate hugged the younger child tightly. ''Course I do. But – but I might not be there mesen.' She glanced at her stepfather. The indulgent smile that had curved his gentle mouth when the excited Rosie had climbed into the trap faded. He looked away and flicked the reins to make the pony walk on.

'What d'ya mean?' The little girl was mystified.

'Me mam might be sending me away to school. I'll only be here in the holidays.'

Rosie blinked rapidly. 'You – you mean you won't come home at night?'

Kate, unable to speak, shook her head.

Rosie, sitting beside her, snuggled closer and took Kate's hand in her small one. She patted it and then held it tightly for the rest of journey to the school. Neither of them spoke again. Not even Rosie could think of anything to say.

Moving day for the Maine family caused great excitement for everyone who lived at the Point.

The Godfreys lent their farm wagon and the two horses – Boxer and Bonnie – to pull it. Jonathan Godfrey drove it to the smithy, helped Walter Maine to load all their belongings and then, with the high load wobbling precariously, drove back along the coast road towards the Point. Later in the afternoon Kate went with her mother in the pony and trap to fetch the rest of the Maine family.

'Enid, you look done in,' Kate heard her mother say in a voice that forbade any argument. 'Ya'll come back to the farm and rest awhile and let the others unload and settle things in. Kate can look after the bairns.'

'But, Mam, I want to . . .' Kate began, but a look from her mother quelled her protest.

It was Saturday afternoon and Danny might be home early from work. She had thought that helping the Maines to move would give her an excuse to go to the Point. Now she had to stay at home and play with Rosie and her two younger brothers.

'I'm three months gone, Esther,' Enid was saying quietly to Kate's mother.

Esther clicked her tongue against her teeth in an expression of exasperation. 'Well, your Walter might have lost his leg in the war, Enid, but he certainly didn't lose owt else, did he?'

Enid snorted with laughter and clapped her hand over her mouth. For a moment the tiredness left her eyes as the two women exchanged a joke that the children could not share.

'You're having 'em a mite too fast for your health, Enid. You're thinner than ya used to be.'

'I reckon it's livin' in the town,' Enid murmured. 'I've never really liked it above the smithy. The smell of the forge never leaves the place.'

At Enid's words Kate could almost hear the sizzling of the iron and smell the burning hoof as Walter shod a horse.

'Well, you're moving back to the Point not a moment too soon to my idea, and ya'll have ya mam nearby to keep an eye on ya.'

'She can't wait to have a brood of little ones running around again.'

Kate watched moodily as the two women smiled at each other.

'Take them into the front garden, Kate,' her mother ordered as she drew the trap to a halt in the yard of Brumbys' Farm. 'But keep them away from the pond at the side of the house, mind.'

It was early evening before Kate took the three children down the lane and over the Hump to the Point. The youngest boy had to be carried and was asleep against Kate's shoulder by the time they arrived at the cottages. His brother dragged his feet with tiredness, but Rosie seemed to have boundless energy, running ahead of them to stand on top of the Hump shouting back, 'Come on, oh, do come on,' then running down the other side of the bank and across the grass towards her new home.

Georgie and Peter Harris were lifting the last heavy box from the cart.

'Now then, our Rosie. Ya've a little bedroom all to ya'sen. Come and see.'

Rosie squealed with delight, clapped her hands and ran into the cottage.

Georgie grinned at Kate. ''Tis only like a big cupboard, but she'll love it.'

Kate smiled.

''Spect ya've had ya hands full with these three all day,' George continued as Enid came out to collect the boys from Kate.

'Thanks ever so for having 'em, Kate,' she said. 'I dun't know what we'd have done with them under us feet all day.'

Kate opened her mouth to reply but Rosie appeared in the doorway. 'Come and see my bedroom, Katie, it's . . .' she paused as her darting eyes caught sight of something beyond Kate and her rosebud mouth shaped itself into an 'oh' of surprise. 'Look, look,' she pointed. 'There's Danny.'

Kate turned to follow the line of Rosie's pointing finger to see Danny free-wheeling down the steep incline of the Hump on a bicycle, his legs sticking straight out on either side. He came rocketing on to the grass, hit a bump and promptly fell off, legs, arms and bicycle all in a heap.

The two girls gave cries of alarm and ran towards him, while Georgie and Peter just stood and laughed.

Kate pulled the huge bicycle away while Rosie squatted down beside Danny. He lay on the grass, his eyes closed, not moving.

'He's not dead, is he?' Rosie whispered.

'Don't be daft, Rosie, he's pretending.' But a cold sliver of fear made her say sharply, 'Danny!'

Still he did not move. Kate flung the bicycle down again, dropped to her knees and bent over him. She took hold of his hand and chafed it. As she bent closer, Danny jerked his head up and planted a kiss on her cheek. Startled, Kate fell backwards, but Rosie shrieked with laughter. 'He kissed you! He kissed you!'

Rosie jumped up and began to pull at his arm. 'Get up, Danny. I want a piggy-back.'

Danny gave an exaggerated groan, but winked at Kate. 'Children!'

He made a big performance of rising, holding his back as if it pained him and bending double. Rosie giggled. 'You're p'tending, like Katie ses. You're p'tending.'

Danny's brown eyes were full of mischief. 'Come on then, up you get.' Obligingly, he bent down so that the little girl could climb on to his back, her chubby arms tight around his neck.

Danny galloped towards the cottages with Rosie bouncing up and down on his back and shrieking with laughter, leaving Kate to pick up his bicycle and wheel it after them.

The Sunday morning of Lilian's christening was fine and bright, but breezy. Scudding clouds made the sunlight fitful, sending shadows running across the fields of waving corn.

'We'll have tea out on the front lawn,' her mother decided. 'Kate, help yar dad fetch the trestle tables from the Grange. Squire said I could borrow them. Then when you come back, you must get changed and ready for church. Jonathan, are your folks going straight to the church?'

Orders and questions came in quick succession from Esther Godfrey's lips, scarcely allowing time for any reply. 'When we get back from church, Kate, I want you to help me carry all the food out into the garden.' Her mother seemed to have been baking during the whole of the previous week and now mountains of pasties and tarts, cakes and plum bread stood ready in the pantry. 'Oh, I do hope it dun't rain,' Esther added, glancing anxiously at the sky.

'Danny says it's going to be fine all day.'

Her mother's green eyes flashed. 'When did you see *him*? I told you not to go to the Point . . .'

'I don't, Mam, honest,' Kate said reasonably, trying to pacify her mother's quick temper. It wasn't much use going there anyway, now he was working, but she kept these thoughts to herself. 'Have you asked the folks from the Point to the christening?'

'The Harrises and the Maines.'

Kate looked up at her mother. 'Not Danny and his mother and father?' As soon as she had let the words slip from her lips, Kate could have bitten off the end of her tongue.

'We dun't have owt to do wi' them.'

'You mean you and Mrs Eland dun't speak. Everyone else does. Dad sees mester in the pub and me an' Danny . . .'

'Aye, you and Danny, you and Danny! That's all I seem to have heard for years.'

'Why dun't you like him now? You used to – to . . .' Kate hesitated. Vague memories, elusive and fleeting, were nudging at her mind. 'You used to make him welcome. When me real dad . . .'

'Stop it! You hear me? I dun't want to speak of him. 'Specially not today.'

'Why, Mam? Just tell me why?'

Suddenly, Esther Godfrey seemed weary. She sighed and turned away, more in sadness than in anger now. 'Dun't ask me, Katie love, please dun't ask me. Ya wouldn't like the answer.'

43

Five

'I'm going with me grandad,' Kate announced firmly and slipped her hand through Will Benson's arm.

'Ya grandad's riding in the trap with me and the baby, Grannie Harris, Enid and Walter,' Esther said. 'It's all arranged. The rest of you will have to walk to the church.'

'What about Rosie? She can't walk all that way.'

'Enid's bairns aren't coming to the church, but they'll come here after.'

'Who's looking after them?' But Kate knew the answer almost before she asked the question.

'The Elands,' was her mother's terse reply.

That meant Rosie would be with Danny. Her two best friends and she could not be with them. I'd rather be playing with them, Kate thought morosely, than going to the christening of a squealing infant!

When the whole party arrived at the church porch, two women were waiting there.

'Jonathan! My dear boy.' The older one of the two women stretched out her arms and enveloped him.

'Hello, Mother.'

Kate watched as her stepfather succumbed to the woman's rapturous hug and then he turned to the younger woman and kissed her on the cheek. 'Hello, Peggy. How are you, love?'

Jonathan Godfrey's tone, always gentle and kindly, had

44

an even deeper note of tenderness when he spoke to his sister, so that Kate stared at the tall, slim woman with interest.

Introductions were made all round.

'I'm so sorry your father couldn't come, Jonathan,' Mrs Godfrey was saying. 'He has a wretched cold and it's settled on his chest. He's cough, cough, cough . . .' She cast her eyes skywards in a gesture of resignation. 'He keeps me awake half the night, too,' she added, but she was smiling as she said it and there was no rancour in her tone.

The party moved into the church and sat at the back near the font while Morning Service continued. Lilian whimpered and grizzled all the way through and when it came to the point of the christening where the vicar splashed water on to her forehead, the baby set up a loud wail that embarrassed Kate. She wished she could rush out of the church. Instead she shrank towards her grandfather, leaning against his arm, to be rewarded by him smiling down at her. Although baby Lilian was as much his grandchild as she was, Kate did not feel her place in Will Benson's affections had been usurped by the new arrival.

'Come on, me little lass,' Will whispered as the party emerged from the church and everyone gathered around Esther and the baby, 'let us slip away. We'll walk back home on the beach, shall we?'

'Oh yes, Grandad,' Kate agreed eagerly, then her expression sobered as she looked down at his polished boots. 'But won't the sand spoil ya boots?'

Will Benson chuckled, 'Mebbe, mebbe so. But they'll shine up again with a bit of elbow grease. Come on, lass, afore an argy-bargy about who's ridin' in the trap starts.'

For Kate it was the best time of the whole day, her walk on the beach with her grandfather.

As they walked at the water's edge towards home, she could see two figures in the distance. As they drew closer,

Kate could see Danny digging in the sand, while Rosie, bare-foot, skipped and danced around him. She saw the child run towards the sea and then heard Rosie shriek with delight, as the waves rushed up the beach towards her. 'Ooh, it's cold. It's freezin'!' The little girl hopped about on the sand, but seconds later she was dancing towards the water once more, daring it to catch her again.

Danny lifted his face to watch Rosie's antics, an affection-ate smile curving his mouth. He caught sight of Kate and his smile broadened. He straightened up and waved to her.

Poised on her toes, Kate said, 'Grandad, I'm just off to see Danny and Rosie.'

To her surprise, her grandfather frowned. 'I dun't think you ought to, lass. Ya mam . . .'

'I'll not be a minute, Grandad, honest. You go on and I'll catch you up afore you get home. You know how fast I can run.'

The old man laughed. 'Aye well – all right, but dun't be long, mind?'

But already Kate was running towards her friends.

'Kate! Kate!' Rosie squealed with delight. 'Danny's build-ing me a sand-castle. Look – with a moat an' all. When the sea comes in, it'll go all round it. In't he clever?'

'Why don't you collect some shells to decorate the sides of the castle, Rosie?' Kate suggested, exchanging a glance with Danny. She had lost count of the number of sand-castles they had built together, digging deep moats and adding shells as windows and doors and turrets. Then standing and watching as the sea slowly demolished their efforts.

As Rosie began to collect stones and shells, Kate said, 'I can't stay. I've got to help with the guests.'

The smile on Danny's face faded and he lowered his gaze. He resumed his digging, piling the sand higher and higher.

Kate stood awkwardly for a moment, suddenly embarrassed because the Elands had not been invited to the christening.

'I'll try and get out later.'

He shrugged his thin shoulders.

Kate bit her lip. She badly wanted to stay and talk to him. She didn't like Danny going quiet on her. It wasn't like him. She glanced towards the sand-dunes. Her grandfather had disappeared. He'd be picking his way across the marsh now. Soon he'd be at Brumbys' Farm and her mother would want to know where she was.

'I wish I could stay now, but I daren't.'

Danny banged the back of the spade against the sides of the castle, flattening the sand. Still he would not look at her again.

Rosie came back clutching several shells to her chest. 'Where shall I put 'em, Danny?'

'On the sides. Look – like this.' He squatted down, and, taking a couple of the shells, he pressed them into the sand-castle.

For a moment Kate stood watching them, feeling excluded from their game.

'I'll – see you later.'

Danny nodded absently. 'Yeah, see ya.'

Kate turned and began to run, her flying feet sending up little showers of sand as she went.

Back at Brumbys' Farm she was set to work to help her mother cater for the party, running from house to front garden and back again so many times until sweat plastered strands of her long hair to her forehead.

'So you're Kate.'

She was standing before Mrs Godfrey, holding out a plate piled high with plum bread. Her stepfather's mother was very smart to Kate's idea. She wore a loose-fitting flowery dress with a full-length coat over it, the sleeves gathered with smocking just above the wrist. From beneath her close-fitting hat, two neat brown curls peeped out. Her shoes were dainty, with pointed toes and a T-bar strap across the top of her foot. Her complexion was pale, made more so by face-powder, and red lipstick accentuated her wide mouth.

The woman took a piece of the plum bread. 'Is this all your mother's baking?' When Kate nodded, she added, 'She'd make her fortune if she opened a shop in the High Street. What do you think, Peg?'

Jonathan's sister nodded. 'It's lovely.'

Kate smiled at her. 'I do like ya frock.' She had been admiring the younger woman's outfit ever since she had first seen Peggy and Mrs Godfrey in the church porch. The dress was low-waisted, the skirt knee-length and made in a blue silky material and was decorated with intricate embroidery. Kate longed to feel it. The cloche hat which Peggy wore, its brim almost hiding her eyes, was trimmed with flowers made out of the same material. She wore a long pearl necklace, one strand tight around her neck, the other dangling down almost to her waist.

'Why, thank you, Kate,' Peggy said in her soft voice.

Kate couldn't take her eyes off the two women in their finery. In comparison, her mother's long black skirt, reaching almost to her ankles, and her crisp, white blouse seemed plain.

'Peggy works in one of the big stores in the High Street,' Mrs Godfrey was saying with an obvious note of pride in her voice. 'She spotted this fabric when it first came in and bought a length.'

Kate's puzzled glance went from one to the other. Peggy smiled. 'Mother's a dressmaker, she made this dress and trimmed the hat.'

Kate gasped. 'Did you mek them flowers?' She pointed at the hat.

'Yes, dear,' Mrs Godfrey said modestly.

'They're lovely,' Kate said, hardly able to take her eyes from them. Her gaze dropped to the face beneath the hat. Peggy was pretty, Kate thought, with a smooth skin and a well-shaped mouth. And she was kind, like her brother, Jonathan, but sometimes when her face fell into repose and she thought no one was watching her, she seemed, to the observant Kate, to have an air of sadness about her.

Mrs Godfrey was leaning towards Kate, smiling and nodding, 'When you come to school in Lincoln you'll have to come and see us and Peggy will take you shopping. There, you'd like that, wouldn't you? You'll love the bustle of the city. There's always something going on. Not like here . . .' The woman glanced over her shoulder across the flat farm fields and shivered slightly. 'Whatever do you find to do here?' she murmured, then added more briskly, 'You'll have such a good time. There's the shops and the markets and the theatre and the pictures. Peggy will show you around, won't you, Peg? You'll love it, Kate, really you will.'

'Of course you must come and see us, Kate.' Peggy's smile was genuine and warm. Dutifully, Kate nodded. Though she knew they meant it kindly, the talk of city life sounded a little frightening. It didn't make her feel any happier about leaving all the things that were familiar, to go to boarding school.

Not one jot.

When all their guests had departed, Jonathan drove his mother and sister back into town to catch the evening train. As they made their farewells, Mrs Godfrey hugged Kate to her, enfolding her in a waft of flowery perfume.

49

'Now, don't forget. When you come to school in September, your Aunty Peg will come to the school and fetch you to our house for tea one Sunday.'

'Thank you,' Kate said politely, and was rewarded by one of her mother's brilliant smiles. 'Thank you very much.'

'Isn't Aunty Peggy married, Mam?' Kate asked as they stood at the gate waving at the trap disappearing along the lane.

'No.'

'She's ever so nice, isn't she?'

'Well, of course, she would be.' Esther smiled, putting her arm about Kate's shoulders as they went back towards the farmhouse. 'She's ya dad's sister.'

Kate giggled inwardly. In her mother's eyes, any relative of Jonathan's couldn't help being nice.

As they went into the scullery, they both heard Lilian's wailing.

'Oh, there she goes!' Esther sighed. 'And there's all the pots to wash . . .'

'I'll do them, Mam. You go and see to her.'

'You're a good girl, Katie, I dun't know what I'd 'ave done without you today. I'll just feed her and then I'll give you a hand.'

Kate stifled a yawn. She was tired, but guessed her mother was even more weary. 'It's all right, Mam, I'll manage.' She picked up a pile of dirty plates and went through to the deep white sink in the back scullery, while her mother sat in the Windsor chair to feed Lilian. Kate would do anything to escape the sight of the baby guzzling at her mother's overflowing breast. She would even face the mountain of washing-up single-handed to avoid seeing the tender expression on her mother's face as she gazed down at the greedy Lilian.

Half an hour later, her stepfather came in through the back door.

'All on your own, Katie? Where's your mother?'

'Upstairs. Lilian won't settle.' She set another of her mother's best cups carefully on the draining-board.

Jonathan picked up a tea-towel and began to dry the pots. He grinned at Kate, the familiar, lopsided smile crinkling his eyes. 'All the excitement of getting herself christened, I expect.'

There was silence between them, the only sounds being the clatter of china as together they washed and dried it, setting it carefully on the kitchen table for Esther to put away herself in the cabinet in her front parlour.

He was an unusual man, Kate mused. Not many men would help with the household chores the way he did.

'Babies – little babies – ' he began hesitantly, 'are not much fun. She'll be different when she's grown a little.'

'I shan't be here that much, shall I?' Kate muttered.

The silence lengthened and she felt he was searching for the right words. 'Kate, you mustn't think . . .'

'At last!' Esther stepped out of the kitchen into the scullery. 'I thought she'd never settle!'

Kate saw the glance that passed between her mother and stepfather.

'You all right, love?' His blue eyes were full of tender concern.

Her mother moved and stood close to him, reached up and, placing her palms against his chest, kissed him gently on the mouth. Still holding the tea-towel in one hand and a plate in the other, his arms went around her and they stood together, oblivious now of Kate's presence. Whatever he had been going to say to her had flown from his mind the moment her mother had stepped into the scullery.

Kate bent her head over the soapy washing-up water, her hair falling forward to hide her tears.

*

51

'It's all settled – you start in two weeks' time.'

Her mother was standing before her dressed in her best costume and pulling off her gloves. 'I've been to Lincoln on the train today and seen the headmistress – Miss Denham. I'm to take you on the Wednesday – the day after the term actually starts. She says that will give everyone else time to have settled back into school.'

Kate felt the colour drain from her face, but no words would come. All she could do was stare at her mother in shock.

But Esther Godfrey, full of her day in the city, of her success with the headmistress of the St Mary's School for Young Ladies, was not even looking at her daughter. Now she was turning away to talk directly to her husband. 'Has the baby been all right? It's a long time to leave her, but I had no choice. It's a good job I've started weaning her.'

'Did you see Mother and Father?'

'Yes – I had a nice dinner with them and a long chat with them about the school. They reckon she'll be fine there, and they'll take her out on a Sunday afternoon. The headmistress said that was when the girls are allowed out with family or friends. Well chaperoned, of course.'

'Peg would fetch her. Did you see Peg? Is she all right?'

'No, she was at work, but I asked after her and she's fine.' She paused and Kate saw the mischievous smile curve her mother's lips. 'I must say, I like your dad. I reckon he took quite a fancy to me.' Almost coquettishly, Esther smoothed tendrils of her hair that were escaping from the combs.

Jonathan caught her by the waist and planted a kiss on her mouth. 'Well, of course he would.'

'He's like you, ain't he? I mean, you're like him.'

'I would like to think so. I admire my father – he's kind and gentle and all his pupils adore him . . .'

'Is he a teacher?' Kate butted in, desperately seeking some kind of hope. 'Will he be there – at the school I'm going to?'

Her mother and stepfather looked round at her, surprise on their faces. They had been so busy planning, deciding her future, that they had forgotten she was even in the room.

Jonathan shook his head, 'No love. He teaches at a boys' school. He won't . . .'

'Then I won't go,' Kate stormed. 'I won't!'

She whirled around, rushed out of the kitchen and through the scullery and dragged open the back door. Then she was running – across the yard, out of the gate, across the lane and up the dunes through the trees – ignoring the shouts of her stepfather behind her.

'Kate! Kate, don't, love. Please don't!'

She stayed in the sandy hollow until the sun had sunk behind the dunes, waiting. Waiting for the time when she knew Danny would be home from work. Then she climbed out of the hollow and, taking a diagonal line across the marsh, came out at the back of the line of four cottages at the Point. She could hear shrieks of laughter coming from the stretch of grass in front of the cottages and recognized Rosie's high-pitched excited chatter organizing her younger brothers in their game. She listened intently. Was Danny there, too?

She moved towards the back door of one of the centre cottages where Danny lived. His mother came out of the little wash-house set at right-angles to the back door and almost dropped the basket of washing she was carrying.

'Why, Kate! You made me jump.' Mrs Eland peered closely through the shadows at her. 'You in bother again, lass?'

Kate shook her head and qualified the negative response

53

by saying, 'Well, not exactly.' There was no doubt she would be in trouble for having stayed out so late. 'Where's Danny?'

She heard Beth Eland's soft sigh. 'He's with his dad up at the headland. They're at the boat.'

As Kate turned away, the older woman said, 'Kate – you – you ought to be finding ya'sen other friends now Danny's working, y'know.'

Kate stood still. Her heart was pounding in her chest as if she had been running a mile. Oh, no! Not Danny's mother too! And it wasn't the first time she'd said as much, either. She turned slowly to stare at Beth. The older woman's brown eyes were troubled. 'It'd be – for the best, lovey,' she added softly.

Was everyone trying to keep her away from Danny? Kate couldn't believe it. She gave a sob and, turning away, began to run. She did not stop until she reached the point of land where the river widened out into the sea.

'Danny. Danny!' she shouted, standing on the grassy headland directly above the muddy river bank. The tide was receding and the Elands' fishing boat was almost stranded on the mud where Robert Eland had moored it earlier in the afternoon at high tide.

She shaded her eyes against the bright gold of the setting sun, low in the western sky. A shadow moved on the boat. 'Katie? What you doing here? Summat wrong?' He clambered over the side and swung his way up the wooden planking of the small jetty that straddled the mud to the boat.

'What's up, Katie?' He peered at her through the gloom and although she could not see the expression in his eyes, she could hear the concern in his voice. It caused a lump in her throat and tears to prickle her eyelids. At least Danny cares, she thought. The words came tumbling from her lips in a jumble, falling over themselves in her eagerness to tell him of her distress.

'Me mam's been to Lincoln – to that school – it's all arranged. I'm to go in two weeks. She's sending me away!' The last was on a wail of despair.

He came and stood in front of her. He put his arms about her and she clung to him, burying her face against his shoulder. They stood on the headland, silhouetted against the red gold of the setting sun. She felt his hands, rough and calloused with the heavy work he now did daily, but surprisingly gentle, stroke her hair. 'Don't cry, Katie. It'll be all right. Perhaps you'll enjoy it when you get there . . .'

'I won't!' Her words were muffled against him but none the less vehement. 'I'll hate it! I'll miss you so much!'

Involuntarily his arms tightened about her. She lifted her face up and tilted her head back and then wound her arms around his neck. They gazed at each other.

'Katie . . .' he began, but whatever he had been going to say, the words remained unspoken for at that moment a shout made them both turn to see Kate's mother, her skirts held high, running towards them. 'Keep away from her, Danny Eland. Dun't you lay a finger on her else I'll . . .'

Kate gasped, shocked to see the rage on her mother's face. Two spots of vivid colour burned in Esther's cheeks and her hair was coming loose from its combs and falling down her back.

She reached them and grasped Kate's arm roughly, jerking her away from Danny.

'Mam, you're hurting. Don't . . .'

'I'll hurt you, me girl, if I ever so much as catch you with him again.'

Kate began to struggle against Esther's grip. This was Danny her mother was talking about; Danny Eland, her life-long friend.

'Mam . . .' she began, but Esther was dragging Kate away from the headland, away from Danny. Kate half-turned back to him, tried to twist out of her mother's grasp. 'Danny . . .' She gave a cry of anguish, but her mother's hold on her arm only tightened.

He made no move. He was standing on the headland, silhouetted against the burnished evening sky, a lonely, bemused figure, as much at a loss to understand what was happening as Kate herself.

Doors were opening in the cottages and faces peering out as Esther Godfrey hustled her daughter homewards. Grannie Harris and next door to her, Mrs Eland, stepped out on to the grass.

As they drew level, Esther shook her fist. 'Keep him away from my girl, Beth Eland. Keep ya bastard away. If ya don't . . .' She paused to drag in a painful, heaving breath. There was menace in her tone as she added more quietly, 'If ya don't – I'll see he knows the reason why!'

Six

The day she had been dreading had arrived.

The summer had passed all too quickly and already it was September. 'I'll miss the Harvest Festival and the Harvest Supper at the Grange.' All her protests were in vain. Her mother was adamant and there was nothing Kate, nor her stepfather, could do about it. Esther Godfrey remained inflexible even in the face of her own father's wrath. From the kitchen Kate had listened as Will Benson had stood in the doorway of the pantry, whilst Esther churned the butter.

'The city's no place for that lass,' he had railed. 'She'll be miserable . . .'

'She will be if you keep putting the idea into her head,' her mother had snapped back.

'But, Esther . . .'

'No "buts", Dad. Kate's going to boarding school for a couple of years and that's that.' The handle of the barrel churn flew round under Esther's angry hand, until they could hear the flip-flop of the thickening butter.

'Huh.' Will Benson turned away from the pantry door. 'Well, I reckon ya'll regret it, lass. Dun't say Ah didn't warn ya.'

'I won't,' Esther said, grimly determined.

Coming back through the kitchen Will took hold of Kate's arm and led her out into the yard. 'Come and see me off,' he whispered. When they were outside he stood before her

57

and put his hands on her shoulders, looking down at her with what looked suspiciously like tears glistening in his eyes.

'Katie love, there's nowt more Ah can do.'

Kate shook her head sadly. 'Dun't worry, Grandad. You tried.'

'Now listen to me, lass. The village where I live – Suddaby – you know it, dun't ya?'

Kate nodded.

'Well, it's between here and Lincoln. If ever you need help, you send me word and I'll come to ya.' He gave her a gentle shake as if to emphasize his words. 'Remember now, won't ya?'

Kate looked up at his worried face, feeling suddenly the older of the two, as if it were her grandfather who needed the reassurance that she would be all right. She forced a smile to her mouth and said as brightly as she could manage. 'I'll remember, Grandad. Dun't you worry. Mebbe me mam's right and I'll love it when I get there.'

They were brave words but there had been a hollow ring to her feigned confidence.

Now it was the morning she must go.

She took a last look around the big bedroom that had been hers alone until now, for only last night her mother had talked of moving the baby into the big room, 'Now that Kate will only be home in the holidays'.

So, already it was no longer 'her' room. Kate's glance roamed over her well-loved toys; the rocking horse standing in the corner, forlorn and neglected for Kate had long since outgrown him. No doubt Lilian would soon be big enough to ride him again and she'd soon have her fingers into all Kate's other toys too; the doll with the china face, the wooden doll's house her stepfather had made for her. The whole of the front opened in two big doors revealing four rooms, hallway and landing. Two miniature pot dolls inhabited the house and the tiny furniture was all made to scale.

The girl turned away and went downstairs feeling strange and awkward in her new school uniform; a long-sleeved winceyette blouse with a tie in the school colours of brown and gold and a brown pleated gym-slip falling straight from her shoulders to just below her knee. The matching braid girdle tied around the waist made her feel bulky and shapeless.

'I feel like a sack of 'tates tied round the middle,' she muttered gloomily. Thick brown woollen stockings held up by suspenders buttoned on to a Liberty bodice made her legs hot and in her sturdy winter boots her feet were sweating.

At the bottom of the stairs she turned to the right and went into the best parlour with its plush chairs and polished brass fender. An organ stood in the corner, but no one ever played it. In the middle of the floor her trunk stood open all neatly packed and ready to be closed when the last-minute things had been added.

Her mother had been sewing for weeks making blouses, pyjamas and even the serge gym-slip. 'Three of everything!' Esther had exclaimed when the list had arrived. 'I can't afford them fancy prices to be buying all ya need ready made. My sewing's as good as anyone's – I'll have to make as many things as I can.'

Now everything was packed in a huge trunk ready to be loaded into the trap. Her stepfather was to drive Kate and her mother to the station in Lynthorpe where they would catch the train to Lincoln. 'Be sure to get a porter to organize taking her trunk up to the school when you get to Lincoln,' he told them.

'I don't need to be tipping no porter to carry something we can carry oursens...' her mother began indignantly.

'Esther,' Jonathan said quietly, 'it won't look good at the

school. Believe me. If you want your daughter to become a "young lady", she's got to start acting like one.'

'Dun't mean she's got to be idle,' her mother muttered but as Jonathan opened his mouth to speak again, she put up her hand palm outwards. 'All right, all right, we'll do as you say.'

And now there was only an hour left before they must leave.

Kate turned and left the parlour and walked back through the narrow hallway, the stairs leading up on her left, and to her right was the front door which opened out on to the garden. Then she passed through the living room, pausing only to glance round, just looking at all the familiar things as if for the last time. The furniture was old-fashioned but everything was polished and sparkling. A red chenille cloth covered the table and red velvet curtains hung at the window. On the mantelpiece brass ornaments shone and twinkled. Slowly she came to the kitchen.

Huge hams from the last time they had killed a pig hung from hooks in the ceiling and to her left was the door leading down two steps into the pantry where all the dairy work and the butter-making was carried out. In the centre stood a plain, scrubbed table and on the far wall was the huge range, the centre of the home almost, Kate thought. It heated the water, boiled and cooked all their food, and its fire warmed them on cold winter days and nights. They even bathed in turn in front of it every Friday night in the tin bath that hung on a peg in the wash-house.

Her mother had let down the clothes airer on the rope from the ceiling and Kate paused a moment to watch her hanging freshly ironed clothes over the wooden slats.

Kate moved on out of the kitchen and through the back scullery. She opened the back door and stepped into the yard.

Her mother's voice followed her. 'Dun't you go getting ya new uniform messed up.'

'No, Mam,' came the automatic reply.

It was a soft, September morning when the heat of the summer was gone and there was a freshness in the air. Kate lifted her head and breathed in all the smells of the farmyard, the scents of home. The cows, the horses, even the pigs and always the breeze carried a hint of the sea as a background perfume.

'Goodbye, Boxer, goodbye, Bonnie.' She patted each of the heavy horses in turn and they nudged at her shoulder over the half-door of their stable. 'I ain't no sugar,' she apologized and added ruefully, 'Not in this stupid dress, I ain't.'

She looked in at the pigs and then wandered round the side of the house past the pond with the huge weeping willow tree bending over and trailing its fronds in the water and round to the front of the house which faced westwards. She stood a moment among the fruit trees laden now with the fruit which usually she helped to pick.

This year she would not be here.

She gazed out across the flat fields beneath the huge expanse of sky. Stooks of corn stood sentinel in the fields waiting to be collected and brought to the farmyard to be stacked. She would not be here to hear the familiar cry, 'Harvest home, harvest home', when her mother placed the last sheaf on the last load. She would not be able to join the gleaners who scoured the fields for every last wisp of corn.

She turned away and went back through the yard and out into the lane. She stood for a moment poised on her toes, holding her breath. She glanced back over her shoulder but there was no one in the yard. Then she began to run.

'I'm sorry, lovey. Danny's not here. He's at work.'

'I was afraid he might be. I – I came to say goodbye.'

'Oh,' Mrs Eland said. 'Oh, I see.' She was looking at Kate with her brown, sad, eyes. Her black hair was drawn severely back from her face into a bun at the nape of her neck. Already there were wisps of grey at her temples even though, Kate guessed, Beth Eland must be a similar age to her mother, – only in her early thirties.

Returning the woman's steady gaze, Kate thought – and not for the first time – that Danny's mother could be really beautiful, as striking as her own mother, if she were to take a little trouble over her appearance. She had a lovely face, with high cheek-bones and dark eyes fringed with long black lashes. Her figure was a little too buxom to be fashionable, but to Kate it made Mrs Eland seem all the more warm and motherly. She was reaching out now and touching Kate's face in a gentle gesture. 'Tek care of ya'sen, lovey.'

Kate nodded and said flatly, 'I'll see you at – Christmas.' It seemed an age away and though Danny's mother said, 'It'll soon be here,' even her tone lacked conviction.

At the cottage next door, Kate found herself swept against Grannie Harris's ample bosom. 'Eh me lass, we'll miss you, all on us. 'Specially Rosie. There's nobody like Kate Hilton in young Rosie's eyes.'

Kate's summer had been spent with Rosie. The child had been her constant companion.

'Let's go and find her. She'd never forgive me if I let you go without seeing her.'

Rosie's tears almost shattered Kate's resolve not to cry. 'Don't go, Katie, don't go 'way. Who'm I going to play with? Who's goin' to take me to school?' She wound her chubby arms around Kate's neck, almost strangling her, and sniffled pitifully.

'I must go, Rosie. Really I must. Me mam'll be waiting

for me,' Kate pulled herself out of the child's grasp, turned and ran.

She could still hear Rosie's sobs as she crested the Hump and plunged down the other side towards home.

'There you are. It's time to go. Mek haste, Kate.' Her mother was dressed in her best costume, with a smart new hat perched on top of her hair which, as always, was piled high on her head, luxuriant and thick – a rich auburn colour like Kate's own. There was not a trace of grey showing in her mother's hair, Kate thought.

Her stepfather was still in his working clothes for he was only coming as far as the station.

'Aren't you going to say goodbye to your sister?'

Dutifully, Kate bent over the cradle and kissed the baby's forehead. Lilian's tiny fingers clutched at Kate's flowing hair and tugged at it.

'Ouch!'

The baby crowed with delight, but when Kate prised open the small hand and stood up, Lilian began to whimper at the removal of her plaything. Kate stood looking down at the child with distaste. She'd rather have little Rosie for a sister any day!

'We're all loaded up,' Jonathan Godfrey came into the kitchen, 'and Enid's just arrived to take Lilian till I get back.' His voice had a forced joviality that did not deceive Kate. But far from upsetting her, it actually comforted her to think that he cared.

As the trap rattled down the lane towards the town, Kate watched Brumbys' Farm become smaller and smaller. She bit down hard upon her lower lip. She refused to let her mother see her cry.

What hurt most of all was that she had not seen Danny.

The one person she loved best in all the world and she had
not even been able to say goodbye to him.

She pushed her hand into the pocket of her coat and felt
the reassuring wrinkled surface of the whelk shell he had
given her.

Seven

The school was a tall grey building set in a row of imposing town houses. From the street, stone steps led up to the heavy front door and the long windows seemed to be watching their approach.

It had been raining when they stepped off the train, and although Esther had tried to hold the umbrella over both of them as they walked from the station, by the time they reached the school Kate's long hair was straggling down her back in untidy wet strands. There was a peculiar fluttering feeling inside her stomach, just below her ribs, like a captive bird struggling to get out.

A maid opened the door; a young girl in a long black dress with a white apron and mob cap covering her short hair. Her face was pale and pinched. She was young enough to be a pupil, but obviously she was not one of them.

'Wait here. I'll tell Miss Denham.'

They were left standing in a hallway that stretched up and up three storeys high. From the centre of the hall the stairs rose to the first floor and divided into two and then again up to the second floor, dividing again. On each level the landings ran around the open square so that even from the topmost floor it was possible to peer down and see who was standing in the hall below.

Kate heard the echo of whispering and looked up to see herself being observed by three pairs of curious eyes, their owners leaning over the balustrade on the second floor.

Somewhere a bell sounded and the three girls scuttled down the stairs to the first floor and disappeared.

The maid returned. 'This way,' and they followed her through a huge oak door at the left-hand side of the hall and into a book-lined study.

From behind a wide, leather-topped desk rose the tallest woman Kate had ever seen. She towered above both Kate and her mother and her height was accentuated even further by her grey hair scraped up from her face into a bun on the top of her head. Miss Denham stood tall and straight-backed, and her shape looked as if her body were trussed up in a corset, moulded by bones and padding, all tightly laced. Her bosom was high and rigid and her waistline, though by no means slim, curved in and then out again to generous hips. Her hairstyle and dress, a grey striped close-fitting gown with a white collar and a small velvet bow at the neck, were out of date for the shapeless fashion of the twenties. But if intimidation of the girls in her charge was her endeavour, then, in Kate's wide eyes, Miss Denham succeeded.

'Good morning, Katharine. I am Miss Denham, and I am the Principal of this school.' The voice was deep, almost masculine, but it fitted the frame from which it issued. Kate felt the woman's cold grey eyes taking in every inch of her appearance from the top of her very wet head right down to the muddy toes of her lace-up boots. The woman was pointing now at Kate's feet.

'I trust, Mrs Godfrey, that you have equipped your daughter with something more appropriate in the way of footwear than – those?'

At her side Kate felt her mother almost bristle with indignation. 'Naturally, Miss Denham, I have – equipped – her with every item on the list of requirements ya gave me.' Esther Godfrey was standing stiffly before the woman and staring fearlessly up at her. In that moment Kate was fiercely

proud of her mother until she remembered that it was her
mother's fault that they were here in the first place!

Miss Denham pulled a bell-rope and before the tassel on
the cord had stopped swinging the little maid appeared in
the doorway.

'Say goodbye to your mother, Katharine, and go with
Mary.'

Kate gave a little gasp, turned and flung her arms around
her mother, pressing her face into Esther Godfrey's bosom.
'Mam, dun't go. Not yet.'

Her mother's arms came tightly around her. She rested
her cheek against Kate's hair. 'Oh, Kate,' she whispered.
'You'll be all right, really you will. Write to us . . .' For an
instant there was a slight tremor in Esther's voice, as if
suddenly she had doubts herself.

'Mrs Godfrey,' Miss Denham's manly voice cut in, 'you
are not helping the child.'

Kate lifted her head and looked up into her mother's
eyes; eyes that were troubled now. 'Mam, please don't leave
me here . . .'

'Katharine!' Miss Denham barked, so that Kate jumped
physically. 'Control yourself. We do not condone such
emotional behaviour here. Now,' the voice quietened a little,
'I repeat, say goodbye to your mother, and pray conduct
yourself with a little more decorum.'

Kate was so shocked that before she really realized what
was happening she was being kissed on the cheek by her
mother and then ushered out of the door by Mary, who shut
the study door with a heavy thud of finality.

'This way, Miss.'

There was nothing Kate could do but follow obediently.

*

The three pairs of inquisitive eyes were staring at her again, this time much closer.

Kate was sitting on a high bed and the three girls were ringed around the end just staring at her.

The long room, with a high ceiling, had five beds down each side. Beside each bed were a small chest of drawers and a narrow wardrobe. There were windows at the end of the room but set so high up in the wall it was impossible to see out of them. They were barred and the little of the glass that could be seen was opaque with grime on the outside so that not even the sky was visible. The floor was bare of any carpet or rugs and was so highly polished that it squeaked under Kate's boots when she walked on it.

'What's your name?' one of the watchers asked at last.

Kate looked at each of the three girls in turn. They were all dressed in similar uniform to her own, yet there was a subtle difference about theirs somehow. They all had short hair, cropped to a length just below their ears.

'Kate. Kate Hilton. What's yours?'

Another spoke but ignored Kate's question. 'Is that your *proper* name? The one you were christened?'

'N-no. I – was christened Katharine, but I'm called Kate.' And Danny calls me Katie, she almost added, but bit her lip to hold back the confidence.

'Huh,' the second girl said scathingly. 'You'll be called Katharine here.'

'And you'll have to have that hair cut.' The third girl spoke for the first time, touching her own neatly cropped hair. 'We all have to have it cut the same way.'

'Or plait it, Isobel. She could have it plaited,' the first one volunteered.

'Not unless she can do it neatly.'

Kate gasped in horror. 'They aren't cuttin' mine!' she said vehemently, but the girls only laughed.

The door opened and a woman entered. She was dressed in what appeared to Kate to be a nurse's uniform. She wore a long navy blue serge dress and a pristine white apron with a bib. Her hair was completely hidden by a starched square of white cloth folded around her head and falling into a triangle at the back.

'Matron – this is the new girl, Katharine Hilton.'

'But she likes to be called Kate.'

The woman's eyebrows almost reached the edge of her cap. 'Really?'

Now four pairs of eyes regarded her.

'Come with me—' the Matron paused and then added with emphasis, 'Katharine.'

The three girls stifled their giggles swiftly as Kate slid slowly off her bed and walked between them towards the Matron.

'Look at her blouse – it's home-made,' came a whisper.

'So's her gym-slip – just look at her boots!'

'Have you unpacked and put your clothes away?' the matron was asking.

'No, me trunk ain't got here yet.'

Another whisper. 'Listen to how she speaks! How common!'

Kate spent the next half-hour in the Matron's room listening to a list of school rules which she knew she would never remember. Then the Matron took her downstairs to the first floor and into a classroom to meet her teacher. When they entered, there were seven other girls in the room, all sitting in a semi-circle around the teacher, sewing. But at once they all stood up and chanted, 'Good afternoon, Matron,' and only sat down again when the Matron had acknowledged their greeting and added, 'You may sit down, girls.'

'Miss Ogden – this is Katharine Hilton. She will be in your class from tomorrow morning.'

The teacher rose and came to greet Kate, stretching out her hands to take Kate's. For the first time since she had arrived at this place, Kate found herself looking into a face that was smiling and welcoming. Miss Ogden was a pretty, dark-haired young woman with a kind smile and merry, dancing eyes. 'Welcome to Class Two, Katharine. We'll introduce you to everyone tomorrow.'

Kate glanced briefly at the other pupils and her heart sank when she saw that the three girls whom she had met half an hour earlier were sitting there, their heads bent demurely over their sewing.

'We'll see you at dinner this evening,' Miss Ogden said as the matron ushered Kate out of the classroom door and continued to show her around the school.

The ground floor consisted of the Principal's study and private sitting room, the dining room and, at the rear of the house, the kitchens where the cook reigned over her kitchen maid and the parlourmaid who had answered the door. On the first floor were three classrooms, an art room and a domestic science room. Upstairs were three large dormitories with ten beds in each, Miss Denham's bedroom and those of her two assistant teachers and the Matron. There was also a small room set aside as the sickroom, whilst up in the attic were the domestic servants' bedrooms.

'There, now you have seen everything, Katharine, I expect you not to get lost. Miss Denham cannot abide unpunctuality either for lessons or meals, or indeed for anything. Dinner is at half-past six. You may go and unpack your trunk which I believe has now arrived from the station.'

With the briefest of nods, she dismissed Kate.

'We speak French at meal-times.' In the dining room, Miss

Denham was towering above her. 'I presume you know a little French?'

'No, Miss, I dun't.'

'She can't speak English properly,' came a voice from somewhere behind her, but Miss Denham chose to ignore the remark.

'You'd better sit next to me this evening, but from tomorrow you will sit at Miss Ogden's table.'

With an outward meekness she did not feel inside, Kate followed the Principal, thinking that she would rather sit near Miss Ogden, French or no French.

Miss Denham's deep voice boomed out above their bowed heads, saying the Grace in French. Then there was a scraping of chairs on the bare wooden floor and everyone sat down.

Two girls from each table went to the serving hatch at the end of the dining room and returned carrying plates with a portion of meat on each. The procedure was repeated until everyone was served. Then, starting with the teacher at the head of each table, the vegetables were passed round and everyone helped themselves. Only when everyone was served was the signal given that they might start eating.

Conversation was not allowed, the rattle of knives and forks being the only sound in the room.

Kate felt the knot in her stomach, just below her ribs, tightening. She took a mouthful of meat and began to chew. The meat was tough and tasteless. Her mouth was dry; she could not swallow it.

'Please may I have a glass of water?'

The Principal spoke but the words were completely unintelligible to Kate. '*En français, s'il te plaît.*'

Kate stared blankly at her. Even sitting down the woman looked tall and imposing, with lips so pursed there was hardly any mouth at all. Further down the table came a stifled giggle which prompted a stony glare from Miss Denham.

There was no way Kate could understand what was being said to her and even less chance of her replying. She bent her head and ate some of the vegetables instead. They had been over-cooked to a mushy pulp. She felt the bile rise into her throat with revulsion. Setting her knife and fork neatly together at the edge of the plate, Kate folded her hands in her lap.

She would eat no more.

'*Mange*!' In the silence of the room, Miss Denham's voice boomed, audible to all.

Kate fixed her gaze upon a picture on the wall opposite to where she was sitting, yet she could feel every eye in the room was turned in her direction. She was aware that only one face was perhaps turned upon her with any expression of sympathy and that was Miss Ogden's, who was seated just below the picture.

'Katharine Hilton, *mange – maintenant*!'

The nervous knot in Kate's stomach hardened into anger. Her green eyes swivelled from the picture and sparked fire.

'I dun't know what you are saying to me. I dun't understand French.'

A shocked gasp reverberated around the room.

Kate stood up, her chair scraping on the wooden floor.

'*Assieds-toi, immédiatement*!'

Kate realized she was probably being ordered to sit down, but she had said she could not understand and now she had to carry it through. She left her place and marched down the length of the room, pulled open the heavy door and went through it. It swung to behind her with an echoing thud. The hall was dark and dismal, with only low wall lights burning. Kate shuddered, lifted her skirt above her knees and scampered up the two flights of stairs to the dormitory.

It was worse there. The long room was in complete darkness with only a glimmer of light coming from the high, barred windows at the far end. Kate rushed towards them. If only she could see out, she might feel better. If she could see the garden, trees, hear the birds . . .

She stood below the windows craning her neck backwards, but all she could see was pale grey light through the grime.

'I can't even see the sky!' she wailed aloud. She leaned her cheek against the wall and sobbed.

It seemed as though she was in the darkness on her own for an age, huddled on her bed, before she heard voices coming up the stairs and along the landing, nearer and nearer.

Then they were in the room. Someone lit the gas light near the door and they were crowding round the end of her bed, gaping at her. Some had expressions of something akin to admiration. 'Fancy walking out like that. I'd never have dared!'

Others with derisory glee. 'You're in for it. Miss Denham wants you in her study. Now!'

And one or two with hostility: 'You'll get us all into trouble if you carry on like that.'

'What can you expect from a country bumpkin? No manners and can't even understand a word of French!'

'Ya'd better go down, likely ya're in fer ca-ane.' It was a cruel impersonation of the Lincolnshire dialect so strong in Kate's speech.

Rage flooded through her again. She dashed away her tears with the back of her hand and swung her legs off the bed. 'I aren't afraid of *her*!'

'Just listen to her! "I aren't!" Wherever did she go to school?'

'A better school than this 'un,' Kate uttered as a parting

shot as she marched out of the room, the sound of their heartless laughter following her down the stairs.

Outside the door of Miss Denham's study, her boldness deserted her. Again the knot of nerves was fluttering just beneath her ribs and rising into her throat. She swallowed and her empty stomach gurgled.

She knocked on the door and on hearing 'Enter' – thankfully spoken in English now – she went in.

Miss Denham sat behind her desk with Miss Ogden standing on one side of her and the Matron on the other. Miss Ogden looked at her sadly, whilst outrage was apparent on the other two faces.

'Katharine Hilton, your behaviour at the dinner table this evening was disgraceful,' Miss Denham began. Kate returned the woman's stare steadfastly, though her insides were churning and her knees were trembling. 'Have you anything to say for yourself?'

'I felt sick, Miss.'

Out of the corner of her eye she saw Miss Ogden's hand flutter briefly towards her, almost as if she wanted to reach out and touch her. 'Oh, you poor child . . .' she heard the teacher mutter, but the gesture of understanding was quelled by a look from the Principal.

Miss Denham turned her cold gaze back upon Kate. 'Normally I would cane you for such behaviour, but because it is your first day here, this time,' there was heavy emphasis on the two words 'this time', 'we will say no more about it. However, you will go straight to your dormitory and to bed instead of participating in games hour before bedtime. You may go.'

Kate went – thankfully. She was relieved to find the dormitory empty, and having paid a visit to the bathroom she undressed and lay down in the narrow, hard bed.

The sounds of the large building were all around her:

voices, footsteps, doors banging, and the chimes of the cathedral clock only a short distance away. When the other girls came to bed, Kate lay with her head buried beneath the covers and pretended to be asleep. No one spoke to her or about her. It was as if she were not even there. When the room was in darkness she lay listening to the breathing of the nine other girls in the room and knew sleep would be impossible. She felt closed in and longed for the cool marsh breezes and the sound of the sea – and Danny.

At the thought of Danny she stuffed the sheet into her mouth to stifle a sob.

Then she remembered the whelk shell; a little piece of home. Quietly, she turned back the covers and swung her feet to the floor. She was half-way between her bed and the wardrobe when light flooded into the room and Kate turned, blinking in the sudden brightness, to see the Matron standing in the doorway.

'What are you doing out of bed, girl?'

The polished floorboards were icy beneath her bare feet. Kate shivered, not so much from cold as from knowing that every girl in the room was wide awake and listening.

'Well?' snapped the Matron.

'I was just getting summat from me coat in the wardrobe.'

Blanket-muffled laughter sounded.

'What is it you want?'

Kate hesitated, searching desperately. 'Me – me hanky.'

'Have you not got a clean one in your bedside drawer?'

'I – dun't know.'

'Oh, very well, but hurry up.'

Trembling now, Kate opened the door of the wardrobe which squeaked loudly in the silence. Praying fervently, she reached into her coat pocket and felt the hard roundness of the whelk shell and beneath it – 'Oh thank you, thank you' – the softness of her white handkerchief.

Fumbling a little, she wrapped the shell in the handkerchief and held it tightly in the palm of her hand before she withdrew it from her pocket. When she turned back to face the Matron, only one corner of the hanky showed in her hand.

The woman nodded briefly and closed the door, plunging the room into darkness once more.

Kate climbed into bed and buried her head beneath the covers to unwrap the shell.

Only then, with the sound of the sea in her ear, did she fall asleep.

Eight

'Katharine Hilton!' Matron's voice rose above the hubbub as the girls scurried to and from the bathroom the next morning. 'Your bath nights are Tuesdays and Fridays, and you will wash your hair each Friday.'

Kate felt the woman's eyes take in the long flowing auburn hair that tumbled untidily down her back, so long that she could almost sit on it.

Her mouth pursed, Matron said, 'You will plait your hair before you come down to breakfast.'

It was an almost impossible task for Kate to plait the long hair herself. She made a valiant effort, although strands escaped and the skeins of hair were woven in and out unevenly. If only her mother's nimble fingers were there; she could plait the length of Kate's hair in seconds.

The day seemed interminable. Kate struggled with the sums and every time she opened her mouth to speak, there came a wave of suppressed giggles around the room. Miss Ogden, helpless to reprimand the covert cruelty, tried to bring comfort to the lonely new girl by praising her sewing, but that only seemed to alienate her further from the other girls.

' "Look at the back of Katharine's work" ', mimicked Isobel, when Miss Ogden left the room for a moment. ' "See how neat it is?" Pity her hair isn't as neat.'

Isobel's two followers giggled dutifully. It was soon obvious to Kate that Isobel Cartwright was a natural ring-leader.

The two girls who were her closest friends – Brenda and Hazel – followed her around and she ordered them about like a mistress giving orders to servants. Isobel had short hair, cut to the regulation length, and yet there seemed a subtle difference in the style. Kate couldn't understand what it was that made it different from all the rest. Then, when school had finished on the Friday afternoon, Isobel was missing. Kate overheard Brenda saying that she had gone out in a car.

'Her mother's taken her out to tea in town – and to have her hair done. They've got a chauffeur. You should have seen him, Hazel. He looked so smart in his grey uniform and peaked cap.'

'However does Isobel get permission to go out in the week?'

Brenda leaned closer, but Kate still heard her whispered words. 'It's probably because her father's a governor of the school. Even Miss Denham doesn't want to upset the Cartwright family!'

'Yes, but to be allowed to go out of school to have her hair done in a salon . .!' Hazel sighed enviously.

The subject of hair made them turn and look at Kate. 'It's your bath night tonight,' Hazel reminded her gleefully. '*And* you've to wash your hair.'

'How do you get it dry?'

'In front of the range,' Kate told them.

The two girls exchanged a glance and then clutched each other as they shook with laughter. 'There's no range here. You'll have to go into the kitchen and put your head in the oven!'

Isobel returned from town with her hair beautifully styled and shining golden. She really was quite a pretty girl, Kate thought charitably, except for a sulky pout to her mouth and a way of holding her head as if she were looking down her nose at everything and everyone. And her cold blue eyes missed nothing.

That evening Kate tiptoed into the bathroom carrying her towel, a huge bar of carbolic soap and a flannel. There was a line of six wash-basins along one wall and two baths in separate cubicles. Sighing with relief, she realized she had the bathroom to herself. She moved into one of the cubicles and looked at the huge cast-iron bath standing on clawed feet and fitted with brass-coloured taps. She'd never seen anything like this before; it was very different from bath-night on a Friday night at home when her mother banished her stepfather from the kitchen and tugged the zinc bath in front of the range, drawing water from the side boiler. Kate and her mother would wash each other's hair before the girl stepped into the bath. Esther, her own hair wrapped in a towel, would pour more hot water into the tub so that it swirled around Kate, warming her. Then she would kneel and soap her daughter's back, talking to her about school or the farm.

Sitting in front of the kitchen range, in the rosy glow of the firelight, had been warm and intimate. It was a time Kate had cherished; a time when she had her mother to herself – even after Lilian had been born.

But this bathroom was so cold that Kate shivered. The floor was bare stone, the walls painted a dull green with only a line of patterned tiles running round the wall just above the bath. Somewhere above her, pipes gurgled noisily as the hot water was pumped up from the boiler in the cellar. She washed her hair in one of the basins first and wound it up in her towel, turban-fashion, on top of her head. Then she moved into one of the cubicles. The bath was so huge that Kate thought if she filled it too full and slipped when climbing in over the high side, she might well drown in it and no one would know.

The bathroom door opened and Isobel looked in. 'Oh, sorry . . .' she began, then, recognizing Kate, added, 'Oh, it's you. What's the matter? Never seen a bath before? You fill it with water, get in and wash your dirty self all over!'

Kate turned her back on the girl and learned over the side of the bath. With nervous fingers she twisted the top of the huge tap and jumped when water gushed out suddenly. She heard Isobel laughing as she went into the next cubicle and ran her own bath.

When the water had reached a depth of about twelve inches, Kate turned off the taps. From the next-door cubicle, the water still gushed into the bath and continued for such a long time that Kate thought it would never stop. As she sat in the water and began to soap herself, she heard the taps being turned off and Isobel splashing. Only a minute or so later, she heard a swish of water as the girl next door stood up and climbed out of the bath. The plug on its chain was pulled out and the water began to empty from the bath. What a waste, Kate thought, me mam would have a ducky fit! Fancy filling a bath up that much and spending about a minute in it and then getting out and emptying it. Isobel wouldn't do that if she had to fill the bath by the bucketful as they did at home. Kate splashed water on to her body to wash off the soap, then put her hands on the top edges of the bath and levered herself up. At that moment, Isobel popped her head round the corner again, dressed in her pyjamas and dressing-gown, ready to leave. Her cool gaze lingered on Kate's slim body, the small breasts scarcely formed and her long legs, thin and coltish. Embarrassed, Kate stood in the bath wishing she had a towel to put around her to cover her nakedness, but the only one she had brought was wrapped around her head.

'You'd better hurry up. We're only allowed ten minutes

each. There's others to bath after you, you know,' the girl
said brusquely.

She turned away and Kate heard the bathroom door open.
From her position in the cubicle, Kate could not see what
Isobel was doing, but the next moment the whole room was
plunged into blackness.

Upon leaving Isobel had turned off the gas-light near the
door, deliberately leaving Kate standing in the bath, shivering
in the darkness.

'Isobel, don't,' she shouted, but the door slammed.

Kate bent and put out her hands trying to find the edge
of the bath. Her feet slipped and she felt herself falling. She
let out a yell as she hit her head with a thud against the
bath and slipped back down into the water, which sloshed
up and down the bath and splashed over the edge on to the
floor. She felt the towel unwind and fall from her head.

'Isobel,' she roared, more angry now than frightened or
hurt. She grabbed the sides of the bath and heaved herself
upright and as she did so, someone pushed open the door
and light from the corridor filtered into the bathroom.

'What on earth are you doing, girl? Did you put this light
off?' Matron snapped as she relit the light to inspect the
bathroom. 'Just look at the mess you are making! Mind you
clear all this up. And where's your towel?'

Kate, her hair plastered to her back and running rivulets
down her body, bent and picked the dripping towel out of
the water.

'Well, you're not going to get very dry on that, are you,
you foolish child?' The matron shook her head impatiently.
'Wait there . . .' She disappeared, and Kate stepped carefully
out of the bath and wrung her wet towel out, twisting it
viciously between her hands, wishing it was Isobel Cartwright's neck.

Matron returned with a towel. 'Here, dry yourself quickly

and let's have no more of this nonsense. And don't go turning lights off until you know how to relight them. Fancy trying to take a bath in the dark!' She shook her head in exasperation and disbelief that anyone could be so stupid.

Kate opened her mouth to retort that the light had been turned out while she was in the bath, but then she closed it again without speaking. She was no tell-tale. She never had been and she wasn't going to start now, however much she hated Isobel Cartwright.

The Matron turned away and left the room, leaving Kate to dry herself and wipe the floor. There was nothing else to use but her own towel which was now not only soaking wet but grubby too.

When she returned to the dormitory, she found all the girls knew of her embarrassment. She glared at Isobel, who smirked as she said, 'Tell Matron, did you?'

'No,' Kate answered shortly. 'I aren't a tell-tale . . .' There were further giggles. 'But I'll get you back, Isobel Cartwright,' she added, wagging her forefinger at the other girl. 'I dun't care how long I have to wait – but one day I'll get you back. You see if I don't!'

'Oooh, I'm sha-aking in me shoes,' Isobel mocked.

Kate turned her back on them all and began to dry her hair, rubbing it vigorously with a towel.

On the first Sunday after her arrival, Kate discovered that all the pupils walked in crocodile fashion up the steep hill to the cathedral for Morning Service, accompanied by the Principal and the two assistant teachers.

The moment she stepped through the huge doors, Kate felt her heart begin to thud. The interior of the holy place was immense! Her hobnailed boots echoed hollowly on the flagstones and she could feel Miss Denham's disapproval boring into her back.

Awe-struck, Kate gazed around her as she took her place in a pew. Stone pillars supported the high arched roof and in front of her the rich wooden carving of the angel choir gave warmth to the austere stonework. Light shone through the stained glass windows, mottling the flagstones.

Unbidden, and for no reason that she could understand, a feeling of peace crept through her. Although she was still sitting among them, for an hour or so she was safe from the taunts of her fellow-pupils and Miss Denham's scolding.

For the first time since she had arrived in Lincoln, Kate felt a sense of security as she gazed around her in wonderment. She forgot her own misfortune as she marvelled at the beauty of the building and listened to the pure voices of the choir, the music reverberating sweetly through the vastness.

Miss Denham walked up and down the aisle twice during the service, her sharp eyes lingering on whisperers, who, reddening, subsided at once.

Kate knelt for the final prayer. 'Please let me go home,' she prayed silently and fervently, squeezing her eyes tightly shut and pressing her hands together so hard her wrists hurt. 'Please make something happen so I can go home . . .'

There was shuffling all around her and she opened her eyes to see that everyone was rising to leave. She sighed and scrambled to her feet. As they filed out of the cathedral, Kate felt bereft as if she were being dragged from a place of sanctuary.

'There's a uniform inspection!' Hazel came running into the dormitory, slamming the door behind her. 'Miss Denham *and*

Matron! They're in "B" Dormitory now. They'll be here next. Quick!'

'Oh help!' wailed one girl down the far end of the dormitory. 'I've lost my house shoes. I'll be for it.'

'I saw a pair in the bathroom last night. Did you leave them there?'

The girl's face brightened. 'Ooh thanks, Hazel. I think I did.' And she scuttled out of the room to retrieve her lost property.

Kate watched all the girls in the room opening drawer after drawer of their bedside cabinets, refolding and tidying the contents. Wardrobe doors were flung open and the clothes hanging there straightened, shoes set neatly beneath.

Brenda was untying the braid girdle around her waist. 'I think my gym-slip's too short. If I loosen my sash will it make it a bit longer?' she asked Isobel.

'It might do,' Isobel said doubtfully.

'Do you think she'll do a gym-slip inspection?'

'Bound to. She always does at the beginning of term.'

'Oooh!' Brenda wailed. 'Does that look better, Isobel?'

Isobel inspected her friend's tunic. 'A bit,' she said, sounding none too hopeful.

The door opened and the girl who had gone to find her shoes came in. 'They're coming,' she hissed.

As the Principal and Matron entered, every girl was standing by her bed, almost to attention. Miss Denham carried a ruler and a pair of scissors.

'Kneel,' Miss Denham commanded.

Mystified, Kate glanced round to see every girl kneeling down, not against the bed as if to pray, but in a line down the centre of the room.

'Katharine . . .' came the warning voice, and swiftly Kate knelt down at the end of the line.

Miss Denham passed down the line, placing the end of

the ruler on the floor and measuring the height of each gym-slip hem from the floor. It was about two inches. Kate glanced down, knowing, with a sinking heart, what she would see. Her own tunic was longer than everyone else's, its hem wrinkling against the bare boards.

She watched as Miss Denham paused in front of Brenda, measuring carefully. Kate could see that the girl was bending her body forward slightly so that the hemline came a little nearer the floor. Miss Denham passed on without comment and Kate could almost hear Brenda's relief.

They were standing before Kate and there was no need for the ruler. 'Stand up, Katharine,' the voice boomed. As she did so, Miss Denham grasped the hem of Kate's gym-slip and, turning it up, inserted the scissors into Esther God-frey's neat stitching and cut the thread. There was a tearing sound as she ripped the hem undone.

'Go down to Miss Ogden's room and ask her to supply you with needle and thread. You will sew up this hem to the correct length tonight. And another thing, Katharine, I am not satisfied with the neatness of your plait. You know the rule, unless you can plait your hair neatly in a single plait down your back, you must have it cut short.'

Kate's face flamed and when the two women had left the room, noise broke out on all sides.

'Phew! That was a close one. I thought I'd had it!' said Brenda.

'She didn't even look at my shoes,' the other girl said petulantly, then cheered up. 'Still, at least I've found them.'

'Ya'd better get goin', Ka-ate,' Isobel mimicked. 'Else ya'll be up 'alf the night a-plaiting yar hair.'

Kate turned and left the room, the sound of their laughter following her along the corridor.

*

85

The days crawled by and she had been at the school two weeks. Two weeks in which she had hardly been able to eat. Fourteen days of sitting beneath Miss Denham's gaze, for the Principal had ordered her to sit beside her for every meal instead of moving to Miss Ogden's table.

Miss Ogden had been the only person to show even a glimmer of kindness, but that was made tentatively, as if she herself feared reprisals should she show too much sympathy towards the new girl. In the classroom Miss Ogden was patient, and Kate felt as if the young teacher would have liked to display more understanding but dared not show favouritism in front of the rest of the class. As for the other girls – led on by the three who had assumed the role of her tormentors, Isobel, Brenda and Hazel – there was not one friendly word from any of them.

Meals were purgatory. Under Miss Denham's glare Kate struggled to eat the unappetizing food, while her stomach churned rebelliously and constantly threatened revolt.

Then came the day of the gooseberries.

Nine

The meal had been going quite well. She had managed to eat all the first course – steak and kidney pie. For once the meat was tender and the pastry not too soggy. But when a bowl of gooseberries was placed before her, Kate looked around for the custard. There was none. She bit her lip and said tentatively to the girl next to her. *'Passez le sugar, sivoo play.'*

'Sucre, sucre,' boomed Miss Denham's voice to her left. *'Tu n'as pas besoin de sucre.'*

Kate looked down at the small green bullets in the dish. Reluctantly, she picked up her spoon and selected two of the gooseberries that looked a little softer than the rest. The moment she put them in her mouth the sourness attacked her taste-buds so that her mouth salivated and her stomach erupted. Before she knew what was happening, she had vomited into the dish in front of her, bringing up all the first course.

Next to her, a girl screamed and pushed back her chair, 'Oh how disgusting!' while Miss Denham rose and grabbed Kate's arm in a vice-like grip and hustled her, still retching, down the room past all the staring faces. Kate found herself dragged through the hallway and pushed into a small lavatory. The door slammed behind her and miserably she leaned over the bowl and retched until there was nothing left to bring up but evil-tasting, yellow bile. Yet still her mouth salivated and her stomach heaved.

At last she leaned against the wall, weak and trembling, a cold sweat breaking out all over her.

A knock came on the door and Miss Ogden's gentle voice said, 'Katharine, are you all right?'

When Kate did not answer, the door opened and pushed against her as she stood behind it. 'Katharine . . .? Oh, my dear girl . . .'

The teacher drew Kate out of the small, dark room. 'Are you feeling better now? Come along, let me take you up to Matron.'

But the Matron was as unsympathetic as Miss Denham. 'Clean yourself up, girl. How dare you create such a disgraceful scene? You're doing it on purpose, just to cause disruption. Change your dress and then you are to report to Miss Denham's study.'

Half an hour later Kate was standing in front of Miss Denham's desk. The Principal rose majestically. 'Come with me.'

Meekly, Kate followed and found herself in the huge dining room being seated at the table once more. All evidence of her humiliation had been removed, but the floor showed damp patches where it had been wiped clean.

A maid entered from the kitchen and placed a plate of food in front of her. It was the first course.

'You will stay here and eat the whole meal again and you will not leave until you have done so.'

Kate watched the woman turn and leave the room. The door closed behind her.

Left alone, without Miss Denham's critical gaze upon her every mouthful, strangely Kate found she could eat – at least the first course – but when another dish of gooseberries came, she hesitated. She picked up her spoon and ate one. The gooseberry itself was just as sour as before but now the juice in which the fruit lay was sweet – much sweeter than before. Someone had realized what was happening and had taken pity on her. Kate felt a warm gratitude towards the unknown person beyond the kitchen door.

When Miss Denham returned, Kate was sitting with two empty plates in front of her.

The woman stood over her. 'There, you see, you can eat it when you try.'

Kate stared back at the woman, deliberately keeping her face expressionless. When dismissed, the young girl stood up and, holding her head high, walked out of the room. There was no way she could win against the authority of this horrible woman, but Kate Hilton was certainly not going to be cowed by her.

But oh, how she longed to be back home running along the beach with Danny panting after her shouting, 'Wait for me, Katie, wait for me!' or to feel the chubby arms of little Rosie Maine winding themselves around her neck and hear her merry voice pleading, 'Come and play with me, Kate.'

Before returning to her classroom Kate went up to the dormitory and felt in the pocket of her coat for the whelk shell, standing several minutes with it pressed against her ear so that even in this dismal, lonely room she might still hear the sound of home.

On the third Sunday, Peggy Godfrey arrived at the school to take Kate out for the afternoon.

Two whole hours of freedom, thought Kate ecstatically. It was her first escape from what she thought of as her prison.

They walked down the hill and along a straight road past a park on the left-hand side until they came to a side street where Mr and Mrs Godfrey lived at number eight. The houses were terraced, with a small frontage outside the bay window and front door. A passage ran between every second house leading to both back yards.

'Kate, how lovely to see you.' Jonathan's mother was smiling a welcome as she opened the front door and Kate found herself stepping straight into the best parlour.

'Come through to the living room, dear. Take no notice of all this.' She laughed and waved her hand to encompass the front room. Kate glanced around as she followed Jonathan's mother. The room was littered with paper patterns and pieces of material. In the centre of the room on a small table stood a sewing machine.

'I use it as my workroom,' Mrs Godfrey was explaining, and Kate remembered that at Lilian's christening Peggy had said her mother was a dressmaker. 'My ladies come here for fittings so I have to have somewhere nice and we never use the front room for anything else except at Christmas.'

Mrs Godfrey led the way through to the back living room, 'Here we are, dear. Look who's come to see us, Henry.'

Kate stepped into the room, where the smell of their recent Sunday dinner still lingered.

'This is Mr Godfrey.' Mrs Godfrey was gesturing towards a man sitting in an easy chair near the fire. He lowered the newspaper he was reading and stood up, and Kate found herself looking into the kindly face of her stepfather. An older face, of course, but the likeness was so astonishing that she could not prevent the words escaping her lips.

'Oh, you're just like me dad.'

The others laughed and Mr Godfrey's deep voice said, 'That's not the first time I've been told that.' He smiled gently down at her, his eyes crinkling just like his son's.

'Sit down, sit down. I hope you can stay to tea, dear,' Mrs Godfrey was saying. 'Peggy has made a trifle, haven't you, Peg?'

Taking off her coat and hat, Peggy nodded.

'And how do you like the school, young Kate?' Mr Godfrey asked.

As she felt the eyes of the three adults upon her, Kate bit on her lower lip to still its sudden trembling. She glanced from one to another and saw the genuine concern written on all their faces; such an expression of friendliness which she had not seen since her arrival in this city.

'It's awful,' she burst out, and the tears held in check for so long now spilled over and flooded down her face. At once Mrs Godfrey pulled her down on to the settee and sat beside her, putting an arm around her shoulders. Shocked, Peggy stood in front of them wringing her hands. Mr Godfrey sat down in his chair again, but laid his newspaper aside and sat forward, his forehead creasing worriedly.

'Tell us all about it, love,' Mrs Godfrey insisted. And out it all came tumbling.

'Well!' and 'Oh, how could they!' and 'I can scarcely believe it!' were the only interruptions they made and when she had finished and leaned her head against Mrs Godfrey's shoulder, it was Peggy who said, 'We can't let her go back there, Mother.'

Mrs Godfrey glanced worriedly at Kate and then at her husband. 'What do you think, Henry?'

Mr Godfrey shook his head, 'It used to have a very good name when Miss Peterson ran it . . .' He paused and Kate saw the glance that passed between husband and wife.

Mrs Godfrey put her arm around Kate, 'Come along and have your tea, dear, and then we'll think what to do.'

As she sat at their tea table, hunger overwhelmed her. There were delicately cut cucumber sandwiches, a trifle with cream, and cakes – a chocolate one with chocolate icing and a sponge cake with jam in the middle.

'Help yourself, dear.'

Six sandwiches, two helpings of trifle and three pieces of cake later, Mrs Godfrey said, 'Better now?'

Kate nodded, feeling comfortably full for the first time in weeks.

'Now,' Mrs Godfrey turned to her husband. 'What ought we to do, Henry?'

'I've been thinking, whilst we've been having tea,' he said slowly. 'I'm afraid we didn't ought to let you stay with us. It wouldn't be right. The school would be angry and your mother wouldn't thank us for interfering. But,' he added hurriedly, 'we'll write to Jonathan – yes, that's what we'll do. We'll tell him everything you've told us and he'll talk to your mother.'

'Couldn't you go and see this – this Miss Denham, Father?' Peggy put in quietly. 'Perhaps she'd listen to you.' She turned to Kate to explain. 'Father's a deputy headmaster at the boys' school in the city.'

Kate nodded. 'I thought it was *his* school I was coming to,' she said simply, but the note of wistfulness was not lost upon the three adults. Mrs Godfrey patted her hand.

'I'd go and see this Miss Denham if I thought it would help,' Mr Godfrey was saying. 'But from what you tell us, Kate, the woman would undoubtedly see it as interference and it could make things even worse for you.'

Kate bowed her head and her long hair fell forward hiding her face. She knew what Mr Godfrey was saying was reasonable; that was exactly how Miss Denham would react. And she doubted whether a letter to her stepfather would help either. He might be sympathetic, but would her mother be?

Slowly Kate rose from the table. 'Thank you for the tea, Mrs Godfrey, it was lovely,' she said in a small voice.

'Now, you can come here any time you like. Every Sunday for your tea. And in the week too, if they'll let you.'

Kate shook back her long hair. 'I dun't think they'll let me come for another two weeks.'

'Well, come whenever you can. We'll be here. Now, Peggy will walk back with you.'

As they walked up the hill, Peggy said, 'I'm sorry you're having to go back. I'd have let you stay with us if it had been up to me. But Father's in a difficult position, being in the teaching profession too. And Mother's afraid of upsetting your mother. She thinks the world of our Jonathan, you know, and doesn't want to do anything that might cause trouble between him and his wife. You do see, don't you, Kate?'

Inwardly Kate sighed. Yes, she did see – only too well!

'Matron wants you, Sicky.'

'You'd better get along to her room instead of standing there gaping.' Her three tormentors – with Isobel Cartwright as the ring-leader – had brought her the command and now they stood close together, their heads bent towards each other, giggling and whispering.

Kate's stomach contracted. She had no choice but to obey the summons. She tucked the shell she was holding under her pillow and slipped off the edge of the high bed. With an exaggerated movement the girls stood back out of her way.

'Dun't get near 'er,' Isobel mimicked. 'She'll be sick all ovver ya.'

'She will be sick when she knows what Matron wants her for.' They all laughed again.

As Kate moved away from her bed, Isobel pounced forward and thrust her hand under the pillow. 'Let's see what you're hiding under here . . .'

Kate whirled around and lunged at the girl, but too late.

93

Isobel held up the whelk shell. 'Look, Sicky's got a pwetty shell. Ah! Here, Brenda, catch.'

Isobel tossed the shell high over Kate's head and Brenda caught it deftly. Kate turned and caught hold of Brenda's arms. 'Give it me!' she cried. 'Give it back. It's mine.'

Brenda threw it to Hazel and the three of them encircled her, throwing it from one to the other.

Kate was almost weeping with frustration. 'You've no right to tek me shell.' The anger welled up in her and she screamed. 'Give it me back!'

The door was flung open and the Matron marched into the room. 'What is all this noise about?'

Immediately Isobel put her hand holding the shell behind her back and turned innocent eyes upon the Matron.

Matron's gaze came to rest upon Kate's hot face and dishevelled hair. 'Katharine Hilton – come with me this instant.'

Without waiting to see if the girl obeyed her, the woman turned and left the room. Kate swung back to Isobel. 'Give me my shell.'

The hand remained behind the girl's back. 'Shell?' the girl drawled, her cold eyes narrowing, 'What shell might that be?'

'You'd better get along to Matron's room else you'll be in more trouble,' Hazel warned.

Kate hesitated, then, casting a vicious glance at Isobel, she muttered through her teeth, 'You wait, Isobel Cartwright, just you wait!'

Pushing Hazel aside, Kate stormed out of the dormitory.

The Matron was standing in the centre of the medical room with a large pair of scissors in her hands. 'Now, my girl. Since you cannot, apparently, keep your hair neatly plaited, it's time we cut it to regulation length.'

Horrified, Kate wheeled around to run from the room but found her way barred by the daunting figure of Miss Denham advancing into the room behind her.

Still in a temper from the girls' teasing, Kate fought back. 'No, no. You aren't going to cut me hair. You've no right. I won't . . .'

The door closed and the immovable figure of Miss Denham leaned against it. 'You, Katharine Hilton, will do exactly as you are told and we will have no more of this wilful behaviour.'

Hardly before Kate knew what was happening, Miss Denham had caught hold of her shoulders and pulled her towards her, enfolding her in a vice-like grip. Kate's face was pressed suffocatingly against the woman's massive bosom. She felt the painful tug on her scalp as the Matron grasped a handful of hair and she heard the scissors cut into her silken curls. Snip, snip, snip and her beautiful auburn tresses slipped to the floor.

When Miss Denham released her, Kate could feel the sudden chill on her neck and she put up her hand to feel the jagged ends brutally cropped just below her ears. Suddenly all the fight went out of her. Her knees gave way and she sank down, reaching out with trembling fingers to touch the shorn locks lying on the floor.

'Get up, Katharine, and sit in a chair whilst I neaten . . .'

Her spirit returned. She scrambled up and struck out at the woman, knocking the scissors out of her hand and sending them slithering across the floor. 'Ya'll not touch me hair – not again.' Her fury gave her strength. She pushed past Miss Denham, dragged open the door and ran. Down the two flights of stairs, through the hall, out of the huge heavy front door and down the steps into the street before anyone could stop her.

On the pavement, poised on the balls of her feet, she

hesitated and glanced back at the grey building towering menacingly above her. Then, her decision made, she picked up her skirts and began to run up the hill towards the cathedral.

Ten

She was wet, cold, hungry – and lost!

Kate had waited in the cathedral until dark, joining the Evensong worshippers and leaving amidst them, hoping that no one would recognize the school uniform and question why she was there on her own – and without coat or hat.

No one did.

She wandered around the precincts of the towering building until she came to a statue of Lord Tennyson. Tired, she sat down and leaned her back against the base.

'What are you doing here, little girl?' The voice spoke directly above her. Kate blinked. For one foolish moment she thought it was the statue speaking to her. Looking round, she saw an elderly man dressed in a long black cassock peering round the corner of the statue.

Kate scrambled up and began to back away from him. Her heart was pounding and at once she was poised on her toes ready for flight. But the man's tone was friendly. 'Don't be afraid. I won't harm you – or be angry. I just wondered – I mean – are you all right? Shouldn't you be going home?'

'Yes,' Kate replied firmly, although he could not fully understand the meaning behind her words. 'That's exactly where I should be – home!'

'Then why . . .?'

'I dun't know which way it is. At least – I know I need to go east, towards the . . .' she stopped. She had been going to say 'towards the sea', but perhaps the old man would question that. It was a long way to the sea. Kate took a deep breath and said, 'I came to Evensong,' which was the truth but not the whole truth,' and when I came out, I didn't know which way to go. So, I was waiting for the stars to come out so I could see the North Star and then I'd know.'

The old man chuckled. 'You seem a very knowledgeable young lady. Finding your way by the stars, eh? Well, well, I never did.'

'Danny,' the very mention of his name brought a lump to her throat, 'he's my friend – he taught me.'

'Did he indeed?' The elderly man glanced upwards into the darkening sky. 'Well, my dear, it's very cloudy tonight. It looks like rain. I don't think you're going to see the stars at all tonight.'

Kate tipped her head backwards, feeling the jagged edges of her newly cropped hair against her neck. She sighed. He was right – there would be neither moon nor stars this night.

She looked back again at the old man. 'Do you know which way is east?' she ventured.

The man nodded. 'Yes, my dear. In fact I'll take you and set you on your way. Once on the road, you just keep straight on.'

They fell into step together and he continued, 'All the main roads which lead into Lincoln were originally built by the Romans and they all lead straight and true towards the cathedral. Now here we are, this will lead you to Wragby Road.' He glanced down at her. 'Is that the one you want?'

Kate hesitated, not wanting to tell the old gentleman a deliberate lie. 'I'm trying to get to Suddaby . . .'

'Suddaby? Why that's miles away . . .'

Kate knew a moment's fear. She'd made a mistake, but she'd had to take the risk to find out the right road.

'Me grandad lives there, he'll be meeting me,' she told him, silently begging forgiveness for the small lie.

'But you have no coat. I really don't like to think of a young girl like you walking all that way alone and in the dark. Won't you . . .?'

'I'll be fine – honest,' she assured him and began to move away.

'Take care, then, my dear. Take care.'

'I will. Thanks, Mester.'

She knew it was a long way to the coast and Fleethaven Point – forty miles or more – but she was not afraid of the distance. All she wanted was to be away from that dreadful school and back home with her family – and with Danny. But she had not, in her moment of precipitate flight, thought of the trouble she would face when she did reach home. For the first time her footsteps slowed. She could almost hear her mother's voice raised in anger and see her stepfather's anxious face.

Then the idea, which had come into her mind as an excuse to the priest, now took root. Her grandad. She would go to her grandad. Hadn't he told her to do just that if she needed help?

And she needed help now.

It was then that she felt the first spots of rain. They were huge droplets, heralding a downpour. Kate looked around anxiously. The city was three miles behind her now and open fields bordered the road on both sides. Only here and there did lights shine into the dusk from the windows of cottages and farmhouses.

She trudged on, bending her face against the rain falling heavily now, quickly soaking through her gym-slip and blouse. The thin-soled house shoes she was wearing offered no protection. She wished she still had her sturdy boots but the matron had thrown them away with a look of disgust upon her face. Kate's hair – what was left of it – was wet through and rivulets of water were running down her neck.

On her left a clutch of farm buildings loomed in the darkness. Holding her breath, Kate tiptoed to the farm gate. Hoping that it was too wet for even the farm dogs to be prowling around, she felt her way stealthily around the wall of the nearest building until she came to an open door. Inside the darkness was even blacker, but as she walked forwards carefully, her hands outstretched in front of her, she felt her feet rustle in straw – deep, dry straw. She took off her wet tunic and spread it out. Then she burrowed beneath the straw and curled up. Although she was still wet and hungry, now at least there was a little warmth. Exhausted, she was asleep in seconds.

She awoke to the sound of rain pounding on the roof and to see daylight filtering through the wooden boards of the barn walls. Scrambling up, she struggled into her damp gymslip. She must go; the farmer might set his dogs on her for trespassing. Opening the barn door a crack, Kate peeped out. There was no one about and she was out of the barn, into the road and running before anyone had seen her.

It was still raining – 'siling' as her grandad would say. At the thought of her grandad, her spirits lifted.

She could almost hear his voice. 'If ya needs me, lass,' he'd told her, 'just send word and Ah'll come.'

Well, she'd do better than that; she was going to him.

It wasn't long before she was soaked. The wet seeped through her clothes and was cold against her skin. She walked briskly in an effort to keep warm, but the wind whipped bitingly across the rolling countryside of the Wolds and she was soon shivering. She was sure she had kept to the main road the old man had shown her but she could not find a signpost that bore the name of Suddaby.

100

It was at that point that she began to be afraid she was lost.

She was taking little running steps every so often and sobs punctuated her rapid breathing. Her head began to ache and her throat was parched; she was hot and then shivering with cold and the next moment sweating again. She looked around for a farmhouse or cottage, but the road stretched ahead through open country. There were no buildings of any kind now, only fields ploughed in neat furrows on either side as far as she could see.

Kate began to pray. 'Oh please, please help me . . .'

She was so tired, her legs ached and . . . Faintly, behind her, came the sound she most wished to hear at this moment; the sound of cart-wheels – a carrier's cart.

'Oh, Grandad, Grandad,' she sobbed thankfully. Turning, she stood watching the carrier approach, knowing what a pathetic, bedraggled creature she must appear to him. The cart slowed and she lifted her eyes to the man on the seat at the front.

'Well, little maid, and what be you a'doin' out on ya own a day like this'n?'

It was not her grandad. If she had not been exhausted and cold and almost on the point of collapse, her common sense would have told her that it would be too much of a coincidence to even hope that it could be her grandfather. This was not his route anyway. But in her confused state, it had seemed like an answer to her prayer.

She stood, bemused, staring up at the carrier's wrinkled face. 'Want a ride, young'un?' he asked kindly. 'Ya fair soaked and no mistake. Ain't ya even got a coat?'

He reached down his gnarled hand and, putting her small, cold hand into his, Kate found herself hoisted on to the seat beside him.

The carrier reached back into his cart. 'Here, wrap ya'sen in this.'

Gratefully, Kate wrapped the waterproof cape around her. The carrier flicked the reins and his two horses moved forward. 'Where be you a'goin'?'

'Suddaby,' Kate answered, speaking for the first time. Her voice was a rasping croak and it hurt her throat to speak. 'Me grandad's the carrier there. He . . .'

'Who? Not old Will Benson?'

Kate nodded and pulled the wrap closer around her. Now she was not walking, she was shivering uncontrollably, and yet her head felt burning hot.

'Well, dun't that beat all! Ah knows old Will real well. Ah'll tek you straight there, young'un, though we've a bit of a ride ahead of us.'

She felt his glance upon her. 'Should you like to ride in the back – under cover? It'd be warmer for ya.'

'Yes, please.'

She lay on a piece of old matting on the floor of his carrier's cart, dozing fitfully. Real sleep was impossible for the jolting of the cart, the rattle of its wheels and the hardness of the floor. She was alternately sweating and shivering, her head ached and there was a growing tightness in her chest. Above her, pans clanged together and pots clinked with every movement.

It seemed as if the journey would never end and then suddenly she felt the cart halt and the carrier was lifting the flap and saying, 'We're here, young 'un, at ya grandad's, but he bain't here. He's out on his rounds, so Mrs Raby, his neighbour, ses.'

Kate roused and pulled herself to the back of the cart. She saw the carrier standing there and with him a tall woman with a grey bun on the top of her head. Sweat prickled her skin and she could not breathe.

Miss Denham! Miss Denham had followed her.
It was then that Kate began to scream.

Their voices were rising and falling, coming and going
around her. She felt herself lifted and carried and then laid
on a sofa.

'Poor mite – she's ill. Ya can see that,' came the
woman's voice.

It was nothing like the voice of Miss Denham. There came
the touch of a work-worn yet caring hand upon her forehead.
That was certainly not Miss Denham. Kate sighed with
thankfulness and closed her eyes. Their conversation floated
around her.

'Who is she?'

'Dunno, really. She ses she's Will Benson's grand-
daughter.'

'Naw. Lass is ramblin'. Him an' his wife never had no
bairns, so how can he have a grandbairn?'

'Dun't ask me – ask him.'

'She must be something to him, though. I'd better look
after her, else Will'll have me guts fer garters.'

Kate shivered and drew her knees up, curling herself into
a ball for warmth. The woman must have noticed for at
once she began issuing orders.

'Get me some kindling fer the fire an' fill the kettle . . .'

'Hang on a mo,' came the carrier's reproachful voice. 'I've
to be on me way. There's me round to see to. I've come out
o' me way to bring her 'ere as it is.'

'Nathaniel Wallis, if this is some relation of Will
Benson's . . .' The words hung in the air like a threat.

'Aye, aye, all right, Millie, you win. I'd not like to get
wrong side o' Will Benson and no mistake.' The man
chuckled and Kate heard his footsteps leave the room.

'Now, me little lass.' The woman was bending over her, a rough kindness in her voice. 'Let's get you out o' them wet things . . .'

In her delirium, Kate imagined it was Mrs Eland helping her out of her wet clothes after her soaking in the sea; Danny's mother who was sponging her face, tucking a warm blanket around her and holding a mug of warm milk to her lips.

Then Danny would soon be home too . . .

'Danny?' she tried to ask and did not recognize her own feeble squeak of a voice.

'There's no Danny here, little lass,' the woman said.

Kate opened her eyes and struggled to focus them. It was not Mrs Eland. Then where . . .?

'Dun't fret. Yar – Will Benson'll soon be home.'

That was it, Kate thought dreamily. Her grandad. She had come to find her grandad.

It seemed only moments later that she heard his voice and then he was there kneeling beside the sofa and stroking her head and saying, 'Oh, me little Katie, me little girl. What have they done to ya?' And Kate knew she was safe at last.

She put her arms round his neck and felt his cool cheek against her hot forehead. 'Ee lass, ya burning up.'

'I've sponged her, Will, and made her drink, but she's poorly. Reckon ya should get her home and tell her folks to get the doctor – ne'er mind the cost.'

'Mebbe she'd better stay here . . .'

Kate gave a whimper at his words. 'No, Grandad. Tek me home. Please – tek me home!'

'All right, lass, all right.' He turned to the woman. 'She'll be all right if we wrap her warm in blankets, won't she?'

'Well . . .' The woman hesitated, reluctant to take responsibility, but as Kate's eyes filled with tears she said, 'I reckon she'll mek 'ersen worse fretting if you dun't tek her home, Will.'

Kate closed her eyes with thankfulness. Soon, soon she would be home. Above her, she heard the woman ask, 'Just who is she, Will? She ses she's yar grand-daughter. I thought she must be rambling, but now I ain't so sure.'

'You mind ya business, Millie Raby, and let me mind mine,' came her grandfather's sharp reply.

'Oh, sorry I spoke, I'm sure. After I've looked after the little lass most o' the afternoon an' all.'

Will sniffed and muttered gruffly, 'I'm sorry, Millie, I meant nowt. But I'm fair worried about her. She's ill. And I'd like to lay me 'ands on who's cut all her lovely hair off. That Ah would!'

Millie Raby's curiosity overcame her pique. 'So you do know her then?'

'Aye, I do,' Will said shortly and then added, 'She is me grand-daughter. She's Esther Everatt's daughter.'

Mrs Raby gave a gasp of surprise. 'Esther . . . Well, I nivver! Esther Everatt! Esther's bastard, is she?'

'No, she's not,' Will's voice thundered, almost shaking the sofa where Kate lay. 'Esther was married a good year afore this little lass was born.'

'Well, I was just remembering about Esther an' how she left this village all sudden-like . . .'

'Well, ya can stop remembering and putting two and two together and mekin' five. Help me get the lass into me cart. I'm tekin' her home where she belongs. An' this time she'll stay there, else Ah'll know the reason why!'

The woman gave a low chuckle. 'Well, Will Benson, they ses as how ya reap what ya sow. It looks to me as if ya wild oats from years back have brought you a bitter harvest.'

'That's where ya wrong, Millie Raby. Wild oats I might

'a sown, but if this little lass is me harvest I couldn't have asked for a greater blessing.'

Kate heard the words of their strange conversation but in her weakened state had no way of knowing if it was all part of her delirium. She was only blissfully aware that her grandfather was here and she was safe, and that he was picking her up tenderly and laying her in blankets in the back of his cart.

'Thank 'ee, Millie. Ah'll not forget ya help this day.'

'Eh, Will . . .' Kate saw the woman put her hand on his arm for a moment. 'We've been neighbours for more years than I care to remember, and I know I'm a nosey old beezum,' she cackled with laughter at the insult to herself, 'but ya secret's safe with me, I promise.'

Through the haze of her drowsiness, Kate heard her grandfather's chuckle. 'Aye, ya not such a bad old stick at that, Millie Raby.'

'Get away wi' ya and get yon lass home.'

This time, despite the rattling of the cart and warm and cosy in a mound of blankets, Kate did sleep, only rousing now and then to call to her grandfather. 'Are we there yet, Grandad?'

'Not far, lass, not far now.'

'Is Danny there, Grandad?'

A pause and then he answered, 'Aye, Danny'll be there.'

'I can't eat the gooseberries, Grandad. Dun't mek me eat the gooseberries.'

'What's that you say, lass, I dun't understand you . . .?'

Kate was asleep again and the next time she awoke she could hear the sea. It was her whelk shell. She was hearing the sea in her shell – the shell Danny had given her. She felt for the pocket of her coat. But she was not wearing her coat.

'Me shell, Grandad. I've lost me shell. Isobel's got me shell . . .'

But now she could smell the salt air and hear the waves across the marsh. It wasn't her shell. It was real.

Then Kate knew she was home.

Will himself carried her from his carrier's cart and into the farmhouse, straight up the stairs and into her own bedroom. Tenderly he laid her on her bed. Her mother and stepfather followed, bewildered and anxious.

'Oh Katie, my darling girl.' Her mother was bending over her, caressing her with gentle, loving hands.

'Mam, dun't be angry, dun't send me back. I dun't mind if you love Lilian more, but please dun't make me go back.' Then Kate began to cough, a tearing sound from deep in her chest.

Her mother's voice was a frantic whisper. 'Dear Lord! What has happened to her? She's so thin and who's cut her hair?'

'Now listen to me, Esther,' Kate heard her grandfather say, 'this lass stays put and if you try to send her away again, ya'll have me to answer to.'

Kate looked up into her mother's face and felt her hand upon her forehead. 'Ya needn't worry, Dad,' Esther was saying. 'But someone'll answer for this. Oh yes, someone will definitely have to answer me a few questions.'

'Mam – I haven't got to go back, have I?'

'No, my love, dun't fret. Ya never going back there.'

Kate closed her eyes. The sound of their voices came and went and she felt herself undressed and put between the sheets with hot bricks wrapped in cloth placed at her feet and on either side of her. As she began to sweat the fever out, she fretted no more. She was home for good. Her mother had promised.

And for all Esther Godfrey's strictness, she never broke her promises.

107

Eleven

She was having strange dreams; she was trying to run but her feet were like lead, her heart was thudding in her chest and she couldn't move. Then it felt as if someone at the end of her bed was lifting her legs.

'Mam, dun't lift me legs. It feels funny. Dun't lift me legs.'

'Katie love, I'm not touching your legs,' came her mother's voice as if from a great distance, and she heard her step-father's gentle voice too. 'It's the fever, Esther. She delirious. Bathe her forehead again.'

Then Kate felt the cool dampness on her forehead and the throbbing eased a little. 'Me shell – she's got me shell. She wouldn't give it back . . .' she murmured.

She awoke once to see Dr Blair's kindly face bending over her as he gently spooned liquid between her lips. 'There, there, my dear. We'll soon have you up and running about again . . .'

She heard him speaking to her mother in his deep voice. 'She'll be fine, Esther, really. It's clear the child hasn't been eating properly and she's exhausted. She obviously got very chilled trying to get home, but there's no real harm done. All she needs is a few days in bed. She'll feel a little weak when she first gets up, but with Fleethaven's good fresh air and your good food . . .'

Then her mother's voice. 'Thank goodness. I – I thought she'd got pneumonia.'

'No – nothing like that, I assure you, but Kate's been very distressed about something, Esther.'

'Yes – and as soon as she's better, I mean to find out exactly what's been going on.'

Another time Kate opened her eyes to see Rosie standing beside her bed clutching a posy of wild flowers. The child's face was unusually solemn, and her voice was only a whisper. 'Katie, I've brought you some flowers – to make you better. Do get better, Katie.'

'Danny? Where's Danny?' Kate croaked. 'Why hasn't he been to see me?'

The child hopped from one foot to the other. 'He – he wanted to come – but he wasn't sure . . .'

'Tell him I want to see him.'

Kate closed her eyes again. When next she opened them, Rosie had gone and her mother was once again sitting beside her bed holding her hand. Every time Kate awoke, her mother was there.

After a couple of days sleeping most of the time, Kate, although still weak, began to feel better. It was her mother who had dark shadows beneath her eyes now.

'Oh Katie,' she said, putting her arms about her daughter and holding her close. 'You had us all frightened. Kate, listen to me a minute. When you were rambling, you said something about me loving Lilian more than you.'

Kate buried her face against her mother's shoulder. 'I dun't remember.'

Her mother stroked the short cropped hair and murmured, 'They say ya speak the truth when you're in that sort of state. But that was not the reason I wanted you to go away to school. I love you dearly. I would never love one of me children more than the other. But a baby takes up a lot of time and attention and I can see it must 'ave felt like that for you, specially because ya'd been the only one for so long.'

109

When the girl did not answer, Esther said, 'Do you under-stand, Katie?'

Against her mother's shoulder she nodded, then drew back and looked into her face. 'Then why did you send me away?'

Esther Godfrey sighed heavily. 'Oh, Katie, there are things you dun't understand . . .'

'Then tell me.'

Her mother avoided Kate's direct gaze and unusually for her she stumbled over her words. 'I was worried – you see you're getting older now – and there are so many dangers for a young girl – a young woman almost . . .'

'Mam, just tell me.'

'I – I was afraid you were getting too close – too involved with – with the boys at the Point.'

'You mean Danny, don't you?'

'Well – yes. He's a young man now and – and young men start to – well – want things from girls.'

Softly Kate said, 'Danny wouldn't hurt me, Mam,' and then added with a little of her old spark, ''Sides, if he tried anything, he'd soon get a kick right where it hurts!'

Kate saw Esther's mouth twitch with laughter, despite the anxiety clouding her eyes. Then her face sobered again. 'Kate, I want you to give me your solemn promise that you will never, ever, let Danny . . . touch you.' Knowing just what a promise meant to her mother, that they were never given lightly, Kate hesitated. 'Why, Mam?' she pressed.

'He – he's not for you, Kate, not in that way. Friends, yes, but there – there can't be anything else.'

'Oh Mam, surely you don't think I'm stupid enough to let anybody – including Danny – touch me before I'm wed. You've drilled that into me ever since – well, as long as I can remember.'

Kate watched her mother's face, saw conflicting emotions

110

crossing it, as if there was a fight going on inside her head. 'What *is* it, Mam?'

'Nothing – nothing. It'll be all right, if ya'll promise me that.'

Kate sensed it wasn't 'nothing'. There was something her mother wasn't telling her. But there was nothing the young girl could do to prise whatever it was out of her mother. Instead she said airily, 'Oh yes, I can promise you that much, Mam.'

For the moment her pledge seemed to satisfy her mother.

What Kate did not voice, and what she had only just realized herself as a result of this conversation with her mother, was a silent vow she made to herself.

One day I'll marry Danny Eland.

It seemed that having gained Kate's promise, her mother's fears regarding Danny were allayed. The very next day Kate heard her voice calling from the bottom of the stairs, 'Kate, Kate you've got a visitor. Up you go.'

She heard footsteps on the stairs and even before the door of her bedroom was pushed wider, she knew it was Danny.

He stood in the doorway, grinning at her, his dark hair tousled, his skin weathered brown and glowing with health. Then she saw the smile fade. 'Oh, Kate – ya pretty hair,' he sympathized, moving into the room and coming to perch on the end of her bed. 'Did ya mam have to cut it off because of the fever?'

Kate shook her head. The nightmare was back; the scissors, the strong arms and her face pressed against Miss Denham's corseted bosom.

'I – I dun't want to talk about it . . .'

His grin was back. Comfortingly he said, 'Well, it'll grow again. 'Sides, it's lovely and curly when it's short, in't it?'

'You're just saying that to cheer me up.' But she too was grinning now. Then the smile wobbled a little. 'Danny – when I ran away from the school, I left the whelk shell you gave me.'

'Dun't worry about that – plenty more on the beach. I'll bring you another.'

'But that was special,' she murmured, leaning back against the pillows, 'it was the biggest you'd ever found – and I've lost it.' Because she was still weak, easy tears filled her eyes.

'Dun't bother ya'sen,' Danny said. 'I'll keep looking till I find another just as big. Hurry up and get better, then we can look together, eh?'

Suddenly, the boarding school was all a horrible nightmare. She was back home and all the days of the rest of her life stretched ahead – with Danny.

Soon Kate was allowed downstairs and with each day she grew stronger. Then came the morning her mother appeared dressed in her best costume with a smart hat perched on the top of her hair.

'I'm off to Lincoln today, Kate, to give that Miss Denham a piece of my mind.'

'Oh, Mam, do – do you think you ought?' Kate quailed at the very thought of her mother standing toe to toe with the enormous, overpowering figure of Miss Denham.

Her mother was smiling down at her, but her green eyes were flashing defiance. She touched Kate's cheek gently with her fingertips. 'Dun't you worry, my love. I've never been frightened of anyone in me life – I ain't likely to start now.'

But Kate was in a state of agitation all day. Her poor stepfather spent the whole time trying to pacify the baby and calm Kate. 'You needn't worry about your mother,' he told her, his lop-sided grin crinkling his eyes. 'She's a match for anyone.'

'You don't know Miss Denham,' Kate muttered, and her insides quivered at the mere thought of the woman.

'I know what might help,' her stepfather said suddenly. He was obviously trying to think of something he could do to take Kate's mind off her mother's trip. He left the kitchen and went through into the living room. Mystified, Kate followed and stood watching as he opened the front of his bureau. He searched beneath a pile of papers.

'I really must get down to filling in these forms about this year's crops for your mother. She hates anything to do with officialdom.' He glanced back over his shoulder, winked at Kate and then continued his search. 'Ah,' he said triumphantly, pulling two sheets of writing paper from the heap. 'Here it is! Right, let's go back into the kitchen where it's warmer. I want you to read this letter.'

Back in the kitchen, he told Kate to sit in his chair by the fire and handed her the letter. 'It's from my mother,' Jonathan told her. 'We received it whilst you were so poorly, but I always intended you should read it when you were stronger.'

Kate unfolded the pages and began to read. The letter was written in a bold flourishing hand and was dated the day of her visit to their home.

> *My dear Jonathan, Kate came to see us today and the poor child is in a dreadful state! She looks thin and pale – nothing like the healthy child we first met at little Lilian's christening. She is obviously very unhappy at that school and if what she told us is true – and I can hardly believe a young girl of her age could make up such tales – then you and Esther should remove her from there at once.*
>
> *We felt we should not interfere directly, but your*

> *father did hear some very disquieting news only last*
> *week, funnily enough. We didn't say anything in*
> *front of young Kate, but we certainly think you and*
> *Esther should think things over very carefully. It*
> *seems this Miss Denham has only been there for a*
> *term. Miss Peterson, the previous Principal – a*
> *lovely woman – was taken ill very suddenly and*
> *sadly died. The appointment of Miss Denham seems*
> *to have been made with unseemly haste and – to*
> *my mind – with disastrous results! Already three*
> *parents have removed their girls from the school.*

Kate raised her head and met her stepfather's eyes. He nodded as if in answer to her unspoken question. 'Of course, you were already home by the time we got this letter. In fact, you were home before the telegram arrived.'

'Telegram?' This was the first Kate had heard about a telegram.

Jonathan sat down in front of her and took her hands in his. Leaning forward he said, gently, 'You were very wrong to run away, you know, Katie. You worried my mother and father – and Peg – very much.'

'How – how did they know?'

'Miss Ogden went to see them that Sunday evening, just after my mother must have written and posted this letter to us. Miss Ogden thought you might have gone there. The school knew their name and address because you'd been allowed to visit their home. They had the police looking for you all over Lincoln throughout the night.'

'The – the police?' Kate felt herself growing red with shame. 'Oh, Dad, I'm sorry. I – I didn't think they'd bother to look for me.'

'Why didn't you write to us, Katie, and tell us what was going on?'

She hung her head, but now there was no long hair to hide behind. 'I didn't think me mam would believe me.'

'We'd have come to see you,' he said softly. 'We both know you would never tell lies. We'd have seen for ourselves,' his glance flickered towards her shorn hair, 'how you were being treated. As for whatever else happened, well, if you ever want to tell us . . .'

Kate shook her head. 'I dun't want to talk about it. Mebbe some time, but not now.'

'I understand,' he said gently.

'I am sorry, Dad.' She looked up at him again, tears brimming her eyes.

He smiled at her and ruffled her short hair. 'We'll say no more about it. You're safely home now and that's all that matters.'

At that moment the baby began to whimper and the whimpers became louder until she was squealing. Jonathan cast a comical look at Kate and went to the cradle to pick Lilian up. Putting her against his shoulder, he patted her back. The baby gave a loud burp and the squealing subsided, but only to a continuous grizzle.

Jonathan nuzzled Lilian's downy head, 'Who's Daddy's pretty little girl, then?' he murmured, but Kate's sharp hearing caught his words and she felt the familiar shaft of jealousy. Jonathan glanced at her and Kate dropped her gaze, afraid that he might read in her eyes the feelings she tried hard, yet failed, to quell.

Jonathan's deep voice came softly. 'I hope she grows up to be like you, Kate. You were a lovely little girl when I first met you. Not that you're not now, of course!'

Kate felt a warm glow spread through her and she raised her face again, the fleeting resentment banished by his affectionate words. 'How old was I?'

'Let me see, you'd be about four. A bright little thing you

115

were, always laughing and chattering. Much the same as you are now – at least, as you were before you went to that wretched school,' he admitted regretfully.

Kate frowned, puzzled. 'But me dad, me—' She stopped, changing the words carefully, conscious of the hurt she might inflict upon her beloved stepfather. 'Me other dad – was here then, wasn't he?'

'He was away at the war. I came to Fleethaven Point to see Grannie Harris when I was on sick leave. Let's think, nineteen-sixteen, it would be. I'd been with her eldest son, Ernie, when he was killed in France and he'd told me all about his home and his family. And about "the Missus at Brumbys' Farm". That's what he called your mother.'

'So you came to see them?' Kate watched the expression on her stepfather's face sober. His eyes took on a faraway look and there was pain in their depths.

'I came to try to bring the Harrises what comfort I could. And then – I stayed for a while. But of course I had to go back eventually. After the war, your father came back. He was very . . . ill, at first.'

'I can just remember him,' Kate said softly. So that was what Danny had meant when he had said Jonathan Godfrey had 'come back' after her father had drowned. But it was all still a little hazy. She didn't quite understand what had happened.

'Did you and me mam . . .?'

At that moment the back door was flung open and her mother called, 'I'm back.' Then she was in the kitchen and the moment for Kate to share further confidences with her stepfather was lost.

He had been quite right; Kate need not have worried. Her mother returned triumphant.

'Ya didn't say that to her, Mam, did ya?' Kate hugged her knees to her chest in delight, imagining the scene as her mother recounted the interview between herself and Miss Denham. Esther Godfrey's eyes still sparkled with the light of battle as she stood, hands on hips, smiling at her daughter. 'Indeed I did, Katie. I told her she was an old beezum!'

'What did she *say*?' Kate's question was high-pitched with excitement, while Jonathan smiled indulgently at his wife, ferocious in the defence of her young.

Esther's grin widened and her eyes twinkled merrily. 'She said she could see where you got your rebellious streak from, and I said, "Well if there's many folk like you in the world, she's going to need it!" ' Her expression softened and she ruffled Kate's short hair. 'I'm glad you've got a bit of my spirit, lass, even if it does mean we clash now and then.'

'Did ya get all me things back? All me clothes I left?'

Esther nodded. 'I left the trunk at the station, though.'

'I'll pick it up tomorrow,' Jonathan promised.

'Oh.' Kate knew there was disappointment showing on her face.

'What is it, love?' her mother prompted.

Kate glanced from one to the other. 'Well, just before I left, three of the girls, they'd got summat of mine and – and they wouldn't give it back . . .'

'Do you mean this?' From her coat pocket, Esther drew out the huge whelk shell.

Kate drew in her breath sharply and, tears glistening in her eyes, she reached out with trembling fingers to take the shell once more into her hands. 'Oh, Mam, thank you. Thank you. Yes, yes, that's it. The whelk shell Danny gave me. Oh, thank goodness you found it. Was it amongst me things?'

'You were rambling about a shell when you were ill and when Danny—' Kate saw her mother glance swiftly at Jonathan and then away again. 'When Danny came to visit you,

117

he told me all about it. I realized it was ... important to you.' Her mother's voice dropped and she gave the faintest of sighs.

There was a pause and Kate prompted, 'And?'

Esther was smiling again, 'When I was taken up to the dormitory to pack your things up, I searched especially for the shell. It wasn't there. So,' Esther continued, enjoying the retelling of her tale, 'I demanded that it be found.'

'Oh Mam, you didn't!' Kate squeaked, but she was laughing with joy at the scene her mother was painting.

'I did,' Esther said firmly, and once more her eyes were sparkling. 'I waited until every girl in your dormitory was fetched from class and made to go through her belongings. And,' she finished triumphantly, 'it was found in the chest of drawers belonging to Isobel Cartwright.'

Kate was not surprised and said so. 'She was one of the three girls who were so horrid.'

'You can forget all about that dreadful place, Katie love, and all the people in it. You won't ever have to see any of them again,' her mother said. 'You're safe home with us now. And I – I won't send you away again.'

Kate bounced up from the chair and hugged her mother. Esther's arms came tightly around her. Everything was all right – her mother really did love her.

And yes, she was safely home; with her mother, her stepfather – and Danny.

Twelve

'Mam – I must go and look at the sea, I just must!'
'Well – all right then. But no paddling, mind. I know you, Kate Hilton. Get a bit of winter sunshine and ya reckon ya can act like it's midsummer!'

Kate grinned at her mother and was rewarded by Esther Godfrey's wonderful smile. 'Eh, but it's good to see you better, love. You're still a bit thin and pale, though. I dun't want you taking risks and getting another chill.'

'I won't, Mam. Just look how I'm muffled up in this coat and scarf – and a hat!' she finished scathingly. Kate had never before worn a hat even when it snowed.

'And don't sit on the wet sand,' her mother shouted after her as Kate went through the farm gate and across the lane. She turned back briefly, smiled and waved. She'd never known her mother fuss so much. But then, she realized, she had never been so ill before; always a robust youngster, she had shaken childhood illnesses off quickly.

Kate climbed the dunes through the trees and at the top stood to look across the marsh towards the far dunes and the sea beyond. With a whoop of delight she ran down the slope and began to run across the marsh, delighting in the feel of the spongy turf beneath her feet, the sharp breeze on her cheeks bringing the colour back to them. To her surprise and disgust, her breathing soon became laboured and she was forced to slow down, even to stop for a few moments to regain her breath.

119

She could no longer run.

She pulled in deep breaths, but it was like trying to breathe in through a feather pillow and there was an ache in her chest. Slowly she threaded her way across the marsh, jumping the meandering streams but having to rest after each exertion. She came to the far dunes and found that she could only climb to the top in three stages, resting twice on the way. But when she gained the beach and saw the sea, it was worth all the effort.

Would she ever run like she used to do? 'Like the wind', as Danny used to say with grudging admiration?

Kate walked slowly along the beach. She even felt the cold more now. Hunched into her thick coat, the woollen scarf around her throat and mouth, she trudged miserably back across the marsh towards the cottages at the Point. She knocked on the Elands' back door and when it opened she found herself enveloped in Beth Eland's embrace, her face pressed against soft, plump breasts.

'Oh lovey, it's so good to see you. How I longed to come and visit you when I heard how ill you was! Ne'er mind, you're here now. Come in near the fire and let me look at you.'

She drew Kate into her warm kitchen and held her at arm's length, her soft brown eyes searching Kate's face. 'Ya still look pale, Katie. Here, tek ya coat off else ya'll not feel the benefit when you go out again. Sit down and have some of my scones, fresh out the oven.'

In a moment, Kate was biting into a thickly buttered scone, the crumbs scattering down her pinafore while Beth stood smiling down at her.

Kate looked up at her. 'Where's Danny? He's not been to see me again. He came that once while I was in bed, but he didn't come no more.'

The smile on the woman's face faltered a little. 'Oh – er – well, yes. He's at work. He – he dun't get much time,

Kate . . .' her eyes flickered away and she fingered the hem of her apron nervously. Then Mrs Eland's face brightened as, seeming to change the subject, she said, 'You sit there, I'll just nip next door and fetch Grannie Harris. She'll want to see you . . .'

'Oh, I see Grannie every day nearly when she comes for the milk and eggs for everyone at the Point.' Kate took another bite, munched a few seconds, swallowed and then said, 'You have ya milk and eggs from us, dun't ya, Mrs Eland?'

Beth's gaze flickered away. 'Um, well, yes.'

Kate stared at her with candid eyes. 'But you never come ya'sen to fetch them, d'ya?'

Beth Eland shook her head, a kind of sadness in the movement.

'Why?' the girl persisted.

'Dun't ask me, Katie,' she whispered. 'Please – dun't ask me.'

It was the same strange reply her mother had once given to a similar question.

There was something odd, Kate thought, realizing something she had always known but had never really thought about before; the fact that in such a small community her mother and Beth Eland never spoke to each other, although each of them was friendly with everyone else. Perhaps they had quarrelled years ago and they were both too proud to make the first step to reconciliation.

Mrs Eland had turned away and was busying herself at the range, stirring something in a cooking pot. Kate jumped up from the stool and went to her, putting her arms around the woman's plump waist and hugging her. She didn't want to upset Danny's mother. Kate liked her – loved her – and not just because she was Danny's mother. Mrs Eland was always so kind and gentle towards her. The woman turned round, holding the girl close once more, her smile as warm as always.

'I'd best get back,' Kate said now. 'It's one of me grandad's days for visiting. Will you tell Danny to call for me on Sunday after dinner?'

The haunted look was back for a moment in the woman's soft brown eyes. 'Aye, all right. I'll tell him,' she promised, but now there was no smile.

'Oh Katie, it's so good to see you looking better.' Bustling between pantry and the living-room table where they were to have dinner the moment Will Benson arrived on his carrier's cart, Esther paused to give Kate a swift hug. As her mother disappeared into the pantry, Kate resumed laying the knives and forks on the table. Emerging once more, carrying a large oval dish for the beef which was still sizzling in the range oven, Esther said, 'You'll soon have to be thinking what you're going to do, though. Do you want to go back to school here?'

Kate shook her head and then glanced at her mother, trying to gauge how what she wanted to tell her might be received. The young girl paused and took a deep breath. 'I'd – like to take a job in town – in the biggest shop there, if I could have a bicycle to get to and from work. And then when classes start at the Evening Institute next autumn, I thought I might learn dressmaking and tailoring. And after that . . .' Her words came faster, tumbling over each other in her enthusiasm.

'You seem to have got it all planned.' Her mother's face – usually so transparent in its expressions – gave no indication of her thoughts. 'Seems eminently sensible to me.' Her stepfather looked round from behind his newspaper and smiled benignly on them both. Esther glanced at him briefly but then her gaze came back to rest on her daughter. Kate felt Esther's scrutiny, but met her mother's gaze squarely. Kate had plans – ambitions. Modest as they might be, the planning of them gave her a thrill of excitement in the pit of her stomach. But she desperately wanted her mother to approve of them.

Kate imagined herself sitting in a room very like Jonathan's mother, Mrs Godfrey – in front of a sewing machine and creating beautiful garments for wealthy ladies. By working in a shop in town she would have the chance to handle and sell fine fabrics. At evening classes she could learn how to turn the fabric into lovely dresses and costumes.

She could hardly wait to begin.

She had now fully recovered from her illness and the terrible experience she had suffered. Her hair had grown a little but at least it was now expertly cut into a neat style and curled prettily around her face. Her complexion was still a little pale for the winter months had not allowed her to be out of doors as much after her illness as she would normally have been, but now her green eyes were shining with excitement at her plans.

Then suddenly her mother was smiling. 'I agree with yar dad. They are sensible plans. I'll have a word with Miss Davenport who works at that big drapery shop, if ya like. She's always been so helpful when I've gone in there.'

'Oh Mam, would you really?' Kate flung her arms about her mother's waist and dragged her into a dance around the kitchen table. 'Oh, thank you, *thank* you!'

Kate's happiness was complete. She was back home at Fleethaven Point. She knew her mam loved her even though baby Lilian took up so much of her attention, and, best of all, she was back with Danny.

*

123

'Danny, do you know why your mam and mine dun't speak to each other?'

'Haven't a clue,' he replied airily and grinned at her.

'Danny – be serious a minute.'

They were walking along the beach as they did now every Sunday afternoon.

'Me – serious?' He flung his arm around her shoulder. 'How can I be serious when I'm that happy to see you looking better, I could burst.'

'Stupid!' She shoved him away, pleased yet shyly embarrassed by his display of affection.

'Ya blushing, Katie Hilton. Ya blushing,' he teased and then dodged out of her way as she aimed a playful cuff at him.

She voiced her thoughts about the strangeness of two people in such a small community deliberately ignoring each other.

Danny wrinkled his brow. 'D'you know, I never thought about it afore. But now you come to mention it, it's always been like that.' His grin broadened. 'Mebbe when they was young they fell out over some bloke.'

Kate regarded him solemnly. Danny had said it as a joke, but Kate was not joking. 'Well, there's summat, an' I'll tell you summat else.'

'What?'

'Whatever the reason is, no one's telling. When I ask questions, they all clam up and say, "Dun't ask, Katie, dun't ask." '

'Well, ya're such a nosey little blighter. If they dun't want to tell ya, that's their business. It's got nowt to do with us and it's not going to come between us.'

He flung his arm around her shoulder again and they walked along in companionable silence.

Somewhere in the universe, sadistic Fate laughed.

Thirteen

1930

'Are ya coming out on me boat?'

Kate skidded to a halt on her bicycle, sending a shower of small stones on to the grass verge. She looked up to see Danny standing on the bank at the side of the lane.

'What? Now? Bit late at this time of day, isn't it?'

'It won't be dark for a couple of hours yet. Oh, do come, Katie.'

He leaped down from the bank into the road and came towards her. In the four years since she had started work in Lynthorpe, they had both altered. At eighteen, Danny was no longer a boy but a man with strong, sunburnt arms and a brown-skinned face that still seemed to be always grinning. He was not very tall, not much taller than Kate, yet his shoulders had broadened. He tried to slick back his hair, but the wind ruffled it into unruly black curls.

Kate's own hair had grown again, falling in waves and curls to her shoulders; and cycling into Lynthorpe every day, whatever the weather, kept her blossoming figure lithe and her skin glowing with health.

Kate looked at Danny closely. There seemed to be an air of excitement about him. Then she remembered. Trying to hide a smile, she said, 'I'm a bit tired for all that rowing . . .'

Triumphantly, Danny interrupted, 'Ya dun't have to row any more.'

Now the laughter was bubbling up inside her, but she

quelled it, allowing Danny his moment of glory. 'I've finished fitting the engine in it.'

'Engine? Really?' She could no longer prevent the smile twitching the corner of her mouth.

He leaned closer. 'You knew!' he accused, but he too was laughing.

'I'm sorry – I didn't want to spoil your surprise, but Dad mentioned it.'

Danny nodded. 'Ya dad's been very good helping us. He's clever with motors – wish I was. Me dad ses we'll keep the oars on board – just in case. Reckon he doesn't trust my mechanical efforts yet.' He paused then added, 'Well, a' ya comin' or not? I've been waiting for you this past half an hour. You're late, aren't ya?'

'Mr Reynolds called me into his office just as I was leaving.'

'Oho – been a naughty girl, have ya?'

''Course not . . .' she began indignantly, then saw his teasing grin. She punched him lightly on his shoulder, feeling the hard muscle beneath her hand.

'So what had you done to have old man Reynolds after ya?' Danny asked her. 'Left a bit of ribbon dangling out of a drawer again?'

Kate giggled as Danny reminded her of the times she had been on the receiving end of one of Mr Reynolds's lectures.

Mr Reynolds was the owner of the drapery store where Kate now worked. He was a short man, always dressed in a black morning jacket with pin-striped trousers. His thin neck poked up out of a stiffly starched collar. His cold blue eyes peered at all his staff through steel-rimmed spectacles which enlarged his eyes and made his scrutiny appear even more critical than it was. He was a martinet; every morning he toured the store and not a thing missed his sharp glance.

'No,' Kate said, her eyes gleaming. 'He's going to promote me.'

'Again? But it's only a couple of months since he put you in charge of a department. Ya'll be manageress of the whole shop soon,' he teased, but he was smiling as he said it.

'He wants me to go into the sewing room – as supervisor. Miss Poole's retiring.'

'But what about the other girls already there? Their noses'll be out o' joint if you're put in over 'em?'

Kate sniffed. 'Quite likely,' she said shortly.

She felt Danny's glance on her. 'Ya're a hard one, Kate Hilton, when it's summat ya want.'

She grinned at him, her eyes sparkling mischievously. 'Me? Hard? I'm an old softy and you know it.'

She didn't confide – not even to Danny – that her unfortunate experience at the school in Lincoln had left her with a sliver of ice in her heart. Never again would she allow herself to be treated as she had been then. Whilst outwardly she was friendly with everyone she met, only with a very few people would she ever drop her guard completely; maybe only with Danny and Rosie Maine.

'Will it mean more money?' he was saying.

'Danny Eland!' She pretended indignation. 'Is that all you can say? Here I am with news of a promotion and all you can think of is money!'

During the four years at Reynolds' Kate had been a quick and eager junior under Miss Davenport's kindly tutelage. Now, at only seventeen, she was in charge of the haberdashery department with a young, gauche school-leaver under her wing. Kate still rode between work and home on her bicycle along the Point road and, just as she had planned, by attending evening classes in Lynthorpe, she was learning dressmaking and tailoring.

It seemed that she possessed a natural talent and before

long she had begun to bring home tiny garments for Lilian, and blouses and skirts for herself and her mother from her classes.

'I can see I'll soon be handing over me sewing machine to you,' her mother had laughed, but there had been pride in her voice. Esther was a fine seamstress, but all her knowledge had come from the aunt who had brought her up. Now she watched with interest as Kate tried out all that she was learning from a professional tailoress. The front parlour at Brumbys' Farm was becoming cluttered with paper patterns and pins and lengths of material.

'Just like home,' Jonathan would tease her fondly, and Kate was reminded once more that it had been the sight of Mrs Godfrey's front room that had sown the seed of ambition in her.

Now Danny was grinning at her, quite unabashed by her pique. 'I was thinking of you being able to save for your bottom drawer.'

'Me – me bottom drawer?'

'Yeah – isn't that what girls call it when they're going to get married?'

'Going to – to get – married?'

He leaned towards her over the handle-bars of her bicycle. Gently he rubbed his nose against hers. 'Well, we'll be getting married one of these fine days, won't we?'

'Well, really!' Kate said, feigning exasperation, but she could not prevent her generous mouth widening into a broad grin. 'If that dun't beat all for a romantic proposal, Danny Eland.'

Suddenly his face was serious and there was a fleeting flash of passion in his dark brown eyes. He reached up and touched her face with strong fingers that were suddenly gentle. 'I've always loved you, Katie Hilton, and I always will. You must know that.'

'Oh Danny,' she breathed, knowing her own green eyes were glowing, mirroring his emotion with the same depth of love and longing.

Their faces were inches apart, coming slowly towards each other, until they could each feel the other's breath on their faces. Their lips met tentatively, trembling on the brink of the unknown; a soft, sweet kiss of innocence.

'Danny – I do love you so,' she murmured. As they drew back, they both heard the distant clip-clopping of a pony's hooves.

'Oh heck! That's me mam coming along the Grange road. Where's she been?'

'It's rent day.'

'Oh – so it is.'

'Quick – give us ya bike . . .'

Danny seized hold of her bicycle and pushed it up the bank and down the other side. Kate scrambled up after him. They crouched down out of sight of her mother who drove past in the pony and trap. Giggling like a couple of children, they parted the grass and watched as she passed within a few feet of them.

'So,' he asked, as they walked down the lane hand-in-hand when Esther was safely out of sight, 'do ya reckon they'll let us get wed soon, or d'ya think we'll have to wait till we're twenty-one?'

'I dun't reckon my mam'll ever agree to it,' Kate said. 'What about yours?'

'Oh, she'll be pleased as punch. She loves you.'

'My mam is fond of you – at least she used to be when we were little, but . . .'

'Aye – aye, she was.'

There was silence between them, then they both spoke at once.

'It's this thing between them . . .'

129

'I remember . . .'

'Sorry – you go first.'

'I was going to say,' Danny said slowly, 'I remember at ya dad's funeral. It's all a bit vague . . .'

Kate nodded but did not interrupt.

'I can remember sitting in the pew in church and watching the coffin in the front of the altar and then when the vicar had finished and ya ma and you and Will Benson came out of the front pew and down the aisle following the coffin as it was taken out . . .'

'Go on,' Kate whispered, prompting.

They had stopped walking and turned to face each other. 'Ya mam stopped – right in front of us. She didn't speak but sort of gestured with her hand that we should walk out behind the three of you. Just as if we were – well – family almost, or at the very least, close friends. And yet now . . .'

'And yet now,' Kate finished for him, 'they don't even speak to each other.'

Danny nodded and they resumed walking hand-in-hand until they came near to Brumbys' Farm.

By silent, mutual consent, they let go of each other's hand. As they reached the farm gate, Danny said, 'We won't tell 'em yet.'

'No, let's keep it our secret for a while.'

They looked at each other, seeing one another in a new way, a different way. Kate felt the thrill of excitement just below her ribs.

Danny loved her.

'I'd best be off,' he murmured, but made no move. 'It is a bit late to go out on the boat now.'

'Yes.' But she too remained exactly where she was. 'We got talking about other things, didn't we?'

They were standing very still, just looking at each other.

'How about Sunday afternoon then?'

'Sunday?' Kate murmured, absently.

'The boat. We'll go out on the boat on Sunday afternoon.'

'Oh yes,' Kate's eyes glowed. 'Sunday afternoon.'

'Me want to come wiv you.'

On the Sunday afternoon after dinner, Lilian stood in front of Kate as she pulled on her boots.

Kate sighed but said levelly, 'Not today. Another time, maybe.'

'Where you goin'?' the child persisted. At four years old, Lilian was an unattractive child with grey, expressionless eyes, mousey, straight hair and a sullen mouth that seemed always to be pouting. She was proving to be a sickly child – totally unlike her robust half-sister. Lilian was always catching cold and Esther was for ever fussing over her youngest chick; something Kate would never have believed possible.

To be fair, though, Kate thought, her mother had hardly ever needed to fuss over her, and on the only occasion when she had been really ill, well, she couldn't fault her mother for the attention she had given her then. Even if it was guilt-based, Kate often thought, remembering the days following her return from the Lincoln school.

'Yes – just where are you going?' her mother asked now.

'We're going to try out the new engine in Danny's boat – well, Mester Eland's boat.'

'Oh, that. I've heard enough about that these past weeks from ya father.'

Her stepfather's face appeared from behind his newspaper. 'Let me know how you get on. Get Danny to show you how to start it and how to steer . . .'

'Now, why would I want to know how to start an engine, or how to steer it, Dad? It was bad enough having to row

131

till we could get the sails up. Now there's a motor in it, I'm just going to lie back and . . .'

'If you ever get stranded out at sea, you might well be glad to know a little about how it works. You should learn, Kate. Any knowledge is useful. You never know when you might . . .'

'Well, it's unlikely I'll ever be out at sea without Danny, and he'll know.'

'Haven't you got some sewing you ought to finish before your class tomorrow night?' Esther put in.

'It's Sunday, Mother, the Lord's day,' Kate answered pertly, mimicking the words Esther herself used so often, but taking the sarcasm out of her tone with a cheeky, infectious grin. 'The Sabbath's not for work. Sunday's for rest and for meeting my – my friends.'

She bit her lip. She would have to be more careful; she had been about to let slip a hint of the change in the relationship between herself and Danny.

Esther's normally generous mouth tightened visibly until it was a hard, straight line. Kate saw her open it to speak, but before the words came, she was out of the kitchen, through the scullery and banging the back door shut behind her. Yet it was not until she had crested the Hump and was running across the stretch of grass between the cottages and the river bank that she was able to forget the disapproval on her mother's face, nor the lonely figure of her little sister, standing staring forlornly after her.

'Kate! Kate!' The sound of her name came bouncing across the breeze and she turned to see Rosie, a long-legged, coltish nine-year-old, galloping across the grass towards her. 'Danny's taking us both out in his dad's boat to try out the engine.'

Kate was disappointed. She would not have Danny to herself. Then, as Rosie linked her arm through hers, Kate felt a stab of guilt. It was impossible to feel irritated with Rosie for many minutes. She was so pretty with her white-gold curls and merry laughter. She was their friend – hers and Danny's. She mustn't be selfish, Kate told herself sharply, wanting to exclude Rosie from their outing just because now there was something extra special between herself and Danny.

After all, she and Danny had the rest of their lives to be alone together. Kate felt an excited flutter just below her ribs. The mere thought filled her with happiness.

Fourteen

She was cycling home along the coast road, singing softly beneath her breath, when she heard a familiar chugging noise behind her. Smiling to herself, Kate braked and jumped off her bicycle, wheeling it on to the grass verge. There was only one person around here who owned a motor car; Squire Marshall. And with his erratic driving on the narrow lane, it was much safer to dismount.

But it was not Squire Marshall at the wheel of a brand-new Austin Twelve; it was Danny. He drew to a halt beside Kate and leaned out through the window, grinning, as she gaped open-mouthed at him.

'Whatever are you doing driving that?'

'You not the only one who's been promoted.' His grin widened.

For the past two weeks Kate had been working as supervisor in the workroom. She even had three girls working under her and, with the added responsibility for their work being properly done as well as her own increased workload, there had been a substantial increase in her pay.

Kate laid her bicycle down in the long grass on the verge and went across the lane to stand beside the vehicle. 'What d'ya mean?'

'Mester Marshall's made me his chauffeur. I'm to look after his car and drive him and his missus wherever they want to go.'

134

Kate shook her head wonderingly. 'Won't you be working on the land any more?'

'Oh yes, but I've always liked motors. He's talking about getting a tractor and a new reaper and 'ee ses he'll put me in charge of all the machinery. It's the sort of job I've allus wanted.'

'Oh, Danny – that's wonderful.' She touched his arm as he leaned through the open window. Then she grinned archly at him. 'Will it mean more money?'

He gaped at her for a moment and then, as he realized she was mocking his own question to her a few weeks back, he poked his head further out of the window and kissed her on the tip of her nose. "Spect so. If we go on like this we'll be able to afford to get wed soon.'

Kate threw back her head, her laughter bouncing on the breeze. 'I dun't reckon a bit of promotion and a few shillings a week more is going to mek us millionaires!'

'Dun't reckon I'd want to be. Mind you, I wouldn't mind a car like this of me own one day.' He ran his hands lovingly round the steering-wheel. 'Would ya like to come for a ride?'

'Did we ought to?' she asked doubtfully.

'Squire wouldn't mind.'

Moments later they were driving towards the town, but when they reached the first houses, Danny turned the motor round and headed back along the coast road. 'Best not be seen.'

'Oh, do let me have a go, Danny. Let me drive it.'

'Well, I aren't sure about that.' Now it was Danny's turn to be doubtful.

'Oh, go on,' she pleaded with her most winning smile. 'I'll be ever so careful and do just what you say. Squire wouldn't mind,' she added coyly echoing Danny's own words.

'Well . . .'

Minutes later she was sitting behind the wheel as Danny was telling her which foot to put on which pedal. 'Press on the clutch-pedal – the left one.' Danny put the gear lever into first gear. 'Now, let it off slowly and at the same time press on the accelerator.' The engine spluttered and the car hopped forward.

'Slowly, I said,' Danny bellowed in her ear.

Kate grinned at him. 'Sorry.'

'Try again . . .'

They moved forward along the lane in a series of jumps and engine stalls, with Kate laughing and Danny shouting at her. At last she seemed to get the hang of it and they were crawling along in first gear, but at least smoothly. 'Now try second gear – press the clutch . . . into neutral . . . rev the accelerator . . . press the clutch again . . .' and he pushed the gear lever into second gear.

The speed was increasing as they approached a gentle bend in the road, the sand-dunes on the left-hand side and on the right a grass verge and then a dyke.

Kate careered across the road towards the verge.

'Turn your wheel. Brake!' Danny shouted.

'Which is the brake?' Kate shouted back, unconsciously pressing down harder on the accelerator. The front wheels bounced on to the grass and the car headed towards the dyke. Danny grabbed the wheel and wrenched it round, but too late. The nearside wheels were on the slope of the dyke bank and the car slid, in slow motion, into the dyke, tipping over on to its side against the opposite bank.

As the car settled itself there was a ghastly silence until Danny, thrown against her and pinning her against the door of the car, said, 'Now look what you've done. I'll get the sack for this.'

Kate was shaking but not too shocked to reply with

asperity, 'Oh, wonderful! Not a word of "Are you all right, Kate?" or "Have you hurt yourself?" '

Danny levered himself off her and started to clamber up out of the car. He glanced back down at her. 'Well – have you?'

There was a slight pause before Kate answered morosely, 'No.'

Danny pushed at the door, now opening at a tilting angle, and heaved himself out. Then he thrust his head and shoulders back inside and held out his hand to her. 'Come on, I'll give you a pull.'

They stood side by side on the bank looking down disconsolately at the car nestling forlornly on its side in the dyke bottom.

'D'ya think our horses could pull it out?' Kate suggested.

'They might.' Danny didn't sound too hopeful.

'I'll bike home and get me dad to come back.'

'What am I going to tell Squire Marshall?'

'*I'll* go and see him,' Kate said airily. 'He likes me – he'll not shout at me.'

'Oh no you won't,' Danny said swiftly. 'I aren't hiding behind a woman's skirts – not even to save me job!'

It was two hours before the Squire's motor car was standing upright on the road once more. The two horses had pulled it from the dyke once Kate's stepfather had attached ropes to the front axle. Now they were all standing in the lane viewing the damage while the two horses champed lazily on the grass verge.

'Whatever were you doing, Danny?' Jonathan was asking.

Kate and Danny exchanged a glance and Kate opened her mouth to explain, but before she could speak Danny said, 'I wasn't concentrating – me nearside wheels hit the verge and

I couldn't seem to steer back on to the lane and afore I knew it – I was in the dyke.'

'Perhaps the steering's gone.' Jonathan was on his knees in front of the vehicle, bending down to look underneath, his head almost touching the ground as he peered between the front wheels. 'If that's the case, then it's not your fault.'

'No such luck,' Danny muttered, but only loud enough for Kate to hear and understand.

Jonathan was reaching underneath the car. 'Looks to me like the axle's bent, that's all.'

'That's all!' Danny echoed wryly. 'It's bad enough.'

Her stepfather was levering himself to his feet. 'See the Squire, Danny, and explain what happened. Tell him I can put it right if he likes.'

Kate saw the hope in Danny's eyes. 'Can you really, Mester?'

She watched the exchange between Danny and her stepfather. The latter was nodding. 'I should be able to – I may need to get some parts, but it shouldn't be too big a job. Come on now, Danny, you get in and steer, and we'll pull it back to Brumbys' Farm.'

As dusk crept over the flat fields, Kate was still waiting for Danny to come back from the Grange. Watching from a bedroom window which faced westwards, she could see the tall chimneys of the Squire's home surrounded by trees. At last she saw a figure walking along the road leading from the Grange back towards the coast road. Lightly she ran down stairs, through the living room and into the kitchen. She paused in the doorway and held her breath. Her mother was bending over the range. Quietly, Kate edged her way towards the door leading into the back scullery, but her mother glanced up and saw her.

'And where do you think you're off to at this time of night, Missy?'

'Danny's just coming back from the Grange. I want to know what the Squire said.' And without waiting for her mother's permission she ran out of the back door.

Really, she thought to herself, I'm almost eighteen and yet I still can't hardly move without her wanting to know what I'm doing.

She hung over the farmyard gate and Danny's shadowy shape loomed up in the dusk. "Ave ya still got ya job then?' she called merrily, confident that the worst Danny would receive from the kindly Squire was a telling off.

'It's all right for you to joke!' Danny muttered morosely. He was walking towards her, but his hands were thrust deep into the pockets of his trousers. Suddenly, he kicked viciously at some loose stones on the road side, sending them pattering on to the grass verge.

A sudden fear clutched at her. 'He didn't – oh, he wouldn't – sack you. Did he?'

'He did! The old bugger bloody well sacked me!'

Kate gasped. Danny rarely resorted to bad language; that he was doing so now, and being so disrespectful to the Squire, shocked her.

And what made it worse – it was all her fault.

Very early the following morning, before going to work, Kate cycled to the Grange. Standing in front of the Squire's huge polished desk, she felt the familiar fluttering just below her ribs that she got when she was nervous.

'What's so urgent, young lady, that I have to be dragged away from my breakfast?'

He was sitting on the opposite side of his desk now, glowering at her. When she had been shown into the book-lined study, he had been sitting in a wing-chair near the long window overlooking the smooth expanse of front lawn, his right foot propped up on a footstool, and a plate of bacon and eggs on a small table to one side. Leaving his meal, he had levered himself up from his chair and hobbled across the room, wincing with every step.

Kate had always liked the Squire, with his bristly white whiskers and red face. As a child, she had thought of him as a jolly Father Christmas and in her sudden concern for him, her nervousness was forgotten for a moment.

'Have you hurt your foot, Squire?'

'Gout,' he said testily. 'That's why I wanted a driver till that silly young fool put my new car in the ditch!'

Her stomach lurched afresh. 'That's what I've come to see you about – Danny Eland.'

The old man grunted and glared up at her. 'Well? What about him?'

Kate took a deep breath. She was taking a big gamble and she knew it. He couldn't hurt Danny any more – he'd already dismissed him. But the Squire was her mother's land-lord. He owned the home they all lived in. If she, Kate, angered him even more . . .

'Well, get on with it.'

'It was all my fault, Squire.' The words came tumbling out in a rush. 'About your motor car, I mean. I was driving it, not Danny. I begged him to let me have a go and – I know he shouldn't have. Oh, Squire – I'm so sorry. Please don't sack Danny. And me dad – he can make it good as new. He's ever so clever with motors and . . .' She was bab-bling now in her agitation.

'Well, I'll be damned!' The look on the Squire's face was so comical that Kate gave a nervous little laugh.

He was shaking his head and staring at her. 'You're so like your mother, Kate, do you know that?'

Now it was Kate's turn to blink in surprise.

'She was only about your age when old Sam Brumby died and she came to see me, standing exactly where you're standing now . . .' His eyes clouded over as if he was seeing not Kate, but her mother, Esther. 'No more than a slip of a girl, she was, but there she stood almost demanding that I grant her the tenancy of Brumbys' Farm. The Brumbys had the tenancy for generations, but there was no family to carry on after Sam.' There was a pause, then the Squire said quietly, 'I always admired your mother for her honesty and it seems you too have that same virtue.'

He smiled at her now, and it was once more the Squire she knew and liked. His eyes twinkled with mischief. 'All right, young lady, I'll see young Danny doesn't lose his job. Mind you, he shouldn't have let you drive it.'

'I know, but . . .'

He held up his hand, palm outwards. 'All right, all right. Just so long as you get your stepfather to fix it up, we'll say no more about it.'

'Oh, thank you, Squire, thank you. But, just one more thing . . .'

'What is it?' he asked resignedly, but his anger was gone now and his eyes were twinkling.

'You – you won't ever let Danny know I came to see you, will you? He'd be cross. He's got his pride, you see.'

The Squire's whiskers twitched. 'All right my dear. It'll be our little secret.'

And as the Squire was rewarded with one of Kate's beaming smiles, he in turn gave her a broad wink.

Fifteen

The following evening Danny was waiting for her in the lane outside Brumbys' Farm when she arrived home from work. It was almost dusk for Kate had been obliged to stay late to finish hemming some velvet curtains by hand with her tiny, neat stitching.

'Guess what?' He came and stood astride the front wheel of her cycle, resting his arms on the handle-bars. He leaned forward and planted a kiss on her mouth. Something had pleased him, Kate thought. He was grinning from ear to ear and forgetting to be cautious right outside the yard gate.

Carefully Kate said, 'You haven't found another job already?'

'Nope – but I've got me old one back.'

Kate gave an exaggerated squeal of delight and hoped it sounded convincing. She flung her arms around Danny's neck and hugged him. He grasped her arms and they were scuffling playfully when a sharp voice rang out in the still night air.

'Kate! Kate – I want you in. Now!'

Danny let go of her as if he had been burned, and sprang away, but Kate merely called back over her shoulder, 'I won't be a minute, Mam.' She leaned her cycle against the gate post and turned back to Danny. Lowering her voice, she said, 'Now, tell me quickly. What happened?'

'Squire sent a message I was to go up to the Grange. I

142

was quaking in me boots, I can tell you, when I went into his study,' Danny said.

So was I! thought Kate, but she said nothing, listening as Danny continued. ' "I was a bit hasty yesterday," ' he ses. "If you can get the motor put right, Eland, you can have your job back." So I told him that ya stepdad reckoned he could fix it, and Squire said, "Godfrey's word is good enough for me. He's a good mechanic." '

Kate's heart warmed to the Squire for his praise of her stepfather.

'Squire said,' Danny's even teeth shone white in the darkness as he grinned, 'ya dad's so clever with mechanical things he's wasted on a farm, even though he comes in handy when we get a problem with the machinery. He put his hand on me shoulder as I was coming out and said, "You could do a lot worse than learn from Jonathan Godfrey." Oh, Katie, I'm that glad to get me job back, I can tell you.'

Kate let out a long sigh too. 'Well, that's all right then.' She moved closer to him, her mouth curving into a smile. 'So when do I get another drive?'

'You don't!' he replied shortly and then, obviously hearing the mischief in her tone, he reached out to grab her arms. 'Oh, you tease, you . . .'

Kate dodged his grasp and squealing with glee, she began to run, across the lane and into the trees on the dunes, glancing back over her shoulder, inviting him to chase her.

Danny was not one to refuse such an invitation. Underfoot, twigs cracked whilst overhead, roosting birds fluttered from their resting place as the two youngsters, their laughter echoing in the stillness of the night, chased each other up and down the dunes like a couple of young puppies.

'Sssh,' Danny said, stopping suddenly. 'What was that?' They stood listening.

Distantly, they heard Esther's voice, 'Kate – Kate!'

Grabbing Danny's hand, Kate whispered, 'Come on, let's go to the beach.'

'You sure, Katie? You'll only mek ya mam madder than ever.'

But Kate was already dragging him up the slope and down on to the marsh. Then they were running towards the easterly dunes, splashing through the creeks in the darkness, skirting the deeper streams. They knew every inch of the marsh and could quite literally find their way in the dark.

Laughing, they flopped down at last in the sandy hollow in the dunes that was their special place. They lay on their backs, close together, just staring up at the vast expanse of darkening sky above them, listening to the musical lap-lap of the waves, somehow louder in the darkness.

Danny raised himself on one elbow and leaned over her. She could feel his breath, soft upon her face. 'When are we going to get married, Katie?'

She touched his face and, with gentle fingers, traced the outline of the features she knew – and loved – so well. She had always loved him. He had been part of her life always, and that was the way she wanted it. It was what they both wanted; to be part of each other's lives for ever.

'As soon as you like, Danny. But I'll have to leave me job. Mr Reynolds dun't – doesn't . . .' she corrected herself. Since her recent promotion she was more than ever conscious of the strong dialect in her speech and was making a determined effort to correct it. She had never felt her speech to be a defect until she had been ridiculed for it at the school in Lincoln. Sometimes, in the dead of night, she still shuddered at the memories of that time and her private humiliations were locked away in the depths of her soul.

'Mr Reynolds', she was saying now, 'doesn't employ married women. I'd have to leave if we got married.'

'Well, I'd want you to anyway.' His head came lower until his mouth brushed her lips. 'You'll have plenty to do looking after me – and the kids!'

Kate giggled and then was lost as his butterfly kiss became more demanding. His arms were around her and he was pressing his strong, muscular body against her. Now she felt his urgency; felt the heat and desire in his kiss.

'No, Danny, no. We mustn't.' Kate pulled away from him suddenly and sat up. She sat with her arms wrapped around her knees drawn up to her chest – a chest that was no longer childishly thin; now her breasts were firm and rounded – and desirable! And Danny wanted her, she knew.

Miserably she buried her face in her skirt. Now Danny would be angry with her, might even hate her, she was thinking. All young men got angry if you didn't let them – well, do things! At least that was what Sheila, one of the young girls in the workroom, said. Sheila was a pert, petite blonde, who wore make-up and high-heeled shoes and short skirts; she seemed to have a different boyfriend every week.

But Esther's warning sounded in Kate's ears so clearly, she might have been standing over them. 'Dun't let him touch you – promise me!'

'I'm sorry,' she muttered. 'But I dun't want to – to . . .'

She felt Danny's touch on her arm and he sat up at the side of her. ''Tis me who should be saying sorry. You're right. We mun't spoil it. We should wait till we're wed.'

She reached out to him in the darkness. 'Oh, Danny,' she breathed. 'I was afraid you'd be cross, that you wouldn't understand . . .'

'Kate – I love you, really love you. I wouldn't do anything to hurt you, or – or upset you.' The grin widened, cheekily, 'But I dun't reckon I can wait for ever.'

'Oh Danny, nor me. Nor me.'

145

She held his beloved face between her hands and gently kissed his lips.

'Just where do you think you've been, Miss? Do you know what time it is? It's half-past ten.' Her mother was waiting at the open back door as Kate came across the yard. Silhouetted against the light from within, Esther stood with her feet set apart and hands on hips. It was a stance that meant trouble.

'Hello, Mam,' Kate said happily. Not even Esther's anger was going to be allowed to spoil things. Danny loved her – and he had got his job back. The Squire had kept his promise. Danny didn't know she had a hand in it – but that was the way she wanted it. She loved him too much to belittle him. She would always let him think that he had regained his job because the Squire valued him and not because she had pleaded his cause.

In her joy, Kate grasped her mother round her slim waist and drew her outside. In the darkness she whirled her mother round the back yard in a merry jig.

'Stop it, Kate . . .' but Esther was laughing in spite of herself. 'Do stop – I'm getting a stitch in me side.' Kate stopped and let go of her. Esther leaned against the pump in the yard, holding her side. 'What's got into you, girl? You're as daft as a brush.'

Kate stretched her arms skywards and threw back her head. 'I'm happy, Mam, that's all. Danny's not going to get the sack and me dad's going to get the job of repairing the Squire's motor. So he'll be happy with his head stuck under a motor car.'

Esther snorted. 'Aye, I might have known – just when harvest is upon us.'

Kate smiled, ''Night, Mam.' And before Esther had a chance to berate her daughter further for her lateness, Kate gave her a peck on the cheek and ran indoors. She was up the stairs, through the nursery where Lilian now slept, and into her own small back room before her mother had got her breath back.

Harvest was upon them. Every evening and on her time off from work, Kate hurried into her outdoor work clothes and ran to the fields. Here, the old traditions survived. Neighbour helped neighbour at harvest and the horses from Brumbys' Farm were in demand.

'I'm not having them new-fangled tractor things in my fields.' Esther vowed, and Kate would see her stepfather smile fondly and hide his disappointment. 'It's bad enough at threshing with the steam engine . . .'

Kate listened to the conversations that were repeated every year and smiled, winking at her stepfather behind her mother's back, knowing he looked forward to the winter days when the huge machine would come into their yard to start the threshing.

'Why don't you persuade Mam to get a tractor?' Kate encouraged her stepfather as they walked out to the fields. 'She would if she knew it would make you happy.'

Jonathan smiled. 'Maybe I will when the horses get too old . . .'

'Oh, there's Danny,' Kate said suddenly, feeling the familiar ripple of pleasure as she saw him standing high on top of the wagon, spreading the sheaves as they were passed up to him by the men below. In the early evening sun, his muscular body, stripped to the waist, glistened with sweat. She began to run, and then, remembering suddenly, glanced back over her shoulder. 'Don't you forget, Dad, when the horses go – it's a tractor we want.' She wagged her finger at him and grinned.

Jonathan smiled too, but then he glanced at Danny and back at her, and she saw the smile fade from his face. 'Kate...' he began, but, filled with the desire to be with Danny, she waved and said, 'See you later, Dad,' and was gone.

Through the bright days of late summer, the two young people were filled with happiness, revelling in the secret they shared, planning their future.

'Mebbe Squire would let us rent a farm of our own one day.'

The look in her eyes softened lovingly. 'Is that what you really want, Danny?'

He wrinkled his forehead. 'I reckon. Would that suit the new Mrs Eland?'

He was teasing yet there was an underlying seriousness. They were deciding their future and he cared about her happiness.

She nodded. 'Oh yes, it'd suit me. I could still do dress-making at home if I wanted.'

'We'd only be tenants, mind. Mebbe he'd let us have Rookery Farm. Tom Willoughby's getting on a bit now and he's no family to carry on after him.'

Kate was doubtful. 'It's more acreage than our farm. Wouldn't you be better staying on the Squire's estate? Maybe one day you could be bailiff.'

She leaned her head against his shoulder as they sat beside a stook, nestling against the sweet-smelling corn and hidden from the inquisitive eyes of the other workers. Danny slipped his arm around her.

'I suppose it wouldn't be a bad job, though I'd sooner have a place of me own. It's not easy to be put in charge of other folk, specially people ya've known all ya life. Ya can soon lose friends.'

She twisted her head to look up at him. 'No ambition,

148

that's your trouble,' but she took any criticism out of her words by planting a kiss on his cheek.

He rested his cheek against her hair. 'I've only one ambition,' he said softly. 'To marry you and live happily ever after . . .'

They sat quietly, watching the sun sink slowly behind the horizon, streaking the sky golden-red.

'It's ya birthday in a couple of days, in't it? Ya eighteenth.'

'Yes. Why?'

'Shall we get engaged on ya birthday?'

Kate sat up and looked at him, her eyes shining. 'Yes, oh yes!'

'Then,' Danny said slowly, 'we'll have to tell them.'

Some of the joy left Kate's face as they regarded each other solemnly. 'Right,' she said firmly, for it was she who had the most difficult task and they both knew it. 'I'll do it tomorrow night when I get home from work.'

'I'll tell my folks, too, then they'll all know at the same time. Okay?'

Kate nodded, feeling the churning of apprehension in her stomach.

'No. No! *No!*' Esther Godfrey's voice rose to an hysterical scream. Kate gaped at her mother, while four-year-old Lilian ran to her father and climbed on to his knee as he sat in the wooden Windsor chair at the side of the range in the kitchen. She flung her arms around his neck and buried her face against his shoulder. Automatically, Jonathan patted the child's back comfortingly, but his attention was not on his young daughter.

'Esther, love, steady on.' To Kate's ears his concerned tone also held a kind of warning. But her mother was in no mood to listen to the voice of reason.

149

'Steady on? Steady on, you say?' Esther leaned on the kitchen table, her palms flat down on the scrubbed surface, her green eyes flashing fire, but there was a stillness about her body that was ominous. 'You will never, never marry Danny Eland.'

'I will. You can't stop me.'

'Oh yes I can, my girl.' Her mother's voice was quiet now, but that very quietness was more menacing than the screaming.

'Esther . . .' came Jonathan's deep voice, but now the two women – mother and daughter – were locked in their private battle of wills and scarcely heard him.

Esther moved suddenly and swiftly towards the door. 'I'll put a stop to this once and for all.'

'Esther – no! You can't. You mustn't!'

She whirled to face her husband. 'Keep out of this, Jonathan. It's nowt to do wi' you.'

She could not have hurt him more if she had slapped him physically. Kate saw her stepfather wince, but his voice was calm as he rose from his chair, still cradling Lilian in his arms. 'Esther – I'm warning you. You'll hurt too many people and do something that can never – ever – be undone.'

Esther flung out her arm, gesturing towards Kate. 'And what do you suggest I do? Let her get on with it, eh?'

'No, but . . .'

'It's got to be stopped, Jonathan. You know it has.' And with that she almost ran from the house.

Kate stared at her stepfather in anguish. 'Dad – what's going on? What *is* it?'

Jonathan sighed and sat down heavily in his chair, shaking his head. 'It looks as if you'll find out very soon now, love.'

'You tell me, Dad.'

'No. It's not my place to do so.'

Kate left the house and ran towards the Point. She crested

the Hump and stood staring at the scene below her. In the distance she could see Danny and his father, Robert Eland, walking away from the cottages up towards the headland where the river joined the sea. The older man had his arm across Danny's shoulders and their heads were slightly inclined towards each other as if they were talking earnestly. At least, as if one were talking and the other listening.

Kate's gaze swivelled and came back to the cottages. She drew in a breath of surprise. Her mother stood outside the Elands' cottage and Beth Eland was in the open doorway, standing quietly while Esther Godfrey flung her arm out in the direction of Danny's departing figure, and then pointed at Beth, stabbing her finger towards the woman's breast to emphasize whatever it was she was saying.

Then Kate felt her heart go out to Danny's mother for suddenly Beth Eland covered her face with her hands and sagged against the door-frame for support. With a shock, Kate noticed that her mother made no move to help Beth, did not even put out her hand to steady her, but appeared only to bend towards her to press home her point even more forcefully.

Kate wanted to run forward, wanted to shout to Danny, wanted to stop whatever it was that was happening.

For all of a sudden, the most dreadful feeling of foreboding flooded through her.

She waited for what seemed an age and yet it could only have been minutes in reality until her mother turned away abruptly, leaving Beth still standing in the doorway, clutching at the door-jamb for support. And although she could not see the woman's face clearly from this distance, Kate knew instinctively that Beth Eland was weeping.

Danny and his father were at the headland, standing side by side, close, yet not touching now. They stood outlined against the sky, just staring out to sea. They did not seem to be speaking now.

Esther was coming towards Kate, her stride swift and purposeful, anger in every movement. Her head was bent and it was not until she began to climb the Hump that Kate saw her glance up and notice her daughter.

They stared at each other for a long moment until Kate burst out, 'You won't stop us, Mam. We love each other, and . . .'

'I warned you, Kate. For years I've been trying to keep you apart. I even tried to get you away from here.'

Kate gasped. 'You mean – you mean – that was why you sent me away to that school? Because of *Danny*?'

Esther nodded. She was quieter now, and strangely there was sadness in her tone as she said, 'I'm sorry, Kate, but you can never marry Danny Eland.'

Tears sprang to Kate's eyes. 'Why, Mam? Please tell me why.'

Kate saw her mother take a deep, unsteady breath. 'Because – he's your half-brother!'

Sixteen

The world revolved. The scene before her danced and blurred. It was like a knife being thrust in just below her ribs. Her heart seemed to stop and then begin to thud painfully. Fear prickled her scalp. She gasped for breath, clutching a hand to her chest, while with trembling fingers she reached out. 'Mam . . .?'

But her mother was walking away, striding down the Hump back towards Brumbys' Farm.

Kate cast a despairing glance towards Danny, still standing on the very point of the land, motionless, just staring out to sea. Matching his stillness, Robert Eland stood silently by his side.

Kate gave a sob, drew in a shuddering breath and ran down the Hump. 'Mam – Mam . . .' She caught up with Esther and grasped her arm roughly, pulling her mother round to face her. 'What do you mean – he's my half-brother? I don't understand.'

Esther's jaw was clenched, her eyes angry, defiant.

'Ya father – Matthew Hilton – got Beth pregnant before he married me.'

Kate gasped and stared at her, eyes wide. 'Didn't – didn't he *know*?'

Esther twisted her arm from Kate's grasp, turned and began to walk swiftly away again. 'No,' she said shortly.

Kate took little running steps to keep up with her. 'But Mam . . .'

Esther put up her hand as if to fend Kate off physically. 'I dun't want to talk of it. You can't marry Danny. Not ever. I've tried to warn you, all these years. But you wouldn't listen. Now you know and there's an end to it.'

Kate stopped and stood watching the slim figure of her mother walking towards the farm, her back rigid, her face turned away from her daughter.

Kate bit down hard upon her lower lip, drawing blood. The pain she caused herself was almost a relief. Then, tears blinding her, she turned towards the dunes and began to run.

'I want to die. I don't want to live any more. Just let me die!'

She was standing at the end of the Spit, at the very tip of the promontory of land that jutted out into the Wash. It was the place where the land, the sea and the sky all seemed to meet. Like the end of the world . . .

The water of a high tide was swirling around her. Dropping to her knees on the shingle, she wrapped her arms around herself. She closed her eyes, screwing up her face in an agony that was a real pain in the pit of her stomach.

'Kate – Kate, don't.'

He was there, picking her up, turning her unresisting body towards him and enveloping her in a fierce embrace. Danny was stroking her hair and murmuring words which made no sense to her, for she was crying hysterically, sobs shaking her body.

'I – don't want – to live – any more.'

'Shush, shush. You must live – for me. What would I do if you were no longer in the same world as me?'

Her arms slipped around his waist and she buried her face against his chest. Beneath his shirt she could feel the rapid beating of his heart. It matched her own.

Her sobs lessened and, muffled against him, she said, 'It isn't true, is it? Tell me it isn't true.'

His hand stroked her hair gently. 'I – can't, Katie. But – oh, how I wish I could!'

She raised her head then and looked up into his troubled face. Tears glistened in his eyes too and he pressed his lips together as if to prevent their trembling. For a long moment they gazed at each other whilst the water lapped at their feet and seagulls screeched mournfully overhead.

Haltingly, she began, 'Me mam won't tell me much, but she said my dad – me real dad – and your mam . . .'

Danny nodded. 'This is going to kill her!' he murmured and then added bitterly, 'Your mam has got a lot to answer for.'

Kate pulled back a little. 'My mam? Why, what has my mam got to do with it?' Her voice became harsher in her frustration at still not being able to understand fully. 'Danny, what do you mean?'

'Me dad ses . . . ' he began and then hesitated, as if suddenly realizing the enormity of the revelation. Robert Eland, the man who had loved him, reared him, been everything to him that anyone could wish for in a father, was not his natural father; was not, in fact, even a blood relative.

In his agitation, Danny ran his strong fingers into his hair and grasped a handful, as if he would pull it out by the roots. He took a deep breath to steady himself and yet, when he spoke, his voice still shook. 'It seems,' he said slowly, as if he still couldn't – or wouldn't – believe what he was telling Kate, 'Your dad – Matthew – and my mam were walking out together when your mother arrived here to work for old Sam Brumby on the farm. Matthew was after anything in skirts, me dad ses.' Still Danny could not break the habit of a lifetime. Robert Eland was, to him, his father. He cleared his throat and went on. 'Matthew chased after Esther and when Sam Brumby died, they got married and he moved into the farm with her – and left me mam pregnant with me.'

Kate gasped. 'Oh, how could he?'

'Evidently – very easily,' Danny said bitterly.

'But yar mam wouldn't . . . I mean . . .' Kate began, then stopped.

They stared at each other. 'I suppose,' he said slowly, 'she was young and – and in love.' His voice dropped to a hoarse whisper. 'Just like us, Katie.'

Kate's eyes widened and she gasped. 'We almost did, didn't we?'

He nodded. 'Thank goodness we stopped in time.'

Kate shivered suddenly as a chill wind blew in from the sea. Her voice broke on a sob. 'I – wish we *had* done it!'

He held her close again, resting his cheek against her ruffled hair. 'Now – we can't – ever.' His arms tightened around her as if he would never let her go.

'I still don't understand it all,' she murmured.

'Nor me. All I know is,' he added grimly, 'what they did has wrecked *our* lives even all this time after.'

'You're only a few months older than me. It can't be true. I won't let it be!'

His tone was flat with misery. 'I – think it is, Katie. If you think about it – looking back – it explains a lot of things.'

'What?'

'Why your mam and mine never speak to each other; why she sent you away to school and why, when that went wrong and you came home, she still tried to keep us apart.'

Kate was silent now. He was right. About everything. And there was something else that even Danny didn't know. The solemn promise which her mother had extracted from her that she would never – ever – let Danny touch her. Behind that promise had been the awful truth her mother had known.

'God, how I hate her!' she muttered through her teeth. 'It's all my mother's fault. If she hadn't come here – if she hadn't married Matthew, then – then . . .'

'Then,' Danny said softly, 'you wouldn't have been born.'

Gently, he cupped her face in his hands. 'Oh, Kate,' he said, his voice deep with emotion, 'we can't ever marry, or be lovers . . .'

'Why? Why not? We could go away where no one knows us. We have different names. We're not related in the eyes of the law.' She was clutching at straws.

'You know we can't!'

She drew back from him suddenly, pushing him away. 'You don't care. You don't love me. Not as I love you. You can't, or you wouldn't be giving in so – so easily.'

He flinched as if her words were physical blows. He caught her by the arms and held her fast so that she could not turn away from him, held her so tightly that she was forced to listen to him. 'Katie, don't say that to me. Not to me. Me dad wouldn't lie to me. He must know . . .'

'Mr Eland, ya mean,' she said cuttingly. 'He's not ya dad, is he? Any more than Mester Godfrey's mine. We've both got *step*dads – now.'

Danny winced and Kate was immediately contrite. She was lashing out blindly in her pain, and hurting the one who was already suffering along with her.

She closed her eyes but fresh tears forced themselves from under her eyelids and coursed down her cheeks. 'Oh, Danny, Danny. I can't bear it. It – hurts so much.' She flung herself against him, wrapping her arms around his waist, burying her head against him again.

'I've always loved you, Katie, and I always will,' he said gently.

'But – but can't we be together? Somehow?' She raised her head to look into his face, her mouth slightly open, hanging on to his words like a drowning woman reaching for the hand of her rescuer, willing him to make it come right.

But Danny could not make it come right; there was only one thing he could promise her and it was all they had left to cling to. With dreadful finality, he said again, 'We can't marry, but they can't stop us loving each other. Not ever, Katie, not *ever*!'

'Oh, lovey, do you hate me?'

The back door of the Elands' cottage had opened to Kate's knock. Beth stood there, her eyes red and swollen. Kate threw herself against the older woman, her arms clasped around Beth's thickening waist, and buried her head against the comforting bosom. She could feel Beth trembling.

'Oh Katie, Katie, can you ever forgive me?'

Kate lifted her head and looked into the older woman's face. She didn't know what to say.

Gently, Beth steered Kate towards the range. She sat down in the chair while Kate sank down on to the rug, her head resting against the older woman's knees. For a long moment Beth stared into the flames and then, in her soft voice, she began, haltingly, to explain. As the memories, both happy and sad, came flooding back, her voice became stronger.

'I loved Matthew,' Beth began simply, 'I think I always had – right from a child . . .'

Like me and Danny, Kate thought bitterly, but she remained silent.

' . . . Even though he was a bit of a flirt . . .' A fond smile curved Beth's mouth. It was a kinder judgment than Robert Eland had given to Danny, and despite all the unhappiness that flirting had caused, Beth still loved Matthew enough to forgive him.

'When Esther arrived at Sam Brumby's farm – well – it was in his nature to try his luck with her. She was a very pretty girl and so fiery, she was a challenge to him. He could never resist a challenge.'

Kate looked up. 'How d'you mean?'

'For a time, Esther would have none of him, but the more she held him off, the more he wanted her.' Beth's voice dropped to a whisper as she admitted, 'That's where I made my mistake . . .'

Kate pressed her cheek closer to Beth's knee but could think of nothing to say.

'She wouldn't give in to him, told him she wouldn't give in to him – nor to any man – till she was wed.'

Kate was silent, knowing all this must have been true. It was her mother's strict code of life – it still was! 'Ya don't give ya'sen to a man till you've a wedding ring on ya finger, girl,' she'd told Kate repeatedly. 'Dun't ever bring a bastard into the world!'

Beth was sighing softly, but continuing. 'Then Sam Brumby died and – to be fair – I don't think ya mam had anywhere else to go.'

'What about me grandad? Why couldn't she go to him?'

Beth looked down at Kate's upturned face. 'Ya'll have to ask ya mam about that, lovey . . .'

'She won't tell me anything.'

'Well, perhaps ya grandad, then. Maybe – maybe he's the one to ask.'

Yes, Kate thought grimly, she would certainly have some questions to ask her grandfather. Intuitively she knew that there was more to all this than even Beth Eland was telling her.

'The Squire would only let her stay on the farm if she

159

were married – so that the tenancy agreement could be in a man's name. So – she and Matthew were married all quick-like. I dun't know to this day how they managed it without any of us knowing.'

'You – you didn't *know*!' Kate was appalled.

'No. I didn't know till Matthew moved his things from – from this very house.'

'He lived here? In this cottage?'

Beth smiled sadly. 'Yes,' she said softly. 'He was born here and lived here with his parents till they both died. Then, for a while, he lived on his own. Of course, Grannie Harris next door and me saw he was all right for food and his washing . . .'

'Where did you live?'

'Next door.' Beth indicated the adjacent cottage on the other side, where her father, Dan Hanley, the coastguard, still lived.

'And Mester Eland?'

Beth's eyes filled with sudden tears. 'On – on a boat on the river bank.' She glanced out of the cottage window to the place on the river bank where the huge hulk of a boat had once rested, shored up on poles and sleepers, half-in, half-out of the water.

Vague pictures, fleeting and disjointed, were flitting through Kate's mind. Memories from childhood that she could glimpse in her mind but not quite hold on to and understand.

'Did Matthew marry her to get the farm, then?'

Beth shook her head. 'No – no, I don't believe he understood what – what ya mam was up to.'

Kate's head jerked up. She felt the coolness of Beth's deep sigh brush her cheek. 'He wanted her – lusted after her and she – she took advantage of that to get him to marry her so she could get the farm.'

'You – you mean it was her fault?'

'In a way but – but try not to be too hard on her, Katie. It's very difficult for us to understand how someone – a young girl of eighteen or so – must have felt with no family, no home. Ask yourself what you would have done in the same circumstances.'

Kate stared up at Beth in surprise. 'You're – you're taking her side.'

'I'm – trying to tell you it fairly. But it's not easy for me.'

'So – all this – all that happened – that's why you never speak to each other. You – you must be very bitter?'

'Oh yes, I'm bitter all right.' Beth's mouth tightened and for a moment there was a flash of fire in her dark brown eyes, but it was gone in a moment as she sighed and added, 'It's funny though, if things had been different – we might have been friends, yar mam and me.' A wry smile twisted the corner of her mouth. 'And despite everything, we always seem to come together if one of us has trouble.'

'How – how d'ya mean?'

'Matthew went off to the war and was reported killed. Ya mam brought me a photograph of him. I – I still have it. It was a kind gesture. I've never forgotten that.'

Kate frowned. 'But I – I thought me dad drowned. Here – at the Point?'

'Matthew came back from the war a broken wreck of a man. Pitiful to see him, it was. Ya mam was wonderful then. She devoted herself to caring for him and he improved beyond what any of us ever thought possible. And that was down to Esther; with her strength and determination, she pulled him through. But she – she sacrificed her own chance of happiness to look after Matthew. I thought then, that somehow, in her own way, she must have loved him to do that.'

'What do you mean, "her own chance of happiness"?'

161

Beth avoided Kate's direct gaze, reluctant to answer. 'She – she'd met Jonathan in the war – when ya dad was away.'

'Oh – I see.' Kate said flatly. She didn't see it all, at least not clearly, but she could sense that Beth would not be drawn on that part any further. 'And me dad – me real dad? *Did* he drown?'

Beth's voice was a hoarse whisper. 'There was a dreadful storm in the winter of nineteen-twenty. Matthew knew the boat we lived on wouldn't stand up to the gales and the surging tide. He – drowned trying to rescue us – his son and – and me.' Beth bowed her head and covered her face with her hands.

Kate gasped. This woman's love for Matthew Hilton was still, even now, as strong as ever. Tentatively Kate put out her hand and touched Beth's arm.

'What about Mester Eland? Where – how does he fit into all this?'

Now there was a tender, loving smile on Beth's mouth, a smile tinged with gratitude. 'He loved me, he'd always loved me. As great a love as any man could have for a woman, Kate. When he knew I was expecting Matthew's child, he married me to give Danny a name.'

Kate's own voice broke. 'He must have loved you very much to do that.'

Beth nodded. 'Oh, he did. He still does. And I have loved him, truly I have, but in – in a very different way to the way I loved Matthew.'

She sighed deeply. 'Robert's been a good husband and a wonderful father to Danny, but he's always been very resentful towards Matthew – and towards your mam. That's why I'm glad to have been able to tell you about it mesen.'

Kate nodded. She was glad too, for the version Danny had heard from Robert Eland treated her mother and father far more harshly than did Beth – the woman who had been hurt most of all. Yet, it was understandable, Robert Eland, too, had suffered.

So it was told – the whole sorry tale. And now Kate understood, if not every little detail, then enough to know that what they said was true.

She and Danny were indeed half-brother and sister.

'Has *she* told you it all, then? What's she said about me, eh? 'Spect I'm the bad woman in it all ...'

'Why ...?' Kate's voice was a whisper, but her eyes held her mother's gaze relentlessly. 'Why didn't you all just tell us the truth? If we'd grown up with it – knowing – we'd have accepted it. Been just friends, been,' the bitterness crept into her tone, 'been brother and sister!'

She was standing facing her mother across the kitchen table.

Esther, hands on hips, her mouth a grim line, said, 'There'd have been no need for you to know, if you'd done as I'd told you ...'

'You didn't want us to know 'cos it was your fault ...'

'Oh aye, I thought as much! Trying to set you against ya own mother ...'

'Who? Danny's mam? Oh no, dun't blame her. She even told me not to think badly of you; said I should understand how it must have been for you with no family and nowhere to go ...'

'She had no right to tell you anything about me ...'

'She stuck up for you, Mother! Her, of all people!'

Esther blinked.

'Yes, that's shocked you, ain't it? And she wouldn't tell me much about you, either. Said I'd to ask you or me grandad.'

'Ya'll do no such thing. Ya'll not say anything to ya grandad. It'll upset him.'

'Then you tell me. Go on, *you* tell me.'

'No,' Esther said through gritted teeth. 'It dun't concern you. You know now all ya need to know, an' that's too much! Ya'll learn no more from me.'

'Well, I'll find out. One day I'll find out everything. As for now – I'm going away. You wanted me gone four years ago, so now you'll get your wish. I'm going!'

Suddenly the fight seemed to drain out of her mother and she sat down heavily on a chair, leaned her elbows on the kitchen table and dropped her head into her hands. 'You don't have to go, Katie. Not now.'

'Oh yes, I do,' Kate leaned towards her mother as if to drive the hurtful shaft in harder. 'I can't stay here – seeing him every day. Not the way we feel about each other. Mother – we're in love. We want – wanted . . .' her voice broke a little as deliberately she changed the tense, 'to get married.'

Esther gave a soft groan. 'I wouldn't have had this happen to you – or Danny – for the world. I tried, really I did, in the only way I could think of to keep you apart. But the harder I tried, the more you seemed drawn to each other . . .' She broke off, raised her head and looked straight at Kate, a sudden urgency in her tone. 'He – he hasn't – touched you, has he?'

There was silence in the kitchen except for the ticking clock and the hissing of the red-hot wood in the grate as Esther waited for the answer that was so important to her, meant everything to her.

Kate stared back at her mother, holding her breath. She had it in her power at this moment to wound her mother deeply; to plunge a knife into her heart in retaliation for the hurt she and Danny were feeling; to punish Esther for the actions of her youth which had brought about this tragedy.

She opened her mouth to speak, to say, 'Yes, yes, yes, he's touched me! We've lain together. We're man and wife in all but name . . .' But she couldn't do it. All the years of love that lay between Kate and her mother, all the values that Esther had instilled into her daughter and Kate's own natural, inborn honesty, would not allow her to tell such a dreadful lie. Slowly, Kate let out the breath she was holding and, with it, some of the resentment against her mother. After all, she had not been solely responsible either for what had happened years ago or for keeping it secret. Danny had been kept in ignorance too. Yet Kate could not blame Beth Eland so much; she had more to risk by telling her son the true circumstances of his birth. She must have feared losing his respect, perhaps even his love.

So, although shreds of resentment against her mother still remained for she believed Esther could, and should, have told her the truth years ago, now Kate said heavily, 'No, Mam. We haven't – done anything.'

'Thank the Lord!' Esther murmured.

Then, as Kate added, 'But I have to go away, Mam. At least, for a while,' all Esther could reply sadly, was, 'Kate, oh, Katie.'

That night as Kate lay in bed, her knees pulled up to her chin, she cradled the whelk shell in her hand.

It was all she had left of Danny; and all she would ever have.

She gave a sob into the darkness as she remembered suddenly, and tears trickled down her cheeks.

Tomorrow was her birthday.

Part Two

Seventeen

'War! Oh no! Not again. Not another one.'
Kate watched in amazement as her mother stood in the middle of the yard, staring at her husband and wringing her hands in agitation. She could not remember having ever seen her so distressed. Angry, yes, many times, but the sight of tears in her mother's green eyes shocked Kate.

Then, at Esther's next words, Kate understood. Her mother had rushed towards Jonathan and was grasping his shoulders, looking up into his face, her eyes wide and afraid. 'You won't go this time, will you?'

Of course! That was it. Kate felt a moment's pity for her mother, usually so strong and sure. For her to be so obviously frightened spoke volumes about the seriousness of the situation.

Jonathan put his arms about his wife and held her close. 'I shouldn't think so, my dear. I'll probably be too old now.'

Esther was clinging to him. 'You can't go – not again. I couldn't bear it. It'll be bad enough all the young fellers having to go . . .'

Now fear clutched at Kate. Feeling sick, she turned away and walked out of the yard and across the lane to the dunes. Under the elder trees it was shady, the breeze rustling the leaves above her. She slipped off her shoes; the sand was cool beneath her feet. The prickly buckthorn bushes were laden with orange berries, bright splashes of colour against the silvery green leaves.

169

Kate climbed the dune and came out on the top above the trees. She stood and looked about her, her glance sweeping the land all around. It was so peaceful; the whispering of the leaves, the trilling song of a soaring skylark, the sudden cry of a gull and the soft splash of the sea were the only sounds to break an absolute quiet.

It seemed strange to be home again. She had been away for almost nine years; nine long years in which so much had happened and yet, perversely, nothing had changed. She had come home frequently; not so much at first when she had been trying to put time and distance between herself and Danny. But recently she had come back to Fleethaven Point more and more until, with war seeming inevitable, she had made the decision to come home.

When she and Danny had learnt why they could never marry, Kate had gone to Lincoln. It seemed ironic, and yet somehow fitting, that she should go back to the place where her mother had tried to send her once before, and where she had been so miserable. She was wretchedly unhappy again, though it was not, she acknowledged, the fault of the beautiful city where she tried to make her home and build a new life. She found comfort in the vast interior of the cathedral and a melancholy catharsis in wandering the streets throbbing with people; yet she felt she was entirely alone. Nor was it the fault of the kindly people who gave her a home; the Godfreys.

At first, Kate had intended to stay only briefly in the small room that had once been her stepfather's in their terraced family home. But an affinity and a friendship sprang up between Peggy Godfrey and the young, unhappy Kate, despite the sixteen years or so between them. Whether her stepfather had told them the circumstances, Kate never knew, but the Godfreys never pried into what had caused Kate's sadness and were gently considerate and made her welcome;

indeed they treated her as another daughter. The weeks grew into months and although at first she made tentative efforts to find herself other lodgings, she could see that the Godfreys' desire for her to stay with them was genuine. She found work in the sewing room of the store where Peggy worked and during the first two years, she returned to Fleethaven Point only twice. She did not see Danny then, but on her third visit, they met accidentally in the lane.

In two years they had changed little in outward appearance, but in their eyes was the sadness they shared.

'You're thinner, Katie,' he had said softly, his brown eyes searching her face.

'You're – not laughing so much,' she'd said.

There had been silence between them as they had stared at one another, each reliving the last time they had been together; that dreadful day.

Then Danny had taken a deep breath. 'We've got to come to terms with it, Katie. Learn to live with it. I dun't want you staying away from here just to avoid seeing me.'

'I don't know which is worse, Danny,' she murmured, 'seeing you – or *not* seeing you.'

'I know. I've done a lot of thinking while you've been away. We can't ever marry . . .' Although there was a wealth of sadness in his tone, there was also a new strength as if the cruel blow had toughened him into manhood. 'But, you know, maybe we have a love far greater even than that. The ties of brother and sister, blood ties, can be even stronger and deeper.'

She listened in silence to his reasoned words, knowing instinctively what torment, what heart-searching, had gone into reaching this sensible acceptance. The hurt was still as deep, but the pain was not so intense. In the two years, Danny had not stopped loving her, but had wrestled with how they might salvage a different kind of love from the wreckage.

So Kate had taken her lead from him, and although she had stayed in Lincoln, she had come home to Fleethaven more often. Little by little the agony eased as they drew strength from each other.

And down the years, Danny's words to her on that fateful day at the end of the Spit were locked within her heart: 'They can't stop us loving each other. Not ever, Katie, not *ever*!'

Now, nine years on, standing on top of the sand-dune, drinking in the sight of the marsh spread before her, Kate was a very different young woman from the distraught girl of eighteen. She had held a responsible position in her work and from that had gained self-confidence. In the Godfreys' home, she had been as happy as it was possible for her to be and she had grown to love their city. But always her heart lay at Fleethaven Point.

How could she ever have thought she could leave this place for good, she thought now. She took a deep, satisfying breath of the fresh, clean air, closed her eyes for a moment and held her face up to the breeze as it ruffled her carefully styled, city hairstyle. Opening her eyes again, she gave a little laugh of exultation and ran down the grassy slope and across the marsh to the beach. She walked at the water's edge, scuffing her toes through the shingle, paddling in the frothy edges of the encroaching waves and gazing across the wide expanse of grey water half expecting to see enemy ships already lying off shore.

This place was in her blood. Its tranquillity enveloped her and welcomed her home. How can we possibly be at war, she thought.

Then, distantly, she heard the rising wail of a siren.

*

'Danny, you won't have to go, will you?'

She had been waiting for him that evening at the junction where the lane leading westwards to the Grange joined the coast road. He came pedalling towards her on his bicycle, the sound of his whistling reaching her long before he did. When he saw her, he took his feet off the pedals and scuffed his boots along the road to slow down.

'Haven't you got those brakes mended yet?' she scolded as he wobbled to a halt, speaking to him as easily and as naturally as if they had seen each other earlier that day and not several weeks ago.

He grinned sheepishly at her. 'Nope – it dun't matter round here. No hills, a' there?' He paused and then added, 'You home for the weekend?'

She shook her head. 'No – I'm back for good.'

'Not afore time neither. You're not a city lass. You dress nice, I'll grant you that . . .'

'Oh thank you, kind sir.' She bobbed a mocking curtsy.

'But you're too pale – and too thin.'

Now she laughed. 'Well, if I can't get my old job back in town, I'll be working on the land, so I'll soon end up as leathery-looking as you.'

Then the teasing stopped; the look that passed between them saying that they both knew what the other was thinking. Without the need for explanation, it was then she asked, 'Danny, you won't have to go, will you?'

His face sobered, the grin fading. 'Farming's what they call a reserved occupation . . .' He hesitated. She held her breath, knowing very well what was coming. 'But I – I might *want* to go, Katie.'

She let out her breath slowly in a deep sigh. She might have known. Someone like Danny wouldn't want to be thought a coward. Not Danny.

She was watching him, seeing, suddenly, the changes the

last nine years had wrought in him. He, too, was thinner in the face, yet his shoulders and chest were if anything even broader and more muscular than ever. Men of his age, she thought, were usually married with two or three little ones. But then, she thought wryly, so were young women of her age!

Neither of them had found a partner. There had been one or two young men in Lincoln who had asked Kate out and sometimes she had gone. But there had never been a second meeting. Either she had politely refused, or a further invitation had not been forthcoming. Perhaps the young men were vaguely aware that they were being compared with the ghost of a love from the past.

As for Danny, he didn't seem interested in any of the young women in the district. He was now Squire Marshall's farm bailiff, well liked and well respected by all those under him, and he still acted as the ailing Squire's personal chauffeur when the old man needed to go anywhere, though gout and increasing infirmity confined the Squire more and more to his home. Mrs Marshall had died in the winter of 1932 and the Squire lived alone with only a few servants to care for him. His son, Arthur, lived in London, taking no interest in the affairs of the small estate and visiting only rarely.

'He's doing very well,' the Squire would tell anyone who would listen. 'Something in the City, you know. A wonderful career . . .' Then the old man's eyes would cloud over and he would sigh, 'I don't know what's to become of the estate, though, when I'm gone.'

'It'll be sold or broken up, you'll see,' Kate's mother would say resentfully to her family in the privacy of their home. 'Young Arthur's for the high life and no mistake! He doesn't want to know what hard work is!'

Jonathan and Kate would exchange a fond smile. Esther could not understand anyone who did not share her love of

174

the land. Her prediction was right, although not quite in the way she would have expected.

The thirties brought their own particular problems for the nation. The Depression hit hard but for Esther Godfrey it brought good fortune. The Squire, rather than see his land go to strangers, decided to offer the three farms which made up the bulk of his estate – Brumbys' Farm, Rookery Farm and Souters' Farm – to the sitting tenants.

'I'd rather see you have the land, Esther, my dear,' he had told Kate's mother, blowing his nose vigorously on a huge handkerchief. 'I know you love Brumbys' Farm.'

Esther's eyes had glowed and the wooden box that held all her savings had been pulled from under her bed and the coins and notes carefully counted. With land at the lowest price anyone could remember, there was just enough for Brumbys' Farm to become Esther's.

Kate still smiled every time she thought of that Sunday morning on one of her visits. Her mother had been as excited as a young girl.

'It'll be mine – really mine – I mean,' she had added swiftly, glancing at Jonathan, 'ours!'

Kate had watched as Jonathan had put his arms around his wife. 'No, my love,' he had said quietly but firmly. 'The papers will be in your name and your name alone.'

'But—'

'But nothing. I won't hear of it being otherwise. You *are* Brumbys' Farm.' He had smoothed back the tendrils of hair from her forehead. 'Your name shall be the first one on the deeds after the Marshalls. There now, won't that be something?'

Esther had nodded, her eyes brimming with tears. 'Yes,' she had whispered. 'Yes, it will.'

Esther had been the only one to take up the Squire's offer. Tom Willoughby, with no family to carry on after him, decided to remain as a tenant for the last few years of his working life.

'I can't see the point of me buying, Esther lass, though I'm glad for you,' the big man had boomed, his red cheeks wobbling with laughter. 'No one deserves it more 'n you. But I only want to work a few more years and what bit o' savings we've got, I want to enjoy. See a bit o' how the other half lives afore I die.' His laughter had boomed out and he had winked saucily at Esther. She had smiled indulgently, trying to understand how anyone could even think of leaving Fleethaven Point. Less than six months after their conversation, Tom's wife, Martha, had died. So now only Tom and his sister-in-law lived at Rookery Farm.

The Souters, whom Kate didn't know very well, for their farm lay to the west of the Squire's estate and was the farthest away from Brumbys', were known to be spendthrifts and had neither the ready money nor the collateral to raise a loan.

So Esther was the only one to buy. At last, she had her reward for all her years of hard work. And now, Kate thought, all that might be snatched away from her mother if their country were plunged once more into war.

But perhaps, Kate thought, our little corner of England will hardly notice the war.

How wrong she was!

Kate walked down the lane towards home, with Danny riding his bike at the side of her, wobbling precariously as he tried to slow his pace to match her walking speed.

'So what are you going to do, now you're back? Get your old job back at old man Reynolds'?'

'I might. Miss Davenport was telling Mam only last week that the workroom supervisor's leaving to get married.'

'Your old job, eh?'

176

'Maybe, but I might be needed to do something a little bit more important.' She glanced at him and added, impishly. 'I could always join up.'

Danny's eyes twinkled with mischief. 'What d'you reckon women could do, eh?'

'Plenty!' she flashed back, just as he had known she would. 'It was the last war that set us free from the kitchen sink. Women worked as VAD nurses, in factories, all sorts . . .'

'Remember it, do you?' He was grinning at her indignation, teasing her fondly.

'No. One of my clients in Lincoln, Mrs Clarkson, was a VAD nurse in the last lot. She loved to talk about it when she came for a fitting. We'll play an even bigger part this time – you'll see!'

'It'll not come to much, I don't reckon. It'll all be over by Christmas.'

Ominously, Kate reminded him, 'That's what they said last time!'

Eighteen

Of course it was not over by Christmas, nor even by well into 1940. The news was not good and as it got worse, Kate began to fear that any day, Danny would say he was volunteering.

The rationing of certain foods sent Esther into a fury. 'What are we supposed to do then? Us that produce the butter and bacon? Ration oursens? Answer me that?'

'They'll tell us, Esther love, just as they'll tell us what crops they want us to plant.'

'Aye, potatoes!' Esther said scathingly. 'Whoever heard of beautiful fields of waving wheat and oats being replaced by 'tates?'

'We must do what we can to help the war effort, love,' Jonathan replied gently.

Then Esther's wonderful smile, like the sun appearing once more, lit up her face. She put her arms about her husband and rested her head against his chest. 'I'll do whatever they want, as long as they don't take you away from me this time.'

Jonathan chuckled softly. 'We'll be in a bad way if they have to call up men of fifty!'

Watching them, Kate smiled fondly, but in her heart she feared for Danny. Conscription had been extended now to include men up to the age of twenty-seven – Danny's age. Would he be called up, Kate anguished, or was he safe as an agricultural worker?

At the beginning of April the enemy invaded Denmark

and Norway and in May they swept through Belgium and also into Holland. Then northern France came under attack.

The menace was coming closer.

'Danny? Where are you going?'

The late May morning was bright, the sun glistening on the water as Kate stood on the river bank, looking down into Robert Eland's fishing boat moored at the end of the wooden jetty. Danny was packing blankets, boxes of food and tins of diesel into the stern.

'Sheerness.'

'*Sheerness*! Whatever for?'

'Me dad had to register the boat because it's just over thirty foot and now it's been commandeered, so I'm takin' it down there mesen.'

'What for?' she repeated.

'I – dunno.'

'Yes, you do. I can tell.'

He continued carrying boxes from the jetty on to the boat. 'There's trouble across the Channel.'

'Is your dad going with you?'

'No, he's got to man the lifeboat. I'm going on me own.'

'Then I'm coming with you.'

'No, you're not . . .'

But she was scrambling down the bank and marching along the wooden planking. He barred her way. 'Tis no place for a woman.'

Kate laughed in his face. 'Oh no? Do you really think I'm going to let you go without *me*!'

'Kate, yar mam . . .'

'Me mam's got nowt to do with it. I'm of age, aren't I?' The dialect, which she had made valiant efforts to smooth out in her working life, came back strongly when she was angry. And she was angry now.

'Well, ya not dressed right.'

'Then I'll go home and get mesen dressed in trousers and warm clothes.'

'Ya'll need oilskins . . .'

She pointed beyond him at the boat bobbing gently on the swell of the river. 'You've always got a spare pair on board. I've seen 'em.'

'Oh, *you*!' Danny said, half exasperated, half amused. 'Ya know too much for ya own good. Go on, then.'

'You'll wait for me? You'll not go without me?'

Now he was grinning broadly. 'I wouldn't dare!'

She was away and running across the turf. At twenty-seven she could still run as fast as she had at fourteen. And for the moment, any dignity which her advancing years and her position as workroom supervisor in the department store in Lynthorpe had brought her, was forgotten.

'Bring more blankets and some food, if you can,' he shouted after her. She did not pause but lifted her hand in acknowledgement that she had heard him.

'And don't forget your . . .'

' . . . gas mask,' she finished for him.

Breathless, she reached Brumbys' Farm to meet Lilian pushing her doll's pram around the yard.

'Shouldn't you be doing something more useful than playing with dolls at your age?' Kate snapped. Lilian, a gawky thirteen-year-old, never failed to irritate Kate. From a whining child she had grown into a sulky, solitary girl who seemed deliberately to shun the company of friends of her own age. To Kate's idea, their mother pampered Lilian, who was never asked to help with the housework or farmwork as Kate had been from a very early age.

'It was different then,' Esther would say when Kate grumbled. 'I was on me own and there was a war on.'

'There's a war on now, for heaven's sake!' Kate would argue.

'But none of our family's involved this time, thank the Lord!'

So what would her mother say, Kate thought now as she raced upstairs to find her warmest clothes, if she knew Kate was about to involve herself deliberately in something to do with the war – even though at the moment she didn't know exactly what?

Dressed in slacks, a thick woollen jumper and grey knitted socks, Kate ran down the narrow stairs carrying three blankets. Swiftly, she packed some bread and cheese into a bag. Sitting in her father's Windsor chair to pull on her wellingtons, she looked up to see Lilian standing in the door watching her. 'Tell Mam I've gone out in the boat with Danny. I don't know how long we'll be gone, but tell her she's not to worry.' Snatching a warm coat from the hook behind the door and stuffing a headscarf and a wool beret into her pocket, Kate turned back to look at her young sister. The girl looked so forlorn standing there, awkward and, even in her own home, somehow lost. Strangely moved to a feeling of tenderness, Kate planted a swift kiss on the girl's forehead. 'You hear, Lilian?'

The girl nodded and then suddenly flung her arms around Kate's waist and buried her head against her. Just as suddenly, she let go and stood back, her face flaming red. Kate wasn't sure which of them was the more embarrassed. She gave the girl a quick grin, said, 'Take care, Lilian,' and was gone.

Funny child, Kate thought as she hurried back to the Point. At her age I'd have been begging to go along too. Lilian hadn't even asked where they were going. Perhaps that was just as well, though, Kate thought shrewdly. But the sudden display of emotion from her sister had surprised Kate.

Danny was standing on the edge of the jetty, the mooring rope already unfastened.

'Hop in and start her up, will ya, Kate?' He grinned suddenly. 'Thank goodness for ya dad and his engines!'

Kate knew the boat and its workings almost as well as Danny did, for she had often gone out to sea with him on her visits home. Good job too, she thought, Mam'll think nothing about it when Lilian tells her.

But she would when Kate did not arrive home that night, she thought with a stab of guilt. Well, she reflected with wry humour, me mam'll just have to break years of silence and go and ask Danny's mother where we are if she's that bothered!

Kate smiled to herself as she guided the boat into the centre of the river and made for the channel which led out through the intertidal marsh and into the North Sea. She doubted very much that even a war would make Esther Godfrey speak to Beth Eland!

They chugged steadily out to sea and turned southwards, following the coastline. It was a long way and would take them a long time to get there.

'I just hope we're in time for whatever it is they want,' Danny said, as they settled themselves for the hours ahead.

'Just look at all them boats!' Danny was standing up in the prow of his boat. It looked as if hundreds of small craft of all shapes and sizes were heading for Sheerness. He turned and looked back at Kate. 'This looks like something big, Kate, I dun't reckon you ought to have come...'

Kate gave him one of her looks and he raised his hand, palm outwards, as if to fend off an impending attack. 'All right, all right...'

She grinned at him but kept her hand firmly on the tiller. 'I never said a word,' she shouted across the breeze.

'No – but ya looked it!'

Somehow they found a place to moor and joined the rest of the boatmen on the quay.

As they walked towards the building where they had to report their arrival, Kate took a beret from her coat pocket and pulled it over her thick hair, tucking stray strands beneath it. In trousers, a bulky jumper and jacket, she could pass for a young boy. Only her luxurious auburn hair gave her away!

Very soon they found out why their boats were needed. The British Expeditionary Forces were virtually trapped on the coast of France at a place called Dunkirk and had to be rescued. Enemy planes were strafing the beaches, and the opposing army was closing in around them. Every available boat was needed to bring the soldiers off the beaches.

One of the boat owners proposed that he should take his own boat across and suddenly there was a chorus of offers. After a brief consultation among the senior officers, they agreed to the suggestion.

Silently the boatmen listened as they heard what their mission was to be; to bring the men off the beaches to ships anchored offshore. Larger boats could bring as many as they were able to carry safely back across the Channel if they wished. It seemed that off the beaches where the soldiers waited, the water was very shallow and some of the larger vessels could get nowhere near the shore.

'It's dangerous,' they were warned. 'The enemy are shelling from inland and there's the Luftwaffe to contend with too ...'

'Kate ...' She felt Danny's grasp upon her arm. 'I really don't think ...'

She looked into his brown eyes, her own almost on a level

with his. 'Danny, ya can't possibly man the boat on ya own *and* rescue people.'

'No, Katie. It'll be dangerous. You're not coming. I won't let you.' His fingers tightened on her arm. 'What if – what if something were to happen to you?'

'Something might happen to you,' she whispered.

They stared at each other and his sigh was cool on her cheek. 'Please, Katie, stay here where it's safe.'

She shook her head. 'No, Danny,' she said with quiet firmness. 'I'm coming. I can't stay here – just waiting – while you're out there. Besides,' she added grinning cheekily, trying to lighten what was a very desperate situation. 'Think I'd let you out alone in France?'

'All right,' he said heavily. 'But if it's really bad I'll put you on one of the big ships.'

Kate grinned. She'd argue that when they got there, she thought, but said nothing.

Pulling her beret down well over her hair, she hovered behind Danny as they formed a queue to sign a form. In the mêlée she managed to scribble her signature and was out and following Danny back to the boat before anyone had realized she was a girl.

The sea was amazingly calm and the weather smiling benignly on their venture. Yet as they drew near the French coast, towed by one of the large vessels to save their precious fuel, the breeze whipped across the water, making the seas choppy.

Ahead now Kate saw a black pall of smoke rising above the town, and heard the thud of gunfire from the shore. Four black lines snaked out into the water. She squinted through the drifting smoke, there was something odd . . .

'Danny!' she clutched his arms. 'Look, those are men standing in the water!'

Lines of soldiers, standing three abreast up to their chests in the freezing water, formed disciplined queues stretching from the shore out towards the boats.

'Poor buggers!' Danny muttered, and Kate knew the sight had affected him deeply for she hardly ever heard Danny swear.

They were released from their tow and Danny started up the engine and steered the boat towards the nearest line of men. From the west came the steady hum of aircraft, growing louder and louder, nearer and nearer. Then they heard the sound of gunfire from three planes coming in low.

'Get down, Kate!' Danny yelled and pushed her into the bottom of the boat. She felt a jagged splinter from the planking dig into her hand.

'Ouch, I've got . . .' But the rest of her words were drowned as a plane passed overhead close to the prow of the boat, bullets splashing into the water directly in front of them. The planes flew off to the east and Kate raised her head. ' . . . a splinter in me hand.'

Danny ran his tongue nervously over his lips and made a valiant attempt to smile, 'If that's all ya get on this little trip, Kate, ya'll be bloody lucky! Come on, they'll be back in a minute. Let's see if we can get a few on board. You steer and I'll help 'em climb in.'

All along the coast the little ships pulled the men from the water, loading their small craft almost to sinking point before they chugged precariously back to the large vessels standing offshore.

Kate steered the boat while Danny helped the soldiers in. When one put his hands on the side, glanced at Kate and then hesitated, Danny said, 'Come on, mate, up with ya.'

'I can't . . .' He nodded towards Kate. 'She's a woman . . .'

'So?'

'I've – lost me trousers, mate. I've nothin' on.'

Danny grinned down at him. 'Born and bred on a farm, mate. You ain't got nothing she's not seen afore.'

There was a ripple of laughter, even amidst all the horror.

'Come on, Bashful Bert,' shouted another soldier waiting in line behind him. 'Get a move on.'

Smiling, Kate averted her gaze to save the poor man's embarrassment and when she looked again, he was wrapping a blanket around himself and grinning sheepishly at her.

'That's all for this time,' Danny shouted. 'We can only take fifteen at a time.'

'Can't we hang on to the side, mate?' one of the soldiers still waiting shouted.

'Sorry,' Danny said firmly. 'We'll capsize and then we'll get no one off. We'll be back as soon as we can ...' he promised, but the look on the faces of those still waiting up to their necks in the water tore at Kate's heart.

Those they had taken on board sat hunched and silent. Their faces were streaked with oil and many had at least four days' growth of beard on their chins. One had a dirty handkerchief tied around one eye, another was only in his vest and underpants and all were wet through and shivering.

Kate opened one of the boxes and passed some bread and cheese and apples round. 'I'm sorry we've nothing hot,' she apologized.

A young soldier – no more than a boy, he seemed to Kate – wolfed the food, stuffing the bread into his mouth.

'How – how long have you been without food?'

'Three days, Miss. We've been on the beach for two, wading out into the water when it looked like a ship was coming, then back to the dunes again when the enemy planes came over ...'

Suddenly Kate's hand seemed frozen on the tiller as a dreadful fear clutched her. This could happen on our beaches! The thought terrified her.

She shuddered, thinking of the peaceful tranquillity of the beach at home; she couldn't imagine Fleethaven Point becoming a place of death with guns blasting and soldiers fleeing for their lives into the dunes and bodies floating in the sea . . .

We can't let it happen, she thought suddenly. We have to help stop it happening – Danny and I. We must.

Until this moment the war had seemed far away; unreal. Oh, they'd read the papers, but it hadn't really affected their small community.

Now – off the beaches of Dunkirk – it was very real.

On their fourth trip back to the lines of waiting men, Danny shouted. 'Give us a hand here, Kate, this one can't help himself. He's about had it.'

'Here – hold this,' she asked one of the soldiers already in the boat.

'Anything you say, Cap'n.' The soldier's face was black with oil, and his clothes were saturated, but he still managed a grin as she handed the tiller over to him and moved down the boat to help Danny.

The man Danny was trying to bring aboard was in a semi-conscious state, almost sinking under the water. 'Give him a shove up, will ya, mate?' Danny asked the man waiting next to him.

'Shouldn't bother,' put in one of the soldiers already in the boat. 'He's only RAF. Where are they, that's what I'd like to know? Ain't seen one of *our* planes all day.'

'Shut up!' said the man next to him. 'He's here, ain't he? He must have been doing something. There's a lot of sky up there. Here, Miss, let me give you a hand.'

The men carefully shuffled position in the boat so that

the friendly soldier moved to Kate's side. 'Come on, mate, let's be having you back to good old Blighty.'

They hauled him into the bottom of the boat where he lay with his eyes closed. The sleeve of his pilot's jacket was ripped open and blood oozed out, mixing with the sea water. Kate took off her scarf and wrapped it round the man's arm, tying it at the back of his neck in a makeshift sling.

'Danny, are there any blankets left?'

'No – we've used 'em all.'

'Here, Miss, take mine,' said the soldier who had helped pull the airman aboard.

'The glamour boys get all the attention,' grumbled the soldier who had already moaned about the RAF.

'Shut it, will you?' muttered the friendly one. 'Else I'll shut it for you.'

The other sniffed. 'All the same – the women . . .'

The other man put his mouth close to the grumbling soldier's ear, but Kate still caught his words. 'This lass had no need to come and save your miserable hide. Risking her life, she is. So shut it!'

Danny turned the boat around and headed out to sea, the small craft low in the water with the weight. Kate bent over the airman and was relieved to hear a low moan escape his lips. She tapped his face with the flat of her hand, not exactly a slap but sharp enough to try and rouse him.

'That's right, Miss,' the friendly one encouraged. 'Don't let 'im go to sleep. The cold will kill him, else.'

Kate put her mouth close to the airman's ear, her whole attention now on the injured man. 'Come on, try to wake up. What's your name?'

She continued to talk to him, gently tapping his cheek to try to rouse him, while in the sky above, enemy aircraft swooped in again from the west, strafing the beaches and sending the waiting soldiers diving for cover in the dunes.

The planes shot off to the east but turned and came back over the water, this time aiming for the small boats loaded with soldiers. Further out to sea, two more planes dropped bombs close to the larger ships waiting for the retreating British Army.

Kate hardly noticed the noise now; she was trying to wrap an already sodden blanket around the airman. She sat down in the bottom of the boat and cradled the man in her lap, wrapping her arms around him and holding him close, rubbing his back to try to warm him.

'I tell you, them glamour boys get all the blooming luck,' the grumbling soldier said again. Kate glanced up at him and opened her mouth to speak, but her words were drowned by a terrific explosion and all heads turned to see the very ship they were making for receive a direct hit. Flames engulfed the bow and black smoke drifted skywards.

'Oh no!' Kate muttered, while the soldiers stared at the rescue ship in grim silence.

Wordlessly, Danny changed course slightly and headed for a smaller boat some distance further out to sea, skirting round the stricken vessel which was now burning fiercely. They could see men jumping back into the sea from which they had just been rescued, but with the present load they carried, Danny could do nothing to help. He steered away, thinking that if they went closer, panic-stricken men would grab their little fishing boat and capsize it.

'We'll see if we can pick some up when we've dropped you lot off,' Danny promised, but no one on board answered him. They just continued to stare at their comrades struggling in the water. As they watched, a figure, his clothes alight, jumped from the vessel into the water. Even above the turmoil they could hear his screams.

'Looks like every man for himself now,' muttered the friendly soldier.

They neared the smaller ship but already they could see that the decks were lined with soldiers.

A ship's officer hung over the side. He cupped his hands and shouted down to Danny as the small boat bobbed against the side, 'We can only take ten maximum.'

In the small boat, heads turned, counting their number. There were eleven soldiers and the airman besides Danny and Kate. The soldiers began to haul themselves up the nets hanging over the side of the ship.

'What about him?' Kate indicated the airman. 'He ought to be taken on board first. He needs medical attention urgently.'

The soldier who had been so scathing about the RAF glanced down as he began to climb. 'Shouldn't bother, miss, he's a gonner anyway.' And with that parting shot, he hauled himself up to safety.

Ten were on board, leaving the airman and the soldier who had been friendly. 'Reckon I'll stay and give you a hand, Miss, if we're to save this lad's life, eh?'

Kate gazed into his craggy face. He was older than the rest – a regular soldier, she thought, rather that a conscript.

'Reckon it's time we introduced ourselves.' He held out a large hand that was blue with cold. 'Gordon Stratford, pleased to meet you, Miss, though I could have wished for better circumstances.'

Kate grinned at him and put her own cold hand briefly into his. 'Kate Hilton, and he's Danny Eland.' She nodded towards Danny, who was manoeuvring the boat around to head back towards the soldiers from the sinking ship.

'We ought to get him roused if we can,' Gordon said. 'He'll slip away if we don't keep him awake.'

Together they struggled with the dead weight of the unconscious airman, trying to get him into a sitting position in the prow of the boat.

The airman's face was gaunt and pale, his eyes closed.

'I've got some rum stowed in that locker,' Kate said. 'Let's try that.'

She held the neck of the bottle to the airman's blue lips and gently tried to ease some of the reviving liquid into his mouth.

'He's a squadron leader,' Gordon said, suddenly. 'Wonder where the rest of his chaps are?'

'Now don't you start, Gordon!' Kate said, but she was smiling, teasing the friendly man who had so generously given up his own chance of immediate rescue to stay to help her and Danny.

Gordon's teeth shone white out of his oil-streaked face. 'No – I'm not like our friend back there.' He jerked his head back towards the ship they had just left. 'The RAF is here all right – I know that – but they've a hell of an area to cover and they won't have a lot of flying time from a fuel point of view when they do get here.'

'Talking about fuel . . .' Kate looked around at the cans Danny had brought. There was only one remaining tin. She glanced at Gordon. 'You go aboard with him the next trip back to a ship,' she said firmly, nodding towards the airman.

Gordon gave her a mock salute. 'Yes, Ma'am.'

While Danny steered the boat back towards the ship that had been hit, Kate chafed the airman's hands, though her own were now as cold as his. Then she rubbed his back again. 'Come on, feller, do wake up,' she murmured as his head lolled against her breast. She wrapped her arms around him again, rocking him as she might a child.

Above the airman's unconscious form, she met Danny's glance as he sat with his hand on the tiller. There was a fleeting look of pain in his eyes. Intuitively, she knew that he had felt a sudden stab of jealousy seeing her with her arms around another man. It was the first time, but it might

191

not be the last, and she could see his inner struggle to come to terms with it. She smiled at Danny, understanding and commiserating. For a brief moment amidst all the chaos, they gazed at each other, and then he gave her a small smile and lifted his shoulders fractionally in a tiny shrug of helpless, reluctant acceptance. Even now, she thought, after all this time, for Danny as well as for her, the pain was never very far away.

'What's all that smoke?' she asked Gordon, watching the huge pall of black smoke ahead of them on the shore billowing and spreading, clouding the coastline for miles until it seemed like dusk, in stark contrast to the bright blue sky over the sea behind them.

'Oil storage tanks. They've been bombed. And the whole town's on fire.'

From out of the smoke hurtled three enemy planes, diving down towards the boats, the rattle of their machine-guns audible even above the engines. Ships' guns were turned on them and those soldiers on the decks who still had rifles pointed them skywards. Even though it was perhaps a futile gesture, nevertheless it was a display of defiance.

Defenceless, Danny, Kate and Gordon watched as the planes swooped directly towards them. Instinctively, Kate's arms tightened around the airman.

It was then that she felt him move. He gave a spluttering cough, then a groan, and opened his eyes.

The planes shot past them, spattering bullets into the water only two feet from the boat, and Kate felt the cold splash of sea water on her cheek. Then they banked away and were gone.

Gordon winked at Kate and said, 'Well now, young feller, back in the land of the living.'

They propped him upright and from the bag, Kate brought out more bread and cheese. 'See if you can get him to eat something – and have some yourself. We're getting close to the men in the water now. I'd better take the tiller for Danny.'

As she turned away to move along the boat, Gordon, his mouth full, said, 'By, this cheese is good. Long time since I tasted proper cheese. You *do* live on a farm, then? Where?'

'Fleethaven Point. It's on the Lincolnshire coast, near the Wash.'

'Good Lord! You come all that way down here?'

'Yes, Danny's boat was commandeered, so he decided to bring it himself. I came too – so here we are.'

'And thank the good Lord for you, lass. For you both – you and your man.'

Yes, she thought wryly, Danny was her man. Still, despite the knowledge of their true relationship, deep in a corner of her heart, locked away, he was still 'her man'.

Nineteen

The little fishing boat all the way from the Wash went back towards the sinking ship, now listing heavily to port and obviously beyond salvage. The men in the water were exhausted. After days and nights on the exposed beaches, under fire from the enemy, then standing in human piers stretching into the cold water of the Channel, they had dared to believe themselves rescued. To be thrown back into the water had sapped the strength and resolve of even these brave men.

Still the enemy aircraft swooped and dived above them. Every three-quarters of an hour or so they were back, splattering bullets across the water and dive-bombing the ships laden with soldiers.

While the men struggled to keep afloat in the water, Danny and Kate went back and forth between the sinking vessel and another rescue ship farther out to sea; so many times that Kate lost count. On the first trip out to the bigger ship, Danny sided with Kate and insisted that Gordon take the young airman aboard and stay with him.

'Ya've done your bit, mate,' Danny said, putting his hand on the older man's arm.

'I don't like leaving you and the young lass to cope.'

'Just stay with him,' Kate said, nodding down at the airman, 'Get him some proper help as soon as you can.'

'I'll do that, Miss, I promise. But you take care, mind.' He shook Danny's hand warmly and, without a trace of embarrassment, kissed Kate's cold cheek. 'I hope we meet again . . .'

They watched Gordon climb a swaying rope ladder, while alongside him, the RAF officer was hoisted aboard on a swinging stretcher. When he was half-way up, they saw Gordon swing round and look out across the water towards the soldiers on the beach running towards the dunes as yet again, enemy aircraft swooped low overhead. For a moment Gordon released one hand-hold, leaned back and looked up at the planes. He shook his fist at them. 'We'll be back, you buggers!' he shouted. 'We'll be back.' Then he turned and continued his climb.

Danny laughed. 'He's a character, in't he?'

'He's a great chap to have around in a crisis,' Kate murmured, half sorry to see Gordon leave them. 'Danny, do you reckon the airman'll make it?'

'I dunno, Kate. He looks bad to me. Come on, let's not stay here – we're sitting ducks!'

Each time they returned to the same ship, Gordon was there, hanging over the ship's rail.

'Your young airman's below,' he shouted down. 'We're in luck – this is a hospital ship. There's a doc on board – and even nurses! He's in good hands now.'

Kate smiled up at him and waved.

Then later, Gordon was still there. 'Come on, mate, come aboard yourselves now. The Captain says we can't take any more and we ought to be on our way before we get hit.'

Danny shook his head. 'There's still men on the beach.'

Gordon shaded his eyes. 'Not so many now – and there's still boats picking them up. Come on board, man. That lass is exhausted.'

Kate felt Danny's eyes on her. 'You go, Kate. I'll manage . . .'

'No!' she said with far more strength than she felt. She

195

was bone-weary, wet, cold and hungry. Her mind kept wandering so that she imagined herself fourteen again and walking across the Wolds in the pouring rain to find her grandfather. Only will-power was keeping her going – as it had then – only sheer determination made her drag her frozen mind back to the present.

But the decision was taken from them, for as Danny revved the engine to head back once more towards the beach, it spluttered twice and died.

'We're out of fuel' he said flatly, as their boat bobbed silently up and down on the waves.

'We'll – get the oars out, then,' Kate said and dragged herself to where they were stowed at the side of the boat.

They were just drifting away from the side of the larger boat, struggling to get the oars in position and aware that Gordon was still watching them anxiously from the deck, when they heard the sound of an enemy plane screaming towards them, a dive-bomber aiming for the laden ship.

'Row, Kate, for God's sake – row!'

Frantically, they pulled on the oars, trying to put distance between themselves and the target. Kate panted and strained at the oars, sobbing with fear and frustration. After all their efforts, all the men they had saved – especially Gordon and the airman – were going to be bombed. Killed or, at best, thrown back into the water.

The Stuka screamed towards them in a steep dive, its black crosses on the top of each wing clearly visible.

One bomb left the aircraft, hurtling down towards them. Then from under the wings, four smaller bombs were released. One landed on the far side of the ship, sending up a plume of water. Another fell between the hospital ship and the little boat trying desperately to escape. It hit the water and exploded, causing such an eruption that the larger ship rocked, sending men slithering about the deck. Only Gordon hung on to the deck rail, fearful for the fate of the little boat.

The vibration thudded through Kate and the surge of water bore their fishing boat aloft, held it suspended for a timeless moment and then plunged it downwards, capsizing it and throwing both Danny and Kate into the sea.

The last thing she remembered hearing was Danny's desperate cry of 'Kate! *Kate!*'

Someone was holding her head above the water. Someone was shouting at her but she could not hear properly for the rushing sound in her ears. Then some kind of strap was being put around her under her armpits and she felt herself being hoisted clear of the water, her legs dangling limply. Then willing hands were reaching out for her, pulling her on to the comparative safety of the deck of the ship. Blankets were wrapped around her and she was being carried.

'Danny?' she croaked. 'Where's Danny?'

'What's she say?' A voice spoke above her.

'Never mind,' said another. 'Get her below – to the doc.'

She was carried below and found herself being placed, with surprising gentleness, on a narrow bed. But no sooner did they set her down than Kate began to struggle. 'No, no. Danny – I must find Danny. He's in the sea. He can't swim.'

'Now, now, young lady.' A man was bending over her. 'I'm a doctor. You just lie still.'

'But Danny – is he safe? Please, I must . . .'

The doctor jerked his head at one of the soldiers who had carried her down, 'See what you can find out. She's obviously very distressed.'

The soldier gave Kate's arm a swift pat. 'Don't worry, Miss. One of our lot dived in when your boat capsized. He got to you first, but he's still looking for – who is it? Danny?'

Weakly, Kate nodded. She sank back against the pillow as exhaustion claimed her.

'That's better. Leave it to the lads. They'll find him.'

Kate closed her eyes and sent up a silent prayer. 'Oh please, dear Lord, please let them find him!'

Later, warm and dry and placed in a bed alongside other casualties aboard the hospital ship, Kate still fretted for news of Danny. The ship was so crowded that the beds in the ward had been pushed close together and men lay on the floor on stretchers or just on blankets.

'It's bloody murder up top,' one of the stretcher bearers said, as they struggled to find a clear space to put down their burden. 'The deck's that crammed, fellers are lying on top of each other.'

It wasn't much better down here, Kate thought ruefully, glancing round. There was scarcely a clear foot of floor space between the soldiers. The nursing sisters of the Queen Alexandra's Nursing Service had to step carefully over patients to tend the wounded. The ward was filled with the sounds of groaning and coughing, and now and then a scream of agony.

Kate raised herself a little. 'Please – do you know if the young man from the little fishing boat has been rescued?'

The stretcher-bearer shrugged his shoulders. 'Sorry, Miss . . .' He turned away and bent over a soldier whose whole face seemed to be a mass of congealed blood, a filthy bandage round his head.

Kate bit her lip. No one seemed to know down here what had happened to Danny and no one had time to go and find out for her.

She became aware that someone in the next bed was watching her. Kate turned her head to find herself looking

into the bluest eyes she had ever seen in a man. His fair
was short and curly, brushed straight back from his br
forehead. His face was lightly tanned yet there were rings
exhaustion around his eyes. His left arm was freshly ba
daged, but instead of a proper white sling, his arm was sti
supported by her scarf.

It was the airman she had cradled in her arms and willed
to live.

He was older than she had thought him to be, but he had
looked young and vulnerable lying unconscious in the bottom
of the fishing boat. Yet, even then, Gordon had said the
insignia on his jacket was quite a high rank. What was it he
had said? Squadron Leader?

She smiled weakly at him. At least now, clean and dry, he
looked more like a member of – what was it the disgruntled
soldier had called the RAF? Oh yes, that was it – the glamour boys.

Kate felt her eyelids close, but she opened them again as
he spoke. His voice was deep, yet a little croaky from his
recent ordeal.

'I want to . . .' he began, but Kate said, 'Don't, please
don't. I just want to know what's happened to Danny . . .'
Her voice broke and she turned her head away towards the
wall so that he should not see her tears. She knew he was
going to start thanking her, maybe telling her how brave
she had been. She didn't want that, because she didn't feel she
had been particularly courageous. She had only come to be
with Danny. How could she explain to the airman that fo
some reason she had not even felt afraid, at least, not for h
own safety. The only fear she felt was to think that all t
carnage could happen in England; that had made her an

Now, however, her terror was very real. She was des
ately frightened for Danny.

Hearing the airman move, she looked back at him

He was struggling to rise from the bed. 'I'll go – and see – what I can find out.'

She put out her hand to stop him. 'No, no, you mustn't. You'll . . .'

'And just what do you think you're up to, young feller?' Gordon's cheerful face appeared round the door. Carefully he stepped between the soldiers on the floor and came towards them. He was soaking wet, his hair plastered down, and rivulets of water were running down his face. The airman sank back on to the bed as Gordon grinned broadly at Kate and said, 'He's okay – we've got him. He's taken in a lot of water. They're pumping him out now. But he'll be all right.'

'Oh, thank God!' she whispered. 'It was you, Gordon, wasn't it?'

'Me – what do you mean? What have I done?' He drew the back of his hand across his eyes and blinked.

'It was you found him, wasn't it? Did you pull me out too?'

The grin widened as he turned away to go and dry off. 'Well, you know what they say? One good turn deserves another . . .'

With that, he was gone.

Gordon appointed himself personal nurse to the three of them – Kate, Danny and Squadron Leader Philip Trent. 'Just don't let on I'm looking after one of the boys in blue,' he grinned, 'or me life won't be worth living.' The nurses, overwhelmed by the numbers, welcomed Gordon's help. Moving among the wounded and exhausted men, the cheerful soldier was as good as a tonic.

An hour or so later, he brought Danny into the cabin, his strong arm under the younger man's shoulder. 'Here you are,

girl. He's all safe and sound. And we're nearly half-way home. Just let's hope that Luftwaffe don't find us!'

Danny grinned sheepishly at Kate. 'I really ought to learn to swim, didn't I?'

'I've been telling you that for years, but do you ever take notice of me?' She was smiling at him, so thankful that he was safe. But she knew if she were to fling her arms around him, as she felt like doing, it would only embarrass him. So her mock admonishment covered their deeper emotions.

He sat down carefully on the bed beside her.

'Are you hurt?' she asked anxiously.

'No – just bruised. How about you?'

'I'm fine. I ought to get off this bed, really. There are far worse than me . . .'

'You lie still, girl,' Gordon ordered, 'You took in a lot of water. 'Sides, you've earned a bed, if anyone has!'

One or two soldiers nearby, less injured than some, heard Gordon and raised a cheer of agreement. Kate felt herself blushing.

Danny grinned at her and then, sobering suddenly, looked up at Gordon. 'Do you know what happened to me boat?'

'Sorry, mate, blown to smithereens.'

Danny closed his eyes and groaned. Kate watched him anxiously. What would Robert Eland say when they returned home? That boat was his livelihood.

As if catching some of their anxiety, Philip Trent asked, 'Is it a great loss to you?'

When Danny didn't answer, Kate explained quietly, 'It's his dad's. He's a fisherman.'

Danny opened his eyes. 'Oh, he'd have come himself, if he could have done, only he had to stay. He's coxswain of our lifeboat . . .'

'Oh, so this rescuing business runs in the family, does it?' Gordon laughed and Danny and Kate smiled. The loss of the boat – even though a big loss to Danny's father – was nothing in comparison to the many lives they had saved.

Robert Eland would understand.

Their homecoming to Fleethaven Point was greeted in differing ways.

'Thoughtless, irresponsible, selfish . . .' Esther Godfrey's tirade went on. 'Fancy just telling our Lilian you were going out in the boat with *him* and then disappearing for nearly a week. We thought you'd been drowned.'

Calmly, Kate said, 'Him? His name's Danny, Mother. And if you'd taken the trouble to ask Mrs Eland – she knew where we were. Well, sort of . . .'

Obviously her private thoughts had been right, Kate realized. Not even the safety of her own daughter had been enough to make Esther Godfrey speak to Beth Eland.

Reluctantly, Esther muttered, 'Ya dad did speak to Mester. He said you'd both gone off down south. We thought it was a pleasure trip and then I find out you've been getting yarsen into *this*!' Esther rattled a daily newspaper under Kate's nose. Plastered all over the front page were dramatic accounts of how an armada of ships of all shapes and sizes had brought back thousands of men from the beaches of Dunkirk.

Kate grinned. 'What – no picture of us on the front page? Well, I'd have thought we warranted that at the very least!'

'I'll have none of your sarcasm, Miss,' her mother snapped, and flung the paper away from her in disgust.

'I suppose you'll be wanting to join up next.'

There was a long silence between them; a waiting silence.

Kate met her mother's fierce gaze. 'I'm thinking about it – yes.'

She saw the colour drain swiftly from her mother's face and Esther put out her hand to steady herself against the table. A small gasp escaped her open lips and her green eyes – so like Kate's own – stared at her daughter.

Kate felt a stab of remorse. She hadn't meant to be quite so blunt, and yet, she had to make her mother understand. She turned and began to pace up and down the kitchen, spreading her hands. 'You don't understand, Mam. It was awful over there. All those soldiers trapped on the beach and in the water – thousands of them. There were bodies too . . .' She gulped and closed her eyes for a moment, then she went on strongly, 'We've all got to do our bit – even the women this time, Mam. We can't let Hitler just walk into our country and take it over. And he will – if we don't stop him. You don't understand, Mam . . .' she said again and then stopped.

Her mother had sunk down into a chair on the opposite side of the kitchen table and was resting her arms on the scrubbed surface. Wearily, she said, 'Yes, I do, Kate. It was the same for me when I went to France after the last war.'

'What? You – you went to France?' Kate could not hide the surprise in her voice, and hearing it, her mother smiled. 'Yes – can you imagine me leaving Fleethaven Point to go all the way to France?'

Kate lowered herself into a chair and faced her mother across the table. 'Tell me about it, Mam?' she asked softly.

There was silence in the kitchen, the only sounds the ticking of the clock and the singing of the kettle on the hob.

'I went out there with the Squire. His eldest son had been killed and he was trying to find his grave. I – went to try to . . . She stopped, glanced swiftly at Kate and then dropped her gaze again. She took a deep breath and continued. 'When I saw their land . . .' Esther's eyes took on a faraway look, as if she were not here in her warm kitchen in 1940 but out on the battlefields of France in 1919, 'absolutely devastated, gouged with trenches as far as you could see. Not a living thing for mile after mile – not a blade of grass; trees, blackened and dead; no birds – only rotting bodies and rats!' She shook her head, murmuring, 'Those poor folk, they can only just have recovered from all that, and now it's happening to them again.' She raised her eyes and met Kate's gaze steadily. 'Oh, I understand all right, Kate, just how you feel. I saw for myself what all our men fought for – and died for – last time. It's just that —' She reached out with fingers that shook slightly to clasp Kate's hands. 'You're my daughter and I – I don't want you to be in danger . . .'

Into Kate's mind came the words 'you'd still have Lilian' but they remained unspoken.

Already, Kate thought, she had said more than enough to hurt her mother.

Esther levered herself up from the table. 'Well, I'spose ya'll do what ya like, whatever I say. But ya'd best go in an' tell ya grandad what you intend.'

'Oh heck!'

The two women looked at each other and the comical expression upon Kate's face at the thought of having to tell her grandfather what she intended, made them both burst out laughing.

Twenty

'Grandad?' Kate opened the door of the front room quietly. Are you awake?' she asked softly.

'Aye, lass. Ah'm allus awake for you. Come in, come in, dun't stand there dithering in the doorway. There's a draught!'

Kate smiled, stepped into the room and closed the door behind her. She sat on a footstool at her grandfather's feet and smiled up at him.

Will Benson now lived at Brumbys' Farm. In the winter of 1936 he had caught influenza and had developed severe bronchitis. Kate smiled as she remembered how it had happened. All the time Will had been really ill, Esther or Jonathan, often with Kate along too when she had been at home, had driven in the pony and trap every day to the village of Suddaby, some thirteen miles inland.

'You're too old to be going about on the front of that carrier's cart any longer,' Esther had railed. 'You're just a stubborn old man who won't realize it's more than time he retired.'

'Shall you retire from the farm, girl, specially now you own it, just 'cos you get old?'

'That's different . . .'

'No, it ain't. What'll I do shut up in me cottage all day with only Minnie Raby and her gossiping tongue for company?'

The next day Esther had returned hands on hips, ready

205

to do battle. 'Me and Jonathan have talked it over. You're coming to live with us at Brumbys' Farm. I'll turn the front parlour into a bed-sitting room for ya. And dun't think I'll let you be idle, 'cos I shan't. Ya can mek ya'sen useful about the farm. And I won't have no argument, it's only right you should come to us. We're yar only family. I won't tek no . . .'

She had stopped as she had heard Will Benson's wheezy laughter. 'I aren't arguing, lass. It's what I want to do.'

'What? Well! Well – I never!' Esther's face had been a picture while Kate had clapped her hand over her mouth to stifle her laughter. But it had gurgled out until she was leaning weakly against the wall. The crafty old devil, Kate had thought, he'd engineered that very cleverly.

So here he was now, installed in the front room that was scarcely ever used anyway; a single bed in one corner and an armchair set in front of the window overlooking the front garden and the flat fields stretching to the setting sun. He had his privacy, yet his family were only a step away, and a little work about the farm when he felt like it kept him feeling useful and needed.

Will Benson was a contented man, it was written on his face for all to see. Yet he was still a force to be reckoned with within the family, which was why Kate found herself sitting at his feet and taking a deep breath before telling him of her plans.

Before she could begin, he said, 'You had us worried, girl. Whatever did you go off for like that with young Danny?'

Kate told him – in far more detail than she had described to her mother – all that had happened to her and Danny since they had set off from Fleethaven Point. She omitted nothing. She told him all about Gordon and the airman and how at the end of it all they'd lost Robert Eland's boat.

When at last she fell silent, she felt Will Benson's gnarled fingers touch her hair. With a catch in his voice he said, 'I'm proud of you, girl. I wish I'd bin there mesen.'

She looked up at him again, holding his gaze with her steady green eyes. 'Grandad, I'm thinking of – of joining up.'

His fingers, still against her hair, trembled slightly. 'Aw, lass. Are ya sure?'

'Oh, Grandad, if you'd seen it out there. Seen our soldiers coming back bedraggled and beaten. And yet,' she added with the ghost of a smile as she thought about Gordon Stratford, 'they didn't act like they were beaten. They were still shaking their fists at the enemy planes and promising to go back.'

'And you reckon you want to lend a hand, eh, lass?'

'I want to "do my bit" as they say.' She smiled up at him, trying to be light-hearted about it, but there was no deceiving the old man.

His face was sober as he asked quietly, 'Danny going too, is he, lass?'

She looked squarely into the watery, faded old eyes. 'I – think so, Grandad.'

Slowly, the old man nodded.

'What did your dad say about the boat?'

'He was very good about it,' Danny answered her. He grinned at her. 'Said he wished he'd been with us.'

She smiled back. 'That's just what me grandad said. Oh, but your dad's so good. He never says much, does he? But he's a wonderful person.'

'Aye,' Danny murmured. 'An' he's been good to me.' There was silence and Kate knew they were both thinking about the same thing; that he wasn't really Danny's father.

'He loves your mam so much. You can see it in his eyes when he looks at her, even now, after all these years.'

'Aye, an' it can't have been easy for him.'

'But she loves him,' Kate reassured him. 'I know she does.'

'Aye, well . . .' They were getting into dangerous waters, touching on a subject that they had not openly discussed for years. Yet always it lay between them.

As if deliberately to change tack, Danny said, 'By the way, can you have a word with Rosie?'

'Rosie?' Kate was surprised. 'What about?'

'She'll be getting herself into trouble if she dun't watch it.' When Kate still looked puzzled, he went on, 'It's them Army lads that's billeted with me grandad.'

Beth Eland's father, Dan Hanley, was the coastguard at Fleethaven Point and, living alone, was the only one with room to spare for the soldiers who manned the gun emplacement on the dunes facing the North Sea.

'Oh.' Now Kate understood. 'What about her mam or Grannie Harris? I'd have thought she could make young Rosie toe the line.'

'She's grown into such a pretty little thing,' Danny murmured.

'All those blonde curls and big blue eyes,' Kate laughed. And Rosie's figure too, she was thinking, all curvey in the right places.

'She's so innocent, though,' Danny was saying. 'Living here at the Point all her life, she ain't had much to do with men. She just won't know . . .'

Kate stifled a snort of laughter. It was Danny who was the innocent one, she thought. If what she had heard was true, then young Rosie Maine knew exactly what she was doing.

When Rosie had turned fifteen, she had found a job in Reynolds' store in Lynthorpe. She was still the same bright chatterbox and, as Danny rightly said, had now blossomed into a very pretty young woman. She was always smiling and friendly and was liked by customers and the other staff as well. It was impossible not to like Rosie Maine, and strangely, even though she was so pretty, she did not seem to cause jealousy. Now, at nineteen, Rosie still had no steady boyfriend but seemed to run a string of them, carefully balancing the attentions of several, never deliberately hurting anyone. When she went dancing in the town on a Saturday night, she was never short of partners. And now her partners were in uniform.

'I'll have a word with her,' Kate promised.

'Aw, thanks, Kate,' Danny said.

It was more than likely, Kate thought wryly, that young Rosie could teach her a thing or two instead of the other way round.

'You're getting yourself a bad name, our Rosie,' Kate said, with some of her mother's bluntness coming to the fore.

The girl fluffed her blonde hair and then smoothed down her skirt with the palms of her hands. 'Oh, Kate, I'm only having a little fun. I'm not doing any harm.'

'It's the harm that might come to you, Rosie, that we're worried about.'

Kate heard the girl draw in her breath sharply. Rosie whirled about to face her. 'We? Who's we?' Suddenly, her eyes were shining with an extra brightness.

'Danny and me.'

'Danny? Danny said something about me? What did he say?'

'He's worried about you – and the soldiers billeted at the Point.'

'Who – Taffy and Don? Don't be daft, our Kate. I'm only friendly with them. They're a nice couple of boys and a long way from home. They're lonely.'

'That's the whole point, Rosie . . .' Kate persisted.

209

'What else did Danny say about me, Kate?'

'Nothing – he just said he was worried about you. We both are.'

Rosie pulled a face and turned away. 'Well, you've no need. I can tek care of mesen, ta. Tell Danny he – he's no need to worry himself about me.'

If she hadn't known her better, Kate could have sworn there was a tearful catch in Rosie's voice.

When Kate reported her talk with Rosie to Danny, far from being reassured, he frowned. 'She's too flirty for her own good, Kate. I've tried having a word with her brothers, Mick and Jimmy, but all Mick can think about is joining up in December when he's eighteen. Not even going to wait for his call-up papers, he ain't.'

There was a deep silence between them as they walked side by side along the beach, close by the water's edge.

'Kate . . .' Danny began, stopped and let out a deep sigh as if he had been holding his breath.

She linked her arm through his. 'Come on, out with it.'

'I – I'm going to volunteer.'

'I know.' She stopped and turned to face him. Checked by her hold on him, he too stopped. Slowly they turned to face each other. She smiled at him and was amused by the look of surprise on his face.

'I guessed you would,' she whispered.

'You – you did?'

She nodded. 'After Dunkirk – I guessed . . . No, that's not quite right, I *knew* you'd want to go.'

His grin was sheepish. 'I thought you'd throw a ducky fit.'

Kate laughed softly. 'Not really, Danny, because I am going to join up too.'

They looked at each other and Danny said quietly, 'Just like our dad did the last time, eh?'

Kate smiled and pressed his arm. Rarely did they speak

of the father they shared, and yet now at this moment, it seemed right to think of him.

They walked on together in silence. A silence that was companionable and yet now held an added poignancy. Not for the first time, they were to be parted. But this time it might mean they never saw each other again. Hardly realizing it, Kate tightened her hold on Danny's arm, and he placed his hand over hers.

At last he said, 'Shall we go and join up – together?'

'Of course – don't you dare go without me!' She aimed a playful punch at his shoulder. 'Where is the nearest recruiting office, by the way? Is it Lincoln?'

'I'm not sure – I'll find out, though.'

'Well, wherever it is, we'll go together,' she said, softly now.

'I reckon it'd be only fair to get hay-making and the harvest over first. I owe the Squire that much. What d'you say?'

Kate nodded. 'Yes, you're right. It looks like being a good one and we're all short-handed as it is. We'll go after harvest.'

They walked back across the marsh and stood on the top of the western dunes to watch the sun set behind Brumbys' Farm, silhouetting the farmhouse and the buildings against the bright orange sky.

The peace of the place they both loved so much wrapped itself around them in its cloak of serenity.

It was difficult to believe at that moment that there was a war going on; that together they had already taken part in it and that in a few months' time they would be caught up in it completely.

She felt an overwhelming sadness. With a certainty she could not explain, Kate knew in that moment that their lives would never be the same again.

Twenty-One

By the end of August, even at Fleethaven Point, the newspaper headlines were beginning to dominate their lives, pushing even the long, exhausting days of harvest into second place.

'Have you seen this?' Danny waved the daily paper under Kate's nose. 'They're getting closer; bombing Midlands towns now, though they're still concentrating on the south-east.'

'Really.' Kate grabbed the paper and scanned the newsprint. She jabbed her finger at the picture of a crashed Heinkel on a British beach. 'They're not getting it all their own way, though.'

'Far from it! The RAF are really coming into their own now.' Danny rubbed his hands together gleefully. 'They reckon there are dog-fights going on over the Kentish coast most of the day.' He ran the tip of his tongue over his lips in excitement. 'I've made up my mind, Katie. It's the RAF for me an' no mistake.'

A picture of the injured airman they had pulled from the sea came into her mind. She shuddered inwardly at the thought that Danny could so easily end up like Philip Trent; baling out over enemy territory, injured and totally dependent on the good-will of complete strangers to rescue him. Resolutely, she pushed such morbid thoughts from her mind. No doubt Philip Trent was back in the air by now, maybe even involved in these dog-fights Danny spoke of. She wondered what had happened to him. Was he still alive?

She hoped so.

Aloud she said, 'Good! Then it's the WAAFs for me.'

'Well, that's it then. We've been an' gone an' done it now,' Danny said as they emerged from the recruiting centre. 'Me in the RAF and you in the WAAFs.' He grinned saucily. 'I hope they know what they're letting themselves in for.'

Playfully, she punched his arm. She felt better now that it was done. There was no going back and her family would just have to accept it.

As if reading her thoughts, Danny said, 'Still thinking about yar mam?'

Kate nodded.

'She had a rough time in the last lot,' he reminded her. 'First Ernie Harris getting killed; yar mother thought a lot about him.'

'I can't remember him. Can you?'

Danny shook his head. 'He was Grannie Harris's eldest. Joined up when he was only sixteen.'

'Me mam never talks about anything to do with the last war. It's as if she wants to forget it all.'

They sauntered back towards the railway station, walking close beside one another but not quite touching, and reminiscing about their childhood, piecing together the snippets they knew of a time they could scarcely remember, yet knowing that what had happened then had shaped their own lives.

'And now we have to do it all again,' Danny said. 'It's sad for the older folk, when you think about it. They called it the "war to end all wars" and yet here we are only twenty odd years later into another. All those families who lost folk in the last war risk losing loved ones this time around. Like Grannie Harris – she easy might, and there'll be plenty of families like her. Ya can understand 'em feeling bitter.'

It was not quite as Kate had imagined. When their papers arrived on the same day about three weeks later, she and Danny were told to report to training camps miles away from each other. Some romantic notion had led her to imagine them arriving together, being kitted out together, training together, working together.

Reality was entirely different.

As she packed a small suitcase – so different from the huge trunk that had been filled with 'three of everything' when she had been leaving home to go to school – she glanced around her bedroom. On the window-sill was the whelk shell. Smiling wryly at her own sentimental foolishness, she popped it into the corner of her suitcase and snapped the lid shut.

They were able to travel as far as Lincoln together but then they had to catch different trains, one going north, one going south.

'Seems as if they're hell-bent on separating us,' Kate grumbled.

'How – was it when ya came to leave?' Danny asked. They had said their goodbyes separately to each set of parents. 'I got the shock of me life when ya mam put her arms round me and gave me a real bear-hug. I reckon there were tears in her eyes.'

Kate stared at him. 'Really?' She shook her head wonderingly. 'She's a strange woman, my mother. I think she's fond of you, deep down, but it takes a war to make her to show it!'

'What about you?' he persisted.

Kate shrugged. 'Almost off-hand really. She just said, "Well, ya off then – tek care of ya'sen" and that was it. Of course,' she added wryly, 'she still has Lilian.'

'Oh, come on, Kate. You're not *still* jealous of that poor kid, are you?'

Kate pulled a grimace. 'No – no, I'm not. If anything, I feel sorry for her. She seems such a lonely child.'

'Not so much a child now. What is she – fourteen?'

'Almost.'

'Well, there you are then. She'll be leaving school in another year.'

Kate shook her head and, mocking her mother's voice, she said, 'Oh no. Our Lilian's clever. Our Lilian's going to university.' She smiled then and added, 'To be fair, the kid is clever and she's happy at the Grammar School – well, as happy as she'd be anywhere. She's so serious all the time – no wonder she hasn't any friends.'

There was a silence, then Kate asked softly, 'What about your mam? Was she all right when you left?'

Danny's eyes were troubled. He nodded, 'She was very brave, but I suppose it must bring back a lot of memories of the last time – seeing the young men off to war, not knowing if they'd ever come back.' He looked at her steadily. 'And young women too, this time. Oh, Katie, do be careful, won't you?'

She nodded. 'You, too, Danny. You too,' she whispered.

There was half an hour before the train Kate had to catch left. In the café they sat across the table from each other, hardly speaking. They'd said everything and yet they'd said nothing. There was so much they could say, so much that still lay between them.

They sat together in an oasis of silence while all around them was the bustle of imminent departure. Most of the men were in uniform, while their families clustered around them; proud, tearful, apprehensive.

They heard the sound of a train approaching the station.

'Come on,' Danny said, getting up. 'That'll be yours.'

Now there was no time left to say anything and suddenly there was so much to say.

'I had so hoped we'd be on the same camp,' She raised her voice to him as they weaved their way through the crowded platform.

'We might be – eventually. They shift people about quite a bit and I think you can apply for – what do they call it – remustering, I think it is. Here, let me put those on the rack for you.'

'What on earth is remustering?' she asked as he heaved her baggage up and then stepped off the train again. They stood on the platform, close but not touching, facing each other.

'It's when you apply to go into a new type of job.'

'You'll write?' Kate said with sudden urgency.

Danny smiled lopsidedly. 'I aren't much of a letter-writer, Katie.'

'That doesn't matter. I just want to hear from you some-times; just to know you're ... safe.'

He nodded. 'All right.'

'And when you get a posting, be sure to let me have your new address?'

Again he nodded.

'And we could try to get leave at the same time, so we can be at home together.' She was babbling now, desperate to put off the moment of parting.

'That might be difficult.'

'Oh, but we could try. Promise me you'll try, Danny ...?' The shrill whistle sounded and doors banged. 'Oh no, not yet ...'

216

'You must get on the train, Katie . . .'

Then suddenly she was in his arms, being held in a fierce hug. 'Katie – take care,' he whispered huskily against her hair. Then he released her suddenly and pushed her towards the train.

Tears blurred her vision so that she stumbled as she stepped into the carriage. The door slammed behind her and by the time she had wrenched open the window, the train was already moving.

She waved frantically, leaning out of the window until billowing smoke hid him from her view.

The moment she entered the sleeping-quarters at the recruitment depot, time seemed to tilt. Kate shuddered. For a moment it was like catapulting back in time into the cheerless dormitory at the boarding school. But then the image faded, for coming towards her, almost bouncing towards her would have been a more apt description, was a plump, jolly-faced girl with short brown hair and laughing hazel eyes.

'Hello, come on in and make yourself at home. We've all just arrived today, so we're still getting to know one another.' Like Kate they were all still in civvies, some dressed in high-heeled shoes and summer dresses, their hair carefully curled, whilst others wore plain, flat-heeled shoes and skirts and cardigans.

'I'm Mavis Nuttall,' the friendly girl was saying, 'and this is Jill Porter, but that's as far as I go, I'm afraid . . .'

The faces in front of her began to introduce themselves one by one but there were so many that after the first few, Kate gave up trying to remember them and merely smiled and nodded.

'What's yours?' asked Mavis.

'Kate. Kate Hilton.'

'You can have this bed between me and Mavis,' Jill offered.

'Shall we all leave our stuff here and go in search of food?' Mavis suggested. 'My stomach says it's tea-time!'

There was general laughter and agreement and a sudden flurry of activity as everyone prepared to leave.

'We'll get settled in later,' Mavis promised cheerily. 'I hear they're pretty strict on tidiness.' She pulled a face. 'And I'm the world's worst. Me mother says my bedroom's like a pig-sty.'

At the mention of pig-sties, Kate felt a sudden surge of longing for home sweep through her. The farm, the Point and all the people there. And Danny – especially Danny. Where was he now, she wondered? What was he doing? Was he feeling as lost and mesmerized by everything as she was at this moment?

The first day seemed to be taken up with various intelligence tests.

'That'll be me on my way out before I've been in a day,' Mavis moaned. 'It's like being back at school.'

Inwardly, Kate shuddered, although she thought she had coped quite well with the tests.

The following day, when they were given their six-digit number, poor Mavis was flustered again. 'Thick as pea soup, me. I'll never remember this.'

Kate laughed. 'Well, you'll have to, else evidently you'll get nothing. No pay, no leave and – no food! You know what the sergeant said – your number's more important than your *name* now.'

'I know,' her new friend wailed, and bent her head over the piece of paper with her number written on it.

The next few days passed in a blur. Form-filling, medical

checks and inoculations, drill and uniform issue. Having queued for their kit of about sixty different items, they staggered back to their quarters.

'Feels like a hundred and sixty when you try to carry it all,' Mavis laughed as she dumped it on her bed and began to sort through it. 'How are we supposed to get all this stuff in this kit-bag?'

'Wear most of it, probably,' Kate suggested.

Mavis gave a shriek of laughter and held up a large pair of navy-blue knickers. 'Have you seen these? Passion-killers, if ever I saw 'em. My *gran* wouldn't be seen dead in a pair like this!'

Kate giggled. 'We'd call them "apple-catchers".'

Mavis blinked. 'Eh?'

Kate sat on the side of the bed and rocked with laughter. 'A pair like that could hold quite a lot . . .'

Puzzled, Mavis looked at the item of underwear again and then, understanding, 'You mean when you're apple-*scrumping*. I've never heard that one before. I see what you mean.' She gave another hoot of laughter. 'I don't reckon you could run very fast with the farmer after you and these full of apples.'

'What on earth are you two laughing about? Share the joke,' Jill called.

In moments, all the girls in the room were convulsed in laughter and, minutes later when their NCO came to give them a demonstration as to how to make their beds in the required manner and how to lay out their kit for inspection, there were still stifled giggles when it came to the folding and laying out of a particular garment!

'Kit inspection first thing tomorrow morning,' the NCO said as she left the room.

Kate surveyed her belongings on her bed. 'What did she say we have to do with our civvies, Mavis?'

219

Her friend was again studying the scrap of paper in her hand. ' . . . Six-five-nine. Er – parcel 'em up to be sent home.'

'Oh yes.' Kate began to fold her clothes. 'Can you remember how to lay out all this kit? I've forgotten what she said already.'

' . . . Five-nine. Nope. Jill's good at that,' Mavis said, nodding towards the girl bending over the bed on the other side of Kate. 'She's promised to go through it again with me tonight.'

'Great! Can I watch too?'

' . . . nine. Got it! At least – I think I have. Yeah, 'course you can. Come on, let go and find the mess.'

'Oh my,' Kate teased, 'we're learning all the names, even if we can't memorize our number!'

Mavis grinned good-naturedly. 'Anything to do with food, Kate, and I can be absolutely *relied* upon to remember it! Come on . . .'

Jill stood at the end of Kate's bed, scrutinizing the kit laid out on it. 'I should refold all your sheets and blankets for a start – they're not very neat. Your greatcoat goes on top of them and your cap on top of that.' She took a side-step and stood at the foot of Mavis's bed. 'Shoes go on the front row – soles uppermost.'

'Oh, I'll never get the hang of it,' Mavis muttered.

'Don't worry, Mave,' Jill said cheerfully, 'neither will Kate by the way she's juggling with her irons and toothbrush. Other way round, Kate. That's it. Where's your button stick? Oh, there it is. It should be on that same row.'

'Seems okay now,' Jill said when the two girls had reshuffled everything to her direction. 'Can you both remember it for tomorrow morning?'

Mavis sighed. 'Not a chance. What about you, Kate?'

'I can remember all the main items, it's the little fiddly things I can't remember where they go.'

'Well, if we do okay with the inspection we get the rest of the morning off,' Jill told them and then spoilt the promise of some free time by adding, 'to finish marking *every* item of kit!'

There were groans all round. 'How do you know all about the lay-out then?' Mavis asked. 'Not that I'm not jolly thankful you do,' she added, anxious not to offend.

Jill shrugged. 'Older brother in the RAF,' she explained. 'He used to practise when he came home. I used to watch him and when the NCO was showing us earlier – well, it was a bit different naturally, but the basic idea seems to be the same.'

'Right,' Mavis said, shuffling all her items of kit into a big heap at the end of her bed. 'Now I'll have a go on my own.'

She began to lay everything out on the bed once more, from the sheets, blankets and bolster at the head of the bed, right down to the shoes – 'Soles uppermost,' Mavis muttered as she worked – at the foot.

Two hours later, just before lights out, Kate and even Mavis could finally lay out their kit perfectly.

After the first three days, it all seemed to get easier. The girls were so friendly; they had so much to talk about because they all came from different places. It was nothing like that awful school, Kate thought. How could she have even thought it the same?

There had been only one occasion when she had been sharply reminded of Miss Denham. The NCO had suddenly said one day, 'Hilton, your hair is too long . . .'

Kate had drawn in her breath sharply and held it, waiting

for the dreadful sound of snipping scissors being brandished. She almost winced in anticipation.

'But as long as you tie it back and keep it firmly under your cap . . .'

Kate let out her breath with relief. School, and all its horrors, faded once more.

On the sixth morning, Mavis, who always seemed to be first with news of any sort, burst into the hut, the buttons on her jacket heaving up and down in her breathlessness. 'Guess where we're all going?'

The other girls turned blank expressions towards her.

'Home,' said one girl with a heartfelt sigh.

'Abroad,' suggested another hopefully.

'Don't be daft – we're not trained yet.'

'My feet think they've had quite enough training,' muttered someone else.

'No idea,' Jill smiled, sensing Mavis's desire to be the bearer of what looked like good news. 'You tell us, Mave.'

'Harrogate!'

'Harrogate?' chorused a dozen voices.

'Why?'

'Whatever for?'

'To finish our training. It seems this recruitment camp is bursting at the seams and we're being shipped off to Harrogate.'

'Wonderful!' said a voice heavy with sarcasm. 'It's a spa town, for heaven's sakes. All the smart folks go there. There are some bee-oo-tiful hotels. Can you imagine us lot red-faced and sweating running along the streets of Harrogate in our passion-killers and gym-shoes?'

'Well, there's a war on,' Mavis countered stoutly. 'They'll have to put up with us.'

'Old biddies tut-tutting and dirty old men leering at us in our WAAF issue underwear.'

'It won't be like that, w-will it?' one girl asked nervously.

'You'll see,' said Winifred, the self-appointed Job's comforter.

It wasn't so bad after all, Kate thought. It was quite a laugh doing drill in the Valley Gardens and learning to march in neat formation up one of the steepest hills. It reminded her of the hill in Lincoln, she mused, leading up to the cathedral. She had *run* up that one, and now, out of all of them, only Kate Hilton arrived at the top with enough breath to say, 'Race you back to the billet . . .'

She and Mavis were lucky in their landlady, who fussed over them like a mother hen. Others could be a bit grim, from the accounts of some of the girls.

Kate smiled as she thought of Winifred's dire warnings. They did have to run along the streets jacketless and in gym-shoes with their lisle stockings rolled down to the ankles, and it caused a bit of a stir among the locals, but their waving was friendly and the children running alongside were joining in rather than mocking.

But on a Sunday, for Church Parade, well, there was a real sense of pride in being seen marching smartly along the wide roads, each wing vying with the others to be the best turned out.

'*It's all lectures, drill and PT,*' Kate wrote in her letter to Danny. '*Then more lectures, drill and PT. Sometimes there's gas mask drill, clothing parades and then more lectures, PT and more drill! Is it the same for you?*' she wanted to know.

'*Yesterday we had a second inoculation and more than half the girls fainted. I have to admit I felt a bit sick but managed not to be.*' Thank goodness, she thought to herself as she wrote the words. She didn't want to give anyone the chance to bestow that awful nickname on her again.

A few days before they were due to leave Harrogate, Kate received a much-delayed letter from home. It was from her stepfather telling her that his father, the kindly Mr Godfrey, had died suddenly in his sleep. *'The funeral is in Lincoln on Friday. Would you be able to come . . .?'* Oh, poor Mrs Godfrey – and Peggy! Her heart went out to them. Friday, her stepfather wrote. Today was Thursday. Could she . . .? She turned the letter over again to read the date at the top and saw that it was dated over ten days earlier. The funeral must have taken place on the previous Friday. Kate immediately sat down to write letters to her stepfather and to Mrs Godfrey and Peggy. Then, with an hour of free time left before tea, she went out to post them.

Needing to be alone, she walked to the edge of the town overlooking the Stray, a vast expanse of smooth parkland. She missed the beach and the sea but the expanse of green before her was a comfort. She sat down on the grass, her chin resting on her knees drawn up to her chest, her arms wrapped around her legs, and watched two children running and chasing each other. They reminded her sharply of herself and Danny at the same age.

The news in her stepfather's letter had saddened her, and suddenly she felt incredibly homesick. It washed over her in waves. She longed for the bite of the east wind off the North Sea, the flat landscape behind, the cries of gulls overhead. Back home they'd be threshing now; the scene was so vivid she could almost smell the dusty chaff and hear the steady throb of the steam engine. Her stepfather would be finding solace up to his elbows in oil and grease, whilst her mother would be teasing him gently, helping to ease his recent loss; 'Great noisy, lumbering thing!' she'd be saying of the engines Jonathan loved.

Oh, why aren't I there, Kate thought suddenly, with Danny feeding the drum and me holding the sacks ready at the other end for the corn . . . ?'

She heard footsteps close by and Mavis's cheerful voice. 'There you are.'

Kate sighed, her moment of solitude – so hard to snatch these days – gone. She stood up, shook the bits of grass from her skirt and smiled at Mavis coming towards her. The plump girl was so extrovert and friendly, never taking offence. It was impossible to feel irritated with Mavis for many minutes.

She linked her arm through Kate's as they walked back towards the town. 'Pay Parade tomorrow and Posting Parade the day after. What have you put in for?'

'Motor Transport.' Kate grinned inwardly remembering her tongue-in-cheek lie when she had been asked if she could drive, especially recalling that the only time she had been behind a wheel she had ended up driving the Squire's motor car into the dyke and had nearly cost Danny his job.

'What about you?'

'R/T operator on an operational station,' the girl replied promptly.

Kate nodded. 'You'll be good at that. A friendly voice over the airwaves is just what the pilots need when they're up there.'

The two friends were lucky; they were posted for further training to the same place, but they had to part from all the other girls they had come to know.

'We might never see any of them again, you know,' Mavis said, unusually sober as they stood together in the train. It was crowded with soldiers and the carriages were stuffy and smoke-filled. The two girls didn't even bother to try to find a seat.

Kate said nothing. Her thoughts were once more with Danny. With all this moving about to different camps to complete her training, she had heard nothing from him, and even anxious letters home to Beth Eland had brought no reply.

The weeks that followed were exhausting but Kate enjoyed the intensive Motor Transport training. She found the lessons in the mornings when they had to learn theory hard – it reminded her too much of school; but in the practical sessions – the driving, the maintenance work and even learning to do minor repairs – Kate was in her element. She became the instructor's star pupil and passed out with the highest marks in all the practical tests. During one of the final tests – driving a convoy at night through the country side where the signposts had been removed and with headlamps dimmed to only a slit of light – Kate was placed at the head of the column of huge lorries.

'You've got three hours,' their instructor told her. 'If you're not back to camp by dawn, we'll send out a spotter plane!' He was grinning as he said it and she knew he was pinning his hopes, and possibly his reputation, on his recruits being first back to the camp. 'Don't forget, only you and the last vehicle have their lights on, everyone else follows the diff-light.'

Kate nodded. At the rear of the vehicles a small light had been fitted to shine down on to the white-painted differential. All the following vehicles would follow her lead. If she went wrong . . .

'Don't forget – I'm relying on you.'

Kate glanced at the clear night sky. She was in luck! Every star shone bright and true for her. Smiling, she revved the noisy engine and pressed her foot down on to the clutch-pedal. She had memorized the route from the map and she set off at a steady speed, glancing frequently into the wing mirror to check that the following vehicles were still there.

In the darkness, she grinned to herself. Oh, Danny, I wish you could see me now driving this great lorry. I wouldn't drive the Squire's new motor into the dyke now!

Two hours and forty-three minutes later, Kate pulled up at the guard-house, every lorry in her convoy following suit.

'Halt! Who goes there?' came the routine inquiry.

'WAAF.' Kate smiled in the darkness.

'Good Lord!' The guard on duty peered at her. 'You back already? We didn't expect you back till first light.' He grinned, stood back and waved them all through. As Kate pulled to a halt in the MT yard, the instructor appeared as she jumped down from the cab.

'Well done! You're first back.' He said no more but the man who had shouted at them, bullied them, despaired of them over the past few weeks, finally put his hand on her shoulder and squeezed it.

That was better than a medal, Kate thought. Later she was to find that the instructor had specially recommended her for promotion and she was immediately upgraded to Aircraftswoman First Class.

Mavis was not so fortunate.

'They keep telling me that I'm too friendly over the radio. That I get too excited when there's a flap on,' she moaned to Kate. 'They say I've got to be calm and efficient at all times. I know they're right. A pilot in trouble doesn't want to hear some hysterical female on the other end of his radio link . . .' She sighed. 'But it's awfully difficult not to yell at a pilot to get out of his burning aircraft instead of trying to find out objectively if it's feasible for him to bring it in to land.'

'You'll get the hang of it, Mave,' Kate encouraged. 'I still think you're just the right sort of person. It's no good having some cold fish who doesn't give a damn.'

'Mmm,' Mavis said doubtfully.

But in the end, Mavis too passed out, not quite at the top of the class like Kate, but well enough to make her ecstatic at becoming a fully-fledged Aircraftswoman Second Class.

'Now keep calm,' Kate teased her. 'You know what they told you.'

'I know, but it's the first time I've passed *anything*!'

'Me too. First time I've ever been good at anything – except perhaps sewing.'

'Sewing? Crikey – not much difference, is there?' Mavis laughed.

Kate laughed too and spread her hands, looking down at them. 'I suppose I'm just practical,' she murmured, 'rather than brainy.' Unbidden, into her mind came a picture of her studious young sister, poring over her school books.

When they heard their postings, she and Mavis were still together.

'Oh, isn't that wonderful? By the way, where is Suddaby? I've never heard of it, have you?'

Kate nodded. 'It's where me grandad used to live before he came to live with us.'

'Really? Evidently it's a new station – an operational bomber station – just being built. Oh, I can't wait! We'll be there from the beginning.' Mavis rubbed her hands together, her face wreathed in smiles. 'Oh, isn't it exciting? Where's the nearest hot spot for night life there, then?'

Kate grinned. 'Suddaby is out in the wilds, miles from anywhere with only birds and the cattle in the fields for company.'

Her friend's face was a picture until she spotted Kate's mischievous smile. 'Oh, you, you're teasing me.'

'Well, a bit maybe. There are one or two market towns within easy reach, but it isn't near a big city.'

'Is it near where you live?'

'Yes, it's about thirteen miles inland from the sea.'

'Oh goody, I've never seen the sea.'

Now it was Kate's turn for her face to register surprise. 'Never seen the sea! You're joking.'

'Nope. I was born, brought up and lived all my life in Leicester. We never had holidays when I was a kid.' Her merry face brightened. 'Why do you think I joined the WAAFs? Thought I'd see the world.'

Kate smiled ruefully on her friend's behalf. 'And the nearest you get is Lincolnshire!'

Mavis shrugged philosophically. 'I don't mind. I'm loving every minute.' She paused, then asked again, 'Well, where is the nearest big city, then?'

'Lincoln,' Kate said quietly and saw Mavis looking at her quizzically.

'You don't look very pleased,' Mavis said, linking her arm through Kate's and pulling her away from the excited chatter of the other girls comparing their postings. 'I'd have thought you'd have been pleased if it's nearer your home.'

Kate made an effort to smile. There were so many memories attached to that city, Kate thought; her childhood and then later, when she and Danny . . . Her mind shied away from that dreadful time. 'Just – a few ghosts, Mave,' she murmured.

'Oh, we'll lay those to rest good and proper, Kate, when we get whooping it up in the town. Poor old Lincoln won't know what's hit it when we get there! You mark my words.'

'See you in Suddaby in a week's time, then,' Mavis was shouting, leaning precariously out of the train as it began to move. A cloud of smoke enveloped her and she was obliged to draw her head into the carriage.

Kate smiled. What a character! She'd been lucky to pal up with Mavis, she thought, as she heaved her kit-bag on to her back and made for another platform to catch her connection to Lynthorpe.

Seven whole days, she thought, with Christmas in the middle. And Danny is sure to be getting leave at the same time, she told herself.

She couldn't wait to get home to see him.

Twenty-Two

'He's not here, lovey.'

'Not – not here? But – he – he must be. He must be getting leave at the end of his training like me, surely? And it's Christmas too!'

Sadly, Beth shook her head as she pulled open the back door wider, silently inviting Kate in. Although it was warm in the kitchen, Kate pushed her hands deeper still into the pockets of her greatcoat, hunching her shoulders.

Suddenly, she felt very cold.

The train journey home had seemed interminable. Standing on draughty platforms, waiting for connections, and then the train had chugged along at what seemed to Kate an inordinately slow pace.

And now Danny was not here.

'Do you know when he's coming?'

Beth shook her head, laying out cups on the table and mashing a pot of tea. 'All I know is he's having extra training so he can fly.'

'Fly! Oh no. He's not going to be a pilot, is he?'

A frown creased Beth's brow. 'No – but he's going to be part of the crew on – on bombers. He said he was going to be – now, what was it? "A tail-end Charlie", that was it.'

Kate sat down suddenly as her legs gave way. 'A rear-gunner – and on bombers!' Kate whispered, then her voice rose shrilly. 'He – he'll be flying over enemy territory. He'll – he'll . . .'

The sight of Beth's white face stilled Kate's outburst and she swallowed hard. She stood up suddenly and went to the older woman, putting her arms about her. Beth laid her head against Kate's shoulder. 'Oh, Kate, I couldn't bear it if – if . . .'

The two women clung together in their mutual fear for Danny's safety.

A little later when she left the Elands' cottage, Kate felt too restless to return home. She set off across the marsh towards the Spit, walking the full length of the promontory of land. She stood at its tip, letting her gaze travel around the expanse of water. The wind whipped across the sea, making the waves choppy, the surface like a huge sheet of corrugated iron. It was grey and cold and so lonely, especially without Danny.

She turned away and retraced her steps towards the beach, wanting to find their hollow in the dunes. But her path was barred by coils of barbed wire, bouncing and rocking in the breeze, stretching along the edge of the dunes. And a huge notice in red lettering proclaimed 'DANGER – MINES'. Kate gasped. They'd blocked off the beach and mined the sand-dunes too.

Thinking back longingly to the days when she and Danny had run barefoot across the smooth, unspoilt sands, for the first time she felt a spurt of hatred for this war.

Close by the concrete pillbox which the army had built for their observers stationed at the Point, she was about to turn away when she heard the unexpected sound of girlish giggles.

Kate's mouth set in a grim line as she marched towards the entrance and peered into the gloomy interior. On a groundsheet, wrapped together in a passionate embrace, were a young man in khaki army uniform and a girl with blonde hair and shapely legs.

'Rosie!' Kate's startled gasp escaped her lips before she could prevent it.

The couple shot apart, the girl pulling down her dress and scrambling to her feet.

Kate turned and stumbled away through the tufts of thick grass.

'Kate! Kate! Wait – please!' There was such desperation in Rosie's voice that Kate stopped. She did not turn around but stood still until Rosie reached her.

Grasping Kate's arm, Rosie begged, 'Please don't tell me dad, Katie. He'd kill me. But it's not what you think. Honest. It's – it's only a bit of fun.'

'It looked like it!' Kate snorted. 'Danny was right about you . . .'

Rosie's eyes widened and in them now was a look of sheer terror. 'Danny? Oh, no – please don't tell Danny. *Please*, Kate. I couldn't bear it if he – if he . . .'

'If he – what?' Kate asked quietly.

Rosie's gaze fell away and her grasp on Kate's arm loosened. 'Nothing. I just don't want you to tell – anyone.'

Kate regarded her thoughtfully. That was understandable she thought reasonably. Yet the thought of Danny knowing of her romping in the sand-dunes had positively terrified Rosie. Kate sighed. 'All right, I won't tell anyone, but as long as you promise me you'll be careful. These lads are lonely and a long way from home, Rosie. They – they might want too much from a pretty girl like you.'

'It's only a kiss and a cuddle, Katie, honest,' Rosie promised.

'Well – just mind it is.'

As she turned away and left Rosie to go back to her young man, Kate couldn't help thinking to herself, 'I sound just like my mother!'

'Please, Kate,' Rosie's plea followed her. 'Please don't tell Danny.'

Kate tried to put on a brave front over Christmas for the sake of her family. They were all so pleased to see her – even Lilian hugged her enthusiastically when she opened the page-to-a-day diary Kate had given her as a Christmas gift.

'It's lovely, Kate. I always keep a diary and never have enough room to write everything in those little ones . . .'

Kate smiled kindly at her sister; the round, childish glasses gave the young girl an owlish look. Her straight hair was cut short to just below her ears. Lilian would have been the perfect pupil for Miss Denham. Kate couldn't imagine what Lilian could possibly have to write about that would fill half a page, let alone a whole one. Overcome with a feeling of pity for the lonely young girl, Kate gave her a swift hug.

'We've invited the two Land Army girls for Christmas dinner,' Esther told Kate. 'Poor things! They're sisters – from Coventry.'

'Oh heck!' Kate said at once, staring at her mother, the unspoken question in her eyes.

Her mother nodded. 'Yes, their home was bombed in that awful raid in November. Their parents were safe, thank God, but the lasses have no home to go back to.'

'How awful!' Kate said. 'Where are they billeted?'

'At the Grange. The Squire's turned it over for the duration. He's taken a small house in the town.' She shook her head, murmuring. 'Poor old Squire – he's not well.'

'Do the girls help here?'

Her mother's impish smile was back. 'Oh, yes. They're surprisingly good too – for townies.'

Kate hid her smile at her mother's innocent tone of condescension.

234

'But I have to watch 'em with ya dad,' Esther added and touched her husband's cheek tenderly.

Kate exchanged an amused glance with her stepfather. As if the idea would even cross his mind, she thought.

So Christmas passed pleasantly enough, but it was not the same without Danny.

Her pen was poised above the white page of the writing pad. Should she tell Danny about Rosie? Kate bit her lip with indecision and then decided to keep her promise to the girl. She sighed. She just hoped young Rosie did know what she was doing else it could all end in tears, as Grannie Harris was fond of saying.

She was sitting in front of the window in the sitting room, her legs curled up in a chair, the writing pad resting on her knee. From time to time she paused, looking up to stare out of the window across the smooth fields towards the Grange, the straight brown furrows white-tipped with the morning frost. In an hour's time, her stepfather would take her to Suddaby in the pony and trap.

'Who needs petrol?' her mother had snorted in contempt, when the rationing had hit so many folks' mode of transport. Jonathan, whose love for motors and engines seemed never to be catered for, at least on Brumbys' Farm, had winked at Kate who had smiled back sympathetically.

A shadow fell across the page of her half-written letter and she looked up to see her grandfather.

'Writing to Danny, lass?' he asked without preamble, and eased his stiff limbs down to sit in the chair beside her. 'You leaving this morning?'

She nodded.

'Ah've got you a little something extra to what I gave ya on Christmas Day, lass,' he said and dropped a package into her lap. 'I expect ya'll be making a lot of new friends and maybe seeing new places and I thought this might come in handy.'

Carefully, Kate unwrapped the square-shaped parcel. It was a Box Brownie camera. 'Oh, Grandad, that's a lovely present. And yes, it will be very nice to have. You make friends with people and then get posted to different places and maybe never see them again.'

Will Benson sniffed. 'That's what Ah thought. Ah got 'em at the shop to put a film in it, lass, so if ya wanted to take a few pictures 'afore ya leave ... And Ah'd like to take one of you in yar smart uniform. Ya'd send it back to me when ya get it developed, would ya?'

'Of course. Thank you, Grandad.' She leaned forward and planted a kiss on his stubbly face.

He sniffed and grunted with embarrassment. Changing the subject, he asked again. 'A' ya writing to Danny?'

'Yes – just to let him know my new address. I haven't heard from him in ages. I expect it's all this moving about. Maybe his letters have got lost. Maybe one day I'll get a bundle arrive all together.'

'Kate . . .' the old man began, paused, and then continued haltingly. 'Katie, it's time to – to let go, lass.'

She avoided looking at him. 'What – what do you mean, Grandad?' The question was unnecessary. In her heart she knew what he meant only too well.

'Don't live ya life hankering after summat – or rather someone – ya can never have.'

'I'm not,' she snapped, and then, feeling guilty for her sharpness, put her hand on his arm. 'Truly I'm not. We're – we're . . .' She took a deep shuddering breath and said the words she had always found so difficult to voice: 'Brother and sister. We know we are. It's just that . . .'

Now she could not put their feelings into words. How

could she explain to her grandfather the love which still lay between her and Danny, a love which she believed would never go away or even be replaced?

Maybe the old man understood, at least in part, for he covered her hand with his wrinkled one. 'I know, lass, I know. But mebbe ya've the chance now to meet other fellers. It's time you were married and settled down and having bairns.'

'Yes, Grandad,' she said dutifully, and forced a smile on to her mouth. She knew her grandfather meant well, but she could not imagine meeting anyone who could take Danny's place in her heart. Not ever.

'ACW Hilton. Ah yes, you're the new driver for the CO, aren't you?'

Kate gasped in surprise. The officer looked up. 'Well? Doesn't that suit?' There was sarcasm in the woman's tone that told Kate immediately that whatever she felt, it would have to suit.

'Oh yes, Ma'am. It – it was just a surprise, that's all. I hadn't been told. I mean—' She floundered, feeling herself going red. 'I mean, I knew I'd be in Motor Transport but I didn't know exactly what I'd be doing.'

'You'll still be in the MT Section and will have to carry out other duties when the CO doesn't need you. The officer in charge of the MT Section is Flying Officer Cooper, but you'll take your day-to-day orders from Flight Sergeant Martin. It seems, however,' the officer added drily, 'that our new Commanding Officer has asked especially for your services.'

'Oh!' This was an even bigger surprise. She could not imagine why.

The officer was looking at her keenly. 'It's a very good

posting, particularly for a new recruit. Just mind you are up to it.'

Kate saluted smartly, some of her confidence returning. 'I'll do my best, Ma'am.'

She was dismissed.

As she left the orderly room, Kate stood for a moment to get her bearings. The airfield was in fact divided by the main road; on one side were all the quarters for the officers and airmen – and the WAAFs – and the administration offices were also sited there. On the opposite side, spread out before her, flat and windswept, was the operational site; the runways, the hangars and control tower and all sorts of buildings whose use Kate had yet to learn.

She drew in a deep breath and held it, revelling in the feel of the wind upon her face and the panorama before her. A small smile curved her mouth as she looked about her. She was so happy to be back in her home county. Before her, beyond the perimeter of the airfield, lay the gently rolling fields of the Wolds. Nearer, she watched a tractor, driven by a WAAF, hauling a bomb-train from the ammunitions dump towards the waiting aircraft. That was a job she might have done. But it seemed as if her new Station Commander had other plans. Now, her main duty would be to familiarize herself with the MT yard and the CO's staff car in particular. Crossing her fingers that it would be a Humber Super Snipe, the same type on which she had done her training, she went in search of the MT Section office.

Flight Sergeant Martin was a kindly, fatherly figure, affectionately known by all in the section as 'Chiefy'. He was bald, apart from tufts of grey, bushy hair which sprouted on either side of his head just above his ears. His eyes twinkled at her from behind round, steel-rimmed spectacles. 'CO wants to see you the minute you arrive. Leave your gear here . . .' He took her outside and pointed in the direction of the building which housed the CO's office. 'Now, you be careful. He's a handsome devil, if ever I saw one,' Chiefy chuckled, a deep, rumbling sound from his round belly.

Waiting in the outer office for her interview with the CO, Kate's confidence ebbed away again and her stomach was churning with nervousness. She was uncomfortably aware of the eyes of the Adjutant upon her.

Then for some reason she suddenly thought about her mother. A picture of Esther Godfrey was in her mind's eye, standing with hands on hips, feet planted firmly a little apart, her strong jawline jutting out resolutely. A small smile twitched at Kate's mouth. No one, as far as she could remember, had ever intimidated her mother; not the Squire, not a headmistress, not authority of any kind. And were she in Kate's place at this very moment, the man beyond that door would hold no fears for Esther Godfrey either. Some of the fluttering under Kate's ribs settled a little.

Something buzzed on the man's desk and he lifted a telephone receiver and listened. 'Sir,' was all he said into the instrument. Replacing the receiver, he looked up at Kate. 'You may go in now.'

Kate stood and marched through the door. As it closed behind her she came to attention in front of the CO's desk and rattled out her rank, name and number.

Then her hand fell away from her forehead in an untidy end to her salute and her lips parted in a gasp.

She was staring straight into the blue eyes of Philip Trent.

Having returned her salute, he at once seemed to relax and become completely 'unofficial'. He came round the desk and held out both his hands to her.

239

'Kate – it's so good to see you again. You look wonderful.'

Hesitating only a moment, but then taking the lead from him, she smiled warmly. 'And you. How are you? How's your arm?'

'Fine. It wasn't broken, thank goodness, only dislocated and a small flesh wound just here.' He indicated a point just below his collarbone. 'It's healed well now.'

They stared at each other, smiling, genuinely pleased to be meeting again.

'Well, this is a coincidence,' she said.

Philip's smile broadened and he shook his head. 'No coincidence, Kate.'

A slight frown furrowed her forehead. 'Why? What do you mean?'

'Do sit down.' He indicated a wooden chair in front of his desk. 'I'll get us some tea.' He leaned forward conspiratorially. 'If anyone asks, we're discussing details of your job as my driver.'

He went towards the door, opened it, issued orders for two teas, closed the door and returned to his desk. Sitting behind it, he smiled across at her again. 'I'd better look all official when the corporal comes in with the tea. Actually, joking apart, we will have to discuss your – er – position as my driver. But first, I want to catch up on what's been happening to you since we last met.'

They looked at each other, remembering Dunkirk, and their faces sobered. 'I'm so glad you're safe,' he said softly. His gaze held hers and for a long moment they just sat staring at each other. Then Philip Trent cleared his throat and seemed to shake himself. His glance fell away and he shuffled some papers on his desk in front of him. 'How's Danny?' he asked softly.

'Fine. He's joined the RAF.'

Philip nodded. 'I know.'

240

'You do?' This was getting more mysterious by the minute.

'I can't believe this is happening.' She shook her head in disbelief. 'What did you mean when you said it wasn't a coincidence?'

He was smiling again, though looking a little sheepish.

'When we get to this exalted position,' he cleared his throat as if poking gentle fun at himself. On looking more carefully, she could see by the four half-inch stripes on his sleeve that he was now a Group Captain. 'It does have its perks,' he was saying. 'We have colleagues in all sorts of posts. And if necessary, we can pull rank to get information.'

Kate still looked puzzled.

'I was pretty sure you – and Danny – would join up after Dunkirk. Not only did I find out that you had, but also where you went for your training and that you'd ended up as an MT driver *and* with a special recommendation for promotion from your instructor,' he added, teasing gently. 'So – I made the right contacts and got you posted here as my personal driver.'

Kate gasped aloud. 'Goodness. Just like that.'

He pulled a face. 'Not really. I had to do a lot of string-pulling. But it worked.' His face clouded momentarily and he leaned towards her. 'You don't – mind?' he asked, suddenly boyish in his anxiety.

Before she could answer, there was a knock at the door and a corporal entered carrying a tray with two cups of tea on it, a small milk jug and sugar bowl. He set it down on the desk and retreated.

The very new station commander was still looking anxiously at his even newer driver. 'Do you mind?' he repeated the moment the door had closed behind the corporal.

'Of course not,' Kate reassured him swiftly. 'I'm really very grateful.' She smiled mischievously as she added, 'I've

already been told by a WAAF officer that it is a very important posting and she hopes I'm up to it!'

Now he laughed aloud as he handed her a cup of tea.
'Oh, you'll be up to it all right, Kate Hilton. There's no
doubt about that, and I'm recommending you be made up
to Leading Aircraftswoman with immediate effect.' His smile
broadened. 'Promotion can come amazingly quickly
sometimes!'

'Thank you,' she whispered, touched by his faith in her.

Then his face sobered. 'There is just something we must
get straight, though . . .'

Kate nodded and, trying to lessen any embarrassment he
might feel considering the debt of gratitude he owed her, she
said, 'I know – this is the last time we can talk like this. In
future we must be – well – official.'

A look of surprise flitted across his face. 'Oh, I hope not,
Kate. No, what I was going to say was that on duty and in
front of others, yes, we must be "official" as you put it.' The
smile lit his face again, 'But I hope that in private we can
still continue to be friends.'

'Well, if you're sure it won't compromise your position in
any way.'

'It won't trouble me. After all,' he puffed out his chest
with mock pride, '*I* am the new Station Commander. My
word is law!'

Kate laughed, but he said quietly and more seriously now,
'No, Kate, all joking apart, it's you who could be compro-
mised, and I wouldn't want that.'

He stood up and Kate followed suit, placing her empty
cup back on the tray. He was moving towards the door and
opening it for her. 'And this is the last time I'll be able
do this for you. I'm afraid you'll have to open it for me
in future.'

She smiled and then, deliberately adopting a bland

expression before leaving his office, she saluted smartly and said, 'Sir!'

Kate threw her kit-bag on to the end bed nearest the big grey stove – Mavis already having laid claim to the bed opposite – and surveyed the rest of the hut. 'Did you have a good Christmas, Mave? There doesn't seem to be many here yet.'

There appeared to be only three other beds occupied besides the one she was now claiming.

'Yes, thanks. There's more arriving later today.' Mavis bounced down on the unoccupied bed next to Kate and lay back with her hands behind her head. 'Two more R/T operators and a meteorologist. You and me are lucky to know each other. I guess for a while we shan't know anyone else. They'll be coming from all over.'

'Mmm,' Kate agreed absently, and sighed. All she hoped was that her recent letter to Danny got delivered to him all right and that he knew where she was. Wouldn't he be surprised that she'd met up again with Philip Trent and that from now on she'd be seeing him every day? She must write at once and tell him . . .

Almost as if reading her thoughts, Mavis said, 'I hear you're the envy of the camp. Landing a job as driver to the dishy CO. Lucky old you!'

Kate just smiled.

'Mind you,' Mavis went on, 'there's a rather nice Flight Sergeant in the Ops Room . . .'

'Oh, Mavis, you're impossible!'

Kate sat down on her bed and pulled out her writing pad.

'Oh, you're not writing to him *again*, are you?' Mavis cast her eyes to the rafters in mock exasperation. 'And you try to tell me he's not your boyfriend!'

Kate said nothing, but bent her head over the page and began to write, 'Dear Danny . . .'

The door of the long hut opened and two newcomers entered. Mavis twisted her head to look towards the door but made no effort to move from the bed.

'Hello there,' she called cheerily. 'Welcome to your new home.' Now she levered herself up on her elbow, swung her legs off the bed and sat up. 'I'm Mavis and this is Kate.'

The two arrivals walked down the length of the hut, a tall, slender girl with sleek blonde hair leading the way with confidence in every stride, while behind her came a smaller, thin girl.

Ignoring Mavis's greeting, the tall girl was complaining loudly in affected tones, 'If I have to endure another Free From Infection inspection just once more . . . it's so humiliating!'

Kate looked up, glancing over the newcomers. Her gaze rested briefly on the thin girl and then was drawn to the other girl. There was something vaguely familiar about her. Kate frowned. The girl nodded stiffly towards Mavis, her only acknowledgement of the friendly greeting.

There was something about the sulky mouth, the tilt of her head as if she were looking down her nose at everything and everyone . . .

Even before the newcomer opened her mouth to speak again, Kate recognized her.

'How do you do?' Her tones were affected and cold. 'This is Edith Brownlow and my name's Isobel Cartwright.'

Twenty-Three

Kate knew she was staring at Isobel Cartwright, but she could not stop herself.

Her stomach was churning. Of all the people she had hoped never to meet again in her life, this girl was top of the list, apart, perhaps, from Miss Denham. Any moment, she expected the girl's petulant mouth to twist into a sneer and hear herself called that dreadful name. 'Why, if it isn't Sicky!'

But Isobel's cool glance flickered over Kate without recognition and she turned her attention to the bed next to Mavis. 'I'll take this one. I see you two have already bagged the ones nearest the stove.'

'First come, first served,' Mavis said airily. She waved her hand towards Kate, making the introductions.

Kate held her breath. Would Isobel remember the name, if not the young girl who had grown up?

Isobel nodded briefly and glanced around, more concerned with her surroundings. 'Well, I don't like being under a window. They're *always* draughty.' She prodded the three-sectioned mattress with her fingers. 'Ugh! I shall have to get Mummy to bring my own bed over from Lincoln. This is disgusting!'

Kate heard Mavis's splutter of laughter which she tried to turn into a cough, but failed.

By contrast, Edith Brownlow was standing uncertainly in the centre of the floor. Kate noticed now, with a stab of pity, that the girl's hair was plastered with an evil-smelling concoction, proclaiming to all that in the medical inspection, Edith must have been found to have head lice.

Kate watched as Isobel glanced coolly towards Edith. 'You'd better take a bed on that side of the hut, Brownlow. *I* don't want to catch nits!'

Obediently and without a word of complaint, Edith took the bed on the opposite side under the window next to Kate and began to unpack her belongings. Kate had a shrewd idea that the girl's bent head was hiding tears. She remembered how she had felt under Isobel Cartwright's scathing jibes.

She went over to Edith. 'Here, let me give you a hand,' Kate said, smiling at the younger girl who was obviously feeling very embarrassed. 'Our corporal's not a bad old stick, actually,' Kate continued, trying to open up a conversation. 'We're lucky – the girls in the next hut have got a battle-axe!'

She kept up a bright chatter while helping the girl to sort out her kit. 'Where are you from?'

'Nottingham.' Edith's voice was no more than a whisper.

'Oh, that's not too far away. You should be able to get home on leave quite easily.'

The girl bent her head again and did not reply. Kate had the feeling that perhaps she had said the wrong thing.

Isobel's complaining voice rose again. 'Where's the bathroom?'

Now Mavis did laugh outright. 'Where on earth did you do your basic training – the Ritz?'

Isobel shot her a vitriolic glance, sat down on her bed and crossed her shapely legs. She was wearing silk stockings, Kate noticed. She doubted if even their easy-going corporal would let Isobel get away with that! From her pocket, Isobel pulled out what looked like a silver cigarette case, opened it, extracted a cigarette and lit it, inhaling deeply.

'Actually,' she drawled, 'we were in an hotel – in Harrogate. At least it was civilized. When we went to the place for our R/T training it was very basic – to say the least! But I thought this would be different. I mean, it's a newly built station.'

Kate couldn't stop herself trotting out the well-worn phrase that was used as an excuse for every short-coming. 'There is a war on, you know . . .' She paused and then added with delicious delight, 'Cartwright!'

Isobel glared at her and instantly Kate regretted drawing her old enemy's attention to her. But Mavis took up the cudgels. 'New it may be, but I suppose they had to get the place banged up and operational as quickly as possible. The new squadron arrives tomorrow complete with Manchesters.'

Kate's interest sharpened. 'Really?' According to something her stepfather had said at Christmas, Danny could be on Manchesters. 'Where are they coming from? What squadron is it?'

'How should I know?' Mavis laughed and added teasingly. '*You* should be able to get all the info – after all, you're closest to the CO.'

'That's true,' she murmured, her mind racing.

'Close to the CO? How come?' Isobel was watching her with renewed interest.

'She's the CO's personal driver,' Mavis told them with a tinge of reflected importance. 'Hand-picked, she was.'

'Really?'

Kate glanced up to see Isobel watching her. On the girl's face there was a rather calculating expression and something else too. Could there possibly be a tinge of respect, Kate thought in surprise. But then, she reminded herself, Isobel Cartwright hasn't realized just who I am – yet!

*

247

More WAAFs arrived over the next two days and soon their hut was fully occupied, with the corporal in charge of them sleeping in the small single room just off the entrance into the hut. After a couple of days they were gradually getting used to being with girls from different parts of the country – from all walks of life.

'God, that woman's useless!' Mavis moaned to Kate as they cut across the grass to the ablutions at six-thirty one morning.

'Who – Edith?'

'Edith? Oh no, not Edith. She's very clever, actually, with the met reports. Seems it's a special interest of hers. No, no, me Lady Isobel Cartwright! I would get lumbered with her on my shift, wouldn't I? Thick as cloud at forty thousand feet, she is!'

Kate felt a moment of sneaking glee to hear Isobel criticized. She bent her head forward so that Mavis should not see the smile on her lips.

'Still,' Mavis added, mellowing a little as her normal generous nature surfaced again, 'she does try, I'll give her that.'

Kate's head shot up. 'Really?' she said, without thinking. 'You do surprise me. I'd have thought she'd think it all beneath her.'

'How on earth she passed out as an R/T operator I don't know. Dave's getting fed up with her already. She comes in for some flak from him, I can tell you.'

'And does she take it?'

'Oh, yes. Hasn't much choice, really, now has she?'

'Suppose not.' Kate paused a moment then asked, 'Who's this Dave?' As they pushed their way into the wash-room, Kate glanced at her friend and saw Mavis's cheeks were a faint shade of pink that had nothing to do with the walk through the frosty morning air. Teasing, she added, 'Do I detect a romance blossoming?'

'Don't be daft, Kate,' Mavis countered, but the pink tinge deepened. 'I've only just met him.'

'Mmm. I can see I shall have to keep my eye on you. Anyway, tell me more about Isobel.'

Mavis launched into a list of mistakes and inefficiencies of which Isobel Cartwright had managed to be guilty in just two shifts. The catalogue was secretly gratifying to Kate, but she hugged the knowledge to herself. She didn't want anyone – not even dear old Mavis – to have the slightest inkling that she knew Isobel.

'How are you getting on with the CO? Is he as nice as he looks?'

'Every bit,' Kate said. Again she made no reference to the fact that she and Group Captain Philip Trent had met before, or that he owed his life to her. It was a secret best kept between the two of them. He had done her an enormous favour in arranging for her to be his driver, but neither of them wanted it common knowledge that he had singled her out for biased treatment.

'Of course, he's a bit old for you, isn't he?'

'Oh, Mavis, really!' Kate laughed. 'The thought never even crossed my mind . . .' But then she remembered his intense gaze across the desk on the day of her arrival. It was more than just a 'thank you for saving my life' look.

'How old do you reckon he is, then?'

'Forty-ish, I should think.'

'Is he married?'

'Oh Mavis, really. I just drive him about – I don't get to know his life history. It's – all very official,' she added, hesitating over the lie.

'I'll find out,' Mavis said confidently and Kate knew she would.

In the seclusion of the staff car, the CO's attitude towards his driver was anything but 'official'.

'Is everything okay in the WAAF quarters? Are you quite comfortable? You can tell me, you know, Kate, quite unofficially. I could try to find you a room in my office block, if you would prefer it.'

She was surprised to hear herself saying. 'Oh no, thank you. I like being with the other girls.' Who would have believed it, she thought, that I could ever come to terms with sleeping in a dormitory of sorts again? 'The only thing is, when you don't need me – there's not much for me to do.' She smiled. 'I can only polish and tinker with this car for so many hours in a day.'

'Well, my demands on your time will no doubt get heavier when we get fully operational, which should be by next week. We shall have two squadrons of bombers here by then. But the station will be very stretched for staff and you may well find yourself being detailed to do other jobs, such as driving the crewbus taking the chaps out to the aircraft when there's an op on. I shall be around myself then anyway.' There was an expression of regret on his face as he met her glance in the rear-view mirror. 'It's the nearest I shall be able to get to flying with them.'

Kate was not surprised; she had known instinctively that Philip would be a fully committed and caring Commanding Officer, nor was she surprised to hear he lamented the fact that his senior post had virtually grounded him.

As she pulled up outside the Control Tower, and was about to jump out of the car to open the rear door for him, he leaned forward and touched her shoulder. 'Are you sure there's nothing you want?'

'Well . . .' she hesitated.

'Go on,' he prompted.

'I – I don't suppose it would be possible to get Danny posted to this station, would it?'

She thought she heard him sigh softly. 'Are you sure it's

250

what you really want, Kate? Wouldn't it be worse for you knowing when he was flying, waiting for his plane to come back?'

She gripped the steering-wheel, her knuckles showing white. 'I – don't know. All I know is that not knowing where he is, or what he's doing, or if he's safe, is unbearable.'

There was a flatness to his voice as he said, 'I'll see what I can do, Kate. But I can't promise anything.'

Before she could move, he had opened the door himself and got out of the car, his long strides taking him towards the building without looking back at her.

Kate bit her lip. Now she did not know whether to wait here for him or go back to the MT yard. Sighing, she got out of the car and followed him. It would be better to hang about waiting for him even if he didn't want her, than to disappear and be missing when he did!

He was in the Met Office on the ground floor talking to Edith who was standing, not exactly to attention, but rigidly upright, answering his questions with a clipped 'Yes, sir,' 'No, sir'.

Kate saw Philip's glance flicker over her but he looked away and concentrated again upon Edith.

Kate went up the concrete stairs to the upper floor. The walls were freshly painted, the top half cream with bottle-green at the bottom. The smell of the paint still lingered. She passed the Signals Room and peeked round the door of the Control Room. Directly in front of her sat Mavis with headphones over her short, springy brown hair. Beside her sat Isobel, leaning forward and listening intently to what Mavis was telling her. There were all sorts of instruments and telephones on the long desk in front of them and on the walls were maps and clocks and blackboards giving local weather conditions and target information. Most interesting of all to Kate was the large operations blackboard with

'SUDDABY' painted in white at the top followed by its call sign, then the squadron numbers and their call signs. In the middle was the word 'RAID' with a blank space for the name to be chalked in each time. Below that was a blank white-painted grid where a WAAF would stand to fill in all the details of each aircraft as it took off on a raid giving the pilot's name, the take-off time and the column everyone watched anxiously: 'RETURN'.

To Kate's left as she stood in the doorway, sat a man at a table. This must be the famous Dave, she thought.

As if feeling her gaze upon him, the Flight Sergeant looked up and grinned at her.

'Hello. Come to see what we get up to here?'

'I'm with the CO,' Kate said. 'He's downstairs.'

Dave winked. 'Thanks for the tip-off.'

At the sound of Kate's voice, Mavis looked around. 'Hello, Kate.' But immediately she turned back to the instruments on her desk.

Dave nodded towards her. 'She's good, is our Mavis. Friend of yours, is she?'

Kate nodded.

At that moment, hearing footsteps on the stairs and seeing Philip appear in the passage behind her, she moved aside to allow him to come into the Control Room.

Standing in the background, she watched while Philip spoke to each person there. As he paused behind Mavis, Kate saw Isobel look up at him, tilting her head coyly, her blue eyes shining and a smile curving her mouth. He spoke briefly to her and then bent over Mavis to talk to her. Kate was amused to see that Isobel bent forward with a semblance of keen concentration. She heard Philip's deep laugh, Mavis's giggle and Isobel's tinkling, affected laughter. As Philip straightened up and turned away to speak to another WAAF on the other side of the room, Isobel glanced at Kate. There

Sow the Seed

was a look of triumph on her face and then, as she continued
to stare at Kate, a slight frown creased her smooth forehead
as if she were trying to draw something out that was nudging
at the depths of her memory, something she could not quite
catch and hold on to. Kate felt the old fluttering just beneath
her ribs.

One of these days, Isobel was going to remember . . .

At that moment they all heard the distinctive sound of
the air-raid siren.

'Right, everybody to the shelters,' Philip said calmly, and
waited until everyone had preceded him out of the room.

'Come on, Mavis, don't hang about,' Dave's voice was
sharp but Kate noticed he made no move himself until Mavis
had pulled off her earphones, pushed on her tin hat, grabbed
her gas mask and followed Isobel who was already heading
for the stairs. Kate felt Philip grasp her arm firmly and propel
her out and across the grass to the trench shelter. The winter
sky hummed and, fascinated, Kate looked up to see two
fighter planes wheeling and diving around each other, guns
spurting death.

'They'll crash into each other,' she gasped.

Beside her, Philip said grimly, 'It happens.'

As it became obvious that the warning had not been for
a bombing raid on the airfield, personnel began to emerge
from the shelters again to stand watching the fight taking
place above them. The aircraft with the circular red, white
and blue emblem of the RAF had the black plane in its
sights. The enemy aircraft twisted and dived, but to no avail;
the British pilot followed his every move as if an invisible
cord tied them together. Suddenly, they saw black smoke
trailing from the enemy plane. Forgetting where they were,
Kate gripped Philip's arm, her horrified gaze watching the
aircraft screaming towards the ground, the smoke slashing
the grey sky. As the plane hit the ground and burst into

253

flames, around her there came the sound of cheering and against the clouds the Spitfire rolled victoriously.

Philip was silent.

'There – there was no parachute, was there?'

'No, Kate,' he answered quietly as they stood together watching the pall of smoke on the far side of the airfield marking wreckage. As fire engines set off across the grass towards it, the all-clear sounded.

Around them there was laughter and congratulation, but Kate could not join in. Despite the fact that she had joined the battle and knew they must fight to the bitter end, nevertheless she could feel no elation at witnessing the death of another human being.

The dead enemy pilot was somebody's son, somebody's brother.

The thought pushed its unwelcome way into her mind; it could so easily have been Danny.

Twenty-Four

The following morning, Kate received a letter from Danny. It was enclosed in a letter from her stepfather. Kate tossed that aside and ripped open the letter from Danny. It was short and didn't tell her very much, but he gave her an address she could write to and he told her he was well and that he would be going home on leave in just over a week. Was there any chance she could get leave at the same time, he asked.

Any chance? Oh, she'd get it if she had to beg on bended knee. Of course, although it wasn't normal procedure, with her unusual relationship with the CO, she could ask Philip personally.

She glanced at her watch. She was due to drive him into Lincoln in about half an hour to catch a train north.

The expression on Philip's face, when he got into the back of the car, was not encouraging. He seemed preoccupied and his eyes were tired. His face looked drawn and strained and the smile, which so altered his expression, was missing. He nodded briefly at her, but sat back in his seat, his shoulders rigid. In the rear mirror she saw him remove his cap and run his hand through his springy, short-cut hair. She could feel the tension in him. Kate bit her lip. She desperately wanted to ask him to approve at least a forty-eight-hour pass for her to coincide with Danny's leave, but above the noise of the large car's engine, it would mean shouting back to him.

She drew into the station and jumped out to open the

door for him. As he bent his head to climb out, she saluted smartly as always, but said softly, 'Sir?'

He straightened up and looked down at her, frowning. 'What is it?' he almost barked at her.

'I – I was wondering how long you w-will be away, sir,' she stammered, deciding instantly that he was in no mood to grant favours, and floundering to think of something – anything – to ask.

'I'll be gone about five days. If you can meet me off the train on Tuesday evening – it gets in about six – I'd be grateful.'

He turned and strode away and Kate found herself saluting to no one in particular.

'Damn!' she muttered to herself as she got back into the car and wove her way out of Lincoln and back towards the station.

'Oh, I can't grant you leave. There's no knowing this far ahead what "Sir" will be doing. You took the job as his driver,' the WAAF officer said sarcastically. 'It's a cushy number, Hilton, so you take the rough with the smooth. You knew you would have to be on call virtually all the time. You'll have to apply through the usual channels.'

So Kate was obliged to reply to Danny's letter explaining the situation. She finished off on a hopeful note. 'I'll do my best though – perhaps I could even ask the CO when he comes back on Tuesday.'

That night as they lay in bed after lights out, Kate was still trying to work out how she was going to wangle some leave to coincide with Danny's. She lay in her narrow bed, feeling the ridges of the three-section 'biscuit' mattress beneath her and staring up with sleepless eyes into the blackness of the rafters. She listened to the steady breathing of the other girls; a cough here, a gentle snore, a murmur there.

Then, above her head she heard a scuffling noise. A noise that was familiar to her and reminded her sharply of home. In the darkness, Kate smiled.

She didn't remember falling asleep, but she awoke with a start to a piercing scream.

Immediately, pandemonium broke out.

'What's the matter?'

'Is it an air-raid?'

'There's a feller in here – must be!'

The door opened and the corporal flashed her torch around the hut. Isobel was standing on her bed shrieking, clutching her nightdress to her.

'Cartwright. Stop that noise at once.'

But the noise did not stop, if anything, the pitch heightened. Isobel was clearly genuinely terrified.

Kate swung her legs out of bed. On bare feet she padded across the wooden floor. Calmly she said, 'May I borrow your torch a mo, Corp?'

Handing it over, the officer said, 'Do you know what's the matter with her, Hilton?'

'I've a good idea.'

Kate left the room for a moment to delve in the cupboard outside the corporal's room. Now some of the other girls were getting decidedly nervous. 'Kate, bring the light back.'

'Won't be a minute. Hang on. Ah, here it is.'

She returned brandishing a broom. 'Now then, mester, let's be 'aving ya.'

'Heavens! Is it a man?' Mavis's voice broke in comically. 'I was only joking – at least I thought I was! '

'Let's just say it's an unwelcome visitor.'

'Something – fell – on my bed and,' Isobel stuttered 'and – ran across my legs!'

Kate turned the torch beam to the roof and ran the beam of light along the rafters. 'Ah,' she smiled her triumph. 'There you are, Mester Rat!'

The whole room erupted in screams. All the girls were now standing on their beds, pressing themselves back against the wall, staring with horrified eyes at the little creature crouching on one of the rafters, its bright eyes shining in the light from the torch. To Kate's amusement, even the corporal took a flying leap on to the nearest bed, nearly knocking the occupant off the other side.

Kate marched towards it and banged the rafter with the broom. The rat scuttled along the beam to the edge of the room, and the girl on the bed beneath squealed, jumped to the floor and leapt on to her neighbour's where bed they clung together, turning frightened eyes upwards.

'He's far more frightened of us than we are of him,' Kate said.

Mavis snorted. 'Wouldn't bank on that, Kate. Get rid of the bloody thing.'

Kate grinned. Mavis rarely swore. In fact few of the girls ever used bad language; the use of it now showed just how terrified they were.

The rat dropped to the floor and ran under the nearest bed. Kate pushed her broom underneath and the animal ran out the other side. Then it ran the full length of the hut.

'Open the door, Corp. It'll run out.'

'Not likely. I'm staying here.'

'Well, if I come down there,' Kate said reasonably, 'it'll run back this way.'

'Well, where is it now?' the corporal asked quaveringly.

'Under the bed opposite where you are.'

'But it might come out when I get on the floor.'

'It won't come for you. They don't come for you unless they're really cornered.'

'Well, for heaven's sake don't corner the bloody thing!' put in Mavis.

The corporal was stepping gingerly off the bed, clutching her nightclothes closely to her. 'J-just bring that broom up here, Hilton.'

'I've told you, if I come any nearer it'll start to run again. Look, Corp, just do it, will you?'

On bare feet the corporal tiptoed towards the door, her eyes fixed on the point where the rat might emerge from under the bed. The occupant of the bed was standing on it, peering with terrified eyes over the edge, convinced the animal would take a flying leap at her.

'Where is it?' she quavered.

'Keep quiet,' Kate ordered, 'else you'll frighten it.'

Mavis smothered an hysterical giggle. '*We'll* frighten *it*! That's a laugh.'

'Ssh!' The rest of the girls hissed.

The door was open and the corporal had never moved so fast in her life back to the safety of the nearest bed.

'And the outer one, Corp.'

'Oh, I can't, Hilton,' she wailed. 'Really I can't.'

Kate sighed. 'Is the door to your room open?'

'Oh Lor'!' the corporal squeaked. 'Yes. I left it open when I came flying in here to find out what all the racket was about.'

'That's why I want you to open the outer door,' Kate said reasonably. 'Oh, never mind, I'll do it myself.'

But as she moved down the room the rat ran out from under the bed. It came to the middle of the floor, stopped and turned wicked eyes upon Kate. It was a huge, brown mangy-looking creature. The frightened girls were whimpering, but clapping their hands over their mouths to keep from screaming out loud. Out of the corner of her eye, Kate saw Isobel slither down the wall on to her bed. 'Mavis – see to Cartwright. She's about to pass out,' Kate said in a matter-of-fact tone.

The rat was on the move again.

It ran first to the right, then to the left, and then seemed to become aware of the open door and went towards it.

'It's gone into your room, Corp. I thought it would.'

There was another wail from the corporal.

'It's all right, we'll soon have him out now.'

And she did. Having opened the outer door, it was a comparatively simple task to shoo the offending animal out into the night.

It took some time for them all to settle back to try to sleep, for they all insisted that Kate should scour the hut with her torch light to ensure there were no more unwelcome visitors.

By morning Isobel had regained her composure and was on the defensive. 'You enjoyed that last night, Hilton, didn't you? You actually enjoyed seeing us all squirm.'

Slowly Kate straightened up from bending over to make her bed to meet Isobel's resentful gaze. She was standing at the foot of the bed glaring at Kate.

Time seemed to take a tilt and, for a fleeting moment, Kate was once more the child in the cold, unfriendly dormitory facing the scathing expression of Isobel Cartwright.

Not this time, you don't, Kate thought. 'Yes, Cartwright,' she said quietly. 'There are people in this world who enjoy teasing others, seeing them squirm, as you put it.' As she was speaking, Kate opened the top drawer of her locker at the side of the bed and reached in. Her fingers closed over the wrinkled roundness of the whelk shell. Without taking her eyes off Isobel's face, she lifted it out and placed it in full view on top of the locker. 'Normally,' she went on softly, 'I'm not one of them.'

Kate saw Isobel's glance flicker towards the shell and become fixed upon it. She watched as a deep red flush crept up the girl's neck and suffused her face.

Isobel's voice was a strangled whisper. 'It *is* you!' They stared at each other, then Isobel said slowly. 'You said you'd get your own back one day, didn't you?'

Kate nodded, her gaze holding the other girl's relentlessly.

'Do . . .' Isobel began and then bit her lip. They were both aware that their conversation was being listened to with interest now by one or two of the others. ' . . . I mean . . .' Isobel was still struggling, but Kate waited, saying nothing. She was not a vindictive girl, but Isobel's taunts had cut deeply all those years ago and in the few days they'd been together again, Kate could see that Isobel had hardly changed. Her unkind attitude towards poor Edith had proved that.

She saw Isobel take in a deep breath. 'Would you agree to call it quits and – and make a fresh start . . .' Again she hesitated and then added, deliberately, ' . . . Kate?'

Kate picked up the shell, put it back in its place and closed the drawer. 'Suits me . . . Isobel.'

She guessed that Isobel found it hard to apologize or even to admit she had been in the wrong, but the expression in the girl's eyes and her muttered 'Thanks,' were enough for Kate. For her, one of the ghosts from the past had been confronted and laid to rest.

Two days later, Mavis said, 'D'you know, Kate, I think m'Lady Isobel is really starting to get the hang of things. She's *really* trying.'

'Very trying, I should think,' Kate laughed.

As they stacked their beds ready for kit inspection, Mavis asked, 'Er, what was all that about the other morning between you and her?'

'Oh, just a – a misunderstanding we had a while back. Best forgotten now.'

At that moment, saving Kate from having to answer more awkward questions, the door opened and the subject of their conversation came in, rubbing her hands together. 'Does this awful place have to be so cold? It must be freezing point in these huts.'

She walked the length of the hut, flapping her arms around herself, and came to stand close to the stove. 'How you can bear to sleep under that window, Kate, beats me.'

'I always liked to be able to see out,' Kate murmured, remembering the high, barred windows of the school dormitory. She glanced at Isobel, but the girl was touching the grey stove. 'It's cold!' she accused. 'Isn't it even lit?'

'Nope,' Mavis said. 'Not allowed to light it till five o'clock tonight.'

Isobel clicked her tongue against her teeth in exasperation and wrapped her arms around herself, tucking her hands under her armpits.

'We could go out and drill,' Mavis suggested impishly.

'No thanks,' Isobel replied shortly. She seemed about to move away and then hesitated and stopped. Her head dropped forward, her eyes downcast, she traced an imaginary pattern on the floor with the toe of her shoe. Without looking up and in a tone quite unlike her normal complaining voice, Isobel said, 'Mavis, I'm very grateful for your help in the Control Room.'

'Eh?" Mavis gawped at the bent head.

'Don't make me repeat it,' Isobel snapped, her tone returning to normal almost immediately. 'It's embarrassing enough for me to say it once!'

'Oh – er – yes.' Mavis was floundering, her plump cheeks turning pink. 'Well – you don't need to say anything, Isobel. We all help each other.'

'Well,' Isobel said, slightly mollified. 'I just wanted you to know I appreciate it, that's all.'

Kate listened to the interchange in amazement. Was Isobel Cartwright actually beginning to behave like a human being?

Mavis, still embarrassed, glanced towards the door as it opened and several girls came in, Edith amongst them. With relief at being given the chance to change the subject, Mavis called, 'What's the weather like, Edith? Is this fog going to lift?'

Edith came towards them, shaking her head. 'No. It looks like it's here for a couple of days at least. All aircraft are grounded. There won't be any operations and,' she smiled and Kate thought immediately how pretty Edith was when she lost her frightened-mouse look, ' . . . there shouldn't be any air-raids from the other side either.'

'Oh, Edith – you clever old thing!' Kate clapped her hands. Edith's cheeks were pink with pleasure as if she were being given the credit for having personally arranged the blanket of fog that lay over the strangely silent airfield. During the last few weeks, the girl had blossomed. Her short hair now gleamed glossily and curled prettily around her face which was not so white and pinched. She was still shy, but thanks to the efforts of Kate and Mavis, she was now included in all the activities and the humiliation surrounding her arrival was forgotten.

'She's not the only one to get nits!' Mavis had said in her blunt, matter-of-fact manner. 'My mother travelled home from London once in a filthy railway carriage and somehow, she got 'em. She nearly went mad! You should have seen us – she had us washing our hair every day for a fortnight – the whole family. Me dad threatened to shave his all off, if she carried on.' Mavis guffawed at the memory.

Isobel had said nothing, but even she made no more sarcastic remarks to Edith, and whilst she made no effort to befriend the girl, she made no objections when Mavis and Kate included Edith in what was fast becoming a foursome.

'So are we all getting a forty-eight-hour?' Isobel drawled now at the news.

'No – but almost as good as.' Mavis's eyes sparkled.

'Come on, Mave,' Kate said, 'we can see you're dying to tell us something.'

'The lads said if the fog didn't lift, they'd put on a dance in the Officers' Mess tomorrow night and we're all invited.'

There were whoops of delight and even Isobel's eyes gleamed.

'Back to earth, girls,' someone shouted from the end of the hut near the door. 'Stand by your beds. They're coming – kit inspection!'

As Isobel moved across to her own bed, she murmured, so that only Kate could hear, 'Have they got their rulers and scissors at the ready? Should we kneel down, do you think?'

Kate spluttered with laughter and Isobel gave her a rare, wide smile. Kate was still trying to stifle her giggles as the NCO and corporal entered the hut, but Isobel stood at the end of her bed, cool, calm and in complete control of her features.

'Shut up, Kate,' Mavis hissed. 'You'll get us all on a fizzer and then there'll be no dance in the Officers' Mess for any of us!'

She would never have believed it possible, Kate thought later, that she could have been laughing so uncontrollably over memories of St Mary's School for Young Ladies! And with – of all people – Isobel Cartwright!

*

As the four of them entered the Mess the following evening, Mavis gasped. 'It's like Christmas!'

The large room had been decorated with trimmings and balloons and at one end, on a raised dais, seven officers were setting up their musical instruments.

Mavis nudged Kate. 'Dave was telling me about them trying to get a band together. I say, he's a bit of all right on the drums, isn't he?'

'Really, Mavis – what about Dave?'

Mavis smiled. 'Oh, he'll do for me all right, but I was thinking about you.'

'Thanks very much – I can find me own fellers, ta!'

The newly formed band struck up, slightly hesitant at first, and then from the floor a young fair-haired Pilot Officer jumped up on to the dais and began to conduct. With more confidence, the players swung into 'We're going to hang out the washing . . .' The room began to fill and soon couples were moving on to the area cleared as a dance-floor.

Soon the girls, outnumbered by the men, were never without a partner. Kate found herself dancing with a tall, dark-haired man who danced woodenly round the floor, not speaking and holding her almost at arm's length. As they danced close to the dais, the fair-haired conductor jumped down and cut in. '''Scuse me, mate . . .' and Kate found herself looking up into his eyes as he took her hand and put his arm around her waist. 'Hello, there. My name's Sandy. What's yours, . pretty WAAF?'

'K-Kate,' she gasped from surprise and now breathlessness too, for they were jigging round the floor at twice the speed of her previous pedestrian partner. 'What – what about the band?'

'Oh, they'll survive ten minutes without going to pieces completely.'

'Are you their conductor?'

'Not officially. I've done a bit in my time and I could see they needed a hand.' He grinned as he added, 'Literally!'

Kate laughed and shook back her hair which tonight she had left long.

'Has anyone ever told you you've got the most beautiful hair?' Sandy said.

'Oh, frequently,' she responded lightly, and although she did not resist when the band began to play 'Over the Rainbow' and Sandy pulled her into his arms again and rested his cheek against her hair, she could not help thinking, 'If only Danny could hold me like this'.

Then resolutely she pushed the thought of Danny Eland from her mind. Sandy seemed a nice boy with his open, honest face and laughing eyes. She'd seen him once or twice around camp when he'd given her a cheeky wink. Perhaps he could be the one to help her forget? Deliberately, she snuggled closer into his arms, closed her eyes and tried to let the soft, dreamy music engulf her.

On Tuesday evening when Kate parked the staff car and went into the station to meet Philip Trent, she found that his train from York had been delayed by an air-raid warning.

'I haven't a clue when it'll get here, Miss,' the ticket-office clerk told her, shrugging indifferently. 'It's getting harder and harder to keep to any sort of timetable these days. Trains come and trains go, Miss, that's all I can promise. But *when* – now that's a different matter.'

Kate pulled a face and then smiled at him. It wasn't this poor man's fault that the war was disrupting all his carefully planned timetables. It must be a nightmare for the railway staff at times, she thought. 'Well, thanks anyway. I'd better hang around. I wouldn't like to be missing when it does get here.'

The man pointed. 'There's a waiting room there and you might just wangle a cup of tea from the ladies over there.'

Kate turned to see that a train had just pulled into the station and a tidal wave of khaki was flowing on to the platform as troops spilled off the train. Set against the wall at the rear of the platform was a long trestle-table on which were numerous cups and a huge tea-urn. Behind the table two women in WVS uniform dispensed tea to the soldiers.

Kate nodded to the clerk. 'Thanks. I'll let the rush subside a little and then I'll see if they've any left.'

Half an hour later, Kate approached the two women. She had been standing a little way off watching them while they handed out cups of tea, always smiling, a cheery word for each soldier, and although the queue stretched right down the platform, they appeared calm and unhurried. But by the time Kate felt she could join the queue the two middle-aged ladies were red-faced and flustered and beads of sweat stood on their foreheads. Kate glanced up the track. There was no sign of the train she awaited, so she left the queue and pushed her way to the end of the table.

'Could you use another pair of hands?' she volunteered. The older of the two women turned to face her and Kate drew in a sharp breath.

She was staring straight into a face she knew. An older, more lined face, but there was no mistaking the gentle features of Miss Ogden.

Twenty-Five

Was she never to be free of that dreadful place, was her first shocked reaction, but when the initial surprise had subsided, Kate realized she was actually quite pleased to see Miss Ogden again.

'You don't remember me, do you?'

Miss Ogden was smiling apologetically. 'I expect you're one of our girls, but you do change so much . . .'

Kate took off her cap and her glorious auburn hair tumbled down to her shoulders.

Miss Ogden gasped. 'Oh! Oh – now I know.' She reached out with hands that trembled slightly. 'My dear Kate. How are you? Oh, I *am* pleased to see you.'

''Ow about a cuppa, darlin'?' a rough voice broke in and, distracted, Miss Ogden's hands fluttered without purpose. 'Oh, yes – er – of course. I'm sorry.'

Behind Kate another group of soldiers had joined the queue, swelling the demand for tea. She slipped behind the table and stood next to Miss Ogden. 'Here, let me help.' Immediately her hands deftly caught up a cup and held it under the tap of the urn. 'Where are you heading, soldier?'

The man grinned at her, showing yellow and misshapen teeth. He tapped the side of his nose. 'Can't tell you that, darlin'. You might be a bloomin' spy!'

Kate laughed gaily. 'Ya think this uniform'd be a good cover, do ya?' Without thinking, she had lapsed into her native dialect.

The man guffawed. 'I take it back. With an accent like that, you're one of us, all right.'

'Thanks.' Kate grinned back, knowing he meant it as a genuine compliment.

For the next ten minutes the three women worked side by side, and when at last the flood had subsided to a trickle, the other helper handed Kate a cup of tea. 'Here you are, me duck, you've earned that.'

Kate accepted it gratefully.

'You go and 'ave a sit down with yer friend, Elsie. I can manage the rest of 'em.'

'Well, if you're sure, Mabel . . .' Miss Ogden said tentatively.

''Course I'm sure – and take yerself a cuppa as well.'

'Oh, I'm so pleased to see you,' Miss Ogden said again, as they sat down in the waiting room together, their hands round the cups and sipping the hot tea. 'You look wonderful and that uniform suits you a treat. I've often thought of you over the years and wondered . . . You had such a rotten time. I've often felt guilty I didn't do more.'

Kate smiled. 'You did as much as you could in the circumstances, I realize that now, and a lot more than anyone else there. Tell me,' she added suddenly. 'Was it you who put the sugar on the second helping of gooseberries that day?'

Shyly, Miss Ogden nodded. 'I couldn't believe she did that to you. I was horrified. I should have said more – done something . . .'

Swiftly, Kate patted the older woman's knee. 'Please, don't worry any more about it. It might have made things even worse if you had.'

Miss Ogden sighed. 'That's true.' She paused, then added, 'I didn't blame you for running away, but I was so worried about you.'

'You went to see my relatives, didn't you?'

269

'Mrs – er – Godfrey, was it?' When Kate nodded, Miss Ogden continued, 'I didn't know if I'd done the right thing, because the poor woman flew into a panic. She said she'd just posted a letter to your people only half an hour beforehand . . .'

'Yes,' Kate murmured, remembering vividly the woman's kind and concerned letter.

'And the next day she sent a telegram and received a reply that you had arrived home.'

Kate grinned ruefully. 'I was wrong to do what I did – I realize that now – but at the time, I didn't think anyone would even care that I had gone.'

Miss Ogden gave a nervous laugh. 'Oh, there was pandemonium that night. But I suspect Miss Denham was more worried about the precious reputation of the school than about your welfare.'

Kate did a swift calculation in her head. Although obviously in the intervening years Miss Ogden had aged, she was nowhere near retirement age. 'Are you still there – at the school?'

Miss Ogden nodded and smiled ruefully. 'No doubt I shall finish my days there.'

They fell silent. Deliberately, Kate refused to ask about Miss Denham. There was nothing she wanted to know about that woman.

She opened her mouth to tell Miss Ogden that she had met up with Isobel Cartwright again too, but then she closed it. If Miss Ogden still felt so guilty even after all this time about the treatment Kate had received at the school, then hearing that she was once again in a kind of dormitory with one of her tormentors might fuel the woman's remorse.

Now Miss Ogden was asking Kate about herself, about her life in the WAAF. Relieved, Kate launched into telling her about driving for the CO and why she came to be waiting on the station.

'And what did you do before joining up...?' Miss Ogden's question was drowned by the arrival of a train.

Kate jumped up. 'I'm sorry, I'd better go. That must be the one I'm waiting for.' Swiftly she took Miss Ogden's hands in hers and squeezed them. 'I'm so glad we've met. Perhaps I'll see you again some time. I often have to bring the CO here.'

'I hope so. Oh, I do hope so, Kate . . .' were Miss Ogden's final words.

When Philip Trent finally stepped off the train which was running over an hour and a half late, climbed into the car and flopped back against the leather seat, Kate did not have the heart to ask him to grant her leave. He looked exhausted. His eyes were dull, with dark shadows beneath them as if he had not slept since leaving five days earlier.

As if to confirm this he said, 'Just get me to my bed, Kate, will you?'

She glanced at him in the rear-view mirror. He was leaning his head back against the leather of the car seat, his eyes closed, his face gaunt with tiredness.

Kate sighed and pressed the starter. The noisy engine burst into life, cutting off any further chance of conversation.

As she drew up outside the CO's quarters, the sirens began to wail and almost immediately they saw enemy aircraft swooping in from the east, low and deadly.

'Out the car, Kate. Quick!'

Kate grabbed her tin hat, opened the door and launched herself from the car.

'I hope you can run – come on.' Philip grasped her arm and began to haul her along, but then Kate began to run –

really run – and he let go of her. When they reached the brick-lined trenches that served as an open-topped shelter, he was a couple of yards behind her. He was grinning as he joined her in the shelter, already crowded with airmen and WAAFs. 'Remind me never to ask you again if you can run!' he said. But his smile faded as, from the comparative safety of the shelter, they watched the enemy aircraft trying to destroy their station. Some aircraft were making a valiant effort to get into the sky, to escape being bombed where they stood on the ground. But the attack had been swift and sudden and the warning had come too late to allow evasive action.

Four planes managed to get into the air, but three on the ground were already in flames. Anti-aircraft guns pumped bullets at the enemy aircraft as they swooped and dived overhead. One enemy plane was hit and came down in a field just off the airfield's limits, bursting into flames on impact.

Horrified, Kate watched as a plane came in low, its black swastika clearly visible. It flew straight towards the control tower. She saw the bomb leave the belly of the aircraft, whistling down towards the tower, where Mavis and Isobel were on duty.

'Oh no!' Kate screamed and jumped up.

'Get down!' Philip shouted at her above the noise, grabbing her arm roughly and pulling her down again.

'But Mavis – and Isobel – they're in there. I know they are.'

Philip got up and pushed his way out of the trench. In an instant, Kate was right behind him.

'Stay there,' he commanded.

'No – I'm coming too . . .'

'Hilton – that's an order.'

Kate hesitated. It was a serious matter to disobey a direct order from her CO. Philip had turned away and began to run across the stretch of grass between the shelter and the control tower. Fire crews and medics were already running in the same direction. She saw Philip raise his arm to direct a crew towards the tower, one corner of which was badly damaged. Another enemy plane swooped low, aiming its nose directly at Philip as he ran. In his urgency to reach the control tower personnel, it was clear he had not even noticed the plane coming directly for him.

Kate screamed at him, 'Philip – look out!' but above the noise and confusion, she knew he could not hear her. She was up and out of the shelter and running after him before she knew what she was doing. The plane, directly in front of him, was coming closer, but the space between herself and Philip was narrowing too. She saw him glance up, see the aircraft, realize that its blazing guns were heading straight for him. He slowed his pace and hesitated, staring up at the plane. In that split second, Kate reached him, grasped his arm and pulled him a yard to the right. They fell to the ground together as the hail of bullets spattered the ground, pitting the earth exactly where he had been standing.

They lay there panting.

'I thought I told you – to – stay there,' he gasped, lying flat on his back.

Kate raised her head to look at him, disbelief on her face.

He got up and held out his hand to haul her to her feet. 'Looks like they're clearing off now. Out of ammo, I expect,' he said grimly.

He stood there for a brief moment amidst all the chaos, still holding her hand, looking down into her eyes. 'Kate Hilton,' he said softly, his voice a caress now, 'are you going to make a habit of saving my life?' Then he squeezed her hand. 'Come on, we'd better find your friends . . .'

The bomb had fallen on one corner of the control tower, demolishing the Signals Room and, below it, the Met Office.

There could easily have been as many as five people in the two rooms at the time, Kate knew. The Control Room, where Mavis and Isobel worked, looked, at first glance, comparatively unscathed, although the glass observation room on the roof was completely shattered and fragments were scattered everywhere.

Figures were staggering from the building, their faces grey with dust and hardly recognizable. Kate saw a tall, plump figure emerge, her arm about a girl whose sleek blonde hair was dishevelled. She had never seen Isobel Cartwright look such a mess.

Kate rushed forward. 'Mavis, are you all right? Isobel?'

'I'm okay,' Mavis gasped, 'but Isobel's got a cut on her face.'

Philip's deep voice spoke suddenly close by. 'Is everybody out of the place?'

'No,' Mavis said. 'We can't find Edith.'

'Where was she?'

'In the Met Room,' Mavis said.

Already people were digging at the rubble. 'Go carefully,' Philip shouted. 'There may be people still alive but trapped.' He turned back to the three girls and, nodding towards the wilting Isobel, said, 'Look after her. I'll have to get back to my office – if it's still standing – and see if I can organize some help. Kate – you stay here. I want you to act as my runner . . .' He paused briefly, and looked at her. Even in the midst of all the devastation, a small smile quirked the corner of his mouth at the aptness of the task he was giving her. No one else he knew could run as fast as Kate Hilton. 'Keep me informed of everything that's going on, will you?'

Kate nodded. 'Yes, sir.'

*

Two hours later they found the bodies; there were three. An airman and two WAAFs. One was Edith.

'She wouldn't have known what hit her, Kate,' Philip said gently, when she burst, breathless, into his office, her eyes wide, her cap stuffed into her pocket and her hair flying free, all protocol forgotten in her agitation.

'Here, sit down . . .' He pushed her firmly into a chair and closed the door between them and the outer office. 'You could do with a drink.' From the drawer of his desk he took a bottle and two glasses.

'Oh, I didn't ought . . .'

'I know, I know,' he said impatiently. 'You're on duty and you didn't ought to drink, specially not with your CO. But this is for medicinal purposes only.' Holding out the glass to her, he added, 'And it's an order. Perhaps it's one you won't mind obeying – for once.'

Kate was still shaking, her hands felt cold and clammy. Seeing Edith's lifeless body, covered in dust, being dragged from the wreckage, had made her feel physically sick.

'No – I mean – I didn't ought to because – because it goes to my head a bit quick.'

'My dear girl, I'm not suggesting you should get roaring drunk.'

'No, but I – I tend to talk too much even when I've only had a little.'

He came and sat on the corner of the desk, just above her. Gently he picked up her hand and put the glass into it, making sure she was gripping it before he let go.

'Well, I'm listening,' he said softly. 'It's no bad thing to talk.' He sighed. 'I wish I had someone to talk to sometimes. I'm finding command is a very lonely occupation.'

She looked up at him, meeting his gaze. Deep in his eyes there was anxiety. Suddenly, she understood the loneliness of his position and all its responsibilities. No wonder he often looked tired and seemed withdrawn.

She had lost a friend in Edith, for whom she would grieve, but Philip had lost several personnel in his charge and at least three aircraft, and his airfield had been shot to pieces. It was his responsibility to get his station operational as soon as possible. And there would undoubtedly be questions asked about whether correct procedures had been observed before and during the raid and, worst of all to face, whether anything could have been done that hadn't been to minimize the damage.

She gulped the liquid in the glass. 'I'm sorry, you must have lots to do, I'll . . .'

He smiled, but it was a sad, forlorn smile. 'That's the better side of being in command. One can delegate, you know. I've done everything I can for the moment.' His eyes clouded. 'I need a few moments myself. Soon I shall have to write some very difficult letters.'

Of course, now there was no question of anyone on the station having any leave, except perhaps on compassionate grounds. And in all truthfulness, Kate could not say that going home to meet Danny fell into that category. But how she longed to lean her head against his shoulder and feel the comfort of his arms around her and tell him just how she felt, knowing he would understand completely.

Philip Trent, in his capacity as Station Commander, decided to attend the funerals of those who had been killed. Clearance was given for Edith's body to be transported home to Nottingham, and the day before her funeral, Philip called Kate into his office.

'I know it's maybe not usual, but you've probably guessed I don't always go by the rule-book.' He grinned at her, and, at ease, she smiled back. 'I want you to drive me to ACW Brownlow's funeral tomorrow, so I was wondering if you'd like to attend the service too?'

'Yes, I would. Thank you.'

He nodded. 'This is where the – er – rule-book gets thrown out of the window. If your two friends would like to come along too, you have my permission to ask them. I can arrange for them to alter their shifts if necessary.'

'Oh, thank you. I'm sure they would like to. The four of us had got quite close.' She was almost surprised to hear herself voicing the fact that she looked upon Isobel Cartwright as a friend. But it was true – now.

Philip nodded again, his face serious. 'I know.' He sighed. 'You make a lot of good friends in this kind of life, all thrown together. But – when something like this happens, well, being close makes it extra painful.'

He really is an understanding man, Kate thought, marvelling as she ran towards the WAAF site and her hut.

'Did he really say that?' Mavis asked incredulously when Kate repeated Philip's offer to her two friends.

Isobel sat on her bed and blew smoke rings into the air, savouring her new packet of cigarettes; it had been pay day the previous day. 'He's different – I'll say that for him,' she observed.

'All the chaps like him too,' Mavis put in. 'Dave says . . .'

Kate and Isobel gave a mocking groan, but Mavis only grinned and went on, 'Dave says they really admire him 'cos he can keep authority and yet be human at the same time.'

Isobel glanced at Kate, sharing the past for a moment. 'Not an easy thing to do,' Isobel murmured.

'So I take it you'll come.'

They both nodded. 'Poor old Edith – it's the least we can do.'

Sadly, Kate sighed. 'It's *all* we can do.'

The car journey to Nottingham was a little strained. Philip, sitting beside Kate in the front, said little, and, taking their cue from him, the two WAAFs in the back seat were silent.

They stood in the rain awaiting the funeral cortège which was already late. Then, as it appeared around the corner, they saw a strange procession walking behind the slow-moving vehicle. A man led the way, lurching from side to side, with a tiny, bird-like woman walking behind him carrying a child of eighteen months or so. Behind her straggled five more children of various ages and sizes. A tall, lanky youth, incongruously still in short trousers; a girl in a coat which was far too big for her, the hem flapping round her ankles; and three smaller children, one with jam smeared across his mouth, another with his nose running and grey socks wrinkled around his ankles. Kate glanced at Isobel, but she was staring fixedly ahead, deliberately ignoring the family.

The man came and stood in front of them. 'You 'ere for our Edie's funeral?' The smell of alcohol wafted into their faces.

'That's right, sir. My name's Trent – your daughter's Commanding Officer.'

The man wiped the back of his hand across his mouth and then proffered it to be shaken. Without a flicker, Philip took it and shook it firmly.

''Ow do?' the man said gruffly, then he jerked his thumb over his shoulder. 'The wife and kids,' he added, rather unnecessarily, Kate thought.

Philip inclined his head towards Mrs Brownlow and her brood. Standing a pace or so behind their CO, the three WAAFs were able to avoid shaking hands with Mr Brownlow, as the party, now complete it seemed, moved towards the church porch. As they fell in behind the coffin, Isobel muttered, 'Now we know why she had nits!'

'Shut up, Iso!' Kate hissed between her teeth as they passed through the porch and into the musty interior of the church.

The service was conducted in a swift, unfeeling monotone. It was obvious that the vicar knew neither Edith nor any member of her family and Kate felt a surge of pity for the girl as her coffin was lowered into the grave. As the party moved away, Edith's father said loudly, 'I told 'er she'd come to no good, joining up. She had a good job – a safe job – in a factory. What did she 'ave to go and join up for? Officers' groundsheets, that's all them WAAFs are. I told 'er.' He glared accusingly at the three girls in uniform as if he held them personally responsible for his daughter's death.

'She wanted to make something of herself, Bert.' The woman looked up at Philip, appealing for support. 'She was a good girl, sir. Not like 'ee's makin' out.'

Philip nodded at the woman, his voice gently sympathetic. 'She was a clever girl, Mrs Brownlow, and well thought of, I promise you. We shall all miss her.'

The woman's eyes filled with tears and she nodded, a swift, pecking movement, hitched up the child in her arms and turned away. The children followed her while Edith's father, with a last baleful glare at the officer and three girls in uniform, sniffed, wiped his hand across his mouth once more, turned away without a glance at his departing family and shuffled off down the road in the opposite direction towards the swinging sign of a pub.

'Good grief! What a family!' Isobel could contain herself no longer as they got back into the car. 'Ooh, sorry, sir.'

'That's all right.' Philip took off his peaked cap and ran his hand through his springy hair. 'Thank goodness that's over. Let's get going, Kate.'

As Kate started the car she heard the gasp of surprise from the back seat at Philip's use of her Christian name. Once out of the city, Philip relaxed and leaned back in the corner of the front seat, half-turned towards the two girls in the back, his arm along the back of the bench seat.

'In the confines of this car, we're unofficial,' he grinned. 'My name's Philip and you're . . .?'

'C-Cartwright and Nuttall,' Mavis stuttered.

In the rear-view mirror, Kate could see Mavis's eyes were nearly popping out of their sockets.

'No, no, Christian names, please.'

'Isobel – and I'm Mavis.'

'Well, Mavis and Isobel, just so long as we're very official when we get back to the station, eh?'

'Oh yes, sir.' Mavis gasped. 'Of course.'

'Now, Kate, if you can find us a quiet, out-of-the-way pub on the way back I'll treat you girls to a spot of lunch.'

The atmosphere relaxed at once and soon Mavis had them in fits of laughter with stories about the antics her young brother had got up to in his efforts to join up at fifteen. 'My mother wanted Dad to leather him, but Dad just smiled and said he wished he could join up again himself. He was in the last lot and got gassed . . .'

Kate was silent, but vague memories of her own father flickered through her mind; hazy pictures of an emaciated figure shaking uncontrollably. In her memories Danny was there and they were walking down the lane at home, one on either side holding the hands of the man they now knew had been the father of the them both.

Over lunch, Kate was amused to notice that Isobel positioned herself next to Philip, engaging him in conversation, tilting her head to one side coyly as she listened, intensely interested in whatever he was saying.

280

'Well, ladies,' he said at last, 'I'm sorry to break this up, but we must be getting back . . .'

'Oh, isn't he *nice*?' Mavis said later, when they had returned to camp.

'Is he married?' Isobel asked, and when Kate glanced at her, she saw a cool, calculating look in Isobel's eyes.

'I can't find out anything,' Mavis said in disgust. 'Even Dave doesn't know, and normally what he *doesn't* know isn't worth knowing! I know he comes from the York area, but honestly, that seems to be all anyone can find out about him.'

'Mmm,' Isobel said and her eyes took on a faraway look.

A week later a letter came from Danny containing anxious inquiries as to Kate's safety. Although he was avoiding putting anything in writing directly, it was obvious he knew about the terrible raid on Suddaby airfield.

'*Please write back at once and let me know you're safe.*' His concern gave her a warm glow, but in contrast the rest of his letter left her with the cold chill of being excluded from a happy event.

'*It was a shame,*' he wrote, '*that you couldn't get leave the same time as me. We had a great time.*'

We, who was 'we'? The next line made it clear.

'*I took Rosie dancing in town, or rather – if I'm truthful – Rosie took me! She really is a great kid and fun to be with. All the fellers are around her like bees round a honeypot, but she danced with me all evening and made an old man feel young again!*'

Kate smiled as she read the letter. Fool! she thought, he's only nine years older than Rosie and yet he talks as if she's still a child. Then her smile faded and her glance went to the window. Her hands, still holding the letter, lay in her lap. She looked out across the gently rolling landscape. But

Rosie was no longer a child. She was a young woman who liked to flirt and have a good time. And she had spent a weekend with Danny.

For the first time in her life, Kate felt a tinge of jealousy towards Rosie Maine.

In her reply posted the same day, Kate promised she would get leave the very next time he did. *'Then we can go home together. I do miss you so, and I've so much to tell you.'* She paused, her pen wavering above the page, knowing that what she was going to write next was unfair, possessive when she had no right to be, and yet she could not help herself.

'And if it doesn't work out and I can't get leave, maybe you could come and stay somewhere near here instead of going home.'

Kate ignored her conscience and posted the letter quickly.

A whole month went by and she did not hear from Danny. Now it was her turn to worry that something might have happened to him.

Twenty-Six

'I know what we ought to do,' Mavis said in her best organizing voice. 'We ought to go to a dance in Lincoln.'

Kate gasped and Isobel looked disdainful. 'Do you think that's appropriate in the circumstances?' Her glance flickered over the empty bed that had been Edith's. No one had arrived yet to fill it.

'Edith wouldn't have wanted us to mope about it. What matters is that we should remember her.'

'I suppose you're right,' Kate said, and even Isobel shrugged.

'If I can fix it up with some of the lads, we'll go into Lincoln next Saturday night. There's bound to be a dance going on somewhere. Dave'll know.' With that Mavis whirled about and was gone from the hut, banging the door behind her, without giving Kate or Isobel any time to argue further.

Kate shook her head, smiling fondly after her friend. Then she reached into her locker for her writing pad.

'*Dear Danny*,' she began. '*My new friend Mavis – you'd like her, she's so jolly – has bullied us into going to a dance in Lincoln on Saturday night. How I wish you were nearer and could go too!*'

Isobel eased her last pair of silk stockings over her shapely legs with tender care. 'If anyone ladders these tonight at the dance, I'll get them put on a charge.' She turned to look at

Kate who was still sitting on her bed. 'Are you getting ready or what?'

'I – I don't think I'll come,' Kate faltered. Most of the girls not on duty were going to the dance in Lincoln, but Kate wasn't in the mood. She'd had no reply from Danny to her last two letters and was just beginning to feel a little uneasy about his safety.

Mavis, hands on hips, came and stood over her. 'Oh yes, you are, my girl, so you'd better look slippy and get ready.'

Adopting that stance, Mavis reminded Kate so sharply of her mother that she burst into laughter. 'Oh, all right then. I'll come.'

She levered herself off the bed, gathered her things together to get washed, put on a clean shirt and brush her uniform.

Mavis had not moved away but was still hovering near Kate's bed. 'I hope you're not going to bawl me out,' she said, chewing the side of her thumb.

'Now what have you done?' Kate said in mild exasperation.

'I've fixed the three of us up with Dave and a couple of his mates.'

'Oh, I'll take Dave, then,' Isobel said airily.

'Keep off, Cartwright. He's mine, and you too, Kate Hilton, with those green eyes of yours.'

'Sounds like you've got the "green eye" over him yourself,' Isobel drawled, and Kate said, 'Oh, I get it! We get the pimply friends, do we? I'd sooner go with Sandy.'

'Eh?'

'You know, the navigator in T-Tommy.'

'Oh yes, I know him. Sorry – he's on leave, evidently.'

Kate pulled a face. 'On second thoughts, then, I reckon I will give it a miss . . .'

heartily, their arms draped casually around a couple of WAAFs, might be flying over enemy territory dropping bombs by this time tomorrow night.

And some would not be coming back.

Kate shuddered. Suddenly, amidst all the jollity, she felt lonely. It was all false, a forced gaiety to hide their fear, their terror of tomorrow. But what else could these brave young men do? Sit around moping, waiting for death in the morning? No, this was their way of being courageous; it was the only way they knew.

The music seemed to grow louder, the laughter became strident; Brian's arm around her was suddenly too tight, the smoky atmosphere oppressive, cloying and stifling. She wanted to push her way through the crowd and escape into the fresh air. A sudden longing for the peace and tranquillity of the end of the Spit overwhelmed her. The desire would not be wholly denied. Kate gave a little sob and thrust herself away from Brian's clutch.

'Hey, what did I do?' he asked, bemused.

'Nothing, nothing,' she mouthed above the noise. She put a hand to her head. 'I must get some – air.'

He grinned stupidly at her, misinterpreting her reasons. Lurching towards her, he grabbed her arm again. 'What a good idea,' he leered.

Kate twisted herself from his grasp. 'No!' She pulled away from him, knocking against the couple dancing nearby. The whole dance-floor was crowded now, there was scarcely room to move.

'Aw, now don't be a spoilsport . . .' he began. Blindly, Kate turned away, but found her face pressed against another blue uniform, the buttons digging into her cheek. Two arms were around her holding her tightly. She gave a cry and began to struggle.

'Kate – it's me . . .'

With a gasp of surprise, she pulled her head back to find herself looking directly into a pair of laughing brown eyes.

'Danny, oh Danny!' And she flung her arms around him.

Behind her, her former dance partner shrugged philosophically. 'Oh well, I know when I'm beaten. Hope you have better luck than I did, mate.'

Danny pushed his way through the throng, with Kate in his wake. When they reached the edge of the floor, he said, 'Come on, let's get out of here,' and together they almost burst through the doors of the hall and out into the open air.

'Whew! I don't think I could have stood another minute!' Danny took great gulps of air. 'It's worse than being in the belly of a Manchester!'

'What are you doing here? How did you know where to find me? How did you get here?'

'Rescuing you, in answer to your first question. And not a moment too soon, by the look of it. As for your second question, you told me in your letter. Forgotten already?' he teased gently. 'And your last question – by truck, like you, I expect.'

'But I thought you were miles away.'

His grin broadened. 'My squadron's just been moved to East Markham.' In the darkness she could not see his face, but she could hear the excitement in his voice. He made no effort to conceal it.

'East Markham! Why, that's only a few miles from Suddaby.'

'I know.' He put his arm casually around her shoulders as they walked along the street. The pavements were wet now with a fine drizzle. 'We'd best get out of this, else we'll end up soaked. There's a pub over there. It might not be too crowded. Let's try it.'

Pushing open the door to the bar, they were met by that unmistakable pub smell, a mixture of beer and smoke. Four old men sat in one corner playing dominoes and the barmaid leaned against the bar examining her long painted nails in close detail. She straightened up as Danny approached the bar, and smiled.

'I was beginning to think I'd 'ave to close up an' go home. All our regulars is at the dance.' She pulled a face and it was obvious the girl wished she were there too. 'What'll it be, love?'

Danny ordered a beer for himself and a shandy for Kate. As he carried them across to her and placed them on a small round table, he jerked his head towards the opposite corner. 'Reminds you of me dad and old Tom Willoughby playing dominoes in their usual corner in the Seagull, dun't it?'

The barmaid had gone back to leaning against the bar and had resumed her nail examination.

Kate smiled as she sipped her drink. 'And you – given half a chance.'

He grinned and then sighed. 'What I'd give sometimes to be safely back at Fleethaven Point playing dominoes with the old 'uns! I had a game with 'em last time I was home.'

'Have – you flown any missions yet?'

He twisted the glass round and round as it stood on the table, staring at it but not really seeing it. The frothy beer slopped from side to side in the glass. 'Yup,' he answered shortly.

'Is it very bad?'

There was silence for a moment. 'Varies.'

She leaned forward. 'Danny. It's me – Kate. You can talk to me about it.'

He sighed deeply. 'It's not that, Katie, you know I'd tell you. But – well – we all like to try to forget about it for a while when we're out. Y'know.'

'Oh, I see,' she said, but her tone indicated the opposite. He was leading a different life now, a life in which she

289

had no part and he was reluctant to tell her about it. She felt resentful.

Sensing her mood, he grinned. 'Come on, Katie. Let's go for a walk up the hill, eh? It's stopped raining.'

Mollified a little, she agreed.

They climbed Steep Hill, their arms linked casually, talking when they felt like it, or just in companionable silence.

'Tell me how things are at home. Have you managed any leave recently?' he asked her.

'No – not since you were there. It was difficult – after the air-raid.' She was silent for a moment, thinking about Rosie, seeing in her mind's eye the girl in the shadows of the pillbox with a soldier.

'You were right about Rosie,' she murmured.

She felt his arm stiffen under hers. 'Rosie? What about Rosie?'

She couldn't see his face in the blackness, but there was a strange note in his tone, almost like a defensiveness.

Kate was silent. She was remembering now Rosie begging her not to tell Danny. Of all people, she didn't want Danny to know. Kate felt guilty, wishing she had kept quiet. She'd had a little too much to drink, that was the trouble; her mouth was apt to say what it liked.

'Kate?' he prompted. He was not going to let it rest there.

'Oh, it's nothing. She just flirts about a bit. You know.'

He stopped and turned to face her, taking hold of her shoulders, peering at her through the darkness. 'No, I don't know. You tell me.'

'I – I caught her in that pillbox the army has built at the Point – with one of the soldiers.'

For a moment, his fingers dug into her arms. Then he let go.

'Well, I'm not having that. Next time I go home, I'll sort her out – an' him, if need be.'

'Oh Danny, don't be stupid. I wish I hadn't told you.'

'I'm glad you did. I wouldn't want to see young Rosie getting 'ersen into trouble.'

'And how are we going to stop her? We're not there.'

'I'll think of something,' Danny muttered.

They walked along in silence, Kate wishing she hadn't let her unruly tongue run away with itself.

'We'd better be getting back to the dance hall. It must be getting late.'

They turned and walked back down the hill, their footsteps echoing hollowly on the cobbles.

When they arrived back at the hall, the caretakers were clearing up. There was no sign of any of their friends.

And worse still – all the transport trucks had disappeared.

Twenty-Seven

'**O**h heck! Now what are we going to do?' Danny muttered, while Kate stared in horror at the spot where the trucks had been parked. There was not a vehicle of any sort to be seen.

'Come on,' Danny said. 'We'll start walking and see if we can hitch a lift.'

'Not likely,' she argued, finding her voice. 'I've tried that once before. I'm not walking all that way . . .'

'What do you mean, you've done it before?' he asked, a belligerent note in his voice. 'When?'

'When I ran away from school – remember? I walked for miles, got soaking wet – and lost! There'll be nothing come along at this time of night to give us a lift. Shouldn't think that carrier of mine's out at this hour – even if he's still around.'

'Don't be daft, Kate. That's years ago. It's a fine night – no rain. You're not a fourteen-year-old kid any more, and besides . . .'

She could hear the amusement in his voice and although she couldn't actually see it, knew he was smiling. 'What?'

'You've got *me* with you this time!'

'Ah well,' she said, laughing and linking her arm through his again. 'That makes all the difference!'

'I don't know what we're laughing for, 'cos there's going to be hell to pay when we get back – it'll be jankers at the very least for both of us.'

'Oh, I'll be all right,' Kate said confidently. 'I'm the CO's pet driver.'

You wouldn't think so, Kate was thinking to herself the next morning as she faced a livid Philip Trent across his desk, or that I'd saved his life – twice!

She was standing to attention, so rigidly that her back began to ache. It was like waiting for sentence to be passed. In this mood he was going to throw the book at her and, most likely, at her section commander too. She and Danny had walked up Steep Hill and out on to the Wragby Road. They'd only had to walk a couple of miles before they had hitched a lift to within two miles of Suddaby camp. Danny left her at the gate and disappeared into the night to get back to his own station. She wondered how he was faring now, up before his own CO!

Kate had reported to the guardroom, praying that it was Isobel's friend on duty. But her luck had run out; the man was a stranger to her and one who obviously stuck rigidly to the rule book.

She had been reported to Chiefy for being half an hour late.

'Oh Kate,' Martin moaned at her, running his hand across his bald pate. 'You would make life difficult. I can hardly confine you to barracks for a couple of days when you're the CO's driver.' He'd sighed and fiddled with his pen on the desk. 'Look, I'll let it go this time. But we'll have to hope the CO doesn't hear about it, or we're both in trouble.'

And now she was standing facing Group Captain Trent and wondering how on earth he had heard about her escapade.

'Everyone else got back on time. Where were you?' Philip barked, his handsome face creased with angry lines.

'We took a walk, sir.'

'We? Who's we?'

'Danny Eland, sir.'

'Oh!' For a moment he seemed nonplussed. 'That's – er – Danny from home?'

'Yes, sir.'

'I – didn't realize he was stationed nearby.'

Kate remained silent, her gaze fixed on the top button of his jacket. Philip ran his hand distractedly through his short, springy hair. 'I was worried sick, Kate. Don't ever do that to me again.'

'What?' she could not prevent the surprise in her tone. His remark – nor the tone in his voice now – was not that of a commanding officer. Then she recollected herself. 'No, sir.'

He stood up and came round the desk. 'You can stop standing there like you're on parade now.'

She relaxed and, for the first time, met his eyes. The anger had gone, but the anxiety still lingered. 'A girl was injured last week walking back to camp in the night. It was an accident, of course, but in the blackout, the driver didn't see her,' he explained softly. 'I couldn't get it out of my mind when I knew you weren't back.'

'How did you know I wasn't back?' she asked in a small voice.

He smiled now, a little sheepishly, Kate thought. 'Oh, I – er – sent for you. Your friends tried to cover for you valiantly, but it was obvious you weren't there and that they didn't know where you were.'

'I'm sorry. Did you want driving somewhere?'

'No,' he said, but did not offer any further explanation.

Kate was thankful that Philip took no further action against her or Flight Sergeant Martin, although it rather surprised her. He had been so very angry at first, yet his fury seemed to stem from anxiety about her safety rather than that she had broken the rules.

She doubted Danny had been so fortunate and she waited anxiously for a letter. But the days went by, a week and then two, and no word came from Danny.

'The Adj has just rung through,' Chiefy bent his head under the raised bonnet of the Humber where Kate was changing the plugs. 'CO's been summoned to a high level meeting at Group HQ. You're likely to be very late back . . .' He grinned at her. '*Officially*, this time!'

'Sir!' Kate smiled and connected the final plug. She packed up her tool kit, wiped her hands on a rag and then sprinted to the wash-room.

Seven hours later she was dozing fitfully in the car parked in the sweeping driveway of Group Headquarters when the sudden sound of someone opening the passenger door and climbing in made her jump.

'Oh, I'm sorry, sir . . .'

'Don't apologize, Kate,' Philip said gently, his voice heavy with tiredness. 'I hope you haven't been sitting here all this time. Have you had something to eat?'

'Oh yes, I've been fine. I only came back to the car about an hour ago when I heard the meeting was breaking up.'

'Yes. Sorry about that, I got caught up with the CO from East Markham. I'm afraid he needs a lift back, Kate. His car broke down on the way here. He'll be here in a minute.'

Wearily, Philip removed his hat and ran his fingers through his thick hair that curled so tightly each curl was like a coiled spring. He leaned his head back against the seat and closed his eyes.

'Er, shouldn't you really sit in the back, sir?' Kate said

hesitantly, reluctant to disturb him, but if they were to have company in the car . . .

His head snapped up and his eyes opened. 'Oh Lord, yes.' As he opened the door and swung his legs out, Kate was sure she heard him mutter, ' . . . and I was so looking forward to sitting in front with you.'

By the time Group Captain Sellick appeared and Kate hopped out to open the door for him, Philip was sitting sedately in the back seat.

'This is very decent of you, Trent.'

'Not at all,' she heard Philip reply as they left Grantham and headed out into the black country road. The moonlight was only fitful as heavy clouds scudded across it. One moment the landscape was bathed in silvery light, the next plunged into pitch blackness. Thank goodness for all that rigorous night driving during training, Kate thought.

Suddenly she slammed both her feet down hard on the brake and the clutch pedal as a black shape loomed up directly in front. The heavy car slithered to the right, throwing the occupants sliding about the back seat.

'What the devil?' she heard one of them mutter as the car came to a halt on the grass verge. Kate half turned her head to see the sorrowful faces of several cows pressed close to the car windows.

'Ahem – it seems they have us surrounded,' Group Captain Sellick said, making no effort to move.

Kate was out of the car and closing the door behind her. 'Come on, cush, cush. Now where have you lot come from, I wonder?' Out in the night air, her eyes became more accustomed to the darkness. She moved among the cows, gently pushing them. 'There, there, girl . . . Ah, now I see.' Dimly, in the fitful moonlight, she could see that the hedge into a nearby field had been trampled down. 'And I see you've

296

brought Dobbin with you too, have you?' she added, laughing softly to herself as she saw a cart-horse amongst the herd.

Slapping the rump of the nearest cow, she turned it and shooed it back towards the opening, all the time murmuring soothing encouragement. Thankfully, she saw the rest of the herd turn and follow the lead of the first cow.

'Want any help?' she heard Philip call.

'Can you get hold of the horse and bring him along?' she called back. 'They've got out of a hole in the hedge here. He must have been in the same field.'

He seemed to hesitate a moment before he said, 'Right.'

It took a good twenty minutes to get all the cows back into the field and lastly the horse, who seemed the most reluctant of all to return.

'Come on, boy,' Kate said, letting him nuzzle her hand. 'I'd have brought a sugar lump if I'd known we were going to meet like this.'

Philip's voice came out of the blackness. 'Oh, I don't mind about the sugar.'

Kate giggled. 'Careful, he might hear you . . .'

'Not him! He's staying safely in the car. You'd never think he was a DFC and yet daren't get in amongst a herd of cows.'

'Can you grab hold of his mane on your side? Come on, boy.' There was a pause while they struggled to get the horse to move. Suddenly it shot forward, through the hole and into the field.

'Thank goodness,' Kate breathed relief. Together they turned to walk back towards the car.

Philip sneezed three times in quick succession. 'Maybe he's getting ready to award *you* the DFC.' Through the darkness she heard his deep chuckle. 'Not the Distinguished Flying Cross, of course. I was thinking more of something like . . . Dispersing Frightening Cows.'

Reaching the car, Kate stifled her laughter. As she started

the engine, Group Captain Sellick asked casually, 'Brought up on a farm, were you, driver?'

'Yes, sir.'

'Ah – that explains it then.'

Beside him, Philip sneezed again – three times.

When they delivered their passenger to East Markham, Kate thought fleetingly that maybe Danny was quite close . . . Then, in the dim light, Kate's attention was caught by the sight of a dark patch on the right side of Philip's face. And he was still sneezing every few minutes. As they pulled away from the gate, she asked with concern, 'Are you all right, sir?'

'Kate – we're on our own now. Drop all this "sir" nonsense. Yes, thanks, I'm fine.' He didn't sound it, she thought. He sounded as if he had suddenly developed a dreadful head cold.

'But – your face . . .?'

'It's only a rash. It was the horse.'

Mystified, she repeated, 'The horse?'

'I get a kind of hay-fever when I get near horses and dogs.'

'Really? Oh, I am sorry. I wouldn't have asked you to help if I'd known.'

'It's nothing. It'll wear off after a time.'

'And the rash on your face . . .?'

'I touched the horse and then my face. It's all part of the allergy.' He grinned. 'Pull over a minute. I think I'll sit up front with you – at least until we get back near camp. I rather like sitting next to you, *Corporal* Hilton.'

'Pardon?'

'Oh yes,' Philip said airily as he got in beside her. 'I've recommended you for promotion. You'll be made up to corporal next week.'

Kate was thankful for the darkness for she knew her face was pink with pleasure.

*

'You should have seen the East Markham CO sitting rigidly in the middle of the back seat, hardly daring to move!' Kate regaled the others with her story later that night. 'And then poor old Ph . . .' Quickly she corrected herself. 'Our poor old CO, when he got out to help me, started sneezing his head off. Seems he gets a type of hay-fever from horses and dogs.'

Mavis was nodding. 'My dad does and so does my younger brother. It can be hereditary, evidently.'

'Really?' Kate said. 'I can't say I've ever heard of it before. I know about ordinary hay-fever of course, but not from animals.'

'Good job you don't get it, Kate, brought up among all the moo-moos and gee-gees, you'd never stop sneezing!' Isobel drawled.

Kate glanced across at Isobel lying languidly on her bed blowing smoke rings into the air. Isobel would never change completely, she thought. The odd snide remark slipped out occasionally. Right now she was probably feeling miffed at the news of Kate's promotion.

Kate smiled to herself. There was a vast difference in one way, though; now Kate was strong enough not to be hurt by anything Isobel said.

The early months of 1941 had been gripped with wintry weather and operations were often cancelled. But with the coming of spring, activity at Suddaby increased. Almost nightly there were bombing raids over enemy territory and Philip never left the station when 'his boys' were away on a raid. Kate was kept busy driving him around the huge airfield; to briefing sessions, watching the ground crews bombing-up, and then later out to dispersal. Often he would ask Kate to drive the bus taking the crews out to the waiting aircraft, climbing aboard the vehicle himself and staying with the airmen until the last moment.

Kate's admiration for the pilots and the other members of the crews grew. They laughed and joked on the bus, as if they were on a jolly works outing, flirting a little with her as they clattered down the steps in their bulky flying jackets and boots.

'See you later, sweetheart.'

'How about a date on Saturday night, gorgeous?'

On one such trip, she met Sandy Petersen again when she drove him and the rest of the crew of T-Tommy out to their aircraft. Sandy, with hair the colour to match his nickname, was a little more persistent in his approach. 'There's a good film on in Lincoln on Friday. If we're not flying would you like to go?'

Kate smiled. 'Yes, thanks, Sandy. I would.'

The smile he gave her as he waved goodbye stayed with her through the long night. She waved as he crossed the tarmac towards the huge bulk of the waiting aircraft. In the dusk she saw him raise his right arm in farewell.

Kate turned the bus around to drive Philip back to the control tower where they went up on to the roof to watch take-off. On clear, fine nights they would stay out in the open, only sheltering in the glass observation room if it were cold or wet.

As the engines of the sixteen Avro Manchesters burst into life and taxied out on to the runways, the ground seemed to vibrate with their throbbing; the whole world seemed filled with noise. They took off, labouring into the night sky, cumbersome with their weight of bombs. Then, for those left behind, came the long hours of dreadful waiting.

'Take me back to my office, would you, Kate? I'll try to get an hour or so shut-eye.'

As she pulled up outside the door of the building housing

the CO's office and was about to open her car door, she felt his hand on her arm.

'Kate . . .' he began, strangely hesitant. 'Would it – would it compromise you too much if I were to ask you to come in and have a drink with me?'

She looked at him through the gloom. 'No – of course not.'

She saw the gleam of his teeth as he smiled. 'Come on, then,' he whispered, gleefully conspiratorial.

'Sit down,' he invited, closing the door of his office and moving to the cabinet where he had a bottle and glasses stowed away. 'I hate these hours when they're away,' he murmured. 'And yet, it's almost worse when they come back and you're counting the aircraft, willing them all back safely and yet knowing . . .'

He left the rest of his sentence unsaid. Placing a drink before her, he sat down in his chair, taking off his cap and running his hand across his forehead, up and through his hair. He let out a deep sigh. 'Oh, Kate, my dear girl, don't get too involved with any of them, will you?'

Kate looked up, a sharp reply on her lips. What business was it of his what she did in her off-duty time? What right had he to give her such advice?

Her mouth set in a rebellious line, she said shortly, 'I won't.'

He sat twirling the glass, watching the swirling liquid. She heard him sigh deeply and then, deliberately changing the subject, he began to ask her about her home, the farm, her family; anything to steer their thoughts away from the squadron at this moment facing flak as they crossed the enemy coast. But not once during the hours they sat together through the long night did he mention his own life or family.

As a pale, watery dawn stretched itself across the flat

fields, they went back to the control tower to await the returning aircraft.

'I'll be on the roof, Kate,' he told her, 'but do you mind taking one of the buses out to meet the crews? One of the other drivers has gone off sick.'

'Of course,' she agreed.

She had often driven the airmen out to their aircraft, but this was the first time she had met their return. When the first plane landed and she drove the bus as near as she could to pick up the crew she was shocked by the sight of them. The laughing, joking boys who had departed now returned exhausted, dirty and silent. Their faces were streaked with grime, their eyes wide with tiredness and they climbed unsteadily into the bus as if every bone in their bodies ached to lie down and rest. Now there was no laughter, no joking, no flirting. They didn't speak to her, didn't even look at her.

Silently she drove them straight to de-briefing and returned to meet another aircraft. By the time the day was fully light, the sky was silent. All the aircraft were back; all, except one.

T-Tommy did not return.

Later that day she drove Philip to Group HQ. As they pulled up outside, he leaned forward from the back seat.

'Kate, I'm sorry about Sandy. I know I have no right to tell you how to run your life but . . .'

'No, you haven't . . .' she began and then, turning to look at him, she saw the tender expression in his eyes, his forehead furrowed with anxiety for her, and her retort died.

His voice was low and hoarse as he added, 'I just don't want to see you get hurt, Kate.'

His concern for her brought a lump to her throat. All she could do was nod.

'Was – was there anything between you and Sandy? I – I overheard him ask you out.'

She shook her head and said flatly, 'No, no there wasn't.' Silently, in her own mind she added sadly, 'There wasn't time.'

She was surprised to see the look of relief that crossed her Commanding Officer's face at her denial of an involvement with the young airman. Thoughtfully, she watched him stride into the building with almost a spring in his step.

Weeks had gone by and she had heard nothing from Danny. Since the loss of Sandy Petersen's aircraft, Kate had become even more aware of just how vulnerable Danny was. Their own aircraft were on ops night after night; East Markham would be no different.

'I'm going to ring East Markham and find out if he's all right!'

Mavis gasped. 'You can't do that, Kate.'

'Why not?'

'They won't like it,' Isobel put in. 'They don't like girls ringing about their boyfriends and if they find out you're a WAAF, they'll take a very dim view.'

'Shan't tell 'em who I am.'

'I doubt they'll tell you anything then.'

'You're allowed to ring the Mess, aren't you?'

Mavis and Isobel exchanged a glance, then Mavis shrugged. 'Don't ask me. If he's on ops they'll tell you absolutely nothing. You can bet your life on it.'

'If that's the case, then I'll know, won't I?' she said reasonably.

'You can't ring from here, you know. It means walking down to the village.'

'Well then, I'll go down to the pub when I'm off duty and ring from there.'

That evening she cajoled the telephone number out of the Adjutant and rang the Airmen's Mess at East Markham. As the receiver was lifted and a voice said 'Hello,' she could hear noisy singing and laughter in the background.

'Is Danny Eland there?'

'Who?' She repeated his name and gave his rank. 'Sorry, I've never heard of him.' He covered the mouthpiece with his hand, but she could still plainly hear him shouting above the racket. 'Anyone know a Danny Eland?'

She heard an answering shout but could not distinguish the words. The man on the other end spoke into the receiver again. 'Seems he's on leave. Got a seventy-two to go home.'

'Home?' Her voice was a strangulated squeak. 'But he – he can't have.'

'Oh – er – sorry. Have I let the cat out of the bag? You mean he's not come home?'

'No – yes – no – oh, never mind,' Kate said, and rang off.

She was seething as she walked back to the huts. How dare he go home – again – and not let her know? Was she taking it for granted that she could never get leave to coincide with his? He hadn't even written to her to give her the chance to try.

Just wait till she saw him again; she wouldn't half give him what-for!

'There's someone to see you.' Mavis cupped her hands around her mouth and yelled at Kate across the stretch of grass between the control tower to which she was headed, and the MT yard where Kate was washing down the staff car.

Kate looked up to see Mavis gesticulating towards the guard-room near the gate. 'Get a move on. It's Danny.'

'Danny!' Kate dropped her cloth into the bucket, hardly

noticing the water that splashed on to her foot, for already she was racing towards the gate.

'Danny. What are you doing here?' In her joy at seeing him her anger with him was swiftly forgotten. But in the next moment her delight turned to apprehension. He looked very solemn and somehow strangely ill at ease. 'Kate,' he said, taking her arm. 'There's something I have to tell you.'

Fear stabbed her. 'Is something wrong at home?'

He hesitated a fraction of a second, but then shook his head. 'Come on, let's go somewhere quiet.'

Having booked in at the guard-room, Danny took her arm and together they walked round the edge of the airfield. It was sultry; the only sound in the stillness was a bee buzzing along the hedgerow.

'Kate – Rosie and I – we're going to get married.'

She stood still, her mouth slightly open. The sun beat down mercilessly, so hot upon her head, that she felt dizzy.

'What? You're not serious, Danny?'

'We've spent a lot of time together lately – when I've been home on leave.'

She thrust her face close to his. 'Yes – when you've been home without me! Now I see why.'

'It's not like that, Kate. Be reasonable.'

'Reasonable, reasonable? You ask me to be reasonable when you're – you're going to get married and to – to *her*? Why are you doing it, Danny? To keep her away from the soldiers? Think she'll be safe, married to you? "Oh, I'll sort her out," you said,' she mimicked bitterly. 'Well, ya've certainly done that, bain't ya?' The dialect was strong now; she was angry. She prodded his shoulder with her forefinger. 'Ya don't have to marry the little bitch to stop her getting 'ersen into trouble, Danny.' She saw him wince and look away from her with a look of disgust on his face. A stab of fear shot through her. She was losing him.

305

'It's not like that, Kate,' he said quietly. 'I'm – very fond of Rosie. I *want* to marry her.'

'You wanted to marry me. Remember?' Her voice rose and she jabbed her finger into her own chest. 'Me!'

Soberly, he nodded, his voice scarcely above a whisper. 'I remember.'

They stared at each other; she, hurt and resentful, he, determined yet with an air of sorrow. In his deep brown eyes there was still a sadness for what might have been, but could never be.

'Don't pity me,' Kate spat at him.

He shook his head. 'Oh, Kate, Kate. Why are you acting like this? I thought you'd be pleased. I thought you loved Rosie . . .'

'I did,' she almost screamed. '*That's* what makes it worse. She was my friend – and she's betrayed me. If you had to get married then I'd rather it be anyone else rather than Rosie. Anyone but Rosie.'

'But – but why? She's still your friend, she loves you dearly. She's going to be so hurt that you . . .'

'I'll never speak to her again, not as long as I live, I won't. I don't even want to see her – not ever.'

'Oh Kate, don't. Please don't say that.' His brown eyes were dark pools of suffering. 'We want you to come to the wedding – you must come . . .'

Kate broke into hysterical laughter. Go to their wedding? How could he be so cruel, she thought, or so stupid? Didn't he understand what this was doing to her? Didn't he know how she felt about him; how much she loved him and always would?

At this precise moment, she wanted to kill Rosie Maine.

Twenty-Eight

Chiefy found her, sloshing water all over the Humber and soaking her feet and legs as well.

'Whatever's got into you, Hilton . . .?' he began, then, coming closer, he realized that she could hardly see what she was doing for the tears streaming down her face.

Kate felt him touch her arm. 'Leave it, love. Come on . . .'

'I can't – I must finish – the car,' she sobbed.

'It's okay. I'll get one of the lads to do it. Come with me.' There was a gentle firmness in his tone that forbade further argument. With a heavy sigh, Kate dropped the cloth into the bucket and turned away.

As they walked back towards the office, Chiefy asked gently, 'Anything I can do to help?'

She shook her head. 'No, no thanks. I'll be fine,' she replied and wondered how she could tell such a lie. She couldn't believe she would ever be 'fine' again.

'Well, go and get a lie-down in your quarters.' He glanced at his watch. 'I can give you an hour, but no more. All right?'

Grateful for his understanding, even though he didn't know what was causing her misery, Kate nodded.

It was almost as bad as before, she thought, as she lay flat on her back on her bed, gazing up at the rafters of the hut, when they had found they were half-brother and sister and that they could never marry.

Now Danny was going to marry Rosie. How could he?

307

How could he do this to her, Kate? Obviously, he no longer felt the same way about her, or else he wouldn't – couldn't – marry someone else. And Rosie! Why, oh why did it have to be Rosie?

The hut was hot and stuffy and now she had a blinding headache. How she longed for the cool, blissful tranquillity at the end of the Spit . . .

'What's up with you? I thought you were out with lover-boy?'

Kate groaned as she rolled over. She had not realized she had fallen asleep. 'Just let me die!' she moaned.

Mavis was bending over her bed in the half-light of evening. 'You ill, Kate?'

She laid her hand against Kate's forehead. 'You do feel a bit hot. Have you reported sick?'

Kate rolled her head from side to side on the pillow.

'Well, come on then . . .'

'Just – leave me alone!' she whimpered.

'Oh sorry, I'm sure.'

The door opened and Isobel marched down towards them, coming to stand beside Mavis to stare down at Kate. 'Oh, you've found her then?'

Mavis turned questioning eyes upon Isobel, who said, 'One of the lads from MT said some bloke came to see her . . .'

'Yes, it was Danny,' Mavis put in. 'You know, the famous Danny we're always hearing about . . .'

'Well, she came back and began throwing water all over the Humber,' Isobel went on. 'To coin his phrase, not mine, she was "bawling her eyes out and making a right pig's ear of it", until Chiefy sent her off duty.'

'Eh?' Mavis stared aghast. 'Oh, heavens! Me putting my great size sevens right in it.'

'As usual,' Isobel murmured, but now they both looked down again at Kate, then they sat either side of her on the bed.

'What's the matter?' Isobel asked.

'Come on, Kate,' Mavis coaxed. 'You can tell us.'

'He's – he's . . .' Fresh tears spurted and Mavis pushed a handkerchief into her hands. 'Getting married!' Kate wailed.

'Married? You – you mean – not to you?'

'Of course she means not to her, idiot, or she wouldn't be blubbering like this, would she?' Isobel snapped.

'Then – who?'

'My – best – friend.'

'Oh hell! That is rough,' Isobel muttered, and for once there was real sympathy in her voice.

'You don't understand . . .' Kate began, then stopped. How could she explain it all to them? It would sound very odd. She was in love with her own half-brother. No – no, she couldn't tell them; certainly not Isobel, even though they were friends now, and not even the easy-going Mavis. It would sound decidedly odd to them.

She made a determined effort and pulled herself upright. 'I'll be – okay, honest,' she sniffed and blew hard into the handkerchief. 'It was just a – a shock. But really, I'd rather not talk about it. Best to try to forget, you know.'

They regarded her seriously for a moment, then, taking their cue from her, Mavis said, 'That's the spirit, girl. Tell you what, we're off duty tonight. If his nibs doesn't want you, we're off down to the pub in the village. All right?'

Kate nodded. Anything, she thought, to blot out her own thoughts right now.

Of course, she couldn't avoid going home – not for ever. She missed seeing her grandad, who wasn't too well now, and her mother and stepfather; even, to her surprise, Lilian. Since she had been away from home, she had begun to feel strangely sorry for Lilian. Detached from home, Kate could see things a little more objectively. Her young sister was a strange girl. She had proved to be clever, academically clever, and Esther's pride in her younger daughter knew no bounds. Two years before war had broken out she had passed the scholarship to go to the local Grammar School.

'University, that's where our Lilian's going when this stupid war's over,' Esther vowed.

'What's the use of a woman going to university?' Will Benson would growl. 'Ya don't need book learning to care for a husband and family?'

'Why shouldn't she go?' Esther would bristle. 'Women ought to have the same chance as men.' And under her breath she would mutter, 'Would have saved me a lot of trouble if Squire'd have thought that years ago and given me the tenancy of the farm straight off! And what about our Kate then? Doin' her bit for the war, ain't she, alongside the fellers?'

'Huh!' Beaten in the same old argument, Will would stamp off to his room slamming the door as he went, leaving Esther triumphant.

But Kate was no longer jealous of her younger sister. In fact, she felt rather sorry for her. It was difficult to live up to the high expectations of proud parents.

'Oh, Kate, it's good to have you home,' Esther said, hugging her. 'Come on in. I've a rabbit pie in the oven and ya grandad's feeling better today. We'll all sit down to dinner together. How've ya been?'

'Not bad, Mam.'

There was a moment's pause as Esther held her at arm's

length and studied her face. Then she sighed gently. 'I can see you've heard the news, then.'

Kate nodded and bit her lip. 'He came to the camp to – to tell me himself.'

'That must have taken a bit o' doing,' Esther murmured, and Kate saw the truth in her words.

'I suppose so.' She sat down in the Windsor chair by the range which still warmed the kitchen and cooked the food. Nothing had changed here at Brumbys' Farm, and in her present state of unhappiness Kate found a reassuring security in that fact. She leaned her head against the back of the chair and closed her eyes. 'Oh Mam, what am I going to do?'

When she opened her eyes, it was to see her mother standing in front of her, hands on her hips. 'Do, lass? What d'ya mean, do?' And then in answer to her own question, she added. 'Ya going to get on with ya life, lass, that's what ya going to do. Meet a nice feller, get married and give me a barrow-load of grand-bairns.'

Kate smiled. Oh, how good it was to be home!

Feigning the submissiveness of childhood, she said, 'Yes, Mam.'

She didn't see Rosie or Beth Eland. She didn't want to see Rosie, not ever. And she couldn't even face Beth – not yet.

'Ya will come home for the wedding, though, Kate, won't ya?' her mother asked.

Kate shook her head. 'I can't, Mam, I just can't.' Then she eyed her mother with amusement – the first flash of genuine humour she had felt recently. 'Don't tell me you're going, Mam? Not to an *Eland* wedding?'

Esther wriggled her shoulders. 'Ya Dad ses I've got to go,'

she smiled self-consciously. 'We allus seem to come together – me an' Beth – for funerals and the like. I 'spose a wedding's as good a reason as any.'

'Well, it's an improvement on funerals!' Kate remarked drily, and her mother had the grace to smile.

'Ya ought to come, Kate. He is ya brother.'

'By heck, you've changed your tune!' Then her tone softened sadly. 'Oh, Mam, if only you'd told us that years ago.'

'I know, lass, I know. Mebbe we should have done.' She sighed. 'But it weren't all my secret, y'know.'

There was silence between them, only the ticking of the clock and the crackling of the wood on the fire in the range.

'I can't come to the wedding, Mam. Really I can't.'

On the day she knew Danny and Rosie were getting married, Kate was safely back at camp, although her mind was anywhere but on her job.

'What is the matter with you today, Kate?' Philip asked her as she took a corner too sharply and the offside wheels bounced on to the grass verge. Even that reminded her sharply of Danny, she thought wryly, and the time they had landed up in a ditch in the Squire's car. Aloud she said, 'Sorry, sir.'

'Is there something the matter?'

'No – no, sir.'

'I've told you not to call me "sir" when we're on our own.'

'No – Philip.'

They fell silent and didn't speak again until she drew up a little way from the camp to allow him to get into the back as had become their habit.

'I shan't need you again today. Get yourself down to the pub in the village with some of your mates and relax a little.'

She forced a weak smile and met his gaze in the rear-view mirror. 'Is that an order – sir?'

She watched the serious expression on his face lighten as he smiled. 'Yes, Corporal Hilton. It's an order.'

'Yes, sir!'

Twenty-Nine

'**S**hut up, Kate, do,' Mavis hissed.

As if from a great distance, Kate heard them arguing over her head as she felt herself being dragged along between them, her stumbling feet seeming to have a will of their own.

'Silly cow'll get us on a fizzer,' Isobel muttered, forgetting her lady-like manner for once. 'Whatever did you let her drink so much for?'

'Don't blame me, you were there too. Or were you too busy chatting up Ron?' Mavis countered.

'We should have known – we should have watched her.'

'He doesn't love me,' Kate wailed. 'He's gone and married . . .'

'Has he got married then?' Isobel hissed at Mavis above Kate's lolling head.

'Yes – today. He rang up again last night to try to get her to go to the wedding. I ask you! Must be a heartless bastard!'

'No – no,' Kate's head came up. 'You've got it wrong, Mave. He does love me, really. He can't marry me, so he's got to marry Rosie. But I didn't want him to get married. 'Specially not – not *Rosie*!'

'What *is* she on about?' Isobel asked.

'Search me,' Mavis said. 'Got this Rosie up the stick by the sound of it.'

'No – no! I – will explain it all,' Kate enunciated carefully. 'Because you're my – my friends now. But you weren't always my friend, were you, Isobel? You – were – very unkind to

314

me at sh-chool, Is-o-bel.' Kate wagged her forefinger in the air at no one in particular seeing as both her arms were being held tightly by the girls on either side of her. 'You used to – call – me Sicky . . . '

As if the memory again prompted the action, she felt the bile rise in her throat. 'I'm gonner be sick!' was all she could mumble before the quantities of beer she had consumed came spewing up into the road.

'Seems I wasn't far wrong either,' Isobel said brutally, but she put her hand on Kate's forehead and held back her long hair while she heaved and retched on to the grass verge.

'Where's her cap?' Isobel asked.

'In my pocket,' Mavis said grimly. 'Oh, heavens! There's something coming!'

Mavis and Isobel looked back over their shoulders as the noise of a vehicle and the pin-pricks of light from its shrouded headlights came towards them.

'Quick, there's a ditch here. Come on, they might not see us.'

'Ugh! There's water in the bottom,' exclaimed the fastidious Isobel.

'Better than being in the guard-room,' Mavis said tartly, shuddering as the cold water covered her ankles.

Kate groaned and slipped from their grasp, splashing on to her knees in the bottom of the ditch.

At that moment the moon, which had been hidden by the clouds, chose to appear, lighting up the countryside with its silver glow.

'Oh hell!' Mavis muttered. 'Now we're for it . . . '

The vehicle slowed as it drew level with the three girls cowering in the ditch and then stopped. As the engine was cut, silence bathed the countryside. Mavis and Isobel held their breath, but Kate, oblivious to what was happening, began to sing.

'There was I waiting at the church, waiting at the church . . .'

Footsteps sounded on the road and then whispered across the grass verge.

'Can't get away to marry you today,' Kate yodelled tunelessly, 'my wife won't – let me!' The final words ended on a high-pitched wail. She threw back her head and looked up into the shadowy face of a tall man standing on the bank directly above them.

'What on earth is going on?'

Kate giggled. 'Why, if it isn't the handsome Groupie!'

Beside her, Isobel groaned, but Mavis was scrambling up out of the ditch. 'Sir – could you just forget you've seen us, please?' She was standing on the bank beside him now. 'Kate's had an awful shock – some sort of family trouble. This isn't like her – really it isn't.'

The silence was all around them again. 'Please, sir, couldn't you – just this once . . .?' Mavis pleaded softly.

Philip Trent's deep voice came gently out of the darkness. 'It's all right, I won't be taking any action over this. I just want to help.' He bent down and stretched out his hand. 'Come on, Kate Hilton. Let's get you back to camp. Maybe I can get her past the guard easier than you two could.'

They couldn't see his face in the darkness, but they could hear the genuine concern in his voice. With him pulling and Isobel pushing, they heaved Kate out of the ditch and between them half-dragged, half-carried her to the jeep he was driving.

'Put her in the back with my coat over her. It's on the back seat. One of you sit with her. The other, come in front with me.'

Hardly able to believe this was actually happening, they obeyed meekly and a few moments later they were heading along the lane back towards camp. Kate was no longer sing-

316

ing – now she was crying. 'I'm sorry. I'm sorry. I didn't mean to . . .'

Her voice faded away and she was quiet.

Isobel leaned forward from the back seat. 'I think she's asleep.'

Philip Trent nodded.

A few yards from the camp gate, he stopped the jeep. 'Look, I hate to do this to you, but if you two get out here and come into camp as normal, I think I can get her past the guards better than if I've got you on board as well.' His deep chuckle made them both smile. As they slid out of the jeep, Mavis said. 'Thank you, sir – for everything.'

'Yes, thank you, sir,' Isobel echoed, 'you've been jolly decent about this.'

'Think nothing of it. But not a word to a soul, mind.'

'No, sir,' they chorused with heartfelt agreement.

Kate was not asleep. Through the mists of alcohol, she had heard everything that was going on, but she couldn't seem to get her mind to work properly. She was muddled and confused. She had never in her life felt like this before; but then never before had she been drunk.

Fortunately for them both, she lay quietly while Philip drove through the gates, pausing to prove his identity to the guard. 'My driver's in the back. We've had a long day . . .'

The soldier on duty glanced into the back of the jeep, then stepped back and saluted smartly. 'Sir!' he barked and the barrier was raised for the vehicle to pass into camp.

It was as if she was waking up in a fog. Her head throbbed abominably when she tried to raise it. She groaned and dropped back against the pillow and a sharp stab of pain shot up the back of her neck and gripped the top of her head.

Somewhere above her a deep voice spoke. 'Oh, surfacing at last, are we?'

Kate opened her eyes and tried to focus on the face bending over her. She blinked rapidly and recognized the face of her commanding officer.

'Oh bloody 'ell!' she muttered and closed her eyes again.

'Such language, young lady!'

'Where am I? What are you doing here?'

'You're in my bed where you've been all night – at least, what was left of it.'

Her eyes flew open. 'Your – *your* bed?'

'Don't look so shocked. I wasn't in it. Taking advantage of a young woman in that state isn't in my line. It's the room behind my office. I like to stay here when there's an op on, so I got it fitted out with the basic necessities. Good job I did. I could hardly have taken you to the CO's house, now could I?'

He sat down carefully on the edge of the bed and leaned over her, resting on his hands placed either side of her. 'Want to talk about it, Kate?' he asked gently.

Kate was just beginning to realize what he had done for her this past night, and at the kindness in his tone easy tears filled her eyes. 'I'm so sorry.'

'It's okay,' he said softly. 'No harm done, as it happens. Your two friends got safely back into camp and – er, Mavis, is it . . .?'

She nodded and he continued. 'Well, Mavis came early this morning and collected your uniform to get it cleaned up. She's just brought it back so you can get up when you like, use my bathroom and then, when you're ready, you can go out through the front office as if you've just been to get your orders for the day. And hopefully . . .' He raised one hand and crossed his fingers, 'No one will be any the wiser for your little escapade.'

She closed her eyes and groaned, imagining what a fool she must have made of herself the previous night. And Philip was being so good about it, even conspiring to sneak her back into camp. She wondered just how many other COs would have done that. No wonder he had said he threw away the rule-book when he felt like it.

'I don't think,' he said slowly, 'you'd better drive today.'

Kate smiled ruefully and put her hand up to her head. 'No, I don't think I better had,' she murmured ungrammatically.

As he got up and turned away, she said, 'You've been very kind. I – don't know how to thank you . . .'

He turned and stood looking down at her. Although his expression was grave, there was a gentle look in his eyes.

'If you remember, Kate Hilton, there have been two occasions when *I* didn't know how to thank *you*. I haven't forgotten, you know.' Then, as if to save them both any further embarrassment, he turned and left the room.

After washing her hair and taking a bath, Kate felt much better, though a little fragile. Dressed in her clean uniform, she waited nervously in Philip's bedroom.

The door opened. 'All clear!' he said in a stage whisper and she went through into his office. 'Parkes has nipped out for lunch so the outer office is empty at the moment. Right now,' he sat down in his chair and steepled his fingers, 'I have to go to East Markham. If you could just drive us out the gate and then in at the other end, I'll drive in between.'

Kate bit her lip and nodded.

'Bring the car round in about an hour. Try to get a bit of lunch . . .' He began, but noticing her turn paler, added, 'If you can face it.'

She smiled thinly and nodded again.

*

319

'Oh, so you are still in the land of the living,' Isobel greeted her as Kate stepped into their hut.

Mavis was hurrying towards her. 'Are you all right? Did he put you on a charge?'

Kate shook her head – and then wished she had not done so for the throbbing increased. She looked at Mavis's troubled face. 'He said you two got back okay. Is that right? You – you didn't get caught?'

Mavis glanced across at Isobel. 'No, he was marvellous. Dropped us off a few yards from the gate and we walked in cool as you like. Oh, wasn't he terrific about it, though?' Mavis said again, a dreamy expression in her eyes.

Kate was relieved. 'That's all right, then.'

'I must say he was jolly decent,' Isobel agreed magnanimously. 'Is he sweet on you or something, Kate?' she added bluntly.

Before Kate could refute such a suggestion, Mavis burst out, 'I jolly well hope not. He's married!' Kate and Isobel stared at her.

'Is he now?' Isobel said softly, but Kate said nothing.

She was surprised at the shaft of disappointment that shot through her. 'How – how do you know?'

'Dave says . . .'

'Ah well, there we have it, then,' Isobel mocked. 'If the fountain of all knowledge says he's married, then married he must be.'

'Shut up, Iso. Dave told me,' Mavis continued patiently. 'He's mates with the Adjutant in the CO's office – Parkes. His *wife* often rings up. Says she's got an aw'fly posh voice. Quite la-di-da.'

Isobel smoothed her blonde hair. 'I'm absolutely devastated,' she said, looking anything but. 'I'd begun to think our lovely CO would be quite a catch. But married – oh dear me no. There's no future in that. Only a lot of heartache.'

Kate glanced at her. How coldly calculating Isobel Cartwright was. There were times when Kate thought the girl had not really changed that much since their school days.

'Excuse me, I've got to go out again. The CO wants driving to East Markham.' She saw the other two exchange a worried glance.

'Will you be all right?' Isobel asked, and there was no mistaking the genuine concern in her tone now. 'I mean – *he's* there, isn't he?'

Instantly Kate regretted her uncharitable thoughts about Isobel.

She managed to give them a wan smile. 'I'll be fine. Danny – Danny won't be there. Don't you remember? He's on honeymoon!'

Safely out of sight of the guard-room, Kate stopped the car and slid from the driver's seat. Philip took her place. 'Don't stand there dithering, get in the front.'

He drove fast but expertly and after a mile or so, she began to relax and some of the guilt for her foolish behaviour began to ebb away. About midway between the two camps, he pulled over on to a wide grass verge on the top of a hill and cut the engine. They sat looking at the scene before them.

She felt his gaze upon her and turned to meet his eyes. They were full of compassion and tenderness. 'Last night wasn't like you, Kate. Not a bit. I know that. Something awful must have happened.'

She looked down at her hands, twisting together in her lap. Tears welled in her eyes and spilled down her cheeks, splashing on to her hands.

'Tell me,' he urged her gently.

So she told him. Everything. From the very beginning, as

far back as she could remember and even before that; about her mother, and Danny's mother; about her father, who was also Danny's father. And about Danny – oh, she told him all about Danny. She cried as she told him, but there was laughter too as she remembered everything. It was like reliving her life again. All the happiness – and then all the sadness.

When she had finished, she found she was lying with her cheek against the rough fabric of his jacket and became aware that his hand was stroking her hair. 'You poor kids,' he murmured.

She became aware of his nearness and sat up, suddenly embarrassed. 'I'm sorry.' She tried to smile, but her mouth quivered. 'I seem to be saying that a lot today.'

His smile was sympathetic. 'Has it helped?'

She nodded, and said, surprise in her tone. 'Yes, yes, I think it has.'

'They say it's good to talk your troubles out. I sometimes wish . . .' He leaned forward and pressed the starter. The engine leapt into life and whatever he had been going to say was drowned in the noise.

'*My dear Kate,*' her stepfather wrote.

I was grieved you could not find it in your heart to attend Danny and Rosie's marriage. On what should have been a happy day for her, the dear girl was heartbroken that you were not there. I know how you feel – and even though these words may deny it – I do understand. But years have passed since you learned the truth and you should by now have come to terms with it. Try to understand, my dear, that life must go forward. You and Danny cannot remain in the safe cocoon of childhood, all in all to each other to the exclusion of all other relationships. It is unhealthy and damaging to you both. A man needs a wife, and you, my dear, should have a husband and

> *children. Danny has done the right thing in breaking free*
> *of those bonds. It does not mean he loves you any the less*
> *– only, perhaps, differently.*

Tears blurred the rest of the words before her eyes. But this
time they were not tears of bitterness over Danny. Kate was
surprised to find how much her gentle stepfather's rebuke
hurt her, made her feel small and petty-minded. She sniffed
and, like a small child, scrubbed the tears away with the
back of her hand.

'*They are away on a short honeymoon – please try to
come home to see your grandfather. He is not too well . . .*'
The letter continued with news about her mother and Lilian
and the farm, but no further mention was made of Danny
or Rosie.

Slowly Kate got up from her bed, biting her lip. She knew
she had hurt Rosie, but until this moment she had not
stopped to think how her absence from their wedding had
hurt so many people. Beth Eland and Enid Maine, Rosie's
mother, too. But more than anything she could not bear to
think that her stepfather was disappointed in her.

She would apply for leave. She was sure that Philip, understanding and kind, and now knowing the full circumstances,
would grant her compassionate leave to go home . . .

'Get down, Grandad, get down! Do you want to be killed?'

The old man was dancing up and down in front of the
window, waving his arms, his bare legs, thin and white,
sticking out from under the flapping tails of his night-shirt.
'You dirty swine! You . . .' But his expletives were drowned
by the roaring of engines as another enemy plane, its swastika
plainly visible, swooped by, low and vicious, strafing the
front of the farmhouse with a shower of bullets. Kate threw

herself at the old man, pushing him to the floor and landing on top of him, knocking the breath out of him. He lay there gasping, but still found the strength to swear volubly. As the plane roared past, there was a rat-a-tat-tat of bullets against the brickwork. Just above them the glass of the window shattered and bullets whistled over their heads to embed themselves in the far wall of the room.

'There, are you satisfied now?' she panted. 'You nearly got us both killed . . .' Her words were drowned by a loud 'crump' which rattled the very foundations of the farmhouse. Every door and window rattled and more glass shattered. Soot billowed from the chimney stack like a black shroud, enveloping them both.

'Oh my God! That's a bomb and it's bloody close.' Now she was scrambling up, oblivious to further danger.

'Kate, don't . . .' he wheezed, struggling to his feet, but she was out of his room and running through the house. There was glass everywhere. It looked as if every window was shattered. As she passed through the living room, soot covered everything. In the kitchen, pots lay smashed on the floor where they'd been vibrated from the shelf and the door stood drunkenly, half off its hinges.

Kate rushed out into the yard. 'Mam! *Mam!*' She looked wildly about her. Hens were rushing to and fro squawking loudly and flapping their wings in the pretence of flight. From the stable came the whinnying of the frightened horses and hooves struck repeatedly at the door.

'Mam – Dad! Where are you?' she yelled. Now there was silence – a deathly silence. The planes, having wrought their havoc, had gone, streaking away across the North Sea to safety.

She ran to the gate and looked up and down the lane. To her right, beyond the Hump, rose a cloud of dust and smoke.

324

'Oh no!' she cried. 'Not the cottages – please, not the cottages.'

Then she was running, running like the wind, her heart pounding, desperately afraid of what she would find.

She had arrived at Brumbys' Farm only half an hour before and hadn't even seen her mother and stepfather. Only her grandfather had been at home, sitting in the chair by the window in his room, still in his night-shirt.

'Ya mam wants me to stay in bed. Me chest is bad, but I 'ate lying in bed. Me elbows get sore. 'Sides, I like to see out the window, across the fields . . .' His old eyes had watered and she knew he must miss being out in the open air when illness confined him to his room. Then he was smiling at her, but the old eyes were still regarding her shrewdly. 'This is a surprise. Couldn't make it for the wedding, I s'pose?'

Kate returned his gaze steadily. Then, finding she was holding her breath, she let it out in a deep sigh. There was no point in even trying to deceive Will Benson. 'I – I couldn't face it, Grandad, but I've been feeling bad about it ever since.'

'Aye, well, lass. I can understand, but I can't excuse ya, 'cos it upset poor Rosie. And Danny.'

'I – just need a bit of time, Grandad. It was such a shock when he – he came to the camp to tell me. I thought I was over it – beginning to lead my own life, but then when Danny came and said he – he was getting married and – and to Rosie . . .'

The gnarled old hand reached out and covered hers, twisting in her lap. 'I know, lass, I know,' he said hoarsely.

'I – I came home to see his mam and Enid . . .'

It was then they had heard the drone of the aircraft coming nearer and nearer . . .

Kate arrived at the top of the Hump and stopped. Before her was a scene of devastation. It was not the cottages, although they had suffered damage. It was the Seagull, which had taken a direct hit. A small incendiary bomb had fallen on one end of the building, slicing rooms in half so that Kate could see the interior, like her own dolls' house when the whole of the front was opened. She could even see the wallpaper on the remaining inner wall of the bedroom. A bed hung precariously half-on, half-off the portion of floor left, teetering on the edge. The bomb had buried itself in the soft earth, making a crater the size of the pond at Brumbys' Farm, and now flames licked at the already half-destroyed building.

Kate absorbed all this in a brief second's pause, then she was flying down the slope towards the building. It was lunchtime opening; there must have been people in the pub. Others were emerging from the cottages and hurrying towards the scene. Kate could see Grannie Harris watching through the broken window of her kitchen, her hand to her mouth. Then two of the soldiers who had been on duty through the previous night and sleeping in Dan Hanley's cottage when the bomb fell, appeared. They were bare-chested, their trousers pulled on hastily. Enid Maine appeared in her doorway, clutching at the door post for support, staring wide-eyed.

Then, suddenly, there was Beth Eland. She came out of her cottage, wrapped a black shawl over her head and walked slowly towards the pub. She didn't run, didn't even hurry. It was as if she were drawn to the scene but was reluctant to reach it.

'Get some water!' Kate shouted to the two soldiers. 'Let's get this fire out first. Get buckets, anything. Form a chain.'

Without realizing it, she was taking charge. All her young life, she had seen how farmers dealt with stack fires and then she had witnessed the calm efficiency on Suddaby Station after an air-raid.

Kate ran to the nearest cottage – Enid's home. 'Look sharp, our Enid, get working the pump in your kitchen filling buckets. Where's the boys? They can help too . . .'

Soon everyone there was helping to transport water to the base of the fire – all except Beth. She stood, a lonely, lost figure, a little way off, just staring at the ravaged building.

Kate grasped her arm. 'Where's Mester Eland? We could do with his help. Is he out fishing?'

Slowly Beth shook her head.

'Where is he, then?'

Beth's gaze was fixed upon the building, mesmerized. Kate shook her arm, trying to bring her out of her stupor. 'Where is he?' she repeated.

Beth's voice was a strangulated whisper. 'In – in the pub.'

'Oh, no!' Kate breathed, then, grasping at straws, she added, 'Maybe he'll be all right. Perhaps he was in the other end of the pub that wasn't hit. Maybe he's just – trapped.'

'He – he'd have been playing dominoes with Tom Willoughby,' Beth whispered.

Kate put her arm around Beth but she could think of nothing more to say now for she knew as well as Beth that the men played dominoes in the corner of the main bar; the end of the building where the bomb had fallen. Kate felt sick in the pit of her stomach. Her stepfather, Jonathan, sometimes played with them too.

'I must go and help,' she whispered. Beth nodded but remained standing where she was; a still, silent, watchful figure, her arms clasped about her body, hugging the shawl closely around her.

I wish I hadn't come home, Kate was thinking. I wish I was anywhere but here.

It was like the time the station had been bombed and Edith's lifeless body had been dragged from the rubble. But this was worse, much worse. This time there were going to

327

be the bodies of people she had known all her life; and among them Robert Eland, the man Danny had called Father all his life.

The fire was out and now they started to move the rubble carefully, praying – but without real hope – that they might find Tom and Robert alive. An air-raid warden and a police constable arrived from Lynthorpe.

'We saw the planes swooping over here and then the bombs.'

'Bombs?' Kate looked up sharply. 'Was there more than this one?'

'Oh aye,' the warden said. 'One fell into a field not far from Souters' Farm. It's not done much damage as the soft ground took the impact and another fell in the lane on the way to town from here – that's why we've been a long time getting here. We had to come right round by the Grange.'

'You – you haven't seen my mother and father, have you?'

'No, love, sorry, I ain't. They missing?'

'I don't know. I've only just got home. I'd only just got into the house and was talking to me grandad when the planes came.'

'The old man all right, is he?'

'Just!' Kate replied wryly. They stood looking at the ruins that had been the pub. The warden sighed. 'I aren't looking forward to this, lass.'

'No.' Kate glanced back over her shoulder and saw that Beth was still standing in the same place, her arms wrapped around herself, just waiting.

At that moment, a figure appeared at the top of the Hump and came plunging down the slope towards them, her hair dishevelled and flying free, her eyes wide with fear, her hand outstretched.

'Oh, Mam!' Kate breathed, and ran to meet her.

Esther gripped her arms, not pausing to express surprise at Kate being there; there was only one thought on her mind. 'Where is he? Where's ya dad? Where's Jonathan?'

Thirty

'Isn't he with you?' Kate realized it was a stupid question immediately she'd spoken.

Her mother shook her head wildly. 'No – no. I've been into town – in the trap. I saw the bombs. I – I thought it was the farm . . .' She gulped painfully. 'I came tearing home – a bomb had landed in the lane – I had to go right round by the Grange to get back.'

'Where is me dad, then?'

Esther was staring with terrified eyes at the ruins of the pub and clinging to Kate, her grip so intense that her fingers dug into Kate's arms. 'He – he said he would tek the cows up to North Marsh Field and then when he came back he – he might walk down the road and have a – game of dominoes at the pub.'

'Esther.' Beth's voice came gently, flat and unemotional. Kate turned and saw her standing just behind them. 'Leave her to me, Katie love. You go and – help.'

Kate eased herself from her mother's grasp and Beth took her place, putting her arm about Esther and holding her close. Never taking her gaze from the heap of rubble, Esther clung to Beth and the two women stood together in silence watching and waiting . . .

They found the landlord first. He had been standing behind the bar when the bomb had come whistling down. With seconds to spare, he had dived under the counter of the bar and, though cut and bruised, he was still alive when the rescuers dug their way to him. The workers continued and more helpers arrived from town. Gently they removed the rubble brick by brick.

'There's someone here. Oh, no . . .'

Kate glanced back towards her mother and Beth. She saw Esther start forward, saw Beth hold her back. Kate saw Beth's lips moving and knew she was talking softly, soothingly to Esther. 'Wait, just wait, Esther. They'll – tell us.'

They had found Tom Willoughby – and Robert Eland.

'They wouldn't have known much about it.' The doctor, who had been one of those to arrive from town, tried to comfort them. 'It would have been very – quick.'

Esther had her arms about Beth, who stood looking down at the lifeless form of her husband. 'Poor Robert,' Beth murmured. 'He didn't deserve that.'

'No – no, he didn't. He was a good man.' Esther patted her arm. Now it was she who must comfort Beth.

The search was continuing and Esther was leading Beth away to her own cottage, while still glancing back anxiously over her shoulder at the devastated building.

Something made Kate glance towards the Hump. 'Mam!' she shouted, and pointed.

Jonathan was standing on the Hump gazing at the horror before him. Esther gave a sob and ran towards him, her arms outstretched. She flew into his arms and clung to him, babbling her relief.

Then, as she told him what had happened, Kate saw her stepfather and her mother go back towards Beth. Jonathan put his arm about Beth and kissed her cheek. Together he and Esther took her to her home.

Kate found that tears were running down her cheeks. 'Here, love, you tek a rest – now ya dad's okay, I shouldn't think there's anyone else in here, is there?'

Kate shook her head. Everyone was accounted for now. The police constable mounted his bicycle. He had the unenviable task of going to Rookery Farm to inform Tom's sister-in-law, Flo Jenkins, of his death.

And Danny, Kate thought. How would they tell Danny? No one knew where he and Rosie had gone on their brief honeymoon. What a dreadful homecoming! Then another thought struck her; a thought that left her sweating with fear for what might have happened.

If Danny had not been on honeymoon with Rosie, he might well have been sitting in the corner of the pub playing dominoes with his stepfather and Tom Willoughby.

'You must come to the funerals, Kate, if you can get leave,' her stepfather said firmly.

Kate bit her lip. 'Dad – I feel so awful now that I didn't come to Danny and Rosie's wedding.'

'What's done is done. But don't make it worse by staying away again.'

It was the worst moment in her life when she stood in the church and looked across at Danny; worse even than when they had found out the truth of their relationship, and that had been bad enough.

She felt sick and wanted to run out, away from them all, out to the end of the Spit. But she was obliged to stand there and watch Beth's white, strained face and see Rosie being the one to take hold of Danny's arm; Rosie comforting Danny when it should have been her, Kate. The longing to step across the aisle and put her arms about him was so strong that she swayed for a moment and had to grip the back of the pew in front of her to stop herself moving towards him. She felt her stepfather's anxious eyes upon her, and she bent her head in the pretence of prayer so that he should not read the expression in her eyes, for she knew her feelings must be plain for all to see.

The congregation knelt in the final prayer and when they rose and began to move out of the church, Kate remained where she was, on her knees, her head bowed, her hands covering her face. She sensed the coffin being carried out first, and knew that the Eland family were following, Beth, Danny – and Rosie, for now she was Mrs Eland.

She felt a light touch on her shoulder and Jonathan's whisper, 'We must go, Kate.'

Slowly she stood up and turned to see Danny going out of the church, one arm around his mother, the other around Rosie.

He did not even glance back at her, and in that moment, Kate had never felt so lonely in her life.

'Will Beth want us at the graveside?' Kate heard her mother whisper to Jonathan as they hesitated outside the porch, their glances going towards where the three figures stood near the freshly dug hole in the churchyard.

'Yes,' Jonathan said firmly and took Esther's arm. 'Come along. You too, Kate.'

The coffin was lowered into the ground and Danny bent to scoop up a handful of earth and scatter it on to the lid. As he straightened up, across the grave his glance met Kate's.

For an instant, the years fell away and they were again two children standing beside Matthew Hilton's grave, the man they now knew had fathered them both. Yet the man they were burying this day had been more of a father to Danny. Poor Danny, she thought, he must have so many conflicting emotions churning inside him, and she wasn't making it any easier. This was not a day for bearing grudges.

The interment ended, and as they began to move away, Kate saw her mother go to Beth's side and take her arm. Together, the two women walked away down the path. Jonathan was speaking to Rosie and, taking her chance, Kate went up to Danny and laid her hand gently on his arm.

He turned swiftly and gripped her hands. 'Kate,' was all he said, but it was enough.

They walked together down the footpath, following the others. She heard him sigh and looked up to see his gaze upon the black-coated figures of his mother and Esther Godfrey ahead of them.

'Strange, isn't it, how those two come together in times of sorrow and yet they can't bring themselves to speak to one another ordinarily?'

Kate was silent. She could have said, 'I know how they feel!' She had made a tentative gesture of reconciliation towards Danny, but even now, Kate admitted guiltily to herself, she could not bring herself to speak to Rosie Eland.

Back at camp it was a little easier, but letters from home renewed the pain.

'*Rosie's living with Beth until after the war and when Danny comes home, the Good Lord willing, the Squire has promised him the tenancy of Rookery Farm, now that poor old Tom has gone. Miss Jenkins has moved into the town – she didn't want to try to run the farm on her own . . .*'

So Kate was kept informed of all the gossip and news from home by her stepfather. Her mother was no letter-writer, but always sent messages via Jonathan. '*Your mother says . . .*' littered every page and Kate would smile fondly as she read the latest instruction from home.

She sat with the letter in her lap and stared out of the window of the hut. So Danny and Rosie would one day live at Rookery Farm, God willing, as her stepfather said, that Danny came through the war. He would work the land he had once dreamed of farming. He would live there with his wife and he would raise his children; all just as he had planned, just as they had planned together so long ago. Only now, his wife was Rosie and not Kate.

She sighed and got up from her bed. It was time to drive one of the lorries taking the crews out to dispersal. The camp had been buzzing with anticipation all day, and Mavis and Isobel expected to be on duty through the night.

'It's something big,' Mavis had told her. 'They're concentrating on the ports and the Rhineland. Night after night, they'll go on – as long as the weather holds.'

At East Markham, they'd be getting ready too. Maybe at this very moment, Danny was climbing into his aircraft, squeezing himself into the rear-gunner's turret.

Kate closed her eyes for a brief moment and groaned aloud. Tears squeezed themselves from beneath her eyelids. Despite everything, she loved him still. 'Dear Father in Heaven, keep him safe,' she prayed. 'Bring him back, just bring him back.'

Thirty-One

'CO wants you – and the car – his office – two minutes.'
'I'm on my way.' Kate scrambled off the bed, pulled her skirt straight and rammed her cap over her long hair, tucking up the stray strands as she ran towards the CO's office.

As she came breathlessly to attention in front of his desk, she noticed at once that Philip's handsome face looked almost grey with fatigue – and something more. His jawline seemed hard, clenched almost, as if he were trying to conceal an anger, and yet at the same time there was an infinite sadness in his blue eyes; today there was no sparkle, no hint of mischief in them.

'I have to go home urgently. Er – family illness,' he said, his voice tight. 'Can you drive me to Lincoln to catch the train?' Suddenly, he leaned forward, resting his elbows on his desk, dropping his head into his hands, his shoulders slumped. 'Oh Kate – Kate! How I wish . . .'

For a long moment there was silence in the room. Kate bit her lip uncertainly. An overwhelming longing to comfort him made her start forward, her hand fluttering towards him to touch him, but in that instant she remembered just who he was and where they were.

'Sir,' she prompted gently. 'Your – your train?'

He lifted his head and looked up at her and, for a long moment, their gaze held. Then he sighed deeply and rose

336

slowly as if his limbs were leaden. 'Let's go,' he said flatly, without a shred of enthusiasm in his voice.

As she saw him on to the train, he said. 'I don't know when I'll be back, Kate, but I'll try to send word for you to meet me.' He looked at her oddly for a moment, opened his mouth as if to say something, then closed it again. Suddenly he clasped her hand briefly. 'Take care of yourself while I'm gone . . .' Then he turned swiftly away from her, leaped on to the train and slammed the door behind him.

Kate was thoughtful as she walked out of the station. His behaviour was puzzling. Mavis had said he was married and yet Philip seemed to avoid mentioning his wife and children – if, indeed, he had any. But if he had been called home on compassionate leave – a man in his position – then someone close to him must be seriously ill.

As she walked along the platform, she saw two women in WVS uniform setting up a trestle-table with a tea-urn, cups and saucers. She looked closely at them but they were strangers; Miss Ogden was not one of them this time.

Outside the station, heavily protected by sandbags piled up either side of the entrance, she moved towards where the staff car was parked. She hesitated. There was no need for her to rush back to camp. Officially, she was off-duty now that she had driven Philip to the city to catch his train. She wouldn't be missed for an hour or so. Kate bit her lip and glanced up the hill towards the cathedral standing sentinel over the city sprawling down the hill beneath it. Almost without her making a conscious decision, her steps took her up High Street and through the Stonebow. As the road began to rise she took a turning to the left in the direction where she believed the school was. All the time she'd lived in Lincoln she had never ventured anywhere near.

It was time to lay to rest a few more ghosts from her childhood.

Margaret Dickinson

She stood before the place where the school had been and gazed at the ruins before her. On either side the buildings, though damaged, were still standing. It looked as if the school had received a direct hit.

A woman came trudging up the hill, carrying a heavy shopping basket, a child dragging at her skirt.

'Excuse me . . .' Kate began.

The woman looked at her with tired, defeated eyes.

'Do – do you know what happened to the school?' Kate nodded towards the demolished building. The woman glanced in the same direction. 'Bomb fell on it,' she explained, rather unnecessarily, Kate thought. 'Awful, it were. My old man's an air-raid warden. Several girls and three teachers were buried. He 'ad to dig 'em out.'

'Were they . . .?'

'Dead? Oh, no – only the headmistress was killed. T'others were hurt, like, but they've got over it.'

'How dreadful!' Kate murmured automatically, but she was thinking, 'Miss Denham is dead.'

'Oh yes,' the tired woman was finding new vigour in her recounting of the event, now she had an interested listener. 'A lovely woman, she was, the headmistress. All the girls loved her . . .'

'Loved her? Miss Denham?'

The woman's gaze was mystified. 'Who? Who did you say? Don't know no Miss Denham. No, the headmistress was called Miss Ogden!'

Kate gasped. 'Oh, no!'

'Knew her, did you?'

Kate nodded, sick at heart. Immediately she felt contrite, ashamed of her moment's fleeting glee at the thought that Miss Denham had been killed. Now she was being punished for her uncharitable thought for unkind Fate had taken the woman who had shown her genuine kindness.

338

Kate continued up towards the cathedral. In the peaceful atmosphere she knelt in prayer for Miss Ogden. Outside again, she walked back down Lindum Hill in a daze, hardly knowing where she was going. Then she found herself in a street she knew very well. In the nine years she had lived in the city she had walked along it hundreds of times to and from work. Kate smiled and quickened her pace.

The door opened upon Peggy. She stared at Kate for a moment and then gave a squeal of delight.

'Kate! I hardly recognized you in your uniform . . .' Peggy flung her arms round her and gave her a swift hug, then stood back, holding Kate by the arms. 'Let me look at you. Oh, you do look smart.' Excited as a young girl, Peggy almost dragged the laughing Kate through into the back room. 'Mother, look who's here!'

Although she passed hurriedly through the front room, there was still time enough for Kate to notice its tidiness with a stab of disappointment; not a paper pattern nor a length of fabric to be seen – not even a stray pin. When she stepped through into the back room, she saw why. Mrs Godfrey was sitting near the fire hunched in her chair.

'Mother's not so well these days, Kate, since we lost Father,' Peggy explained softly, and Kate nodded, understanding. The whole family had mourned the kind and gentle man. 'But she keeps cheerful,' Peggy was saying, 'and she loves visitors.'

Indeed, it seemed to be true, for at the sight of her, Mrs Godfrey's wrinkled face seemed to light up. 'Why, my lovely Kate. Come in and sit down. Make a cup of tea, Peg, there's a dear. I can't get about now, it's my legs. What I'd do without our Peg, I don't know,' and her gaze went fondly to her daughter.

The time flew by as they chatted. Mrs Godfrey wanted to know all about the family at Fleethaven Point and Kate found herself telling the two women all about the bombs, and even, though haltingly at first, about Danny's marriage to Rosie. As she talked she was surprised to find it became easier.

'I've just been up the hill – to look at the school.'

'Really?' Peggy could not hide the surprise in her voice.

'I met Miss Ogden on the station a while back, handing out cups of tea to the soldiers. She was kind to me when I was there—' Kate gave a wry laugh. 'She was the only one who was, mind you.'

'Ah yes, poor Miss Ogden. She took over as Principal seven or eight years ago now.'

'What – what happened to Miss Denham?'

'She retired. Went to live in the country with her sister who'd also been a headmistress somewhere.'

So Miss Denham was living somewhere comfortably in retirement, whilst poor Miss Ogden was dead.

Sometimes, Kate thought bitterly, Fate really got it wrong!

'Drive the long way round, Kate,' Philip said as he got in beside her on his return. 'If everything's all right, I'm in no hurry to get back. I seem to have been away a lot longer than a week.'

'Everything's fine. There was an op on last night and everyone got back safely. Well – more or less,' she grinned. 'B-Baker's undercarriage jammed and he had to do a belly-landing. Honestly, Jeff landed that kite as if it were a glider.'

'He's a great pilot.' There was a pause and then he added softly, 'And how about you? Are *you* all right?'

'Yes, thanks, I'm fine.'

It was already dark as she drove up the hill and out on to the Wragby road. About five miles from Suddaby, in open country, Philip said, 'Pull in over there, Kate. Let's take a breather.'

She drew the car to a halt on the wide grass verge. Below them the ground sloped away across fields of ripening corn, almost ready for harvesting, yet in the light from the full, bright moon in a clear sky the countryside seemed different shades of grey. With a shock, Kate realized it was almost a year since she and Danny had joined up.

'A bomber's moon, Kate,' Philip murmured, interrupting her thoughts. 'I wonder where they're headed for tonight?'

'Who? Us – or them?'

He gave a wry laugh. 'Both! It's mad, isn't it? It's all absolutely mad. A waste of young lives.'

'But, sir . . .'

'Oh, don't get me wrong. I'm as patriotic as the next man and I know full well what we have to do. But – oh, dear Lord – just sometimes I get so sick and tired, so desperately tired, of seeing all those fine young men flying off into the sky and knowing that by the law of averages some aren't going to come back.'

'I know – I feel exactly the same sometimes.'

'I thought you did,' he said, so quietly that she almost didn't catch his words. In the car, side by side, there was an intimacy between them that had nothing to do with a commanding officer and his driver.

Kate was emboldened to ask softly, the use of his Christian name coming naturally at this moment, 'And how about you, Philip? How are things with your family?'

He gave a long, deep sigh. 'So-so,' he replied, his tone non-committal.

Kate stared at him but his face was in heavy shadow and she could not read his expression. Questions buzzed around her brain, but Philip volunteered no more and she could hardly pursue the matter.

He pulled a pipe from his pocket and began to pack it, more, it seemed, to give his hands something to do, rather than because he needed to smoke it. 'You don't mind, do you?' he asked her, indicating the pipe.

'No – no, of course not.'

'I suppose,' he said in staccato clauses between puffs, 'we had – better be – getting back.'

As she started the engine and eased the car off the grass verge and down the incline, Philip said suddenly, 'Am I imagining things, or is that aircraft?'

Kate opened her mouth to answer, but at that moment a small bomb fell into the road about two hundred yards in front of them. The whole world seemed to explode in a flash and Kate gave a cry and swerved. The car bounced across the grass verge and settled, nose-first, into a ditch. Kate groaned and thought, irrationally at such a moment, there I go again falling back into my bad ways!

'Out the car, quick!' Philip was out of his side and scrambling round to the driver's side. He tugged at the door. 'Open the door, Kate.'

'I can't – it's stuck.'

'Slide across to the other side,' he shouted, and struggled back round the car again. He bent and reached in to grasp her hand and pull her out. She fell out of the car into his arms.

'You're not hurt, are you?'

'No – no . . .'

'Come on then, we must get away from this car. If a bomb drops on this, we'll be toast.'

He grabbed her hand and pulled her after him, thrusting a way through the hedge and into the cornfield. They waded through the waist-high corn until they were almost in the centre of the field and well away from the car. Above them, the sound of an aircraft came steadily nearer.

'Down, Kate, down!' Even as he spoke, Philip pushed her to the ground and flung himself on top of her, his body shielding hers, his hands covering her head protectively.

The bomb fell a hundred yards from them, and the earth shook beneath them. Soil erupted and spattered down all around, and they could smell the burning cordite. Kate gave a shriek and put her arms round Philip's back, burying her face into his neck. The noise of the plane was growing fainter, yet they lay there tense and waiting for the sound of more bombers.

'I think,' Philip murmured, 'they've gone.' They could smell the burning crater but now there was a beautiful silence, the whispering wind rippling through the corn and the pitiful cries of birds, disturbed from sleep and flying in disorientated circles above them, the only sounds. Philip shifted his weight a little, but made no effort to get up. He put his right arm under her neck and the other around her waist and bent his face towards her. 'Oh, Kate, Kate . . .' Then he was kissing her, gently at first and then with increasing urgency.

Her arms were about his neck and she twisted her body towards him. She felt him unbutton her jacket and suddenly his hand was warm and gentle on her breast. His fingertips, trembling slightly, caressed her nipple which hardened immediately under his touch. Her lips parted and his kiss became deeper, probing, yet tender.

'Oh, Kate, I love you, I need you . . .'

She was returning his kisses with matching ardour, drowning in the new sensations her body was experiencing, lost to all sense and reason, awakened from innocence to the sensations of passion . . .

'Oh, I wish we could stay here for ever,' he murmured,

cradling her head against his chest as he lay on his back looking up at the moon and stars. She was quiet, a gentle smile playing on her lips, savouring the tumult of emotions, enjoying the aftermath of an ecstasy she had never even guessed existed between a man and a woman. His fingers were stroking her hair, touching her cheek, and then he lifted his head to kiss the top of hers, nuzzling his face against her hair. 'My dearest Kate.' Then as her silence lengthened, there was an anxious question in his voice. 'Kate?'

She did not speak but lifted her head, seeking his mouth. She heard him groan deep in his throat. It was the answer he sought. His arms came strongly about her, pulling her on top of him.

They made love again, slowly, savouring every moment, every touch, until desire claimed them once more.

'I suppose we shall have to go,' he said reluctantly, some time later. He got up and held out his hands to help her up. Standing, he pulled her close to him, searching her face, pale in the moonlight. Gently he bent down and kissed her forehead and then her mouth. Kate put her arms about his waist, hugging him to her. It had happened so suddenly, and yet so naturally; she had no regrets.

They had begun to walk across the field, their arms about each other, when they heard the sound of an approaching vehicle.

'Come on, we'd better hurry. If they spot the car, they might stop.'

They reached the edge of the field as the RAF policeman got out of his jeep and slid down the sloping grass verge towards the staff car, nose first in the ditch.

'It's okay, we're here,' Philip called, holding aside the hedge for Kate to squeeze through.

A torch was shone in their faces and then flicked off quickly. 'Oh, sorry, sir. Are either of you hurt?'

'No, we're fine. There was an air-raid. A bomb fell on the road in front of us and we landed up in the ditch and then took cover in the field. We thought it safest to get right away from the car.'

'Of course, sir. Can I give you a lift back?'

'Yes, please. I just want my bag out of the car . . .'

'I'll get it, sir.'

He held open the door of his jeep for Kate and Philip to climb in, closed the door, retrieved Philip's bag and returned to his own vehicle. 'If you say there's been a bomb up ahead, sir, I'd better go another way. Is that all right, sir?'

'Fine.' The jeep's engine burst into life and under cover of its noise, Philip whispered, 'Take as long as you like.' In the darkness, he reached for Kate's hand and held it until they had passed through the gates of Suddaby Station.

The next morning, with a fresh staff car, Kate drew up outside the CO's office. Before she could get out of the car to open the rear door for him, Philip came bounding out and got into the front seat of the car, slamming the door and grinning at her. For one dreadful moment she thought he was going to kiss her there and then in front of the whole station, but instead, he leaned back against the leather seat, stretched his long legs, and gave a self-satisfied sigh.

'Drive.'

'Sir – shouldn't you – er – sit in the back?'

'Drive! Into the country.'

An impish smile curved her mouth. 'Where?' she asked in an innocent tone. 'To the nearest cornfield?'

'Shameless hussy!' But he was smiling fondly at her as he said it.

Confused now, she bent to touch the starter button. 'Sir – you really shouldn't look at me like that.'

'Can't help it,' he said, never taking his gaze from her. 'I don't know when I last felt so happy.'

She gave a little gasp of surprise and turned to look back at him, but the look on his face told her that his words were genuine.

She had never seen him looking so relaxed and contented. His face looked years younger and, with the lines of worry smoothed from his forehead and a sparkle in his eyes, he was even more handsome than ever.

'Go back to where we parked last night and, no, I don't mean the cornfield. The top of the hill, you know where I mean?'

Kate nodded.

'We can sit and talk there, yet I think we can see the road in both directions if anyone comes along.'

She pulled carefully on to the wide grass verge, bringing the car to a halt and pulled on the brake. As she switched off the engine, Philip reached for her hand, raised it to his lips and kissed each one of her fingers slowly and deliberately. A thrill of pleasure ran through her and she knew she was blushing.

'Kate – I want you to know that this is not just a wartime fling. I've been falling in love with you for ages, oh, maybe ever since that first moment I opened my eyes and saw you bending over me in the little boat off the beach at Dunkirk. I don't know. I wanted to see you again and all the time I was making inquiries to see if you'd joined up and then pulling strings to have you posted as my driver. Well . . .' He shrugged his wide shoulders. 'All I know is I had the strangest – compulsion – to see you, to be with you, even though I also had the feeling that it might be – well, dangerous.'

346

'Dangerous?'

A cloud came over his new-found happiness. His eyes were filled with sadness as he said hoarsely, 'I want to be honest with you . . . I don't want to hurt you . . .'

'What is it, Philip?' she encouraged, guessing what he was trying to say.

'I'm – married.'

'I know,' she said, and the look on his face was so comical that she laughed, leaned across and kissed his cheek.

'You know?' he said incredulously.

'Mmm – Mavis!'

'Oh – Mavis,' he echoed, and a wry smile curved his mouth briefly.

'Yes. What Mavis doesn't know, Mavis will make it her business to find out,' she smiled, and added, so that he would not get the wrong idea about her friend, 'but it's not malicious nosiness. Not with her, anyway.'

'No, I know that.' He sighed. 'I'm glad you do know. I spent half last night reliving . . .' he looked at her and his eyes darkened with desire at the mere memory, 'the cornfield – and the rest of the night feeling a real heel because it had happened.'

'Well, there's no need to feel a heel. I'm a big girl. I knew you were married but it doesn't take a genius to see you're not exactly happy, or presumably your wife – and children if you have any – would be here with you, living in the CO's house.'

'You – don't know it all then? You don't know about my – daughter?'

'No, I don't know anything other than that you are married.'

He looked down at her hand, still resting quietly in his, then he raised it again and held it against his cheek.

'I must tell you . . .'

347

'You don't have to,' she cut in quickly.

'I – want to,' he said firmly. He was thoughtful for a long moment and then he began to tell her about his life before he had known her.

'I'm from a Forces family and so is my wife. My father was a Brigadier in the last war. Of course, he wanted me to join his old regiment and he was rather cut up when I opted for the youngest service, even though I decided to make a career in the RAF. My wife too was from a long line of serving officers and our parents were friends – still are, which makes it all the more difficult. Grace and I were thrown together and soon it became expected that we should marry. I think both of us got caught up in it and carried along without making any conscious decision for ourselves. I was – still am – very fond of Grace and never wanted to hurt her . . .' He hesitated and then began again on a different tack. 'We have a daughter, Lizzie. She – she was born with serious physical handicaps and the prognosis is that she won't reach her teens.'

'Oh, Philip!' Kate whispered, and tears filled her eyes.

'Grace has devoted her life to the child, whereas I – well – I can't do very much, not unless I leave the RAF and devote myself to her in the same way. But Grace's devotion has become almost an obsession. I think her own mother has filled her mind with the thought that the abnormalities must come from my side, when in truth I don't think there's blame to be attached to either of us. It just – happened.'

The words came unbidden to Kate's lips and were voiced before she really realized she was saying them. 'Some people find it easier to deal with life's cruelties if they can find someone to blame.' She heard the words almost as if someone else were speaking them.

'I suppose so,' Philip said heavily. 'Grace's mother moved in with us and sort of – took over.'

'And pushed you out and the more distant you became, the more they blamed you.'

He looked at her wonderingly. 'You *do* understand, don't you?'

She said nothing but gave his hand a little squeeze.

'Oh, Kate, what am I going to do? What are we going to do?'

Sensibly, she said, 'We'll take it day by day, just like everyone else is having to do in this war, and when it's all over – well, we'll see then, won't we?'

She smiled at him as he leaned forward to kiss her mouth. As his lips touched hers, desire ran through her like a shock wave.

When she went back to her hut in the early evening, the letter was lying on her bed. At once she recognized Danny's sloping handwriting on the envelope.

With a jolt Kate realized that during the last twenty-four hours she had not once thought of Danny Eland.

Thirty-Two

S o, Rosie was to have Danny's child.

Kate sat on the bed, waiting for the hurt to come. Rosie is having Danny's baby, she told herself, and tightened the muscles in her stomach, waiting.

She felt nothing. All she could see in her mind's eye was Rosie's happy face, her dancing golden curls, and Danny's proud grin stretching from ear to ear. And just fancy, Beth a grandma! How pleased she would be.

Kate had the strangest feeling that she was gripping Danny's hand tightly, hanging on to it like someone drowning. Then gradually, she felt as if she were loosening her hold, not completely, but just starting to let go; beginning to let Danny go.

She stood up, folded his letter and put it back into the envelope, opened the drawer of her locker and tucked it behind the whelk shell.

Slowly she closed the drawer.

'Do you know,' Philip said, a comical expression on his face, 'I'm running out of excuses for us to drive out of camp.'

Kate giggled, then her face sobered. 'We shall have to be careful. I wouldn't want to see your career damaged.'

'What about you? I don't want to see you hurt.' He sighed heavily. 'Oh, Kate, I love you so but I wish things could be different.'

350

'They couldn't be so very different, even if you weren't married,' she said directly, but the gentleness of her tone took away the bluntness of her words. 'We still wouldn't be able to meet openly. Me a lowly corporal and you a Group Captain!'

'Yes. Isn't it ridiculous?'

'It seems so, but the powers-that-be must have had their reasons for setting such rules. I suppose they had the undermining of discipline in mind.'

He nodded. 'Well, not all girls would be as understanding as you, Kate. Some would try to take advantage.'

She giggled again. 'Oh, I take advantage of you – whenever I get the chance.'

'Kate!' he exclaimed, pretending to be shocked, but in truth enjoying her admission that she enjoyed their lovemaking as much as he did. He put his arm along the back of the seat and caressed her neck. The tingling sensation his touch caused made her swerve slightly.

'I think you'd better stop that unless you want to end up in the ditch again,' she said.

They laughed together.

Their love affair continued through the winter months of 1941. As its intensity grew, it was inevitable that they could not hide it from everyone. Though they tried to be circumspect in public, strove valiantly to be strictly CO and driver in front of others, there was the light of love in their eyes when they looked at each other, such a spring in their steps as they hurried to drive away from the camp to be alone for a few snatched moments, that soon, someone must notice and the tongues would start wagging.

At the Christmas dance in the Officers' Mess, Philip came towards Kate and she went into his arms as if it were the most natural thing in the world. They danced together the whole evening. He did not dance with any other girl – not even the senior WAAF officer there – and when he led Kate to a table, brought her a drink and sat down with her, all the other airmen and officers shrugged their shoulders and turned their thoughts away from even thinking of asking the CO's beautiful driver for a dance.

But for some, the sight of Group Captain Philip Trent monopolizing the company of Corporal Kate Hilton was not so easily forgotten.

'Kate – you'll get yourself into bother.' Mavis, with Isobel one pace behind as if to back her, was standing at the foot of her bed the following morning.

'Eh?' Kate glanced up from the letter she was writing home, and could see at once by their faces that they had guessed. 'I don't know what you're talking about.'

'Oh yes, you do. You don't usually tell lies, Kate Hilton.'

Kate felt herself colouring. No, she didn't. She had always been a very truthful person, but this time it was not just herself she was trying to protect.

As if reading her thoughts, Isobel murmured, 'You see, Mave, her trouble is that she's not a tell-tale. I can vouch for that.'

'And don't say it's none of our business . . .' Mavis began, as they came and sat on her bed, one either side of her.

'. . . Because it is,' finished Isobel.

'You'd make a good double act,' Kate said, trying to steer them off the topic. 'Ever thought of applying to ENSA?'

'It's got to stop, Kate,' Isobel said. 'You'll get into awful trouble – and so will he. He might lose his whole career and he's a nice bloke.'

'Too nice,' Mavis said.

'You've got it wrong. We're just good friends . . .'

Isobel snorted. 'Now, where have I heard that before?'

Mavis leaned closer, whispering even though there was no one else in the hut to overhear. 'I told you before, Kate, he's married. If there is anything going on, you're both running a terrible risk.'

'It's not as if he is a flier,' Isobel resorted to shock tactics, 'and any day might be his last.'

'We're trying to make you see sense,' Mavis said. 'We both know how upset you were over Danny and no one more than us wanted you to meet a nice feller and fall in love, but did you *have* to pick the CO *and* a married man?'

'Not very sensible, was it?' Isobel added.

'I've told you,' Kate tried to insist. 'There's nothing . . .'

'Well, it ought to stop – now!' Isobel said ruthlessly, totally disbelieving Kate's protests, and Mavis added, 'Don't say we didn't warn you.'

'Kate – come in.' Philip moved to pull down the blackout blinds on his office window, then came and locked the door behind her. He took her in his arms.

'Darling, there's something I have to tell you.'

Fear clutched her stomach. What had happened? Was it something awful?

'You know, don't you, that the two squadrons on this station are switching to the new Lancaster bomber?'

She nodded.

'Well,' he went on slowly, his blue gaze never leaving her face, 'so are East Markham.'

Kate stared at him, running her tongue over lips that were suddenly dry.

'The Lanc is too heavy for Markham's grass runways. So they're closing East Markham temporarily to lay new concrete runways . . .'

'And?' Kate prompted, although now she was beginning to guess what was coming.

'. . . and their squadrons are being moved elsewhere – again only temporarily. Kate,' his fingers gently traced the outline of her face, 'Danny's squadron is coming here.'

She found she had been holding her breath. Now she let it out slowly and smiled. 'That's all right,' she said.

He searched her face. 'I didn't know how you would feel. I mean, I know you once asked me to see if I could wangle a posting here for him, but – well – that was before he got married and before – us.'

'I'll be fine,' she promised him softly, and some of the anxiety was smoothed from Philip's face.

Kate was pleased Danny was coming to Suddaby. She would have the chance to talk to him, to explain why she had not attended the wedding. If she could talk to him – alone – she knew she could make him understand. Soon, everything between them would be all right again; it would be as it had always been.

But she could not go home. Even yet, she could not face Rosie – especially a heavily pregnant Rosie.

The day the Lancasters arrived at Suddaby, there was great excitement.

'Heavens! They're big!' Mavis gasped, as, along with Kate and Isobel, they stood on the peritrack watching.

'Who? The Lancs – or the fellers?' Kate grinned.

Mavis's laughter bounced on the breeze. She rubbed her hands together, 'Well, if the crews are as good as their aircraft – wheel 'em out!'

'Mavis, really! What about the wonderful Dave?'

Mavis turned pink. 'I can still look, can't I?'

'Is it serious with you two, then?' Isobel asked, but Mavis

only grinned and said, 'Can't hear you above the racket, Iso, old thing.'

The aircraft taxied past them, several with symbols and pictures painted on them just below the cockpit. A shapely female proclaimed M-Mother and the three girls pointed and laughed.

'Well, if that's someone's mother, I'm a Dutchman.'

'Look, there's P-Pluto,' Mavis pointed. Behind it came another, D-Doggo, depicting a bulldog with an enemy plane – the swastika plainly visible – crushed in its massive jaw.

'Aren't they wonderful?' Mavis said, her admiring glance following the aircraft. 'Four Rolls Royce Merlin engines and they can carry over twenty thousand pounds of bombs.'

'I don't know how they get 'em into the air. They're massive!'

'Well, you just watch, sunshine. They will – and tonight if this weather holds.'

Kate gasped. 'So soon? But they've only just got here.'

'War won't wait for them to be pampered. That reminds me, Iso, we might have to do double shift tonight. With all these extra kites here, we're going to be a bit busy. And if it's long-range, they're going to be very low on fuel by the time they get back.'

Isobel groaned. 'Then I'm off to get a bit of shut-eye now.'

Mavis and Isobel turned and walked back across the grass towards the camp gate and the road leading to the WAAF site, leaving Kate staring at the new arrivals and wondering just which aircraft was Danny's.

Throughout the day the airfield hummed with activity. The arrival of an additional squadron and all its attendant personnel put an additional strain on the new airfield's resources. And now, with the rumour spreading that the night's op was to be 'a big one', there was an air of tension and scarcely concealed excitement.

'I must go to Group HQ,' Philip told her, 'for a meeting with the AOC.'

'Sir,' Kate responded dutifully, but beneath her breath she muttered a frustrated 'Damn!' She was so anxious to see Danny before he flew that night, but now she was to be away from the station for most of the day.

At Group Headquarters, Kate found herself with little to do while she waited for Philip. It was always the same, she thought. He was involved in lengthy conferences and meetings whilst she wandered from room to room, feeling in the way, on the edge of all the activity yet unable to take part.

Kate sat watching a WAAF Flight Officer who was analysing the photographs from the previous night's raid ready for the meeting called by the Air Officer Commanding.

'Do you know what tonight's target is?' Kate asked her.

The WAAF officer looked up and smiled. 'Not yet. We should be getting the signal from Bomber Command any time. The weather's exceptionally good just now, so it'll probably be something big.'

Kate nodded, but her thoughts were back at Suddaby. She just had to see Danny before take-off that night.

As the WAAF officer had predicted, when the signal came through it was a 'maximum effort raid'; the Ruhr.

Back on station, Kate drove Philip immediately to briefing.

'Would it be all right if – if I came in? I'll sit right at the back out of the way.'

He looked at her. 'Danny?' he asked softly.

She smiled tremulously and whispered, 'You're far too observant, Group Captain Trent.'

He smiled, but there was still a sadness in his eyes, though whether it was for her or for himself, she couldn't be sure.

'You'll have to pretend you're dispensing tea or something, Kate. I really can't get you admitted to the briefing. I'm sorry.' His apology was genuine; she realized at once that she had put him in a very difficult position by even asking for such a favour.

She forced a smile on to her mouth and said brightly, 'I understand. I'll go and help Christine.'

He nodded and at the doorway, they parted; he strode into the briefing room whilst Kate slipped into a tiny room at the side where a WAAF was pouring out cups of tea from a huge urn. Christine glanced up, but seeing that it was the CO's WAAF driver she made no demur about Kate's presence. Almost everyone on the camp now allowed her admittance even to the most sensitive of areas, recognizing that the CO trusted the discretion of his driver implicitly. The knowledge warmed her.

Outside the aircraft were being fuelled from the huge tankers and the armourers would be loading up the bomb trains; twelve 500-pounders and one 4000-pound bomb for each Lancaster. It was a physically demanding and sometimes dangerous job.

By the time the aircrews were filing into briefing, their aircraft would be standing ready at dispersal, fuelled, tested and bombed up.

As the crews trooped in, Kate scanned their faces eagerly through the hatch from the tiny kitchen. No one even glanced in her direction; their eyes went immediately to the large wall map showing their target. By the time most of the chairs were filled and the men came to attention as the Station and Squadron Commanders entered, Kate had still not spotted Danny. As the briefing began, she searched among the heads, trying to pick out his black hair, but then as the man from the

Met Office opened the proceedings, Kate found her attention
captivated. Unobserved, she was able to eavesdrop on the
whole procedure. It was impossible to be oblivious to the tension in the room, the feeling of a peculiar excitement. In
front of her the airmen were making notes, their whole
attention focused on the man pointing at the weather map,
transferring all the information in front of them to their own
maps and charts.

'Over the target, conditions should be fair . . . over base
on return, clear . . .'

The Met man stepped down and the Flying Control Officer stepped up to give details of the runway to be used and
take off times. The intelligence officer fascinated Kate and she
found herself gripping the edge of the hatch as she leaned
forward to listen to him giving route details, where the aircraft, once over enemy territory, might encounter flak and
where they might expect to be intercepted by enemy night
fighters.

Then came the Squadron Commander and lastly she
watched Philip as he addressed his men, emphasizing the
importance of accurate navigation and time-keeping. There
were to be a great number of aircraft all heading in the
same direction . . . Everyone in the room synchronized their
watches and finally Philip wished them all good luck.

As the CO left the dais and marched between the ranks
of men, Kate scuttled out of the building. By the time Philip
emerged she was standing with the car door open in readiness. Only when they were in the staff car did he ask, 'Did
you manage to see him?'

'No,' she said, unable to keep the tremor from her voice.
He leaned forward from the back seat as she added, 'But
I've only just realized, he'll be at the other briefing, won't
he? He's a rear-gunner.'

The radio operators and gunners had a separate briefing.

'Oh Kate, I'm sorry. I hadn't realized he was a gunner. I haven't had chance to meet everyone yet. Tell you what – drop me off at my office. You might just catch them drawing their flying kit. But can you be sure to be back to pick me up in time to take me out to dispersal?'

'Oh, thank you. Yes, of course I will.'

Minutes later, Kate was hovering outside Parachute Section waiting for the crews to emerge.

If only she could just see him, talk to him . . .

'Kate! Kate!' Suddenly there he was, coming towards her, a bulky figure in his sheepskin flying jacket and leather boots, his parachute slung carelessly over one shoulder. But the cheeky grin was the same as ever.

'Danny, oh Danny . . .' For a moment her vision blurred as tears filled her eyes. Then she was reaching out and he was taking her hands in his.

'I had to see you, I want to tell you . . .'

'Eland,' came a deep voice behind them and they both glanced round. 'Time to go.'

'Sir,' Danny responded and turning back, squeezed Kate's hands quickly. 'I'm sorry, Katie . . .'

'But, Danny, I have to talk to you, I have to explain . . .'

'Later, Katie, when I get back.'

For a desperate moment she clung to his hands, but he pulled himself free, smiled a rueful apology and hurried after the rest of his crew.

'Danny, Danny . . .' she called, running after him. 'Which – which is your plane, please tell me?'

She had to know which aircraft he was in; she had to be able to watch for it coming back.

He turned back briefly, raised his hand in a wave, and called, 'D-Doggo . . . I'll see you when I get back.'

359

Thirty-Three

Kate watched him walk away from her. There was still an hour to take-off, but the crews needed to go out to their aircraft, for all the cockpit checks and starting the engines of forty aircraft – more now a third squadron had arrived – would take up every minute of that time.

As she saw Danny climb into the back of a covered lorry, Kate turned towards the staff car. It was time to pick up Philip.

She watched take-off from the roof of the control tower as she had done so many times before alongside Philip. This time it was different; this time Danny was out there some-where, hunched in his lonely rear turret, the most vulnerable position in the whole aircraft to enemy night fighters. The huge aircraft, cumbersome with their weight of bombs and fuel, taxied from the various dispersal points, forming up to take off in orderly, timed intervals. At the end of the runway, each aircraft waited for the controller's red light to switch to green before revving its engines and beginning its lumber-ing, heart-stopping take-off. The noise of over two hundred Merlin engines filled the night air, as one by one they trundled down the runway, gathering speed, faster and faster, till Kate found she was holding her breath, willing each one into the air. The end of the runway came nearer and nearer until it seemed impossible they would make it. Then, just as her knuckles were turning white as she gripped the rail, the aircraft would lift unwillingly into the air, its undercarriage immediately raised. Silhouetted against the darkening sky, the bombers were like a flock of predatory birds carrying death and destruction in their bellies.

From this distance, she could not see which was D-Doggo, but it did not stop her praying, 'Oh, please let him come back safely – let them all come back safely . . .'

Soon they'd be flying over the coast, maybe over Flee-thaven Point. Would Danny be thinking of Rosie far below, blissfully ignorant of the danger he was in, when she, Kate, knew only too well?

In the control tower, in a pool of light, the personnel on duty – Mavis and Isobel among them – began to plot the movement of the aircraft.

As the sound of the last aircraft faded into the distance, Kate felt a light touch on her shoulder and turned to see Philip's concerned face. 'Come on, Kate,' he said gently. 'We'll go back to my office.'

She nodded. 'I'll drop you off and then – then I want to go back to my hut . . .'

She hesitated as she saw the pain flit across his face, and added swiftly, 'I need my coat, but I'll come back if – if you want me to.'

His voice was husky as he said, 'Of course I want you to.'

She took Philip to his office, leaving the staff car parked outside, for they would need it once more in the cold light of dawn as the Lancasters struggled home. She walked out of the airfield's main gate and across the road to the WAAF site. Inside the hut she pulled on her greatcoat, feeling sud-denly cold. About to turn away, she paused and, with fingers which trembled slightly, pulled open the drawer of her locker. The whelk shell nestled against her pile of clean handker-chiefs. Hesitating only a moment, she picked it up and slipped it into the pocket of her coat. It was their talisman and during the long night ahead she was going to need it. There was nothing to do now but wait!

When the first aircraft were due back the airfield beacon was switched on. How glad the crews would be to see it flashing the signal SB; Suddaby, home and safety. As the first planes began to land, Kate and Philip were back in the Control Room. While Philip stood quietly behind the R/T operator, Kate sat in the shadows in one corner, listening and watching in fascination as the personnel worked. There was an air of deliberate calm, and yet the atmosphere crackled with tension. A WAAF began to fill in the landing times of the returning aircraft on the huge board. Kate's glance kept coming back time and again to D-Doggo.

There was no need for radio silence now the raid was over, and Mavis and Isobel began calling up the aircraft. One by one the planes landed. There were anxious moments when one aircraft had to do an emergency landing because its undercarriage was damaged, and another limped in on only two engines. As always, the fire crews stood ready and raced towards the aircraft as it slewed off the runway and on to the grass. There was another crisis when two planes wanted to come in at the same time because they were dangerously low on fuel and were given permission to land, one immediately after the other.

Kate felt the sweat prickle the back of her neck and marvelled at her two friends for their composed efficiency and the way they kept their voices calm and professional when giving directions to the aircrew. Long gone were any criticisms that Mavis was too excitable. Now, she nursed down a lame aircraft, soothed the momentary panic of a young pilot on his first op and juggled expertly with the

extra aircraft stacking above the airfield, all demanding
runway space at once, it seemed to Kate.

Now, there were only three Suddaby aircraft and four
from the visiting East Markham squadron to come in.

Philip was bending down in front of her. 'I must go across
to de-briefing . . .' he began, and as she made to rise to take
him across in the car, he put his hand briefly on hers. 'You
stay here, if you want to,' he whispered.

'If you're sure . . .?' She looked up into his eyes, but in
the dim light, his expression was difficult to read. He gave
her hand a swift squeeze, straightened up, turned away and
was gone.

Huddled in the corner, she watched and waited, feeling
even more alone now that Philip had left.

The radio fell silent, yet Mavis and Isobel were still vigil-
ant. They would not relax until all the aircraft were in, or . . .
Kate shuddered, suddenly realizing what her two friends
dealt with every day. Waiting and listening for the planes to
come back. Sometimes, waiting in vain.

The waiting was becoming unbearable. Quietly, Kate slipped out of the Control Room.

The vehicles were drawing up outside de-briefing and she
watched the young airmen walking towards the building,
their young faces lined with tension and grey with exhaustion. It was so hard to believe that these were the same men
who laughed and drank and made merry in the pub and the
dance hall. Then, they looked as if they didn't have a care
in the world, whereas now . . .

Tentatively, she touched the arm of a pilot officer passing
close by her. 'Excuse me, are you from the East Markham
squadron?'

His glance took in her WAAF uniform. Guardedly, he
nodded.

'Do you – know Danny Eland?'

'Yes,' he said briefly.

'Is – is he safe?'

The young man, his eyes glazed with tiredness, shrugged. 'Sorry – can't say. I mean – I don't know. I don't know yet who's back – and who's not,' he added significantly.

There was another aircraft approaching the runway, its engines coughing and spluttering. Any moment it would be out of fuel. Lower and lower it dropped until its huge tyres hit the runway with a squeal and it was racing along the concrete. In the darkness Kate could not see its name and she shivered in the cold morning, waiting, still waiting . . .

The crew were piling out of the crewbus and walking towards her. She moved forward a step.

'Danny?' she whispered, but the men were strangers. It was not Danny's crew.

She swallowed the fear rising in her throat and looked anxiously towards the east, willing there to be another plane in view. But the dawning sky was empty and silent.

She went into the building where de-briefing was taking place; the crews, drinking tea, were moving from one WAAF interrogator to another as they gave their various reports. Kate felt the fear in the pit of her stomach, as she glanced around the room. There was no sign of Danny, nor of any other member of his crew.

She repeated her question. 'Are you from East Markham? Do you know what's happened to D-Doggo?'

'No, sorry. Three aircraft went down over the target. Maybe . . .'

She turned away; she didn't want to hear.

Across the room, she saw Philip, moving among the crews, glance at her. Kate bit her lip. She shouldn't be here, really. But he did not look angry, only worried.

She left the building and ran, her heart thumping, back towards the control tower. Breathless, she ran up the stairs and burst into the Control Room. She paused in the doorway, her hand still holding the door-handle, her frightened eyes going at once to the blackboard.

There were two names still on the board: P-Pluto and D-Doggo. Dragging her terrified gaze from the board, she met Dave's sympathetic eyes. Instead of being annoyed with her for charging into the Control Room, he rose, came towards her and led her gently to a chair in the corner. 'Sit there, love, I'll get you a cuppa.'

The room, which only half an hour ago had seemed chaotic, a nerve centre of activity, was now silent. Only crackles and whistles emitted from the radio, no pilot's voice requesting permission to land, no voice giving the call-sign 'D-Doggo here'.

She had to face the truth; Danny was missing.

Mavis and Isobel were sitting in front of their radio control panels and Kate sensed they could not bring themselves to say anything, or even look at her.

Kate started up as footsteps sounded hollowly on the concrete stairs outside. Then Philip came into the Control Room. He glanced immediately at the board, just as she had done, and then his gaze came around slowly to rest upon her huddled miserably in the corner.

Ignoring the rule-book once more and how it would look to those in the Control Room, Philip touched her shoulder, his voice firm yet infinitely tender. 'Come on, Kate.'

Stiffly, Kate eased her aching limbs from their locked position and, with his arm about her shoulders, allowed herself to be guided down the narrow stairs.

Outside, to the east, the sky was growing lighter. Dawn would be casting its soft glow over Fleethaven, she thought, silhouetting the cottages, rousing the sleepy occupants to another day. Soon, at home, they would be rising, her mother first, then Jonathan, and the day's work would begin.

And Beth. In her cottage she would be first to rise, perhaps taking Rosie a cup of tea in bed. Perhaps they would speak of Danny. Of course they would speak of Danny. But did they know, could they guess, the agony she, Kate, was going through at this very moment? Did they, too, watch the sky night after night, hearing the aircraft droning overhead, and wonder if somewhere in the vast dark sky was Danny up there? Did they lie awake waiting, listening for the return?

Walking along beside Philip, she thrust her hands deep into her pockets and felt the whelk shell. She gripped it until the point dug into her palm. Was this really all she would have left of Danny now? She would keep it with her always, she vowed, until he was safely home . . .

In the seclusion of his office, Philip took her in his arms. She clung to him, burying her head against his smart commanding officer's uniform, her tears making mottled damp patches on his shoulder. Her held her tightly, stroking her hair, but saying nothing.

She drew back a little and looked up at him, his features blurred through her tears. 'I'll have to go home,' she stuttered. 'I must t-tell – Rosie.'

Gently he wiped the tears from her face, but could not stem the flow.

His voice was flat and heavy as he said quietly, 'Yes, my dear. I'll arrange it for you.'

Thirty-Four

'Why, Katie love!' The joy on Beth Eland's face at seeing her was unmistakable, but then she saw Kate's solemn face, the anxiety in her eyes. Beth's hand flew to cover her mouth which formed a silent 'oh'. Then she reached out and drew Kate into the kitchen.

'What is it?'

Kate looked into the older woman's face. Gently, she took hold of her hand and said, 'Is Rosie here?'

Beth nodded. 'She – she's lying down. She gets very tired. She's only a few weeks to go . . .'

'Can you fetch her?'

Beth nodded, her eyes anxious, an ill-concealed terror growing in them.

Rosie came into the kitchen, her young face flushed from sleep, her blonde curls tousled, her body swollen with child. She paused in the doorway as she met Kate's steady gaze. Kate held out her arms to Rosie, and the girl gave a little cry and with surprising swiftness covered the distance between them. They clasped each other, Kate leaning forward over Rosie's bulge. The girl drew back with a nervous laugh of embarrassment and glanced down at her stomach. 'Gets in the way a bit, dun't it?'

'Sit down, Rosie,' Kate said, and Beth stood quietly beside her daughter-in-law's chair. Instinctively, the girl put up her hand and caught hold of Beth's. Then their eyes met Kate's.

She took a deep breath, trying to still the sick feeling

that was rising in her stomach. 'You know that Danny was stationed at East Markham and I'm at Suddaby.'

They nodded, their gaze never leaving her face.

'East Markham has been closed temporarily for concrete runways to be constructed...' She paused again. 'And Danny's squadron has been moved to Suddaby.'

Rosie's face brightened. 'Oh, how lovely! You'll be together. I *am* pleased.'

Kate bit her lip. There was not a trace of jealousy in Rosie's tone. She was genuinely happy to think that Kate and Danny would be together. 'Isn't that wonderful, Mother?' Rosie smiled up at Beth, but the older woman's gaze never left Kate's face.

'Have you seen him, Katie?' Rosie chattered on brightly, her joy at thinking they had met twisting like a knife in Kate's heart. She pulled in another deep breath. This was even harder than she had imagined it would be. 'They arrived two days ago but I only saw him very briefly. I – I didn't have a chance to talk to him – not properly.' Here her voice almost quavered. She had wanted so desperately to speak to him, to explain, to make up their quarrel. Now she might never have the chance.

'That same night all the aircraft from Suddaby and the squadron from East Markham – they – they all had to go on a big operation...'

She was going round in circles, avoiding the moment when she must tell them the awful news. And they were waiting so patiently, so trustingly, not firing questions at her or demanding that she hurry up. Yet surely they must realize...

'My two friends are R/T operators and I was allowed to sit in the Control Room and – and watch for the planes to come in. Only – only – oh, Rosie...' Tears filled her eyes and their faces became blurred in front of her. 'Danny's aircraft didn't c-come back.'

There was silence in the room save for the clock ticking and the kettle humming on the hob, and outside a lone seagull cried mournfully. For a long moment the two women stared at Kate, and then Rosie's face crumpled and she let out a cry that pierced Kate's heart, for it echoed her own foreboding. She went and knelt before the girl, grasping her hands as they twisted in her lap, while Beth stood by, not moving, as if she had not really taken in the dreadful news.

'Listen, Rosie, listen. His plane has been posted missing, but that doesn't mean he's – he's dead. He could have baled out. Anything. You mustn't give up hope. None of us.' She looked up at Beth in mute appeal for help, but Beth was stunned. Woodenly, she moved to sit in the Windsor chair that had been her husband's. The husband she had lost so recently. And now perhaps she had lost her son. Beth gripped the wooden arms tightly and stared unseeingly in front of her.

Kate scrambled to her feet. Grannie Harris, next door, she'd fetch her. Then she remembered. Poor Grannie Harris could hardly walk now and spent most of her day in a bed under the kitchen window, so, as she said herself, she could 'still look out an' see what's going on'.

Kate bit her lip. Rosie was rocking backwards and forwards, wailing horribly, a high-pitched noise that went right through Kate.

There was only one person she could fetch to help; her mother, Esther Godfrey.

What was it Danny had said, she thought wryly as she ran back towards Brumbys' Farm, her feet flying across the turf. 'They never speak to one another, but when there's trouble, real trouble, they come together.' Well, Kate thought, there was 'real trouble' now right enough.

'Of course I'll come at once,' Esther said without hesitation and only paused to issue instructions to her husband.

'I'll manage the milking, Esther love, you go,' Jonathan said calmly.

'Poor Beth,' Esther murmured as she hurried along the lane beside Kate. 'To lose her husband *and* her son so close together, to say nothing of . . .'

'We don't know he's dead yet, Mam. That's what I'm trying to get them to believe.'

Her mother eyes were sharp as she looked into Kate's face. 'Do *you* believe it?'

'I've got to,' Kate muttered, 'else I'll go out me head an' all.'

They couldn't stop Rosie crying. They tried everything – comforting her, talking to her, hugging her, even, in the end, Esther being quite firm with her. But to no avail. She sat rocking, her arms around her bulging stomach, sobbing at first, then wailing loudly and then leaning back exhausted against the back of the chair, the tears just pouring silently down her cheeks.

Where they failed with Rosie, Esther succeeded with Beth. For a couple of hours she had sat in the chair on the opposite side of the range, gripping the arms until her knuckles showed white, staring ahead of her at nothing in particular.

At last, Esther, after trying soothing words of sympathy which didn't work, stood in front of Beth. Her feet set apart, hands on hips, Esther Godfrey went into action.

'Now look here, Beth Eland, this ain't no good. You've lost a good man, I know that, and you're worried sick about young Danny. But as Kate says, we've got to hope for him yet. Now you mun think on yar grand-bairn. Ya've got to help us with Rosie . . .' Esther stood a moment watching Beth for any sign of a response. There was none.

Kate saw her mother glance across at her, raising her shoulders in a gesture of helplessness. 'I'm sorry, Katie,' she murmured. 'There's nothing for it. There's one way to bring her out of it, but it's – it's a bit brutal.'

Kate watched Beth for a moment. The woman was in a kind of trance. 'Do whatever you have to, Mam.'

Esther took a deep breath and leaned forwards, her face close to Beth's. 'It's yar grand-bairn, Beth – yours and *Matthew's*!'

Kate winced. Her mother had not been underestimating her own harsh tactics, but when Kate saw Beth blink and begin to focus her eyes upon Esther towering over her, she knew her mother had been right.

Now Beth's hands loosened their panic-stricken grip on the chair and she reached towards Esther, who clasped her hands and chafed them between her own. 'That's it, Beth. Come on, lass.'

Kate stifled a half-hysterical giggle. To hear her mother call Beth Eland 'lass' was comical and yet, she thought, perhaps they do still see each other as girls. Girls who might, once upon a time, have been friends.

'Oh, Esther.' Beth spoke for the first time since Kate had broken the news to them. 'How am I to bear it?'

Esther just patted her hand, unable, for once, to think of anything to say.

Kate's attention swivelled suddenly back to Rosie as the girl gave a gasp that was nothing to do with weeping. Rosie was bending over and clutching her stomach. 'Oh – it hurts!'

'Mam . . .' Kate began, but already Esther had turned from Beth back to Rosie.

'Where, lass?'

'Here.' Rosie smoothed her hands round her abdomen and down her groin. 'It's all right,' she sniffled, 'it's going off now.'

Esther watched her for a moment as the girl relaxed, sat

371

up again and leaned back in the chair. Then Esther glanced back at Beth. 'Is everything ready?' she asked quietly.

Kate watched as Beth's eyes widened, but understanding immediately, the woman nodded. 'In the other room . . .' She nodded to the door leading out of the kitchen to the only other downstairs room in the cottage. 'Rosie sleeps in there. We—' She hesitated and then corrected herself. 'I – sleep in the little room upstairs.' So fresh was Beth's widowhood that she still sometimes forgot.

'Kate – run and tell yar dad to fetch either the doctor or the midwife. It dun't matter which, but I want one of 'em to take a look at her. She's had a bad shock and with all this crying, she could be going into labour. I aren't as practised as Grannie Harris – I could use a little advice.'

Kate was off and running, and, having delivered her breathless message, was soon sprinting back towards the row of cottages at the Point.

Esther had got Rosie into the other room and had made her lie on the bed by the time Kate arrived back, just in time to hear the girl give another scream, her eyes wide with fear.

'Oh – it hurts. I dun't want it, if it's going to hurt like this.'

'There's not a lot ya can do about it now, lass. Ya can't leave it in there for ever,' Esther said briskly, but not unkindly. She turned to look at Kate hovering uncertainly in the doorway. 'Wash yar hands well, Kate, and come and help, will ya? Beth, get the kettle going. I could use a cup 'o tea, if nothing else.'

Kate hesitated for a fraction of a second, recoiling at the irony of the situation. She had hated Rosie for marrying Danny and now here she was being forced to help her bring his child into the world. Really, she thought, scrubbing her hands under the pump over the sink, life isn't fair!

When she went back into the bedroom, Rosie was rolling

from side to side on the bed, clutching her stomach and squealing.

Kate went to stand beside her, feeling helpless and inadequate.

'Let's get her clothes off and get her into her nightdress before the doc or the nurse comes,' Esther said.

'No – leave me alone,' Rosie said petulantly. 'I want Danny!' and she began wailing again.

Gradually, by alternately coaxing and being firm with her, Esther and Kate got her undressed.

'Mam, the bed's all wet.'

'Oh heck, 'er waters have broken. Go an' tell Beth . . .'

But at that moment Beth opened the door. 'Esther, Jonathan's here. He says the doctor's out on his rounds and the nurse is with a woman and can't leave her for about an hour . . .'

'Well, someone'll have to come, 'er waters have broken.'

Beth disappeared for a moment and they heard the deep rumble of Jonathan's voice, the outer door open and close, and Beth came back into the room, her worried eyes going immediately to the girl still writhing in agony on the bed.

'He – he's gone back to town to get someone to come.'

Kate saw the look that passed between her mother and Beth – a long look of shared memories from which Kate was excluded. 'Least it's not snowing this time,' Esther murmured, and the two women smiled a little sadly at each other.

'I don't want it!' Rosie was screaming. 'I don't *want* it!'

Kate, still standing beside the bed, bent over her. Something inside her snapped. ''Course you want it. It's Danny's baby. Don't you dare say you don't want Danny's baby, Rosie Eland!' she yelled back at Rosie, while out the corner of her eye she saw her mother nodding her approval.

'That's it, lass, get her good and mad, then she might do bit o' work.'

Rosie's screams were stilled in shock. She gazed up at Kate with big round eyes, her lips parted in a gasp of surprise.

'That's better,' Esther encouraged. 'Now, just try to calm down a bit, lass, and do as I tell you. Mebbe I bain't a midwife, but I've brought plenty of calves and piglets into the world. A babby can't be that different. Prop her up against the pillows, spread your legs open, Rosie. That's it – now ya forming, lass.'

'Oh – oh!' Rosie gasped, and held out her hand to Kate. 'Katie – it – hurts!'

'It's all right, Rosie,' Kate said gently now. 'Hang on to me, grip as hard as you like if it helps, but do what me mam tells you. Please, Rosie, for – for Danny.'

Rosie pressed her lips together and nodded. 'I'll try, Katie.'

'Next time you feel a pain swelling, Rosie, try a little push,' Esther said.

Rosie nodded. 'Oh, it's – starting again.'

'Push, Rosie.'

Gripping Kate's hand, Rosie pushed, and Kate found herself straining too.

Together they were going to bring Danny's child into the world.

Thirty-Five

'I wish that midwife would come,' Esther murmured. 'The head's born, so the rest won't be long.'

'Oh – oh,' squeaked Rosie as pain engulfed her once more.

'Push, push,' said Kate and her mother in unison.

'I – am! Ooh . . .'

'There!' Esther was triumphant, as if she had done it all herself. 'Beth, quick, come and see! Rosie, lass, you have a son.'

Rosie was weeping with relief now and Kate found that tears were coursing down her own face as she cradled Rosie's head against her and wiped the strands of blonde hair, wet with sweat, from her forehead.

It was at that moment that the midwife walked through the door.

'Oh Kate, I'm all mixed up. I don't know whether I'm happy or – or sad.'

Rosie was sitting up in bed now, propped against pillows with her son in her arms, flushed and triumphant, yet her eyes still filled with ready tears.

'Be happy, Rosie. It's what Danny would want,' Kate said softly, and touched the soft wispy black hair on the baby's head tenderly.

'You – you don't believe he's dead, do you?'

Kate shook her head. 'No, I—' she began and then corrected herself, conscious of Rosie's feelings. 'We'd know. We'd feel it.'

Rosie shifted the baby in her arms. 'Do – do you want to hold him, Kate?'

Kate smiled and held out her arms. 'Yes, please, Rosie.'

Sitting holding Danny's son in her arms was the strangest feeling. Danny's child; a child that might – had circumstances been different – so easily have been hers. She felt a protectiveness towards the tiny baby boy, a closeness and a flood of love.

'What are you going to call him?' Kate asked.

'Robert – after Danny's father.'

Kate nodded and said softly, 'Beth will like that.' Although she knew the facts, Rosie didn't seem to remember so readily that Robert Eland had not been Danny's natural father. But then, she was that much younger than Danny and Kate and had not even the haziest memory of Matthew Hilton. It was quite natural that Rosie should always think of Robert Eland as Danny's father.

Tears glistened in Kate's own eyes as she looked up at Rosie again. 'I've just realized – I'm his aunt.'

Rosie's eyes widened as now she, too, remembered. 'Of course you are – I was forgetting. Yes – his *only* aunt.'

She was, Kate thought. Although Rosie was the eldest of five children, all the others were boys.

'Kate – er—' Rosie twisted the sheet in her fingers. 'Can I ask you something?'

'Mmm,' Kate said absently, her attention back on the baby who was beginning to stir. He whimpered and Rosie took him back into her arms and offered him her breast.

'Would you – I'd love it if you – and I know it's what Danny would – want . . .'

Kate looked up and grinned. 'Yes, of course I will.'

Rosie's eyes widened. 'Will what? I haven't asked you yet?'

'Be his godmother.'

'How did you know that was what I was going to ask?'

'Well, you were, weren't you?'

Rosie nodded and the tiny room was suddenly filled with their laughter.

For the first time, Kate was reluctant to return to Suddaby, and yet she was anxious to see Philip again. She had so much to tell him. She could talk to Philip for he knew all about her. She longed to tell him how she had made up with Rosie and how the birth of their baby had, in a strange way, helped her.

As she stepped off the train, she saw him waiting on the platform, standing tall and dignified in his uniform, a slight frown creasing his forehead. It gave her a shock to see him there. Yet a thrill of pleasure ran through her seeing him unexpectedly; it was as if her own eagerness to see him had brought him there.

As she walked towards him, she reasoned with herself. His being here is nothing to do with you, she told herself sharply. He'll have come to catch a train . . .

'Kate!' He was coming towards her, his hands outstretched, and, oblivious of onlookers, he took her in his arms and held her close. 'Oh, Kate, how I've missed you.'

She clung to him, feeling the warmth and the strength of him.

They drew apart reluctantly. She was embarrassed by his public display, but he was grinning with happiness at seeing her again and obviously didn't care what anyone else was thinking.

'Are you catching a train?'

'Eh? Oh no, just meeting one.'

'You – you mean, you came to meet me?' she gasped.

377

'Yes. I've missed you so much. I couldn't wait any longer. I was even rash enough to ask Mavis what train you might be on. I've only been waiting on this draughty station for two hours!'

Lost for words, Kate just stared at him, her mouth half-open.

'You don't mind, do you?' It was the same question he'd asked her when he'd engineered her posting as his driver.

'Well, of course not, but . . .'

'Then stop dithering, woman,' the grin was back, 'and let's get to the car and into the countryside where I can kiss you properly.'

They hurried out of the station and Kate drove recklessly up the hill out of the city. A few miles from Suddaby she turned the car down a bumpy track leading deep into a wooded area that had become their secret hideaway. They were hungry for each other, desperate with desire that their separation had fuelled . . .

Afterwards they sat together in the back seat of the car, cool beneath the shadows of the trees with only the sounds of the breeze whispering through the leaves and of birdsong from the high branches.

Philip glanced at his watch. 'We'd better be making a move soon.'

'Is there an operation on tonight?' she asked.

'No, we've been stood down. Widespread fog is forecast. But I have been away from the station rather a long time on unofficial business,' he chuckled. 'I ought to be getting back.'

'Has everything been all right?' she asked. 'No more air raids?'

'No – we've had a very quiet time. Some might say too quiet.' He paused and then asked, gently, 'How were things at home?'

Kate sighed. 'Poor Rosie. She was hysterical. She went into labour and I stayed with her all the time.'

His arms tightened around her. 'It must have been very difficult for you.'

'No,' she said, and there was still surprise in her voice. 'It helped – really it did. Funny, isn't it, after all the fuss I made? Although maybe it's also because I have you now,' she added realistically.

'Oh, Kate.' His voice was hoarse and he buried his face against her hair.

'There hasn't—' she began hesitantly. 'You haven't heard anything about – about Danny's aircraft?' She felt compelled to ask and yet she knew the answer. Philip would have told her at once if there had been news of any sort.

He held her close and said softly, 'No, my dear. I'm so sorry, but we've heard nothing.'

They sat quietly together in the peace of the woodland for a few moments longer, then Philip kissed her gently and sighed regretfully. 'I'm sorry, darling, but we really must go.'

Kate reached for her jacket and got out of the back seat of the car.

'Oh no!' she groaned as she noticed that the car was lurching drunkenly to one side. 'We've got a puncture.'

Philip got out of the car and stood looking down at the flat tyre. He ran his hand distractedly through his short hair. 'Oh, hell! We can hardly explain away being stuck in the middle of the wood. Now what are we going to do?'

'Do? Change the wheel, of course.'

He looked at her blankly for a moment and then shook his head and frowned. 'I'm sorry, but I can't . . .'

Mischievously, she gave him a mock salute. 'Oh, but I can – sir! What *do* you think they taught us in MT training?'

His worried expression cleared a little. 'Can you really . . .?'

'Just stand back – and watch!'

In what seemed an incredibly short space of time, Kate had whipped off the huge wheel and replaced it with the spare.

'Well, well,' Philip grinned as they got back into the car. 'You really are a young lady full of surprises. Mind you, if I'd stopped to think for a moment, I should have realized it would have been part of your training,' and he added with endearing honesty, 'I suppose part of me can't get used to the idea of a woman being able to change a huge wheel like that a darn sight quicker than I could.'

As they bounced over the rough track through the trees back towards the road, Kate giggled as he muttered, 'But thank goodness you could, else we might have had some awkward explaining to do.'

When they drove through the gates into the station, with Philip sitting circumspectly in the back seat, she could feel him taking on the mantle of Commanding Officer once more. He seemed to be two people; the serious, dedicated Group Captain who carried the awesome responsibility for the station with strength and yet compassion. And then there was the man she knew when they were alone; the man who loved her and needed her to love him.

Two days later, he called her into his office. 'Come in – close the door.'

She stood before his desk. His face was tired, the lines of weariness etched deeply. 'I've done all I can to find out about Danny.' He shook his head sadly. 'But there's nothing. His plane hasn't been found and there's no report of him being a prisoner.'

'Is there anything about any other member of the same

crew? Something that might give a clue as to what happened to their plane?'

Philip shook his head. 'Nothing. It's as if they've disappeared completely. Still, at least there's hope. Usually when this happens, it's that their aircraft has crashed in enemy territory and they're hiding out with resistance workers. I don't want you to build up false hopes, though, and I'd advise you not to say anything to his family. Living amongst it, I know you understand better.'

Kate nodded. 'Yes, you're right. And I hope you're right about Danny too.'

Philip looked at her solemnly. 'So do I, Kate. So do I.'

They spent every possible moment they could together, but it became more difficult as Philip's responsibilities increased. Now he had three squadrons under his overall command on a station purpose-built for two. Although it was only a temporary measure that one of the East Markham squadrons be housed at Suddaby, nevertheless it threw a strain on the smaller station. Frequently, Philip slept in the little room behind his office, rather than go to his official quarters. He was so committed, Kate thought. He was there at every take-off and waiting through the long night until every aircraft was back, or at least until those who had not returned were posted 'missing'. And then he would hunch his shoulders into his coat and return alone to his office to write those awful letters to the families of the missing crews.

'We have a free afternoon off, Kate,' he whispered from the back seat of the car as they drove out of the gate one morning for a routine visit to Group HQ. 'A whole four hours with nothing to do. Where shall we go?'

'I don't know. Where do you want to go?'

'How about you take me to your home? I'd love to see where you live.'

Kate gasped. 'Home! But – but do you think we should?'

Philip shrugged. 'Why not? We'll be careful. I won't hug and kiss you in front of them, though I'd like to.'

She laughed. 'But it's not quite the thing for the Commanding Officer to spend the afternoon with his driver, is it?'

'No, I suppose not.' He was thoughtful for a moment. 'Isn't Fleethaven Point a restricted area?'

'Ye-es. The Army's got men posted at the Point. There's a gun emplacement there.'

'Well, then, that's it. I've come to inspect the site officially. Something to do with balloons, if anyone asks. Yes, that's it.' The decision made, he sat back in his seat, a self-satisfied look on his face.

The rule-book out the window once more, Kate thought, and laughing, told him, 'You're impossible!'

In the rear-view mirror she saw him grinning at her.

'Mam, Dad – this is Group Captain Trent. He's the CO.'

Philip held out his hand. 'Pleased to meet you, Mrs Godfrey – Mr Godfrey. Please call me Philip. When we're away from camp, Kate and I call each other by our Christian names, but we have to be very official on duty.'

Kate sensed her mother's eyes upon her and felt the flush of embarrassment creeping up her neck. 'Careful,' Kate's glance said silently to Philip, 'me mam's no fool.' Aloud, she said, 'Please sit down, sir – I mean, Philip. I'll just go and see me grandad. Is he up, Mam?'

'Oh aye, he's up. Fighting fit, he is. He'll outlive the lot of us.' Esther busied herself laying cups and saucers on the table.

382

Kate turned to leave the living room to go through to the front room, but at that moment the door opened and Will Benson came in. 'Ah thought I 'eard voices,' he said, as Kate kissed the white stubble on his chin.

The introductions were made again and soon Kate began to relax as Philip chatted comfortably with her stepfather and grandfather.

'Well,' he said at last, standing up, 'we'd better take a look at the Point, Kate.'

'Ya'll spoil yar shoes, young feller, traipsing across the sand. Lend him yar boots, Jonathan.'

When Philip had squeezed his size nine feet into Jonathan's size eight boots, and Kate had put on her own pair of wellingtons, they set off down the lane towards the Point. The moment they were out of sight of the farmhouse, Philip pulled her into his arms.

'No,' she gasped. 'Someone might come along the lane . . .' But she found herself returning his kiss, unable to resist him. Once over the Hump, they walked apart again.

'Oh Kate,' he murmured. 'All this secrecy, it's driving me mad. How I wish . . .'

'Kate – Kate!'

They both looked up to see Rosie hurrying towards them. 'Have you heard something about Danny?'

Kate shook her head. 'Oh, Rosie, I'm sorry, no. This is my commanding officer. We – he's here on official business.'

Rosie's eyes widened fearfully. 'Not – about Danny?'

Philip smiled, reassuring her quickly. 'No, no. We've heard nothing. I'm sorry,' he added, gently sympathetic.

Rosie's mouth quivered, but she tried to smile bravely. 'Oh well, I suppose no news is good news. Have you time to see the baby, Kate?'

Kate glanced up at Philip, who nodded. 'May I come too?'

Shyly, Rosie nodded and led the way into Beth Eland's cottage.

As she held Danny's son, Kate felt Philip looking at her and glanced up to meet his gaze. There was a strange mixture of emotions on his face, but suddenly his jaw hardened and he turned away. 'I'm sorry, Kate, we must go. Goodbye, Mrs Eland – Rosie,' he said, courteous as ever although it was evident he wished to be gone from the cottage.

Swiftly, Kate placed the baby back in Rosie's arms, kissed her and Beth and followed Philip.

He was striding ahead of her and she had to run to catch up with him. He walked fast with long, angry strides so that every so often she was obliged to take a little running step to stay by his side.

Philip neither glanced at her nor spoke to her.

Whatever is the matter, Kate thought.

He stood on the sand-dunes, his gaze scanning the coastline and out to sea, then without a word he marched back towards the Hump. They said a brief goodbye to Esther, Jonathan and her grandfather.

As always in front of others, she opened the car door for Philip to get into the back seat, but even when they were once more driving through the countryside, he made no suggestion that she should pull over so that he could sit beside her in the front.

They drove all the way back to camp in silence.

Thirty-Six

Later that evening, Kate went to Philip's office. His strange behaviour towards her had distressed her. What *had* she done to make him ill-tempered? It was so unlike him. He was serious and preoccupied sometimes, but with all his responsibilities she could understand that. This afternoon had been different.

There was a strip of light showing under the door. Tentatively she knocked, and when bidden, she entered and closed the door behind her. Coming smartly to attention, she saluted.

'Well?' he barked.

Her courage almost failed her. 'Sir – could we – be *off* duty for a moment?'

He glared at her and then suddenly groaned and dropped his face into his hands. 'Oh, Kate, I'm sorry.'

She was round the desk and kneeling beside him. 'Whatever was the matter? I couldn't understand . . .'

'Couldn't you?' He raised his head to look at her, a half-smile on his mouth. 'Just good old-fashioned jealousy, my darling.'

'Why?'

'When you were holding the baby – his baby – you were looking down at it with such love in your eyes, as if – as if you were longing that it was yours . . .' His voice dropped to a hoarse whisper. 'Yours – and Danny's.'

Kate felt a flood of tenderness for him as she cupped his

385

face in her hands and gently lifted his head to make him look at her. 'Once, that would have been true. But not now, not since – you. Yes, I love that little baby – as my nephew. I still love Danny – and I always will – but in the way I should have done all along, as my brother!'

'Really?'

'Really. And that's because of you. If I hadn't known you, I would still be clinging to Danny, hating Rosie and probably bitter against a poor, innocent baby. Oh, there's a tinge of regret and sadness, I admit. You can't kill the past, obliterate it as if it had never happened. It did happen; Danny and I fell in love before we knew of our relationship and we were devastated. But time and other people – you and Rosie – have helped to heal the wounds. The scars are still there, probably always will be. But now we can, both Danny *and* me, go forward. In the last few months, I've done a lot of growing up.' She sighed and added musingly, 'It might sound daft, but – but it was as if I was locked into being a seven-teen-year-old, clinging desperately to what might have been. They all tried to tell me – me mam, Dad and even *Danny*'s mother, but it wasn't until I – I found I could love someone else that I began to realize and understand that they were right.'

She sat back on her heels and said softly, 'There's only one thing I'm so sad about.'

'What's that?'

'I may never get the chance to tell Danny all this.'

Now it was his turn to reassure her. 'You will. I know you will.'

'Philip, I do love you. I don't think you'll ever really understand how much you've helped me, and come to mean to me.'

'Oh my dear – do you realize that's the first time you've actually said it?'

'Is it?' she said in surprise. 'I hadn't realized.' Then she giggled deliciously. 'But then I always did believe that actions speak louder than words.'

'You're wicked. Do you know that? Deliciously, gloriously *wicked*!'

She was glad to see he was smiling again and that their easy friendship was restored.

'The Yanks are coming, the Yanks are coming,' Mavis trilled, dancing up and down the hut. 'Now we'll show 'em just who's going to win this war. With our Lancs and their bombers, we'll really sock it to 'em!'

Since the attack on Pearl Harbor a few months earlier, Britain had no longer been alone; now she had a powerful ally and everyone was far more optimistic about the eventual outcome. Even so, they all knew the end of the war was still a long way off.

The weeks turned into months and still there was no news of Danny. As far as his squadron were concerned he became another statistic. Not forgotten, but gone, and there was no time, not yet, for indulging in mourning. There were too many to mourn.

For the WAAFs the ghosts of the young men lost still haunted the station. 'Do you remember Jim or Bill or Nick . . .?' was often whispered in the darkness of the hut. It kept the memories of the brave young men alive and the girls liked to think that their lost friends would be pleased that someone thought of them still.

'CO wants you and the car at his office now.' The corporal popped her head round the door of the hut.

'Now?' Kate echoed in surprise.

The corporal nodded and shrugged. 'Must be something important for him to be going somewhere this late. You'd better hop to it.'

Minutes later, Kate pulled up in the staff car outside Philip's office and opened the back door for him to climb in. She saluted smartly, but he waved her aside and went round and sat in the front passenger's seat.

Kate got back into the car. 'Sir . . .?'

He was sitting staring straight in front. 'It doesn't matter any more, Kate,' he said quietly. 'Just drive into the countryside, darling. I have to talk to you.'

Fear leaped in her breast as she bent and pressed the starter. As they paused at the gate to register their departure, she couldn't fail to notice the guard's glance into the car and the slight raising of his eyebrows. But Philip just sat passively beside her.

What had he meant – it didn't matter now? Had their affair been found out? Was there trouble brewing for him – and her too? Was this what he wanted to tell her?

She drove the few miles to their favourite spot. Her hands were clammy with nervousness on the steering-wheel.

She switched off the engine and half-turned to face him. Slowly he turned to look at her. He seemed to be taking in every tiny detail of her face as if to commit it to memory; as if it was important that he should know every line of it.

'You do know how very much I love you, don't you, Kate?' he said at last, his voice deep with emotion.

Her heart was thumping, beads of sweat standing out on her forehead. 'Yes,' she whispered, hoarsely. 'Whatever is it, Philip? Tell me – please!'

'I – I have to go home . . .'

'Is that all?' She almost laughed with relief but then it died immediately as she saw him shaking his head.

'I mean – I have to go home – for good.'

She was silent now, just staring at him in shock.

He took a deep breath and then let it out slowly in a sigh. 'Lizzie – my daughter – is critically ill. She – she won't live longer than a few months.'

'Oh, Philip.' At once she was all compassion. 'How dreadful! I'm so sorry.' The words seemed inadequate, but what else could she say?

'I'm – being posted to a station near home. My-in-laws have pulled strings and got it arranged. I wish they had consulted me first, but I suppose they felt they were helping. For once, Grace really seems to need me . . .'

She looked into his troubled eyes. With deep intuition she said, 'And you need to be with her – with Grace – too, don't you? And with Lizzie?'

He nodded. 'But what about you, Kate? I don't want you to think – I mean I don't want you to be hurt . . .' he said, anguished.

'It's all right,' Kate said. She heard the words come out of her mouth as if it were someone else speaking; so calm, so understanding. Yet inside, there was a fluttering of panic just below her ribs and her heart was crying out; 'Not again, oh, not again!' She wanted to throw herself against him, beg him not to leave her, not to go. But one look at the torment in Philip's face made her draw on all her reserves of strength for his sake. The poor man was being torn in two. And she did understand what he must be feeling for his daughter. Only a few weeks ago she would not have done so, but to her own amazement, holding Danny's son in her arms had wrought changes in Kate. There had still been the poignant longing that this child should have been hers – and Danny's – and yet there had been so much more. So this, she had thought, was what having children was all about. Holding a tiny, helpless, scrap of humanity in her arms, knowing it

389

was totally dependent on its parents, well, somehow it was sobering and in one moment banished all selfishness.

And that was what Philip must feel for his child, perhaps even more so for a 'less than perfect' mite. She had only ever thought of Grace Trent as a shadowy figure, who, by her devotion to her daughter, had shut Philip out of her life. But now, Kate felt pity for Grace – and pangs of guilt thrust their way through her emotions. She couldn't let Philip shoulder all the blame or start feeling guilty about her too.

'I knew what I was doing – what I was getting into when we began our affair . . .' She tried to reassure him.

She saw him wince. 'It's not an "affair",' he said harshly. He was angry now and she was surprised how much her words had hurt him. 'It's not a sordid affair, Kate.'

'All right, all right.' She tried to placate him swiftly. 'I didn't mean it the way it sounded. Right now, your place is with your wife and little girl. But I'll wait, Philip. However, long it takes. Just remember I'm here – waiting.' She touched the back of his hand and he turned it over quickly and grasped her fingers in such a tight grip that it was painful.

'Kate . . .' he whispered hoarsely. 'I do love you so very much. Bless you for understanding.'

'I can only guess at what your wife must be going through. You must – be with her.' Though she was weeping inside, Kate kept her voice strong for Philip's sake. She wondered if he knew how much it cost her to encourage him to leave.

'Poor Grace,' he said heavily. 'It's not her fault. She's borne the brunt of looking after Lizzie. Poor little Lizzie. I was so proud and happy the night she was born. I always wanted a daughter . . .'

'It's no one's *fault*, Philip. Please don't feel so badly.'

He closed his eyes and groaned deeply. 'But I do. You've been so hurt before and here I am hurting you again.'

That, Kate thought, she could not deny. 'You're hurting too, aren't you?' she murmured.

'Oh yes. My dearest girl – you'll never know just how much.'

Gently he drew her against him and they sat together, just holding each other closely, staring out of the car window at the blackness of the night, the only light being from the stars millions of miles away, and the new moon, a curved slit of light.

'My mother would say we're unlucky – seeing the new moon through glass,' Kate said.

'At this precise moment,' Philip said sadly, 'I'd have to agree with her.'

His departure, once arranged, was swift. They only managed to snatch one brief meeting when their lovemaking was tinged with sadness and a terrible fear that this was the last time they would ever see each other.

'I'll write to you, Kate.'

'How – how can I write to you?'

'I'll send you my address at the new station. Somehow we must keep in touch. We must! After a time, I'll see if I can get you posted to where I am,' he vowed urgently. 'Oh, Kate, I'll miss you so . . .'

The whole station was sorry to see him go; he had been a kind and caring CO, maintaining authority through the strength of his personality, because people really liked him.

'May we take a photograph, sir?' Mavis rushed up with Kate's camera in her hands as Philip came out of his office for the last time. Kate, holding the car door open, bit her lip, but Philip smiled easily and nodded. As his batman put his kit-bag and briefcase into the boot of the car, Philip came and stood beside Kate. 'I'd better have one with my best driver,' he murmured so that only she could hear. 'Expert at changing wheels and driving into ditches – and positively whizzo in a cornfield.'

Instead of reducing her to helpless giggles, his words made the tears spring to her eyes.

'Thanks, sir,' Mavis chirped. 'We'll send you one when they're developed.'

'Thank you, Mavis.' With a last wave to those standing around who had come to see him off, he got into the back seat of the car. Kate bit down firmly on her lip and managed to stop the tears running down her face, at least until they were past the guard-room.

They all missed him, and none more so than Kate.

Three days after his departure, when she got up in the morning, she was sick for the first time.

Thirty-Seven

'So,' Isobel said, sitting down on the bed beside her, 'how long do you think you can keep this little secret?'

'I – don't know what you mean!'

Mavis came and stood in front of her. 'Oh, come off it, Kate. We're not daft.' There were only the three of them in the hut so they had no need to lower their voices. 'Throwing up every morning for the past fortnight. You're in the family way, aren't you?'

Kate's shoulders sagged and she nodded.

Isobel clicked her tongue against her teeth in exasperation. 'I can hardly believe you could be so daft, Kate Hilton. Born and bred on a farm and you *still* get caught! Didn't you get him to – well, you know – take precautions?'

'He did – at least . . .' She hesitated, remembering a few weeks previously when, after being separated for a few days, there had been a desperate urgency to their lovemaking, which had been wonderful. Kate felt her cheeks grow warm at the mere memory; she could not, even now, regret a moment.

'I see,' Isobel's voice was heavy with sarcasm now, 'most of the time he did, except when he got carried away in the heat of the moment, eh?'

'Something like that,' Kate murmured. Isobel was far too astute at times.

'What are you going to do about it?' she was saying.

'Do? What do you mean – do?'

'Well, are you going to get rid of it?'

'No! No – I'm not. I might have made a mistake – but I aren't going to do anything like that.' In her distress, her dialect was strong again.

'Why not?' Isobel insisted, while Mavis bit her lip. 'You'll be thrown out of the WAAFs. Look, Kate, there's places you can go. We don't mean a back street job, not now . . .'

'No!' she said with finality.

Her two friends glanced at each other. Isobel's mouth was a tight line. 'Don't be stupid, Kate. You don't want to be burdened with a kid. An *illegitimate* kid!' she added brutally. 'What'll your family say?'

Kate winced. What indeed? she thought.

'Don't be so hard on her, Iso,' Mavis put in. 'Maybe she – she wants to keep it.'

''Course she doesn't . . .'

'Will you two please stop talking about me as if I'm not here *and* trying to decide my future? I'm not getting rid of the baby. It's my baby – and I'm keeping it!'

Isobel was looking at her strangely. 'Do you think you *ought* to keep it? I mean . . .'

'What do you mean, Isobel?'

'Well, if it's Danny's . . .'

'It isn't!' Kate snapped, then, more quietly but equally firmly, she added, 'and don't go asking whose it is, because I aren't telling you. Or anyone else, for that matter.'

'You don't need to – not any more,' Isobel said pointedly, but Kate chose deliberately not to pursue it any further.

'If you're sure . . .' Mavis began tentatively.

'I am,' Kate said with far more confidence than she felt inside.

'Then,' Mavis continued, 'we'll stick by you, won't we, Iso?'

'I suppose so,' Isobel said grudgingly. 'I still think you're wrong, but it's your choice.' Getting up off the bed, she delivered a parting shot. 'Well, I wouldn't be in your shoes going home to tell your folks.'

Kate shuddered and at the thought of her mother, her insides quivered. Ever since the realization had come upon her, telling her mother was the thing she dreaded most.

'You trollop! You whore!' Esther Godfrey drew back her right hand and slapped Kate's face hard. 'How could you do that to *me*? After all I've taught you. Ain't I told you time and again – you dun't let a feller touch you till you've a wedding ring on ya finger . . .?' The tirade went on and all Kate could do was stand there and take it. It brought Jonathan running in from the yard and Will Benson hobbling through from his room. They arrived at the split second when Esther delivered her physical blow.

'Esther . . .' Jonathan was shocked and Will demanded, 'What's up? What's going on?'

Esther swung round to face her father. 'What's up? *She's* what's up. Up the stick, that's what's up. In the blood, ain't it?' she accused, so that the old man wavered slightly and grasped at the table for support.

'Esther – you've said enough . . .' Jonathan began.

'Oh no, I ain't. I ain't started yet.' She turned back to Kate, thrusting her face close to her daughter's white one, in which the only colour was two red fingermarks along Kate's jawline left by Esther's stinging blow.

'Who is it? Is he going to marry you?'

Kate, too numb to speak, shook her head.

Esther stared at her for a moment, long and hard. 'Don't tell me – it's *him*!'

Kate blinked. 'W-who?'

'Danny. It's Danny's, ain't it? Yar bastard's *his*.'

395

'No.' Kate shook her head, so violently that her hair swung from side to side. 'No – I promise you that. It's not his.'

'Then – who?'

'I can't tell you . . .'

'You little trollop . . .' Esther began again.

Jonathan caught hold of his wife, putting his arms around her. 'Esther, just calm down . . .'

But she was struggling against him, her glare never leaving Kate's face. 'Do you mean,' she spat, 'you don't know who the father is?'

Kate gasped. 'Of course I know. But – I can't tell you.'

'Why?'

'Well then – I won't.'

Now mother and daughter glared at each other, some of Kate's spirit returning. She faced the three of them and raised her head high. 'I've made a mistake, I don't deny. And I'm sorry to have caused you pain. But I won't – involve the father, nor get rid of the child . . .'

'Why won't he marry you?'

'Because he – he can't.' Her voice dropped to a whisper but the three listeners in the room heard plainly. 'He's already married.'

Suddenly the fight seemed to drain out of Esther. She sagged against Jonathan as she looked at her father. 'History repeatin' itsen',' she murmured, and then closed her eyes and groaned.

Then, for Kate, came the worst shock of all. Esther turned in her husband's arms, buried her face against his chest and began to cry, great tearing, rending sobs as if her heart would break.

Tears blurred Kate's vision and blindly, she turned and ran from the house; across the yard and the lane, under the elder trees and up the slope of the dunes, then down the other

side and across the open marsh, as always seeking the sanctuary of the lonely beach.

But it was barred to her. Coils of barbed wire still blocked
her way on to the east dunes. She wandered back to the
westerly dunes and sat down amidst the thick spiky marram
grass beneath the elder trees. Hugging her legs to her, she
dropped her head to rest on her knees.

Her mind was a blank, refusing to take in the scene she
had just caused. She had known her mother would be angry
and upset, but Esther had been unrestrained and undignified
in her wild fury. Her mother had always had a quick temper,
and even as a child Kate had often felt the sharpness of her
hand, though always on her legs. But never before had Esther
smacked her across the face like that; not even when she
had caught her with Danny. Kate could still feel her jaw
smarting now.

She sat huddled in the dunes for a long time, until the cold
seeped through her clothing and she shivered. She looked up
to see that the sun had disappeared behind Brumbys' Farm.
Stiffly, Kate stood up. She hesitated for a moment, undecided
whether to go home or to go to the Point to see Beth and
Rosie. She sighed. She wasn't ready to tell them yet, nor
could she stay out here all night – though she wished she
could!

As she crossed the yard and went towards the back door,
she could hear the sounds of evening milking coming from
the cowshed. She bit her lip and paused, listening. Now she
could hear her father's deep tones, talking soothingly to the
cows as he milked them. As she moved to the shed and
opened the half-door, Jonathan straightened up and came
towards her. He held out his arms to her and wordlessly, she
went into them. He held her close and stroked her hair, just
as he had in her childhood.

'Oh Kate, love. Don't think too harshly of your mother. She – she has reasons why she reacted so badly.'

Kate drew back and looked up at him, straining through the dimness of the shed to see his face. 'It's not what I think of her, it's what she thinks of me!'

'She'll come around. Give her time.'

Jonathan was wrong. Esther did not 'come around'. She said no more to Kate, indeed, she virtually ignored her presence. Although she laid a place for her at the table and served her meals, she refused to speak to her elder daughter and pointedly avoided even looking at her. Lilian sat silently at the table, her eyes downcast. Immediately meals were finished, the younger girl would leave the table and shut herself in her bedroom with her books, taking refuge from the storms within the household and refusing to take sides.

When Kate's seventy-two-hour pass was almost up and she had to return to camp, she had still not found the courage to see Beth and Rosie.

They'll know soon enough, she thought, as she repacked her bag for leaving.

'You ready, lass? I'm taking you back to camp.'

'Oh, Grandad, I don't think . . .'

'No, Dad,' began her mother. 'You didn't ought . . .'

'I'll have no arguments . . .' He whipped round with surprising agility to frown at his daughter. 'From either of you! And dun't *you* start, neither.' He wagged his finger at Jonathan sitting in his chair before the range, calmly reading the newspaper.

Jonathan glanced up. 'I wasn't going to.' He smiled. 'Do you good to get out a bit instead of sitting here all day being waited on hand and foot.' But the words were said in fun and the old man exchanged a grin with his son-in-law.

'Come on then, Kate, let's be off.'

Outside the pony and trap waited in the yard and when they were both settled in the back, Will slapped the reins and the pony moved forward. Once in the lane with the distance lengthening between them and the farm, above the rattle of the wheels, he said, 'I aren't going to ask a lot of questions, lass, and I aren't going to preach at ya. But there's one thing I've got to know. Was it true what ya told ya mam? Ya bairn's not Danny's, is it?'

Kate tucked her hand through her grandfather's arm and held it tightly. 'No, Grandad, I promise you that. It's not Danny's.' There was a note of wistfulness in her voice, almost as if she wished the baby were his, but her grandfather had no such feelings. 'Thank the Lord for that!' he muttered.

Kate sighed. Once, she had longed to be the mother of Danny's children, and even now, despite her newfound love for Philip, still not a day went by without her thinking of Danny, longing to know if he was alive and safe.

The wind whipped coolly against her face and her gaze travelled unseeingly around the vast flatness of the landscape as the trap rattled along the lanes. She was remembering Beth Eland's words – so long ago now – and yet she could still hear them on the wind. 'You and Danny will probably always love each other. No one can stop you doing that. But somewhere there will be another love for each of you, and it will be a different kind of love to the one you'll always carry for one another.'

Now, since loving Philip with a passionate, physical love, she had indeed learned the difference between the loves in her life. Danny would always be her first love, an innocent and pure emotion that would never die, never be replaced, maybe, in some ways, never be equalled. But it was true what Beth had tried to tell her; there were many kinds of love and now she had experienced quite another with Philip. Her longing for him, for his arms about her, was a physical ache, a passionate, bodily longing, so strong at times she almost blushed. Now Philip Trent was gone from her life, without knowing he had fathered her child. And at this moment, it would be grossly unfair of her to add to his burdens by telling him.

As they neared Suddaby, Kate said, 'You don't need to go through the village Grandad, if you take the next right turn . . .'

'There's summat I want to show you. Ya don't think I've come all this way just for the good of me health, do ya?'

Puzzled, Kate said, 'Well, I just thought you wanted to bring me back to camp . . .'

He sniffed. 'Well, I did, of course, but I wanted to talk to you and tell you summat it's high time ya knew. Something mebbe you should have been told years ago . . .'

'I don't understand. What's all the mystery? What is it I don't know?'

'All in good time, Katie, all in good time.'

He guided the trap through the village. 'That's where I used to live.' He pointed with the whip to the middle cottage of a row of six. 'That's where you came when you ran away from school. D'ya remember?'

Kate shook her head. 'Not really. I mean, I remember running away and being given a lift by a carrier, and some woman looking after me.'

'Aye, that was Minnie Raby. Dead and gone now, she is, God rest her.'

'She wasn't that old, was she?'

'No, younger than me.' He laughed wheezily. 'I'm a stubborn old bugger. Ya mam's allus reckoning she'll have to knock me on the head to mek me lie down.'

He did not stop the trap near his former home but carried on along the village street towards the church, where he pulled the trap to a halt and climbed down stiffly. 'Come on, lass,' he ordered, holding out his gnarled hand to help her down.

The iron gate to the churchyard squeaked as he pushed it open. Will sniffed. ''Spect this'll be disappearing soon – for the war effort,' he remarked to no one in particular.

Kate followed her grandfather's bent form as he walked up the path towards the church porch. But instead of going into the building he moved on and turned on to the grass between the gravestones. He came to a place and stopped. Kate moved to stand beside him and saw in front of her two white headstones, identical in size and shape but with an unmarked plot between the two.

'That's where I'm to be buried when I go, Kate. Ya mam's promised me to see to it.'

Kate read the inscriptions on the two headstones. One was Will's wife, Rebecca Benson, who had died in 1919.

But Will was pointing to the companion headstone. 'That's ya grandmother, Kate.'

Kate gave a startled gasp and stared at him. Slowly she turned her gaze back to the graves. She bent closer and read. 'In loving memory of Constance Everatt who fell asleep 9th June 1893, aged nineteen years. The Lord giveth and the Lord taketh away.'

'Ya mam was born . . .' Will's voice shook a little, 'out of wedlock.' He couldn't bring himself to use the name her mother used so scathingly. Of herself, it seemed, Kate realized with a sudden shock.

Esther Everatt had been born a bastard.

Suddenly – everything fell into place.

'I loved Connie,' Will was saying simply and he drew the back of his hand, now thin and bony, the skin paper-thin, across his eyes which suddenly watered. It was difficult to imagine this bent old man standing in the draughty church-yard being young and virile; virile enough to sire a bastard on a younger girl.

'Rebecca were a good wife and I didn't mean to hurt her. We never had any children, Rebecca an' me, and then after a few years she didn't like that side of married life . . .' He ran the back of his hand across his mouth. 'Connie were a young lass in the village. I – couldn't help mesen, Kate. I just couldn't help mesen . . .' His voice faded away and he was lost, looking back down the years to a time when he had known a brief time of passionate happiness. 'She were a lovely girl, a lovely girl.'

'What happened?' It was Kate now whose voice was a husky whisper.

'She – died giving birth to Esther.'

'And then?' she prompted gently. She wanted to know it all. It was important that she knew everything.

He sighed heavily. 'Poor little lass. She was brought up by Connie's older sister, Hannah. She was married to George. A nice chap, but slow. They had seven bairns of their own. But she was a shrew of a woman and only took Esther in out of duty to her dead sister. She never showed young Esther a shred of affection and never let her forget the facts of her birth. So ya see, ya mam does understand, knows only too well, but from the other side, lass, from the other side of things. She knows what it's like to *be* the bastard. That's why she fought like a she-cat for her own place, that's why she married Matthew Hilton when he offered. And he did ask her, Kate.' Will's voice was firm now. 'Whatever anyone tries to tell you different, Matthew did want to marry her. He was mad to have her, 'cos she wouldn't give hersen to him without a wedding band, see? It was only when he found out afterwards that he'd left

Beth Hanley pregnant with Danny that he was resentful towards ya mam and tried to put the blame on her. And her only fault was that she wanted to be respectable and have a home she could call her own. That was her only fault, Kate, her *only* fault.'

'And that's why she's so mad at me,' Kate murmured, her gaze still on her grandmother's headstone, 'for bringing another bastard into the world.'

They were silent, then Kate put her hand through the crook of his arm again. Hugging him to her, she said, 'I'm so glad you've told me everything, Grandad. It helps me understand things a lot better. And why my mother's – well, like she is.'

'We don't realize,' he murmured, 'when we're young and foolish how the mistakes we make are going to affect those who come after us . . .'

'But you don't regret having loved Connie, do you?'

He pursed his frail mouth and shook his head. 'Never, I'll never regret that.'

'Or having Esther?' she asked, suddenly feeling the wiser one of the two.

Again he shook his head. 'I'm proud to be her father.'

'Well, then,' Kate said rationally. 'I'm going to be proud to have my child. I'll look after it, love it and never regret having it.'

'What about the father, lass, can he really not marry you?'

Kate looked down again at Connie's grave, sharing for a moment the same feelings she must have known so long ago. 'No, Grandad, he can't,' she told Will simply. 'There are other – complications.'

'Does he know about . . .?'

'I can't tell him, Grandad. It – wouldn't be fair.'

'So, ya've to bear it on ya own then?' He looked back

down at the gravestone and his whispered words were more of an apology to the love of his youth than sympathy with Kate in her present similar, predicament. 'Aw, lass, I'm sorry, so sorry.'

Thirty-Eight

Kate missed Philip more than she would have believed possible. She longed to have his arms about her, to rest her head against his shoulder and to be able to tell him about the child. She needed his reassuring strength, too, to cope with her fears for Danny. But Philip had burdens enough of his own.

It seemed particularly cruel that she should lose both the men in her life so suddenly – and when she needed them most. She felt a young girl again; alone and lost, with no one to turn to for help.

The man who took his place as Station Commander was older than Philip. Thin, with a balding head and wearing steel-rimmed spectacles, he was tall, but stooped slightly and was very round-shouldered. He was also thin-lipped and humourless, so that the pleasure Kate had enjoyed as Philip's driver – quite apart from her more personal relationship with him – was gone. This man showed no concern for her as a human being and he extended that lack of concern to all the personnel on the station.

If he had shown a caring attitude towards his aircrews then Kate could have forgiven his brusque treatment of her. As it was, his indifference was universal.

'He'll not last,' Mavis said. 'You can't have the man at the top as cold as ice. He's not human.'

'Well, for the first time, I'm quite pleased I'll be leaving before long,' Kate said feelingly. 'I hate the job now.'

'You wouldn't have liked whoever came in *his* place, now would you?' Isobel said reasonably. 'Mind you, I have to agree – this one's a bastard.'

Hearing her friend use the word as an insult made Kate shudder inwardly. Instinctively she put her hands protectively over her stomach, feeling the growing roundness. It was what her mother was and it was what her mother called the child she was carrying.

'When are you planning to leave?' Mavis asked.

Kate's two friends had been as good as their promise; even Isobel had relented and they helped her whenever they could. Although her driving work was not heavy, if she was suddenly asked to do something that might be harmful for her or the child, one of them would step in immediately and cover for her.

Kate smiled thinly. 'I'll have to see Ma'am soon. My skirt's getting too tight for me now. I'll be showing before long.'

'Are you going home?' Isobel asked.

'I—' Kate hesitated. 'I'm not sure. Me mam's mad as hell. I've got a seventy-two-hour pass this weekend. I'm going home to see – well – how the land lies.'

And, she thought to herself, this time I'll have to tell Rosie and Danny's mam.

Kate entered through the back door and put her bag down in the scullery. As she stepped into the kitchen, her mother looked up from where she was rolling out pastry on the kitchen table. Lilian sat at one end, her school books open on the scrubbed surface.

'Oh, it's you, is it?' Esther said, and banged the rolling pin down hard upon the pastry.

Lilian's glance went immediately to Kate's stomach. With a mumbled 'Hello', the girl lowered her eyes, her face red

406

with embarrassment, and concentrated on the exercise book lying open in front of her. Her pen moved swiftly across the page as she wrote.

'Hello, Mam – Lilian,' Kate said brightly and moved round the table to kiss her mother's cheek.

But Esther leaned away. 'Dun't you "mam" me, me girl, coming in here all brazen and bold as ya like. You're no daughter of mine. Thought I made that clear last time you come.'

Kate gasped. She had known her mother was furious but she hadn't realized just how deep her outrage was. Like Jonathan, Kate had believed that given time her mother would at least stand by her.

She made to move towards the door leading into the hall and to her grandfather's room.

'And dun't go whining to him. I've telled 'em both, I ain't having you back home. Ya've made ya bed, ya can lie on it!'

Kate swung round. 'Is that what you'd have wanted folks to say to your mother – if she'd lived?'

Esther's mouth pursed and she rolled the pastry viciously until it was too thin and tore. She gave a click of exasperation and bundled it up into a ball again to begin rolling it out once more. 'So I was right. That's where he took you that last time, did he? Meant you knowing all about my shame. As if that excuses you.'

More gently now, Kate said, shaking her head in disbelief, 'I'd have thought you'd be more understanding, that's all.'

'Understanding? Expect me to understand when me mother died and left me to the mercy of me Aunt Hannah all me young life till I was old enough to get out and come here? Aye, an' me troubles didn't end there, did they? I got mesen a whole lot more with Matthew Hilton and Beth – and Danny.'

'Your mother couldn't help dying, Mam,' Kate said

quietly. 'She'd have loved you and looked after you if she'd lived.'

'Aye, well, mebbe so . . .' for a moment there was a fleeting uncertainty about Esther, as if she would dearly like to believe what Kate was saying, and yet the resentment surrounding the circumstances of her own birth was too deep-rooted to forgive the years of hardship it had caused.

'And *him*,' she flung out her hand towards the direction of Will Benson's room, 'even he didn't acknowledge me as his daughter till after his wife 'ad died.'

'Well, he couldn't really, could he? But he's always cared about you, always been on your side. He explained more about – well, how things happened here. It made me see things . . .'

'I dun't need no one to mek excuses for me. I dun't need no one on my side, 'cept p'raps yar dad . . .' She paused and then added pointedly, 'Yar *step*dad.'

Kate came back and stood on the opposite side of the table, leaning across it. 'Mam, why are you still so bitter?'

'I wasn't – at least, I thought I wasn't. But you – this—' She jabbed a floury finger towards Kate's stomach. 'It's brought it all back. Everything I've tried to live down, everything I've tried to do to make sure you never made the same mistake. All for nothing! It's in the blood. It must be.' She nodded her head towards Lilian. ''Spect she'll do the same, an' all.'

Lilian's head snapped up, goaded at last. 'Oh no, I won't, Mam. I've got more sense than that. Besides, I'm staying on at school, going to better myself and get an education. Go to university, if I can. I'm not going to wreck my life . . .' She stopped short of actually voicing the words, but they hung in the air between them, ' . . . like Kate!'

'There you are, see?' Esther said triumphantly. 'At least

one of me daughters 'as got a bit of sense, a bit of my ambition.'

Kate looked at Lilian; at the short-cropped mousy hair, the owlish spectacles she wore, the smug expression on her plain face. Rather than feeling resentful towards her younger sister, Kate pitied her. She could visualize Lilian, with that attitude, being lonely all her life.

Kate sighed and turned away. There was no point in continuing to argue. She walked out of the house and stood in the yard. She pulled her coat closely around her and her collar up against the blustery wind which swept in from the sea, even today when it was supposed to be summer. She looked around, but could not see her stepfather. She pushed her hands deep into her pockets and felt the whelk shell. Since the night Danny had gone missing, she had carried it everywhere with her.

She sighed again. She'd better get it over; she would go and see Beth – and Rosie.

'Why, lovey, how grand it is to see you.'

The greeting was the same as ever from Danny's mother. Rosie hugged her warmly and smiled brightly, though the worry never quite left her eyes. Kate was saddened to see that Rosie was no longer the bouncy chatterbox; Danny's disappearance had caused that.

They can't know about me, Kate thought, as she allowed herself to be ushered into the kitchen and pressed into the chair near the range. Kate looked around. 'Where's – the baby?'

'Robbie's asleep in the back garden,' Rosie said. 'Me Uncle Georgie brought one of those big baby cars home. He's buried in it, poor little mite.' She held back the curtain at the kitchen window and Kate looked out to see a black perambulator in the middle of the strip of grass outside the window. It was so deep that only the covers were visible. From here she could see no sign of the baby in its depths.

'He'll wake up soon. Always hungry, he is. I'll fetch him in then for you to see him. He's growing so fast, ain't he, Nan? We call her Nan now. She loves being a grandma, don't you?'

Beth smiled gently, her brown eyes soft with love for her grandson. Then, in her quiet, concerned way, she asked Kate, 'How've you been then, lovey?'

Kate glanced from one to the other of them. Did they know? They were looking at her, but their expressions gave nothing away.

'Er – well . . .' She hesitated, twisting her hands together in her lap.

Beth touched her hand lightly. 'It's all right, Katie, we know about the bairn.'

The gentleness in her tone touched Kate more deeply than her own mother's wrath. Tears sprang into her eyes and there was such a lump in her throat that for a moment she couldn't speak.

She brushed the tears away from her eyes with the back of her hand, like a child. 'I'm sorry. It's just that – me mam's that mad . . .'

'Oh, we know all about yar mam being mad,' Beth said grimly. 'I've heard her.'

'She's told you?'

Beth shook her head. 'Oh, no. She's not speaking to me again now. I heard her through the wall when she comes to see Grannie Harris next door. Ranting and raving, she was, one day. I could hear ev'ry word.'

Kate sighed with resignation. 'I might have known you two wouldn't be speaking again by now! I really thought it might be different – I mean, after the bomb, and then how she came at once to Rosie when Robbie was born. Didn't need asking twice . . .'

Beth nodded. 'She's a strange woman, ya mother. She was kindness itself when Robert was killed, I can't deny that. But – well – we've had this all our lives. There's that much between us. We can't be friends – not ever – but, whenever there's trouble, we can't be enemies either.' She smiled a little self-consciously and added, 'I s'pose I'm as much to blame as she is. In the early years, it was me who was bitter towards her.' She shrugged, but the years could not be shrugged off so easily. 'Never mind about that now, lass. What about you?'

'I – I don't know. I'll have to leave the WAAFs soon, and me mam, it seems, doesn't want me to come home.'

The two women gasped, their eyes wide. 'Not want you to come home?' they chorused in surprise.

'Oh, she's going too far this time,' Beth muttered, at once like a mother hen with ruffled feathers. 'I'll go and tell her what I think . . .'

'No – no, don't,' Kate said swiftly. 'I've caused enough trouble. Besides,' she added, and although she spoke bravely, she couldn't keep the doubt from her tone, 'I'm hoping Dad will be able to bring her round in time.'

Her feathers smoothed a little, Beth said, 'Well, if anyone can make her see sense, it's Jonathan . . .'

From the garden came a wail and Rosie rushed out to bring in her son. 'Here you are.' She came back in and placed the baby in Kate's arms. 'Here's ya Auntie Kate to see you.' And Kate found herself looking down into the solemn brown gaze of Danny's son.

The baby gazed back at her and then a broad smile stretched across his chubby face and his fat little hands wavered towards her face.

'Oh, Rosie, he's lovely!' she exclaimed, and the little fellow's mother and grandmother stood watching, beaming proudly.

'I won't have her here and that's an end to it.'

'Very well,' Jonathan said, his mouth tight and a deep frown on his forehead. 'If that's your final word, Esther, so be it. But I think you're wrong – and I think you'll regret it.'

'Where would you've been if ya Aunt Hannah had said the same all them years back?' Will Benson raged. 'Answer me that!'

'A lot better off, probably,' Esther retorted, unrelenting.

'Don't talk daft, girl,' her father snapped back.

Despite the family quarrel Kate had caused, she almost laughed to hear her mother addressed as 'girl'. But then, she supposed, to a parent their child is always a child.

'Ya'd have been in the workhouse but for her,' Will went on.

'It weren't no better than the workhouse. I might have fared better there.'

'Oh, Esther, that's not fair . . .' Jonathan began.

'What do you know about it?' She rounded on him. 'You've always had a loving, close family. A mother, a father *and* a sister. You're spoilt with family! I was nothing but a skivvy to the lot of them and never allowed to forget the circumstances of my birth. Never! "Me sister's bastard!" – that's what me aunt used to call me.' She turned then on Kate. 'That's why I'm bitter. I'm bitter for what you're doing to an unborn mite with no choice in the matter. It's not the poor bairn I'm against, it's you for causing it. You should have known better.'

Jonathan was staring at Esther.

'And what's up with you?' She rounded on him.

'Nothing. Nothing at all. You've just given me what could be a very good idea,' he said thoughtfully.

'What?'

'Ah – now that, for the moment, is my secret.'

He got up from the kitchen table and went through into the living room. They heard him open his bureau in the corner of the room, heard the rustle of paper and the scrape of a chair, and then there was silence. Intrigued, Kate peeped through the doorway into the room.

His head bent, her stepfather was seated at the table, busily writing a letter.

Thirty-Nine

A week after her return to camp, during which she had expected that each day she might be summonsed to Ma'am's office to be confronted with the words, 'You're pregnant, Hilton, aren't you?', Kate received a letter from her stepfather, containing one from his sister Peggy, in Lincoln.

In his letter, Jonathan merely said, '*I think, my dear, that the enclosed letter will be the answer for you, at least for the time being . . .*'

Kate unfolded it and began to read.

'*My dear Jonathan, Of course Kate can come back to us. We should love to have her – it will be like old times – and she would be company for mother, who although still lively in her mind, is increasingly confined to the house and, indeed, to her sofa.*' Did Peggy really understand what she was offering, Kate wondered. Would Mrs Godfrey be so happy to have her if she knew she was going to be an unmarried mother? But as she read on it became clear that Peggy and her mother understood the situation exactly.

'*As you know, since Father died, Mother has slept downstairs in the living room, and so Kate, and her little one when it arrives, could have Mother's bedroom upstairs. I'm still in my own room anyway, so it won't be putting us about at all! And there's still the tiny bedroom Kate had before, when the little one gets older . . .*' Peggy, bless her, seemed to be offering Kate a long-term home, not just a temporary stop-gap. '*Besides,*' she went on, '*it will be lovely for Mother*

414

*to have more company in the day when I have to be at work
– she gets very lonely. Do give Kate our best love and tell
her to come and see us as soon as she can and we can talk
everything over . . .'*

The words blurred now for tears were coursing down her
cheeks. How kind they were, even making it sound as if she,
Kate, would be doing them a favour.

Mavis came thundering down the hut. 'Kate – what's up?
Is it bad news . . .?' The wooden slats creaked as she dropped
her weight on to the bed at the side of Kate.

Kate shook her head. 'No – no,' she sobbed. 'Just the
opposite.'

Then she told Mavis what had happened when she had
gone home and then about the letter she had just received.

'Well, that's all right, then,' Mavis said in her matter-of-
fact manner. 'I thought there was something wrong – all
that blubbering.'

Kate smiled and wiped away her tears. Dear friend though
Mavis was, she could not be expected to understand the
relief that Jonathan's letter had brought to her. Her mother's
initial reaction had been expected, but Kate had not believed
that Esther Godfrey would turn her face away from her own
daughter quite so heartlessly and so completely. Kate had
suddenly felt very alone; the only people who were on her
side were powerless to help her – her grandad, old and
increasingly infirm and dependent upon Esther, Beth Eland
and Rosie and even, she had thought, her stepfather. But
Jonathan Godfrey was nothing if not resourceful, and for
once he had acted without reference to Esther.

Whether her mother approved or disapproved, she had
no way of knowing for neither Jonathan nor Peggy mentioned Esther in their letters.

Two days later, Kate was able to hitch a lift into Lincoln
and go to see Peggy and Mrs Godfrey.

'It really is so kind of you,' she began hesitantly, after the first flurries of welcome were over and she had been seated near the fire opposite Mrs Godfrey, a cup of tea balanced on her lap. 'Are you sure you really don't mind? I mean, the neighbours . . .'

Mrs Godfrey laughed. 'There's a lot worse goes on down this street behind the lace curtains than you bringing a baby into the world, my dear. But if it troubles you, you can always wear a wedding ring and call yourself Mrs Hilton. There's lots of women on their own now with this war on, and no one bothers to ask questions any more. But we're not worried one way or the other, are we, Peggy love?'

Peggy was standing beside Kate, looking down at her thoughtfully. 'No, Mother, we're not,' she said absently.

Suddenly she sat down beside Kate and looked her full in the face. 'Kate, you're obviously still troubled as to what we think of you and how it will reflect upon us, aren't you?'

Kate glanced down at the liquid in her cup. 'Well, yes, you see, me mam . . .'

'We know about your mother – Jonathan told us just enough to enable us to put two and two together . . .'

' . . . And make five,' put in Mrs Godfrey.

Kate smiled wanly. 'She – she was so upset. It's always been so important to her, you see. In her eyes, I've done just about the worst thing I could have done.'

For a moment there was silence in the room. Peggy was still watching Kate then she took a deep breath and seemed to come to a decision. Kate saw her glance at her mother and raise her eyebrows as if seeking approval for something she was about to do.

'It's up to you, love,' the older woman said quietly, obviously understanding her daughter's meaning.

Peggy turned back to Kate and smiled gently. 'You won't remember much about the last war, you'd only be little. I was a young girl of eighteen when I met Michael. He worked with Jonathan and they volunteered together. We – fell very much in love, and we knew that any day he might be sent to France. So, we were going to get married – with the blessing of both our parents, even though we'd only known each other three months. The date was set and everything arranged and then his unit was posted overseas at short notice and all leave cancelled. He begged and pleaded with the authorities to allow him just a few days to get back here so that we could get married by special licence before he went. But he couldn't get leave. He had to – to go without even seeing me again.' Peggy's hands were twisting in her lap now, but her voice remained strong and there was a tender smile on her lips as though her story brought back happy memories as well as the sad times. 'A few weeks after he'd gone, I – I found I was carrying his child.'

Kate gasped. 'Oh Peggy . . .'

'I got three letters from him before he was killed on the Somme and I never got the chance to tell him he was to be a father. Maybe it was for the best in a way, because I was dreadfully ill after we'd heard he'd been killed and I – I lost the baby.' There was a haunted look in her eyes now.

'Did – did me dad know?'

'Not at the time,' Mrs Godfrey put in. 'When Jonathan came home wounded, Peg was over the worst, except that she was thin and dreadfully unhappy. He was worried enough about her, as it was. But after the war, when he was home for good, well, we told him then.'

'So you see, Kate,' Peggy said softly, 'we do understand. I would have given anything – anything – if I could have kept that baby and brought it up – wedding ring or no wedding ring. I would have had something left of Michael.'

Kate eyes went to Mrs Godfrey. As if reading her unspoken question, the woman nodded. 'Yes, her father and

I stood by her,' she said softly. 'We'd have brought the little one up, if it had lived.'

The lump in Kate's throat was so large, she found it impossible to speak.

'So,' Peggy said gently, 'we feel – Mother and me – that it's as if we've been given a second chance. Do you see?'

Kate nodded. 'Yes,' she whispered. 'And I'm so very grateful.'

Mrs Godfrey suddenly slapped her hand on to her lap, rattling the cup in the saucer.

'Careful, Mother, you'll spill that.' Peggy jumped up to rescue the wobbling cup.

'I've just had a wonderful idea.' Mrs Godfrey beamed at the other two. 'When you leave the WAAFs, Kate, why don't you start dressmaking again?'

'Oh, but I couldn't expect you to look after the baby all day while I go out to work . . .'

'I don't mean that. I mean here, in the front room, just like I used to do. There's folks crying out for it now, wanting their old clothes made over because of the rationing. They still knock on my door even now, at my age, asking if I "couldn't just sew this seam up, Mrs Godfrey . . ." You know they do, Peg.'

'Well, it's whether Kate wants to . . .'

As Peggy turned back to look at her, Kate knew the answer was plainly written in her shining eyes and her wide smile. 'Want to! Oh, I'd love it. It was the sight of your room when I visited from school that made me take up sewing and dressmaking in the first place.'

'Was it really?' Mrs Godfrey laughed aloud. 'Well, who would have thought it, all my clutter inspiring you like that!'

Peggy was smiling too. 'Well, that's settled then.'

Indeed, everything seemed to be settled very satisfactorily, Kate thought as she waited for the transport back to camp.

For the first time in months, she dared to feel a tinge of hope. Suddenly, she felt a flutter beneath her ribs and, smiling, she put her hand over the place. Her child had moved for the first time.

She would see Ma'am first thing in the morning, she decided.

'Well, you're not the first and I don't expect you'll be the last!' Ma'am was tight-lipped and disapproving, but had become resigned to the fact that in her position in charge of a clutch of women, this kind of interview was bound to happen. 'But I must say, I am surprised at you, Hilton. You had a wonderful job as personal driver to the CO, one which you've kept despite a change at the top.' The shrewd eyes were regarding her keenly.

Kate made no comment but kept rigidly to attention, her gaze unflinchingly on the top button on Ma'am's jacket.

The officer sighed. 'Very well, dismissed.'

Outside, the air cooling her hot cheeks, Kate let out a sigh. Now the only thing she had to face was the gossip spreading round the camp . . .

'Think you can run the gauntlet of the pub tonight, Kate?' Mavis asked cheerily. 'Me and Isobel have actually got a night off together. Thought we'd take you out for a farewell drink . . .' She grinned. 'Well, in your case, orange juice.'

Kate threw her shoe at Mavis, who ducked smartly. The shoe sailed across two beds, landed on the floor and skidded under the third. Kate padded across the floor after it and, panting against her tight waistband, bent to retrieve the shoe. 'Yes, I suppose so. Does everyone know now?'

Mavis shrugged. 'Shouldn't let it worry you – 'sides, me and Isobel will be there.'

'Oh well, then. I'll have no trouble,' Kate laughed.

She needn't have worried; everyone was far more wrapped up in their own worries or bent on having a good time before tomorrow's op than worrying if a silly little WAAF was pregnant.

Kate was sorry to say goodbye to Mavis and Isobel, but apart from that, leaving was easy. There had been no word from Philip; in one way she was disappointed and hurt, yet in another, it was a relief. Since making her decision not to tell him about the child, she had been worried what she would do if he wrote to her. But with every day that passed without a letter, her decision not only seemed right, but also easier to carry through. And with Philip gone, she really had no reason to regret leaving the WAAFs.

'You won't get rid of us as easy as this though, will she, Iso? We'll come and visit you.'

'Even if it's only to bring those ghastly bootees you're trying to knit, Mave,' Isobel drawled. 'Poor child!' she added, but now there was no malicious bite to Isobel's teasing.

Mavis laughed good-humouredly. 'You're right there, Iso. I'll never win prizes for knitting and that's a fact!'

They walked with her to the gate and helped her into the back of the lorry which was taking her into Lincoln. Kate waved as the lorry drew away, but then her glance went beyond them, taking a last look at the station that had been her home for over eighteen months. So much had happened here and she had made so many friends, she mused, as she watched the two waving figures grow smaller and smaller. She had fallen in love with Philip and known a very different kind of love that had obliterated the unhappy childhood romance, so cruelly shattered.

Danny . . . Her mind shied away from thinking about him. But she couldn't – not for ever. Where was he, her beloved brother? Was he alive? He must be. Surely she'd know – she would feel it – if he wasn't? What was it he had said all those years ago? 'What would I do if you were no longer in the same world as me?'

She thought of Rosie waiting in the tiny cottage at Flee-thaven Point with the son Danny had never seen.

Kate ran her hand over her stomach.

Oh Danny, her heart cried silently. I wish you were here for me to tell you about this.

How am I going to get through it without you?

Kate was surprised how quickly she settled in the terraced house with Mrs Godfrey and Peggy. For appearances she wore a ring on the third finger of her left hand and when giving her name she just said Kate Hilton and left it to others to add the 'Mrs' themselves.

Soon several ladies were coming to Mrs Godfrey's front parlour with their sewing or dressmaking demands. All were Mrs Godfrey's former clients and word soon spread that there was a very clever little dressmaker back in business at number eight. Kate enjoyed the work, even though as the months passed she found it increasingly difficult to bend over her bulge to operate the sewing machine.

'You've done Mother a power of good,' Peggy told her.

'Have I? How?' Kate asked, surprised.

'Now she can't get about, while I was at work she used to get so lonely before you came. Oh, she'd have a few visitors, but not like now when your clients pop through for a bit of a chat about the old days. She's loving every minute of it.'

Kate pulled a face. 'She might not when there's a squalling infant keeping her awake half the night.'

Peggy's expression softened. 'You'll see – she'll make the world's best doting grandmother – oh no, wait a bit, *great*-grandmother.'

How kind they were to her, Kate thought, she was very lucky, but she was saddened by the thought that the coming child's true grandmother wanted nothing to do with it.

'Peggy! Peggy!'

Kate knocked on the bedroom door. From inside she heard the squeak of bedsprings and the door opened.

'What is it?'

'Pains. I've got pains, Peg. Here . . .' Kate clutched her groin and gasped, doubling over as another spasm gripped her.

'How often are they coming?'

'I – don't know.'

'Right – back to bed and I'll . . .'

At that moment the siren began to wail.

Forty

'I'll phone for the midwife from next door. Joe's an ARP Warden so they've got a telephone.' As she spoke, Peggy was already stripping off her nightdress and struggling back into her clothes.

'What about getting your mother into the shelter?' Kate shouted above the noise.

Peggy laughed. 'If I were to get her in, Kate, it would be the first time. She never goes.'

'Oooh—' Kate let out a yowl and thought, now I know why Rosie was squealing so much.

'Is it bad? They're coming a bit close together for my liking.'

'No – no – not that bad,' Kate lied bravely. 'I just squeaked because they take you by surprise a bit.'

Peggy ran lightly downstairs while Kate staggered back to the big bedroom and heaved herself back on to the bed. She lay there propped up against the pillows, her knees drawn up, her legs apart, trying to remember all the things her mother had instructed Rosie to do.

And all the while the siren wailed.

By the time Peggy's footsteps came pounding back up the stairs, Kate's pains had increased in intensity and frequency.

'About every three and a half minutes,' Kate told her calmly.

'Oh dear.' Peggy ran her hand distractedly through her hair. 'Kate – I can't get through. The lines must be down and Joe's out because of the raid . . . '

'Don't worry,' Kate said. Despite the pain, a strange calm seemed to spread through her. 'It can't be very different to calves and piglets being born and I've seen enough of those.'

'But I haven't,' Peggy wailed. 'I don't know what to do . . . '

'I was there when Rosie had . . . ' Kate gasped as another pain clenched her abdomen, 'her – her son. I think I can remember what me mam did.' For a moment a feeling of intense longing swept over her; oh, how she would love it to be Esther standing beside the bed at this very moment! Dearly as she loved Peggy, she was not at this moment inspiring Kate with confidence and composure. Indeed, it was the patient who was having to calm the nurse.

As the wave of pain subsided, trying to lighten the situation, Kate smiled and said, 'Shouldn't you be boiling water or something, Peg?'

Peggy stood at the end of her bed, her eyes wild, wringing her hands. 'Oh Kate . . .'

'Peg – Peg! What's happening?' Mrs Godfrey's anxious voice drifted up from the room below.

Peggy hurried to the door and shouted down the stairs. 'It's coming – and I don't know what to do, Mother . . . '

Kate heard the older woman's voice. 'Just calm down, Peg. Rita's here, she's coming up . . . '

Footsteps sounded on the stairs and as Rita, their next-door neighbour, came into the bedroom, Kate panted hard as a spasm of pain began and swelled, until she was gripping the mattress beneath her.

'Well, you're well on, by the look of you,' Rita smiled down at Kate. 'I'm just off on me bike to find our Joe. He'll get the midwife for you.' She turned to Peggy. 'Don't worry,

424

Peg, just keep mopping her brow and try to get her to relax when the pains come. And pant hard, Kate, don't push yet, else you might tear yourself.'

'Oh, Rita,' Peg began again. 'Can't you stay? I'll go and find Joe.'

'No, Peg. I know all the places he might be better'n you.'

'Do be quick, won't you?'

Rita laughed as she left the room and ran lightly down the stairs. 'I'll do me best, if Hitler'll let me . . .'

'I wish I could get you to the Maternity Home, but I don't know anyone with any petrol.'

'It's not fair to – to ask anyone – in an air raid, Peg.' Kate panted.

'Oh, they wouldn't mind that . . .'

As if to refute Peggy's statement about the generosity of their neighbours and their brave disregard for safety if called upon, they heard the whine of a bomb and then there was a terrific blast. The house shuddered and the windows rattled.

'I think,' Kate said with wry humour, 'I'd rather stay here, if you don't mind, Peg.'

'What's happening?' came Mrs Godfrey's voice from below. 'Is she all right?'

'Tell her I'm fine. I think the pains are not as bad at the moment.'

Peggy relayed the message and then came back to stand nervously at the side of the bed. 'I am sorry I'm not being much use, Kate,' she said. Kate reached out and clasped Peggy's hand. 'Of course you are, Peg . . . We – we'll do it together. We'll manage – bombs or no bombs.'

For a while Kate's labour eased. 'I think it's taking a rest before the final push,' she joked, and Peggy smiled thinly.

When the pains began again, strongly and more frequently, Peggy seemed calmer, although she kept casting anxious glances towards the open bedroom door and straining to hear the sound of footsteps above the noise of the raid going on all over the city.

'They're here,' came Mrs Godfrey's voice at last. 'Rita's found the midwife.'

Tears of relief streamed down Peggy's face. 'Oh, thank goodness – we'll be all right now, Kate.'

Kate did not reply. For the moment, her eyes screwed up with effort and her face growing redder by the second, she was too busy . . .

Peggy, happy now under the midwife's guidance, bustled up and downstairs, fetching and carrying whatever was needed. Rita was dispatched to the kitchen to make a cup of tea and Mrs Godfrey sat on her sofa downstairs, her hands folded placidly in her lap, waiting to hear the first cry of the newborn baby from the bedroom above her.

Outside the bombs continued to whistle down. They heard another one quite close and as it landed the ground shook and the glass in the bedroom window cracked. But the midwife just stood at the side of the bed, her hand resting lightly on Kate's stomach. She didn't even flinch.

Fancy bringing a child into a world like this, Kate thought. I should have been more careful, I should have . . . 'Aaah . . .'

'You're doing fine. Not much longer now,' came the soothing voice.

Kate's daughter was born just as the all-clear sounded. It seemed like a good omen.

'Oh, she's lovely, Mrs Hilton – just perfect,' said the midwife as she laid the child in Kate's arms.

Kate's eyes roamed over the tiny form, counting fingers and toes and drinking in the look of her child.

'What's that mark on her left cheek?'

'Oh, just a little birth-pressure mark – it will soon fade,' the nurse said casually, used to reassuring worried mothers.

Kate wasn't so sure.

On the left side of the baby's face, just on the line of the jaw, were marks in the shape of two tiny fingers.

Remembering, Kate could almost feel again the stinging slap Esther had dealt her on the side of her face in exactly the same place as the marks on her baby's.

'Oh, she's beautiful,' Peggy cooed as she bent over the cradle the following day. 'Isn't she good? I quite expected her to be bawling loudly.'

Kate lay back against the pillows. The first euphoria of the birth had deserted her and now she felt rather tired and strangely lonely, even though Peggy and Mrs Godfrey were ecstatic in their delight in the newest member of their household.

'What are you going to call her?'

Kate hesitated and then she began to laugh, a little hysterically, so that Peggy patted her hand in alarm. 'Don't, Kate, don't,' she beseeched.

Tears poured down Kate's face. 'I'm sorry, I'm not usually so emotional. I don't know what's the matter with me.'

'It's just all the excitement,' Peggy soothed.

Calmer now, Kate watched the baby sleeping placidly in the cradle. If only Peggy knew how she had agonized over the naming of her baby.

Peggy, misreading Kate's silence, said, 'Well, you'll have to think of one now. You have to register her soon, you know.'

'Yes,' Kate whispered, still staring at her daughter. She would love to call her daughter Philippa, but how could she? So far she had managed to keep the father's identity secret, although she felt that Isobel and Mavis had guessed the truth. But she knew her two loyal friends would keep silent, and that was the way she wanted it. She loved Philip enough to want to protect him and spare him any further distress.

And if she could not call her daughter after him, then there was really only one other name she would consider.

The interview with the Registrar was a little embarrassing, as he went through the questions.

'... And what is the surname by which the child is to be known?' the man asked, writing with meticulous care as Kate answered each question.

'Hilton.'

'Name and surname of mother?'

'Katharine Hilton.'

'No, Mrs Hilton, I need your maiden name.'

When she did not answer immediately, he looked up over his steel-rimmed spectacles.

She returned his gaze steadfastly and said quietly, 'Hilton is my only name. I'm not married, Mr Forbes.'

'Ah – I see,' he said evenly, giving no indication in his tone as to his feelings on such a matter. 'Then I presume we cannot fill in the father's name on the certificate. In these circumstances,' he went on to inform her, 'it is necessary for the father to be present at the time of registration to give his consent for his name to be on the certificate.'

Kate nodded. 'I understand,' she said huskily. Clearing her throat nervously, she said, more strongly, 'I'm afraid it's – not possible.'

He said no more but filled in the other details, and a few moments later, Kate left the room with her daughter's birth certificate in her hand.

Born on the sixteenth day of January, 1943
Danielle Hilton.

Forty-One

Kate could imagine the furore her choice of name would cause at Fleethaven Point. She didn't care. She wanted to call her baby after Danny and she would not apologize to anyone for having done so. How she wished with all her heart that Danny could see the little girl she had named after him. Mindful, however, of the feelings of others, Kate decided that the little girl would be known as Ella.

At home in the little terraced house, Mrs Godfrey fussed over the infant. 'Leave her with me, Kate. She'll be right as ninepence here in her crib. Go and have a lie down, dear. You look exhausted. You really didn't ought to be sewing again yet.'

'Oh, I'm fine really. I didn't sleep too well last night.'

'Really? I didn't hear her crying.'

'Oh no, she only woke the once to be fed. She's a good little thing. No – it was just that – well, after I fed her I couldn't get off again.'

Mrs Godfrey eyed her sympathetically. Kate knew the older woman understood some of the thoughts going through Kate's mind. 'Peg's written last weekend to tell Jonathan, so – your mother will know.'

Kate nodded, biting her lip. She forced a smile. 'I didn't expect to hear anything.'

She bent over the baby, asleep in the cradle. The child was a sweet little thing, with tiny features and downy fair hair. The birthmark along her jawline was fading a little and

429

only deepened in colour when the child screwed up her face and cried. It seemed a cruel twist of fate, Kate thought, that the innocent child should bear the mark of Esther's wrath.

Mrs Godfrey sniffed disapprovingly and rocked the cradle with her hand as it stood at the side of her sofa. 'Well, I'd have expected better from our Jonathan.'

Mavis and Isobel arrived on the doorstep bearing gifts for the baby.

'Sorry we haven't been before,' they explained. 'We wanted to come together and couldn't seem to organize leave at the same time.'

'They can't manange without us, you know,' Mavis joked.

While Isobel sat and chatted to Mrs Godfrey and nursed Ella, Mavis drew Kate into the front room. She fished a letter out of her bag.

'This arrived for you at camp last week. I – didn't want to post it on to you. I wanted to make sure you got it.'

Kate took the letter as Mavis said, 'It arrived in the mail from a station up north – in Yorkshire.' When Kate did not answer, Mavis persisted, 'The CO went up to Yorkshire, didn't he?'

'So he did, Mave,' Kate murmured, and composing her face, she looked up again and smiled. 'I expect it's just a friendly letter.'

'Oh, most probably,' Mavis said, with more than a hint of sarcasm. Kate felt her friend's shrewd gaze upon her face. ''Spect he doesn't know you've left, does he?' she remarked pointedly.

Slipping the letter into the pocket of her wrap-around apron, Kate said firmly, 'No, and I don't want him to know either.' She saw Mavis open her mouth to say something more, but before she could do so, Kate linked her arm through hers and pulled her back into the living room. 'Come on, Auntie Mavis, it's time you nursed your god-daughter.'

Mavis's eyes widened. 'God-daughter? You mean – you mean you want *me* to be her godmother?' Her face was growing pink with pleasure.

Kate smiled at her. 'Yes, you and Iso, if you will. And Peggy too.'

'Oh, I'd love it. I've never been a godmother.' She paused, then asked, 'Er, aren't you supposed to have two godmothers and one god*father* for a girl?'

The smile faded from Kate's face. 'Yes,' she nodded, 'but there's only one person I would want as her godfather – and – and he's not here just now.'

'You – you mean – Danny?'

Kate's voice was a whisper, 'Yes.'

'Oh. Oh, I see,' Mavis murmured. It was obvious that her friend did not see at all. In fact she was more perplexed than ever. Kate watched Mavis looking down at the child in Isobel's arms, her forehead creased and chewing the side of her thumb. Kate could almost read the thoughts running through Mavis's mind. Kate had been in love with Danny Eland, but he had married someone else. They believed Kate and Philip Trent had been lovers, yet when her child was born, Kate had called her Danielle and now she was admitting that the only man she would want as a godfather was Danny Eland. It was all too much for Mavis to take in.

It was exactly what Kate wanted, although she felt a little guilty at deliberately trying to turn away suspicion from Philip and back on to Danny.

Later, in the privacy of her bedroom, Kate read Philip's letter. It was carefully worded so that to the uninformed eye, it would be a friendly letter from a superior officer to his one-time driver for whom he had an affectionate regard. But

431

to Kate there were hidden references that told her his feelings had not changed.

'... I expect Lincolnshire is looking a little wintry at the moment – no fields of rippling ripe corn ... My current driver is not nearly so efficient at changing a wheel in the dark ...'

He remembered everything that had happened and between the lines, Kate could detect his longing for her. There was a paragraph in which there was more than a hint of anxiety. 'I have written twice before, but have not had a reply from you. Perhaps you did not get the letters?' No, she had not received his letters and had begun to think his silence meant the end of their affair. And then came his final words.

'... Kate, we must meet. I shall be attending a big meeting in Grantham the week after next. If you're still the new CO's driver, you should be bringing him ...'

Kate closed her eyes and groaned. She had dreaded something like this happening. Now he was going to find out she had left the WAAFs and, most probably, why! But if he had to know, then he should hear it from her, and not from any other garbled source.

'... We could meet on the Wednesday about four, at the station, if you could manage it,' Philip suggested.

'Heavens!' Kate murmured, as she turned over his letter and re-read the date. 'That's only the day after tomorrow.'

Her mind worked feverishly. She'd have to find a way to go and meet him. Now she knew he wanted to see her again, she would have to tell him about his baby daughter. 'Oh dear,' she agonized. 'I hope I'm doing the right thing.'

Luckily for Kate, Wednesday was the day when Peggy, on her half-day off from work, took complete charge of Ella. 'Much as you love her,' Peggy had told Kate from the very first week, 'you need a break. Besides,' she had smiled down tenderly at the infant, 'I want her to myself for just a few hours . . .'

So on Wednesdays, Kate was free to wander into town, to shop, to go to the cinema, or even to go home to Flee-thaven Point if she had wanted. Thank goodness Philip had suggested a Wednesday, she thought; she didn't even need to tell Mrs Godfrey or Peggy where she was going . . .

The biting February wind whipped along the platform as she waited for him, pulling her coat around her. Then suddenly there he was, striding towards her, and she felt tears prickle her eyes at the sight of his tall, lean figure. He grasped her hands in his, enveloping her cold hands in his huge warm grasp. 'Kate . . .' he whispered. 'Oh my dear, don't cry.'

She tried to laugh through the tears she could no longer hide. How could she explain, so quickly, that she was still a little emotional after the birth of her daughter? *Their* daughter.

Philip tucked her hand through his arm. 'Come on – let's see if we can find the famous British Restaurant,' he said, trying to make her laugh. 'How have you been? How are things at the station? I want to hear everything that's been going on since I left.'

Kate swallowed nervously, realizing what a shock for him her news was going to be. As they walked, she glanced up at him. His face seemed thinner and there were dark shadows beneath his eyes. He looks desperately tired, she thought. Even his voice sounded weary as if he were having to force himself to speak cheerfully. 'I've only just realized what's different about you,' he said as he sat down opposite her in a secluded corner of the restaurant. 'You're not in uniform.'

Kate drew in a deep breath. 'Oh – er – no. I'll explain –

433

in a minute . . .' She bit her lip. Before she told him anything, there was something she must know first. Leaning forward across the table, she said softly, 'Philip, how are things with you? I mean – with Lizzie?'

The look of pain that was suddenly in his eyes shocked her in its intensity. 'Oh, Kate. That's partly why I asked you to meet me. I wanted to see you, of course. You'll never know how desperately I've missed you all these weeks and months . . .'

And I you, she thought, but for the moment she remained silent.

'But . . .' He was strangely, unnervingly hesitant now, and Kate found she was holding her breath. Intuitively, she knew suddenly that she did not really want to hear what Philip was about to say.

He reached across the table and took her hands in his. 'My daughter died three weeks ago. She suffered greatly during the final weeks and it has been a dreadful time for the whole family. Grace is distraught and needs me to be with her . . .'

How cruel it was, Kate thought, that Philip believed he had lost his only child, when in truth, he now had another. But she could not tell him now. Enough time when he had grieved for Lizzie and his wife was strong again. Oh yes, Kate promised him silently. One day you'll know you have an adorable, perfect daughter. One day, when the time is right and you can rejoice whole-heartedly, I will tell you.

'Poor Grace,' she heard him saying, dragging her wandering thoughts back to the present, 'after being so strong all these years while caring for Lizzie, she's gone to pieces now.'

Now Kate knew what it felt like to be a mother, she

spared a compassionate thought for the unknown woman who was Philip's wife.

She squeezed his hands and whispered, 'Philip – I'm so sorry.'

'You do understand.' His blue eyes, clouded with misery, searched her face. 'I can't bear the thought that I might lose you, but I must stay with Grace for a while.'

'Of course I understand. I told you when you left, I would be waiting. It's just going to be a little longer, that's all.' Her words were brave, but inside her something died. Would he ever come back to her?

As if reading her thoughts, he said urgently, 'One day, we'll be together. I promise you, Kate.'

He was a man of honour who was compelled, at this moment, to put duty before his own happiness; yet she knew he would not make such a promise lightly. She knew he truly believed he would be able to keep his pledge.

As they walked back towards the station, he said again, 'You never did say why you're not in uniform.'

Kate's heart hammered. 'Oh, I – er – thought it might be less conspicuous for you. Me being', her voice broke a little, 'a lowly corporal meeting a Group Captain.' And when he said, 'That was thoughtful of you, darling,' she hated her lie all the more.

'I'll write to you,' he said suddenly.

'Oh er, yes, c-could you send the letters to my relatives in Lincoln? I'll give you their address.' She felt her cheeks grow hot as he glanced down at her.

'Of course, if you'd rather.'

'Only your letter took several days to reach me and – and I never did get the other two you mentioned. Besides . . .' I might as well make it convincing now I've started, she told herself. 'There are too many prying eyes at the camp . . .'

'That's true. You can write to me, though, at my new station. There's no problem my end.'

When they parted two hours later on the platform, he said, 'We'll try to meet again . . .'

For a moment she clung to him and then, tears blinding her, she turned away and stumbled on to the train. As it pulled away, Kate sat huddled in the corner of the carriage, unable to bring herself to wave goodbye to him.

Forty-Two

Every day, Kate watched for the postman until even Mrs Godfrey remarked upon it. 'Are you expecting a letter, dear?'

'No . . . yes . . .' Kate sighed. 'Not really.'

'Still hoping to hear from your mam?' Mrs Godfrey asked gently.

Kate sighed heavily and forced a wry smile.

Mrs Godfrey shook her head. 'I really don't know what the woman can be thinking of. I'm sorry, Kate. I know she's your mother, but honestly . . .'

Kate shrugged her shoulders in sad agreement. She could not tell even the kindly Mrs Godfrey everything that was locked away in her heart. She seemed to have lost everyone; Danny, Philip, and even her family at Fleethaven Point. If asked, she would have been hard-pressed to say which loss hurt the most.

The following day, they heard footsteps coming down the passage at the side of the house to the back door.

'Now, who can that be, just as we're sitting down to dinner?' Mrs Godfrey grumbled, but without real rancour as she, more than anyone else in the house, loved visitors to call and relieve the monotony of her day.

The latch on the back gate clicked and through the living-room window which looked out over the back yard, they saw Jonathan and Rosie appear.

Kate gave a squeal of delight and rushed to open the door. 'Dad – and Rosie!'

There was much hugging and kissing and cooing over the baby before Kate could bring herself to ask the two questions uppermost in her mind. 'How's me mam?' and 'Is there any news of Danny?'

In answer to the first question, Jonathan pursed his mouth and shook his head, apology in his eyes. 'Kate dear, I've tried everything I can think of, but she won't budge. I begged her to come today but she refused. Your grandfather would have come, but he's chesty this winter and travelling is so uncertain just now.'

Kate nodded. 'I understand. I've taken some photographs of Ella with the camera he gave me. I'll sort out one or two for you to take back.'

'He'd like that, and maybe if your mother sees a picture of her grand-daughter . . .'

Kate forced a smile. 'Maybe, Dad, maybe,' but her tone did not hold much hope.

It was then she asked, 'And Danny? Have you heard anything?'

Rosie's mouth quivered and her eyes filled with easy tears. 'Not a word, Kate. He must – be . . .'

'No!' The rebuttal came out sharper than she intended. 'No, Rosie, don't say that. Don't even think it!'

Kate picked up the baby. 'Come upstairs with us, Rosie, while I change her.'

Leaving Jonathan chatting to his mother, Kate and Rosie went upstairs to the large bedroom which Kate shared with her child.

'Are you really happy here, Kate?'

'As happy as I can be, Rosie,' Kate said honestly, 'in the

438

circumstances. The Godfreys have been wonderful. I don't know what I'd have done without them.'

Rosie bit her lip. 'We all feel bad about ya mam's attitude.' She giggled. 'Did ya know Danny's mam went and had a big row with her? You should have seen 'em, standing toe to toe in the yard of Brumbys' Farm going at each other hammer and tongs. Just words, like, I don't mean it got to fisticuffs.'

'Thank goodness for that,' Kate said, feeling once more the stinging slap on her cheek. 'Even so, I'm sorry they had a quarrel over me. I didn't want to be the cause of more resentment between them. There's enough already!'

Rosie shrugged. 'I reckon they both enjoyed it really. Danny's mam came back her eyes sparkling and her cheeks red. I think they both got a lot of things off their chests they've been harbouring for years. Mebbe they'll start speaking to each other now.'

Kate laughed and said wryly, 'I shouldn't hold your breath waiting for that to happen, Rosie!'

Rosie smiled. 'No, mebbe you're right.' Then her smile faded. 'I seem to spend me life waiting.'

'I know, love, I know.'

Rosie sat down on Kate's bed watching the baby kicking in her high-sided cot. 'Poor Danny. He's got a son he's never seen and now a niece he doesn't even know about.'

Kate sat beside her, putting her arm around the girl. Rosie leaned her head against Kate's shoulder, drawing strength. Her action reminded Kate sharply of their childhood.

'You must believe he's still alive, Rosie. I do,' she said firmly.

'I'll try, Kate. But if he isn't – I really don't know how I'm going to live out the rest of my life without him.'

Silently, Kate thought, 'I know just how you feel, Rosie.'

*

The weeks of winter turned into spring. Despite the deprivations of war, Ella thrived and the little terraced house was a haven for Kate. She received letters frequently from her stepfather with loving messages from her grandfather. But no word came from her mother or from her sister, Lilian.

There was still no news of Danny, and no more letters from Philip either.

Then suddenly, one morning while she was busy sewing, she heard Mrs Godfrey's voice raised in alarm. 'Kate, Kate, come quick . . .'

Fearful that something was wrong with either the old lady or Ella, Kate hurried through to the back room to find Mrs Godfrey waving a yellow envelope at her. 'It's one of those dreadful telegrams. It's addressed to you and the lad's waiting for a reply.'

With trembling fingers, Kate tore open the thin envelope and unfolded the single sheet of paper. There was no name or address of the sender and the message just said, '*Meet me Grantham station. Thursday the twenty-fifth.*'

Kate gasped. Philip. It must be from Philip. He wanted to see her again. He was trying to keep the promise he had made to her.

'Well, what is it?' Mrs Godfrey asked.

'It's nothing – I mean, it's not bad news . . .' She went to the back door to tell the boy that there was no reply. Closing the back door, her eyes still on the piece of paper in her hand she walked back into the room to stand uncertainly beside Mrs Godfrey's sofa.

'Who's it from, then?'

'I – it doesn't say . . .' Kate hesitated. This time she had no choice but to take Mrs Godfrey partially into her confidence. 'I – I think it's from Ella's father.'

'Oh!'

'He – wants me to meet him – in Grantham, the day after tomorrow.'

'Do you want to go?'

Kate met the older woman's gaze and nodded, knowing her eyes were shining her answer.

'Then go, my dear. I can mind Ella until Peg gets home from work. She can put her to bed.'

'Are you sure?' Kate asked diffidently.

'Of course I am. The little one's taken well to the bottle and it's time you had a day out and I'm sure . . .' the older woman wriggled her shoulders as if she too shared Kate's excitement, ' . . . you'd like to see your young man again.'

Deeply moved by the woman's understanding, Kate bent and kissed the wrinkled cheek. 'Oh, you're so good to me!'

The old lady flapped her hand and shooed Kate back to her sewing, but the pink tinge on her face told Kate she was touched by the younger woman's display of affection.

She was standing, huddled into her thick coat, on the draughty station at Grantham staring up the track – just waiting.

'Wouldn't you be better in the waiting room, Miss?' a porter – only a young boy – asked.

'What? Oh, no – no thanks. His . . . The train should be here in a minute. I don't want to miss it.'

The young boy nodded knowingly. 'Your feller coming home on leave, is he, Miss?'

She nodded. She didn't want to go into explanations.

'We get a lot of reunions and partin's on this station. Breaks ya heart sometimes, miss. Specially when they're leavin'. Might never come back again, see.'

Kate swallowed the lump in her throat as she remembered the last time she had seen Danny; she had not thought then that it might be the last time she would see him. Yet when she had left Philip on this very platform only a few weeks ago, she had been only too aware that they could be parting for ever. She should have trusted him, she castigated herself, she should have had more faith in his love for her.

'When's the next train due in from the north?' she asked.

The boy shrugged his shoulders. 'Difficult to say. There should be one in about an hour. Why don't you wait in the waiting room, Miss. It'd be warmer in there.'

'I'm fine – really. To tell you the truth, I can't settle to sit down.'

A train came drew in from the south and passengers spilled on to the opposite platform. Kate hardly glanced across the tracks, her gaze intent on the empty track curving northwards out of the station. Behind her there came the clatter of footsteps as passengers from the train made their way over the tracks and on to the platform where she was waiting and towards the main exit. There was laughter and chatter as people greeted each other. Then, with a great deal of hissing and puthering smoke, the train pulled out of the station again to continue its journey. The noises faded and there was silence once more.

She heard her name spoken softly. 'Kate?' and again, 'Katie.'

For a fleeting moment, she felt devastated; that was not Philip's voice. He had not come.

But in the next instant her heart soared. She knew that voice – oh, how well she knew that voice! Hardly daring to believe it, she turned around slowly to stare at the man limping towards her, muffled in an RAF greatcoat; a short, stocky man, his black hair ruffled by the breeze . . .

As tears filled her eyes, his image blurred and wavered like a mirage so that for a moment she didn't know if what she was seeing was real. She reached out and felt him grasp her hands in his and then – she knew he was real.

'Danny!' she gasped, and the tears spilled down her cheeks. 'Oh, thank God you're safe!'

Their questions were tumbling over each other until he said, 'Come on, let's find somewhere warm and a cup o' tea.'

Once in the tea-room, sitting opposite each other over the small table, cocooned from the other travellers in their own little space, they began to talk.

'Are you really all right? Why are you limping? What happened?' her questions came again.

Danny winked at her and grinned widely. 'I'm fine, honest. Oh, me leg's bad though, but that's all. That's why I've been repatriated.'

'Repatriated? Were – were you captured then?'

'We'd reached the target, dropped our bombs and were banking away when we were hit. The pilot nursed the kite for several miles but I think we all knew we couldn't make it back home. Anyway, he was doin' his best to get as near to the coast as he could when one of the engines caught fire. He kept flying to give us all time to bale out, but I couldn't get to me 'chute . . .'

Kate felt herself going hot at the thought; she well knew that the rear-gunner could not wear his parachute in the confines of his turret.

'Well, there I was swivelling the turret so I could get out and take me chances by jumping just before the 'plane crashed. And do you know what happened? The whole rear turret fell off! And guess what?'

Wordlessly, Kate shook her head.

'It landed in a tree! I smashed me leg up badly, and because I tried to evade capture for two days, I didn't get proper medical attention. It'll never be right again.'

'But you're alive,' Kate said.

Danny pulled a face. 'If that tree hadn't been there, I wouldn't be.'

'Then thank goodness it was.'

They sat in silence for a moment, then she asked, 'How come they've let you go?'

'The leg won't mend properly. They know I'll be no good for any more fighting so . . . here I am. Mind you, I made 'em think me leg was a lot worse than it is. Reckon I deserve a medal for me acting!'

'Oh Danny.' She laughed and then wanted to know, 'How did you get back?'

'Through Sweden.'

There was another pause while they just sat looking at each other across the table, drinking in the sight of each other.

Then he asked gently. 'How've you been, Kate? Why aren't you in uniform? Aren't you in the WAAFs any more?'

She circled the cup with her hands and glanced down at it. She shook her head. 'No. I – had to leave.'

'*Had* to leave? Why?'

'I – got pregnant.'

'Pregnant!' he burst out, so loudly that one or two people nearby looked across. Some smiled, thinking that a young husband was hearing the joyous news for the first time; others curious in case there was a shotgun wedding about to be arranged.

'Sssh,' she hissed.

'Shush be damned! Who is it? I'll bloody kill him!'

'Danny – don't. It's not like that. Just calm down – and listen.'

'Well,' he said, but his tone was not encouraging, 'I'm listening.'

'I've grown up a lot since – well – since I last saw you . . .'

His mouth was tight as if he would like to refute that

444

particular statement, but he held back any retort and let her continue. 'There was someone on our station – don't ask me who 'cos I'm not going to tell you. We had an affair. I loved him, Danny. Not in the same way I once loved you, but . . .'

She saw his eyes soften as if the memory of their young, innocent love still hurt him too.

' . . . but I did love him – I still do.'

'Why don't you get married then?'

'He – he'd already gone when I found I was pregnant.'

'Gone? Do you mean – he was killed?' Danny asked gently now and reached across the table to take her hand.

Kate shook her head. 'No – no, he's already married.'

'Oh, Kate.' There was reproach and yet sympathy too in his tone.

Her head jerked up. 'I know you must think badly of me. But I'm not sorry. I have a beautiful baby girl whom I love dearly and things – well – they're working out.'

'But you're not living at home, are you?'

'No – and that reminds me; was it you sent that telegram?'

''Course it was. Who did you think it was from?'

She smiled. 'I – I thought it was from – Ella's father. You didn't put a name on it.'

Now he looked suddenly boyishly self-conscious. 'I thought you'd know who it was from. 'Course I didn't know about the other bloke in your life, now did I?' He was teasing her now and the brief anger had gone. 'I sent one to – to Rosie too, so they'll know I'm on me way home.' His embarrassment deepened. 'But I wanted to see you first. After all, Rosie's got me for the rest of me life . . .' His voice was a hoarse whisper and Kate knew then that deep down, he still felt about her as he always had, but knew also that life had to go on. They could not cling morbidly to the past and their smashed childhood dreams. He squeezed her hand tightly and she returned the gesture. They sat holding hands across the table.

'So – how did you find out where I was?' she prompted.

'Mavis. As soon as I landed in England, I rang Suddaby. Some stuck-up woman on the switchboard said you weren't there anymore, but that's all she would say. So I rang back again a bit later and got hold of Mavis. She told me you were staying with the Godfreys.' He grinned. 'But that's all *she* would tell me. You've got some very loyal friends.'

'Good old Mavis,' Kate murmured and inside she was bubbling with laughter to think just how confused Mavis would be feeling now.

'Why aren't you at home, then?'

'Me mam won't have anything to do with me now – because of the baby.'

'Huh!' Danny grunted expressively. 'I might have known.'

Kate sighed. 'Oh, it's not that simple. Me grandad explained a lot of things to me. I'll tell you all about it sometime. Not now, but sometime.'

'But you're all right with the Godfreys? You're happy there?' She nodded, but he was not convinced. 'You sure? I can't imagine you living in a city for ever.'

'Oh, I'm getting more used to it. I take the baby out in the pram to the Arboretum and up the hill to the cathedral.' She smiled. 'I love that cathedral – I really do. And sometimes we get right out of the city into the countryside. Besides, I'm so lucky to be able to work from Mrs Godfrey's front room. What I'd have done without her and Peg, I don't know.'

He nodded and was thoughtful for a moment. Then he looked up. 'What do you call her?'

'Who?'

'Ya baby?'

446

'Oh,' Now it was Kate's turn to be embarrassed. 'I hope you don't mind – I called her Danielle.'

He stared at her for a moment and then threw back his head and laughed. 'You little devil! That'll set the tongues wagging again.'

'You're not angry, are you?'

'No, 'course I'm not. I'm tickled pink. I'll come over and see her as soon as I can . . .' He seemed reluctant to speak of his home, of Rosie and their child. But then she realized, he would think they were still enemies.

People were beginning to leave the tea-room and Danny glanced up at the clock. 'Me train'll be leaving in a minute. Come to the platform with me, will ya? How are you getting back to Lincoln?'

'I can get a train in about half an hour, I think.'

On the platform, he kissed her cheek. 'Thanks for coming – even if you did think it was some other feller!'

'I'm so very thankful it was you.' If fate could only allow one of the men in her life to come back, she thought, then it had to be Danny. She touched his face gently with her fingertips. 'Go home, Danny. Go home to Rosie – and your son.'

The astonished look on his face was almost comical. She nodded in answer to his unspoken question. 'When you were missing – we helped each other, supported each other. I was there when Robbie was born. Rosie and I, we – got close again.'

He put his arms around her, pulling her close and resting his cheek against her hair. 'Thank you,' he said simply.

They stood, just holding each other, then he asked softly, 'What's he like, this son of mine?'

'He's got brown eyes and black hair, just like his father.' Her voice broke a little as she added, 'He'll break a few hearts too . . .'

His arms tightened about her momentarily and then a whistle sounded shrilly, reverberating down the platform. There was a sudden flurry of activity all around them. Last-minute travellers dashed on to the platform and jumped aboard. Lovers tore themselves apart, reaching out with extended fingers, touching until the very last moment.

Reluctantly, Danny drew back and held her from him at arm's length. For a long moment he looked deep into her eyes. 'Take care of yourself, Katie Hilton. And your little lass. If you ever – ever need me, you know where I am.'

She nodded, not trusting herself to speak. His words from their childhood echoed down the years: 'I'll always care for you, Katie Hilton, dun't ever forget that'.

His arms came fiercely around her once more and for a timeless moment, she clung to him. Then he turned away and climbed aboard the train, pulling the door to behind him with a thud. He pushed down the window and leaned out. As the train pulled away, he was still waving.

'God bless and keep you,' she whispered, as his face became smaller and smaller until she could no longer see it through the blur of her tears. She watched until the train was out of sight and then turned and walked across the empty platform, her footsteps echoing eerily in the stillness.

Hunching her shoulders and hugging her coat around her, she plunged her hands deep into her pockets and, once more, she felt the wrinkled surface of the whelk shell.

And remembering, she smiled.

REAP THE HARVEST

Following the disastrous floods of 1953, Ella Hilton is compelled to live at Brumby's Farm with her grandmother, Esther, and is soon acutely aware of the mysteries surrounding her family's past.

As Ella grows up and falls in love herself, the story of three generations of women – Esther, Kate and Ella – comes full circle and history seems destined to repeat itself in tragedy.

In the final part of this glorious Lincolnshire trilogy, Margaret Dickinson brings the 1950s vividly to life in a story of secrets and love, buried under years of pride and misunderstanding.